DEAD IN DIXIE

DEAD IN DIXIE

SFBC
FANTASY

DEAD UNTIL DARK Copyright © 2001 by Charlaine Harris Schulz

Publication History: Ace Books mass market, May 2001
Ace Trade paperback, July 2009

LIVING DEAD IN DALLAS Copyright © 2002 by Charlaine Harris Schulz

Publication History: Ace Books mass market, April 2002
Ace Hardcover, January 2009
Ace Trade paperback, August 2009

CLUB DEAD Copyright © 2003 by Charlaine Harris Schulz

Publication History: Ace Books mass market, May 2003
Ace Trade paperback, September 2009
Ace Hardcover, March 2010

First SFBC Fantasy Printing: May 2003
Second SFBC Fantasy Edition: July 2010

Published by arrangement with
The Berkley Publishing Group
A Division of Penguin Putnam Inc.
375 Hudson Street
New York, New York 10014

Visit The SFBC online at *http://www.sfbc.com*

ISBN # 978-1-61664-557-1

Printed in the United States of America.

Contents

Introduction

WHEN I FIRST heard that SFBC was going to do a Sookie omnibus, I was absolutely delighted. Having the first three Sookie adventures in one book seemed like a great idea, and I've been pleased to sign many, many copies of "Dead in Dixie" over the years.

It feels like a long time since the first Sookie Stackhouse books ("Dead Until Dark," "Living Dead in Dallas," and "Club Dead") appeared on the shelves. My life has changed considerably since then, and the books have taken on a whole new life in their reinterpretation as a television show, "True Blood," created by the wonderful talent of Alan Ball. Thanks to Alan, Sookie has become more popular than I'd ever imagined possible.

When I consider how close the books came to not being published at all, Sookie's current popularity seems all the more amazing. I'd reached a crossroads in my career, which was firmly stuck in the midlist. I created the world Sookie lives in because I wanted to write books that crossed genres. This was way before the term "urban fantasy" was created to denote the crop that sprang up after the success of Laurell K. Hamilton, myself, and many other writers who excel in this vigorous and wildly creative field.

The first few editors who read "Dead Until Dark" were not enthusiastic, to put it mildly. It was a book they thought would be difficult to market, impossible to shelve, and all around a bad idea. Finally, after two years, John Morgan (then a junior editor at Ace) asked his boss, Ginjer Buchanan, if they could take a chance on the book, and Ginjer agreed.

To the amazement of almost everyone, "Dead Until Dark" really took off. John Morgan was in touch with my agent (Joshua Bilmes) within a couple of months of the book's publication, anxious to sign me for two more. I was delighted for two reasons: first, the book was selling well, and second, I would get to revisit Sookie's world and continue her adventures. After "Living Dead In Dallas" came out, John was back in touch with Joshua because Ace wanted three more books. After many years, I was on the right track, and I had some job security.

Readers are often dismayed about the hardships Sookie endures in the course of her pursuit of true love and financial stability. I can only defend myself by saying that Sookie can take anything I can dish out, as she's proved over and over. She makes many mistakes and she takes a lot of licks, but she remains loyal, honest, brave, and strong. I wish I were more like her.

I'm often asked why I think Sookie has become so popular. I usually answer, somewhat flippantly, that if I knew that I would have done it much sooner.

Why do people enjoy reading about a telepathic barmaid from a small town in Louisiana? I think it's because she's down-to-earth, and because she's so resilient. She's the living exemplar of the awful saying, "If life hands you lemons, made lemonade." Sookie makes a lot of lemonade.

If you haven't read about the world of Bon Temps, Louisiana, before, I hope you will enjoy reading about it now. Maybe this reissue of "Dead in Dixie" will entertain you, and we'll get to see you in the bar at Merlotte's again.

—CHARLAINE HARRIS

DEAD UNTIL DARK

*My thanks and appreciation go to the people
who thought this book
was a good idea—
Dean James, Toni L. P. Kelner
and
Gary and Susan Nowlin*

Chapter 1

I'D BEEN WAITING for the vampire for years when he walked into the bar.

Ever since vampires came out of the coffin (as they laughingly put it) four years ago, I'd hoped one would come to Bon Temps. We had all the other minorities in our little town—why not the newest, the legally recognized undead? But rural northern Louisiana wasn't too tempting to vampires, apparently; on the other hand, New Orleans was a real center for them—the whole Anne Rice thing, right?

It's not that long a drive from Bon Temps to New Orleans, and everyone who came into the bar said that if you threw a rock on a street corner you'd hit one. Though you better not.

But I was waiting for my own vampire.

You can tell I don't get out much. And it's not because I'm not pretty. I am. I'm blond and blue-eyed and twenty-five, and my legs are strong and my bosom is substantial, and I have a waspy waistline. I look good in the warm-weather waitress outfit Sam picked for us: black shorts, white T, white socks, black Nikes.

But I have a disability. That's how I try to think of it.

The bar patrons just say I'm crazy.

Either way, the result is that I almost never have a date. So little treats count a lot with me.

And he sat at one of my tables—the vampire.

I knew immediately what he was. It amazed me when no one else turned around to stare. They couldn't tell! But to me, his skin had a little glow, and I just knew.

I could have danced with joy, and in fact I did do a little step right there by the bar. Sam Merlotte, my boss, looked up from the drink he was mixing and gave me a tiny smile. I grabbed my tray and pad and went over to the vampire's table. I hoped that my lipstick was still even and my ponytail was still neat. I'm kind of tense, and I could feel my smile yanking the corners of my mouth up.

He seemed lost in thought, and I had a chance to give him a good once-over before he looked up. He was a little under six feet, I estimated. He had thick brown hair, combed straight back and brushing his collar, and his long sideburns seemed curiously old-fashioned. He was pale, of course; hey, he was dead, if you believed the old tales. The politically correct theory, the one the vamps themselves publicly backed, had it that this guy was the victim of a virus that left him apparently dead for a couple of days and thereafter allergic to sunlight, silver, and garlic. The details depended on which newspaper you read. They were all full of vampire stuff these days.

Anyway, his lips were lovely, sharply sculpted, and he had arched dark brows. His nose swooped down right out of that arch, like a prince's in a Byzantine mosaic. When he finally looked up, I saw his eyes were even darker than his hair, and the whites were incredibly white.

"What can I get you?" I asked, happy almost beyond words.

He raised his eyebrows. "Do you have the bottled synthetic blood?" he asked.

"No, I'm so sorry! Sam's got some on order. Should be in next week."

"Then red wine, please," he said, and his voice was cool and clear, like a stream over smooth stones. I laughed out loud. It was too perfect.

"Don't mind, Sookie, mister, she's crazy," came a familiar voice from the booth against the wall. All my happiness deflated, though I could feel the smile still straining my lips. The vampire was staring at me, watching the life go out of my face.

"I'll get your wine right away," I said, and strode off, not even looking at Mack Rattray's smug face. He was there almost every night, he and his wife Denise. I called them the Rat Couple. They'd done their best to make me miserable since they'd moved into the rent trailer at Four Tracks Corner. I had hoped that they'd blow out of Bon Temps as suddenly as they'd blown in.

When they'd first come into Merlotte's, I'd very rudely listened in to their thoughts—I know, pretty low-class of me. But I get bored like everyone else, and though I spend most of my time blocking out the thoughts of other people that try to pass through my brain, sometimes I just give in. So I knew some things about the Rattrays that maybe no one else did. For one thing, I knew they'd been in jail, though I didn't know why. For another, I'd read the nasty thoughts Mack Rattray had entertained about yours truly. And then I'd heard in Denise's thoughts that she'd abandoned a baby she'd had two years before, a baby that wasn't Mack's.

And they didn't tip, either.

Sam poured a glass of the house red wine, looking over at the vampire's table as he put it on my tray.

When Sam looked back at me, I could tell he too knew our new customer was undead. Sam's eyes are Paul Newman blue, as opposed to my own hazy blue gray. Sam is blond, too, but his hair is wiry and his blond is almost a sort of hot red gold. He is always a little sunburned, and though he looks slight in his clothes, I have seen him unload trucks with his shirt off, and he has plenty of upper body strength. I never listen to Sam's thoughts. He's my boss. I've had to quit jobs before because I found out things I didn't want to know about my boss.

But Sam didn't comment, he just gave me the wine. I checked the glass to make sure it was sparkly clean and made my way back to the vampire's table.

"Your wine, sir," I said ceremoniously and placed it carefully on the table exactly in front of him. He looked at me again, and I stared into his lovely eyes while I had the chance. "Enjoy," I said proudly. Behind me, Mack Rattray yelled, "Hey, Sookie! We need another pitcher of beer here!" I sighed and turned to take the empty pitcher from the Rats' table. Denise was in fine form tonight, I noticed, wearing a halter top and short shorts, her mess of brown hair floofing around her head in fashionable tangles. Denise wasn't truly pretty, but she was so flashy and confident that it took awhile to figure that out.

A little while later, to my dismay, I saw the Rattrays had moved over to the vampire's table. They were talking at him. I couldn't see that he was responding a lot, but he wasn't leaving either.

"Look at that!" I said disgustedly to Arlene, my fellow waitress. Arlene is redheaded and freckled and ten years older than me, and she's been married four times. She has two kids, and from time to time, I think she considers me her third.

"New guy, huh?" she said with small interest. Arlene is currently dating Rene Lenier, and though I can't see the attraction, she seems pretty satisfied. I think Rene was her second husband.

"Oh, he's a vampire," I said, just having to share my delight with someone.

"Really? Here? Well, just think," she said, smiling a little to show she appreciated my pleasure. "He can't be too bright, though, honey, if he's with the Rats. On the other hand, Denise is giving him quite a show."

I figured it out after Arlene made it plain to me; she's much better at sizing up sexual situations than I am due to her experience and my lack.

The vampire was hungry. I'd always heard that the synthetic blood the Japanese had developed kept vampires up to par as far as nutrition, but didn't really satisfy their hunger, which was why there were "Unfortunate Incidents" from time to time. (That was the vampire euphemism for the bloody slaying of a human.) And here was Denise Rattray, stroking her throat, turning her neck from side to side . . . what a *bitch*.

My brother, Jason, came into the bar, then, and sauntered over to give me a hug. He knows that women like a man who's good to his family and also kind to the disabled, so hugging me is a double whammy of recommendation. Not that Jason needs many more points than he has just by being himself. He's handsome. He can sure be mean, too, but most women seem quite willing to overlook that.

"Hey, sis, how's Gran?"

"She's okay, about the same. Come by to see."

"I will. Who's loose tonight?"

"Look for yourself." I noticed that when Jason began to glance around there was a flutter of female hands to hair, blouses, lips.

"Hey. I see DeeAnne. She free?"

"She's here with a trucker from Hammond. He's in the bathroom. Watch it."

Jason grinned at me, and I marvelled that other women could not see the selfishness of that smile. Even Arlene tucked in her T-shirt when Jason came in, and after four husbands she should have known a little about evaluating men. The other waitress I worked with, Dawn, tossed her hair and straightened her back to make her boobs stand out. Jason gave her an amiable wave. She pretended to sneer. She's on the outs with Jason, but she still wants him to notice her.

I got really busy—everyone came to Merlotte's on Saturday night for some portion of the evening—so I lost track of my vampire for a while. When I next had a moment to check on him, he was talking to Denise. Mack was looking at him with an expression so avid that I became worried.

I went closer to the table, staring at Mack. Finally, I let down my guard and listened.

Mack and Denise had been in jail for vampire draining.

Deeply upset, I nevertheless automatically carried a pitcher of beer and some glasses to a raucous table of four. Since vampire blood was supposed to temporarily relieve symptoms of illness and increase sexual potency, kind of like prednisone and Viagra rolled into one, there was a huge black market for genuine, undiluted vampire blood. Where there's a market there are suppliers; in this case, I'd just learned, the scummy Rat Couple. They'd formerly trapped vampires and drained them, selling the little vials of blood for as much as $200 apiece. It had been the drug of choice for at least two years now. Some buyers went crazy after drinking pure vampire blood, but that didn't slow the market any.

The drained vampire didn't last long, as a rule. The drainers left the vampires staked or simply dumped them out in the open. When the sun came up, that was all she wrote. From time to time, you read about the tables being turned when the vampire managed to get free. Then you got your dead drainers.

Now my vampire was getting up and leaving with the Rats. Mack met my eyes, and I saw him looking distinctly startled at the expression on my face. He turned away, shrugging me off like everyone else.

That made me mad. Really mad.

What should I do? While I struggled with myself, they were out the door. Would the vampire believe me if I ran after them, told him? No one else did. Or if by chance they did, they hated and feared me for reading the thoughts concealed in people's brains. Arlene had begged me to read her fourth husband's mind when he'd come in to pick her up one night because she was pretty certain he was thinking of leaving her and the kids, but I wouldn't because I wanted to keep the one friend I had. And even Arlene hadn't been able to ask me directly because that would be admitting I had this gift, this curse. People couldn't admit it. They had to think I was crazy. Which sometimes I almost was!

So I dithered, confused and frightened and angry, and then I knew I just had to act. I was goaded by the look Mack had given me—as if I was negligible.

I slid down the bar to Jason, where he was sweeping DeeAnne off her feet. She didn't take much sweeping, popular opinion had it. The trucker from Hammond was glowering from her other side.

"Jason," I said urgently. He turned to give me a warning glare. "Listen, is that chain still in the back of the pickup?"

"Never leave home without it," he said lazily, his eyes scanning my face for signs of trouble. "You going to fight, Sookie?"

I smiled at him, so used to grinning that it was easy. "I sure hope not," I said cheerfully.

"Hey, you need help?" After all, he was my brother.

"No, thanks," I said, trying to sound reassuring. And I slipped over to Arlene. "Listen, I got to leave a little early. My tables are pretty thin, can you cover for me?" I didn't think I'd ever asked Arlene such a thing, though I'd covered for her many times. She, too, offered me help. "That's okay," I said. "I'll be back in if I can. If you clean my area, I'll do your trailer."

Arlene nodded her red mane enthusiastically.

I pointed to the employee door, to myself, and made my fingers walk, to tell Sam where I was going.

He nodded. He didn't look happy.

So out the back door I went, trying to make my feet quiet on the gravel. The employee parking lot is at the rear of the bar, through a door leading into the storeroom. The cook's car was there, and Arlene's, Dawn's, and mine. To my right, the east, Sam's pickup was sitting in front of his trailer.

I went out of the gravelled employee parking area onto the blacktop that surfaced the much larger customer lot to the west of the bar. Woods surrounded the clearing in which Merlotte's stood, and the edges of the parking lot were mostly gravel. Sam kept it well lit, and the surrealistic glare of the high, parking lot lights made everything look strange.

I saw the Rat Couple's dented red sports car, so I knew they were close.

I found Jason's truck at last. It was black with custom aqua and pink swirls on the sides. He sure did love to be noticed. I pulled myself up by the tailgate and rummaged around in the bed for his chain, a thick length of links that he carried in case of a fight. I looped it and carried it pressed to my body so it wouldn't chink.

I thought a second. The only halfway private spot to which the Rattrays could have lured the vampire was the end of the parking lot where the trees actually overhung the cars. So I crept in that direction, trying to move fast and low.

I paused every few seconds and listened. Soon I heard a groan and the faint sounds of voices. I snaked between the cars, and I spotted them right where I'd figured they'd be. The vampire was down on the ground on his back, his face contorted in agony, and the gleam of chains crisscrossed his wrists and ran down to his ankles. Silver. There were two little vials of blood already on the ground beside Denise's feet, and as I watched, she fixed a new Vacutainer to the needle. The tourniquet above his elbow dug cruelly into his arm.

Their backs were to me, and the vampire hadn't seen me yet. I loosened the coiled chain so a good three feet of it swung free. Who to attack first? They were both small and vicious.

I remembered Mack's contemptuous dismissal and the fact that he never left me a tip. Mack first.

I'd never actually been in a fight before. Somehow I was positively looking forward to it.

I leapt out from behind a pickup and swung the chain. It thwacked across Mack's back as he knelt beside his victim. He screamed and jumped up. After a glance, Denise set about getting the third Vacutainer plugged. Mack's hand dipped down to his boot and came up shining. I gulped. He had a knife in his hand.

"Uh-oh," I said, and grinned at him.

"You crazy bitch!" he screamed. He sounded like he was looking forward to using the knife. I was too involved to keep my mental guard up, and I had a clear flash of what Mack wanted to do to me. It drove me really crazy. I went for him with every intention of hurting him as badly as I could. But he was ready for me and jumped forward with the knife while I was swinging the chain. He sliced at my arm and just missed it. The chain, on its recoil, wrapped around his skinny neck like a lover. Mack's yell of triumph turned into a gurgle. He dropped the knife and clawed at the links with both hands. Losing air, he dropped to his knees on the rough pavement, yanking the chain from my hand.

Well, there went Jason's chain. I swooped down and scooped up Mack's knife, holding it like I knew how to use it. Denise had been lunging forward, looking like a redneck witch in the lines and shadows of the security lights.

She stopped in her tracks when she saw I had Mack's knife. She cursed and railed and said terrible things. I waited till she'd run down to say, "Get. Out. Now."

Denise stared holes of hate in my head. She tried to scoop up the vials of blood, but I hissed at her to leave them alone. So she pulled Mack to his feet. He was still making choking, gurgling sounds and holding the chain. Denise kind of dragged him along to their car and shoved him in through the passenger's side. Yanking some keys from her pocket, Denise threw herself in the driver's seat.

As I heard the engine roar into life, suddenly I realized that the Rats now had another weapon. Faster than I've ever moved, I ran to the vampire's head and panted, "Push with your feet!" I grabbed him under the arms and yanked back with all my might, and he caught on and braced his feet and shoved. We were just inside the tree line when the red car came roaring down at us. Denise missed us by less than a yard when she had to swerve to avoid hitting a pine. Then I heard the big motor of the Rats' car receding in the distance.

"Oh, wow," I breathed, and knelt by the vampire because my knees wouldn't hold me up any more. I breathed heavily for just a minute, trying to get hold of myself. The vampire moved a little, and I looked over. To my horror, I saw wisps of smoke coming up from his wrists where the silver touched them.

"Oh, you poor thing," I said, angry at myself for not caring for him instantly. Still trying to catch my breath, I began to unwind the thin bands of silver, which all seemed to be part of one very long chain. "Poor baby," I whispered, never thinking until later how incongruous that sounded. I have agile fingers, and I released his wrists pretty quickly. I wondered how the Rats had distracted him while they got into position to put them on, and I could feel myself reddening as I pictured it.

The vampire cradled his arms to his chest while I worked on the silver wrapped around his legs. His ankles had fared better since the drainers hadn't troubled to pull up his jeans legs and put the silver against his bare skin.

"I'm sorry I didn't get here faster," I said apologetically. "You'll feel better in a minute, right? Do you want me to leave?"

"No."

That made me feel pretty good until he added, "They might come back, and I can't fight yet." His cool voice was uneven, but I couldn't exactly say I'd heard him panting.

I made a sour face at him, and while he was recovering, I took a few precautions. I sat with my back to him, giving him some privacy. I know how unpleasant it is to be stared at when you're hurting. I hunkered down on the pavement, keeping watch on the parking lot. Several cars left, and others came in, but none came down to our end by the woods. By the movement of the air around me, I knew when the vampire had sat up.

He didn't speak right away. I turned my head to the left to look at him. He was closer than I'd thought. His big dark eyes looked into mine. His fangs had retracted; I was a little disappointed about that.

"Thank you," he said stiffly.

So he wasn't thrilled about being rescued by a woman. Typical guy.

Since he was being so ungracious, I felt I could do something rude, too, and I listened to him, opening my mind completely.

And I heard . . . nothing.

"Oh," I said, hearing the shock in my own voice, hardly knowing what I was saying. "I *can't hear you*."

"Thank you!" the vampire said, moving his lips exaggeratedly.

"No, no . . . I can hear you speak, but . . ." and in my excitement, I did something I ordinarily would never do, because it was pushy, and personal, and revealed I was disabled. I turned fully to him and put my hands on both sides of his white face, and I looked at him intently. I focused with all my energy. *Nothing*. It was like having to listen to the radio all the time, to stations you didn't get to select, and then suddenly tuning in to a wavelength you couldn't receive.

It was heaven.

His eyes were getting wider and darker, though he was holding absolutely still.

"Oh, excuse me," I said with a gasp of embarrassment. I snatched my hands away and resumed staring at the parking lot. I began babbling about Mack and Denise, all the time thinking how marvelous it would be to have a companion I could not hear unless he chose to speak out loud. How beautiful his silence was.

". . . so I figured I better come out here to see how you were," I concluded, and had no idea what I'd been saying.

"You came out here to rescue me. It was brave," he said in a voice so seductive it would have shivered DeeAnne right out of her red nylon panties.

"Now you cut that out," I said tartly, coming right down to earth with a thud.

He looked astonished for a whole second before his face returned to its white smoothness.

"Aren't you afraid to be alone with a hungry vampire?" he asked, something arch and yet dangerous running beneath the words.

"Nope."

"Are you assuming that since you came to my rescue that you're safe, that I harbor an ounce of sentimental feeling after all these years? Vampires often turn on those who trust them. We don't have human values, you know."

"A lot of humans turn on those who trust them," I pointed out. I can be practical. "I'm not a total fool." I held out my arm and turned my neck. While he'd been recovering, I'd been wrapping the Rats' chains around my neck and arms.

He shivered visibly.

"But there's a juicy artery in your groin," he said after a pause to regroup, his voice as slithery as a snake on a slide.

"Don't you talk dirty," I told him. "I won't listen to that."

Once again we looked at each other in silence. I was afraid I'd never see him again; after all, his first visit to Merlotte's hadn't exactly been a success. So I was trying to absorb every detail I could; I would treasure this encounter and rehash it for a long, long time. It was rare, a prize. I wanted to touch his skin again. I couldn't remember how it felt. But that would be going beyond some boundary of manners, and also maybe start him going on the seductive crap again.

"Would you like to drink the blood they collected?" he asked unexpectedly. "It would be a way for me to show my gratitude." He gestured at the stoppered vials lying on the blacktop. "My blood is supposed to improve your sex life and your health."

"I'm healthy as a horse," I told him honestly. "And I have no sex life to speak of. You do what you want with it."

"You could sell it," he suggested, but I thought he was just waiting to see what I'd say about that.

"I wouldn't touch it," I said, insulted.

"You're different," he said. "What are you?" He seemed to be going through a list of possibilities in his head from the way he was looking at me. To my pleasure, I could not hear a one of them.

"Well. I'm Sookie Stackhouse, and I'm a waitress," I told him. "What's your name?" I thought I could at least ask that without being presuming.

"Bill," he said.

Before I could stop myself, I rocked back onto my butt with laughter. "The vampire Bill!" I said. "I thought it might be Antoine, or Basil, or Langford! Bill!" I hadn't laughed so hard in a long time. "Well, see ya, Bill. I got to get back to work." I could feel the tense grin snap back into place when I thought of Merlotte's. I put my hand on Bill's shoulder and pushed up. It was rock hard, and I was on my feet so fast I had to stop myself from stumbling. I examined my socks to make sure their cuffs were exactly even, and I looked up and down my outfit to check for wear and tear during the fight with the Rats. I dusted off my bottom since I'd been sitting on the dirty pavement and gave Bill a wave as I started off across the parking lot.

It had been a stimulating evening, one with a lot of food for thought. I felt almost as cheerful as my smile when I considered it.

But Jason was going to be mighty angry about the chain.

*   *   *

AFTER WORK THAT night, I drove home, which is only about four miles south from the bar. Jason had been gone (and so had DeeAnne) when I got back to work, and that had been another good thing. I was reviewing the evening as I drove to my grandmother's house, where I lived. It's right before Tall Pines cemetery, which lies off a narrow two-lane parish road. My great-great-great grandfather had started the house, and he'd had ideas about privacy, so to reach it you had to turn off the parish road into the driveway, go through some woods, and then you arrived at the clearing in which the house stood.

It's sure not any historic landmark, since most of the oldest parts have been ripped down and replaced over the years, and of course it's got electricity and plumbing and insulation, all that good modern stuff. But it still has a tin roof that gleams blindingly on sunny days. When the roof needed to be replaced, I wanted to put regular roofing tiles on it, but my grandmother said no. Though I was paying, it's her house; so naturally, tin it was.

Historical or not, I'd lived in this house since I was about seven, and I'd visited it often before then, so I loved it. It was just a big old family home, too big for Granny and me, I guess. It had a broad front covered by a screened-in porch, and it was painted white, Granny being a traditionalist all the way. I went through the big living room, strewn with battered furniture arranged to suit us, and down the hall to the first bedroom on the left, the biggest.

Adele Hale Stackhouse, my grandmother, was propped up in her high bed, about a million pillows padding her skinny shoulders. She was wearing a long-sleeved cotton nightgown even in the warmth of this spring night, and her bedside lamp was still on. There was a book propped in her lap.

"Hey," I said.

"Hi, honey."

My grandmother is very small and very old, but her hair is still thick, and so white it almost has the very faintest of green tinges. She wears it kind of rolled against her neck during the day, but at night it's loose or braided. I looked at the cover of her book.

"You reading Danielle Steele again?"

"Oh, that woman can sure tell a story." My grandmother's great pleasures were reading Danielle Steele, watching her soap operas (which she called her "stories") and attending meetings of the myriad clubs she'd belonged to all her adult life, it seemed. Her favorites were the Descendants of the Glorious Dead and the Bon Temps Gardening Society.

"Guess what happened tonight?" I asked her.

"What? You got a date?"

"No," I said, working to keep a smile on my face. "A vampire came into the bar."

"Ooh, did he have fangs?"

I'd seen them glisten in the parking lot lights when the Rats were draining him, but there was no need to describe that to Gran. "Sure, but they were retracted."

"A vampire right here in Bon Temps." Granny was as pleased as punch. "Did he bite anybody in the bar?"

"Oh, no, Gran! He just sat and had a glass of red wine. Well, he ordered it, but he didn't drink it. I think he just wanted some company."

"Wonder where he stays."

"He wouldn't be too likely to tell anyone that."

"No," Gran said, thinking about it a moment. "I guess not. Did you like him?"

Now that was kind of a hard question. I mulled it over. "I don't know. He was real interesting," I said cautiously.

"I'd surely love to meet him." I wasn't surprised Gran said this because she enjoyed new things almost as much as I did. She wasn't one of those reactionaries who'd decided vampires were damned right off the bat. "But I better go to sleep now. I was just waiting for you to come home before I turned out my light."

I bent over to give Gran a kiss, and said, "Night night."

I half-closed her door on my way out and heard the click of the lamp as she turned it off. My cat, Tina, came from wherever she'd been sleeping to rub against my legs, and I picked her up and cuddled her for a while before putting her out for the night. I glanced at the clock. It was almost two o'clock, and my bed was calling me.

My room was right across the hall from Gran's. When I first used this room, after my folks had died, Gran had moved my bedroom furniture from their house so I'd feel more homey. And here it was still, the single bed and vanity in white-painted wood, the small chest of drawers.

I turned on my own light and shut the door and began taking off my clothes. I had at least five pair of black shorts and many, many white T-shirts, since those tended to get stained so easily. No telling how many pairs of white socks were rolled up in my drawer. So I didn't have to do the wash tonight. I was too tired for a shower. I did brush my teeth and wash the makeup off my face, slap on some moisturizer, and take the band out of my hair.

I crawled into bed in my favorite Mickey Mouse sleep T-shirt, which came almost to my knees. I turned on my side, like I always do, and I relished the silence of the room. Almost everyone's brain is turned off in the wee hours of the night, and the vibrations are gone, the intrusions do not have to be repelled. With such peace, I only had time to think of the vampire's dark eyes, and then I fell into the deep sleep of exhaustion.

BY LUNCHTIME THE next day I was in my folding aluminum chaise out in the front yard, getting browner by the second. I was in my favorite white strapless two-piece, and it was a little roomier than last summer, so I was pleased as punch.

Then I heard a vehicle coming down the drive, and Jason's black truck with its pink and aqua blazons pulled up to within a yard of my feet.

Jason climbed down—did I mention the truck sports those high tires?—to stalk toward me. He was wearing his usual work clothes, a khaki shirt and pants, and he had his sheathed knife clipped to his belt, like most of the county road workers did. Just by the way he walked, I knew he was in a huff.

I put my dark glasses on.

"Why didn't you tell me you beat up the Rattrays last night?" My brother threw himself into the aluminum yard chair by my chaise. "Where's Gran?" he asked belatedly.

"Hanging out the laundry," I said. Gran used the dryer in a pinch, but she really liked hanging the wet clothes out in the sun. Of course the clothesline was in the backyard, where clotheslines should be. "She's fixing country-fried steak and sweet potatoes and green beans she put up last year, for lunch," I added, knowing that would distract Jason a little bit. I hoped Gran stayed out back. I didn't want her to hear this conversation. "Keep your voice low," I reminded him.

"Rene Lenier couldn't wait till I got to work this morning to tell me all about it. He was over to the Rattrays' trailer last night to buy him some weed, and Denise drove up like she wanted to kill someone. Rene said he liked to have gotten killed, she was so mad. It took both Rene and Denise to get Mack into the trailer, and then they took him to the hospital in Monroe." Jason glared at me accusingly.

"Did Rene tell you that Mack came after me with a knife?" I asked, deciding attacking was the best way of handling this. I could tell Jason's pique was due in large part to the fact that he had heard about this from someone else.

"If Denise told Rene, he didn't mention it to me," Jason said slowly, and I saw his handsome face darken with rage. "He came after you with a knife?"

"So I had to defend myself," I said, as if it were matter-of-fact. "And he took your chain." This was all true, if a little skewed.

"I came in to tell you," I continued, "but by the time I got back in the bar, you were gone with DeeAnne, and since I was fine, it just didn't seem worth tracking you down. I knew you'd feel obliged to go after him if I told you about the knife," I added diplomatically. There was a lot more truth in that, since Jason dearly loves a fight.

"What the hell were you doing out there anyway?" he asked, but he had relaxed, and I knew he was accepting this.

"Did you know that, in addition to selling drugs, the Rats are vampire drainers?"

Now he was fascinated. "No . . . so?"

"Well, one of my customers last night was a vampire, and they were draining him out in Merlotte's parking lot! I couldn't have that."

"There's a vampire here in Bon Temps?"

"Yep. Even if you don't want a vampire for your best friend, you can't let trash like the Rats drain them. It's not like siphoning gas out of a car. And they would have left him out in the woods to die." Though the Rats hadn't told me their intentions, that was my bet. Even if they'd put him under cover so he could survive the day, a drained vampire took at least twenty years to recover, at least that's what one had said on *Oprah*. And that's if another vampire took care of him.

"The vampire was in the bar when I was there?" Jason asked, dazzled.

"Uh-huh. The dark-haired guy sitting with the Rats."

Jason grinned at my epithet for the Rattrays. But he hadn't let go of the night before, yet. "How'd you know he was a vampire?" he asked, but when he looked at me, I could tell he was wishing he had bitten his tongue.

"I just knew," I said in my flattest voice.

"Right." And we shared a whole unspoken conversation.

"Homulka doesn't have a vampire," Jason said thoughtfully. He tilted his face back to catch the sun, and I knew we were off dangerous ground.

"True," I agreed. Homulka was the town Bon Temps loved to hate. We'd been rivals in football, basketball, and historical significance for generations.

"Neither does Roedale," Gran said from behind us, and Jason and

I both jumped. I give Jason credit, he jumps up and gives Gran a hug everytime he sees her.

"Gran, you got enough food in the oven for me?"

"You and two others," Gran said. Our grandmother smiled up at Jason. She was not blind to his faults (or mine), but she loved him. "I just got a phone call from Everlee Mason. She was telling me you hooked up with DeeAnne last night."

"Boy oh boy, can't do anything in this town without getting caught," Jason said, but he wasn't really angry.

"That DeeAnne," Gran said warningly as we all started into the house, "she's been pregnant one time I know of. You just take care she doesn't have one of yours, you'll be paying the rest of your life. Course, that may be the only way I get great-grandchildren!"

Gran had the food ready on the table, so after Jason hung up his hat we sat down and said grace. Then Gran and Jason began gossiping with each other (though they called it "catching up") about people in our little town and parish. My brother worked for the state, supervising road crews. It seemed to me like Jason's day consisted of driving around in a state pickup, clocking off work, and then driving around all night in his own pickup. Rene was on one of the work crews Jason oversaw, and they'd been to high school together. They hung around with Hoyt Fortenberry a lot.

"Sookie, I had to replace the hot water heater in the house," Jason said suddenly. He lives in my parents' old house, the one we'd been living in when they died in a flash flood. We lived with Gran after that, but when Jason got through his two years of college and went to work for the state, he moved back into the house, which on paper is half mine.

"You need any money on that?" I asked.

"Naw, I got it."

We both make salaries, but we also have a little income from a fund established when an oil well was sunk on my parents' property. It played out in a few years, but my parents and then Gran made sure the money was invested. It saved Jason and me a lot of struggle, that padding. I don't know how Gran could have raised us if it hadn't been for that money. She was determined not to sell any land, but her own income is not much more than social security. That's one reason I don't get an apartment. If I get groceries when I'm living with her, that's reasonable, to her; but if I buy groceries and bring them to her house and leave them on her table and go home to my house, that's charity and that makes her mad.

"What kind did you get?" I asked, just to show interest.

He was dying to tell me; Jason's an appliance freak, and he wanted to describe his comparison shopping for a new water heater in detail. I listened with as much attention as I could muster.

And then he interrupted himself. "Hey Sook, you remember Maudette Pickens?"

"Sure," I said, surprised. "We graduated in the same class."

"Somebody killed Maudette in her apartment last night."

Gran and I were riveted. "When?" Grand asked, puzzled that she hadn't heard already.

"They just found her this very morning in her bedroom. Her boss tried to call her to find out why she hadn't shown up for work yesterday and today and got no answer, so he rode over and got the manager up, and they unlocked the place. You know she had the apartment across from DeeAnne's?" Bon Temps had only one bona fide apartment complex, a three-building, two-story U-shaped grouping, so we knew exactly where he meant.

"She got killed there?" I felt ill. I remembered Maudette clearly. Maudette had had a heavy jaw and a square bottom, pretty black hair and husky shoulders. Maudette had been a plodder, never bright or ambitious. I thought I recalled her working at the Grabbit Kwik, a gas station/convenience store.

"Yeah, she'd been working there for at least a year, I guess," Jason confirmed.

"How was it done?" My grandmother had that squnched, give-it-to-me-quick look with which nice people ask for bad news.

"She had some vampire bites on her—uh—inner thighs," my brother said, looking down at his plate. "But that wasn't what killed her. She was strangled. DeeAnne told me Maudette liked to go to that vampire bar in Shreveport when she had a couple of days off, so maybe that's where she got the bites. Might not have been *Sookie's* vampire."

"Maudette was a fang-banger?" I felt queasy, imagining slow, chunky Maudette draped in the exotic black dresses fang-bangers affected.

"What's that?" asked Gran. She must have missed *Sally-Jessy* the day the phenomenon was explored.

"Men and women that hang around with vampires and enjoy being bitten. Vampire groupies. They don't last too long, I think, because they want to be bitten too much, and sooner or later they get that one bite too many."

"But a bite didn't kill Maudette." Gran wanted to be sure she had it straight.

"Nope, strangling." Jason had begun finishing his lunch.

"Don't you always get gas at the Grabbit?" I asked.

"Sure. So do a lot of people."

"And didn't you hang around with Maudette some?" Gran asked.

"Well, in a way of speaking," Jason said cautiously.

I took that to mean he'd bedded Maudette when he couldn't find anyone else.

"I hope the sheriff doesn't want to talk to you," Gran said, shaking her head as if indicating "no" would make it less likely.

"What?" Jason was turning red, looking defensive.

"You see Maudette in the store all the time when you get your gas, you so-to-speak date her, then she winds up dead in an apartment you're familiar with," I summarized. It wasn't much, but it was something, and there were so few mysterious homicides in Bon Temps that I thought every stone would be turned in its investigation.

"I ain't the only one who fills the bill. Plenty of other guys get their gas there, and all of them know Maudette."

"Yeah, but in what sense?" Gran asked bluntly. "She wasn't a prostitute, was she? So she will have talked about who she saw."

"She just liked to have a good time, she wasn't a pro." It was good of Jason to defend Maudette, considering what I knew of his selfish character. I began to think a little better of my big brother. "She was kinda lonely, I guess," he added.

Jason looked at both of us, then, and saw we were surprised and touched.

"Speaking of prostitutes," he said hastily, "there's one in Monroe specializes in vampires. She keeps a guy standing by with a stake in case one gets carried away. She drinks synthetic blood to keep her blood supply up."

That was a pretty definite change of subject, so Gran and I tried to think of a question we could ask without being indecent.

"Wonder how much she charges?" I ventured, and when Jason told us the figure he'd heard, we both gasped.

Once we got off the topic of Maudette's murder, lunch went about as usual, with Jason looking at his watch and exclaiming that he had to leave just when it was time to do the dishes.

But Gran's mind was still running on vampires, I found out. She came into my room later, when I was putting on my makeup to go to work.

"How old you reckon the vampire is, the one you met?"

"I have no idea, Gran." I was putting on my mascara, looking wide-eyed and trying to hold still so I wouldn't poke myself in the eye, so my voice came out funny, as if I was trying out for a horror movie.

"Do you suppose . . . he might remember the War?"

I didn't need to ask which war. After all, Gran was a charter member of the Descendants of the Glorious Dead.

"Could be," I said, turning my face from side to side to make sure my blush was even.

"You think he might come to talk to us about it? We could have a special meeting."

"At night," I reminded her.

"Oh. Yes, it'd have to be." The Descendants usually met at noon at the library and brought a bag lunch.

I thought about it. It would be plain rude to suggest to the vampire that he ought to speak to Gran's club because I'd saved his blood from Drainers, but maybe he would offer if I gave a little hint? I didn't like to, but I'd do it for Gran. "I'll ask him the next time he comes in," I promised.

"At least he could come talk to me and maybe I could tape his recollections?" Gran said. I could hear her mind clicking as she thought of what a coup that would be for her. "It would be so interesting to the other club members," she said piously.

I stifled an impulse to laugh. "I'll suggest it to him," I said. "We'll see."

When I left, Gran was clearly counting her chickens.

I HADN'T THOUGHT of Rene Lenier going to Sam with the story of the parking lot fight. Rene'd been a busy bee, though. When I got to work that afternoon, I assumed the agitation I felt in the air was due to Maudette's murder. I found out different.

Sam hustled me into the storeroom the minute I came in. He was hopping with anger. He reamed me up one side and down the other.

Sam had never been mad with me before, and soon I was on the edge of tears.

"And if you think a customer isn't safe, you tell me, and I'll deal with it, not you," he was saying for the sixth time, when I finally realized that Sam had been scared for me.

I caught that rolling off him before I clamped down firmly on "hearing" Sam. Listening in to your boss led to disaster.

It had never occurred to me to ask Sam—or anyone else—for help.

"And if you think someone is being harmed in our parking lot, your next move is to call the police, not step out there yourself like a vigilante," Sam huffed. His fair complection, always ruddy, was redder than ever, and his wiry golden hair looked as if he hadn't combed it.

"Okay," I said, trying to keep my voice even and my eyes wide open so the tears wouldn't roll out. "Are you gonna fire me?"

"No! No!" he exclaimed, apparently even angrier. "I don't want to lose you!" He gripped my shoulders and gave me a little shake. Then he stood looking at me with wide, crackling blue eyes, and I felt a surge of heat rushing out from him. Touching accelerates my disability, makes it imperative that I hear the person touching. I stared right into his eyes for a long moment, then I remembered myself, and I jumped back as his hands dropped away.

I whirled and left the storeroom, spooked.

I'd learned a couple of disconcerting things. Sam desired me; and I couldn't hear his thoughts as clearly as I could other people's. I'd had waves of impressions of how he was feeling, but not thoughts. More like wearing a mood ring than getting a fax.

So, what did I do about either piece of information?

Absolutely nothing.

I'd never looked on Sam as a beddable man before—or at least not beddable by me—for a lot of reasons. But the simplest one was that I never looked at anyone that way, not because I don't have hormones—boy, do I have hormones—but they are constantly tamped down because sex, for me, is a disaster. Can you imagine knowing everything your sex partner is thinking? Right. Along the order of "Gosh, look at that mole . . . her butt is a little big . . . wish she'd move to the right a little . . . why doesn't she take the hint and . . . ?" You get the idea. It's chilling to the emotions, believe me. And during sex, there is simply no way to keep a mental guard up.

Another reason is that I like Sam for a boss, and I like my job, which gets me out and keeps me active and earning so I won't turn into the recluse my grandmother fears I'll become. Working in an office is hard for me, and college was simply impossible because of the grim concentration necessary. It just drained me.

So, right now, I wanted to mull over the rush of desire I'd felt from him. It wasn't like he'd made me a verbal proposition or thrown me down on the storeroom floor. I'd felt his feelings, and I could ignore them if I chose. I appreciated the delicacy of this, and wondered if Sam had touched me on purpose, if he actually knew what I was.

I took care not be alone with him, but I have to admit I was pretty shaken that night.

THE NEXT TWO nights were better. We fell back into our comfortable relationship. I was relieved. I was disappointed. I was also run off my feet since Maudette's murder sparked a business boom at Merlotte's. All sorts of rumors were buzzing around Bon Temps, and the Shreveport news team did a little piece on Maudette Picken's grisly death. Though I didn't attend her funeral, my grandmother did, and she said the church was jam-packed. Poor lumpy Maudette, with her bitten thighs, was more interesting in death than she'd ever been in life.

I was about to have two days off, and I was worried I'd miss connecting with the vampire, Bill. I needed to relay my grandmother's request. He hadn't returned to the bar, and I began to wonder if he would.

Mack and Denise hadn't been back in Merlotte's either, but Rene Lenier and Hoyt Fortenberry made sure I knew they'd threatened me with horrible things. I can't say I was seriously alarmed. Criminal trash like the Rats roamed the highways and trailer parks of America, not smart enough or moral enough to settle down to productive living. They never made a positive mark on the world, or amounted to a hill of beans, to my way of thinking. I shrugged off Rene's warnings.

But he sure enjoyed relaying them. Rene Lenier was small like Sam, but where Sam was ruddy and blond, Rene was swarthy and had a bushy headful of rough, black hair threaded with gray. Rene often came by the bar to drink a beer and visit with Arlene because (as he was fond of telling anyone in the bar) she was his favorite ex-wife. He had three. Hoyt Fortenberry was more of a cipher than Rene. He was neither dark nor fair, neither big nor little. He always seemed cheerful and always tipped decent. He admired my brother Jason far beyond what Jason deserved, in my opinion.

I was glad Rene and Hoyt weren't there the night the vampire returned.

He sat at the same table.

Now that the vampire was actually in front of me, I felt a little shy. I found I'd forgotten the almost imperceptible glow of his skin. I'd exaggerated his height and the clear-cut lines of his mouth.

"What can I get you?" I asked.

He looked up at me. I had forgotten, too, the depth of his eyes. He didn't smile or blink; he was so immobile. For the second time, I relaxed into his silence. When I let down my guard, I could feel my face relax. It was as good as getting a massage (I am guessing).

"What are you?" he asked me. It was the second time he'd wanted to know.

"I'm a waitress," I said, again deliberately misunderstanding him. I could feel my smile snap back into place again. My little bit of peace vanished.

"Red wine," he ordered, and if he was disappointed I couldn't tell by his voice.

"Sure," I said. "The synthetic blood should come in on the truck tomorrow. Listen, could I talk to you after work? I have a favor to ask you."

"Of course. I'm in your debt." And he sure didn't sound happy about it.

"Not a favor for me!" I was getting miffed myself. "For my grandmother. If you'll be up—well, I guess you will be—when I get off work at one-thirty, would you very much mind meeting me at the employee door at the back of the bar?" I nodded toward it, and my ponytail bounced around my shoulders. His eyes followed the movement of my hair.

"I'd be delighted."

I didn't know if he was displaying the courtesy Gran insisted was the standard in bygone times, or if he was plain old mocking me.

I resisted the temptation to stick out my tongue at him or blow a raspberry. I spun on my heel and marched back to the bar. When I brought him his wine, he tipped me 20 percent. Soon after that, I looked over at his table only to realize he'd vanished. I wondered if he'd keep his word.

Arlene and Dawn left before I was ready to go, for one reason and another; mostly because all the napkin holders in my area proved to be half-empty. As I retrieved my purse from the locked cabinet in Sam's office, where I stow it while I work, I called good-bye to my boss. I could hear him clanking around in the men's room, probably trying to fix the leaky toilet. I stepped into the ladies' room for a second to check my hair and makeup.

When I stepped outside I noticed that Sam had already switched off the customer parking lot lights. Only the security light on the electricity pole in front of his trailer illuminated the employee parking lot. To the amusement of Arlene and Dawn, Sam had put in a yard and planted boxwood in front of his trailer, and they were constantly teasing him about the neat line of his hedge.

I thought it was pretty.

As usual, Sam's truck was parked in front of his trailer, so my car was the only one left in the lot.

I stretched, looking from side to side. No Bill. I was surprised at how disappointed I was. I had really expected him to be courteous, even if his heart (did he have one?) wasn't in it.

Maybe, I thought with a smile, he'd jump out of a tree, or appear with a poof! in front of me draped in a red-lined black cape. But nothing happened. So I trudged over to my car.

I'd hoped for a surprise, but not the one I got.

Mack Rattray jumped out from behind my car and in one stride got close enough to clip me in the jaw. He didn't hold back one little bit, and I went down onto the gravel like a sack of cement. I let out a yell when I went down, but the ground knocked all the air out of me and some skin off of me, and I was silent and breathless and helpless. Then I saw Denise, saw her swing back her heavy boot, had just enough warning to roll into a ball before the Rattrays began kicking me.

The pain was immediate, intense, and unrelenting. I threw my arms over my face instinctively, taking the beating on my forearms, legs, and my back.

I think I was sure, during the first few blows, that they'd stop and hiss warnings and curses at me and leave. But I remember the exact moment I realized that they intended to kill me.

I could lie there passively and take a beating, but I would not lie there and be killed.

The next time a leg came close I lunged and grabbed it and held on for my life. I was trying to bite, trying to at least mark one of them. I wasn't even sure whose leg I had.

Then, from behind me, I heard a growl. Oh, no, they've brought a dog, I thought. The growl was definitely hostile. If I'd had any leeway with my emotions, the hair would have stood up on my scalp.

I took one more kick to the spine, and then the beating stopped.

The last kick had done something dreadful to me. I could hear my own breathing, stertorous, and a strange bubbling sound that seemed to be coming from my own lungs.

"What the hell is that?" Mack Rattray asked, and he sounded absolutely terrified.

I heard the growl again, closer, right behind me. And from another direction, I heard a sort of snarl. Denise began wailing, Mack was cursing. Denise yanked her leg from my grasp, which had grown very weak. My arms flopped to the ground. They seemed to be beyond my control. Though my vision was cloudy, I could see that my right arm was broken. My face felt wet. I was scared to continue evaluating my injuries.

Mack began screaming, and then Denise, and there seemed to be all kinds of activity going on around me, but I couldn't move. My only view was my broken arm and my battered knees and the darkness under my car.

Some time later there was silence. Behind me, the dog whined. A cold nose poked my ear, and a warm tongue licked it. I tried to raise my hand to pet the dog that had undoubtedly saved my life, but I couldn't. I could hear myself sigh. It seemed to come from a long way away.

Facing the fact, I said, "I'm dying." It began to seem more and more real to me. The toads and crickets that had been making the most of the night had fallen silent at all the activity and noise in the parking lot, so my little voice came out clearly and fell into the darkness. Oddly enough, soon after that I heard two voices.

Then a pair of knees covered in bloody blue jeans came into my view. The vampire Bill leaned over so I could look into his face. There was blood smeared on his mouth, and his fangs were out, glistening white against his lower lip. I tried to smile at him, but my face wasn't working right.

"I'm going to pick you up," Bill said. He sounded calm.

"I'll die if you do," I whispered.

He looked me over carefully. "Not just yet," he said, after this evaluation. Oddly enough, this made me feel better; no telling how many injuries he'd seen in his lifetime, I figured.

"This will hurt," he warned me.

It was hard to imagine anything that wouldn't.

His arms slid under me before I had time to get afraid. I screamed, but it was a weak effort.

"Quick," said a voice urgently.

"We're going back in the woods out of sight," Bill said, cradling my body to him as if it weighed nothing.

Was he going to bury me back there, out of sight? After he'd just rescued me from the Rats? I almost didn't care.

It was only a small relief when he laid me down on a carpet of pine needles in the darkness of the woods. In the distance, I could see the glow of the light in the parking lot. I felt my hair trickling blood, and I felt the pain of my broken arm and the agony of deep bruises, but what was most frightening was what I didn't feel.

I didn't feel my legs.

My abdomen felt full, heavy. The phrase "internal bleeding" lodged in my thoughts, such as they were.

"You will die unless you do as I say," Bill told me.

"Sorry, don't want to be a vampire," I said, and my voice was Weak and thready.

"No, you won't be," he said more gently. "You'll heal. Quickly. I have a cure. But you have to be willing."

"Then trot out the cure," I whispered. "I'm going." I could feel the pull the grayness was exerting on me.

In the little part of my mind that was still receiving signals from the world, I heard Bill grunt as if he'd been hurt. Then something was pressed up against my mouth.

"Drink," he said.

I tried to stick out my tongue, managed. He was bleeding, squeezing to encourage the flow of blood from his wrist into my mouth. I gagged. But I wanted to live. I forced myself to swallow. And swallow again.

Suddenly the blood tasted good, salty, the stuff of life. My unbroken arm rose, my hand clamped the vampire's wrist to my mouth. I felt better with every swallow. And after a minute, I drifted off to sleep.

When I woke up, I was still in the woods, still lying on the ground. Someone was stretched out beside me; it was the vampire. I could see his glow. I could feel his tongue moving on my head. He was licking my head wound. I could hardly begrudge him.

"Do I taste different from other people?" I asked.

"Yes," he said in a thick voice. "What are you?"

It was the third time he'd asked. Third time's the charm, Gran always said.

"Hey, I'm not dead," I said. I suddenly remembered I'd expected to check out for good. I wiggled my arm, the one that had been broken. It was weak, but it wasn't flopping any longer. I could feel my legs, and I wiggled them, too. I breathed in and out experimentally and was pleased with the resulting mild ache. I struggled to sit up. That proved to be quite an effort, but not an impossibility. It was like my first fever-free day after I'd had pneumonia as a kid. Feeble but blissful. I was aware I'd survived something awful.

Before I finished straightening, he'd put his arms under me and cradled me to him. He leaned back against a tree. I felt very comfortable sitting on his lap, my head against his chest.

"What I am, is telepathic," I said. "I can hear people's thoughts."

"Even mine?" He sounded merely curious.

"No. That's why I like you so much," I said, floating on a sea of pinkish well-being. I couldn't seem to be bothered with camouflaging my thoughts.

I felt his chest rumble as he laughed. The laugh was a little rusty. "I can't hear you at all," I blathered on, my voice dreamy. "You have no idea how peaceful that is. After a lifetime of blah, blah, blah, to hear . . . nothing."

"How do you manage going out with men? With men your age, their only thought is still surely how to get you into bed."

"Well, I don't. Manage. And frankly, at any age, I think their goal is get a woman in bed. I don't date. Everyone thinks I'm crazy, you know, because I can't tell them the truth; which is, that I'm driven crazy by all these thoughts, all these heads. I had a few dates when I started working at the bar, guys who hadn't heard about me. But it was the same as always. You can't concentrate on being comfortable with a guy, or getting a head of steam up, when you can hear they're wondering if you dye your hair, or thinking that your butt's not pretty, or imagining what your boobs look like."

Suddenly I felt more alert, and I realized how much of myself I was revealing to this creature.

"Excuse me," I said. "I didn't mean to burden you with my problems. Thank you for saving me from the Rats."

"It was my fault they had a chance to get you at all," he said. I could tell there was rage just under the calm surface of his voice. "If I had had the courtesy to be on time, it would not have happened. So I owed you some of my blood. I owed you the healing."

"Are they dead?" To my embarrassment, my voice sounded squeaky.

"Oh, yes."

I gulped. I couldn't regret that the world was rid of the Rats. But I had to look this straight in the face, I couldn't dodge the realization that I was sitting in the lap of a murderer. Yet I was quite happy to sit there, his arms around me.

"I should worry about this, but I'm not," I said, before I knew what I was going to say. I felt that rusty laugh again.

"Sookie, why did you want to talk to me tonight?"

I had to think back hard. Though I was miraculously recovered from the beating physically, I felt a little hazy mentally.

"My grandmother is real anxious to know how old you are," I said hesitantly. I didn't know how personal a question that was to a vampire. The vampire in question was stroking my back as though he were soothing a kitten.

"I was made vampire in 1870, when I was thirty human years old." I looked up; his glowing face was expressionless, his eyes pits of blackness in the dark woods.

"Did you fight in the War?"

"Yes."

"I have the feeling you're gonna get mad. But it would make her and her club so happy if you'd tell them a little bit about the War, about what it was really like."

"Club?"

"She belongs to Descendants of the Glorious Dead."

"Glorious dead." The vampire's voice was unreadable, but I could tell, sure enough, he wasn't happy.

"Listen, you wouldn't have to tell them about the maggots and the infections and the starvation," I said. "They have their own picture of the War, and though they're not stupid people—they've lived through other wars—they would like to know more about the way people lived then, and uniforms and troop movements."

"Clean things."

I took a deep breath. "Yep."

"Would it make you happy if I did this?"

"What difference does that make? It would make Gran happy, and since you're in Bon Temps and seem to want to live around here, it would be a good public relations move for you."

"Would it make you happy?"

He was not a guy you could evade. "Well, yes."

"Then I'll do it."

"Gran says to please eat before you come," I said.

Again I heard the rumbling laugh, deeper this time.

"I'm looking forward to meeting her now. Can I call on you some night?"

"Ah. Sure. I work my last night tomorrow night, and the day after I'm off for two days, so Thursday would be a good night." I lifted my arm to look at my watch. It was running, but the glass was covered with dried blood. "Oh, yuck," I said, wetting my finger in my mouth and cleaning the watch face off with spit. I pressed the button that illuminated the hands, and gasped when I saw what time it was.

"Oh, gosh, I got to get home. I hope Gran went to sleep."

"She must worry about you being out so late at night by yourself," Bill observed. He sounded disapproving. Maybe he was thinking of Maudette? I had a moment of deep unease, wondering if in fact Bill had known her, if she'd invited him to come home with her. But I rejected the idea because I was stubbornly unwilling to dwell on the odd, awful, nature of Maudette's life and death; I didn't want that horror to cast a shadow on my little bit of happiness.

"It's part of my job," I said tartly. "Can't be helped. I don't work nights all the time, anyway. But when I can, I do."

"Why?" The vampire gave me a shove up to my feet, and then he rose easily from the ground.

"Better tips. Harder work. No time to think."

"But night is more dangerous," he said disapprovingly.

He ought to know. "Now don't you go sounding like my grandmother," I chided him mildly. We had almost reached the parking lot.

"I'm older than your grandmother," he reminded me. That brought the conversation up short.

After I stepped out of the woods, I stood staring. The parking lot was as serene and untouched as if nothing had ever happened there, as if I hadn't been nearly beaten to death on that patch of gravel only an hour before, as if the Rats hadn't met their bloody end.

The lights in the bar and in Sam's trailer were off.

The gravel was wet, but not bloody.

My purse was sitting on the hood of my car.

"And what about the dog?" I said.

I turned to look at my savior.

He wasn't there.

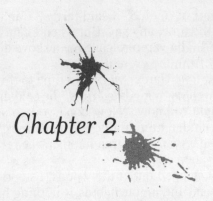

Chapter 2

I GOT UP very late the next morning, which was not too surprising. Gran had been asleep when I got home, to my relief, and I was able to climb into my bed without waking her.

I WAS DRINKING a cup of coffee at the kitchen table and Gran was cleaning out the pantry when the phone rang. Gran eased her bottom up onto the stool by the counter, her normal chatting perch, to answer it.

"*Hel*-lo," she said. For some reason, she always sounded put out, as if a phone call were the last thing on earth she wanted. I knew for a fact that wasn't the case.

"Hey, Everlee. No, sitting here talking to Sookie, she just got up. No, I haven't heard any news today. No, no one called me yet. What? What tornado? Last night was clear. Four Tracks Corner? It did? No! No, it did not! Really? Both of 'em? Um, um, um. What did Mike Spencer say?"

Mike Spencer was our parish coroner. I began to have a creepy feeling. I finished my coffee and poured myself another cup. I thought I was going to need it.

Gran hung up a minute later. "Sookie, you are not going to believe what has happened!"

I was willing to bet I would believe it.

"What?" I asked, trying not to look guilty.

"No matter how smooth the weather looked last night, a tornado must have touched down at Four Tracks Corner! It turned over that rent trailer in the clearing there. The couple that was staying in it, they both got killed, trapped under the trailer somehow and crushed to a pulp. Mike says he hasn't seen anything like it."

"Is he sending the bodies for autopsy?"

"Well, I think he has to, though the cause of death seems clear enough, according to Stella. The trailer is over on its side, their car is halfway on top of it, and trees are pulled up in the yard."

"My God," I whispered, thinking of the strength necessary to accomplish the staging of that scene.

"Honey, you didn't tell me if your friend the vampire came in last night?"

I jumped in a guilty way until I realized that in Gran's mind, she'd changed subjects. She'd been asking me if I'd seen Bill every day, and now, at last, I could tell her yes—but not with a light heart.

Predictably, Gran was excited out of her gourd. She fluttered around the kitchen as if Prince Charles were the expected guest.

"Tomorrow night. Now what time's he coming?" she asked.

"After dark. That's as close as I can get."

"We're on daylight saving time, so that'll be pretty late." Gran considered. "Good, we'll have time to eat supper and clear it away beforehand. And we'll have all day tomorrow to clean the house. I haven't cleaned that area rug in a year, I bet!"

"Gran, we're talking about a guy who sleeps in the ground all day," I reminded her. "I don't think he'd ever look at the rug."

"Well, if I'm not doing it for him, then I'm doing it for me, so I can feel proud," Gran said unanswerably. "Besides, young lady, how do you know where he sleeps?"

"Good question, Gran. I don't. But he has to keep out of the light and he has to keep safe, so that's my guess."

Nothing would prevent my grandmother from going into a house-proud frenzy, I realized very shortly. While I was getting ready for work, she went to the grocery and rented a rug cleaner and set to cleaning.

On my way to Merlotte's, I detoured north a bit and drove by the Four Tracks Corner. It was a crossroads as old as human habitation of the area. Now formalized by road signs and pavement, local lore said it was the intersection of two hunting trails. Sooner or later, there would be ranch-style houses and strip malls lining the roads, I guessed, but for now it was woods and the hunting was still good, according to Jason.

Since there was nothing to prevent me, I drove down the rutted path that led to the clearing where the Rattrays' rented trailer had stood. I stopped my car and stared out the windshield, appalled. The trailer, a very small and old one, lay crushed ten feet behind its original location. The Rattrays' dented red car was still resting on one end of the accordian-pleated mobile home. Bushes and debris were littered around the clearing, and the woods behind the trailer showed signs of a great force passing through; branches snapped off, the top of one pine hanging down by a thread of bark. There were clothes up in the branches, and even a roast pan.

I got out slowly and looked around me. The damage was simply incredible, especially since I knew it hadn't been caused by a tornado; Bill the vampire had staged this scene to account for the deaths of the Rattrays.

An old Jeep bumped its way down the ruts to come to a stop by me.

"Well, Sookie Stackhouse!" called Mike Spencer, "What you doing here, girl? Ain't you got work to go to?"

"Yes, sir. I knew the Rat—the Rattrays. This is just an awful thing." I thought that was sufficiently ambiguous. I could see now that the sheriff was with Mike.

"An awful thing. Yes, well. I did hear," Sheriff Bud Dearborn said as climbed down out of the Jeep, "that you and Mack and Denise didn't exactly see eye to eye in the parking lot of Merlotte's, last week."

I felt a cold chill somewhere around the region of my liver as the two men ranged themselves in front of me.

Mike Spencer was the funeral director of one of Bon Temps' two funeral homes. As Mike was always quick and definite in pointing out, anyone who wanted could be buried by Spencer and Sons Funeral Home; but only white people seemed to want to. Likewise, only people of color chose to be buried at Sweet Rest. Mike himself was a heavy middle-aged man with hair and mustache the color of weak tea, and a fondness for cowboy boots and string ties that he could not wear when he was on duty at Spencer and Sons. He was wearing them now.

Sheriff Dearborn, who had the reputation of being a good man, was a little older than Mike, but fit and tough from his thick gray hair to his heavy shoes. The sheriff had a mashed-in face and quick brown eyes. He had been a good friend of my father's.

"Yes, sir, we had us a disagreement," I said frankly in my downhomiest voice.

"You want to tell me about it?" The sheriff pulled out a Marlboro and lit it with a plain, metal lighter.

And I made a mistake. I should have just told him. I was supposed to be crazy, and some thought me simple, too. But for the life of me, I could see no reason to explain myself to Bud Dearborn. No reason, except good sense.

"Why?" I asked.

His small brown eyes were suddenly sharp, and the amiable air vanished.

"Sookie," he said, with a world of disappointment in his voice. I didn't believe in it for a minute.

"I didn't do this," I said, waving my hand at the destruction.

"No, you didn't," he agreed. "But just the same, they die the week after they have a fight with someone, I feel I should ask questions."

I was reconsidering staring him down. It would feel good, but I didn't think feeling good was worth it. It was becoming apparent to me that a reputation for simplicity could be handy.

I may be uneducated and unworldly, but I'm not stupid or unread.

"Well, they were hurting my friend," I confessed, hanging my head and eyeing my shoes.

"Would that be this vampire that's living at the old Compton house?" Mike Spencer and Bud Dearborn exchanged glances.

"Yes, sir." I was surprised to hear where Bill was living, but they didn't know that. From years of deliberately not reacting to things I heard that I didn't want to know, I have good facial control. The old Compton house was right across the fields from us, on the same side of the road. Between our houses lay only the woods and the cemetery. How handy for Bill, I thought, and smiled.

"Sookie Stackhouse, your granny is letting you associate with that vampire?" Spencer said unwisely.

"You can sure talk to her about that," I suggested maliciously, hardly able to wait to hear what Gran would say when someone suggested she wasn't taking care of me. "You know, the Rattrays were trying to drain Bill."

"So the vampire was being drained by the Rattrays? And you stopped them?" interrupted the sheriff.

"Yes," I said and tried to look resolute.

"Vampire draining *is* illegal," he mused.

"Isn't it murder, to kill a vampire that hasn't attacked you?" I asked.

I may have pushed the naivete a little too hard.

"You know damn good and well it is, though I don't agree with that law. It is a law, and I will uphold it," the sheriff said stiffly.

"So the vampire just let them leave, without threatening vengeance? Saying anything like he wished they were dead?" Mike Spencer was being stupid.

"That's right." I smiled at both of them and then looked at my watch. I remembered the blood on its face, my blood, beaten out of me by the Rattrays. I had to look through that blood to read the time.

"Excuse me, I have to get to work," I said. "Good-bye, Mr. Spencer, Sheriff."

"Good-bye, Sookie," Sheriff Dearborn said. He looked like he had more to ask me, but couldn't think of how to put it. I could tell he wasn't totally happy with the look of the scene, and I doubted any tornado had shown up on radar anywhere. Nonetheless, there was the trailer, there was the car, there were the trees, and the Rattrays had been dead under them. What could you decide but that the tornado had killed them? I guessed the bodies had been sent for an autopsy, and I wondered how much could be told by such a procedure under the circumstances.

The human mind is an amazing thing. Sheriff Dearborn must have known that vampires are very strong. But he just couldn't imagine how strong one could be: strong enough to turn over a trailor, crush it. It was even hard for me to comprehend, and I knew good and well that no tornado had touched down at Four Corners.

The whole bar was humming with the news of the deaths. Maudette's murder had taken a backseat to Denise and Mack's demises. I caught Sam eyeing me a couple of times, and I thought about the night before and wondered how much he knew. But I was scared to ask in case he hadn't seen anything. I knew there were things that had happened the night before that I hadn't yet explained to my own satisfaction, but I was so grateful to be alive that I put off thinking of them.

I'd never smiled so hard while I toted drinks, I'd never made change so briskly, I'd never gotten orders so exactly. Even ol' bushy-haired Rene didn't slow me down, though he insisted on dragging me into his long-winded conversations every time I came near the table he was sharing with Hoyt and a couple of other cronies.

Rene played the role of crazy Cajun some of the time, though any Cajun accent he might assume was faked. His folks had let their heritage fade. Every woman he'd married had been hard-living and wild. His brief hitch with Arlene had been when she was young and childless, and she'd told me that from time to time she'd done things then that curled her hair to think about now. She'd grown up since then, but Rene hadn't. Arlene was sure fond of him, to my amazement.

Everyone in the bar was excited that night because of the unusual happenings in Bon Temps. A woman had been murdered, and it was a mystery; usually murders in Bon Temps are easily solved. And a couple had died violently by a freak of nature. I attributed what happened next to that excitement. This is a neighborhood bar, with a few out of towners who pass through on a regular basis, and I've never had much problem with unwanted attention. But that night one of the men at a table next to Rene and Hoyt's, a heavy blond man with a broad, red face, slid his hand up the leg of my shorts when I was bringing their beer.

That doesn't fly at Merlotte's.

I thought of bringing the tray down on his head when I felt the hand removed. I felt someone standing right behind me. I turned my head and saw Rene, who had left his chair without my even realizing it. I followed his arm down and saw that his hand was gripping the blond's and squeezing. The blond's red face was turning a mottled mixture.

"Hey, man, let go!" the blond protested. "I didn't mean nothing."

"You don't touch anyone who works here. That's the rule." Rene might be short and slim, but anyone there would have put his money on our local boy over the beefier visitor.

"Okay, okay."

"Apologize to the lady."

"To Crazy Sookie?" His voice was incredulous. He must have been here before.

Rene's hand must have tightened. I saw tears spring into the blond's eyes.

"I'm sorry, Sookie, okay?"

I nodded as regally as I could. Rene let go of the man's hand abruptly and jerked his thumb to tell the guy to take a hike. The blond lost no time throwing himself out the door. His companion followed.

"Rene, you should have let me handle that myself," I said to him very quietly when it seemed the patrons had resumed their conversations. We'd given the gossip mill enough grist for at least a couple of days. "But I appreciate you standing up for me."

"I don't want no one messing with Arlene's friend," Rene said matter-of-factly. "Merlotte's is a nice place, we all want to keep it nice. 'Sides, sometimes you remind me of Cindy, you know?"

Cindy was Rene's sister. She'd moved to Baton Rouge a year or two ago. Cindy was blond and blue-eyed: beyond that I couldn't think of a similarity. But it didn't seem polite to say so. "You see Cindy much?" I asked. Hoyt and the other man at the table were exchanging Shreveport Captains scores and statistics.

"Every so now and then," Rene said, shaking his head as if to say he'd like it to be more often. "She works in a hospital cafeteria."

I patted him on the shoulder. "I gotta go work."

When I reached the bar to get my next order, Sam raised his eyebrows at me. I widened my eyes to show how amazed I was at Rene's intervention, and Sam shrugged slightly, as if to say there was no accounting for human behavior.

But when I went behind the bar to get some more napkins, I noticed he'd pulled out the baseball bat he kept below the till for emergencies.

GRAN KEPT ME busy all the next day. She dusted and vacuumed and mopped, and I scrubbed the bathrooms—did vampires even need to use the bathroom? I wondered, as I chugged the toilet brush around the bowl. Gran had me vacuum the cat hair off the sofa. I emptied all the trash cans. I polished all the tables. I wiped down the washer and the dryer, for goodness's sake.

When Gran urged me to get in the shower and change my clothes, I realized that she regarded Bill the vampire as my date. That made me feel a little odd. One, Gran was so desperate for me to have a social life that even a vampire was eligible for my attention; two, that I had some feelings that backed up that idea; three, that Bill might accurately read all this; four, could vampires even do it like humans?

I showered and put on my makeup and wore a dress, since I knew Gran would have a fit if I didn't. It was a little blue cotton-knit dress with tiny daisies all over it, and it was tighter than Gran liked and shorter than Jason deemed proper in his sister. I'd heard that the first time I'd worn it. I put my little yellow ball earrings in and wore my hair pulled up and back with a yellow banana clip holding it loosely.

Gran gave me one odd look, which I was at a loss to interpret. I could have found out easily enough by listening in, but that was a terrible thing to do to the person you lived with, so I was careful not to. She herself was wearing a skirt and blouse that she often wore to the Descendants of the Glorious Dead meetings, not quite good enough for church, but not plain enough for everyday wear.

I was sweeping the front porch, which we'd forgotten, when he came. He made a vampire entrance; one minute he wasn't there, and the next he was, standing at the bottom of the steps and looking up at me.

I grinned. "Didn't scare me," I said.

He looked a little embarrassed. "It's just a habit," he said, "appearing like that. I don't make much noise."

I opened the door. "Come on in," I invited, and he came up the steps, looking around.

"I remember this," he said. "It wasn't so big, though."

"You remember this house? Gran's gonna love it." I preceded him into the living room, calling Gran as I went.

She came into the living room very much on her dignity, and I realized for the first time she'd taken great pains with her thick white hair, which was smooth and orderly for a change, wrapped around her head in a complicated coil. She had on lipstick, too.

Bill proved as adept at social tactics as my grandmother. They greeted, thanked each other, complimented, and finally Bill ended up sitting on the couch and, after carrying out a tray with three glasses of peach tea, my Gran sat in the easy chair, making it clear I was to perch by Bill. There was no way to get out of this without being even more obvious, so I sat by him, but scooted forward to the edge, as if I might hop up at any moment to get him a refill on his, the ritual glass of iced tea.

He politely touched his lips to the edge of the glass and then set it down. Gran and I took big nervous swallows of ours.

Gran picked an unfortunate opening topic. She said, "I guess you heard about the strange tornado."

"Tell me," Bill said, his cool voice as smooth as silk. I didn't dare look at him, but sat with my hands folded and my eyes fixed to them.

So Gran told him about the freak tornado and the deaths of the Rats. She told him the whole thing seemed pretty awful, but cut-and-dried, and at that I thought Bill relaxed just a millimeter.

"I went by yesterday on my way to work," I said, without raising my gaze. "By the trailer."

"Did you find it looked as you expected?" Bill asked, only curiosity in his voice.

"No," I said. "It wasn't anything I could have expected. I was really . . . amazed."

"Sookie, you've seen tornado damage before," Gran said, surprised.

I changed the subject. "Bill, where'd you get your shirt? It looks nice." He was wearing khaki Dockers and a green-and-brown striped golfing shirt, polished loafers, and thin, brown socks.

"Dillard's," he said, and I tried to imagine him at the mall in Monroe, perhaps, other people turning to look at this exotic creature with his glowing skin and beautiful eyes. Where would he get the money to pay with? How did he wash his clothes? Did he go into his coffin naked? Did he have a car or did he just float wherever he wanted to go?

Gran was pleased with the normality of Bill's shopping habits. It gave me another pang of pain, observing how glad she was to see my supposed suitor in her living room, even if (according to popular literature) he was a victim of a virus that made him seem dead.

Gran plunged into questioning Bill. He answered her with courtesy and apparent goodwill. Okay, he was a *polite* dead man.

"And your people were from this area?" Gran inquired.

"My father's people were Comptons, my mother's people Loudermilks," Bill said readily. He seemed quite relaxed.

"There are lots of Loudermilks left," Gran said happily. "But I'm afraid old Mr. Jessie Compton died last year."

"I know," Bill said easily. "That's why I came back. The land reverted to me, and since things have changed in our culture toward people of my particular persuasion, I decided to claim it."

"Did you know the Stackhouses? Sookie says you have a long history." I thought Gran had put it well. I smiled at my hands.

"I remember Jonas Stackhouse," Bill said, to Gran's delight. "My folks were here when Bon Temps was just a hole in the road at the edge of the frontier. Jonas Stackhouse moved here with his wife and his four children when I was a young man of sixteen. Isn't this the house he built, at least in part?"

I noticed that when Bill was thinking of the past, his voice took on a different cadence and vocabulary. I wondered how many changes in slang and tone his English had taken on through the past century.

Of course, Gran was in genealogical hog heaven. She wanted to know all about Jonas, her husband's great-great-great-great-grandfather. "Did he own slaves?" she asked.

"Ma'am, if I remember correctly, he had a house slave and a yard slave. The house slave was a woman of middle age and the yard slave a very big young man, very strong, named Minas. But the Stackhouses mostly worked their own fields, as did my folks."

"Oh, that is exactly the kind of thing my little group would love to hear! Did Sookie tell you . . ." Gran and Bill, after much polite dosi-doing, set a date for Bill to address a night meeting of the Descendants.

"And now, if you'll excuse Sookie and me, maybe we'll take a walk. It's a lovely night." Slowly, so I could see it coming, he reached over and took my hand, rising and pulling me to my feet, too. His hand was cold and hard and smooth. Bill wasn't quite asking Gran's permission, but not quite not, either.

"Oh, you two go on," my grandmother said, fluttering with happiness. "I have so many things to look up. You'll have to tell me all the local names you remember from when you were . . ." and here Gran ran down, not wanting to say something wounding.

"Resident here in Bon Temps," I supplied helpfully.

"Of course," the vampire said, and I could tell from the compression of his lips that he was trying not to smile.

Somehow we were at the door, and I knew that Bill had lifted me and moved me quickly. I smiled, genuinely. I like the unexpected.

"We'll be back in a while," I said to Gran. I didn't think she'd noticed my odd transition, since she was gathering up our tea glasses.

"Oh, you two don't hurry on my account," she said. "I'll be just fine."

Outside, the frogs and toads and bugs were singing their nightly rural opera. Bill kept my hand as we strolled out into the yard, full of the smell of new-mown grass and budding things. My cat, Tina, came out of the shadows and asked to be tickled, and I bent over and scratched her head. To my surprise, the cat rubbed against Bill's legs, an activity he did nothing to discourage.

"You like this animal?" he asked, his voice neutral.

"It's my cat," I said. "Her name is Tina, and I like her a lot."

Without comment, Bill stood still, waiting until Tina went on her way into the darkness outside the porch light.

"Would you like to sit in the swing or the lawn chairs, or would you like to walk?" I asked, since I felt I was now the hostess.

"Oh, let's walk for a while. I need to stretch my legs."

Somehow this statement unsettled me a little, but I began moving down the long driveway in the direction of the two-lane parish road that ran in front of both our homes.

"Did the trailer upset you?"

I tried to think how to put it.

"I feel very . . . hmmm. Fragile. When I think about the trailer."

"You knew I was strong."

I tilted my head from side to side, considering. "Yes, but I didn't realize the full extent of your strength," I told him. "Or your imagination."

"Over the years, we get good at hiding what we've done."

"So. I guess you've killed a bunch of people."

"Some." Deal with it, his voice implied.

I clasped both hands behind my back. "Were you hungrier right after you became a vampire? How did that happen?"

He hadn't expected that. He looked at me. I could feel his eyes on me even though we were now in the dark. The woods were close around us. Our feet crunched on the gravel.

"As to how I became a vampire, that's too long a story for now," he said. "But yes, when I was younger—a few times—I killed by accident. I was never sure when I'd get to eat again, you understand? We were always hunted, naturally, and there was no such thing as artificial blood. And there were not as many people then. But I had been a good man when I was alive—I mean, before I caught the virus. So I tried to be civilized about it, select bad people as my victims, never feed on children. I managed never to kill a child, at least. It's so different now. I can go to the all-night clinic in any city and get some synthetic blood, though it's disgusting. Or I can pay a whore and get enough blood to keep going for a couple of days. Or I can glamor someone, so they'll let me bite them for love and then forget all about it. And I don't need so much now."

"Or you can meet a girl who gets head injuries," I said.

"Oh, you were the dessert. The Rattrays were the meal."

Deal with it.

"Whoa," I said, feeling breathless. "Give me a minute."

And he did. Not one man in a million would have allowed me that time without speaking. I opened my mind, let my guards down completely, relaxed. His silence washed over me. I stood, closed my eyes, breathed out the relief that was too profound for words.

"Are you happy now?" he asked, just as if he could tell.

"Yes," I breathed. At that moment I felt that no matter what this creature beside me had done, this peace was priceless after a lifetime of the yammering of other minds inside my own.

"You feel good to me, too," he said, surprising me.

"How so?" I asked, dreamy and slow.

"No fear, no hurry, no condemnation. I don't have to use my glamor to make you hold still, to have a conversation with you."

"Glamor?"

"Like hypnotism," he explained. "All vampires use it, to some extent or another. Because to feed, until the new synthetic blood was developed, we had to persuade people we were harmless . . . or assure them they hadn't seen us at all . . . or delude them into thinking they'd seen something else."

"Does it work on me?"

"Of course," he said, sounding shocked.

"Okay, do it."

"Look at me."

"It's dark."

"No matter. Look at my face." And he stepped in front of me, his hands resting lightly on my shoulders, and looked down at me. I could see the faint shine of his skin and eyes, and I peered up at him, wondering if I'd begin to squawk like a chicken or take my clothes off.

But what happened was . . . nothing. I felt only the nearly drug-like relaxation of being with him.

"Can you feel my influence?" he asked. He sounded a little breathless.

"Not a bit, I'm sorry," I said humbly. "I just see you glow."

"You can see that?" I'd surprised him again.

"Sure. Can't everyone?"

"No. This is strange, Sookie."

"If you say so. Can I see you levitate?"

"Right here?" Bill sounded amused.

"Sure, why not? Unless there's a reason?"

"No, none at all." And he let go of my arms and began to rise.

I breathed a sigh of pure rapture. He floated up in the dark, gleaming like white marble in the moonlight. When he was about two feet off the ground, he began hovering. I thought he was smiling down at me.

"Can all of you do that?" I asked.

"Can you sing?"

"Nope, can't carry a tune."

"Well, we can't all do the same things, either." Bill came down slowly and landed on the ground without a thump. "Most humans are squeamish about vampires. You don't seem to be," he commented.

I shrugged. Who was I to be squeamish about something out of the ordinary? He seemed to understand because, after a pause, during which we'd resumed walking, Bill said, "Has it always been hard for you?"

"Yes, always." I couldn't say otherwise, though I didn't want to whine. "When I was very small, that was worst, because I didn't know how to put up my guard, and I heard thoughts I wasn't supposed to hear, of course, and I repeated them like a child will. My parents didn't know what to do about me. It embarrassed my father, in particular. My mother finally took me to a child psychologist, who knew exactly what I was, but she just couldn't accept it and kept trying to tell my folks I was reading their body language and was very observant, so I had good reason to imagine I heard people's thoughts. Of course, she couldn't admit I was literally *hearing people's thoughts* because that just didn't fit into her world.

"And I did poorly in school because it was so hard for me to concentrate when so few others were. But when there was testing, I would test very high because the other kids were concentrating on their own papers . . . that gave me a little leeway. Sometimes my folks thought I was lazy for not doing well on everyday work. Sometimes the teachers thought I had a learning disability; oh, you wouldn't believe the theories. I must have had my eyes and ears tested every two months, seemed like, and brain scans . . . gosh. My poor folks paid through the nose. But they never could accept the simple truth. At least outwardly, you know?"

"But they knew inside."

"Yes. Once, when my dad was trying to decide whether to back a man who wanted to open an auto parts store, he asked me to sit with him when the man came to the house. After the man left, my dad took me outside and looked away and said, 'Sookie, is he telling the truth?' It was the strangest moment."

"How old were you?"

"I must've been less than seven 'cause they died when I was in the second grade."

"How?"

"Flash flood. Caught them on the bridge west of here."

Bill didn't comment. Of course, he'd seen deaths piled upon deaths.

"Was the man lying?" he asked after a few seconds had gone by.

"Oh, yes. He planned to take Daddy's money and run."

"You have a gift."

"Gift. Right." I could feel the corners of my mouth pull down.

"It makes you different from other humans."

"You're telling me." We walked for a moment in silence. "So you don't consider yourself human at all?"

"I haven't for a long time."

"Do you really believe you've lost your soul?" That was what the Catholic Church was preaching about vampires.

"I have no way of knowing," Bill said, almost casually. It was apparent that he'd brooded over it so often it was quite a commonplace thought to him. "Personally, I think not. There is something in me that isn't cruel, not murderous, even after all these years. Though I can be both."

"It's not your fault you were infected with a virus."

Bill snorted, even managing to sound elegant doing that. "There have been theories as long as there have been vampires. Maybe that one is true." Then he looked as if he was sorry he'd said that. "If what makes a vampire is a virus," he went on in a more offhand manner, "it's a selective one."

"How do you become a vampire?" I'd read all kinds of stuff, but this would be straight from the horse's mouth.

"I would have to drain you, at one sitting or over two or three days, to the point of your death, then give you my blood. You would lie like a corpse for about forty-eight hours, sometimes as long as three days, then rise and walk at night. And you would be hungry."

The way he said "hungry" made me shiver.

"No other way?"

"Other vampires have told me humans they habitually bite, day after day, can become vampires quite unexpectedly. But that requires consecutive, deep, feedings. Others, under the same conditions, merely become anemic. Then again, when people are near to death for some other reason, a car accident or a drug overdose, perhaps, the process can go . . . badly wrong."

I was getting the creepies. "Time to change the subject. What do you plan on doing with the Compton land?"

"I plan on living there, as long as I can. I'm tired of drifting from city to city. I grew up in the country. Now that I have a legal right to exist, and I can go to Monroe or Shreveport or New Orleans for synthetic blood or prostitutes who specialize in our kind, I want to stay here. At least see if it's possible. I've been roaming for decades."

"What kind of shape is the house in?"

"Pretty bad," he admitted. "I've been trying to clean it out. That I can do at night. But I need workmen to get some repairs done. I'm not bad at carpentry, but I don't know a thing about electricity."

Of course, he wouldn't.

"It seems to me the house may need rewiring," Bill continued, sounding for all the world like any other anxious homeowner.

"Do you have a phone?"

"Sure," he said, surprised.

"So what's the problem with the workmen?"

"It's hard to get in touch with them at night, hard to get them to meet with me so I can explain what needs doing. They're scared, or they think it's a prank call." Frustration was evident in Bill's voice, though his face was turned away from me.

I laughed. "If you want, I'll call them," I offered. "They know me. Even though everyone thinks I'm crazy, they know I'm honest."

"That would be a great favor," Bill said, after some hesitation. "They could work during the day, after I'd met with them to discuss the job and the cost."

"What an inconvenience, not being able to get out in the day," I said thoughtlessly. I'd never really considered it before.

Bill's voice was dry. "It certainly is."

"And having to hide your resting place," I blundered on.

When I felt the quality of Bill's silence, I apologized.

"I'm sorry," I said. If it hadn't been so dark, he would have seen me turn red.

"A vampire's daytime resting place is his most closely guarded secret," Bill said stiffly.

"I apologize."

"I accept," he said, after a bad little moment. We reached the road and looked up and down it as if we expected a taxi. I could see him clearly by the moonlight, now that we were out of the trees. He could see me, too. He looked me up and down.

"Your dress is the color of your eyes."

"Thank you." I sure couldn't see him *that* clearly.

"Not a lot of it, though."

"Excuse me?"

"It's hard for me to get used to young ladies with so few clothes on," Bill said.

"You've had a few decades to get used to it," I said tartly. "Come on, Bill! Dresses have been short for forty years now!"

"I liked long skirts," he said nostalgically. "I liked the underthings women wore. The petticoats."

I made a rude noise.

"Do you even have a petticoat?" he asked.

"I have a very pretty beige nylon slip with lace," I said indignantly. "If you were a human guy, I'd say you were angling for me to talk about my underwear!"

He laughed, that deep, unused chuckle that affected me so strongly. "Do you have that slip on, Sookie?"

I stuck out my tongue at him because I knew he could see me. I edged the skirt of my dress up, revealing the lace of the slip and a couple more inches of tanned me.

"Happy?" I asked.

"You have pretty legs, but I still like long dresses better."

"You're stubborn," I told him.

"That's what my wife always told me."

"You were married."

"Yes, I became a vampire when I was thirty. I had a wife, and I had five living children. My sister, Sarah, lived with us. She never wed. Her young man was killed in the war."

"The Civil War."

"Yes. I came back from the battlefield. I was one of the lucky ones. At least I thought so at the time."

"You fought for the Confederacy," I said wonderingly. "If you still had your uniform and wore it to the club, the ladies would faint with joy."

"I hadn't much of a uniform by the end of the war," he said grimly. "We were in rags and starving." He seemed to shake himself. "It had no meaning for me after I became vampire," Bill said, his voice once again chilly and remote.

"I've brought up something that upset you," I said. "I am sorry. What should we talk about?" We turned and began to stroll back down the driveway toward the house.

"Your life," he said. "Tell me what you do when you get up in the morning."

"I get out of bed. Then I make it up right away. I eat breakfast. Toast, sometimes cereal, sometimes eggs, and coffee—and I brush my teeth and shower and dress. Sometimes I shave my legs, you know. If it's a workday, I go in to work. If I don't go in until night, I might go shopping, or take Gran to the store, or rent a movie to watch, or sunbathe. And I read a lot. I'm lucky Gran is still spry. She does the wash and the ironing and most of the cooking."

"What about young men?"

"Oh, I told you about that. It's just impossible."

"So what will you do, Sookie?" he asked gently.

"Grow old and die." My voice was short. He'd touched on my sensitive area once too often.

To my surprise, Bill reached over and took my hand. Now that we'd made each other a little angry, touched some sore spots, the air seemed somehow clearer. In the quiet night, a breeze wafted my hair around my face.

"Take the clip out?" Bill asked.

No reason not to. I reclaimed my hand and reached up to open the clip. I shook my head to loosen my hair. I stuck the clip in his pocket, since I hadn't any. As if it was the most normal thing in the world, Bill began running his fingers through my hair, spreading it out on my shoulders.

I touched his sideburns, since apparently touching was okay. "They're long," I observed.

"That was the fashion," he said. "It's lucky for me I didn't wear a beard as so many men did, or I'd have it for eternity."

"You never have to shave?"

"No, luckily I had just shaven." He seemed fascinated with my hair. "In the moonlight, it looks silver," he said very quietly.

"Ah. What do you like to do?"

I could see a shadow of a smile in the darkness.

"I like to read, too." He thought. "I like the movies . . . of course, I've followed their whole inception. I like the company of people who lead ordinary lives. Sometimes I crave the company of other vampires, though most of them lead very different lives from mine."

We walked in silence for a moment.

"Do you like television?"

"Sometimes," he confessed. "For a while I taped soap operas and watched them at night when I thought I might be forgetting what it was like to be human. After a while I stopped, because from the examples I saw on those shows, forgetting humanity was a good thing." I laughed.

We walked into the circle of light around the house. I had half-expected Gran to be on the porch swing waiting for us, but she wasn't. And only one dim bulb glowed in the living room. Really, Gran, I thought, exasperated. This was just like being brought home from a first date by a new man. I actually caught myself wondering if Bill would try to kiss me or not. With his views on long dresses, he would probably think it was out of line. But as stupid as kissing a vampire might seem, I realized that was what I really wanted to do, more than anything.

I got a tight feeling in my chest, a bitterness, at another thing I was denied. And I thought, Why not?

I stopped him by pulling gently on his hand. I stretched up and lay my lips on his shining cheek. I inhaled the scent of him, ordinary but faintly salty. He was wearing a trace of cologne.

I felt him shudder. He turned his head so his lips touched mine. After a moment, I reached to circle his neck with my arms. His kiss deepened, and I parted my lips. I'd never been kissed like this. It went on and on until I thought the whole world was involved in this kiss in the vampire's mouth on mine. I could feel my breathing speeding up, and I began to want other things to happen.

Suddenly Bill pulled back. He looked shaken, which pleased me no end. "Good night, Sookie," he said, stroking my hair one last time.

"Good night, Bill," I said. I sounded pretty quavery myself. "I'll try to call some electricians tomorrow. I'll let you know what they say."

"Come by the house tomorrow night—if you're off work?"

"Yes," I said. I was still trying to gather myself.

"See you then. Thanks, Sookie." And he turned away to walk

through the woods back over to his place. Once he reached the darkness, he was invisible.

I stood staring like a fool, until I shook myself and went inside to go to bed.

I spent an indecent amount of time lying awake in bed wondering if the undead could actually do—it. Also, I wondered if it would be possible to have a frank discussion with Bill about that. Sometimes he seemed very old-fashioned, sometimes he seemed as normal as the guy next door. Well, not really, but pretty normal.

It seemed both wonderful and pathetic to me that the one creature I'd met in years that I'd want to have sex with was actually not human. My telepathy limited my options severely. I could have had sex just to have it, sure; but I had waited to have sex I could actually enjoy.

What if we did it, and after all these years I discovered I had no talent for it? Or maybe it wouldn't feel good. Maybe all the books and movies exaggerated. Arlene, too, who never seemed to understand that her sex life was not something I wanted to hear about.

I finally got to sleep, to have long, dark dreams.

The next morning, between fielding Gran's questions about my walk with Bill and our future plans, I made some phone calls. I found two electricians, a plumber, and some other service people who gave me phone numbers where they could be reached at night and made sure they understood that a phone call from Bill Compton was not a prank.

Finally, I was lying out in the sun turning toasty when Gran carried the phone out to me.

"It's your boss," she said. Gran liked Sam, and he must have said something to make her happy because she was grinning like a Cheshire cat.

"Hi, Sam," I said, maybe not sounding too glad because I knew something had gone wrong at work.

"Dawn didn't make it in, cher," he said.

"Oh . . . *hell*," I said, knowing I'd have to go in. "I kind of have plans, Sam." That was a first. "When do you need me?"

"Could you just come in from five to nine? That would help out a lot."

"Am I gonna get another full day off?"

"What about Dawn splitting a shift with you another night?"

I made a rude noise, and Gran stood there with a stern face. I knew I'd get a lecture later. "Oh, all right," I said grudgingly. "See you at five."

"Thanks, Sookie," he said. "I knew I could count on you."

I tried to feel good about that. It seemed like a boring virtue. You can always count on Sookie to step in and help because she doesn't have a life!

Of course, it would be fine to get to Bill's after nine. He'd be up all night, anyway.

Work had never seemed so slow. I had trouble concentrating enough to keep my guard intact because I was always thinking about Bill. It was lucky there weren't many customers, or I would have heard unwanted thoughts galore. As it was, I found out Arlene's period was late, and she was scared she was pregnant, and before I could stop myself I gave her a hug. She stared at me searchingly and then turned red in the face.

"Did you read my mind, Sookie?" she asked, warning written in her voice. Arlene was one of the few people who simply acknowledged my ability without trying to explain it or categorizing me as a freak for possessing such an ability. She also didn't talk about it often or in any normal voice, I'd noticed.

"Sorry, I didn't mean to," I apologized. "I'm just not focused today."

"All right, then. You stay out from now on, though." And Arlene, her flaming curls bobbing around her cheeks, shook her finger in my face.

I felt like crying. "Sorry," I said again and strode off into the storeroom to collect myself. I had to pull my face straight and hold in those tears.

I heard the door open behind me.

"Hey, I said I was sorry, Arlene!" I snapped, wanting to be left alone. Sometimes Arlene confused telepathy with psychic talent. I was scared she'd ask me if she was really pregnant. She'd be better off buying an early home pregnancy kit.

"Sookie." It was Sam. He turned me around with a hand on my shoulder. "What's wrong?"

His voice was gentle and pushed me much closer to tears.

"You should sound mean so I won't cry!" I said.

He laughed, not a big laugh, a small one. He put an arm around me. "What's the matter?" He wasn't going to give up and go away.

"Oh, I . . ." and I stopped dead. I'd never, ever explicitly discussed my problem (that's how I thought of it) with Sam or anyone else. Everyone in Bon Temps knew the rumors about why I was strange, but no one seemed to realize that I had to listen to their mental clatter nonstop, whether I wanted to or not—every day, the yammer yammer yammer . . .

"Did you hear something that bothered you?" His voice was quiet and matter-of-fact. He touched the middle of my forhead, to indicate he knew exactly how I could "hear."

"Yes."

"Can't help it, can you?"

"Nope."

"Hate it, don't you, cher?"

"Oh, yes."

"Not your fault then, is it?"

"I try not to listen, but I can't always keep my guard up." I felt a tear I hadn't been able to quell start trickling down my cheek.

"Is that how you do it? How do you keep your guard up, Sookie?"

He sounded really interested, not as though he thought I was a basket case. I looked up, not very far, into Sam's prominent, brilliant blue eyes.

"I just . . . it's hard to describe unless you can do it . . . I pull up a fence—no, not a fence, it's like I'm snapping together steel plates—between my brain and all others."

"You have to hold the plates up?"

"Yes. It takes a lot of concentration. It's like dividing my mind all the time. That's why people think I'm crazy. Half my brain is trying to keep the steel plates up, and the other half might be taking drink orders, so sometimes there's not a lot left over for coherent conversation." What a gush of relief I was feeling, just being able to talk about it.

"Do you hear words or just get impressions?"

"Depends on who I'm listening to. And their state. If they're drunk, or really disturbed, it's just pictures, impressions, intentions. If they're sober and sane it's words and some pictures."

"The vampire says you can't hear him."

The idea of Bill and Sam having a conversation about me made me feel very peculiar. "That's true," I admitted.

"Is that relaxing to you?"

"Oh, *yes*." I meant it from my heart.

"Can you hear me, Sookie?"

"I don't want to try!" I said hastily. I moved to the door of the storeroom and stood with my hand on the knob. I pulled a tissue from my shorts pocket and patted the tear track off my cheek. "I'll have to quit if I read your mind, Sam! I like you, I like it here."

"Just try it sometime, Sookie," he said casually, turning to open a carton of whiskey with the razor-edged box cutter he kept in his pocket. "Don't worry about me. You have a job as long as you want one."

I wiped down a table Jason had spilled salt on. He'd been in earlier to eat a hamburger and fries and down a couple of beers.

I was turning over Sam's offer in my mind.

I wouldn't try to listen to him today. He was ready for me. I'd wait when he was busy doing something else. I'd just sort of slip in and give him a listen. He'd invited me, which was absolutely unique.

It was kind of nice to be invited.

I repaired my makeup and brushed my hair. I'd worn it loose, since Bill had seemed to like that, and a darn nuisance it had been all evening. It was just about time to go, so I retrieved my purse from its drawer in Sam's office.

THE COMPTON HOUSE, like Gran's, was set back from the road. It was a bit more visible from the parish road than hers, and it had a view of the cemetery, which her house didn't. This was due (at least in part) to the Compton house's higher setting. It was on top of a knoll and it was fully two-storied. Gran's house had a couple of spare bedrooms upstairs, and an attic, but it was more like half a top story.

At one point in the family's long history, the Comptons had had a very nice house. Even in the dark, it had a certain graciousness. But I knew in the daylight you could see the pillars were peeling, the wood siding was crooked, and the yard was simply a jungle. In the humid warmth of Louisiana, yard growth could get out of hand mighty quick, and old Mr. Compton had not been one to hire someone to do his yard work. When he'd gotten too feeble, it had simply gone undone.

The circular drive hadn't gotten fresh gravel in many years, and my car lurched to the front door. I saw that the house was all lit up, and I began to realize that the evening would not go like last evening. There was another car parked in front of the house, a Lincoln Continental, white with a dark blue top. A blue-on-white bumper sticker read VAMPIRES SUCK. A red and yellow one stated HONK IF YOU'RE A BLOOD DONOR! The vanity plate read, simply, FANGS 1.

If Bill already had company, maybe I should just go on home.

But I had been invited and was expected. Hesitantly, I raised my hand and knocked.

The door was opened by a female vampire.

She glowed like crazy. She was at least five feet eleven and black. She was wearing spandex. An exercise bra in flamingo pink and matching calf-length leggings, with a man's white dress shirt flung on unbuttoned, constituted the vampire's ensemble.

I thought she looked cheap as hell and most likely absolutely mouthwatering from a male point of view.

"Hey, little human chick," the vampire purred.

And all of a sudden I realized I was in danger. Bill had warned me repeatedly that not all vampires were like him, and he had moments when he was not so nice, himself. I couldn't read this creature's mind, but I could hear cruelty in her voice.

Maybe she had hurt Bill. Maybe she was his lover.

All of this passed through my mind in a rush, but none of it showed on my face. I've had years of experience in controlling my face. I could feel my bright smile snap on protectively, my spine straightened, and I said cheerfully, "Hi! I was supposed to drop by tonight and give Bill some information. Is he available?"

The female vampire laughed at me, which was nothing I wasn't used to. My smile notched up a degree brighter. This critter radiated danger the way a light bulb gives off heat.

"This little human gal here says she has some information for you, Bill!" she yelled over her (slim, brown, beautiful) shoulder.

I tried not to let relief show in any way.

"You wanna see this little thing? Or shall I just give her a love bite?"

Over my dead body, I thought furiously, and then realized it might be just that.

I didn't hear Bill speak, but the vampire stood back, and I stepped into the old house. Running wouldn't do any good; this vamp could undoubtedly bring me down before I'd gone five steps. And I hadn't laid eyes on Bill, and I couldn't be sure he was all right until I saw him. I'd brave this out and hope for the best. I'm pretty good at doing that.

The big front room was crammed with dark old furniture and people. No, not people, I realized after I'd looked carefully; two people, and two more strange vampires.

The two vampires were both male and white. One had a buzz cut and tattoos on every visible inch of his skin. The other was even taller than the woman, maybe six foot four, with a head of long rippling dark hair and a magnificent build.

The humans were less impressive. The woman was blond and plump, thirty-five or older. She was wearing maybe a pound too much makeup. She looked as worn as an old boot. The man was another story. He was lovely, the prettiest man I'd ever seen. He couldn't have been more than twenty-one. He was swarthy, maybe Hispanic, small and fine-boned. He wore denim cut-offs and nothing else. Except for makeup. I took that in my stride, but I didn't find it appealing.

Then Bill moved and I saw him, standing in the shadows of the dark hall leading from the living room to the back of the house. I looked at him, trying to get my bearings in this unexpected situation. To my dismay, he didn't look at all reassuring. His face was very still, absolutely impenetrable. Though I couldn't believe I was even thinking it, it would have been great at that point to have had a peek into his mind.

"Well, we can have a wonderful evening now," the long-haired male vampire said. He sounded delighted. "Is this a little friend of yours, Bill? She's so fresh."

I thought of a few choice words I'd learned from Jason.

"If you'll just excuse me and Bill a minute," I said very politely, as if this was a perfectly normal evening, "I've been arranging for workmen for the house." I tried to sound businesslike and impersonal, though wearing shorts and a T-shirt and Nikes does not inspire professional respect. But I hoped I conveyed the impression that nice people I encountered in the course of my working day could not possibly hold any threat of danger.

"And we heard Bill was on a diet of synthetic blood only," said the tattooed vampire. "Guess we heard wrong, Diane."

The female vampire cocked her head and gave me a long look. "I'm not so sure. She looks like a virgin to me."

I didn't think Diane was talking hymens.

I took a few casual steps toward Bill, hoping like hell he would defend me if worst came to worst, but finding myself not absolutely sure. I was still smiling, hoping he would speak, would move.

And then he did. "Sookie is mine," he said, and his voice was so cold and smooth it wouldn't have made a ripple in the water if it had been a stone.

I looked at him sharply, but I had enough brains to keep my mouth shut.

"How good you been taking care of our Bill?" Diane asked.

"None of your fucking business," I answered, using one of Jason's words and still smiling. I said I had a temper.

There was a sharp little pause. Everyone, human and vampire, seemed to examine me closely enough to count the hairs on my arms. Then the tall male began to rock with laughter and the others followed suit. While they were yukking it up, I moved a few feet closer to Bill. His dark eyes were fixed on me—*he* wasn't laughing—and I got the distinct feeling he wished, just as much as I did, that I could read his mind.

He was in some danger, I could tell. And if he was, then I was.

"You have a funny smile," said the tall male thoughtfully. I'd liked him better when he was laughing.

"Oh, Malcolm," said Diane. "All human women look funny to you."

Malcolm pulled the human male to him and gave him a long kiss. I began to feel a little sick. That kind of stuff is private. "This is true," Malcolm said, pulling away after a moment, to the small man's apparent disappointment. "But there is something rare about this one. Maybe she has rich blood."

"Aw," said the blond woman, in a voice that could blister paint, "That's just crazy Sookie Stackhouse."

I looked at the woman with more attention. I recognized her at last, when I mentally erased a few miles of hard road and half the makeup. Janella Lennox had worked at Merlotte's for two weeks until Sam had fired her. She'd moved to Monroe, Arlene had told me.

The male vampire with the tattoos put his arm around Janella and rubbed her breasts. I could feel the blood drain out of my face. I was disgusted. It got worse. Janella, as lost to decency as the vampire, put her hand on his crotch and massaged.

At least I saw clearly that vampires can sure have sex.

I was less than excited about that knowledge at the moment.

Malcolm was watching me, and I'd showed my distaste.

"She's innocent," he said to Bill, with a smile full of anticipation.

"She's mine," Bill said again. This time his voice was more intense. If he'd been a rattlesnake his warning could not have been clearer.

"Now, Bill, you can't tell me you've been getting everything you need from that little thing," Diane said. "You look pale and droopy. She ain't been taking good care of you."

I inched a little closer to Bill.

"Here," offered Diane, whom I was beginning to hate, "have a taste of Liam's woman or Malcolm's pretty boy, Jerry."

Janella didn't react to being offered around, maybe because she was too busy unzipping Liam's jeans, but Malcolm's beautiful boyfriend, Jerry, slithered willingly over to Bill. I smiled as though my jaws were going to crack as he wrapped his arms around Bill, nuzzled Bill's neck, rubbed his chest against Bill's shirt.

The strain in my vampire's face was terrible to see. His fangs slid out. I saw them fully extended for the first time. The synthetic blood was not answering all Bill's needs, all right.

Jerry began licking a spot at the base of Bill's neck. Keeping my guard up was proving to be more than I could handle. Since three present were vampires, whose thoughts I couldn't hear, and Janella was fully occupied, that left Jerry. I listened and gagged.

Bill, shaking with temptation, was actually bending to sink his fangs into Jerry's neck when I said, "No! He has the Sino-virus!"

As if released from a spell, Bill looked at me over Jerry's shoulder. He was breathing heavily, but his fangs retracted. I took advantage of the moment by taking more steps. I was within a yard of Bill, now.

"Sino-AIDS," I said.

Alcoholic and heavily drugged victims affected vampires temporarily, and some of them were said to enjoy that buzz; but the blood of a human with full-blown AIDS didn't, nor did sexually transmitted diseases, or any other bugs that plagued humans.

Except Sino-AIDS. Even Sino-AIDS didn't kill vampires as surely as the AIDS virus killed humans, but it left the undead very weak for nearly a month, during which time it was comparatively easy to catch and stake them. And every now and then, if a vampire fed from an infected human more than once, the vampire actually died— redied?—without being staked. Still rare in the United States, Sino-AIDS was gaining a foothold around ports like New Orleans, with sailors and other travelers from many countries passing through the city in a partying mood.

All the vampires were frozen, staring at Jerry as if he were death in disguise; and for them, perhaps, he was.

The beautiful young man took me completely by surprise. He turned and leapt on me. He was no vampire, but he was strong, evidently only in the earliest stages of the virus, and he knocked me against the wall to my left. He circled my throat with one hand and lifted the other to punch me in the face. My arms were still coming up to defend myself when Jerry's hand was seized, and his body froze.

"Let go of her throat," Bill said in such a terrifying voice that I was scared myself. By now, the scares were just piling up so quickly I didn't think I'd ever feel safe again. But Jerry's fingers didn't relax, and I made a little whimpering sound without wanting to at all. I slewed my eyes sideways, and when I looked at Jerry's gray face, I realized that Bill was holding his hand, Malcolm was gripping his legs, and Jerry was so frightened he couldn't grasp what was wanted of him.

The room began to get fuzzy, and voices buzzed in and out. Jerry's mind was beating against mine. I was helpless to hold him out. His mind was clouded with visions of the lover who had passed the virus to Jerry, a lover who had left him for a vampire, a lover Jerry himself had murdered in a fit of jealous rage. Jerry was seeing his death coming from the vampires he had wanted to kill, and he was not satisfied that he had extracted enough vengeance with the vampires he had already infected.

I could see Diane's face over Jerry's shoulder, and she was smiling. Bill broke Jerry's wrist.

He screamed and collapsed on the floor. The blood began surging into my head again, and I almost fainted. Malcolm picked Jerry up and carried him over to the couch as casually as if Jerry were a rolled-up rug. But Malcolm's face was not as casual. I knew Jerry would be lucky if he died quickly.

Bill stepped in front of me, taking Jerry's place. His fingers, the fingers that had just broken Jerry's wrist, massaged my neck as gently as my grandmother's would have done. He put a finger across my lips to make sure I knew to keep silent.

Then, his arm around me, he turned to face the other vampires.

"This has all been very entertaining," Liam said. His voice was as cool as if Janella wasn't giving him a truly intimate massage there on the couch. He hadn't troubled himself to budge during the whole incident. He had newly visible tattoos I could never in this world have imagined. I was sick to my stomach. "But I think we should be driving back to Monroe. We have to have a little talk with Jerry when he wakes up, right, Malcolm?"

Malcolm heaved the unconscious Jerry over his shoulder and nodded at Liam. Diane looked disappointed.

"But fellas," she protested. "We haven't found out how this little gal knew."

The two male vampires simultaneously switched their gaze to me. Quite casually, Liam took a second off to reach a climax. Yep, vampires could do it, all right. After a little sigh of completion, he said, "Thanks, Janella. That's a good question, Malcolm. As usual, our Diane has cut to the quick." And the three visiting vampires laughed as if that was a very good joke, but I thought it was a scary one.

"You can't speak yet, can you, sweetheart?" Bill gave my shoulder a squeeze as he asked, as if I couldn't get the hint.

I shook my head.

"I could probably make her talk," Diane offered.

"Diane, you forget," Bill said gently.

"Oh, yeah. She's yours," Diane said. But she didn't sound cowed or convinced.

"We'll have to visit some other time," Bill said, and his voice made it clear the others had to leave or fight him.

Liam stood, zipped up his pants, gestured to his human woman.

"Out, Janella, we're being evicted." The tattoos rippled across his heavy arms as he stretched. Janella ran her hands along his ribs as if she just couldn't get enough of him, and he swatted her away as lightly as if she'd been a fly. She looked vexed, but not mortified as I would have been. This was not new treatment for Janella.

Malcolm picked up Jerry and carried him out the front door without a word. If drinking from Jerry had given him the virus, Malcolm was not yet impaired. Diane went last, slinging a purse over her shoulder and casting a bright-eyed glance behind her.

"I'll leave you two lovebirds on your own, then. It's been fun, honey," she said lightly, and she slammed the door behind her.

The minute I heard the car start up outside, I fainted.

I'd never done so in my life, and I hoped never to again, but I felt I had some excuse.

I seemed to spend a lot of time around Bill unconscious. That was a crucial thought, and I knew it deserved a lot of pondering, but not just at that moment. When I came to, everything I'd seen and heard rushed back, and I gagged for real. Immediately Bill bent me over the edge of the couch. But I managed to keep my food down, maybe because there wasn't much in my stomach.

"Do vampires act like that?" I whispered. My throat was sore and bruised where Jerry had squeezed it. "They were horrible."

"I tried to catch you at the bar when I found out you weren't at home," Bill said. His voice was empty. "But you'd left."

Though I knew it wouldn't help a thing, I began crying. I was sure Jerry was dead by now, and I felt I should have done something about that, but I couldn't have kept silent when he was about to infect Bill. So many things about this short episode had upset me so deeply that I didn't know where to begin being upset. In maybe fifteen minutes I'd been in fear of my life, in fear for Bill's life (well—existence), made to witness sex acts that should be strictly private, seen my potential sweetie in the throes of blood lust (emphasis on lust), and nearly been choked to death by a diseased hustler.

On second thought, I gave myself full permission to cry. I sat up and wept and mopped my face with a handkerchief Bill handed me. My curiosity about why a vampire would need a handkerchief was just a little flicker of normality, drenched by the flood of my nervous tears.

Bill had enough sense not to put his arms around me. He sat on the floor, and had the grace to keep his eyes averted while I mopped myself dry.

"When vampires live in nests," he said suddenly, "they often become more cruel because they egg each other on. They see others like themselves constantly, and so they are reminded of how far from being human they are. They become laws unto themselves. Vampires like me, who live alone, are a little better reminded of their former humanity."

I listened to his soft voice, going slowly through his thoughts as he made an attempt to explain the unexplainable to me.

"Sookie, our life is seducing and taking and has been for centuries, for some of us. Synthetic blood and grudging human acceptance isn't going to change that overnight—or over a decade. Diane and Liam and Malcolm have been together for fifty years."

"How sweet," I said, and my voice held something I'd never heard from myself before: bitterness. "Their golden wedding anniversary."

"Can you forget about this?" Bill asked. His huge dark eyes came closer and closer. His mouth was about two inches from mine.

"I don't know." The words jerked out of me. "Do you know, I didn't know if you could do it?"

His eyebrows rose interrogatively. "Do . . . ?"

"Get—" and I stopped, trying to think of a pleasant way to put it. I'd seen more crudity this evening than I'd seen in my lifetime, and I didn't want to add to it. "An erection," I said, avoiding his eyes.

"You know better now." He sounded like he was trying not to be amused. "We can have sex, but we can't make children or have them. Doesn't it make you feel better, that Diane can't have a baby?"

My fuses blew. I opened my eyes and looked at him steadily. "Don't—you—laugh—at—me."

"Oh, Sookie," he said, and his hand rose to touch my cheek.

I dodged his hand and struggled to my feet. He didn't help me, which was a good thing, but he sat on the floor watching me with a still, unreadable face. Bill's fangs had retracted, but I knew he was still suffering from hunger. Too bad.

My purse was on the floor by the front door. I wasn't walking very steadily, but I was walking. I pulled the list of electricians out of a pocket and lay it on a table.

"I have to go."

He was in front of me suddenly. He'd done one of those vampire things again. "Can I kiss you good-bye?" he asked, his hands down at his sides, making it so obvious he wouldn't touch me until I said green light.

"No," I said vehemently. "I can't stand it after them."

"I'll come see you."

"Yes. Maybe."

He reached past me to open the door, but I thought he was reaching for me, and I flinched.

I spun on my heel and almost ran to my car, tears blurring my vision again. I was glad the drive home was so short.

Chapter 3

THE PHONE WAS ringing. I pulled my pillow over my head. Surely Gran would get it? As the irritating noise persisted, I realized Gran must be gone shopping or outside working in the yard. I began squirming to the bed table, not happy but resigned. With the headache and regrets of someone who has a terrible hangover (though mine was emotional rather than alcohol induced) I stretched out a shaky hand and grabbed the receiver.

"Yes?" I asked. It didn't come out quite right. I cleared my throat and tried again. "Hello?"

"Sookie?"

"Um-hum. Sam?"

"Yeah. Listen, cher, do me a favor?"

"What?" I was due to work today anyway, and I didn't want to hold down Dawn's shift and mine, too.

"Go by Dawn's place, and see what she's up to, would you? She won't answer her phone, and she hasn't come in. The delivery truck just pulled up, and I got to tell these guys where to put stuff."

"Now? You want me to go now?" My old bed had never held on to me harder.

"Could you?" For the first time, he seemed to grasp my unusual mood. I had never refused Sam anything.

"I guess so," I said, feeling tired all over again at the very idea. I wasn't too crazy about Dawn, and she wasn't too crazy about me. She was convinced I'd read her mind and told Jason something she'd been thinking about him, which had cause him to break up with her. If I took that kind of interest in Jason's romances, I'd never have time to eat or sleep.

I showered and pulled on my work clothes, moving sluggishly. All my bounce had gone flat, like soda with the top left off. I ate cereal and brushed my teeth and told Gran where I was going when I tracked her down; she'd been outside planting petunias in a tub by the back door. She didn't seem to understand exactly what I meant, but smiled and waved anyway. Gran was getting a little more deaf every week, but I realized that was no great wonder since she was seventy-eight. It was marvelous that she was so strong and healthy, and her brain was sound as a bell.

As I went on my unwelcome errand, I thought about how hard it must have been for Gran to raise two more children after she'd already raised her own. My father, her son, had died when I was seven and Jason ten. When I'd been twenty-three, Gran's daughter, my Aunt Linda, had died of uterine cancer. Aunt Linda's girl, Hadley, had vanished into the same subculture that had spawned the Rattrays even before Aunt Linda had passed away, and to this day we didn't know if Hadley realizes her mother is dead. That was a lot of grief to get through, yet Gran had always been strong for us.

I peered through my windshield at the three small duplexes on one side of Berry Street, a run-down block or two that ran behind the oldest part of downtown Bon Temps. Dawn lived in one of them. I spotted her car, a green compact, in the driveway of one of the better-kept houses, and pulled in behind it. Dawn had already put a hanging basket of begonias by her front door, but they looked dry. I knocked.

I waited for a minute or two. I knocked again.

"Sookie, you need some help?" The voice sounded familiar. I turned around and shielded my eyes from the morning sun. Rene Lenier was standing by his pickup, parked across the street at one of the small frame houses that populated the rest of the neighborhood.

"Well," I began, not sure if I needed help or not, or if I did that Rene could supply it. "Have you seen Dawn? She didn't come to work today, and she never called in yesterday. Sam asked me to stop by."

"Sam should come do his own dirty work," Rene said, which perversely made me defend my boss.

"Truck came in, had to be unloaded." I turned and knocked again. "Dawn," I yelled. "Come let me in." I looked down at the concrete porch. The pine pollen had begun falling two days ago. Dawn's porch was solid yellow. Mine were the only footprints. My scalp began to prickle.

I barely registered the fact that Rene stood awkwardly by the door to his pickup, unsure whether to stay or go.

Dawn's duplex was a one-story, quite small, and the door to the other half was just feet away from Dawn's. Its little driveway was empty, and there were no curtains at the windows. It looked as though Dawn was temporarily out of a neighbor. Dawn had been proud enough to hang curtains, white with dark gold flowers. They were drawn, but the fabric was thin and unlined, and Dawn hadn't shut the cheap one-inch aluminum blinds. I peered in and discovered the living room held only some flea-market furniture. A coffee mug sat on the table by a lumpy recliner and an old couch covered with a hand-crocheted afghan was pushed against the wall.

"I think I'll go around back," I called to Rene. He started across the street as though I'd given him a signal, and I stepped off the front porch. My feet brushed the dusty grass, yellow with pine pollen, and I knew I'd have to dust off my shoes and maybe change my socks before work. During pine pollen season, everything turns yellow. Cars, plants, roofs, windows, all are powdered with a golden haze. The ponds and pools of rainwater have yellow scum around the edges.

Dawn's bathroom window was so discreetly high that I couldn't see in. She'd lowered the blinds in the bedroom, but hadn't closed them tightly. I could see a little through the slats. Dawn was in bed on her back. The bedclothes were tossed around wildly. Her legs were spraddled. Her face was swollen and discolored, and her tongue protruded from her mouth. There were flies crawling on it.

I could hear Rene coming up behind me.

"Go call the police," I said.

"What you say, Sookie? You see her?"

"Go *call the police!*"

"Okay, okay!" Rene beat a hasty retreat.

Some female solidarity had made me not want Rene to see Dawn like that, without Dawn's consent. And my fellow waitress was far beyond consenting.

I stood with my back to the window, horribly tempted to look again in the futile hope I'd made a mistake the first time. Staring at the duplex next door to Dawn's, maybe a scant six feet away, I wondered how its tenants could have avoided hearing Dawn's death, which had been violent.

Here came Rene again. His weatherbeaten face was puckered into an expression of deep concern, and his bright brown eyes looked suspiciously shiney.

"Would you call Sam, too?" I asked. Without a word, he turned and trudged back to his place. He was being mighty good. Despite his tendency to gossip, Rene had always been one to help where he saw a need. I remembered him coming out to the house to help Jason hang

Gran's porch swing, a random memory of a day far different from this.

The duplex next door was just like Dawn's, so I was looking directly at its bedroom window. Now a face appeared, and the window was raised. A tousled head poked out. "What you doing, Sookie Stackhouse?" asked a slow, deep, male voice. I peered at him for a minute, finally placing the face, while trying not to look too closely at the fine, bare chest underneath.

"JB?"

"Sure thing."

I'd gone to high school with JB du Rone. In fact, some of my few dates had been with JB, who was lovely but so simple that he didn't care if I read his mind or not. Even under today's circumstances, I could appreciate JB's beauty. When your hormones have been held in check as long as mine, it doesn't take much to set them off. I heaved a sigh at the sight of JB's muscular arms and pectorals.

"What you doing out here?" he asked again.

"Something bad seems to have happened to Dawn," I said, not knowing if I should tell him or not. "My boss sent me here to look for her when she didn't come to work."

"She in there?" JB simply scrambled out of the window. He had some shorts on, cut-offs.

"Please don't look," I asked, holding up my hand and without warning I began crying. I was doing that a lot lately, too. "She looks so awful, JB."

"Aw, honey," he said, and bless his country heart, he put an arm around me and patted me on the shoulder. If there was a female around who needed comforting, by God, that was a priority to JB du Rone.

"Dawn liked 'em rough," he said consolingly, as if that would explain everything.

It might to some people, but not to unworldly me.

"What, rough?" I asked, hoping I had a tissue in my shorts pocket. I looked up at JB to see him turn a little red.

"Honey, she liked . . . aw, Sookie, you don't need to hear this."

I had a widespread reputation for virtue, which I found somewhat ironic. At the moment, it was inconvenient.

"You can tell me, I worked with her," I said, and JB nodded solemnly, as if that made sense.

"Well, honey, she liked men to—like, bite and hit her." JB looked weirded out by this preference of Dawn's. I must have made a face because he said, "I know, I can't understand why some people like that, either." JB, never one to ignore an opportunity to make hay, put both arms around me and kept up the patting, but it seemed to concentrate on the middle of my back (checking to see if I was wearing a bra) and then quite a bit lower (JB liked firm rear ends, I remembered.)

A lot of questions hovered on the edge of my tongue, but they remained shut inside my mouth. The police got there, in the persons of Kenya Jones and Kevin Prior. When the town police chief had partnered Kenya and Kevin, he'd been indulging his sense of humor, the town figured, for Kenya was at least five foot eleven, the color of bitter chocolate, and built to weather hurricanes. Kevin possibly made it up to five foot eight, had freckles over every visible inch of his pale body, and had the narrow, fatless build of a runner. Oddly enough, the two K's got along very well, though they'd had some memorable quarrels.

Now they both looked like cops.

"What's this about, Miss Stackhouse?" Kenya asked. "Rene says something happened to Dawn Green?" She'd scanned JB while she talked, and Kevin was looking at the ground all around us. I had no idea why, but I was sure there was a good police reason.

"My boss sent me here to find out why Dawn missed work yesterday and hadn't shown up today," I said. "I knocked on her door, and she didn't answer, but her car was here. I was worried about her, so I started around the house looking in the windows, and she's in there." I pointed behind them, and the two officers turned to look at the window. Then they looked at each other and nodded as if they'd had a whole conversation. While Kenya went over to the window, Kevin went around to the back door.

JB had forgotten to pat while he watched the officers work. In fact, his mouth was a little open, revealing perfect teeth. He wanted to go look through the window more than anything, but he couldn't shoulder past Kenya, who pretty much took up whatever space was available.

I didn't want my own thoughts any more. I relaxed, dropping my guard, and listened to the thoughts of others. Out of the clamor, I picked one thread and concentrated on it.

Kenya Jones turned back to stare through us without seeing us. She was thinking of everything she and Kevin needed to do to keep the investigation as textbook perfect as Bon Temps patrol officers could. She was thinking she'd heard bad things about Dawn and her liking for rough sex. She was thinking that it was no surprise Dawn had met a bad end, though she felt sorry for anyone who ended up with flies crawling on her face. Kenya was thinking she was sorry she'd eaten that extra doughnut that morning at the Nut Hut because it might come back up and that would shame her as a black woman police officer.

I tuned in to another channel.

JB was thinking about Dawn getting killed during rough sex just a few feet away from him, and while it was awful it was also a little exciting and Sookie was still built wonderful. He wished he could screw her right now. She was so sweet and nice. He was pushing away the humiliation he'd felt when Dawn had wanted him to hit her, and he couldn't, and it was an old humiliation.

I switched.

Kevin came around the corner thinking that he and Kenya better not botch any evidence and that he was glad no one knew he'd ever slept with Dawn Green. He was furious that someone had killed a woman he knew, and he was hoping it wasn't a black man because that would make his relationship with Kenya even more tense.

I switched.

Rene Lenier was wishing someone would come and get the body out of the house. He was hoping no one knew he'd slept with Dawn Green. I couldn't spell out his thoughts exactly, they were very black and snarled. Some people I can't get a clear reading on. He was very agitated.

Sam came hurrying toward me, slowing down when he saw JB was touching me. I could not read Sam's thoughts. I could feel his emotions (right now a mix of worry, concern, and anger) but I could not spell out one single thought. This was so fascinating and unexpected that I stepped out of JB's embrace, wanting to go up to Sam and grab his arms and look into his eyes and really probe around in his head. I remembered when he'd touched me, and I'd shied away. Now he *felt* me in his head and though he kept on walking toward me, his mind flinched back. Despite his invitation to me, he hadn't known I would see he was different from others: I picked up on that until he shut me down.

I'd never felt anything like it. It was like an iron door slamming. In my face.

I'd been on the point of reaching out to him instinctively, but my hand dropped to my side. Sam deliberately looked at Kevin, not at me.

"What's happening, Officer?" Sam asked.

"We're going to break into this house, Mr. Merlotte, unless you have a master key."

Why would Sam have a key?

"He's my landlord," JB said in my ear, and I jumped.

"He is?" I asked stupidly.

"He owns all three duplexes."

Sam had been fishing in his pocket, and now he came up with a bunch of keys. He flipped through them expertly, stopping at one and singling it out, getting it off the ring and handing it to Kevin.

"This fits front and back?" Kevin asked. Sam nodded. He still wasn't looking at me.

Kevin went to the back door of the duplex, out of sight, and we were all so quiet we could hear the key turn in the lock. Then he was in the bedroom with the dead woman, and we could see his face twist when the smell hit him. Holding one hand across his mouth and nose, he bent over the body and put his fingers on her neck. He looked out the window then and shook his head at his partner. Kenya nodded and headed out to the street to use the radio in the patrol car.

"Listen, Sookie, how about going to dinner with me tonight?" JB asked. "This has been tough on you, and you need some fun to make up for it."

"Thanks, JB." I was very conscious of Sam listening. "It's really nice of you to ask. But I have a feeling I'm going to be working extra hours today."

For just a second, JB's handsome face was blank. Then comprehension filtered in. "Yeah, Sam's gotta hire someone else," he observed. "I got a cousin in Springhill needs a job. Maybe I'll give her a call. We could live right next door to each other, now."

I smiled at him, though I am sure it was a very weak smile, as I stood shoulder to shoulder with the man I'd worked with for two years.

"I'm sorry, Sookie," he said quietly.

"For what?" My own voice was just as low. Was he going to acknowledge what had passed between us—or rather, failed to pass?

"For sending you to check on Dawn. I should have come myself. I was sure she was just shacked up with someone new and needed a reminder that she was supposed to be working. The last time I had to come get her, she yelled at me so much I just didn't want to deal with it again. So like a coward, I sent you, and you had to find her like that."

"You're full of surprises, Sam."

He didn't turn to look at me or make any reply. But his fingers folded around mine. For a long moment, we stood in the sun with people buzzing around us, holding hands. His palm was hot and dry, and his fingers were strong. I felt I had truly connected with another human. But then his grip loosened, and Sam stepped over to talk with the detective, who was emerging from his car, and JB began asking me how Dawn had looked, and the world fell back into its same old groove.

The contrast was cruel. I felt tired all over again, and remembered the night before in more detail than I wanted to. The world seemed a bad and terrible place, all its denizens suspect, and I the lamb wandering through the valley of death with a bell around my neck. I stomped over to my car and opened the door, sank sideways into the seat. I'd be standing plenty today; I'd sit while I could.

JB followed me. Now that he'd rediscovered me, he could not be detached. I remembered when Gran had had high hopes for some permanent relationship between us, when I'd been in high school. But talking to JB, even reading his mind, was as interesting as a kindergarten primer was to an adult reader. It was one of God's jokes that such a dumb mind had been put in such an eloquent body.

He knelt before me and took my hand. I found myself hoping that some smart rich lady would come along and marry JB and take care of him and enjoy what he had to offer. She would be getting a bargain.

"Where are you working now?" I asked him, just to distract myself.

"My dad's warehouse," he said.

That was the job of last resort, the one JB always returned to when he got fired from other jobs for doing something lamebrained, or for not showing up, or for offending some supervisor mortally. JB's dad ran an auto parts store.

"How are your folks doing?"

"Oh, fine. Sookie, we should do something together."

Don't tempt me, I thought.

Someday my hormones were going to get the better of me and I'd do something I'd regret; and I could do worse than do it with JB. But I would hold out and hope for something better. "Thanks, honey," I said. "Maybe we will. But I'm kind of upset right now."

"Are you in love with that vampire?" he asked directly.

"Where did you hear that?"

"Dawn said so." JB's face clouded as he remembered Dawn was dead. What Dawn had said, I found on scanning JB's mind, was "That new vampire is interested in Sookie Stackhouse. I'd be better for him. He needs a woman who can take some rough treatment. Sookie would scream if he touched her."

It was pointless being mad at a dead person, but briefly I indulged myself by doing just that.

Then the detective was walking toward us, and JB got to his feet and moved away.

The detective took JB's position, squatting on the ground in front of me. I must look in bad shape.

"Miss Stackhouse?" he asked. He was using that quiet intense voice many professionals adopt in a crisis. "I'm Andy Bellefleur." The Bellefleurs had been around Bon Temps as long as there'd been a Bon Temps, so I wasn't amused at a man being "beautiful flower." In fact, I felt sorry for whoever thought it was amusing as I looked down at the block of muscle that was Detective Bellefleur. This particular family member had graduated before Jason, and I'd been one class behind his sister Portia.

He'd been placing me, too. "Your brother doing okay?" he asked, his voice still quiet, not quite as neutral. It sounded like he'd had a run-in or two with Jason.

"The little I see of him, he's doing fine," I answered.

"And your grandmother?"

I smiled. "She's out planting flowers this morning."

"That's wonderful," he said, doing that sincere head shake that's supposed to indicate admiring amazement. "Now, I understand that you work at Merlotte's?"

"Yes."

"And so did Dawn Green?"

"Yes."

"When was the last time you saw Dawn?"

"Two days ago. At work." I already felt exhausted. Without shifting my feet from the ground or my arm from the steering wheel, I lay my head sideways on the headrest of the driver's seat.

"Did you talk to her then?"

I tried to remember. "I don't think so."

"Were you close to Miss Green?"

"No."

"And why did you come here today?"

I explained about working for Dawn yesterday, about Sam's phone call this morning.

"Did Mr. Merlotte tell you why he didn't want to come here himself?"

"Yes, a truck was there to unload. Sam has to show the guys where to put the boxes." Sam also did a lot of the unloading himself, half the time, to speed up the process.

"Do you think Mr. Merlotte had any relationship with Dawn?"

"He was her boss."

"No, outside work."

"Nope."

"You sound pretty positive."

"I am."

"Do you have a relationship with Sam?"

"No."

"Then how are you so sure?"

Good question. Because from time to time I'd heard thoughts that indicated that if she didn't hate Sam, Dawn sure as hell wasn't real fond of him? Not too smart a thing to tell the detective.

"Sam keeps everything real professional at the bar," I said. It sounded lame, even to me. It just happened to be the truth.

"Did you know anything about Dawn's personal life?"

"No."

"You weren't friendly?"

"Not particularly." My thoughts drifted as the detective bent his head in thought. At least that was what it looked like.

"Why is that?"

"I guess we didn't have anything in common."

"Like what? Give me an example."

I sighed heavily, blowing my lips out in exasperation. If we didn't have anything in common, how could I give him an example?

"Okay," I said slowly. "Dawn had a real active social life, and she liked to be with men. She wasn't so crazy about spending time with women. Her family is from Monroe, so she didn't have family ties here. She drank, and I don't. I read a lot, and she didn't. That enough?"

Andy Bellefleur scanned my face to see if I was giving him attitude. He must have been reassured by what he saw.

"So, you two didn't ever see each other after working hours?"

"That's correct."

"Doesn't it seem strange to you that Sam Merlotte asked you to check on Dawn, then?"

"No, not at all," I said stoutly. At least, it didn't seem strange now, after Sam's description of Dawn's tantrum. "This is on my way to the bar, and I don't have children like Arlene, the other waitress on our shift. So it would be easier for me." That was pretty sound, I thought. If I said Dawn had screamed at Sam the last time he'd been here, that would give exactly the wrong impression.

"What did you do after work two days ago, Sookie?"

"I didn't come to work. I had the day off."

"And your plan for that day was—?"

"I sunbathed and helped Gran clean house, and we had company."

"Who would that be?"

"That would be Bill Compton."

"The vampire."

"Right."

"How late was Mr. Compton at your house?"

"I don't know. Maybe midnight or one."

"How did he seem to you?"

"He seemed fine."

"Edgy? Irritated?"

"No."

"Miss Stackhouse, we need to talk to you more at the station house. This is going to take awhile, here, as you can see."

"Okay, I guess."

"Can you come in a couple of hours?"

I looked at my wristwatch. "If Sam doesn't need me to work."

"You know, Miss Stackhouse, this really takes precedence over working at a bar."

Okay, I was pissed off. Not because he thought murder investigations were more important than getting to work on time; I agreed with him, there. It was his unspoken prejudice against my particular job.

"You may not think my job amounts to much, but it's one I'm good at, and I like it. I am as worthy of respect as your sister, the lawyer, Andy Bellefleur, and don't you forget it. I am not stupid, and I am not a slut."

The detective turned red, slowly and unattractively. "I apologize," Andy said stiffly. He was still trying to deny the old connection, the shared high school, the knowledge of each other's family. He was thinking he should have been a detective in another town, where he could treat people the way he thought a police officer should.

"No, you'll be a better detective here if you can get over that attitude," I told him. His gray eyes flared wide in shock, and I was childishly glad I'd rocked him, though I was sure I would pay for it sooner or later. I always did when I gave people a peek at my disability.

Mostly, people couldn't get away from me fast enough when I'd given them a taste of mind reading, but Andy Bellefleur was fascinated. "It's true, then," he breathed, as if we were somewhere alone instead of sitting in the driveway of a rundown duplex in rural Louisiana.

"No, forget it," I said quickly. "I can just tell sometimes by the way people look what they're thinking."

He deliberately thought about unbuttoning my blouse. But I was wary now, back to my normal state of barricaded seige, and I did no more than smile brightly. I could tell I wasn't fooling him, though.

"When you're ready for me, you come to the bar. We can talk in the storeroom or Sam's office," I said firmly and swung my legs into the car.

The bar was buzzing when I got there. Sam had called Terry Bellefleur, Andy's second cousin if I recalled correctly, in to watch the bar while he talked to the police at Dawn's place. Terry had had a bad war in Vietnam, and he existed narrowly on government disability of some kind. He'd been wounded, captured, held prisoner for two years, and now his thoughts were most often so scary that I was extra special careful when I was around him. Terry had a hard life, and acting normal was even harder for him than it was for me. Terry didn't drink, thank God.

Today I gave him a light kiss on the cheek while I got my tray and scrubbed my hands. Through the window into the little kitchen I could see Lafayette Reynold, the cook, flipping burgers and sinking a basket of fries into hot oil. Merlotte's serves a few sandwiches, and that's all. Sam doesn't want to run a restaurant, but a bar with some food available.

"What was that for, not that I'm not honored," Terry said. He'd raised his eyebrows. Terry was redhaired, though when he needed a shave, I could tell his whiskers were gray. Terry spent a lot of time outside, but his skin never exactly tanned. It got a rough, reddened look, which made the scars on his left cheek stand out more clearly. That didn't seem to bother Terry. Arlene had been to bed with Terry one night when she'd been drinking, and she'd confided in me that Terry had many scars even worse than the one on his cheek.

"Just for being here," I said.

"It true about Dawn?"

Lafayette put two plates on the serving hatch. He winked at me with a sweep of his thick, false lashes. Lafayette wears a lot of makeup. I was so used to him I never thought of it any more, but now his eye shadow brought the boy, Jerry, to my mind. I'd let him go with the three vampires without protest. That had probably been wrong, but realistic. I couldn't have stopped them from taking him. I couldn't have gotten the police to catch up with them in time. He was dying anyway, and he was taking as many vampires and humans with him as he could; and he was already a killer himself. I told my conscience this would be the last talk we'd have about Jerry.

"Arlene, burgers up," Terry called, jerking me back into the here and how. Arlene came over to grab the plates. She gave me a look that said she was going to pump me dry at the first chance she got. Charlsie Tooten was working, too. She filled in when one of the regular women got sick or just didn't show. I hoped Charlsie would take Dawn's place full-time. I'd always liked her.

"Yeah, Dawn's dead," I told Terry. He didn't seem to mind my long pause.

"What happened to her?"

"I don't know, but it wasn't peaceful." I'd seen blood on the sheets, not a lot, but some.

"Maudette," Terry said, and I instantly understood.

"Maybe," I said. It sure was possible that whoever had done in Dawn was the same person who'd killed Maudette.

Of course, everyone in Renard Parish came in that day, if not for lunch, then for an afternoon cup of coffee or a beer. If they couldn't make their work schedule bend around that, they waited until they clocked out and came in on their way home. Two young women in our town murdered in one month? You bet people wanted to talk.

Sam returned about two, with heat radiating off his body and sweat trickling down his face from standing out in the shadeless yard at the crime scene. He told me that Andy Bellefleur had said he was coming to talk to me again soon.

"I don't know why," I said, maybe a tad sullenly. "I never hung around with Dawn. What happened to her, did they tell you?"

"Someone strangled her after beating on her a little," Sam said. "But she had some old tooth marks, too. Like Maudette."

"There are lots of vampires, Sam," I said, answering his unspoken comment.

"Sookie." His voice was so serious and quiet. It made me remember how he'd held my hand at Dawn's house, and then I remembered how he'd shut me out of his mind, known I was probing, known how to keep me out. "Honey, Bill is a good guy, for a vampire, but he's just not human."

"Honey, neither are you," I said, very quietly but very sharply. And I turned my back on Sam, not exactly wanting to admit why I was so angry with him, but wanting him to know it nonetheless.

I worked like a demon. Whatever her faults, Dawn had been efficient, and Charlsie just couldn't keep up with the pace. She was willing, and I was sure she'd catch up with the rhythm of the bar, but for tonight, Arlene and I had to take up the slack.

I earned a ton of money in tips that evening and on into the night when people found out I'd actually discovered the body. I just kept my face solemn and got through it, not wanting to offend customers who just wanted to know what everyone else in town wanted to know.

On my way home, I allowed myself to relax a little. I was exhausted. The last thing I expected to see, after I turned into the little drive through the woods that led to our house, was Bill Compton. He was leaning against a pine tree waiting for me. I drove past him a little, almost deciding to ignore him. But then I stopped.

He opened my door. Without looking him in the eyes, I got out. He seemed comfortable in the night, in a way I never could be. There were too many childhood taboos about the night and the darkness and things that went bump.

Come to think of it, Bill was one of those things. No wonder he felt at ease.

"Are you going to look at your feet all night, or are you going to talk to me?" he asked in a voice that was just above a whisper.

"Something happened you should know about."

"Tell me." He was trying to do something to me: I could feel his power hovering around me, but I batted it away. He sighed.

"I can't stand up," I said wearily. "Let's sit on the ground or something. My feet are tired."

In answer, he picked me up and set me on the hood of the car. Then he stood in front of me, his arms crossed, very obviously waiting.

"Tell me."

"Dawn was murdered. Just like Maudette Pickens."

"Dawn?"

Suddenly I felt a little better. "The other waitress at the bar."

"The redheaded one, the one who's been married so often?"

I felt a lot better. "No, the dark-haired one, the one who kept bumping into your chair with her hips to get you to notice her."

"Oh, that one. She came to my house."

"Dawn? When?"

"After you left the other night. The night the other vampires were there. She's lucky she missed them. She was very confident of her ability to handle anything."

I looked up at him. "Why is she so lucky? Wouldn't you have protected her?"

Bill's eyes were totally dark in the moonlight. "I don't think so," he said.

"You are . . ."

"I'm a vampire, Sookie. I don't think like you. I don't care about people automatically."

"You protected me."

"You're different."

"Yeah? I'm a waitress, like Dawn. I come from a plain family, like Maudette. What's so different?"

I was in a sudden rage. I knew what was coming.

His cool finger touched the middle of my forehead. "Different," he said. "You're not like us. But you're not like them, either."

I felt a flare of rage so intense it was almost divine. I hauled off and hit him, an insane thing to do. It was like hitting a Brink's armored truck. In a flash, he had me off the car and pinned to him, my arms bound to my sides by one of his arms.

"No!" I screamed. I kicked and fought, but I might as well have saved the energy. Finally I sagged against him.

My breathing was ragged, and so was his. But I didn't think it was for the same reason.

"Why did you think I needed to know about Dawn?" He sounded so reasonable, you'd think the struggle hadn't happened.

"Well, Mr. Lord of Darkness," I said furiously, "Maudette had old bite marks on her thighs, and the police told Sam that Dawn had bite marks, too."

If silence can be characterized, his was thoughtful. While he was mulling, or whatever vampires do, his embrace loosened. One hand began rubbing my back absently, as if I was a puppy who had whimpered.

"You imply they didn't die from these bites."

"No. From strangulation."

"Not a vampire, then." His tone put it beyond question.

"Why not?"

"If a vampire had been feeding from these women, they would have been drained instead of strangled. They wouldn't have been wasted like that."

Just when I was beginning to be comfortable with Bill, he'd say something so cold, so vampirey, I had to start all over again.

"Then," I said wearily, "either you have a crafty vampire with great self-control, or you have someone who's determined to kill women who've been with vampires."

"Hmmm."

I didn't feel very good about either of those choices.

"Do you think I'd do that?" he asked.

The question was unexpected. I wriggled in his pinioning embrace to look up at him.

"You've taken great care to point out how heartless you are," I reminded him. "What do you really want me to believe?"

And it was so wonderful not to know. I almost smiled.

"I could have killed them, but I wouldn't do it here, or now," Bill said. He had no color in the moonlight except for the dark pools of his eyes and the dark arches of his brows. "This is where I want to stay. I want a home."

A vampire, yearning for home.

Bill read my face. "Don't pity me, Sookie. That would be a mistake." He seemed willing me to stare into his eyes.

"Bill, you can't glamor me, or whatever you do. You can't enchant me into pulling my T-shirt down for you to bite me, you can't convince me you weren't ever here, you can't do any of your usual stuff. You have to be regular with me, or just force me."

"No," he said, his mouth almost on mine. "I won't force you."

I fought the urge to kiss him. But at least I knew it was my very own urge, not a manufactured one.

"So, if it wasn't you," I said, struggling to keep on course, "then Maudette and Dawn knew another vampire. Maudette went to the vampire bar in Shreveport. Maybe Dawn did, too. Will you take me there?"

"Why?" he asked, sounding no more than curious.

I just couldn't explain being in danger to someone who was so used to being beyond it. At least at night. "I'm not sure Andy Bellefleur will go to the trouble," I lied.

"There are still Bellefleurs here," he said, and there was something different in his voice. His arms hardened around me to the point of pain.

"Yes," I said. "Lots of them. Andy is a police detective. His sister, Portia, is a lawyer. His cousin Terry is a veteran and a bartender. He substitutes for Sam. There are lots of others."

"Bellefleur . . ."

I was getting crushed.

"Bill," I said, my voice squeaky with panic.

He loosened his grip immediately. "Excuse me," he said formally.

"I have to go to bed," I said. "I'm really tired, Bill."

He set me down on the gravel with scarcely a bump. He looked down at me.

"You told those other vampires that I belonged to you," I said.

"Yes."

"What exactly did that mean?"

"That means that if they try to feed on you, I'll kill them," he said. "It means you are my human."

"I have to say I'm glad you did that, but I'm not really sure what being your human entails," I said cautiously. "And I don't recall being asked if that was okay with me."

"Whatever it is, it's probably better than partying with Malcolm, Liam, and Diane."

He wasn't going to answer me directly.

"Are you going to take me to the bar?"

"What's your next night off?"

"Two nights from now."

"Then, at sunset. I'll drive."

"You have a car?"

"How do you think I get places?" There might have been a smile on his shining face. He turned to melt into the woods. Over his shoulder he said, "Sookie. Do me proud."

I was left standing with my mouth open.

Do him proud indeed.

Chapter 4

Half the patrons of Merlotte's thought Bill had had a hand in the markings on the women's bodies. The other 50 percent thought that some of the vampires from bigger towns or cities had bitten Maudette and Dawn when they were out barhopping, and they deserved what they got if they wanted to go to bed with vampires. Some thought the girls had been strangled by a vampire, some thought they had just continued their promiscuous ways into disaster.

But everyone who came into Merlotte's was worried that some other woman would be killed, too. I couldn't count the times I was told to be careful, told to watch my friend Bill Compton, told to lock my doors and not let anyone in my house. . . . As if those were things I wouldn't do, normally.

Jason came in for both commiseration and suspicion as a man who'd "dated" both women. He came by the house one day and held forth for a whole hour, while Gran and I tried to encourage him to keep going with his work like an innocent man would. But for the first time in my memory, my handsome brother was really worried. I wasn't exactly glad he was in trouble, but I wasn't exactly sorry, either. I know that was small and petty of me.

I am not perfect.

I am so not-perfect that despite the deaths of two women I knew, I spent a substantial amount of time wondering what Bill meant about doing him proud. I had no idea what constituted appropriate dress for visiting a vampire bar. I wasn't about to dress in some kind of stupid costume, as I'd heard some bar visitors did.

I sure didn't know anyone to ask.

I wasn't tall enough or bony enough to dress in the sort of spandex outfit the vampire Diane had worn.

Finally I pulled a dress from the back of my closet, one I'd had little occasion to wear. It was a Nice Date dress, if you wanted the personal interest of whoever was your escort. It was cut square and low in the neck and it was sleeveless. It was tight and white. The fabric was thinly scattered with bright red flowers with long green stems. My tan glowed and my boobs showed. I wore red enamel earrings and red high-heeled screw-me shoes. I had a little red straw purse. I put on light makeup and wore my wavy hair loose down my back.

Gran's eyes opened wide when I came out of my room.

"Honey, you look beautiful," she said. "Aren't you going to be a little cold in that dress?"

I grinned. "No, ma'am, I don't think so. It's pretty warm outside."

"Wouldn't you like to wear a nice white sweater over that?"

"No, I don't think so." I laughed. I had pushed the other vampires far enough back in my mind to where looking sexy was okay again. I was pretty excited about having a date, though I had kind of asked Bill myself and it was more of a fact-finding mission. That, too, I tried to forget, so I could just enjoy myself.

Sam called me to tell me my paycheck was ready. He asked if I'd come in and pick it up, which I usually did if I wasn't going to work the next day.

I drove to Merlotte's feeling a little anxious at walking in dressed up.

But when I came in the door, I got the tribute of a moment of stunned silence. Sam's back was to me, but Lafayette was looking through the hatch and Rene and JB were at the bar. Unfortunately, so was my brother, Jason, whose eyes opened wide when he turned to see what Rene was staring at.

"You lookin' good, girl!" called Lafayette enthusiastically. "Where you get that dress?"

"Oh, I've had this old thing forever," I said mockingly, and he laughed.

Sam turned to see what Lafayette was gawking at, and his eyes got wide, too.

"God almighty," he breathed. I walked over to ask for my check, feeling very self-conscious.

"Come in the office, Sookie," he said, and I followed him to his small cubicle by the storeroom. Rene gave me a half-hug on my way by him, and JB kissed my cheek.

Sam rummaged through the piles of paper on top of his desk, and finally came up with my check. He didn't hand it to me, though.

"Are you going somewhere special?" Sam asked, almost unwillingly.

"I have a date," I said, trying to sound matter-of-fact.

"You look great," Sam said, and I saw him swallow. His eyes were hot.

"Thank you. Um, Sam, can I have my check?"

"Sure." He handed it to me, and I popped it in my purse.

"Good-bye, then."

"Good-bye." But instead of indicating I should leave, Sam stepped over and smelled me. He put his face close to my neck and inhaled. His brilliant blue eyes closed briefly, as if to evaluate my odor. He exhaled gently, his breath hot on my bare skin.

I stepped out of the door and left the bar, puzzled and interested in Sam's behavior.

When I got home a strange car was parked in front of the house. It was a black Cadillac, and it shone like glass. Bill's. Where did they get the money to buy these cars? Shaking my head, I went up the steps to the porch and walked in. Bill turned to the door expectantly; he was sitting on the couch talking to Gran, who was perched on one arm of an old overstuffed chair.

When he saw me, I was sure I'd overdone it, and he was really angry. His face went quite still. His eyes flared. His fingers curved as if he were scooping something up with them.

"Is this all right?" I asked anxiously. I felt the blood surge up into my cheeks.

"Yes," he said finally. But his pause had been long enough to anger my grandmother.

"Anyone with a brain in his head has got to admit that Sookie is one of the prettiest girls around," she said, her voice friendly on the surface but steel underneath.

"Oh, yes," he agreed, but there was a curious lack of inflection in his voice.

Well, screw him. I'd tried my best. I stiffened my back, and said, "Shall we go, then?"

"Yes," he said again, and stood. "Good-bye, Mrs. Stackhouse. It was a pleasure seeing you again."

"Well, you two have a good time," she said, mollified. "Drive careful, Bill, and don't drink too much."

He raised an eyebrow. "No, ma'am."

Gran let that sail right on past.

Bill held my car door open as I got in, a carefully calculated series of maneuvers to keep as much of me as possible in the dress. He shut the door and got in on the driver's side. I wondered who had taught him to drive a car. Henry Ford, probably.

"I'm sorry I'm not dressed correctly," I said, looking straight ahead of me.

We'd been going slowly on the bumpy driveway through the woods. The car lurched to a halt.

"Who said that?" Bill asked, his voice very gentle.

"You looked at me as though I'd done something wrong," I snapped.

"I'm just doubting my ability to get you in and out without having to kill someone who wants you."

"You're being sarcastic." I still wouldn't look.

His hand gripped the back of my neck, forced me to turn to him.

"Do I look like I am?" he asked.

His dark eyes were wide and unblinking.

"Ah . . . no," I admitted.

"Then accept what I say."

The ride to Shreveport was mostly silent, but not uncomfortably so. Bill played tapes most of the way. He was partial to Kenny G.

Fangtasia, the vampire bar, was located in a suburban shopping area of Shreveport, close to a Sam's and a Toys 'R' Us. It was in a shopping strip, which was all closed down at this hour except for the bar. The name of the place was spelled out in jazzy red neon above the door, and the facade was painted steel gray, a red door providing color contrast. Whoever owned the place must have thought gray was less obvious than black because the interior was decorated in the same colors.

I was carded at the door by a vampire. Of course, she recognized Bill as one of her own kind and acknowledged him with a cool nod, but she scanned me intently. Chalky pale, as all Caucasian vampires are, she was eerily striking in her long black dress with its trailing sleeves. I wondered if the overdone "vampire" look was her own inclination, or if she'd just adopted it because the human patrons thought it appropriate.

"I haven't been carded in years," I said, fishing in my red purse for my driver's license. We were standing in a little boxy entrance hall.

"I can no longer tell human ages, and we must be very careful we serve no minors. In any capacity," she said with what was probably meant to be a genial smile. She cast a sideways look at Bill, her eyes flicking up and down him with an offensive interest. Offensive to me, at least.

"I haven't seen you in a few months," she said to him, her voice as cool and sweet as his could be.

"I'm mainstreaming," he explained, and she nodded.

"WHAT WERE YOU telling her?" I whispered as we walked down the short hall and through the red double doors into the main room.

"That I'm trying to live among humans."

I wanted to hear more, but then I got my first comprehensive look at Fangtasia's interior. Everything was in gray, black, and red. The walls were lined with framed pictures of every movie vampire who had shown fangs on the silver screen, from Bela Lugosi to George Hamilton to Gary Oldman, from famous to obscure. The lighting was dim, of course, nothing unusual about that; what was unusual was the clientele. And the posted signs.

The bar was full. The human clients were divided among vampire groupies and tourists. The groupies (fang-bangers, they were called) were dressed in their best finery. It ranged from the traditional capes and tuxes for the men to many Morticia Adams ripoffs among the females. The clothes ranged from reproductions of those worn by Brad Pitt and Tom Cruise in *Interview with the Vampire* to some modern outfits that I thought were influenced by *The Hunger.* Some of the fang-bangers were wearing false fangs, some had painted trickles of blood from the corners of their mouths or puncture marks on their necks. They were extraordinary, and extraordinarily pathetic.

The tourists looked like tourists anywhere, maybe more adventurous than most. But to enter into the spirit of the bar, they were nearly all dressed in black like the fang-bangers. Maybe it was part of a tour package? "Bring some black for your exciting visit to a real vampire bar! Follow the rules, and you'll be fine, catching a glimpse of this exotic underworld."

Strewn among this human assortment, like real jewels in a bin of rhinestones, were the vampires, perhaps fifteen of them. They mostly favored dark clothes, too.

I stood in the middle of the floor, looking around me with interest and amazement and some distaste, and Bill whispered, "You look like a white candle in a coal mine."

I laughed, and we strolled through the scattered tables to the bar. It was the only bar I'd ever seen that had a case of warmed bottled blood on display. Bill, naturally, ordered one, and I took a deep breath and ordered a gin and tonic. The bartender smiled at me, showing me that his fangs had shot out a little at the pleasure of serving me. I tried to smile back and look modest at the same time. He was an American Indian, with long coal black straight hair and a craggy nose, a straight line of a mouth, and a whippy build.

"How's it going, Bill?" the bartender asked. "Long time, no see. This your meal for the night?" He nodded toward me as he put our drinks on the bar before us.

"This is my friend Sookie. She has some questions to ask."

"Anything, beautiful woman," said the bartender, smiling once again. I liked him better when his mouth was the straight line.

"Have you seen this woman, or this one, in the bar?" I asked, drawing the newspaper photos of Maudette and Dawn from my purse. "Or this man?" With a jolt of misgiving, I pulled out my brother's picture.

"Yes to the women, no to the man, though he looks delicious," said the bartender, smiling at me again. "Your brother, perhaps?"

"Yes."

"What possibilities," he whispered.

It was lucky I'd had extensive practice in face control. "Do you remember who the women hung around with?"

"That's something I wouldn't know," he replied quickly, his face closing down. "That's something we don't notice, here. You won't, either."

"Thank you," I said politely, realizing I'd broken a bar rule. It was dangerous to ask who left with whom, evidently. "I appreciate your taking the time."

He looked at me consideringly. "That one," he said, poking a finger at Dawn's picture, "she wanted to die."

"How do you know?"

"Everyone who comes here does, to one extent or another," he said so matter-of-factly I could tell he took that for granted. "That is what we are. Death."

I shuddered. Bill's hand on my arm drew me away to a just-vacated booth. Underscoring the Indian's pronouncement, at regular intervals wall placards proclaimed, "No biting on premises." "No lingering in the parking lot." "Conduct your personal business elsewhere." "Your patronage is appreciated. Proceed at your own risk."

Bill took the top off the bottle with one finger and took a sip. I tried not to look, failed. Of course he saw my face, and he shook his head.

"This is the reality, Sookie," he said. "I need it to live."

There were red stains between his teeth.

"Of course," I said, trying to match the matter-of-fact tone of the bartender. I took a deep breath. "Do you suppose I want to die, since I came here with you?"

"I think you want to find out why other people are dying," he said. But I wasn't sure that was what he really believed.

I didn't think Bill had yet realized that his personal position was precarious. I sipped my drink, felt the blossoming warmth of the gin spread through me.

A fang-banger approached the booth. I was half-hidden by Bill, but still, they'd all seen me enter with him. She was frizzy-haired and boney, with glasses that she stuffed in a purse as she walked over. She bent across the table to get her mouth about two inches from Bill.

"Hi, dangerous," she said in what she hoped was a seductive voice. She tapped Bill's bottled blood with a fingernail painted scarlet. "I have the real stuff." She stroked her neck to make sure he got the point.

I took a deep breath to control my temper. I had invited Bill to this place; he hadn't invited me. I could not comment on what he chose to do here, though I had a surprisingly vivid mental image of leaving a slap mark on this hussy's pale, freckled cheek. I held absolutely still so I wouldn't give Bill any cues about what I wanted.

"I have a companion," Bill said gently.

"She doesn't have any puncture marks on her neck," the girl observed, acknowledging my presence with a contemptuous look. She might as well have said "Chicken!" and flapped her arms like wings. I wondered if steam was visibly coming out of my ears.

"I have a companion," Bill said again, his voice not so gentle this time.

"You don't know what you're missing," she said, her big pale eyes flashing with offense.

"Yes, I do," he said.

She recoiled as if I'd actually done the slapping, and stomped off to her table.

To my disgust, she was only the first of four. These people, men and women, wanted to be intimate with a vampire, and they weren't shy about it.

Bill handled all of them with calm aplomb.

"You're not talking," he said, after a man of forty had left, his eyes actually tearing up at Bill's rejection.

"There's nothing for me to say," I replied, with great self-control.

"You could have sent them on their way. Do you want me to leave you? Is there someone else here who catches your fancy? Long

Shadow, there at the bar, would love to spend time with you, I can tell."

"Oh, for God's sake, no!" I wouldn't have felt safe with any of the other vampires in the bar, would have been terrified they were like Liam or Diane. Bill had turned his dark eyes to me and seemed to be waiting for me to say something else. "I do have to ask them if they've seen Dawn and Maudette in here, though."

"Do you want me with you?"

"Please," I said, and sounded more frightened than I'd wanted to. I'd meant to ask like it would be a casual pleasure to have his company.

"The vampire over there is handsome; he has scanned you twice," he said. I almost wondered if he was doing a little tongue biting himself.

"You're teasing me," I said uncertainly after a moment.

The vampire he'd indicated was handsome, in fact, radiant; blond and blue-eyed, tall and broad shouldered. He was wearing boots, jeans, and a vest. Period. Kind of like the guys on the cover of romance books. He scared me to death.

"His name is Eric," said Bill.

"How old is he?"

"Very. He's the oldest thing in this bar."

"Is he mean?"

"We're all mean, Sookie. We're all very strong and very violent."

"Not you," I said. I saw his face close in on itself. "You want to live mainstream. You're not gonna do antisocial stuff."

"Just when I think you're too naive to walk around alone, you say something shrewd," he said, with a short laugh. "All right, we'll go talk to Eric."

Eric, who, it was true, had glanced my way once or twice, was sitting with a female vampire who was just as lovely as he. They'd already repelled several advances by humans. In fact, one lovelorn young man had already crawled across the floor and kissed the female's boot. She'd stared down at him and kicked him in the shoulder. You could tell it had been an effort for her not to kick him in the face. Tourists flinched, and a couple got up and left hurriedly, but the fang-bangers seemed to take this scene for granted.

At our approach, Eric looked up and scowled until he realized who the intruders were.

"Bill," he said, nodding. Vampires didn't seem to shake hands.

Instead of walking right up to the table, Bill stood a careful distance away, and since he was gripping my arm above my elbow, I had to stop, too. This seemed to be the courteous distance with this set.

"Who's your friend?" asked the female. Though Eric had a slight accent, this woman talked pure American, and her round face and sweet features would have done credit to a milkmaid. She smiled, and her fangs ran out, kind of ruining the image.

"Hi, I'm Sookie Stackhouse," I said politely.

"Aren't you sweet," Eric observed, and I hoped he was thinking of my character.

"Not especially," I said.

Eric stared at me in surprise for a moment. Then he laughed, and the female did, too.

"Sookie, this is Pam and I am Eric," the blond vampire said. Bill and Pam gave each other the vampire nod.

There was a pause. I would have spoken, but Bill squeezed my arm.

"My friend Sookie would like to ask a couple of questions," Bill said.

The seated vampires exchanged bored glances.

Pam said, "Like how long are our fangs, and what kind of coffin do we sleep in?" Her voice was laced with contempt, and you could tell those were tourist questions that she hated.

"No, ma'am," I said. I hoped Bill wouldn't pinch my arm off. I thought I was being calm and courteous.

She stared at me with amazement.

What the hell was so startling? I was getting a little tired of this. Before Bill could give me any more painful hints, I opened my purse and took out the pictures. "I'd like to know if you've seen either of these women in this bar." I wasn't getting Jason's picture out in front of this female. It would've been like putting a bowl of milk in front of a cat.

They looked at the pictures. Bill's face was blank. Eric looked up. "I have been with this one," he said coolly, tapping Dawn's picture. "She liked pain."

Pam was surprised Eric had answered me, I could tell by her eyebrows. She seemed somehow obligated to follow his example. "I have seen both of them. I have never been with them. This one," she flicked her finger at Maudette's picture, "was a pathetic creature."

"Thank you very much, that's all of your time I need to take," I said, and tried to turn to leave. But Bill still held my arm imprisoned.

"Bill, are you quite attached to your friend?" Eric asked.

It took a second for the meaning to sink in. Eric the Hunk was asking if I could be borrowed.

"She is mine," Bill said, but he wasn't roaring it as he had to the nasty vampires from Monroe. Nonetheless, he sounded pretty darn firm.

Eric inclined his golden head, but he gave me the once-over again. At least he started with my face.

Bill seemed to relax. He bowed to Eric, somehow including Pam in the gesture, backed away for two steps, finally permitting me to turn my back to the couple.

"Gee whiz, what was that about?" I asked in a furious whisper. I'd have a big bruise the next day.

"They're older than I am by centuries," Bill said, looking very vampirey.

"Is that the pecking order? By age?"

"Pecking order," Bill said thoughtfully. "That's not a bad way to put it." He almost laughed. I could tell by the way his lip twitched.

"If you had been interested, I would have been obliged to let you go with Eric," he said, after we'd resumed our seats and had a belt from our drinks.

"No," I said sharply.

"Why didn't you say anything when the fang-bangers came to our table trying to seduce me away from you?"

We weren't operating on the same wave level. Maybe social nuances weren't something vampires cared about. I was going to have to explain something that couldn't really bear much explaining.

I made a very unladylike sound out of sheer exasperation.

"Okay," I said sharply. "Listen up, Bill! When you came to my house, I had to invite you. When you came here with me, I had to invite you. You haven't asked me out. Lurking in my driveway doesn't count, and asking me to stop by your house and leave a list of contractors doesn't count. So it's always been me asking you. How can I tell you that you have to stay with me, if you want to go? If those girls will let you suck their blood—or that guy, for that matter—then I don't feel I have a right to stand in your way!"

"Eric is much better looking than I am," Bill said. "He is more powerful, and I understand sex with him is unforgettable. He is so old he only needs to take a sip to maintain his strength. He almost never kills any more. So, as vampires go, he's a good guy. You could still go with him. He is still looking at you. He would try his glamor on you if you were not with me."

"I don't want to go with Eric," I said stubbornly.

"I don't want to go with any of the fang-bangers," he said.

We sat in silence for a minute or two.

"So we're all right," I said obscurely.

"Yes."

We took a few moments more, thinking this over.

"Want another drink?" he asked.

"Yes, unless you need to get back."

"No, this is fine."

He went to the bar. Eric's friend Pam left, and Eric appeared to be counting my eyelashes. I tried to keep my gaze on my hands, to indicate modesty. I felt power tweaks kind of flow over me and had an uneasy feeling Eric was trying to influence me. I risked a quick peek, and sure enough he was looking at me expectantly. Was I supposed to pull off my dress? Bark like a dog? Kick Bill in the shins? Shit.

Bill came back with our drinks.

"He's gonna know I'm not normal," I said grimly. Bill didn't seem to need an explanation.

"He's breaking the rules just attempting to glamorize you after I've told him you're mine," Bill said. He sounded pretty pissed off. His voice didn't get hotter and hotter like mine would have, but colder and colder.

"You seem to be telling everyone that," I muttered. Without doing anything about it, I added silently.

"It's vampire tradition," Bill explained again. "If I pronounce you mine, no one else can try to feed on you."

"Feed on me, that's a delightful phrase," I said sharply, and Bill actually had an expression of exasperation for all of two seconds.

"I'm protecting you," he said, his voice not quite as neutral as usual.

"Had it occurred to you that I—"

And I stopped short. I closed my eyes. I counted to ten.

When I ventured a look at Bill, his eyes were fixed on my face, unblinking. I could practically hear the gears mesh.

"You—don't need protection?" he guessed softly. "You are protecting—me?"

I didn't say anything. I can do that.

But he took the back of my skull in his hand. He turned my head to him as though I were a puppet. (This was getting to be an annoying habit of his.) He looked so hard into my eyes that I thought I had tunnels burned into my brain.

I pursed my lips and blew into his face. "Boo," I said. I was very uncomfortable. I glanced at the people in the bar, letting my guard down, listening.

"Boring," I told him. "These people are boring."

"Are they, Sookie? What are they thinking?" It was a relief to hear his voice, no matter that his voice was a little odd.

"Sex, sex, sex." And that was true. Every single person in that bar had sex on the brain. Even the tourists, who mostly weren't thinking about having sex with the vampires themselves, but were thinking about the fang-bangers having sex with the vampires.

"What are you thinking about, Sookie?"

"Not sex," I answered promptly and truthfully. I'd just gotten an unpleasant shock.

"Is that so?"

"I was thinking about the chances of us getting out of here without any trouble."

"Why were you thinking about that?"

"Because one of the tourists is a cop in disguise, and he just went to the bathroom, and he knows that a vampire is in there, sucking on the neck of a fang-banger. He's already called the police on his little radio."

"Out," he said smoothly, and we were out of the booth swiftly and moving for the door. Pam had vanished, but as we passed Eric's table, Bill gave him some sign. Just as smoothly, Eric eased from his seat and rose to his magnificent height, his stride so much longer than ours that he passed out the door first, taking the arm of the bouncer and propelling her outside with us.

As we were about to go out the door, I remembered the bartender, Long Shadow, had answered my questions willingly, so I turned and jabbed my finger in the direction of the door, unmistakably telling him to leave. He looked as alarmed as a vampire can look, and as Bill yanked me through the double doors, he was throwing down his towel.

Outside, Eric was waiting outside by his car—a Corvette, naturally.

"There's going to be a raid," Bill said.

"How do you know?"

Bill stuck on that one.

"Me," I said, getting him off the hook.

Eric's wide blue eyes shone even in the gloom of the parking lot. I was going to have to explain.

"I read a policeman's mind," I muttered. I snuck a look to see how Eric was taking this, and he was staring at me the same way the Monroe vampires had. Thoughtful. Hungry.

"That's interesting," he said. "I had a psychic once. It was incredible."

"Did the psychic think so?" My voice was tarter than I'd meant it to be.

I could hear Bill's indrawn breath.

Eric laughed. "For a while," he answered ambiguously.

We heard sirens in the distance, and without further words Eric and the bouncer slid into his car and were gone into the night, the car seeming quieter than others' cars, somehow. Bill and I buckled up hastily, and we were leaving the parking lot by one exit just as the police were coming in by another. They had their vampire van with them, a special prisoner transport with silver bars. It was driven by two cops who were of the fanged persuasion, and they sprang out of their van and reached the club door with a speed that rendered them just blurs on my human vision.

We had driven a few blocks when suddenly Bill pulled into the parking lot of yet another darkened strip mall.

"What—?" I began, but got no further. Bill had unclipped my seat belt, moved the seat back, and grabbed me before I had finished my sentence. Frightened that he was angry, I pushed against him at first, but I might as well have been heaving against a tree. Then his mouth located mine, and I knew what he was.

Oh, boy, could he kiss. We might have problems communicating on some levels, but this wasn't one of them. We had a great time for maybe five minutes. I felt all the right things moving through my body in waves. Despite the awkwardness of being in the front seat of a car, I managed to be comfortable, mostly because he was so strong and considerate. I nipped his skin with my teeth. He made a sound like a growl.

"Sookie!" His voice was ragged.

I moved away from him, maybe half an inch.

"If you do that any more I'll have you whether you want to be had or not," he said, and I could tell he meant it.

"You don't want to," I said finally, trying not to make it a question.

"Oh, yes, I want to," and he grabbed my hand and showed me.

Suddenly, there was a bright rotating light beside us.

"The police," I said. I could see a figure get out of the patrol car and start toward Bill's window. "Don't let him know you're a vampire, Bill," I said hastily, fearing fallout from the Fangtasia raid. Though most police forces loved having vampires join them on the job, there was a lot of prejudice against vampires on the street, especially as part of a mixed couple.

The policeman's heavy hand rapped on the window.

Bill turned on the motor, hit the button that lowered the window. But he was silent, and I realized his fangs had not retracted. If he opened his mouth, it would be really obvious he was a vampire.

"Hello, officer," I said.

"Good evening," the man said, politely enough. He bent to look in the window. "You two know all the shops here are closed, right?"

"Yes, sir."

"Now, I can tell you been messing around a little, and I got nothing against that, but you two need to go home and do this kind of thing."

"We will." I nodded eagerly, and Bill managed a stiff inclination of his head.

"We're raiding a bar a few blocks back," the patrolman said casually. I could see only a little of his face, but he seemed burly and middle-aged. "You two coming from there, by any chance?"

"No," I said.

"Vampire bar," the cop remarked.

"Nope. Not us."

"Let me just shine this light on your neck, miss, if you don't mind."

"Not at all."

And by golly, he shone that old flashlight on my neck and then on Bill's.

"Okay, just checking. You two move on now."

"Yes, we will."

Bill's nod was even more curt. While the patrolman waited, I slid back over to my side and clipped my seat belt, and Bill put the car in gear and backed up.

Bill was just infuriated. All the way home he kept a sullen (I guess) silence, whereas I was inclined to view the whole thing as funny.

I was cheerful at finding Bill wasn't indifferent to my personal attractions, such as they were. I began to hope that someday he would want to kiss me again, maybe longer and harder, and maybe even—we could go further? I was trying not to get my hopes up. Actually, there was a thing or two that Bill didn't know about me, that no one knew, and I was very careful to try to keep my expectations modest.

When he got me back to Gran's, he came around and opened my door, which made me raise my eyebrows; but I am not one to stop a courteous act. I assumed Bill did realize I had functioning arms and the mental ability to figure out the door-opening mechanism. When I stepped out, he backed up.

I was hurt. He didn't want to kiss me again; he was regretting our earlier episode. Probably pining after that damn Pam. Or maybe even

Long Shadow. I was beginning to see that the ability to have sex for several centuries leaves room for lots of experimentation. Would a telepath be so bad to add to his list?

I kind of hunched my shoulders together and wrapped my arms across my chest.

"Are you cold?" Bill asked instantly, putting his arm around me. But it was the physical equivalent of a coat, he seemed to be trying to stay as far away from me as the arm made possible.

"I am sorry I have pestered you. I won't ask you for any more," I said, keeping my voice even. Even as I spoke I realized that Gran hadn't set up a date for Bill to speak to the Descendants, but she and Bill would just have to work that out.

He stood still. Finally he said, "You—are—incredibly—naive." And he didn't even add that codicil about shrewdness, like he had earlier.

"Well," I said blankly. "I am?"

"Or maybe one of God's fools," he said, and that sounded a lot less pleasant, like Quasimodo or something.

"I guess," I said tartly, "you'll just have to find out."

"It had better be me that finds out," he said darkly, which I didn't understand at all. He walked me up to the door, and I was sure hoping for another kiss, but he gave me a little peck on the forehead. "Good night, Sookie," he whispered.

I rested my cheek against his for a moment. "Thanks for taking me," I said, and moved away quickly before he thought I was asking for something else. "I'm not calling you again." And before I could lose my determination, I slipped into the dark house and shut the door in Bill's face.

Chapter 5

I CERTAINLY HAD a lot to think about the next couple of days. For someone who was always hoarding new things to keep from being bored, I'd stored enough up to last me for weeks. The people in Fangtasia, alone, were food for examination, to say nothing of the vampires. From longing to meet one vampire, now I'd met more than I cared to know.

A lot of men from Bon Temps and the surrounding area had been called in to the police station to answer a few questions about Dawn Green and her habits. Embarrassingly enough, Detective Bellefleur took to hanging around the bar on his off-hours, never drinking more alcohol than one beer, but observing everything that took place around him. Since Merlotte's was not exactly a hotbed of illegal activity, no one minded too much once they got used to Andy being there.

He always seemed to pick a table in my section. And he began to play a silent game with me. When I came to his table, he'd be thinking something provocative, trying to get me to say something. He didn't seem to understand how indecent that was. The provocation was the point, not the insult. He just wanted me to read his mind again. I couldn't figure out why.

Then, maybe the fifth or sixth time I had to get him something, I guess it was a Diet Coke, he pictured me cavorting with my brother. I was so nervous when I went to the table (knowing to expect something, but not knowing exactly what) that I was beyond getting angry and into the realm of tears. It reminded me of the less sophisticated tormenting I'd taken when I was in grade school.

Andy had looked up with an expectant face, and when he saw tears an amazing range of things ran across his face in quick succession: triumph, chagrin, then scalding shame.

I poured the damn coke down his shirt.

I walked right past the bar and out the back door.

"What's the matter?" Sam asked sharply. He was right on my heels.

I shook my head, not wanting to explain, and pulled an aging tissue out of my shorts pocket to mop my eyes with.

"Has he been saying ugly things to you?" Sam asked, his voice lower and angrier.

"He's been thinking them," I said helplessly, "to get a rise out of me. He knows."

"Son of a bitch," Sam said, which almost shocked me back to normal. Sam didn't curse.

Once I started crying, it seemed like I couldn't stop. I was getting my crying time done for a number of little unhappinesses.

"Just go on back in," I said, embarrassed at my waterworks. "I'll be okay in just a minute."

I heard the back door of the bar open and shut. I figured Sam had taken me at my word. But instead, Andy Bellefleur said, "I apologize, Sookie."

"That's Miss Stackhouse to you, Andy Bellefleur," I said. "It seems to me like you better be out finding who killed Maudette and Dawn instead of playing nasty mind games with me."

I turned around and looked at the policeman. He was looking horribly embarrassed. I thought he was sincere in his shame.

Sam was swinging his arms, full of the energy of anger.

"Bellefleur, sit in someone else's area if you come back," he said, but his voice held a lot of suppressed violence.

Andy looked at Sam. He was twice as thick in the body, taller by two inches. But I would have put my money on Sam at that moment, and it seemed Andy didn't want to risk the challenge either, if only from good sense. He just nodded and walked across the parking lot to his car. The sun glinted on the blond highlights in his brown hair.

"Sookie, I'm sorry," Sam said.

"Not your fault."

"Do you want to take some time off? We're not so busy today."

"Nope. I'll finish my shift." Charlsie Tooten was getting into the swing of things, but I wouldn't feel good about leaving. It was Arlene's day off.

We went back into the bar, and though several people looked at us curiously as we entered, no one asked us what had happened. There was only one couple sitting in my area, and they were busy eating and had glasses full of liquid, so they wouldn't be needing me. I began putting up wineglasses. Sam leaned against the workspace beside me.

"Is it true that Bill Compton is going to speak to the Descendants of the Glorious Dead tonight?"

"According to my grandmother."

"Are you going?"

"I hadn't planned on it." I didn't want to see Bill until he called me and made an appointment to see me.

Sam didn't say anything else then, but later in the afternoon, as I was retrieving my purse from his office, he came in and fiddled with some papers on his desk. I'd pulled out my brush and was trying to get a tangle out of my ponytail. From the way Sam dithered around, it seemed apparent that he wanted to talk to me, and I felt a wave of exasperation at the indirection men seemed to take.

Like Andy Bellefleur. He could just have asked me about my disability, instead of playing games with me.

Like Bill. He could just have stated his intentions, instead of this strange hot-cold thing.

"So?" I said, more sharply than I'd intended.

He flushed under my gaze.

"I wondered if you'd like to go to the Descendants meeting with me and have a cup of coffee afterward."

I was flabbergasted. My brush stopped in midswoop. A number of things ran through my mind, the feel of his hand when I'd held it in front of Dawn Green's duplex, the wall I'd met in his mind, the unwisdom of dating your boss.

"Sure," I said, after a notable pause.

He seemed to exhale. "Good. Then I'll pick you up at your house at seven-twenty or so. The meeting starts at seven-thirty."

"Okay. I'll see you then."

Afraid I'd do something peculiar if I stayed longer, I grabbed my purse and strode out to my car. I couldn't decide whether to giggle with glee or groan at my own idiocy.

It was five-forty-five by the time I got home. Gran already had supper on the table since she had to leave early to carry refreshments to the Descendants meeting, which was held at the Community Building.

"Wonder if he could have come if we'd had it in the fellowship hall of Good Faith Baptist?" Gran said out of the blue. But I didn't have a problem latching on to her train of thought.

"Oh, I think so," I said. "I think that idea about vampires being scared of religious items isn't true. But I haven't asked him."

"They do have a big cross hung up in there," Gran went on.

"I'll be at the meeting after all," I said. "I'm going with Sam Merlotte."

"Your boss, Sam?" Gran was very surprised.

"Yes, ma'am."

"Hmmm. Well, well." Gran began smiling while she put the plates on the table. I was trying to think of what to wear while we ate our sandwiches and fruit salad. Gran was excited about the meeting, about listening to Bill and introducing him to her friends, and now she was in outer space somewhere (probably around Venus) since I actually had a date. With a human.

"We'll be going out afterward," I said, "so I guess I'll get home maybe an hour after the meeting's over." There weren't that many places to have coffee in Bon Temps. And those restaurants weren't exactly places you'd want to linger.

"Okay, honey. You just take your time." Gran was already dressed, and after supper I helped her load up the cookie trays and the big coffee urn she'd bought for just such events. Gran had pulled her car around to the back door, which saved us a lot of steps. She was happy as she could be and fussed and chattered the whole time we were loading. This was her kind of night.

I shed my waitress clothes and got into the shower lickety-split. While I soaped up, I tried to think of what to wear. Nothing black and white, that was for sure; I had gotten pretty sick of the Merlotte's waitress colors. I shaved my legs again, didn't have time to wash my hair and dry it, but I'd done it the night before. I flung open my closet and stared. Sam had seen the white flowered dress. The denim jumper wasn't nice enough for Gran's friends. Finally I yanked out some khaki slacks and a bronze silk blouse with short sleeves. I had brown leather sandals and a brown leather belt that would look good. I hung a chain around my neck, stuck in some big gold earrings, and I was ready. As if he'd timed it, Sam rang the doorbell.

There was a moment of awkwardness as I opened the door.

"You're welcome to come in, but I think we just have time—"

"I'd like to sit and visit, but I think we just have time—"

We both laughed.

I locked the door and pulled it to, and Sam hurried to open the door of his pickup. I was glad I'd worn pants, as I pictured trying to get up in the high cab in one of my shorter skirts.

"Need a boost?" he asked hopefully.

"I think I got it," I said, trying not to smile.

We were silent on the way to the Community Building, which

was in the older part of Bon Temps; the part that predated the War. The structure was not antebellum, but there had actually been a building on that site that had gotten destroyed during the War, though no one seemed to have a record of what it had been.

The Descendants of the Glorious Dead were a mixed bunch. There were some very old, very fragile members, and some not quite so old and very lively members, and there were even a scattering of middle-aged men and women. But there were no young members, which Gran had often lamented, with many significant glances at me.

Mr. Sterling Norris, a longtime friend of my grandmother's and the mayor of Bon Temps, was the greeter that night, and he stood at the door shaking hands and having a little conversation with everyone who entered.

"Miss Sookie, you look prettier every day," Mr. Norris said. "And Sam, we haven't seen you in a coon's age! Sookie, is it true this vampire is a friend of yours?"

"Yes, sir."

"Can you say for sure that we're all safe?"

"Yes, I'm sure you are. He's a very nice . . . person." Being? Entity? If you like the living dead, he's pretty neat?

"If you say so," Mr. Norris said dubiously. "In my time, such a thing was just a fairy tale."

"Oh, Mr. Norris, it's still your time," I said with the cheerful smile expected of me, and he laughed and motioned us on in, which was what was expected of him. Sam took my hand and sort of steered me to the next to last row of metal chairs, and I waved at my grandmother as we took our seats. It was just time for the meeting to start, and the room held maybe forty people, quite a gathering for Bon Temps. But Bill wasn't there.

Just then the president of Descendants, a massive, solid woman by the name of Maxine Fortenberry, came to the podium.

"Good evening! Good evening!" she boomed. "Our guest of honor has just called to say he's having car trouble and will be a few minutes late. So let's go on and have our business meeting while we're waiting for him."

The group settled down, and we got through all the boring stuff, Sam sitting beside me with his arms crossed over his chest, his right leg crossed over the left at the ankle. I was being especially careful to keep my mind guarded and face smiling, and I was a little deflated when Sam leaned slightly to me and whispered, "It's okay to relax."

"I thought I was," I whispered back.

"I don't think you know how."

I raised my eyebrows at him. I was going to have a few things to say to Mr. Merlotte after the meeting.

Just then Bill came in, and there was a moment of sheer silence as those who hadn't seen him before adjusted to his presence. If you've never been in the company of a vampire before, it's a thing you really have to get used to. Under the flourescent lighting, Bill really looked much more unhuman than he did under the dim lighting in Merlotte's, or the equally dim lighting in his own home. There was no way he could pass for a regular guy. His pallor was very marked, of course, and the deep pools of his eyes looked darker and colder. He was wearing a lightweight medium-blue suit, and I was willing to bet that had been Gran's advice. He looked great. The dominant line of the arch of his eyebrow, the curve of his bold nose, the chiseled lips, the white hands with their long fingers and carefully trimmed nails . . . He was having an exchange with the president, and she was charmed out of her support hose by Bill's close-lipped smile.

I didn't know if Bill was casting a glamor over the whole room, or if these people were just predisposed to be interested, but the whole group hushed expectantly.

Then Bill saw me. I swear his eyebrows twitched. He gave me a little bow, and I nodded back, finding no smile in me to give him. Even in the crowd, I stood at the edge of the deep pool of his silence.

Mrs. Fortenberry introduced Bill, but I don't remember what she said or how she skirted the fact that Bill was a different kind of creature.

Then Bill began speaking. He had notes, I saw with some surprise. Beside me, Sam leaned forward, his eyes fixed on Bill's face.

". . . we didn't have any blankets and very little food," Bill was saying calmly. "There were many deserters."

That was not a favorite fact of the Descendants, but a few of them were nodding in agreement. This account must match what they'd learned in their studies.

An ancient man in the first row raised his hand.

"Sir, did you by chance know my great-grandfather, Tolliver Humphries?"

"Yes," Bill said, after a moment. His face was unreadable. "Tolliver was my friend."

And just for a moment, there was something so tragic in his voice that I had to close my eyes.

"What was he like?" quavered the old man.

"Well, he was foolhardy, which led to his death," said Bill with a wry smile. "He was brave. He never made a cent in his life that he didn't waste."

"How did he die? Were you there?"

"Yes, I was there," said Bill wearily. "I saw him get shot by a Northern sniper in the woods about twenty miles from here. He was slow because he was starved. We all were. About the middle of the morning, a cold morning, Tolliver saw a boy in our troop get shot as he lay in poor cover in the middle of a field. The boy was not dead, but painfully wounded. But he could call to us, and he did, all morning. He called to us to help him. He knew he would die if someone didn't."

The whole room had grown so silent you could hear a pin drop.

"He screamed and he moaned. I almost shot him myself, to shut him up, because I knew to venture out to rescue him was suicide. But I could not quite bring myself to kill him. That would be murder, not war, I told myself. But later I wished I had shot him, for Tolliver was less able than I to withstand the boy's pleading. After two hours of it, he told me he planned to try to rescue the boy. I argued with him. But Tolliver told me that God wanted him to attempt it. He had been praying as we lay in the woods.

"Though I told Tolliver that God did not wish him to waste his life foolishly—that he had a wife and children praying for his safe return at home—Tolliver asked me to divert the enemy while he attempted the boy's rescue. He ran out into the field like it was a spring day and he was well rested. And he got as far as the wounded boy. But then a shot rang out, and Tolliver fell dead. And, after a time, the boy began screaming for help again."

"What happened to him?" asked Mrs. Fortenberry, her voice as quiet as she could manage to make it.

"He lived," Bill said, and there was tone to his voice that sent shivers down my spine. "He survived the day, and we were able to retrieve him that night."

Somehow those people had come alive again as Bill spoke, and for the old man in the front row there was a memory to cherish, a memory that said much about his ancestor's character.

I don't think anyone who'd come to the meeting that night was prepared for the impact of hearing about the Civil War from a survivor. They were enthralled; they were shattered.

When Bill had answered the last question, there was thunderous applause, or at least it was as thunderous as forty people could make it. Even Sam, not Bill's biggest fan, managed to put his hands together.

Everyone wanted to have a personal word with Bill afterward except me and Sam. While the reluctant guest speaker was surrounded by Descendants, Sam and I sneaked out to Sam's pickup. We went to the Crawdad Diner, a real dive that happened to have very good food. I wasn't hungry, but Sam had key lime pie with his coffee.

"That was interesting," Sam said cautiously.

"Bill's speech? Yes," I said, just as cautiously.

"Do you have feelings for him?"

After all the indirection, Sam had decided to storm the main gate.

"Yes," I said.

"Sookie," Sam said, "You have no future with him."

"On the other hand, he's been around a while. I expect he'll be around for a another few hundred years."

"You never know what's going to happen to a vampire."

I couldn't argue with that. But, as I pointed out to Sam, I couldn't know what was going to happen to me, a human, either.

We wrangled back and forth like this for too long. Finally, exasperated, I said, "What's it to you, Sam?"

His ruddy skin flushed. His bright blue eyes met mine. "I like you, Sookie. As friend or maybe something else sometime . . ."

Huh?

"I just hate to see you take a wrong turn."

I looked at him. I could feel my skeptical face forming, eyebrows drawn together, the corner of my mouth tugging up.

"Sure," I said, my voice matching my face.

"I've always liked you."

"So much that you had to wait till someone else showed an interest, before you mentioned it to me?"

"I deserve that." He seemed to be turning something over in his mind, something he wanted to say, but hadn't the resolution.

Whatever it was, he couldn't come out with it, apparently.

"Let's go," I suggested. It would be hard to turn the conversation back to neutral ground, I figured. I might as well go home.

It was a funny ride back. Sam always seemed on the verge of speaking, and then he'd shake his head and keep silent. I was so aggravated I wanted to swat him.

We got home later than I'd thought. Gran's light was on, but the rest of the house was dark. I didn't see her car, so I figured she'd parked in back to unload the leftovers right into the kitchen. The porch light was on for me.

Sam walked around and opened the pickup door, and I stepped

down. But in the shadow, my foot missed the running board, and I just sort of tumbled out. Sam caught me. First his hands gripped my arms to steady me, then they just slid around me. And he kissed me.

I assumed it was going to be a little good-night peck, but his mouth just kind of lingered. It was really more than pleasant, but suddenly my inner censor said, "This is the boss."

I gently disengaged. He was immediately aware that I was backing off, and gently slid his hands down my arms until he was just holding hands with me. We went to the door, not speaking.

"I had a good time," I said, softly. I didn't want to wake Gran, and I didn't want to sound bouncy.

"I did, too. Again sometime?"

"We'll see," I said. I really didn't know how I felt about Sam.

I waited to hear his truck turn around before I switched off the porch light and went into the house. I was unbuttoning my blouse as I walked, tired and ready for bed.

Something was wrong.

I stopped in the middle of the living room. I looked around me.

Everything looked all right, didn't it?

Yes. Everything was in its proper place.

It was the smell.

It was a sort of penny smell.

A coppery smell, sharp and salty.

The smell of blood.

It was down here with me, not upstairs where the guest bedrooms sat in neat solitude.

"Gran?" I called. I hated the quavering in my voice.

I made myself move, I made myself go to the door of her room. It was pristine. I began switching on lights as I went through the house.

My room was just as I'd left it.

The bathroom was empty.

The washroom was empty.

I switched on the last light. The kitchen was . . .

I screamed, over and over. My hands were fluttering uselessly in the air, trembling more with each scream. I heard a crash behind me, but couldn't be concerned. Then big hands gripped me and moved me, and a big body was between me and what I'd seen on the kitchen floor. I didn't recognize Bill, but he picked me up and moved me to the living room where I couldn't see any more.

"Sookie," he said harshly, "Shut up! This isn't any good!"

If he'd been kind to me, I'd have kept on shrieking.

"Sorry," I said, still out of my mind. "I am acting like that boy."

He stared at me blankly.

"The one in your story," I said numbly.

"We have to call the police."

"Sure."

"We have to dial the phone."

"Wait. How did you come here?"

"Your grandmother gave me a ride home, but I insisted on coming with her first and helping her unload the car."

"So why are you still here?"

"I was waiting for you."

"So, did you see who killed her?"

"No. I went home, across the cemetery, to change."

He was wearing blue jeans and Grateful Dead T-shirt, and suddenly I began to giggle.

"That's priceless," I said, doubling over with the laughter.

And I was crying, just as suddenly. I picked up the phone and dialled 911.

Andy Bellefleur was there in five minutes.

J ASON CAME AS soon as I reached him. I tried to call him at four or five different places, and finally reached him at Merlotte's. Terry Bellefleur was bartending for Sam that night, and when he'd gotten back from telling Jason to come to his grandmother's house, I asked Terry if he'd call Sam and tell him I had troubles and couldn't work for a few days.

Terry must have called Sam right away because Sam was at my house within thirty minutes, still wearing the clothes he'd worn to the meeting that night. At the sight of him I looked down, remembering unbuttoning my blouse as I walked through the living room, a fact I'd completely lost track of; but I was decent. It dawned on me that Bill must have set me to rights. I might find that embarrassing later, but at the moment I was just grateful.

So Jason came in, and when I told him Gran was dead, and dead by violence, he just looked at me. There seemed to be nothing going on behind his eyes. It was as if someone had erased his capacity for absorbing new facts. Then what I'd said sank in, and my brother sank to his knees right where he stood, and I knelt in front of him. He put his arms around me and lay his head on my shoulder, and we just stayed there for a while. We were all that was left.

Bill and Sam were out in the front yard sitting in lawn chairs, out of the way of the police. Soon Jason and I were asked to go out on the porch, at least, and we opted to sit outside, too. It was a mild evening, and I sat facing the house, all lit up like a birthday cake, and the people that came and went from it like ants who'd been allowed at the party. All this industry surrounding the tissue that had been my grandmother.

"What happened?" Jason asked finally.

"I came in from the meeting," I said very slowly. "After Sam pulled off in his truck. I knew something was wrong. I looked in every room." This was the story of How I Found Grandmother Dead, the official version. "And when I got to the kitchen I saw her."

Jason turned his head very slowly so his eyes met mine. "Tell me."

I shook my head silently. But it was his right to know. "She was beaten up, but she had tried to fight back, I think. Whoever did this cut her up some. And then strangled her, it looked like."

I could not even look at my brother's face. "It was my fault." My voice was nothing more than a whisper.

"How do you figure that?" Jason said, sounding nothing more than dull and sluggish.

"I figure someone came to kill me like they killed Maudette and Dawn, but Gran was here instead."

I could see the idea percolate in Jason's brain.

"I was supposed to be home tonight while she was at the meeting, but Sam asked me to go at the last minute. My car was here like it would be normally because we went in Sam's truck. Gran had parked her car around back while she was unloading, so it wouldn't look like she was here, just me. She had given Bill a ride home, but he helped her unload and went to change clothes. After he left, whoever it was . . . got her."

"How do we know it wasn't Bill?" Jason asked, as though Bill wasn't sitting right there beside him.

"How do we know it wasn't anyone?" I said, exasperated at my brother's slow wits. "It could be anyone, anyone we know. I don't think it was Bill. I don't think Bill killed Maudette and Dawn. And I do think whoever killed Maudette and Dawn killed Grandmother."

"Did you know," Jason said, his voice too loud, "that Grandmother left you this house all by yourself?"

It was like he'd thrown a bucket of cold water in my face. I saw Sam wince, too. Bill's eyes got darker and chillier.

"No. I just always assumed you and I would share like we did on the other one." Our parents' house, the one Jason lived in now.

"She left you all the land, too."

"Why are you saying this?" I was going to cry again, just when I'd been sure I was dry of tears now.

"She wasn't fair!" he was yelling. "It wasn't fair, and now she can't set it right!"

I began to shake. Bill pulled me out of the chair and began walking with me up and down the yard. Sam sat in front of Jason and began talking to him earnestly, his voice low and intense.

Bill's arm was around me, but I couldn't stop shaking.

"Did he mean that?" I asked, not expecting Bill to answer.

"No," he said. I looked up, surprised.

"No, he couldn't help your grandmother, and he couldn't handle the idea of someone lying in wait for you and killing her instead. So he had to get angry about something. And instead of getting angry with you for not getting killed, he's angry about things. I wouldn't let it worry me."

"I think it's pretty amazing that you're saying this," I told him bluntly.

"Oh, I took some night school courses in psychology," said Bill Compton, vampire.

And, I couldn't help thinking, hunters always study their prey. "Why would Gran leave me all this, and not Jason?"

"Maybe you'll find out later," he said, and that seemed fine to me.

Then Andy Bellefleur came out of the house and stood on the steps, looking up at the sky as if there were clues written on it.

"Compton," he called sharply.

"No," I said, and my voice came out as a growl.

I could feel Bill look down at me with the slight surprise that was a big reaction, coming from him.

"Now it's gonna happen," I said furiously.

"You *were* protecting me," he said. "You thought the police would suspect me of killing those two women. That's why you wanted to be sure they were accessible to other vampires. Now you think this Bellefleur will try to blame your grandmother's death on me."

"Yes."

He took a deep breath. We were in the dark, by the trees that lined the yard. Andy bellowed Bill's name again.

"Sookie," Bill said gently, "I am sure you were the intended victim, as sure as you are."

It was kind of a shock to hear someone else say it.

"And I didn't kill them. So if the killer was the same as their killer, then I didn't do it, and he will see that. Even if he is a Bellefleur."

We began walking back into the light. I wanted none of this to be. I wanted the lights and the people to vanish, all of them, Bill, too. I wanted to be alone in the house with my grandmother, and I wanted her to look happy, as she had the last time I'd seen her.

It was futile and childish, but I could wish it nonetheless. I was lost in that dream, so lost I didn't see harm coming until it was too late.

My brother, Jason, stepped in front of me and slapped me in the face.

It was so unexpected and so painful that I lost my balance and staggered to the side, landing hard on one knee.

Jason seemed to be coming after me again, but Bill was suddenly in front of me, crouched, and his fangs were out and he was scary as hell. Sam tackled Jason and brought him down, and he may have whacked Jason's face against the ground once for good measure.

Andy Bellefleur was stunned at this unexpected display of violence. But after a second he stepped in between our two little groups on the lawn. He looked at Bill and swallowed, but he said in a steady voice, "Compton, back off. He won't hit her again."

Bill was taking deep breaths, trying to control his hunger for Jason's blood. I couldn't read his thoughts, but I could read his body language.

I couldn't exactly read Sam's thoughts, but I could tell he was very angry.

Jason was sobbing. His thoughts were a confused and tangled blue mess.

And Andy Bellefleur didn't like any of us and wished he could lock every freaking one of us up for some reason or another.

I pushed myself wearily to my feet and touched the painful spot of my cheek, using that to distract me from the pain in my heart, the dreadful grief that rolled over me.

I thought this night would never end.

THE FUNERAL WAS the largest ever held in Renard Parish. The minister said so. Under a brilliant early summer sky, my grandmother was buried beside my mother and father in our family plot in the ancient cemetery between the Comptons' house and Gran's house.

Jason had been right. It was my house, now. The house and the twenty acres surrounding it were mine, as were the mineral rights. Gran's money, what there was, had been divided fairly between us, and Gran had stipulated that I give Jason my half of the home our parents had lived in, if I wanted to retain full rights to her house. That was easy to do, and I didn't want any money from Jason for that half, though my lawyer looked dubious when I told him that. Jason would just blow his top if I mentioned paying me for my half; the fact that I was part-owner had never been more than a fantasy to him. Yet Gran leaving her house to me outright had come as a big shock. She had understood him better than I had.

It was lucky I had income other than from the bar, I thought heavily, trying to concentrate on something besides her loss. Paying taxes on the land and house, plus the upkeep of the house, which Gran had assumed at least partially, would really stretch my income.

"I guess you'll want to move," Maxine Fortenberry said when she was cleaning the kitchen. Maxine had brought over devilled eggs and ham salad, and she was trying to be extra helpful by scrubbing.

"No," I said, surprised.

"But honey, with it happening right here . . ." Maxine's heavy face creased with concern.

"I have far more good memories of this kitchen than bad ones," I explained.

"Oh, what a good way to look at it," she said, surprised. "Sookie, you really are smarter than anyone gives you credit for being."

"Gosh, thanks, Mrs. Fortenberry," I said, and if she heard the dry tone in my voice she didn't react. Maybe that was wise.

"Is your friend coming to the funeral?" The kitchen was very warm. Bulky, square Maxine was blotting her face with a dishtowel. The spot where Gran had fallen had been scrubbed by her friends, God bless them.

"My friend. Oh, Bill? No, he can't."

She looked at me blankly.

"We're having it in the daytime, of course."

She still didn't comprehend.

"He can't come out."

"Oh, of course!" She gave herself a light tap on the temple to indicate she was knocking sense into her head. "Silly me. Would he really fry?"

"Well, he says he would."

"You know, I'm so glad he gave that talk at the club, that has really made such a difference in making him part of the community."

I nodded, abstracted.

"There's really a lot of feeling about the murders, Sookie. There's really a lot of talk about vampires, about how they're responsible for these deaths."

I looked at her with narrowed eyes.

"Don't you go all mad on me, Sookie Stackhouse! Since Bill was so sweet about telling those fascinating stories at the Descendants meeting, most people don't think he could do those awful things that were done to those women." I wondered what stories were making the rounds, and I shuddered to think. "But he's had some visitors that people didn't much like the looks of."

I wondered if she meant Malcolm, Liam, and Diane. I hadn't much liked their looks either, and I resisted the automatic impulse to defend them.

"Vampires are just as different among themselves as humans are," I said.

"That's what I told Andy Bellefleur," she said, nodding vehemently. "I said to Andy, you should go after some of those others, the ones that don't want to learn how to live with us, not like Bill Compton, who's really making an effort to settle in. He was telling me at the funeral home that he'd gotten his kitchen finished, finally."

I could only stare at her. I tried to think of what Bill might make in his kitchen. Why would he need one?

But none of the distractions worked, and finally I just realized that for a while I was going to be crying every whipstitch. And I did.

At the funeral Jason stood beside me, apparently over his surge of anger at me, apparently back in his right mind. He didn't touch me or talk to me, but he didn't hit me, either. I felt very alone. But then I realized as I looked out over the hillside that the whole town was grieving with me. There were cars as far as I could see on the narrow drives through the cemetery, there were hundreds of dark-clad folks around the funeral-home tent. Sam was there in a suit (looking quite unlike himself), and Arlene, standing by Rene, was wearing a flowered Sunday dress. Lafayette stood at the very back of the crowd, along with Terry Bellefleur and Charlsie Tooten; the bar must be closed! And all Gran's friends, all, the ones who could still walk. Mr. Norris wept openly, a snowy white handkerchief held up to his eyes. Maxine's heavy face was set in graven lines of sadness. While the minister said what he had to, while Jason and I sat alone in family area in the uneven folding chairs, I felt something in me detach and fly up, up into the blue brilliance: and I knew that whatever had happened to my grandmother, now she was at home.

The rest of the day went by in a blur, thank God. I didn't want to remember it, didn't want to even know it was happening. But one moment stood out.

Jason and I were standing by the dining room table in Gran's house, some temporary truce between us. We greeted the mourners, most of whom did their best not to stare at the bruise on my cheek.

We glided through it, Jason thinking that he would go home and have a drink after, and he wouldn't have to see me for a while and then it would be all right, and me thinking almost exactly the same thing. Except for the drink.

A well-meaning woman came up to us, the sort of woman who has thought over every ramification of a situation that was none of her business to start with.

"I am so sorry for you kids," she said, and I looked at her; for the life of me I couldn't remember her name. She was a Methodist. She had three grown children. But her name ran right out the other side of my head.

"You know it was so sad seeing you two there alone today, it made me remember your mother and father so much," she said, her face creasing into a mask of sympathy that I knew was automatic. I glanced at Jason, looked back to the woman, nodded.

"Yes," I said. But I heard her thought before she spoke, and I began to blanch.

"But where was Adele's brother today, your great uncle? Surely he's still living?"

"We're not in touch," I said, and my tone would have discouraged anyone more sensitive than this lady.

"But her only brother! Surely you . . ." and her voice died away as our combined stare finally sank home.

Several other people had commented briefly on our Uncle Bartlett's absence, but we had given the "this is family business" signals that cut them right off. This woman—what was her name?—just hadn't been as quick to read them. She'd brought a taco salad, and I planned to throw it right into the garbage when she'd left.

"We do have to tell him," Jason said quietly after she left. I put my guard up; I had no desire to know what he was thinking.

"You call him," I said.

"All right."

And that was all we said to each other for the rest of the day.

Chapter 6

I STAYED AT home for three days after the funeral. It was too long; I needed to go back to work. But I kept thinking of things I just had to do, or so I told myself. I cleaned out Gran's room. Arlene happened to drop by, and I asked her for help, because I just couldn't be in there alone with my grandmother's things, all so familiar and imbued with her personal odor of Johnson's baby powder and Campho-Phenique.

So my friend Arlene helped me pack everything up to take to the disaster relief agency. There'd been tornadoes in northern Arkansas the past few days, and surely some person who had lost everything could use all the clothes. Gran had been smaller and thinner than I, and besides that her tastes were very different, so I wanted nothing of hers except the jewelry. She'd never worn much, but what she wore was real and precious to me.

It was amazing what Gran had managed to pack into her room. I didn't even want to think about what she'd stored in the attic: that would be dealt with later, in the fall, when the attic was bearably cool and I'd time to think.

I probably threw away more than I should have, but it made me feel efficient and strong to be doing this, and I did a drastic job of it. Arlene folded and packed, only putting aside papers and photographs, letters and bills and cancelled checks. My grandmother had never used a credit card in her life and never bought anything on time, God bless her, which made the winding-up much easier.

Arlene asked about Gran's car. It was five years old and had very little mileage. "Will you sell yours and keep hers?" she asked. "Yours is newer, but it's small."

"I hadn't thought," I said. And I found I couldn't think of it, that cleaning out the bedroom was the extent of what I could do that day.

At the end of the afternoon, the bedroom was empty of Gran. Arlene and I turned the mattress and I remade the bed out of habit. It was an old four-poster in the rice pattern. I had always thought her bedroom set was beautiful, and it occurred to me that now it was mine. I could move into the bigger bedroom and have a private bath instead of using the one in the hall.

Suddenly, that was exactly what I wanted to do. The furniture I'd been using in my bedroom had been moved over here from my parents' house when they'd died, and it was kid's furniture; overly feminine, sort of reminiscent of Barbies and sleepovers.

Not that I'd ever had many sleepovers, or been to many.

Nope, nope, nope, I wasn't going to fall into that old pit. I was what I was, and I had a life, and I could enjoy things; the little treats that kept me going.

"I might move in here," I told Arlene as she taped a box shut.

"Isn't that a little soon?" she asked. She flushed red when she realized she'd sounded critical.

"It would be easier to be in here than be across the hall thinking about the room being empty," I said. Arlene thought that through, crouched beside the cardboard box with the roll of tape in her hand.

"I can see that," she agreed, with a nod of her flaming red head.

We loaded the cardboard boxes into Arlene's car. She had kindly agreed to drop them by the collection center on her way home, and I gratefully accepted the offer. I didn't want anyone to look at me knowingly, with pity, when I gave away my grandmother's clothes and shoes and nightgowns.

When Arlene left, I hugged her and gave her a kiss on the cheek, and she stared at me. That was outside the bounds our friendship had had up till now. She bent her head to mine and we very gently bumped foreheads.

"You crazy girl," she said, affection in her voice. "You come see us, now. Lisa's been wanting you to baby-sit again."

"You tell her Aunt Sookie said hi to her, and to Coby, too."

"I will." And Arlene sauntered off to her car, her flaming hair puffing in a waving mass above her head, her full body making her waitress outfit look like one big promise.

All my energy drained away as Arlene's car bumped down the driveway through the trees. I felt a million years old, alone and lonely. This was the way it was going to be from now on.

I didn't feel hungry, but the clock told me it was time to eat. I went into the kitchen and pulled one of the many Tupperware containers from the refrigerator. It held turkey and grape salad, and I liked it, but I sat there at the table just picking at it with a fork. I gave up, returning it to the icebox and going to the bathroom for a much-needed shower. The corners of closets are always dusty, and even a housekeeper as good as my grandmother had been had not been able to defeat that dust.

The shower felt wonderful. The hot water seemed to steam out some of my misery, and I shampooed my hair and scrubbed every inch of skin, shaving my legs and armpits. After I climbed out, I plucked my eyebrows and put on skin lotion and deodorant and a spray to untangle my hair and anything else I could lay my hands on. With my hair trailing down my back in a cascade of wet snarls, I pulled on my nightshirt, a white one with Tweety Bird on the front, and I got my comb. I'd sit in front of the television to have something to watch while I got my hair combed out, always a tedious process.

My little burst of purpose expired, and I felt almost numb.

The doorbell rang just as I was trailing into the living room with my comb in one hand and a towel in the other.

I looked through the peephole. Bill was waiting patiently on the porch.

I let him in without feeling either glad or sorry to see him.

He took me in with some surprise: the nightshirt, the wet hair, the bare feet. No makeup.

"Come in," I said.

"Are you sure?"

"Yes."

And he came in, looking around him as he always did. "What are you doing?" he asked, seeing the pile of things I'd put to one side because I thought friends of Gran's might want them: Mr. Norris might be pleased to get the framed picture of his mother and Gran's mother together, for example.

"I cleaned out the bedroom today," I said. "I think I'll move into it." Then I couldn't think of anything else to say. He turned to look at me carefully.

"Let me comb out your hair," he said.

I nodded indifferently. Bill sat on the flowered couch and indicated the old ottoman positioned in front of it. I sat down obediently, and he scooted forward a little, framing me with his thighs. Starting at the crown of my head, he began teasing the tangles out of my hair.

As always, his mental silence was a treat. Each time, it was like putting the first foot into a cool pool of water when I'd been on a long, dusty hike on a hot day.

As a bonus, Bill's long fingers seemed adept at dealing with the thick mane of my hair. I sat with my eyes closed, gradually becoming tranquil. I could feel the slight movements of his body behind me as he worked with the comb. I could almost hear his heart beating, I thought, and then realized how strange an idea that was. His heart, after all, didn't.

"I used to do this for my sister, Sarah," he murmured quietly, as if he knew how peaceful I'd gotten and was trying not to break my mood. "She had hair darker than yours, even longer. She'd never cut it. When we were children, and my mother was busy, she'd have me work on Sarah's hair."

"Was Sarah younger than you, or older?" I asked in a slow, drugged voice.

"She was younger. She was three years younger."

"Did you have other brothers or sisters?"

"My mother lost two in childbirth," he said slowly, as if he could barely remember. "I lost my brother, Robert, when he was twelve and I was eleven. He caught a fever, and it killed him. Now they would pump him full of penicillin, and he would be all right. But they couldn't then. Sarah survived the war, she and my mother, though my father died while I was soldiering; he had what I've learned since was a stroke. My wife was living with my family then, and my children . . ."

"Oh, Bill," I said sadly, almost in a whisper, for he had lost so much.

"Don't, Sookie," he said, and his voice had regained its cold clarity.

He worked on in silence for a while, until I could tell the comb was running free through my hair. He picked up the white towel I'd tossed on the arm of the couch and began to pat my hair dry, and as it dried he ran his fingers through it to give it body.

"Mmmm," I said, and as I heard it, it was no longer the sound of someone being soothed.

I could feel his cool fingers lifting the hair away from my neck and then I felt his mouth just at the nape. I couldn't speak or move. I exhaled slowly, trying not to make another sound. His lips moved to my ear, and he caught the lobe of it between his teeth. Then his tongue darted in. His arms came around me, crossing over my chest, pulling me back against him.

And for a miracle I only heard what his body was saying, not those niggling things from minds that only foul up moments like this. His body was saying something very simple.

He lifted me as easily as I'd rotate an infant. He turned me so I was facing him on his lap, my legs on either side of his. I put my arms around him and bent a little to kiss him. It went on and on, but after a while Bill settled into a rhythm with his tongue, a rhythm even someone as inexperienced as I could identify. The nightshirt slid up to the tops of my thighs. My hands began to rub his arms helplessly. Strangely, I thought of a pan of caramels my grandmother had put on the stove for a candy recipe, and I thought of the melted, warm sweet goldenness of them.

He stood up with me still wrapped around him. "Where?" he asked.

And I pointed to my grandmother's former room. He carried me in as we were, my legs locked around him, my head on his shoulder, and he lay me on the clean bed. He stood by the bed and in the moonlight coming in the unshaded windows, I saw him undress, quickly and neatly. Though I was getting great pleasure from watching him, I knew I had to do the same; but still a little embarrassed, I just drew off the nightshirt and tossed it onto the floor.

I stared at him. I'd never seen anything so beautiful or so scary in my life.

"Oh, Bill," I said anxiously, when he was beside me in the bed, "I don't want to disappoint you."

"That's not possible," he whispered. His eyes looked at my body as if it were a drink of water on a desert dune.

"I don't know much," I confessed, my voice barely audible.

"Don't worry. I know a lot." His hands began drifting over me, touching me in places I'd never been touched. I jerked with surprise, then opened myself to him.

"Will this be different from doing it with a regular guy?" I asked.

"Oh, yes."

I looked up at him questioningly.

"It'll be better," he said in my ear, and I felt a twinge of pure excitement.

A little shyly, I reached down to touch him, and he made a very human sound. After a moment, the sound became deeper.

"Now?" I asked, my voice ragged and shaking.

"Oh, yes," he said, and then he was on top of me.

A moment later he found out the true extent of my inexperience.

"You should have told me," he said, but very gently. He held himself still with an almost palpable effort.

"Oh, please don't stop!" I begged, thinking that the top would fly off my head, something drastic would happen, if he didn't go on with it.

"I have no intention of stopping," he promised a little grimly. "Sookie . . . this will hurt."

In answer, I raised myself. He made an incoherent noise and pushed into me.

I held my breath. I bit my lip. Ow, ow, ow.

"Darling," Bill said. No one had ever called me that. "How are you?" Vampire or not, he was trembling with the effort of holding back.

"Okay," I said inadequately. I was over the sting, and I'd lose my courage if we didn't proceed. "Now," I said, and I bit him hard on the shoulder.

He gasped, and jerked, and he began moving in earnest. At first I was dazed, but I began to catch on and keep up. He found my response very exciting, and I began to feel that something was just around the corner, so to speak—something very big and good. I said, "Oh, please, Bill, please!" and dug my nails in his hips, almost there, almost there, and then a small shift in our alignment allowed him to press even more directly against me and almost before I could gather myself I was flying, flying, seeing white with gold streaks. I felt Bill's teeth against my neck, and I said, "Yes!" I felt his fangs penetrate, but it was a small pain, an exciting pain, and as he came inside me I felt him draw on the little wound.

We lay there for a long time, from time to time trembling with little aftershocks. I would never forget his taste and smell as long as I lived, I would never forget the feel of him inside me this first time—my first time, ever—I would never forget the pleasure.

Finally Bill moved to lie beside me, propped on one elbow, and he put his hand over my stomach.

"I am the first."

"Yes."

"Oh, Sookie." He bent to kiss me, his lips tracing the line of my throat.

"You could tell I don't know much," I said shyly. "But was that all right for you? I mean, about on a par with other women at least? I'll get better."

"You can get more skilled, Sookie, but you can't get any better." He kissed me on the cheek. "You're wonderful."

"Will I be sore?"

"I know you'll think this is odd, but I don't remember. The only virgin I was ever with was my wife, and that was a century and a half ago . . . yes, I recall, you will be very sore. We won't be able to make love again, for a day or two."

"Your blood heals," I observed after a little pause, feeling my cheeks redden.

In the moonlight, I could see him shift, to look at me more directly. "So it does," he said. "Would you like that?"

"Sure. Wouldn't you?"

"Yes," he breathed, and bit his own arm.

It was so sudden that I cried out, but he casually rubbed a finger in his own blood, and then before I could tense up he slid that finger up inside me. He began moving it very gently, and in a moment, sure enough, the pain was gone.

"Thanks," I said. "I'm better now."

But he didn't remove his finger.

"Oh," I said. "Would you like to do it again so soon? Can you do that?" And as his finger kept up its motion, I began to hope so.

"Look and see," he offered, a hint of amusement in his sweet dark voice.

I whispered, hardly recognizing myself, "Tell me what you want me to do."

And he did.

I WENT BACK to work the next day. No matter what Bill's healing powers were, I was a little uncomfortable, but boy, did I feel powerful. It was a totally new feeling for me. It was hard not to feel—well, cocky is surely the wrong word—maybe incredibly smug is closer.

Of course, there were the same old problems at the bar—the cacophony of voices, the buzzing of them, the persistence. But somehow I seemed better able to tone them down, to tamp them into a pocket. It was easier to keep my guard up, and I felt consequently more relaxed. Or maybe since I was more relaxed—boy, was I more relaxed—it was easier to guard? I don't know. But I felt better, and I was able to accept the condolences of the patrons with calm instead of tears.

Jason came in at lunch and had a couple of beers with his hamburger, which wasn't his normal regimen. He usually didn't drink during the work day. I knew he'd get mad if I said anything directly, so I just asked him if everything was okay.

"The chief had me in again today," he said in a low voice. He looked around to make sure no one else was listening, but the bar was sparsely filled that day since the Rotary Club was meeting at the Community Building.

"What is he asking you?" My voice was equally low.

"How often I'd seen Maudette, did I always get my gas at the place she worked. . . . Over and over and over, like I hadn't answered those questions seventy-five times. My boss is at the end of his patience, Sookie, and I don't blame him. I been gone from work at least two days, maybe three, with all the trips I been making down to the police station."

"Maybe you better get a lawyer," I said uneasily.

"That's what Rene said."

Then Rene Lenier and I saw eye to eye.

"What about Sid Matt Lancaster?" Sidney Matthew Lancaster, native son and a whiskey sour drinker, had the reputation of being the most aggressive trial lawyer in the parish. I liked him because he always treated me with respect when I served him in the bar.

"He might be my best bet." Jason looked as petulant and grim as a lovely person can. We exchanged a glance. We both knew Gran's lawyer was too old to handle the case if Jason was ever, God forbid, arrested.

Jason was far too self-absorbed to notice anything different about me, but I'd worn a white golf shirt (instead of my usual round-necked T-shirt) for the protection of its collar. Arlene was not as unaware as my brother. She'd been eyeing me all morning, and by the time the three o'clock lull hit, she was pretty sure she'd got me figured out.

"Girl," she said, "you been having fun?"

I turned red as a beet. "Having fun" made my relationship with Bill lighter than it was, but it was accurate as far as it went. I didn't know whether to take the high road and say, "No, making love," or keep my mouth shut, or tell Arlene it was none of her business, or just shout, "Yes!"

"Oh, Sookie, who is the man?"

Uh-oh. "Um, well, he's not . . ."

"Not local? You dating one of those servicemen from Bossier City?"

"No," I said hesitantly.

"Sam? I've seen him looking at you."

"No."

"Who, then?"

I was acting like I was ashamed. Straighten your spine, Sookie Stackhouse, I told myself sternly. Pay the piper.

"Bill," I said, hoping against hope that she'd just say, "Oh, yeah."

"Bill," Arlene said blankly. I noticed Sam had drifted up and was listening. So was Charlsie Tooten. Even Lafayette stuck his head through the hatch.

"Bill," I said, trying to sound firm. "You know. Bill."

"Bill Auberjunois?"

"No."

"Bill . . . ?"

"Bill Compton," Sam said flatly, just as I opened my mouth to say the same thing. "Vampire Bill."

Arlene was flabbergasted, Charlsie Tooten immediately gave a little shriek, and Lafayette about dropped his bottom jaw.

"Honey, couldn't you just date a regular human fella?" Arlene asked when she got her voice back.

"A regular human fella didn't ask me out." I could feel the color fix in my cheeks. I stood there with my back straight, feeling defiant and looking it, I'm sure.

"But, sweetie," Charlsie Tooten fluted in her babyish voice, "honey . . . Bill's, ah, got that virus."

"I know that," I said, hearing the distinct edge in my voice.

"I thought you were going to say you were dating a black, but you've gone one better, ain't you, girl?" Lafayette said, picking at his fingernail polish.

Sam didn't say anything. He just stood leaning against the bar, and there was a white line around his mouth as if he were biting his cheek inside.

I stared at them all in turn, forcing them to either swallow this or spit it out.

Arlene got through it first. "All right, then. He better treat you good, or we'll get our stakes out!"

They were all able to laugh at that, albeit weakly.

"And you'll save a lot on groceries!" Lafayette pointed out.

But then in one step Sam ruined it all, that tentative acceptance, by suddenly moving to stand beside me and pull the collar of my shirt down.

You could have cut the silence of my friends with a knife.

"Oh, shit," Lafayette said, very softly.

I looked right into Sam's eyes, thinking I'd never forgive him for doing this to me.

"Don't you touch my clothes," I told him, stepping away from him and pulling the collar back straight. "Don't tend to my personal life."

"I'm scared for you, I'm worried about you," he said, as Arlene and Charlsie hastily found other things to do.

"No you're not, or not entirely. You're mad as hell. Well listen, buddy. You *never got in line*."

And I stalked away to wipe down the formica on one of the tables. Then I collected all the salt shakers and refilled them. Then I checked the pepper shakers and the bottles of hot peppers on each table and booth, the Tabasco sauce, too. I just kept working and kept my eyes in front of me, and gradually, the atmosphere cooled down.

Sam was back in his office doing paperwork or something, I didn't care what, as long as he kept his opinions to himself. I still felt like he'd ripped the curtain off a private area of my life when he'd exposed my neck, and I hadn't forgiven him. But Arlene and Charlsie had found make-work, as I'd done, and by the time the after-work crowd began trickling in, we were once again fairly comfortable with one another.

Arlene came into the women's room with me. "Listen, Sookie, I got to ask. Are vampires all everyone says they are, in the lover department?"

I just smiled.

Bill came into the bar that evening, just after dark. I'd worked late since one of the evening waitresses had had car trouble. One minute he wasn't there, and the next minute he was, slowing down so I could see him coming. If Bill had any doubts about making our relationship public, he didn't show them. He lifted my hand and kissed it in a gesture that performed by anyone else would have seemed phony as hell. I felt the touch of his lips on the back of my hand all the way down to my toes, and I knew he could tell that.

"How are you this evening?" he whispered, and I shivered.

"A little . . ." I found I couldn't get the words out.

"You can tell me later," he suggested. "When are you through?"

"Just as soon as Susie gets here."

"Come to my house."

"Okay." I smiled up at him, feeling radiant and light-headed.

And Bill smiled back, though since my nearness had affected him, his fangs were showing, and maybe to anyone else but me the effect was a little—unsettling.

He bent to kiss me, just a light touch on the cheek, and he turned to leave. But just at that moment, the evening went all to hell.

Malcolm and Diane came in, flinging the door open as if they were making a grand entrance, and of course, they were. I wondered where Liam was. Probably parking the car. It was too much to hope they'd left him at home.

Folks in Bon Temps were getting accustomed to Bill, but the

flamboyant Malcolm and the equally flamboyant Diane caused quite a stir. My first thought was that this wasn't going to help people get used to Bill and me.

Malcolm was wearing leather pants and a kind of chain-mail shirt. He looked like something on the cover of a rock album. Diane was wearing a one-piece lime green bodysuit spun out of Lycra or some other very thin, stretchy cloth. I was sure I could count her pubic hairs if I so desired. Blacks didn't come into Merlotte's much, but if any black was absolutely safe there, it was Diane. I saw Lafayette goggling through the hatch in open admiration, spiced by a dollop of fear.

The two vampires shrieked with feigned surprise when they saw Bill, like demented drunks. As far as I could tell, Bill was not happy about their presence, but he seemed to handle their invasion calmly, as he did almost everything.

Malcolm kissed Bill on the mouth, and so did Diane. It was hard to tell which greeting was more offensive to the customers in the bar. Bill had better show distaste, and quick, I thought, if he wanted to stay in good with the human inhabitants of Bon Temps.

Bill, who was no fool, took a step back and put his arm around me, dissociating himself from the vampires and aligning himself with the humans.

"So your little waitress is still alive," Diane said, and her clear voice was audible through the whole bar. "Isn't that amazing."

"Her grandmother was murdered last week," Bill said quietly, trying to subdue Diane's desire to make a scene.

Her gorgeous lunatic brown eyes fixed on me, and I felt cold.

"Is that right?" she said and laughed.

That was it. No one would forgive her now. If Bill had been trying to find a way to entrench himself, this would be the scenario I would write. On the other hand, the disgust I could feel massing from the humans in the bar could backlash and wash over Bill as well as the renegades.

Of course . . . to Diane and her friends, Bill was the renegade.

"When's someone going to kill you, baby?" She ran a fingernail under my chin, and I knocked her hand away.

She would have been on me if Malcolm hadn't grabbed her hand, lazily, almost effortlessly. But I saw the strain show in the way he was standing.

"Bill," he said conversationally, as if he wasn't exerting every muscle he had to keep Diane still, "I hear this town is losing its unskilled service personnel at a terrible rate. And a little bird in Shreveport tells me you and your friend here were at Fangtasia asking questions about what vampire the murdered fang-bangers might have been with."

"You know that's for us to know, no one else," Malcolm continued, and all of a sudden his face was so serious it was truly terrifying. "Some of us don't want to go to—baseball—games and . . ." (here he was searching his memory for something disgustingly human, I could tell) "barbecues! We are Vampire!" He invested the word with majesty, with glamor, and I could tell a lot of the people in the bar were falling under his spell. Malcolm was intelligent enough to want to erase the bad impression he knew Diane had made, all the while showering contempt on those of us it had been made on.

I stomped on his instep with every ounce of weight I could muster. He showed his fangs at me. The people in the bar blinked and shook themselves.

"Why don't you just get outta here, mister," Rene said. He was slouched at the bar with his elbows flanking a beer.

There was moment when things hung in the balance, when the bar could have turned into a bloodbath. None of my fellow humans seemed to quite comprehend how strong vampires were, or how ruthless. Bill had moved in front of me, a fact registered by every citizen in Merlotte's.

"Well, if we're not wanted . . ." Malcolm said. His thick-muscled masculinity warred with the fluting voice he suddenly affected. "These good people would like to eat meat, Diane, and do human things. By themselves. Or with our former friend Bill."

"I think the little waitress would like to do a very human thing with Bill," Diane began, when Malcolm caught her by the arm and propelled her from the room before she could cause more damage.

The entire bar seemed to shudder collectively when they were out the door, and I thought I better leave, even though Susie hadn't shown up yet. Bill waited for me outside; when I asked him why, he said he wanted to be sure they'd really left.

I followed Bill to his house, thinking we'd gotten off relatively lightly from the vampire visitation. I wondered why Diane and Malcolm had come; it seemed odd to me that they would be cruising so far from home and decide, on a whim, to drop in Merlotte's. Since they were making no real effort at assimilation, maybe they wanted to scotch Bill's prospects.

The Compton house was visibly different from the last time I'd been in, the sickening evening I'd met the other vampires.

The contractors were really coming through for Bill, whether because they were scared not to or because he was paying well, I didn't know. Maybe both. The living room was getting a new ceiling and the new wallpaper was white with a delicate flowered pattern. The hardwood floors had been cleaned, and they shone as they must have originally. Bill led me to the kitchen. It was sparse, naturally, but bright and cheerful and had a brand-new refrigerator full of bottled synthetic blood (yuck).

The downstairs bathroom was opulent.

As far as I knew, Bill never used the bathroom; at least for the primary human function. I stared around me in amazement.

The space for this grand bathroom had been achieved by including what had formerly been the pantry and about half the old kitchen.

"I like to shower," he said, pointing to a clear shower stall in one corner. It was big enough for two grownups and maybe a dwarf or two. "And I like to lie in warm water." He indicated the centerpiece of the room, a huge sort of tub surrounded by an indoor deck of cedar, with steps on two sides. There were potted plants arranged all around it. The room was as close to being in the middle of a very luxurious jungle as you could get in northern Louisiana.

"What is that?" I asked, awed.

"It's a portable spa," Bill said proudly. "It has jets you can adjust individually so each person can get the right force of water. It's a hot tub," he simplified.

"It has seats," I said, looking in. The interior was decorated around the top with green and blue tiles. There were fancy controls on the outside.

Bill turned them, and water began to surge.

"Maybe we can bathe together?" Bill suggested.

I felt my cheeks flame, and my heart began to pound a little faster.

"Maybe now?" Bill's fingers tugging at my shirt where it was tucked into my black shorts.

"Oh, well . . . maybe." I couldn't seem to look at him straight when I thought of how this—okay, man—had seen more of me than I'd ever let anyone see, including my doctor.

"Have you missed me?" he asked, his hands unbuttoning my shorts and peeling them down.

"Yes," I said promptly because I knew that to be true.

He laughed, even as he knelt to untie my Nikes. "What did you miss most, Sookie?"

"I missed your silence," I said without thinking at all.

He looked up. His fingers paused in the act of pulling the end of the bow to loosen it.

"My silence," he said.

"Not being able to hear your thoughts. You just can't imagine, Bill, how wonderful that is."

"I was thinking you'd say something else."

"Well, I missed that, too."

"Tell me about it," he invited, pulling my socks off and running his fingers up my thigh, tugging off the panties and shorts.

"Bill! I'm embarrassed," I protested.

"Sookie, don't be embarrassed with me. Least of anyone, with me." He was standing now, divesting me of my shirt and reaching behind me to unsnap my bra, running his hands over the marks the straps had made on my skin, turning his attention to my breasts. He toed off his sandals at some point.

"I'll try," I said, looking at my own toes.

"Undress me."

Now that I could do. I unbuttoned his shirt briskly and eased it out of his pants and off his shoulders. I unbuckled his belt and began to work on the waist button of his slacks. It was stiff, and I had quite a job.

I thought I was going to cry if the button didn't cooperate more. I felt clumsy and inept.

He took my hands and led them up to his chest. "Slow, Sookie, slow," he said, and his voice had gone soft and shivery. I could feel myself relaxing almost inch by inch, and I began to stroke his chest as he'd stroked mine, twining the curly hair around my fingers and gently pinching his flat nipples. His hand went behind my head and pressed gently. I hadn't known men liked that, but Bill sure did, so I paid equal attention to the other one. While I was doing that, my hands resumed work on the damn button, and this time it came undone with ease. I began pushing down his pants, sliding my fingers inside his Jockeys.

He helped me down into the spa, the water frothing around our legs.

"Shall I bathe you first?" he asked.

"No," I said breathlessly. "Give me the soap."

Chapter 7

THE NEXT NIGHT Bill and I had an unsettling conversation. We were in his bed, his huge bed with the carved headboard and a brand-new Restonic mattress. His sheets were flowered like his wallpaper, and I remember wondering if he liked flowers printed on his possessions because he couldn't see the real thing, at least as they were meant to be seen . . . in the daylight.

Bill was lying on his side, looking down at me. We'd been to the movies; Bill was crazy about movies with aliens, maybe having some kindred feeling for space creatures. It had been a real shoot-em-up, with almost all the aliens being ugly, creepy, bent on killing. He'd fumed about that while he'd taken me out to eat, and then back to his place. I'd been glad when he'd suggested testing the new bed.

I was the first to lie on it with him.

He was looking at me, as he liked to do, I was learning. Maybe he was listening to my heart pounding, since he could hear things I couldn't, or maybe he was watching my pulse throb, because he could see things I couldn't, too. Our conversation had strayed from the movie we'd seen to the nearing parish elections (Bill was going to try to register to vote, absentee ballot), and then to our childhoods. I was realizing that Bill was trying desperately to remember what it had been like to be a regular person.

"Did you ever play 'show me yours' with your brother?" he asked. "They now say that's normal, but I will never forget my mother beating the tarnation out of my brother Robert after she found him in the bushes with Sarah."

"No," I said, trying to sound casual, but my face tightened, and I could feel the clenching of fear in my stomach.

"You're not telling the truth."

"Yes, I am." I kept my eyes fixed on his chin, hoping to think of some way to change the topic. But Bill was nothing if not persistent.

"Not your brother, then. Who?"

"I don't want to talk about this." My hands contracted into fists, and I could feel myself begin to shut down.

But Bill hated being evaded. He was used to people telling him whatever he wanted to know because he was used to using his glamor to get his way.

"Tell me, Sookie." His voice was coaxing, his eyes big pools of curiosity. He ran his thumbnail down my stomach, and I shivered.

"I had a . . . funny uncle," I said, feeling the familiar tight smile stretch my lips.

He raised his dark arched brows. He hadn't heard the phrase.

I said as distantly as I could manage, "That's an adult male relative who molests his . . . the children in the family."

His eyes began to burn. He swallowed; I could see his Adam's apple move. I grinned at him. My hands were pulling my hair back from my face. I couldn't stop it.

"And someone did this to you? How old were you?"

"Oh, it started when I was real little," and I could feel my breathing begin to speed up, my heart beat faster, the panicky traits that always came back when I remembered. My knees drew up and pressed together. "I guess I was five," I babbled, talking faster and faster, "I know you can tell, he never actually, ah, screwed me, but he did other stuff," and now my hands were shaking in front of my eyes where I held them to shield them from Bill's gaze. "And the worst thing, Bill, the worst thing," I went on, just unable to stop, "is that every time he came to visit, I always knew what he was going to do because I could read his mind! And there wasn't anything I could do to stop it!" I clamped my hands over my mouth to make myself shut up. I wasn't supposed to talk about it. I rolled over onto my stomach to conceal myself, and held my body absolutely rigid.

After a long time, I felt Bill's cool hand on my shoulder. It lay there, comforting.

"This was before your parents died?" he said in his usual calm voice. I still couldn't look at him.

"Yes."

"You told your mama? She did nothing?"

"No. She thought I was dirty minded, or that I'd found some book at the library that taught me something she didn't feel I was ready to know." I could remember her face, framed in hair about two shades darker than my medium blond. Her face pinched with distaste. She had come from a very conservative family, and any public display of affection or any mention of a subject she thought indecent was flatly discouraged.

"I wonder that she and my father seemed happy," I told my vampire. "They were so different." Then I saw how ludicrous my saying that was. I rolled over to my side. "As if we aren't," I told Bill, and tried to smile. Bill's face was quite still, but I could see a muscle in his neck jumping.

"Did you tell your father?"

"Yes, right before he died. I was too embarrassed to talk to him about it when I was younger; and Mother didn't believe me. But I couldn't stand it anymore, knowing I was going to see my great-uncle Bartlett at least two weekends out of every month when he drove up to visit."

"He still lives?"

"Uncle Bartlett? Oh, sure. He's Gran's brother, and Gran was my dad's mother. My uncle lives in Shreveport. But when Jason and I went to live with Gran, after my parents died, the first time Uncle Bartlett came to her house I hid. When she found me and asked me why, I told her. And she believed me." I felt the relief of that day all over again, the beautiful sound of my grandmother's voice promising me I'd never have to see her brother again, that he would never never come to the house.

And he hadn't. She had cut off her own brother to protect me. He'd tried with Gran's daughter, Linda, too, when she was a small girl, but my grandmother had buried the incident in her own mind, dismissed it as something misunderstood. She had told me that she'd never left her brother alone with Linda at any time after that, had almost quit inviting him to her home, while not quite letting herself believe that he'd touched her little girl's privates.

"So he's a Stackhouse, too?"

"Oh, no. See, Gran became a Stackhouse when she married, but she was a Hale before." I wondered at having to spell this out for Bill. He was sure Southern enough, even if he was a vampire, to keep track of a simple family relationship like that.

Bill looked distant, miles away. I had put him off with my grim nasty little story, and I had chilled my own blood, that was for sure.

"Here, I'll leave," I said and slid out of bed, bending to retrieve my clothes. Quicker than I could see, he was off the bed and taking the clothes from my hands.

"Don't leave me now," he said. "Stay."

"I'm a weepy ol' thing tonight." Two tears trickled down my cheeks, and I smiled at him.

His fingers wiped the tears from my face, and his tongue traced their marks.

"Stay with me till dawn," he said.

"But you have to get in your hidey hole by then."

"My what?"

"Wherever you spend the day. I don't want to know where it is!" I held up my hands to emphasize that. "But don't you have to get in there before it's even a little light?"

"Oh," he said, "I'll know. I can feel it coming."

"So you can't oversleep?"

"No."

"All right. Will you let me get some sleep?"

"Of course I will," he said with a gentlemanly bow, only a little off mark because he was naked. "In a little while." Then, as I lay down on the bed and held out my arms to him, he said, "Eventually."

SURE ENOUGH, IN the morning I was in the bed by myself. I lay there for a little, thinking. I'd had little niggling thoughts from time to time, but for the first time the flaws in my relationship with the vampire hopped out of their own hidey hole and took over my brain.

I would never see Bill in the sunlight. I would never fix his breakfast, never meet him for lunch. (He could bear to watch me eat food, though he wasn't thrilled by the process, and I always had to brush my teeth afterward very thoroughly, which was a good habit anyway.)

I could never have a child by Bill, which was nice at least when you thought of not having to practice birth control, but . . .

I'd never call Bill at the office to ask him to stop on the way home for some milk. He'd never join the Rotary, or give a career speech at the high school, or coach Little League Baseball.

He'd never go to church with me.

And I knew that now, while I lay here awake—listening to the birds chirping their morning sounds and the trucks beginning to rumble down the road while all over Bon Temps people were getting up and putting on the coffee and fetching their papers and planning their day—that the creature I loved was lying somewhere in a hole underground, to all intents and purposes dead until dark.

I was so down by then that I had to think of an upside, while I cleaned up a little in the bathroom and dressed.

He seemed to genuinely care for me. It was kind of nice, but unsettling, not to know exactly how much.

Sex with him was absolutely great. I had never dreamed it would be that wonderful.

No one would mess with me while I was Bill's girlfriend. Any hands that had patted me in unwanted caresses were kept in their owner's laps, now. And if the person who'd killed my grandmother had killed her because she'd walked in on him while he was waiting for me, he wouldn't get another try at me.

And I could relax with Bill, a luxury so precious I could not put a value on it. My mind could range at will, and I would not learn anything he didn't tell me.

There was that.

It was in this kind of contemplative mood that I came down Bill's steps to my car.

To my amazement, Jason was there sitting in his pickup.

This was not exactly a happy moment. I trudged over to his window.

"I see it's true," he said. He handed me a Styrofoam cup of coffee from the Grabbit Quik. "Get in the truck with me."

I climbed in, pleased by the coffee but cautious overall. I put my guard up immediately. It slipped back into place slowly and painfully, like wiggling back into a girdle that was too tight in the first place.

"I can't say nothing," he told me. "Not after the way I lived my life these past few years. As near as I can tell, he's your first, isn't he?"

I nodded.

"He treat you good?"

I nodded again.

"I got something to tell you."

"Okay."

"Uncle Bartlett got killed last night."

I stared at him, the steam from the coffee rising between us as I pried the lid off the cup. "He's dead," I said, trying to understand it. I'd worked hard never to think of him, and here I thought of him, and the next thing I heard, he was dead.

"Yep."

"Wow." I looked out the window at the rosy light on the horizon. I felt a surge of—freedom. The only one who remembered besides me, the only one who'd enjoyed it, who insisted to the end that I had initiated and continued the sick activities he thought were so gratifying . . . he was *dead*. I took a deep breath.

"I hope he's in hell," I said. "I hope every time he thinks of what he did to me, a demon pokes him in the butt with a pitchfork."

"God, Sookie!"

"He never messed with you."

"Damn straight!"

"Implying what?"

"Nothing, Sookie! But he never bothered anyone but you that I know of!"

"Bullshit. He molested Aunt Linda, too."

Jason's face went blank with shock. I'd finally gotten through to my brother. "Gran told you that?"

"Yes."

"She never said anything to me."

"Gran knew it was hard for you, not seeing him again when she could tell you loved him. But she couldn't let you be alone with him, because she couldn't be a hundred percent sure girls were all he wanted."

"I've seen him the past couple of years."

"You have?" This was news to me. It would have been news to Gran, too.

"Sookie, he was an old man. He was so sick. He had prostate trouble, and he was feeble, and he had to use a walker."

"That probably slowed him down chasing the five-year-olds."

"Get over it!"

"Right! Like I could!"

We glared at each other over the width of the truck seat.

"So what happened to him?" I asked finally, reluctantly.

"A burglar broke into his house last night."

"Yeah? And?"

"And broke his neck. Threw him down the stairs."

"Okay. So I know. Now I'm going home. I gotta shower and get ready for work."

"That's all you're saying?"

"What else is there to say?"

"Don't want to know about the funeral?"

"No."

"Don't want to know about his will?"

"No."

He threw up his hands. "All right," he said, as if he'd been arguing a point very hard with me and realized that I was intractable.

"What else? Anything?" I asked.

"No. Just your great-uncle dying. I thought that was enough."

"Actually, you're right," I said, opening the truck door and sliding out. "That was enough." I raised my cup to him. "Thanks for the coffee, brother."

IT WASN'T TILL I got to work that it clicked.

I was drying a glass and really not thinking about Uncle Bartlett, and suddenly my fingers lost all strength.

"Jesus Christ, Shepherd of Judea," I said, looking down at the broken slivers of glass at my feet. "Bill had him killed."

I DON'T KNOW why I was so sure I was right; but I was, the minute the idea crossed my mind. Maybe I had heard Bill dialing the phone when I was half-asleep. Maybe the expression on Bill's face when I'd finished telling him about Uncle Bartlett had rung a silent warning bell.

I wondered if Bill would pay the other vampire in money, or if he'd repay him in kind.

I got through work in a frozen state. I couldn't talk to anyone about what I was thinking, couldn't even say I was sick without someone asking me what was wrong. So I didn't speak at all, I just worked. I tuned out everything except the next order I had to fill. I drove home trying to feel just as frozen, but I had to face facts when I was alone.

I freaked out.

I had known, really I had, that Bill certainly had killed a human or two in his long, long, life. When he'd been a young vampire, when he'd needed lots of blood, before he'd gained control of his needs sufficiently to exist on a gulp here, a mouthful there, without actually killing anyone he drank from . . . he'd told me himself there'd been a death or two along the way. And he'd killed the Rattrays. But they'd have done me in that night in back of Merlotte's, without a doubt, if Bill hadn't intervened. I was naturally inclined to excuse him those deaths.

How was the murder of Uncle Bartlett different? He'd harmed me, too, dreadfully, made my already difficult childhood a true nightmare. Hadn't I been relieved, even pleased, to hear he'd been found dead? Didn't my horror at Bill's intervention reek of hypocrisy of the worst sort?

Yes. No?

Tired and incredibly confused, I sat on my front steps and waited in the darkness, my arms wrapped around my knees. The crickets were singing in the tall grass when he came, arriving so quietly and quickly I didn't hear him. One minute I was alone with the night, and the next, Bill was sitting on the steps beside me.

"What do you want to do tonight, Sookie?" His arm went around me.

"Oh, Bill." My voice was heavy with despair.

His arm dropped. I didn't look up at his face, couldn't have seen it through the darkness, anyway.

"You should not have done it."

He didn't bother with denying it at least.

"I am glad he's dead, Bill. But I can't . . ."

"Do you think I would ever hurt you, Sookie?" His voice was quiet and rustling, like feet through dry grass.

"No. Oddly enough, I don't think you would hurt me, even if you were really mad at me."

"Then . . . ?"

"It's like dating the Godfather, Bill. I'm scared to say anything around you now. I'm not used to my problems being solved that way."

"I love you."

He'd never said it before, and I might almost have imagined it now, his voice was so low and whispery.

"Do you, Bill?" I didn't raise my face, kept my forehead pressed against my knees.

"Yes, I do."

"Then you have to let my life get lived, Bill, you can't alter it for me."

"You wanted me to alter it when the Rattrays were beating you."

"Point taken. But I can't have you trying to fine-tune my day-today life. I'm gonna get mad at people, people are gonna get mad at me. I can't worry about them being killed. I can't live like that, honey. You see what I'm saying?"

"Honey?" he repeated.

"I love you," I said. "I don't know why, but I do. I want to call you all those gooshy words you use when you love someone, no matter how stupid it sounds since you're a vampire. I want to tell you you're my baby, that I'll love you till we're old and gray—though that's not gonna happen. That I know you'll always be true to me—hey, that's not gonna happen either. I keep running up against a brick wall when I try to tell you I love you, Bill." I fell silent. I was all cried out.

"This crisis came sooner than I thought it would," Bill said from the darkness. The crickets had resumed their chorus, and I listened to them for a long moment.

"Yeah."

"What now, Sookie?"

"I have to have a little time."

"Before . . . ?"

"Before I decide if the love is worth the misery."

"Sookie, if you knew how different you taste, how much I want to protect you . . ."

I could tell from Bill's voice that these were very tender feelings he was sharing with me. "Oddly enough," I said, "that's what I feel about you. But I have to live here, and I have to live with myself, and I have to think about some rules we gotta get clear between us."

"So what do we do now?"

"I think. You go do whatever you were doing before we met."

"Trying to figure out if I could live mainstream. Trying to think of who I'd feed on, if I could stop drinking that damn synthetic blood."

"I know you'll—feed on someone else besides me." I was trying very hard to keep my voice level. "Please, not anyone here, not anyone I have to see. I couldn't bear it. It's not fair of me to ask, but I'm asking."

"If you won't date anyone else, won't bed anyone else."

"I won't." That seemed an easy enough promise to make.

"Will you mind if I come into the bar?"

"No. I'm not telling anyone we're apart. I'm not talking about it."

He leaned over, I could feel the pressure on my arm as his body pressed against it.

"Kiss me," he said.

I lifted my head and turned, and our lips met. It was blue fire, not orange-and-red flames, not that kind of heat: blue fire. After a second, his arms went around me. After another, my arms went around him. I began to feel boneless, limp. With a gasp, I pulled away.

"Oh, we can't, Bill."

I heard his breath draw in. "Of course not, if we're separating," he said quietly, but he didn't sound like he thought I meant it. "We should definitely not be kissing. Still less should I want to throw you back on the porch and fuck you till you faint."

My knees were actually shaking. His deliberately crude language, coming out in that cold sweet voice, made the longing inside me surge even higher. It took everything I had, every little scrap of self-control, to push myself up and go in the house.

But I did it.

*   *   *

IN THE FOLLOWING week, I began to craft a life without Gran and without Bill. I worked nights and worked hard. I was extra careful, for the first time in my life, about locks and security. There was a murderer out there, and I no longer had my powerful protector. I considered getting a dog, but couldn't decide what kind I wanted. My cat, Tina, was only protection in the sense that she always reacted when someone came very near the house.

I got calls from Gran's lawyer from time to time, informing me about the progress of winding up her estate. I got calls from Bartlett's lawyer. My great-uncle had left me twenty thousand dollars, a great sum for him. I almost turned down the legacy. But I thought again. I gave the money to the local mental health center, earmarking it for the treatment of children who were victims of molestation and rape.

They were glad to get it.

I took vitamins, loads of them, because I was a little anemic. I drank lots of fluids and ate lots of protein.

And I ate as much garlic as I wanted, something Bill hadn't been able to tolerate. He said it came out through my pores, even, when I had garlic bread with spaghetti and meat sauce one night.

I slept and slept and slept. Staying up nights after a work shift had me rest-deprived.

After three days I felt restored, physically. In fact, it seemed to me that I was a little stronger than I had been.

I began to take in what was happening around me.

The first thing I noticed was that local folks were really pissed off at the vampires who nested in Monroe. Diane, Liam, and Malcolm had been touring bars in the area, apparently trying to make it impossible for other vampires who wanted to mainstream. They'd been behaving outrageously, offensively. The three vampires made the escapades of the Louisiana Tech students look bland.

They didn't seem to ever imagine they were endangering themselves. The freedom of being out of the coffin had gone to their heads. The right to legally exist had withdrawn all their constraints, all their prudence and caution. Malcolm nipped at a bartender in Bogaloosas. Diane danced naked in Farmerville. Liam dated an underage girl in Shongaloo, and her mother, too. He took blood from both. He didn't erase the memory of either.

Rene was talking to Mike Spencer, the funeral director, in Merlotte's one Thursday night, and they hushed when I got near. Naturally, that caught my attention. So I read Mike's mind. A group of local men were thinking of burning out the Monroe vampires.

I didn't know what to do. The three were, if not exactly friends of Bill, at least sort of coreligionists. But I loathed Malcolm, Diane, and Liam just as much as anyone else. On the other hand; and boy—there always was another hand, wasn't there?—it just went against my grain to know ahead of the fact about premeditated murders and just sit on my hands.

Maybe this was all liquor talking. Just to check, I dipped into the minds of the people around me. To my dismay, many of them were thinking about torching the vampire's nest. But I couldn't track down the origin of the idea. It felt as though the poison had flowed from one mind and infected others.

There wasn't any proof, any proof at all, that Maudette and Dawn and my grandmother had been killed by a vampire. In fact, rumor had it that the coroner's report might show evidence against that. But the three vampires were behaving in such a way that people wanted to blame them for something, wanted to get rid of them, and since Maudette and Dawn were both vampire-bitten and habitues of vampire bars, well, folks just cobbled that together to pound out a conviction.

Bill came in the seventh night I'd been alone. He appeared at his table quite suddenly. He wasn't by himself. There was a boy with him, a boy who looked maybe fifteen. He was a vampire, too.

"Sookie, this is Harlen Ives from Minneapolis," Bill said, as if this were an ordinary introduction.

"Harlen," I said, and nodded. "Pleased to meet you."

"Sookie." He bobbed his head at me, too.

"Harlen is in transit from Minnesota to New Orleans," Bill said, sounding positively chatty.

"I'm going on vacation," Harlen said. "I've been wanting to visit New Orleans for years. It's just a mecca for us, you know."

"Oh . . . right," I said, trying to sound matter of fact.

"There's this number you can call," Harlen informed me. "You can stay with an actual resident, or you can rent a . . ."

"Coffin?" I asked brightly.

"Well, yes."

"How nice for you," I said, smiling for all I was worth. "What can I get you? I believe Sam has restocked the blood, Bill, if you'd like some? It's flavored A neg, or we've got the O positive."

"Oh, A negative, I think," Bill said, after he and Harlen had a silent communication.

"Coming right up!" I stomped back to the cooler behind the bar and pulled out two A neg's, popped the tops, and carted them back on a tray. I smiled the whole time, just like I used to.

"Are you all right, Sookie?" Bill asked in a more natural voice after I'd plonked their drinks down in front of them.

"Of course, Bill," I said cheerily. I wanted to break the bottle over Bill's head. Harlen, indeed. Overnight stay. Right.

"Harlen would like to drive over to visit Malcolm, later," Bill said, when I came to take the empties and ask if they wanted a refill.

"I'm sure Malcolm would love to meet Harlen," I said, trying not to sound as bitchy as I felt.

"Oh, meeting Bill has just been super," Harlen said, smiling at me, showing fangs. Harlen knew how to do bitch, all right. "But Malcolm is absolutely a legend."

"Watch out," I said to Bill. I wanted to tell him how much peril the three nesting vampires had put themselves into, but I didn't think it'd come to a head just yet. And I didn't want to spell it out because Harlen was sitting there, batting his baby blues at me and looking like a teen sex symbol. "Nobody's too happy with those three, right now," I added, after a moment. It was not an effectual warning.

Bill just looked at me, puzzled, and I spun on my heel and walked away.

I came to regret that moment, regret it bitterly.

AFTER BILL AND Harlen had left, the bar buzzed even harder with the kind of talk I'd heard from Rene and Mike Spencer. It seemed to me like someone had been lighting fire, keeping the anger level stoked up. But for the life of me I couldn't discover who it was, though I did some random listening, both mental and physical. Jason came into the bar, and we said hello, but not much more. He hadn't forgiven me for my reaction to Uncle Bartlett's death.

He'd get over it. At least he wasn't thinking about burning anything, except maybe creating some heat in Liz Barrett's bed. Liz, even younger than me, had curly short brown hair and big brown eyes and an unexpectedly no-nonsense air about her that made me think Jason might have met his match. After I'd said good-bye to them after their pitcher of beer was empty, I realized that the anger level in the bar had escalated, that the men were really serious about doing something.

I began to be more than anxious.

As the evening wore on, the activity in the bar grew more and more frenetic. Less women, more men. More table-hopping. More drinking. Men were standing, instead of sitting. It was hard to pin down, since there wasn't any big meeting, really. It was by word-of-mouth, whispered from ear to ear. No one jumped on the bar and screamed, "Whatta ya say, boys? Are we gonna put up with those monsters in our midst? To the castle!" or anything like that. It was just that, after a time, they all began drifting out, standing in huddled groups out in the parking lot. I looked out one of the windows at them, shaking my head. This wasn't good.

Sam was uneasy, too.

"What do you think?" I asked him, and I realized this was the first time I'd spoken to him all evening, other than "Pass the pitcher," or "Give me another margarita."

"I think we've got a mob," he said. "But they'll hardly go over to Monroe now. The vampires'll be up and about until dawn."

"Where is their house, Sam?"

"I understand it's on the outskirts of Monroe on the west side—in other words, closest to us," he told me. "I don't know for sure."

I drove home after closing, half hoping I'd see Bill lurking in my driveway so I could tell him what was afoot.

But I didn't see him, and I wouldn't go to his house. After a long hesitation, I dialed his number, but got only his answering machine. I left a message. I had no idea what the three nesting vampires' phone was listed under, if they had a phone at all.

As I pulled off my shoes and removed my jewelry—all silver, take that, Bill!—I remember worrying, but I wasn't worrying enough. I went to bed and quickly to sleep in the bedroom that was now mine. The moonlight streamed in the open shades, making strange shadows on the floor. But I only stared at them for a few minutes. Bill didn't wake me that night, returning my call.

BUT THE PHONE did ring, early in the morning, after daylight.

"What?" I asked, dazed, the receiver pressed to my ear. I peered at the clock. It was seven-thirty.

"They burned the vampires' house," Jason said. "I hope yours wasn't in it."

"What?" I asked again, but my voice was panicked now.

"They burned the vampires' house outside of Monroe. After sunrise. It's on Callista Street, west of Archer."

I remembered Bill saying he might take Harlen over there. Had he stayed?

"No." I said it definitely.

"Yes."

"I have to go," I said, hanging up the phone.

IT SMOLDERED IN the bright sunlight. Wisps of smoke trailed up into the blue sky. Charred wood looked like alligator skin. Fire trucks and law enforcement cars were parked helter-skelter on the lawn of the two-story house. A group of the curious stood behind yellow tape.

The remains of four coffins sat side by side on the scorched grass. There was a body bag, too. I began to walk toward them, but for the longest time they seemed to be no closer; it was like one of those dreams where you can never reach your goal.

Someone grabbed my arm and tried to stop me. I can't remember what I said, but I remember a horrified face. I trudged on through the debris, inhaling the smell of burned things, wet charred things, a smell that wouldn't leave me the rest of my life.

I reached the first coffin and looked in. What was left of the lid was open to the light. The sun was coming up; any moment now it would kiss the dreadful thing resting on soggy, white silk lining.

Was it Bill? There was no way to tell. The corpse was disintegrating bit by bit even as I watched. Tiny fragments flaked off and blew into the breeze, or disappeared in a tiny puff of smoke where the sun's rays began to touch the body.

Each coffin held a similar horror.

Sam was standing by me.

"Can you call this murder, Sam?"

He shook his head. "I just don't know, Sookie. Legally, killing the vampires is murder. But you'd have to prove arson first, though I don't think that'd be very hard." We could both smell gasoline. There were men buzzing around the house, climbing here and there, yelling to each other. It didn't appear to me that these men were conducting any serious crime-scene investigation.

"But this body here, Sookie." Sam pointed to the body bag on the grass. "This was a real human, and they have to investigate. I don't think any member of that mob ever realized there might be a human in there, ever considered anything besides what they did."

"So why are you here, Sam?"

"For you," he said simply.

"I won't know if it's Bill all day, Sam."

"Yes, I know."

"What am I supposed to do all day? How can I wait?"

"Maybe some drugs," he suggested. "What about sleeping pills or something?"

"I don't have anything like that," I said. "I've never had trouble sleeping."

This conversation was getting odder and odder, but I don't think I could have said anything else.

A big man was in front of me, the local law. He was sweating in the morning heat, and he looked like he'd been up for hours. Maybe he'd been on the night shift and had to stay on when the fire started. When men I knew had started the fire.

"Did you know these people, miss?"

"Yes, I did. I'd met them."

"Can you identify the remains?"

"Who could identify that?" I asked incredulously.

The bodies were almost gone now, featureless and disintegrating. He looked sick. "Yes, ma'am. But the person."

"I'll look," I said before I had time to think. The habit of being helpful was mighty hard to break.

As if he could tell I was about to change my mind, the big man knelt on the singed grass and unzipped the bag. The sooty face inside was that of a girl I'd never met. I thanked God.

"I don't know her," I said, and felt my knees give. Sam caught me before I was on the ground, and I had to lean against him.

"Poor girl," I whispered. "Sam, I don't know what to do."

The law took part of my time that day. They wanted to know everything I knew about the vampires who had owned the house, and I told them, but it didn't amount to much. Malcolm, Diane, Liam. Where they'd come from, their age, why they'd settled in Monroe, who their lawyers were; how would I know anything like that? I'd never even been to their house before.

When my questioner, whoever he was, found out that I'd met them through Bill, he wanted to know where Bill was, how he could contact him.

"He may be right there," I said, pointing to the fourth coffin. "I won't know till dark." My hand rose of its own volition and covered my mouth.

Just then one of the firemen started to laugh, and his companion, too. "Southern fried vampires!" the shorter one hooted to the man who was questioning me. "We got us some Southern fried vampires here!"

He didn't think it was so damn funny when I kicked him. Sam pulled me off and the man who'd been questioning me grabbed the fireman I'd attacked. I was screaming like a banshee and would have gone for him again if Sam had let go.

But he didn't. He dragged me toward my car, his hands just as strong as bands of iron. I had a sudden vision of how ashamed my grandmother would have been to see me screaming at a public servant, to see me physically attack someone. The idea pricked my crazy hostility like a needle puncturing a balloon. I let Sam shove me into the passenger's seat, and when he started the car and began backing away, I let him drive me home while I sat in utter silence.

We got to my house all too soon. It was only ten o'clock in the morning. Since it was daylight savings time I had at least ten plus hours to wait.

Sam made some phone calls while I sat on the couch staring ahead of me. Five minutes had passed when he came back into the living room.

"Come on, Sookie," he said briskly. "These blinds are filthy."

"What?"

"The blinds. How could you have let them go like this?"

"What?"

"We're going to clean. Get a bucket and some ammonia and some rags. Make some coffee."

Moving slowly and cautiously, afraid I might dry up and blow away like the bodies in the coffins, I did as he bid me.

Sam had the curtains down on the living-room windows by the time I got back with the bucket and rags.

"Where's the washing machine?"

"Back there, off the kitchen," I said, pointing.

Sam went back to the washroom with an armful of curtains. Gran had washed those not a month ago, for Bill's visit. I didn't say a word.

I lowered one of the blinds, closed it, and began washing. When the blinds were clean, we polished the windows themselves. It began raining about the middle of the morning. We couldn't get the outside. Sam got the long-handled dust mop and got the spider webs out of the corners of the high ceiling, and I wiped down the baseboards. He took down the mirror over the mantel, dusted the parts that we couldn't normally reach, and then we cleaned the mirror and rehung it. I cleaned the old marble fireplace till there wasn't a trace of winter's fire left. I got a pretty screen and put it over the fireplace, one painted with magnolia blossoms. I cleaned the television screen and had Sam lift it so I could dust underneath. I put all the movies back in their own boxes and labeled what I'd taped. I took all the cushions off the couch and vacuumed up the debris that had collected beneath them, finding a dollar and five cents in change. I vacuumed the carpet and used the dust mop on the wood floors.

We moved into the dining room and polished everything that could be polished. When the wood of the table and chairs was gleaming, Sam asked me how long it'd been since I'd done Gran's silver.

I hadn't ever polished Gran's silver. We opened the buffet to find that, yes, it certainly needed it. So into the kitchen we carried it, and we found the silver polish, and we polished away. The radio was on, but I gradually realized that Sam was turning it off every time the news began.

We cleaned all day. It rained all day. Sam only spoke to me to direct me to the next task.

I worked very hard. So did he.

By the time the light was growing dim, I had the cleanest house in Renard Parish.

Sam said, "I'm going now, Sookie. I think you want to be alone."

"Yes," I said. "I want to thank you some time, but I can't thank you now. You saved me today."

I felt his lips on my forehead and then a minute later I heard the door slam. I sat at the table while the darkness began to fill the kitchen. When I almost could not see, I went outside. I took my big flashlight.

It didn't matter that it was still raining. I had on a sleeveless denim dress and a pair of sandals, what I'd pulled on that morning after Jason had called me.

I stood in the pouring warm rain, my hair plastered to my skull and my dress clinging wetly to my skin. I turned left to the woods and began to make my way through them, slowly and carefully at first. As Sam's calming influence began to evaporate, I began to run, tearing my cheeks on branches, scratching my legs on thorny vines. I came out of the woods and began to dash through the cemetery, the beam of the flashlight bobbing before me. I had thought I was going to the house on the other side, the Compton house: but then I knew Bill must be here, somewhere in this six acres of bones and stones. I stood in the center of the oldest part of the graveyard, surrounded by monuments and modest tombstones, in the company of the dead.

I screamed, "Bill Compton! Come out now!"

I turned in circles, looking around in the near-blackness, knowing even if I couldn't see him, Bill would be able to see me, if he could see anything—if he wasn't one of those blackened, flaking atrocities I'd seen in the front yard of the house outside Monroe.

No sound. No movement except the falling of the gentle drenching rain.

"Bill! Bill! Come out!"

I felt, rather than heard, movement to my right. I turned the beam of the flashlight in that direction. The ground was buckling. As I watched, a white hand shot up from the red soil. The dirt began to heave and crumble. A figure climbed out of the ground.

"Bill?"

It moved toward me. Covered with red streaks, his hair full of dirt, Bill took a hesitant step in my direction.

I couldn't even go to him.

"Sookie," he said, very close to me, "why are you here?" For once, he sounded disoriented and uncertain.

I had to tell him, but I couldn't open my mouth.

"Sweetheart?"

I went down like a stone. I was abruptly on my knees in the sodden grass.

"What happened while I slept?" He was kneeling by me, bare and streaming with rain.

"You don't have clothes on," I murmured.

"They'd just get dirty," he said sensibly. "When I'm going to sleep in the soil, I take them off."

"Oh. Sure."

"Now you have to tell me."

"You have to not hate me."

"What have you done?"

"Oh my God, it wasn't me! But I could have warned you more, I could have grabbed you and made you listen. I tried to call you, Bill!"

"What has happened?"

I put one hand on either side of his face, touching his skin, realizing how much I would have lost, how much I might yet lose.

"They're dead, Bill, the vampires from Monroe. And someone else with them."

"Harlen," he said tonelessly. "Harlen stayed over last night, he and Diane really hit if off." He waited for me to finish, his eyes fixed on mine.

"They were burned."

"On purpose."

"Yes."

He squatted beside me in the rain, in the dark, his face not visible to me. The flashlight was gripped in my hand, and all my strength had ebbed away. I could feel his anger.

I could feel his cruelty.

I could feel his hunger.

He had never been more completely vampire. There wasn't anything human in him.

He turned his face to the sky and howled.

I thought he might kill someone, the rage rolling off him was so great. And the nearest person was me.

As I comprehended my own danger, Bill gripped my upper arms. He pulled me to him, slowly. There was no point in struggling, in fact I sensed that would only excite Bill more. Bill held me about an inch from him, I could almost smell his skin, and I could feel the turmoil in him, I could taste his rage.

Directing that energy in another way might save me. I leaned that inch, put my mouth on his chest. I licked the rain off, rubbed my cheek against his nipple, pressed myself against him.

The next moment his teeth grazed my shoulder, and his body, hard and rigid and ready, shoved me so forcefully I was suddenly on my back in the mud. He slid directly into me as if he were trying to reach through me to the soil. I shrieked, and he growled in response, as though we were truly mud people, primitives from caves. My hands, gripping the flesh of his back, felt the rain pelting down and the blood under my nails, and his relentless movement. I thought I would be plowed into this mud, into my grave. His fangs sank into my neck.

Suddenly I came. Bill howled as he reached his own completion, and he collapsed on me, his fangs pulling out and his tongue cleaning the puncture marks.

I had thought he might kill me without even meaning to.

My muscles would not obey me, even if I had known what I wanted to do. Bill scooped me up. He took me to his house, pushing open the door and carrying me straight through into the large bathroom. Laying me gently on the carpet, where I spread mud and rainwater and a little streak of blood, Bill turned on the warm water in the spa, and when it was full he put me in and then got in himself. We sat on the seats, our legs trailing out in the warm frothing water that became discolored quickly.

Bill's eyes were staring miles away.

"All dead?" he said, his voice nearly inaudible.

"All dead, and a human girl, too," I said quietly.

"What have you been doing all day?"

"Cleaning. Sam made me clean my house."

"Sam," Bill said thoughtfully. "Tell me, Sookie. Can you read Sam's mind?"

"No," I confessed, suddenly exhausted. I submerged my head, and when I came up, Bill had gotten the shampoo bottle. He soaped my hair and rinsed it, combed it as he had the first time we'd made love.

"Bill, I'm sorry about your friends," I said, so exhausted I could hardly get the words out. "And I am so glad you are alive." I slid my arms around his neck and lay my head on his shoulder. It was hard as a rock. I remember Bill drying me off with a big white towel, and I remember thinking how soft the pillow was, and I remember him sliding into bed beside me and putting his arm around me. Then I fell into sleep.

In the small hours of the morning, I woke halfway to hear someone moving around the room. I must have been dreaming, and it must have been bad, because I woke with my heart racing. "Bill?" I asked, and I could hear the fear in my voice.

"What's wrong?" he asked, and I felt the bed indent as he sat on the edge.

"Are you all right?"

"Yes, I was just out walking."

"No one's out there?"

"No, sweetheart." I could hear the sound of cloth moving over skin, and then he was under the sheets with me.

"Oh, Bill, that could have been you in one of those coffins," I said, the agony still fresh in my mind.

"Sookie, did you ever think that could have been you in the body bag? What if they come here, to burn this house, at dawn?"

"You have to come to my house! They won't burn my house. You can be safe with me," I said earnestly.

"Sookie, listen: because of me you could die."

"What would I lose?" I asked, hearing the passion in my voice. "I've had the best time since I met you, the best time of my life!"

"If I die, go to Sam."

"Passing me along already?"

"Never," he said, and his smooth voice was cold. "Never." I felt his hands grip my shoulders; he was on one elbow beside me. He scooted a little closer, and I could feel the cool length of his body.

"Listen, Bill," I said. "I'm not educated, but I'm not stupid. I'm not real experienced or worldly, either, but I don't think I'm naive." I hoped he wasn't smiling in the dark. "I can make them accept you. I can."

"If anyone can, you will," he said. "I want to enter you again."

"You mean—? Oh, yeah. I see what you mean." He'd taken my hand and guided it down to him. "I'd like that, too." And I sure would, if I could survive it after the pounding I'd taken in the graveyard. Bill had been so angry that now I felt battered. But I could also feel that liquidy warm feeling running through me, that restless excitement to which Bill had addicted me. "Honey," I said, caressing him up and down his length, "honey." I kissed him, felt his tongue in my mouth. I touched his fangs with my own tongue. "Can you do it without biting?" I whispered.

"Yes. It's just like a grand finale when I taste your blood."

"Would it be almost as good without?"

"It can never be as good without, but I don't want to weaken you."

"If you wouldn't mind," I said tentatively. "It took me a few days to feel up to par."

"I've been selfish . . . you're just so good."

"If I'm strong, it'll be even better," I suggested.

"Show me how strong you are," he said teasingly.

"Lie on your back. I'm not real sure how this works, but I know other people do it." I straddled him, heard his breathing quicken. I was glad the room was dark and outside the rain was still pouring. A flash of lightening showed me his eyes, glowing. I carefully maneuvered into what I hoped was the correct position, and guided him inside me. I had great faith in instinct, and sure enough it didn't play me false.

Chapter 8

TOGETHER AGAIN, MY doubts at least temporarily drenched by the fear I'd felt when I'd thought I might have lost him, Bill and I settled into an uneasy routine.

If I worked nights, I would go over to Bill's house when I finished, and usually I spent the rest of the night there. If I worked days, Bill would come to my house after sunset, and we would watch TV, or go to the movies, or play Scrabble. I had to have every third night off, or Bill had to refrain from biting those nights; otherwise I began to feel weak and draggy. And there was the danger, if Bill fed on me too much . . . I kept chugging vitamins and iron until Bill complained about the flavor. Then I cut back on the iron.

When I slept at night, Bill would go do other stuff. Sometimes he read, sometimes he wandered the night; sometimes he'd go out and do my yard work under the illumination of the security lights.

If he ever took blood from anyone else, he kept it secret, and he did it far from Bon Temps, which was what I had asked.

I say this routine was uneasy because it seemed to me that we were waiting. The burning of the Monroe nest had enraged Bill and (I think) frightened him. To be so powerful when awake and so helpless when asleep had to be galling.

Both of us were wondering if public feeling against vampires would abate now that the worst troublemakers in the area were dead.

Though Bill didn't say anything directly, I knew from the course our conversation took from time to time that he was worried about my safety with the murderer of Dawn, Maudette, and my grandmother still at large.

If the men of Bon Temps and the surrounding towns thought

burning out the Monroe vampires would set their minds at ease about the murders, they were wrong. Autopsy reports from the three victims finally proved they had their full complement of blood when they were killed. Furthermore, the bite marks on Maudette and Dawn had not only looked old, they were proved to be old. The cause of their deaths was strangulation. Maudette and Dawn had had sex before they'd died. And afterward.

Arlene and Charlsie and I were cautious about things like going out into the parking lot by ourselves, making sure our homes were still locked tight before we entered them, trying to notice what cars were around us as we drove. But it's hard to keep careful that way, a real strain on the nerves, and I am sure we all lapsed back into our sloppy ways. Maybe it was more excusable for Arlene and Charlsie, since they lived with other people, unlike the first two victims; Arlene with her kids (and Rene Lenier, off and on), and Charlsie with her husband, Ralph.

I was the only one who lived alone.

Jason came into the bar almost every night, and he made a point of talking to me every time. I realized he was trying to heal whatever breach lay between us, and I responded as much as I could. But Jason was drinking more, too, and his bed had as many occupants as a public toilet, though he seemed to have real feelings for Liz Barrett. We worked cautiously together on settling the business of Gran's estate and Uncle Bartlett's, though he had more to do with that than I. Uncle Bartlett had left Jason everything but my legacy.

Jason told me one night when he'd had an extra beer that he'd been back to the police station twice more, and it was driving him crazy. He'd talked to Sid Matt Lancaster, finally, and Sid Matt had advised Jason not to go to the police station any more unless Sid Matt went with him.

"How come they keep hauling you in?" I asked Jason. "There must be something you haven't told me. Andy Bellefleur hasn't kept after anybody else, and I know Dawn and Maudette both weren't too picky about who came home with them."

Jason looked mortified. I'd never seen my beautiful older brother look as embarrassed.

"Movies," he mumbled.

I bent closer to be sure I'd heard him right. "Movies?" I said, incredulously.

"Shhh," he hissed, looking guilty as hell. "We made movies."

I guess I was just as embarrassed as Jason. Sisters and brothers don't need to know everything about each other. "And you gave them a copy," I said tentatively, trying to figure out just how dumb Jason had been.

He looked off in another direction, his hazy blue eyes romantically shiny with tears.

"Moron," I said. "Even allowing for the fact that you couldn't know how this was gonna come to public light, what's gonna happen when you decide to get married? What if one of your ex-flames mails a copy of your little tango to your bride-to-be?"

"Thanks for kicking me when I'm down, Sis."

I took a deep breath. "Okay, okay. You've quit making these little videos, right?"

He nodded emphatically. I didn't believe him.

"And you told Sid Matt all about it, right?"

He nodded less firmly.

"And you think that's why Andy is on your case so much?"

"Yeah," Jason said morosely.

"So, if they test your semen and it isn't a match for what was inside Maudette and Dawn, you're clear." By now, I was as shifty-faced as my brother. We had never talked about semen samples before.

"That's what Sid Matt says. I just don't trust that stuff."

My brother didn't trust the most reliable scientific evidence that could be presented in a court. "You think Andy's going to fake the results?"

"No, Andy's okay. He's just doing his job. I just don't know about that DNA stuff."

"Moron," I said, and turned away to get another pitcher of beer for four guys from Ruston, college students on a big night out in the boonies. I could only hope Sid Matt Lancaster was good at persuasion.

I spoke to Jason once more before he left Merlotte's. "Can you help me?" he asked, turning up to me a face I hardly recognized. I was standing by his table, and his date for the night had gone to the ladies' room.

My brother had never asked me for help before.

"How?"

"Can't you just read the minds of the men who come in here and find out if one of them did it?"

"That's not as easy as it sounds, Jason," I said slowly, thinking as I went along. "For one thing, the man would have to be thinking of his crime while he sat here, at the exact moment I listened in. For another thing, I can't always read clear thoughts. Some people, it's just like listening to a radio, I can hear every little thing. Other people, I just get a mass of feelings, not spelled out; it's like hearing someone talk in their sleep, see? You can hear they're talking, you can tell if they're upset or happy, but you can't hear the exact words. And then other times, I can hear a thought, but I can't trace it to its source if the room is crowded."

Jason was staring at me. It was the first time we had talked openly about my disability.

"How do you stop from going crazy?" he asked, shaking his head in amazement.

I was about to try to explain putting up my guard, but Liz Barrett returned to the table, newly lipsticked and fluffed. I watched Jason resume his woman-hunting persona like shrugging on a heavy coat, and I regretted not getting to talk to him more when he was by himself.

That night, as the staff got ready to leave, Arlene asked me if I could baby-sit for her the next evening. It would be an off-day for both of us, and she wanted to go to Shreveport with Rene to see a movie and go out to eat.

"Sure!" I said. "I haven't kept the kids in a while."

Suddenly Arlene's face froze. She half-turned to me, opened her mouth, thought the better of speaking, then thought again. "Will . . . ah . . . will Bill be there?"

"Yes, we'd planned on watching a movie. I was going to stop by the video rental place, tomorrow morning. But I'll get something for the kids to watch instead." Abruptly, I caught her meaning. "Whoa. You mean you don't want to leave the kids with me if Bill's gonna be there?" I could feel my eyes narrow to slits and my voice drop down to its angry register.

"Sookie," she began helplessly, "honey, I love you. But you can't understand, you're not a mother. I can't leave my kids with a vampire. I just can't."

"No matter that I'm there, and I love your kids, too? No matter that Bill would never in a million years harm a child." I slung my purse over my shoulder and stalked out the back door, leaving Arlene standing there looking torn. By golly, she ought to be upset!

I was a little calmer by the time I turned onto the road to go home, but I was still riled up. I was worried about Jason, miffed at Arlene, and almost permanently frosted at Sam, who was pretending these days that I was a mere acquaintance. I debated whether to just go home rather than going to Bill's; decided that was a good idea.

It was a measure of how much he worried about me that Bill was at my house about fifteen minutes after I should have been at his.

"You didn't come, you didn't call," he said quietly when I answered the door.

"I'm in a temper," I said. "A bad one."

Wisely he kept his distance.

"I apologize for making you worry," I said after a moment. "I won't do that again." I strode away from him, toward the kitchen. He followed behind, or at least I presumed he did. Bill was so quiet you never knew until you looked.

He leaned against the door frame as I stood in the middle of the kitchen floor, wondering why I'd come in the room, feeling a rising tide of anger. I was getting pissed off all over again. I really wanted to throw something, damage something. This was not the way I'd been brought up, to give way to destructive impulses like that. I contained it, screwing my eyes shut, clenching my fists.

"I'm gonna dig a hole," I said, and I marched out the back door. I opened the door to the tool shed, removed the shovel, and stomped to the back of the yard. There was a patch back there where nothing ever grew, I don't know why. I sunk the shovel in, pushed it with my foot, came up with a hunk of soil. I kept on going. The pile of dirt grew as the hole deepened.

"I have excellent arm and shoulder muscles," I said, resting against the shovel and panting.

Bill was sitting in a lawn chair watching. He didn't say anything.

I resumed digging.

Finally, I had a really nice hole.

"Were you going to bury anything?" Bill asked, when he could tell I was done.

"No." I looked down at the cavity in the ground. "I'm going to plant a tree."

"What kind?"

"A live oak," I said off the top of my head.

"Where can you get one?"

"At the Garden Center. I'll go sometime this week."

"They take a long time to grow."

"What difference would that make to you?" I snapped. I put the shovel up in the shed, then leaned against it, suddenly exhausted.

Bill made as if to pick me up.

"I am a *grown woman*," I snarled. "I can walk into the house on my own."

"Have I done something to you?" Bill asked. There was very little loving in his voice, and I was brought up short. I had indulged myself enough.

"I apologize," I said. "Again."

"What has made you so angry?"

I just couldn't tell him about Arlene.

"What do you do when you get mad, Bill?"

"I tear up a tree," he said. "Sometimes I hurt someone."

Digging a hole didn't seem so bad. It had been sort of constructive. But I was still wired—it was just more of a subdued buzz than a high-frequency whine. I cast around restlessly for something to affect.

Bill seemed adept at reading the symptoms. "Make love," he suggested. "Make love with me."

"I'm not in the right mood for love."

"Let me try to persuade you."

It turned out he could.

At least it wore off the excess energy of anger, but I still had a residue of sadness that sex couldn't cure. Arlene had hurt my feelings. I stared into space while Bill braided my hair, a pastime that he apparently found soothing.

Every now and then I felt like I was Bill's doll.

"Jason was in the bar tonight," I said.

"What did he want?"

Bill was too clever by far, sometimes, at reading people.

"He appealed to my mind-reading powers. He wanted me to scan the minds of the men who came into the bar until I found out who the murderer was."

"Except for a few dozen flaws, that's not a bad idea."

"You think?"

"Both your brother and I will be regarded with less suspicion if the murderer is in jail. And you'll be safe."

"That's true, but I don't know how to go about it. It would be hard, and painful, and boring, to wade through all that stuff trying to find a little bit of information, a flash of thought."

"Not any more painful or hard than being suspected of murder. You're just accustomed to keeping your gift locked up."

"Do you think so?" I began to turn to look at his face, but he held me still so he could finish braiding. I'd never seen keeping out of people's minds as selfish, but in this case I supposed it was. I would have to invade a lot of privacy. "A detective," I murmured, trying to see myself in a better light than just nosey.

"Sookie," Bill said, and something in his voice made me take notice. "Eric has told me to bring you to Shreveport again."

It took me a second to remember who Eric was. "Oh, the big Viking vampire?"

"The very old vampire," Bill said precisely.

"You mean, he ordered you to bring me there?" I didn't like the sound of this at all. I'd been sitting on the side of the bed, Bill behind me, and now I turned to look in his face. This time he didn't stop me. I stared at Bill, seeing something in his face that I'd never seen before. "You *have* to do this," I said, appalled. I could not imagine someone giving Bill an order. "But honey, I don't want to go see Eric."

I could see that made no difference.

"What is he, the Godfather of vampires?" I asked, angry and incredulous. "Did he give you an offer you couldn't refuse?"

"He is older than me. More to the point, he is stronger."

"Nobody's stronger than you," I said stoutly.

"I wish you were right."

"So is he the head of Vampire Region Ten, or something?"

"Yes. Something like that."

Bill was always closemouthed about how vampires controlled their own affairs. That had been fine with me, until now.

"What does he want? What will happen if I don't go?"

Bill just sidestepped the first question. "He'll send someone—several someones—to get you."

"Other vampires."

"Yes." Bill's eyes were opaque, shining with his difference, brown and rich.

I tried to think this through. I wasn't used to being ordered around. I wasn't used to no choices at all. It took my thick skull several minutes to evaluate the situation.

"So, you'd feel obliged to fight them?"

"Of course. You are mine."

There was that "mine" again. It seemed he really meant it. I sure felt like whining, but I knew it wouldn't do any good.

"I guess I have to go," I said, trying not to sound bitter. "This is just plain old blackmail."

"Sookie, vampires *aren't like humans.* Eric is using the best means to achieve his goal, which is getting you to Shreveport. He didn't have to spell all this out; I understood it."

"Well, I understand it now, but I hate it. I'm between a rock and hard place! What does he want me for, anyway?" An obvious answer popped right into my mind, and I looked at Bill, horrified. "Oh, no, I won't do that!"

"He won't have sex with you or bite you, not without killing me." Bill's glowing face lost all vestiges of familiarity and became utterly alien.

"And he knows that," I said tentatively, "so there must be another reason he wants me in Shreveport."

"Yes," Bill agreed, "but I don't know what it is."

"Well, if it doesn't have to do with my physical charms, or the unusual quality of my blood, it must have to do with my . . . little quirk."

"Your gift."

"Right," I said, sarcasm dripping from my voice. "My precious gift." All the anger I thought I'd eased off my shoulders came back to sit like a four-hundred-pound gorilla. And I was scared to death. I wondered how Bill felt. I was even scared to ask that.

"When?" I asked instead.

"Tomorrow night."

"I guess this is the downside of nontraditional dating." I stared over Bill's shoulder at the pattern of the wallpaper my grandmother had chosen ten years ago. I promised myself that if I got through this, I would repaper.

"I love you." His voice was just a whisper.

This wasn't Bill's fault. "I love you, too," I said. I had to stop myself from begging, Please don't let the bad vampire hurt me, please don't let the vampire rape me. If I was between a rock and a hard place, Bill was doubly so. I couldn't even begin to estimate the self-control he was employing. Unless he really was calm? Could a vampire face pain and this form of helplessness without some inner turmoil?

I searched his face, the familiar clear lines and white matte complexion, the dark arches of his brows and proud line of his nose. I observed that Bill's fangs were only slightly extended, and rage and lust ran them full out.

"Tonight," he said. "Sookie . . ." His hands began urging me to lie beside him.

"What?"

"Tonight, I think, you should drink from me."

I made a face. "Ick! Don't you need all your strength for tomorrow night? I'm not hurt."

"How have you felt since you drank from me? Since I put my blood inside you?"

I mulled it over. "Good," I admitted.

"Have you been sick?"

"No, but then I almost never am."

"Have you had more energy?"

"When you weren't taking it back!" I said tartly, but I could feel my lips curve up in a little smile.

"Have you been stronger?"

"I—yes, I guess I have." I realized for the first time how extraordinary it was that I'd carried in a new chair, by myself, the week before.

"Has it been easier to control your power?"

"Yes, I did notice that." I'd written it off to increased relaxation.

"If you drink from me tonight, tomorrow night you will have more resources."

"But you'll be weaker."

"If you don't take much, I'll recoup during the day when I sleep. And I may have to find someone else to drink from tomorrow night before we go."

My face filled with hurt. Suspecting he was doing it and knowing were sure two different things.

"Sookie, this is for us. No sex with anyone else, I promise you."

"You really think all this is necessary."

"Maybe necessary. At least helpful. And we need all the help we can get."

"Oh, all right. How do we do this?" I had only the haziest recollection of the night of the beating, and I was glad of it.

He looked at me quizzically. I had the impression he was amused. "Aren't you excited, Sookie?"

"At drinking blood from you? Excuse me, that's not my turn-on."

He shook his head, as if that was beyond his understanding. "I forget," he said simply. "I forget how it is to be otherwise. Would you prefer neck, wrist, groin?"

"Not groin," I said hastily. "I don't know, Bill. Yuck. Whichever."

"Neck," he said. "Lie on top of me, Sookie."

"That's like sex."

"It's the easiest way."

So I straddled him and gently let myself down. This felt very peculiar. This was a position we used for lovemaking and nothing else.

"Bite, Sookie," he whispered.

"I can't do that!" I protested.

"Bite, or I'll have to use a knife."

"My teeth aren't sharp like yours."

"They're sharp enough."

"I'll hurt you."

He laughed silently. I could feel his chest moving beneath me.

"Damn." I breathed, and steeling myself, I bit his neck. I did a good job because there was no sense prolonging this. I tasted the metallic blood in my mouth. Bill groaned softly, and his hands brushed my back and continued down. His fingers found me.

I gave a gasp of shock.

"Drink," he said raggedly, and I sucked hard. He groaned, louder, deeper, and I felt him pressing against me. A little ripple of madness went through me, and I attached myself to him like a barnacle, and he entered me, began moving, his hands now gripping my hip bones. I drank and saw visions, visions all with a background of darkness, of white things coming up from the ground and going hunting, the thrill of the run through the woods, the prey panting ahead and the excitement of its fear; pursuit, legs pumping, hearing the thrumming of blood through the veins of the pursued . . .

Bill made a noise deep in his chest and convulsed inside me. I raised my head from his neck, and a wave of dark delight carried me out to sea.

This was pretty exotic stuff for a telepathic barmaid from northern Louisiana.

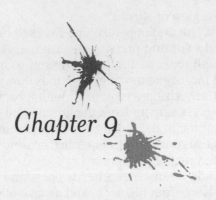

Chapter 9

I WAS GETTING ready by sunset the next day. Bill had said he was going to feed somewhere before we went, and as upset as the idea made me, I had to agree it made sense. He was right about how I'd feel after my little informal vitamin supplement the night before, too. I felt super. I felt very strong, very alert, very quick-witted, and oddly enough, I also felt very pretty.

What would I wear for my own little interview with a vampire? I didn't want to look like I was trying to be sexy, but I didn't want to make a fool of myself by wearing a shapeless gunnysack, either. Blue jeans seemed to be the answer, as they so often are. I put on white sandals and a pale blue scoop-neck tee. I hadn't worn it since I'd started seeing Bill because it exposed his fang marks. But Bill's "ownership" of me, I figured, could not be too strongly reinforced tonight. Remembering the cop last time checking my neck, I tucked a scarf in my purse. I thought again and added a silver necklace. I brushed my hair, which seemed at least three shades lighter, and let it ripple down my back.

Just when I was really having to struggle with picturing Bill with somebody else, he knocked. I opened the door and we stood looking at each other for a minute. His lips had more color than normal, so he'd done it. I bit my own lips to keep from saying anything.

"You did change," he said first.

"You think anyone else'll be able to tell?" I hoped not.

"I don't know." He held out his hand, and we walked to his car. He opened my door, and I brushed by him to climb in. I stiffened.

"What's wrong?" he asked, after a moment.

"Nothing," I said, trying to keep my voice even, and I sat in the passenger's seat and stared straight ahead of me.

I told myself I might as well be mad at the cow who had given him his hamburger. But somehow the simile just didn't work.

"You smell different," I said after we'd been on the highway for a few minutes. We drove for a few minutes in silence.

"Now you know how I will feel if Eric touches you," he told me. "But I think I'll feel worse because Eric will enjoy touching you, and I didn't much enjoy my feeding."

I figured that wasn't totally, strictly, true; I know I always enjoy eating even if I'm not served my favorite food. But I appreciated the sentiment.

We didn't talk much. We were both worried about what was ahead of us. All too soon, we were parking at Fangtasia again, but this time in the back. As Bill held open the car door, I had to fight an impulse to cling to the seat and refuse to get out. Once I made myself emerge, I had another struggle involving my intense desire to hide behind Bill. I gave a kind of gasp, took his arm, and we walked to the door like we were going to a party we were anticipating with pleasure.

Bill looked down at me with approval.

I fought an urge to scowl at him.

He knocked on the metal door with FANGTASIA stencilled on it. We were in a service and delivery alley that ran behind all the stores in the little strip mall. There were several other cars parked back there, Eric's sporty red convertible among them. All the vehicles were high-priced.

You won't find a vampire in a Ford Fiesta.

Bill knocked, three quick, two spaced apart. The Secret Vampire Knock, I guess. Maybe I'd get to learn the Secret Handshake.

The beautiful blond vampire opened the door, the female who'd been at the table with Eric when I'd been to the bar before. She stood back without speaking to let us enter.

If Bill had been human, he would have protested at how tightly I was holding his hand.

The female was in front of us more quickly than my eyes could follow, and I started. Bill wasn't surprised at all, naturally. She led us through a storeroom disconcertingly similar to Merlotte's and into a little corridor. We went through the door on our right.

Eric was in the small room, his presence dominating it. Bill didn't exactly kneel to kiss his ring, but he did nod kind of deep. There was another vampire in the room, the bartender, Long Shadow; he was in fine form tonight, in a skinny-strap tee and weight-lifting pants, all in deep green.

"Bill, Sookie," Eric greeted us. "Bill, you and Sookie know Long Shadow. Sookie, you remember Pam." Pam was the blond female. "And this is Bruce."

Bruce was a human, the most frightened human I'd ever seen. I had considerable sympathy with that. Middle-aged and paunchy, Bruce had thinning dark hair that curved in stiff waves across his scalp. He was jowly and small-mouthed. He was wearing a nice suit, beige, with a white shirt and a brown-and-navy patterned tie. He was sweating heavily. He was in a straight chair across the desk from Eric. Naturally, Eric was in the power chair. Pam and Long Shadow were standing against the wall across from Eric, by the door. Bill took his place beside them, but as I moved to join him, Eric spoke again.

"Sookie, listen to Bruce."

I stood staring at Bruce for a second, waiting for him to speak, until I understood what Eric meant.

"What exactly am I listening for?" I asked, knowing my voice was sharp.

"Someone has embezzled about sixty thousand dollars from us," Eric explained.

Boy, somebody had a death wish.

"And rather than put all our human employees to death or torture, we thought perhaps you would look into their minds and tell us who it was."

He said "death or torture" as calmly as I said, "Bud or Old Milwaukee."

"And then what will you do?" I asked.

Eric seemed surprised.

"Whoever it is will give our money back," he said simply.

"And then?"

His big blue eyes narrowed as he stared at me.

"Why, if we can produce proof of the crime, we'll turn the culprit over to the police," he said smoothly.

Liar, liar, pants on fire. "I'll make a deal, Eric," I said, not bothering to smile. Winsome did not count with Eric, and he was far from any desire to jump my bones. At the moment.

He smiled, indulgently. "What would that be, Sookie?"

"If you really do turn the guilty person over to the police, I'll do this for you again, whenever you want."

Eric cocked an eyebrow.

"Yeah, I know I'd probably have to anyway. But isn't it better if I come willing, if we have good faith with each other?" I broke into a sweat. I could not believe I was bargaining with a vampire.

Eric actually seemed to be thinking that over. And suddenly, I was in his thoughts. He was thinking he could make me do what he wanted, anywhere, anytime, just by threatening Bill or some human I loved. But he wanted to mainstream, to keep as legal as he could, to keep his relations with humans aboveboard, or at least as aboveboard as vampire–human dealings could be. He didn't want to kill anyone if he didn't have to.

It was like suddenly being plunged into a pit of snakes, cold snakes, lethal snakes. It was only a flash, a slice of his mind, sort of, but it left me facing a whole new reality.

"Besides," I said quickly, before he could see I'd been inside his head, "how sure are you that the thief is a human?"

Pam and Long Shadow both moved suddenly, but Eric flooded the room with his presence, commanding them to be still.

"That's an interesting idea," he said. "Pam and Long Shadow are my partners in this bar, and if none of the humans is guilty, I guess we'll have to look at them."

"Just a thought," I said meekly, and Eric looked at me with the glacial blue eyes of a being who hardly remembers what humanity was like.

"Start now, with this man," he commanded.

I knelt by Bruce's chair, trying to decide how to proceed. I'd never tried to formalize something that was pretty chancy. Touching would help; direct contact clarified the transmission, so to speak. I took Bruce's hand, found that too personal (and too sweaty) and pushed back his coat cuff. I took hold of his wrist. I looked into his small eyes.

I didn't take the money, who took it, what crazy fool would put us in danger like this, what will Lillian do if they kill me, and Bobby and Heather, why did I work for vampires anyway, it's sheer greed, and I'm paying for it, God I'll never work for these things again how can this crazy woman find out who took the fucking money why doesn't she let go of me what is she is she a vampire, too, or some kind of demon her eyes are so strange I should have found out earlier that the money was missing and found out who took it before I even said anything to Eric . . .

"Did you take the money?" I breathed, though I was sure I already knew the answer.

"No," Bruce groaned, sweat running down his face, and his thoughts, his reaction to the question, confirmed what I'd heard already.

"Do you know who did?"

"I wish."

I stood, turned to Eric, shook my head. "Not this guy," I said.

Pam escorted poor Bruce out, brought the next interrogee.

My subject was a barmaid, dressed in trailing black with lots of cleavage on display, her ragged strawberry blond hair straggling down her back. Of course, working at Fangtasia would be a dream job for a fang-banger, and this gal had the scars to prove she enjoyed her perks. She was confident enough to grin at Eric, foolish enough to take the wooden chair with some confidence, even crossing her legs like Sharon Stone—she hoped. She was surprised to see a strange vampire and a new woman in the room, and not pleased by my presence, though Bill made her lick her lips.

"Hey, sweetie," she said to Eric, and I decided she must have no imagination at all.

"Ginger, answer this woman's questions," Eric said. His voice was like a stone wall, flat and implacable.

Ginger seemed to understand for the first time that this was a time to be serious. She crossed her ankles this time, sat with her hands on the tops of her thighs, and assumed a stern face. "Yes, master," she said, and I thought I was going to barf.

She waved an imperious hand at me, as if to say, "Begin, fellow vampire server." I reached down for her wrist, and she flung my hand away. "Don't touch me," she said, almost hissing.

It was such an extreme reaction that the vampires tensed up, and I could feel that crackling the air in the room.

"Pam, hold Ginger still," Eric commanded, and Pam appeared silently behind Ginger's chair, leaning over and putting her hands on Ginger's upper arms. You could tell Ginger struggled some because her head moved around, but Pam held her upper body in a grip that kept the girl's body absolutely immobile.

My fingers circled her wrist. "Did you take the money?" I asked, staring into Ginger's flat brown eyes.

She screamed, then, long and loud. She began to curse me. I listened to the chaos in the girl's tiny brain. It was like trying to walk over a bombed site.

"She knows who did," I said to Eric. Ginger fell silent then, though she was sobbing. "She can't say the name," I told the blond vampire. "He has bitten her." I touched the scars on Ginger's neck as if that needed more illustration. "It's some kind of compulsion," I reported, after I'd tried again. "She can't even picture him."

"Hypnosis," Pam commented. Her proximity to the frightened girl had made Pam's fangs run out. "A strong vampire."

"Bring in her closest friend," I suggested.

Ginger was shaking like a leaf by then with thoughts she was compelled not to think pressing her from their locked closet.

"Should she stay, or go?" Pam asked me directly.

"She should go. It'll only scare someone else."

I was so into this, so into openly using my strange ability, that I didn't look at Bill. I felt that somehow if I looked at him, it would weaken me. I knew where he was, that he and Long Shadow had not moved since the questioning had begun.

Pam hauled the trembling Ginger away. I don't know what she did with the barmaid, but she came returned with another waitress in the same kind of clothes. This woman's name was Belinda, and she was older and wiser. Belinda had brown hair, glasses, and the sexiest pouting mouth I'd ever seen.

"Belinda, what vampire has Ginger been seeing?" Eric asked smoothly once Belinda was seated, and I was touching her. The waitress had enough sense to accept the process quietly, enough intelligence to realize she had to be honest.

"Anyone that would have her," Belinda said bluntly.

I saw an image in Belinda's mind, but she had to think the name.

"Which one from here?" I asked suddenly, and then I had the name. My eyes sought his corner before I could open my mouth, and then he was on me, Long Shadow, vaulting over the chair holding Belinda to land on top of me as I crouched in front of her. I was bowled over backward into Eric's desk, and only my upflung arms saved me from his teeth sinking into my throat and ripping it out. He bit my forearm savagely, and I screamed; at least I tried to, but with so little air left from the impact it was more like an alarmed choking noise.

I was only conscious of the heavy figure on top of me and the pain of my arm, my own fear. I hadn't been frightened that the Rats were going to kill me until almost too late, but I understood that to keep his name from leaving my lips, Long Shadow was ready to kill me instantly, and when I heard the awful noise and felt his body press even harder on me I didn't have any idea what it meant. I'd been able to see his eyes over the top of my arm. They were wide, brown, crazed, icy. Suddenly they dulled and seemed to almost flatten. Blood gushed out of Long Shadow's mouth, bathing my arm. It flowed into my open mouth, and I gagged. His teeth relaxed, and his face fell in on itself. It began to wrinkle. His eyes turned into gelatinous pools. Handfuls of his thick black hair fell on my face.

I was shocked beyond moving. Hands gripped my shoulders and began pulling me out from under the decaying corpse. I pushed with my feet to scrabble back faster.

There wasn't an odor, but there was gunk, black and streaky, and the absolute horror and disgust of watching Long Shadow deconstruct with incredible speed. There was a stake sticking out of his back. Eric stood watching, as we all were, but he had a mallet in his hand. Bill was behind me, having pulled me out from under Long Shadow. Pam was standing by the door, her hand gripping Belinda's arm. The waitress looked as rocky as I must have.

Even the gunk began to vanish in smoke. We all stood frozen until the last wisp was gone. The carpet had a kind of scorched mark on it.

"You'll have to get you an area rug," I said, completely out of the blue. Honest to God, I couldn't stand the silence any more.

"Your mouth is bloody," Eric said. All the vampires had fully extended fangs. They'd gotten pretty excited.

"He bled onto me."

"Did any go down your throat?"

"Probably. What does that mean?"

"That remains to be seen," Pam said. Her voice was dark and husky. She was eyeing Belinda in a way that would have made me distinctly nervous, but Belinda seemed to be preening, incredibly. "Usually," Pam went on, her eyes on Belinda's pouty lips, "we drink from humans, not the other way around."

Eric was looking at me with interest, the same kind of interest that Pam had in Belinda. "How do things look to you now, Sookie?" he asked in such a smooth voice you'd never think he'd just executed an old friend.

How *did* things look to me now? Brighter. Sounds were clearer, and I could hear better. I wanted to turn and look at Bill, but I was scared to take my eyes off Eric.

"Well, I guess Bill and me'll go now," I said, as if no other process was possible. "I did that for you, Eric, and now we get to go. No retaliation for Ginger and Belinda and Bruce, okay? We agreed." I started toward the door with an assurance I was far from feeling. "I'll just bet you need to go see how the bar is doing, huh? Who's mixing the drinks, tonight?"

"We got a substitute," Eric said absently, his eyes never leaving my neck. "You smell different, Sookie," he murmured, taking a step closer.

"Well, remember now, Eric, we had a deal," I reminded him, my smile broad and tense, my voice snapping with good cheer. "Bill and I are going home now, aren't we?" I risked a glance behind me at Bill. My heart sank. His eyes were open wide, unblinking, his lips drawn back in a silent snarl to expose his extended fangs. His pupils were dilated enormously. He was staring at Eric.

"Pam, get out of the way," I said, quietly but sharply. Once Pam was distracted from her own blood lust, she evaluated the situation in one glance. She swung open the office door and propelled Belinda through it, stood beside it to usher us out. "Call Ginger," I suggested, and the sense of what I was saying penetrated Pam's fog of desire. "Ginger," she called hoarsely, and the blond girl stumbled from a door down the hall. "Eric wants you," Pam told her. Ginger's face lit up like she had a date with David Duchovny, and she was in the room and rubbing against Eric almost as fast as a vampire could have. As if he'd woken from a spell, Eric looked down at Ginger when she ran her hands up his chest. As he bent to kiss her, Eric looked at me over her head. "I'll see you again," he said, and I pulled Bill out the door as quick as a wink. Bill didn't want to go. It was like trying to tow a log. But once we were out in the hall he seemed to be a little more aware of the need to get out of there, and we hurried from Fangtasia and got into Bill's car.

I looked down at myself. I was bloodstained and wrinkled, and I smelled funny. Yuck. I looked over at Bill to share my disgust with him, but he was looking at me in an unmistakable way.

"No," I said forcefully. "You start this car and get out of here before anything else happens, Bill Compton. I tell you flat, I'm not in the mood."

He scooted across the seat toward me, his arms scooping me up before I could say anything else. Then his mouth was on mine, and after a second his tongue began licking the blood from my face.

I was really scared. I was also really angry. I grabbed his ears and pulled his head away from mine using every ounce of strength I possessed, which happened to be more than I thought I had.

His eyes were still like caves with ghosts dwelling in their depths. "Bill!" I shrieked. I shook him. "Snap out of it!"

Slowly, his personality seeped back into his eyes. He drew a shuddering sigh. He kissed me lightly on the lips.

"Okay, can we go home now?" I asked, ashamed that my voice was so quavery.

"Sure," he said, sounding none too steady himself.

"Was that like sharks scenting blood?" I asked, after a fifteen-minute silent drive that almost had us out of Shreveport.

"Good analogy."

He didn't need to apologize. He'd been doing what nature dictated, as least as natural as vampires got. He didn't bother to. I would kind of liked to have heard an apology.

"So, am I in trouble?" I asked finally. It was two in the morning, and I found the question didn't bother me as much as it should have.

"Eric will hold you to your word," Bill said. "As to whether he will leave you alone personally, I don't know. I wish . . ." but his voice trailed off. It was the first time I'd heard Bill wish for anything.

"Sixty thousand dollars isn't a lot of money to a vampire, surely," I observed. "You all seem to have plenty of money."

"Vampires rob their victims, of course," Bill said matter-of-factly. "Early on, we take the money from the corpse. Later, when we're more experienced, we can exert enough control to persuade a human to give us money willingly, then forget it's been done. Some of us hire money managers, some of us go into real estate, some of us live on the interest from our investments. Eric and Pam went in together on the bar. Eric put up most of the money, Pam the rest. They had known Long Shadow for a hundred years, and they hired him to be bartender. He betrayed them."

"Why would he steal from them?"

"He must have had some venture he needed the capital for," Bill said absently. "And he was in a mainstreaming position. He couldn't just go out and kill a bank manager after hypnotizing him and persuading the man to give him the money. So he took it from Eric."

"Wouldn't Eric have loaned it to him?"

"If Long Shadow hadn't been too proud to ask, yes," Bill said.

We had another long silence. Finally I said, "I always think of vampires as smarter than humans, but they're not, huh?"

"Not always," he agreed.

When we reached the outskirts of Bon Temps, I asked Bill to drop me off at home. He looked sideways at me, but didn't say anything. Maybe vampires were smarter than humans, after all.

Chapter 10

THE NEXT DAY, when I was getting ready for work, I realized I was definitely off vampires for a while. Even Bill.

I was ready to remind myself I was a human.

The trouble was, I had to notice that I was a changed human.

It wasn't anything major. After the first infusion of Bill's blood on the night the Rats had beaten me, I'd felt healed, healthy, stronger. But not markedly different. Maybe more—well, sexier.

After my second draft of Bill's blood, I'd felt really strong, and I'd been braver because I'd had more confidence. I felt more secure in my sexuality and its power. It seemed apparent I was handling my disability with more aplomb and capability.

I'd had Long Shadow's blood by accident. The next morning, looking in the mirror, my teeth were whiter and sharper. My hair looked lighter and livelier, and my eyes were brighter. I looked like a poster girl for good hygiene, or some healthy cause like taking vitamins or drinking milk. The savage bite on my arm (Long Shadow's last bite on this earth, I realized) was not completely healed, but it was well on its way.

Then my purse spilled as I picked it up, and my change rolled under the couch. I held up the end of the couch with one hand while with the other I retrieved the coins.

Whoa.

I straightened and took a deep breath. At least the sunlight didn't hurt my eyes, and I didn't want to bite everyone I saw. I'd enjoyed my breakfast toast, rather than longing for tomato juice. I wasn't turning into a vampire. Maybe I was sort of an enhanced human?

Life had sure been simpler when I hadn't dated.

When I got to Merlotte's, everything was ready except for slicing the lemons and limes. We served the fruit both with mixed drinks and with tea, and I got out the cutting board and a sharp knife. Lafayette was tying on his apron as I got the lemons from the big refrigerator.

"You highlighted your hair, Sookie?"

I shook my head. Under the enveloping white apron, Lafayette was a symphony of color; he was wearing a fuschia thin-strap tee, dark purple jeans, red thong sandals, and he had sort of raspberry eye shadow on.

"It sure looks lighter," he said skeptically, raising his own plucked brows.

"I've been out in the sun a lot," I assured him. Dawn had never gotten along with Lafayette, whether because he was black or because he was gay, I didn't know . . . maybe both. Arlene and Charlsie just accepted the cook, but didn't go out of their ways to be friendly. But I'd always kind of liked Lafayette because he conducted what had to be a tough life with verve and grace.

I looked down at the cutting board. All the lemons had been quartered. All the limes had been sliced. My hand was holding the knife, and it was wet with juices. I had done it without knowing it. In about thirty seconds. I closed my eyes. My God.

When I opened them, Lafayette was staring from my face to my hands.

"Tell me I didn't just see that, girlfriend," he suggested.

"You didn't," I said. My voice was cool and level, I was surprised to note. "Excuse me, I got to put these away." I put the fruit in separate containers in the big cooler behind the bar where Sam kept the beer. When I shut the door, Sam was standing there, his arms crossed across his chest. He didn't look happy.

"Are you all right?" he asked. His bright blue eyes scanned me up and down. "You do something to your hair?" he said uncertainly.

I laughed. I realized that my guard had slid into place easily, that it didn't have to be a painful process. "Been out in the sun," I said.

"What happened to your arm?"

I looked down at my right forearm. I'd covered the bite with a bandage.

"Dog bit me."

"Had it had its shots?"

"Sure."

I looked up at Sam, not too far, and it seemed to me his wiry, curly, red-blond hair snapped with energy. It seemed to me I could hear his heart beating. I could feel his uncertainly, his desire. My body responded instantly. I focussed on his thin lips, and the rich smell of his aftershave filled my lungs. He moved two inches closer. I could feel the breath going in and out of his lungs. I knew his penis was stiffening.

Then Charlsie Tooten came in the front door and slammed it behind her. We both took a step away from each other. Thank God for Charlsie, I thought. Plump, dumb, good-natured, and hardworking, Charlsie was a dream employee. Married to Ralph, her high school sweetheart, who worked at one of the chicken processing plants, Charlsie had a girl in the eleventh grade and a married daughter. Charlsie loved to work at the bar so she could get out and see people, and she had a knack for dealing with drunks that got them out the door without a fight.

"Hi, you two!" she called cheerfully. Her dark brown hair (L'Oreal, Lafayette said) was pulled back dramatically to hang from the crown of her head in a cascade of ringlets. Her blouse was spotless and the pockets of her shorts gaped since the contents were too packed. Charlsie was wearing sheer black support hose and Keds, and her artificial nails were a sort of burgundy red.

"That girl of mine is expecting. Just call me Grandma!" she said, and I could tell Charlsie was happy as a clam. I gave her the expected hug, and Sam patted her on the shoulder. We were both glad to see her.

"When is the baby due?" I asked, and Charlsie was off and running. I didn't have to say anything for the next five minutes. Then Arlene trailed in, makeup inexpertly covering the hickeys on her neck, and she listened to everything all over again. Once my eyes met Sam's, and after a little moment, we looked away simultaneously.

Then we began serving the lunchtime crowd, and the incident was over.

Most people didn't drink much at lunchtime, maybe a beer or a glass of wine. A hefty proportion just had iced tea or water. The lunch crowd consisted of people who happened to be close to Merlotte's when the lunch hour came, people who were regulars and thought of it naturally, and the local alcoholics for whom their lunchtime drink was maybe the third or fourth. As I began to take orders, I remembered my brother's plea.

I listened in all day, and it was gruelling. I'd never spent the day listening; I'd never let my guard down for so long. Maybe it wasn't as painful as it had been; maybe I felt cooler about what I was hearing. Sheriff Bud Dearborn was sitting at a table with the mayor, my grandmother's friend Sterling Norris. Mr. Norris patted me on the shoulder, standing up to do so, and I realized it was the first time I'd seen him since Gran's funeral.

"How are you doing, Sookie?" he asked in a sympathetic voice. He was looking poorly, himself.

"Just great, Mr. Norris. Yourself?"

"I'm an old man, Sookie," he said with an uncertain smile. He didn't even wait for me to protest. "These murders are wearing me down. We haven't had a murder in Bon Temps since Darryl Mayhew shot Sue Mayhew. And there wasn't no mystery about that."

"That was . . . what? Six years ago?" I asked the sheriff, just to keep standing there. Mr. Norris was feeling so sad at seeing me because he was thinking my brother was going to be arrested for murder, for killing Maudette Pickens, and the mayor reckoned that meant Jason had most likely also killed Gran. I ducked my head to hide my eyes.

"I guess so. Let's see, I remember we were dressed up for Jean-Anne's dance recital . . . so that was . . . yes, you're right, Sookie, six years ago." The sheriff nodded at me with approval. "Jason been in today?" he asked casually, as if it were a mere afterthought.

"No, haven't seen him," I said. The sheriff told me he wanted iced tea and a hamburger; and he was thinking of the time he'd caught Jason with his Jean-Anne, making out like crazy in the bed of Jason's pickup truck.

Oh, Lord. He was thinking Jean-Anne was lucky she hadn't been strangled. And then he had a clear thought that cut me to the quick: Sheriff Dearborn thought, These girls are all bottom-feeders, anyway.

I could read his thought in its context because the sheriff happened to be an easy scan. I could feel the nuances of the idea. He was thinking, "Low-skill jobs, no college, screwing vampires . . . bottom of the barrel."

Hurt and angry didn't begin to describe how I felt at this assessment.

I went from table to table automatically, fetching drinks and sandwiches and clearing up the remainders, working as hard as I usually did, with that awful smile stretching my face. I talked to twenty people I knew, most of whom had thoughts as innocent as the day is long. Most customers were thinking of work, or tasks they had to get done at home, or some little problem they needed to solve, like getting the Sears repairman to come work on the dishwasher or getting the house clean for weekend company.

Arlene was relieved her period had started.

Charlsie was immersed in pink glowing reflections on her shot at immortality, her grandchild. She was praying earnestly for an easy pregnancy and safe delivery for her daughter.

Lafayette was thinking that working with me was getting spooky. Policeman Kevin Pryor was wondering what his partner Kenya was doing on her day off. He himself was helping his mother clean out the tool shed and hating every minute of it.

I heard many comments, both aloud and unspoken, about my hair and complexion and the bandage on my arm. I seemed more desirable to more men, and one woman. Some of the guys who'd gone on the vampire burning expedition were thinking they didn't have a chance with me because of my vampire sympathies, and they were regretting their impulsive act. I marked their identities in my mind. I wasn't going to forget they could have killed my Bill, even though at the moment the rest of the vampire community was low on my list of favorite things.

Andy Bellefleur and his sister, Portia, were having lunch together, something they did at least once every week. Portia was a female version of Andy: medium height, blocky build, determined mouth and jaw. The resemblance between brother and sister favored Andy, not Portia. She was a very competent lawyer, I'd heard. I might have suggested her to Jason when he was thinking he'd need an attorney, if she'd not been female . . . and I'd been thinking about Portia's welfare more than Jason's.

Today the lawyer was feeling inwardly depressed because she was educated and made good money, but never had a date. That was her inner preoccupation.

Andy was disgusted with my continued association with Bill Compton, interested in my improved appearance, and curious about how vampires had sex. He also was feeling sorry he was probably going to arrest Jason. He was thinking that the case against Jason was not much stronger than that against several other men, but Jason was the one who looked the most scared, which meant he had something to hide. And there were the videos, which showed Jason having sex— not exactly regular, garden-variety sex—with Maudette and Dawn.

I stared at Andy while I processed his thoughts, which made him uneasy. Andy really did know what I was capable of. "Sookie, you going to get that beer?" he asked finally, waving a broad hand in the air to make sure he had my attention.

"Sure, Andy," I said absently, and got one out of the cooler. "You need any more tea, Portia?"

"No, thanks, Sookie," Portia said politely, patting her mouth with her paper napkin. Portia was remembering high school, when she would have sold her soul for a date with the gorgeous Jason Stackhouse. She was wondering what Jason was doing now, if he had a thought in his head that would interest her—maybe his body would be worth the sacrifice of intellectual companionship? So Portia hadn't seen the tapes, didn't know of their existence; Andy was being a good cop.

I tried to picture Portia with Jason, and I couldn't help smiling. That would be an experience for both of them. I wished, not for the first time, that I could plant ideas as well as reap them.

By the end of my shift, I'd learned—nothing. Except that the videos my brother had so unwisely made featured mild bondage, which caused Andy to think of the ligature marks around the victims' necks.

So, taken as a whole, letting my head open for my brother had been a futile exercise. All I'd heard tended to make me worry more and didn't supply any additional information that might help his cause.

A different crowd would come in tonight. I had never come to Merlotte's just for fun. Should I come in tonight? What would Bill do? Did I want to see him?

I felt friendless. There was no one I could talk to about Bill, no one who wouldn't be halfway shocked I was seeing him in the first place. How could I tell Arlene I was blue because Bill's vampire buddies were terrifying and ruthless, that one of them had bitten me the night before, bled into my mouth, been staked on top of me? This was not the kind of problem Arlene was equipped to handle.

I couldn't think of anyone who was.

I couldn't recall anyone dating a vampire who wasn't an indiscriminate vampire groupie, a fang-banger who would go with just any bloodsucker.

By the time I left work, my enhanced physical appearance no longer had the power to make me confident. I felt like a freak.

I puttered around the house, took a short nap, watered Gran's flowers. Toward dusk, I ate something I'd nuked in the microwave. Wavering up until the last moment about going out, I finally put on a red shirt and white slacks and some jewelry and drove back to Merlotte's.

It felt very strange entering as a customer. Sam was back behind the bar, and his eyebrows went up as he marked my entrance. Three waitresses I knew by sight were working tonight, and a different cook was grilling hamburgers, I saw through the serving hatch.

Jason was at the bar. For a wonder, the stool next to him was empty, and I eased onto it.

He turned to me with his face set for a new woman: mouth loose and smiling, eyes bright and wide. When he saw it was me, his expression underwent a comical change. "What the hell are you doing here, Sookie?" he asked, his voice indignant.

"You'd think you weren't glad to see me," I remarked. When Sam paused in front of me, I asked him for a bourbon and coke, without meeting his eyes. "I did what you told me to do, and so far nothing," I whispered to my brother. "I came in here tonight to try some more people."

"Thanks, Sookie," he said, after a long pause. "I guess I didn't realize what I was asking. Hey, is something different about your hair?"

He even paid for my drink when Sam slid it in front of me.

We didn't seem to have much to talk about, which was actually okay, since I was trying to listen to the other customers. There were a few strangers, and I scanned them first, to see if they were possible suspects. It didn't seem they were, I decided reluctantly. One was thinking hard about how much he missed his wife, and the subtext was that he was faithful to her. One was thinking about it being his first time here, and the drinks were good. Another was just concentrating on sitting up straight and hoping he could drive back to the motel.

I'd had another drink.

Jason and I had been swapping conjectures about how much the lawyer's fees would be when Gran's estate was settled. He glanced at the doorway and said, "Uh-oh."

"What?" I asked, not turning to see what he was looking at.

"Sis, the boyfriend's here. And he's not alone."

My first idea was that Bill had brought one of his fellow vampires with him, which would have been upsetting and unwise. But when I turned, I realized why Jason had sounded so angry. Bill was with a human girl. He had a grip on her arm, she was coming on to him like a whore, and his eyes were scanning the crowd. I decided he was looking for my reaction.

I got off the barstool and decided another thing.

I was drunk. I seldom drank at all, and two bourbon and cokes consumed within minutes had made me, if not knee-walking drunk, at least tipsy.

Bill's eyes met mine. He hadn't really expected to find me here. I couldn't read his mind as I had Eric's for an awful moment, but I could read his body language.

"Hey, Vampire Bill!" Jason's friend Hoyt called. Bill nodded politely in Hoyt's direction, but began to steer the girl—tiny, dark—in my direction.

I had no idea what to do.

"Sis, what's his game?" Jason said. He was working up a head of steam. "That gal's a fang-banger from Monroe. I knew her when she liked humans."

I still had no idea what to do. My hurt was overwhelming, but my pride kept trying to contain it. I had to add a dash of guilt to that emotional stew. I hadn't been where Bill had expected me to be, and I hadn't left him a note. Then again—on the other hand (my fifth or sixth)—I'd had a lot of shocks the night before at the command performance in Shreveport; and only my association with him had obliged me to go to *that* shindig.

My warring impulses held me still. I wanted to pitch myself on her and beat the shit out of her, but I hadn't been brought up to brawl in barrooms. (I also wanted to beat the shit out of Bill, but I might as well go bang my head on the wall for the all the damage it would do him.) Then, too, I wanted to burst into tears because my feelings were hurt—but that would be weak. The best option was not to show anything because Jason was ready to launch into Bill, and all it needed was some action from me to squeeze his trigger.

Too much conflict on top of too much alcohol.

While I was enumerating all these options, Bill had approached, wending his way through the tables, with the woman in tow. I noticed the room was quieter. Instead of watching, I was being watched.

I could feel my eyes well with tears while my hands fisted. Great. The worst of both responses.

"Sookie," Bill said, "this is what Eric dropped off at my doorstep." I could hardly understand what he was saying.

"So?" I said furiously. I looked right into the girl's eyes. They were big and dark and excited. I kept my own lids wide apart, knowing if I blinked the tears would flow.

"As a reward," Bill said. I couldn't understand how he felt about this.

"Free *beverage*?" I said, and couldn't believe how venomous my voice sounded.

Jason put his hand on my shoulder. "Steady, girl," he said, his voice as low and mean as mine. "He ain't worth it."

I didn't know what Bill wasn't worth, but I was about to find out. It was almost exhilarating to have no idea what I was about to do, after a lifetime of control.

Bill was regarding me with sharp attention. Under the flourescents over the bar, he looked remarkably white. He hadn't fed from her. And his fangs were retracted.

"Come outside and talk," he said.

"With her?" I was almost growling.

"No," he said. "With me. I have to send her back."

The distaste in his voice influenced me, and I followed Bill out-

side, keeping my head up and not meeting any eyes. He kept ahold of
the girl's arm, and she was practically walking on her toes to keep up.
I didn't know Jason was coming with us until I turned to see him behind me as we passed into the parking lot. Outside, people were coming and going, but it was marginally better than the crowded bar.

"Hi," the girl said chattily. "My name's Desiree. I think I've met
you before, Jason."

"What are you doing here, Desiree?" Jason asked, his voice quiet.
You could almost believe he was calm.

"Eric sent me over here to Bon Temps as a reward for Bill," she
said coyly, looking at Bill from the corners of her eyes. "But he seems
less than thrilled. I don't know why. I'm practically a special vintage."

"Eric?" Jason asked me.

"A vampire from Shreveport. Bar owner. Head honcho."

"He left her on my doorstep," Bill told me. "I didn't ask for her."

"What are you going to do?"

"Send her back," he said impatiently. "You and I have to talk."

I gulped. I felt my fingers uncurl.

"She needs a ride back to Monroe?" Jason asked.

Bill looked surprised. "Yes. Are you offering? I need to talk to
your sister."

"Sure," Jason said, all geniality. I was instantly suspicious.

"I can't believe you're refusing me," Desiree said, looking up at
Bill and pouting. "No one has ever turned me down before."

"Of course I am grateful, and I'm sure you are, as you put it, a
special vintage," Bill said politely. "But I have my own wine cellar."

Little Desiree stared at him blankly for a second before comprehension slowly lit her brown eyes. "This woman yours?" she asked,
jerking her head at me.

"She is."

Jason shifted nervously at Bill's flat statement.

Desiree gave me a good looking over. "She's got funny eyes," she
finally pronounced.

"She's my sister," Jason said.

"Oh. I'm sorry. You're much more . . . normal." Desiree gave Jason the up-and-down, and seemed more pleased with what she saw.
"Hey, what's your last name?"

Jason took her hand and began leading her toward his pickup.
"Stackhouse," he was saying, giving her the full eye treatment, as they
walked away. "Maybe on the way home, you can tell me a little about
what you do . . ."

I turned back to Bill, wondering what Jason's motive was for this generous act, and met Bill's gaze. It was like walking into a brick wall.

"So, you want to talk?" I asked harshly.

"Not here. Come home with me."

I scuffed the gravel with my shoe. "Not your house."

"Then yours."

"No."

He raised his arched brows. "Where then?"

Good question.

"My folks' pond." Since Jason was going to be giving Miss Dark and Tiny a ride home, he wouldn't be there.

"I'll follow you," he said briefly, and we parted to go to our respective cars.

The property where I'd spent my first few years was to the west of Bon Temps. I turned down the familiar gravel driveway and parked at the house, a modest ranch that Jason kept up pretty well. Bill emerged from his car as I slid from mine, and I motioned him to follow me. We went around the house and down the slope, following a path set with big paving stones. In a minute we were at the pond, man-made, that my dad had put in our backyard and stocked, anticipating fishing with his son in that water for years.

There was a kind of patio overlooking the water, and on one of the metal chairs was a folded blanket. Without asking me, Bill picked it up and shook it out, spreading it on the grass downslope from the patio. I sat on it reluctantly, thinking the blanket wasn't safe for the same reasons meeting him in either home wasn't safe. When I was close to Bill, what I thought about was being even closer to him.

I hugged my knees to me and stared off across the water. There was a security light on the other side of the pond, and I could see it reflected in the still water. Bill lay on his back next to me. I could feel his eyes on my face. He laced his fingers together across his ribs, ostentatiously keeping his hands to himself.

"Last night frightened you," he said neutrally.

"Weren't you just a little scared?" I asked, more quietly than I'd thought I would.

"For you. A little for myself."

I wanted to lie on my stomach but worried about getting that close to him. When I saw his skin glow in the moonlight, I yearned to touch him.

"It scared me that Eric can control our lives while we're a couple."

"Do you not want to be a couple anymore?"

The pain in my chest was so bad I put my hand over it, pressing the area above my breast.

"Sookie?" He was kneeling by me, an arm around me.

I couldn't answer. I had no breath.

"Do you love me?" he asked.

I nodded.

"Why do you talk of leaving me?"

The pain made its way out through my eyes in the form of tears.

"I'm too scared of the other vampires and the way they are. What will he ask me to do next? He'll try to make me do something else. He'll tell me he'll kill you otherwise. Or he'll threaten Jason. And he can do it."

Bill's voice was as quiet as the sound of a cricket in the grass. A month ago, I might not have been able to hear it. "Don't cry," he told me. "Sookie, I have to tell you unwelcome facts."

The only welcome thing he could have told me at that point was that Eric was dead.

"Eric is intrigued by you now. He can tell you have mental powers that most humans don't have, or ignore if they know they possess them. He anticipates your blood is rich and sweet." Bill's voice got hoarse when he said that, and I shivered. "And you're beautiful. You're even more beautiful now. He doesn't realize you have had our blood three times."

"You know that Long Shadow bled onto me?"

"Yes. I saw."

"Is there anything magic about three times?"

He laughed, that low, rumbly, rusty laugh. "No. But the more vampire blood you drink, the more desirable you become to our kind, and actually, more desirable to anyone. And Desiree thought she was a vintage! I wonder what vampire said that to her."

"One that wanted to get in her pants," I said flatly, and he laughed again. I loved to hear him laugh.

"With all this telling me how lovely I am, are you saying that Eric, like, lusts for me?"

"Yes."

"What's to stop him from taking me? You say he's stronger than you."

"Courtesy and custom, first of all."

I didn't snort, but I came close.

"Don't discount that. We're all observant of custom, we vampires. We have to live together for centuries."

"Anything else?"

"I am not as strong as Eric, but I'm not a new vampire. He might get badly hurt in a fight with me, or I might even win if I got lucky."

"Anything else?"

"Maybe," Bill said carefully, "you yourself."

"How so?"

"If you can be valuable to him otherwise, he may leave you alone if he knows that is your sincere wish."

"But I don't want to be valuable to him! I don't want to ever see him again!"

"You promised Eric you'd help him again," Bill reminded me.

"If he turned the thief over to the police," I said. "And what did Eric do? He staked him!"

"Possibly saving your life in the process."

"Well, I found his thief!"

"Sookie, you don't know much about the world."

I stared at him, surprised. "I guess that's so."

"Things don't turn out . . . even." Bill stared out into the darkness. "Even I think sometimes I don't know much, anymore." Another gloomy pause. "I have only once before seen one vampire stake another. Eric is going beyond the limits of our world."

"So, he's not too likely to take much notice of that custom and courtesy you were bragging about earlier."

"Pam may keep him to the old ways."

"What is she to him?"

"He made her. That is, he made her vampire, centuries ago. She comes back to him from time to time and helps him do whatever he is doing at the moment. Eric's always been something of a rogue, and the older he gets the more willful he gets." Calling Eric willful seemed a huge understatement to me.

"So, have we talked our way around in circles?" I asked.

Bill seemed to be considering. "Yes," he confirmed, a tinge of regret in his voice. "You don't like associating with vampires other than myself, and I have told you we have no choice."

"How about this Desiree thing?"

"He had someone drop her off on my doorstep, hoping I would be pleased he'd sent me a pretty gift. Also, it would test my devotion to you if I drank from her. Perhaps he poisoned her blood somehow, and her blood would have weakened me. Maybe she would just have been a crack in my armor." He shrugged. "Did you think I had a date?"

"Yes." I felt my face harden, thinking about Bill walking in with the girl.

"You weren't at home. I had to come find you." His tone wasn't accusatory, but it wasn't happy, either.

"I was trying to help Jason out by listening. And I was still upset from last night."

"Are we all right now?"

"No, but we're as all right as we can get," I said. "I guess no matter who I cared for, it wouldn't always go smooth. But I hadn't counted on obstacles this drastic. There's no way you can ever outrank Eric, I guess, since age is the criterion?"

"No," said Bill. "Not outrank . . ." and he suddenly looked thoughtful. "Though there may be something I can do along those lines. I don't want to—it goes against my nature—but we would be more secure."

I let him think.

"Yes," he concluded, ending his long brood. He didn't offer to explain, and I didn't ask.

"I love you," he said, as if that was the bottom line to whatever course of action he was considering. His face loomed over me, luminous and beautiful in the half-darkness.

"I feel the same about you," I said, and put my hands against his chest so he wouldn't tempt me. "But we have too much against us right now. If we can pry Eric off our backs, that would help. And another thing, we have to stop this murder investigation. That would be a second big piece of trouble off our backs. This murderer has the deaths of your friends to answer for, and the deaths of Maudette and Dawn to answer for." I paused, took a deep breath. "And the death of my grandmother." I blinked back tears. I'd gotten adjusted to Gran not being in the house when I came home, and I was getting used to not talking to her and sharing my day with her, but every now and then I had a stab of grief so acute it robbed me of breath.

"Why do you think the same killer is responsible for the Monroe vampires being burned?"

"I think it was the murderer who planted this idea, this vigilante thing, in the men in the bar that night. I think it was the murderer who went from group to group, egging the guys on. I've lived here all my life, and I've never seen people around here act that way. There's got to be a reason they did this time."

"He agitated them? Fomented the burning?"

"Yes."

"Listening hasn't turned up anything?"

"No," I admitted glumly. "But that's not to say tomorrow will be the same."

"You're an optimist, Sookie."

"Yes, I am. I have to be." I patted his cheek, thinking how my optimism had been justified since he had entered my life.

"You keep on listening, since you think it may be fruitful," he said. "I'll work on something else, for now. I'll see you tomorrow evening at your place, okay? I may . . . no, let me explain then."

"All right." I was curious, but Bill obviously wasn't ready to talk.

On my way home, following the taillights of Bill's car as far as my driveway, I thought of how much more frightening the past few weeks would have been if I hadn't had the security of Bill's presence. As I went cautiously down the driveway, I found myself wishing Bill hadn't felt he had to go home to make some necessary phone calls. The few nights we'd spent apart, I wouldn't say I'd been exactly writhing with fear, but I'd been very jumpy and anxious. At the house by myself, I spent lots of time going from locked window to locked door, and I wasn't used to living that way. I felt disheartened at the thought of the night ahead.

Before I got out of my car, I scanned the yard, glad I'd remembered to turn on the security lights before I left for the bar. Nothing was moving. Usually Tina came running when I'd been gone, anxious to get in the house for some cat kibble, but tonight she must be hunting in the woods.

I separated my house key from the bunch on my key ring. I dashed from the car to the front door, inserted and twisted the key in record time, and slammed and locked the door behind me. This was no way to live, I thought, shaking my head in dismay; and just as I completed that idea, something hit the front door with a thud. I shrieked before I could stop myself.

I ran for the portable phone by the couch. I punched in Bill's number as I went around the room pulling down the shades. What if the line was busy? He'd said he was going home to use the phone!

But I caught him just as he walked in the door. He sounded breathless as he picked up the receiver. "Yes?" he said. He always sounded suspicious.

"Bill," I gasped, "there's someone outside!"

He crashed the phone down. A vampire of action.

He was there in two minutes. Looking out into the yard from a slightly lifted blind, I glimpsed him coming into the yard from the woods, moving with a speed and silence a human could never equal. The relief of seeing him was overwhelming. For a second I felt ashamed at calling Bill to rescue me: I should have handled the situation myself. Then I thought, Why? When you know a practically invincible being who professes to adore you, someone so hard to kill it's next to impossible, someone preternaturally strong, that's who you're gonna call.

Bill investigated the yard and the woods, moving with a sure, silent grace. Finally he came lightly up the steps. He bent over something on the front porch. The angle was too acute, and I couldn't tell what it was. When he straightened, he had something in his hands, and he looked absolutely . . . expressionless.

This was very bad.

I went reluctantly to the front door and unlocked it. I pushed out the screen door.

Bill was holding the body of my cat.

"Tina?" I said, hearing my voice quaver and not caring at all. "Is she dead?"

Bill nodded, one little jerk of his head.

"What—how?"

"Strangled, I think."

I could feel my face crumple. Bill had to stand there holding the corpse while I cried my eyes out.

"I never got that live oak," I said, having calmed a little. I didn't sound very steady. "We can put her in that hole." So around to the backyard we went, poor Bill holding Tina, trying to look comfortable about it, and me trying not to dissolve again. Bill knelt and lay the little bundle of black fur at the bottom of my excavation. I fetched the shovel and began to fill it in, but the sight of the first dirt hitting Tina's fur undid me all over again. Silently, Bill took the shovel from my hands. I turned my back, and he finished the awful job.

"Come inside," he said gently when it was finished.

We went in the house, having to walk around to the front because I hadn't yet unlocked the back.

Bill patted me and comforted me, though I knew he hadn't ever been crazy about Tina. "God bless you, Bill," I whispered. I tightened my arms around him ferociously, in a sudden convulsion of fear that he, too, would be taken from me. When I'd gotten the sobs reduced to hiccups, I looked up, hoping I hadn't made him uncomfortable with my flood of emotion.

Bill was furious. He was staring at the wall over my shoulder, and his eyes were glowing. He was the most frightening thing I'd ever seen in my life.

"Did you find anything out in the yard?" I asked.

"No. I found traces of his presence. Some footprints, a lingering scent. Nothing you could bring into court as proof," he went on, reading my mind.

"Would you mind staying here until you have to go to . . . get away from the sun?"

"Of course." He stared at me. He'd fully intended to do that whether or not I agreed, I could tell.

"If you still need to make phone calls, just make them here. I don't care." I meant if they were on my phone bill.

"I have a calling card," he said, once again astonishing me. Who would have thought?

I washed my face and took a Tylenol before I put on my nightgown, sadder than I'd been since Gran had been killed, and sadder in different way. The death of a pet is naturally not in the same category as the death of a family member, I chided myself, but it didn't seem to affect my misery. I went through all the reasoning I was capable of and came no closer to any truth except the fact that I'd fed and brushed and loved Tina for four years, and I would miss her.

Chapter 11

MY NERVES WERE raw the next day. When I got to work and told Arlene what had happened, she gave me a hard hug, and said, "I'd like to kill the bastard that did that to poor Tina!" Somehow, that made me feel a lot better. Charlsie was just as sympathetic, if more concerned with the shock to me rather than the agonized demise of my cat. Sam just looked grim. He thought I should call the sheriff, or Andy Bellefleur, and tell one of them what had happened. I finally did call Bud Dearborn.

"Usually these things go in cycles," Bud rumbled. "Ain't nobody else reported a pet missing or dead, though. I'm afraid it sounds like some kind a personal thing, Sookie. That vampire friend of yours, he like cats?"

I closed my eyes and breathed deeply. I was using the phone in Sam's office, and he was sitting behind the desk figuring out his next liquor order.

"Bill was at home when whoever killed Tina threw her on my porch," I said as calmly as I could. "I called him directly afterward, and he answered the phone." Sam looked up quizzically, and I rolled my eyes to let him know my opinion of the sheriff's suspicions.

"And he told you the cat was strangled," Bud went on ponderously.

"Yes."

"Do you have the ligature?"

"No. I didn't even see what it was."

"What did you do with the kitty?"

"We buried her."

"Was that your idea or Mr. Compton's?"

"Mine." What else would we have done with Tina?

"We may come dig your kitty up. If we had had the ligature and the cat, maybe we could see if the method of strangulation matched the method used in killing Dawn and Maudette," Bud explained ponderously.

"I'm sorry. I didn't think about that."

"Well, it don't matter much. Without the ligature."

"Okay, good-bye." I hung up, probably applying a little more pressure than the receiver required. Sam's eyebrows lifted.

"Bud is a jerk," I told him.

"Bud's not a bad policeman," Sam said quietly. "None of us here are used to murders that are this sick."

"You're right," I admitted, after a moment. "I wasn't being fair. He just kept saying 'ligature' like he was proud he'd learned a new word. I'm sorry I got mad at him."

"You don't have to be perfect, Sookie."

"You mean I get to screw up and be less than understanding and forgiving, from time to time? Thanks, boss." I smiled at him, feeling the wry twist to my lips, and got up off the edge of his desk where I'd been propped to make my phone call. I stretched. It wasn't until I saw the way Sam's eyes drank in that stretch that I became self-conscious again. "Back to work!" I said briskly and strode out of the room, trying to make sure there wasn't a hint of sway to my hips.

"Would you keep the kids for a couple of hours this evening?" Arlene asked, a little shyly. I remembered the last time we'd talked about my keeping her kids, and I remembered the offense I'd taken at her reluctance to leave her kids with a vampire. I hadn't been thinking like a mother would think. Now, Arlene was trying to apologize.

"I'd be glad to." I waited to see if Arlene would mention Bill again, but she didn't. "When to when?"

"Well, Rene and I are gonna go to the movies in Monroe," she said. "Say, six-thirty?"

"Sure. Will they have had supper?"

"Oh, yeah, I'll feed 'em. They'll be excited to see their aunt Sookie."

"I look forward to it."

"Thanks," Arlene said. She paused, almost said something else, then appeared to think again. "See you at six-thirty."

I got home about five, most of the way driving against the sun, which was glaring like it was staring me down. I changed to a blue-and-green knit short set, brushed my hair and secured it with a banana clip. I had a sandwich, sitting uneasily by myself at the kitchen table.

The house felt big and empty, and I was glad to see Rene drive up with Coby and Lisa.

"Arlene's having trouble with one of her artificial nails," he explained, looking embarrassed at having to relay this feminine problem. "And Coby and Lisa were raring to get over here." I noticed Rene was still in his work clothes—heavy boots, knife, hat, and all. Arlene wasn't going to let him take her anywhere until he showered and changed.

Coby was eight and Lisa was five, and they were hanging all over me like big earrings when Rene bent to kiss them good-bye. His affection for the kids gave Rene a big gold star in my book, and I smiled at him approvingly. I took the kids' hands to lead them back to the kitchen for some ice cream.

"We'll see you about ten-thirty, eleven," he said. "If that's all right." He put his hand on the doorknob.

"Sure," I agreed. I opened my mouth to offer to keep the kids for the night, as I'd done on previous occasions, but then I thought of Tina's limp body. I decided that tonight they'd better not stay. I raced the kids to the kitchen, and a minute or two later I heard Rene's old pickup rattling down the driveway.

I picked up Lisa. "I can hardly lift you anymore, girl, you're getting so big! And you, Coby, you shaving yet?" We sat at the table for a good thirty minutes while the children ate ice cream and rattled off their list of achievements since we'd last visited.

Then Lisa wanted to read to me, so I got out a coloring book with the color and number words printed inside, and she read those to me with some pride. Coby, of course, had to prove he could read much better, and then they wanted to watch a favorite show. Before I knew it, it was dark.

"My friend is coming over tonight," I told them. "His name is Bill."

"Mama told us you had a special friend," Coby said. "I better like him. He better be nice to you."

"Oh, he is," I assured the boy, who had straightened and thrust out his chest, ready to defend me if my special friend wasn't nice enough in Coby's estimation.

"Does he send you flowers?" Lisa asked romantically.

"No, not yet. Maybe you can kind of hint I'd like some?"

"Ooo. Yeah, I can do that."

"Has he asked you to marry him?

"Well, no. But I haven't asked him, either."

Naturally, Bill picked that moment to knock.

"I have company," I said, smiling, when I answered the door.

"I can hear," he said.

I took his hand and led him into the kitchen.

"Bill, this is Coby and this young woman is Lisa," I said formally.

"Good, I've been wanting to meet you," Bill said, to my surprise. "Lisa and Coby, is it all right with you if I keep company with your aunt Sookie?"

They eyed him thoughtfully. "She isn't really our aunt," Coby said, testing the waters. "She's our mom's good friend."

"Is that right?"

"Yes, and she says you don't send her flowers," Lisa said. For once, her little voice was crystal clear. I was so glad to realize that Lisa had gotten over her little problem with her *r*'s. Really.

Bill looked sideways at me. I shrugged. "Well, they asked me," I said helplessly.

"Hmmm," he said thoughtfully. "I'll have to mend my ways, Lisa. Thank you for pointing that out to me. When is Aunt Sookie's birthday, do you know?"

I could feel my face flushing. "Bill," I said sharply. "Cut it out."

"Do you know, Coby?" Bill asked the boy.

Coby shook his head, regretfully. "But I know it's in the summer because the last time Mama took Sookie to lunch in Shreveport for her birthday, it was summertime. We stayed with Rene."

"You're smart to remember that, Coby," Bill told him.

"I'm smarter than that! Guess what I learned in school the other day." And Coby was off and running.

Lisa eyed Bill with great attention the whole time Coby spoke, and when Coby was finished, she said, "You look real white, Bill."

"Yes," he said, "that's my normal complexion."

The kids exchanged glances. I could tell they were deciding that "normal complexion" was an illness, and it wouldn't be too polite to ask more questions. Every now and then children show a certain tactfulness.

Bill, initially a little stiff, began to get more and more flexible as the evening wore on. I was ready to admit I was tired by nine, but he was still going strong with the kids when Arlene and Rene came by to pick them up at eleven.

I'd just introduced my friends to Bill, who shook their hands in an absolutely normal way, when another caller arrived.

A handsome vampire with thick black hair combed into an improbable wavy style strolled up out of the woods as Arlene was bundling the kids into the truck, and Rene and Bill were chatting. Bill waved a casual hand at the vampire, and he raised one in return, joining Bill and Rene as if he'd been expected.

From the front porch swing, I watched Bill introduce the two, and the vampire and Rene shook hands. Rene was gaping at the newcomer, and I could tell he felt he'd recognized him. Bill looked meaningfully at Rene and shook his head, and Rene's mouth closed on whatever comment he'd been going to make.

The newcomer was husky, taller than Bill, and he wore old jeans and an "I Visited Graceland" T-shirt. His heavy boots were worn at the heel. He carried a squirt bottle of synthetic blood in one hand and took a swig from time to time. Mr. Social Skills.

Maybe I'd been cued by Rene's reaction, but the more I looked at the vampire, the more familiar he seemed. I tried mentally warming up the skin tone, adding a few lines, making him stand straighter and investing his face with some liveliness.

Oh my God.

It was the man from Memphis.

Rene turned to go, and Bill began steering the newcomer up to me. From ten feet away, the vampire called, "Hey, Bill tells me someone killed your cat!" He had a heavy Southern accent.

Bill closed his eyes for a second, and I just nodded speechlessly.

"Well, I'm sorry about that. I like cats," the tall vampire said, and I clearly got the idea he didn't mean he liked to stroke their fur. I hoped the kids weren't picking up on that, but Arlene's horrified face appeared in the truck window. All the good will Bill had established had probably just gone down the drain.

Rene shook his head behind the vampire's back and climbed into the driver's seat, calling a good-bye as he started up the engine. He stuck his head out the window for a long last look at the newcomer. He must have said something to Arlene because she appeared at her window again, staring for all she was worth. I saw her mouth drop open in shock as she looked harder at the creature standing beside Bill. Her head disappeared into the truck, and I heard a screech as the truck pulled away.

"Sookie," Bill said warningly, "this is *Bubba*."

"Bubba," I repeated, not quite trusting my ears.

"Yep, Bubba," the vampire said cheerfully, goodwill radiating from his fearsome smile. "That's me. Pleased to meetcha."

I shook hands with him, making myself smile back. Good God Almighty, I never thought I'd be shaking hands with *him*. But he'd sure changed for the worse.

"Bubba, would you mind waiting here on the porch? Let me explain our arrangement to Sookie."

"That's all right with me," Bubba said casually. He settled on the swing, as happy and brainless as a clam.

We went into the living room, but not before I'd noticed that when Bubba had made his appearance, much of the night noise—bugs, frogs—had simply stopped. "I had hoped to explain this to you before Bubba got here," Bill whispered. "But I couldn't."

I said, "Is that who I think it is?"

"Yes. So now you know at least some of the sighting stories are true. But *don't* call him by his name. Call him Bubba! Something went wrong when he came over—from human to vampire—maybe it was all the chemicals in his blood."

"But he was really dead, wasn't he?"

"Not . . . quite. One of us was a morgue attendant and a big fan, and he could detect the tiny spark still left, so he brought him over, in a hurried manner."

"Brought him over?"

"Made him vampire," Bill explained. "But that was a mistake. He's never been the same from what my friends tell me. He's as smart as a tree trunk, so to make a living he does odd jobs for the rest of us. We can't have him out in public, you can see that."

I nodded, my mouth hanging open. Of course not. "Geez," I murmured, stunned at the royalty in my yard.

"So remember how stupid he is, and how impulsive . . . don't spend time alone with him, and don't ever call him anything but Bubba. Also, he likes pets, as he told you, and a diet of their blood hasn't made him any the more reliable. Now, as to why I brought him here . . ."

I stood with my arms across my chest, waiting for Bill's explanation with some interest.

"Sweetheart, I have to go out of town for a while," Bill said.

The unexpectedness of this completely disconcerted me.

"What . . . why? No, wait. I don't need to know." I waved my hands in front of me, shooing away any implication that Bill was obligated to tell me his business.

"I'll tell you when I get back," he said firmly.

"So where does your friend—Bubba—come in?" Though I had a nasty feeling I already knew.

"Bubba is going to watch you while I'm gone," Bill said stiffly.

I raised my eyebrows.

"All right. He's not long on . . ." Bill cast around. ". . . anything," he finally admitted. "But he's strong, and he'll do what I tell him, and he'll make sure no one breaks into your house."

"He'll stay out in the woods?"

"Oh, yes," Bill said emphatically. "He's not even supposed to come up and speak to you. At dark, he'll just find a place from which he can see the house, and he'll watch all night."

I'd have to remember to close my blinds. The idea of the dim vampire peering in my windows was not edifying.

"You really think this is necessary?" I asked helplessly. "You know, I don't remember you asking me."

Bill sort of heaved, his version of taking a deep breath. "Sweetheart," he began in an overly patient voice, "I am trying very hard to get used to the way women want to be treated now. But it isn't natural to me, especially when I fear you are in danger. I'm trying to give myself peace of mind while I'm gone. I wish I didn't have to go, and it isn't what I want to do, but what I have to do, for us."

I eyed him. "I hear you," I said finally. "I'm not crazy about this, but I am afraid at night, and I guess . . . well, okay."

Frankly, I don't think it mattered a damn whether I consented or not. After all, how could I make Bubba leave if he didn't want to go? Even the law enforcement people in our little town didn't have the equipment to deal with vampires, and if they were faced with this particular vampire, they'd just stand and gape for long enough for him to tear them apart. I appreciated Bill's concern, and I figured I better have the good grace to thank him. I gave him a little hug.

"Well, if you have to go off, you just be careful while you're gone," I said, trying not to sound forlorn. "Do you have a place to stay?"

"Yes. I'll be in New Orleans. There was a room open at the Blood in the Quarter."

I'd read an article about this hotel, the first in the world that catered exclusively to vampires. It promised complete security, and so far it had delivered. It was right smack dab in the middle of the French Quarter, too. And at dusk it was absolutely surrounded by fang-bangers and tourists waiting for the vampires to come out.

I began to feel envious. Trying not to look like a wistful puppy who's being pushed back in the door when its owners leave, I yanked my smile back into place. "Well, you have a good time," I said brightly. "Got your packing done? The drive should take a few hours, and it's already dark."

"The car is ready." I understood for the first time that he had delayed leaving to spend time with me and Arlene's kids. "I had better leave." He hesitated, seemed to be searching for the right words. Then he held out his hands to me. I took them, and he pulled a little, just exerted a tiny pressure. I moved into his embrace. I rubbed my face against his shirt. My arms circled him, pressed him into me.

"I'll miss you," he said. His voice was just a breath in the air, but I heard him. I felt him kiss the top of my head, and then he stepped away from me and out the front door. I heard his voice on the front porch as he gave Bubba some last minute directions, and I heard the squeak of the swing as Bubba got up.

I didn't look out the window until I heard Bill's car going down the driveway. Then I saw Bubba sauntering into the woods. I told myself, as I took my shower, that Bill must trust Bubba since he'd left him guarding me. But I still wasn't sure who I was more afraid of: the murderer Bubba was watching for, or Bubba himself.

At work the next day, Arlene asked me why the vampire had been at my house. I wasn't surprised that she'd brought it up.

"Well, Bill had to go out of town, and he worries, you know . . ." I was hoping to let it drop at that. But Charlsie had drifted up (we weren't at all busy: the Chamber of Commerce was having a lunch and speaker at Fins and Hooves, and the Ladies' Prayers and Potatoes group were topping their baked potatoes at old Mrs. Bellefleur's huge house). "You mean," Charlsie said with starry eyes, "that your man got you a personal bodyguard?"

I nodded reluctantly. You could put it that way.

"That's so romantic," Charlsie sighed.

You could look at it that way.

"But you should see him," Arlene told Charlsie, having held her tongue as long as she could. "He's exactly like—!"

"Oh, no, not when you talk to him," I interrupted. "He's not at all the same." That was true. "And he really doesn't like it when he hears that name."

"Oh," said Arlene in a hushed voice, as if Bubba could be listening in the broad daylight.

"I do feel safer with Bubba in the woods," I said, which was more or less true.

"Oh, he doesn't stay in the house?" Charlsie asked, clearly a little disappointed.

"God, no!" I said, then mentally apologized to God for taking his name in vain. I was having to do that a lot lately. "No, Bubba stays in the woods at night, watching the house."

"Was that true about the cats?" Arlene looked squeamish.

"He was just joking. Not a great sense of humor, huh?" I was lying through my teeth. I certainly believed Bubba enjoyed a snack of cat blood.

Arlene shook her head, unconvinced. It was time to change the subject. "Did you and Rene have fun on your evening out?" I asked.

"Rene was so good last night, wasn't he?" she said, her cheeks pink.

A much-married woman, blushing. "You tell me." Arlene enjoyed a little ribald teasing.

"Oh, you! What I mean, he was real polite to Bill and even that Bubba."

"Any reason why he wouldn't be?"

"He has kind of a problem with vampires, Sookie." Arlene shook her head. "I know, I do, too," she confessed when I looked at her with raised eyebrows. "But Rene really has some prejudice. Cindy dated a vampire for a while, and that just made Rene awful upset."

"Cindy okay?" I had a great interest in the health of someone who'd dated a vamp.

"I haven't seen her," Arlene admitted, "but Rene goes to visit every other week or so. She's doing well, she's back on the right track. She has a job in a hospital cafeteria."

Sam, who'd been standing behind the bar loading the refrigerator with bottled blood, said, "Maybe Cindy would like to move back home. Lindsey Krause quit the other shift because she's moving to Little Rock."

That certainly focussed our attention. Merlotte's was becoming seriously understaffed. For some reason, low-level service jobs had dropped in popularity in the last couple of months.

"You interviewed anyone else?" Arlene asked.

"I'll have to go through the files," Sam said wearily. I knew that Arlene and I were the only barmaids, waitresses, servers, whatever you wanted to call us, that Sam had hung on to for more then two years. No, that wasn't true; there was Susanne Mitchell, on the other shift. Sam spent lots of time hiring and occasionally firing. "Sookie, would you have a look through the file, see if there's anyone there you know has moved, anyone already got a job, anyone you really recommend? That would save me some time."

"Sure," I said. I remembered Arlene doing the same thing a couple of years ago when Dawn had been hired. We had more ties to the community than Sam, who never seemed to join anything. Sam had been in Bon Temps for six years now, and I had never met anyone who seemed to know about Sam's life prior to his buying the bar here.

I settled down at Sam's desk with the thick file of applications. After a few minutes, I could tell I was really making a difference. I had three piles: moved, employed elsewhere, good material. Then I added a fourth and fifth stack: a pile for people I couldn't work with because I couldn't stand them, and a pile for the dead. The first form on the fifth pile had been filled out by a girl who'd died in a car accident last Christmas, and I felt sorry for her folks all over again when I saw her name at the top of the form. The other application was headed "Maudette Pickens."

Maudette had applied for a job with Sam three months before her death. I guess working at Grabbit Kwik was pretty uninspiring. When I glanced over the filled-in blanks and noticed how poor Maudette's handwriting and spelling had been, it made me feel pitiful all over again. I tried to imagine my brother thinking of having sex with this woman—and filming it—was a worthwhile way to spend his time, and I marvelled at Jason's strange mentality. I hadn't seen him since he'd driven off with Desiree. I hoped he'd gotten home in one piece. That gal was a real handful. I wished he'd settle down with Liz Barrett: she had enough backbone to hold him up, too.

Whenever I thought about my brother lately, it was to worry. If only he hadn't known Maudette and Dawn so well! Lots of men knew them both, apparently, both casually and carnally. They'd both been vampire bitten. Dawn had liked rough sex, and I didn't know Maudette's proclivities. Lots of men got gas and coffee at the Grabbit Kwik, and lots of men came in to get a drink here, too. But only my stupid brother had recorded sex with Dawn and Maudette on film.

I stared at the big plastic cup on Sam's desk, which had been full of iced tea. "The Big Kwencher from Grabbit Kwik" was written in neon orange on the side of the green cup. Sam knew them both, too. Dawn had worked for him, Maudette had applied for a job here.

Sam sure didn't like *me* dating a vampire. Maybe he didn't like *anyone* dating a vampire.

Sam walked in just then, and I jumped like I'd been doing something bad. And I had, in my book. Thinking evil of a friend was a bad thing to do.

"Which is the good pile?" he asked, but he gave me a puzzled look.

I handed him a short stack of maybe ten applications. "This gal, Amy Burley," I said, indicating the one on top, "has experience, she's only subbing at the Good Times Bar, and Charlsie used to work with her there. So you could check with Charlsie first."

"Thanks, Sookie. This'll save me some trouble."

I nodded curtly in acknowledgment.

"Are you all right?" he asked. "You seem kind of distant today."

I looked at him closely. He looked just like he always did. But his mind was closed to me. How could he do that? The only other mind completely closed to me was Bill's, because of his vampire state. But Sam was sure no vampire.

"Just missing Bill," I said deliberately. Would he lecture me about the evils of dating a vampire?

Sam said, "It's daytime. He couldn't very well be here."

"Of course not," I said stiffly, and was about to add, "He's out of town." Then I asked myself if that was a smart thing to do when I had even a hint of suspicion in my heart about my boss. I left the office so abruptly that Sam stared after me in astonishment.

When I saw Arlene and Sam having a long conversation later that day, their sidelong glances told me clearly that I was the topic. Sam went back to his office looking more worried than ever. But we didn't have any more chitchat the rest of the day.

Going home that evening was hard because I knew I'd be alone until morning. When I'd been alone other evenings, I'd had the reassurance that Bill was just a phone call away. Now he wasn't. I tried to feel good about being guarded once it was dark and Bubba crawled out of whatever hole he'd slept in, but I didn't manage it.

I called Jason, but he wasn't home. I called Merlotte's, thinking he might be there, but Terry Bellefleur answered the phone and said Jason hadn't been in.

I wondered what Sam was doing tonight. I wondered why he never seemed to date much. It wasn't for want of offers, I'd been able to observe many times.

Dawn had been especially aggressive.

That evening I couldn't think of anything that pleased me.

I began wondering if Bubba was the hitman—hitvampire?—Bill had called when he wanted Uncle Bartlett bumped off. I wondered why Bill had chosen such a dimwitted creature to guard me.

Every book I picked up seemed wrong, somehow. Every television show I tried to watch seemed completely ridiculous. I tried to read my *Time* and became incensed at the determination to commit suicide that possessed so many nations. I pitched the magazine across the room.

My mind scrabbled around like a squirrel trying to get out of a cage. It couldn't light on anything or be comfortable anywhere.

When the phone rang, I jumped a foot.

"Hello?" I said harshly.

"Jason's here now," Terry Bellefleur said. "He wants to buy you a drink."

I thought uneasily about going out to the car, now that it was dark; about coming home to an empty house, at least a house I would have to hope was empty. Then I scolded myself because, after all, there would be someone watching the house, someone very strong, if very brainless.

"Okay, I'll be there in a minute," I said.

Terry simply hung up. Mr. Chatterbox.

I pulled on a denim skirt and a yellow T-shirt and, looking both ways, crossed the yard to my car. I'd left on every outside light, and I unlocked my car and scooted inside quick as a wink. Once inside the car, I relocked my door.

This was sure no way to live.

I AUTOMATICALLY PARKED in the employee lot when I got to Merlotte's. There was a dog pawing around the Dumpster, and I patted him on the head when I went in. We had to call the pound about once a week to come get some stray or dumped dogs, so many of them pregnant it just made me sick.

Terry was behind the bar.

"Hey," I said, looking around. "Where's Jason?"

"He ain't here," Terry said. "I haven't seen him this evening. I told you so on the phone."

I gaped at him. "But you called me after that and said he had come in."

"No, I didn't."

We stared at each other. Terry was having one of his bad nights, I could tell. His head was writhing around on the inside with the snakes of his army service and his battle with alcohol and drugs. On the outside, you could see he was flushed and sweating despite the air conditioning, and his movements were jerky and clumsy. Poor Terry.

"You really didn't?" I asked, in as neutral a tone as possible.

"Said so, didn't I?" His voice was belligerent.

I hoped none of the bar patrons gave Terry trouble tonight.

I backed out with a conciliatory smile.

The dog was still at the back door. He whined when he saw me.

"Are you hungry, fella?" I asked. He came right up to me, without the cringing I'd come to expect from strays. As he moved more into the light, I saw that this dog had been recently abandoned, if his glossy coat was any indicator. He was a collie, at least mostly. I started to step into the kitchen to ask whoever was cooking if they had any scraps for this guy, but then I had a better idea.

"I know bad ol' Bubba is at the house, but maybe you could come in the house with me," I said in that baby voice I use with animals when I think nobody's listening. "Can you pee outside, so we don't make a mess in the house? Hmmm, boy?"

As if he'd understood me, the collie marked the corner of the Dumpster.

"Good fella! Come for a ride?" I opened my car door, hoping he wouldn't get the seats too dirty. The dog hesitated. "Come on, sugar, I'll give you something good to eat when we get to my place, okay?" Bribery was not necessarily a bad thing.

After a couple more looks and a thorough sniffing of my hands, the dog jumped onto the passenger seat and sat looking out the windshield like he'd committed himself to this adventure.

I told him I appreciated it, and I tickled his ears. We set off, and the dog made it clear he was used to riding.

"Now, when we get to the house, buddy," I told the collie firmly, "we're gonna make tracks for the front door, okay? There's an ogre in the woods who'd just love to eat you up."

The dog gave an excited yip.

"Well, he's not gonna get a chance," I soothed him. It sure was nice to have something to talk to. It was even nice he couldn't talk back, at least for the moment. And I didn't have to keep my guard up because he wasn't human. Relaxing. "We're gonna hurry."

"Woof," agreed my companion.

"I got to call you something," I said. "How about . . . Buffy?"

The dog growled.

"Okay. Rover?"

Whine.

"Don't like that either. Hmmm." We turned into my driveway.

"Maybe you already have a name?" I asked. "Let me check your neck." After I turned off the engine, I ran my fingers through the thick hair. Not even a flea collar. "Someone's been taking bad care of you, sweetie," I said. "But not anymore. I'll be a good mama." With that last inanity, I got my house key ready and opened my door. In a flash, the dog pushed past me and stood in the yard, looking around him alertly. He sniffed the air, and a growl rose in his throat.

"It's just the good vampire, sugar, the one that's guarding the house. You come on inside." With some constant coaxing, I got the dog to come into the house. I locked the door behind us instantly.

The dog padded all around the living room, sniffing and peering. After watching him for a minute to be sure he wasn't going to chew on anything or lift his leg, I went to the kitchen to find something for him to eat. I filled a big bowl with water. I got another plastic bowl Gran had kept lettuce in, and I put the remains of Tina's cat food and some leftover taco meat in it. I figured if you'd been starving, that would be acceptable. The dog finally worked his back to the kitchen and headed for the bowls. He sniffed at the food and raised his head to give me a long look.

"I'm sorry. I don't have any dog food. That's the best I could come up with. If you want to stay with me, I'll get some Kibbles 'N Bits." The dog stared at me for a few more seconds, then bent his head to the bowl. He ate a little meat, took a drink, and looked up at me expectantly.

"Can I call you Rex?"

A little growl.

"What about Dean?" I asked. "Dean's a nice name." A pleasant guy who helped me at a Shreveport bookstore was named Dean. His eyes looked kind of like this collie's, observant and intelligent. And Dean was a little different; I'd never met a dog named Dean. "I'll bet you're smarter than Bubba," I said thoughtfully, and the dog gave his short, sharp bark.

"Well, come on, Dean, let's get ready for bed," I said, quite enjoying having something to talk to. The dog padded after me into the bedroom, checking out all the furniture very thoroughly. I pulled off the skirt and tee, put them away, and stepped out of my panties and unhooked my bra. The dog watched me with great attention while I pulled out a clean nightgown and went into the bathroom to shower. When I stepped out, clean and soothed, Dean was sitting in the doorway, his head cocked to one side.

"That's to get clean, people like to have showers," I told him. "I know dogs don't. I guess it's a human thing." I brushed my teeth and pulled on my nightgown. "You ready for sleep, Dean?"

In answer, he jumped up on the bed, turned in a circle, and lay down.

"Hey! Wait a minute!" I'd certainly talked myself into that one. Gran would have a fit if she could know a dog was on her bed. Gran had believed animals were fine as long as they spent the night out-

side. Humans inside, animals outside, had been her rule. Well, now I
had a vampire outside and a collie on my bed.

I said, "You get down!" and pointed at the rug.

The collie, slowly, reluctantly, descended from the bed. He eyed
me reproachfully as he sat on the rug.

"You stay there," I said sternly and got in the bed. I was very
tired, and not nearly so nervous now that the dog was here; though
what help I expected him to be in case of an intruder, I didn't know,
since he didn't know me well enough to be loyal to me. But I would
accept any comfort I could find, and I began to relax into sleep. Just
as I was drifting off, I felt the bed indent under the weight of the collie. A narrow tongue gave my cheek a swipe. The dog settled close to
me. I turned over and patted him. It was sort of nice having him here.

The next thing I knew, it was dawn. I could hear the birds going to
town outside, chirping up a storm, and it felt wonderful to be snuggled
in bed. I could feel the warmth of the dog through my nightgown; I must
have gotten hot during the night and thrown off the sheet. I drowsily
patted the animal's head and began to stroke his fur, my fingers running idly through the thick hair. He wriggled even closer, sniffed my
face, put his arm around me.

His *arm*?

I was off the bed and shrieking in one move.

In my bed, Sam propped himself on his elbows, sunny side up,
and looked at me with some amusement.

"Oh, ohmyGod! Sam, how'd you get here? What are you doing?
Where's Dean?" I covered my face with my hands and turned my
back, but I'd certainly seen all there was to see of Sam.

"Woof," said Sam, from a human throat, and the truth stomped
over me in combat boots.

I whirled back to face him, so angry I felt like I was going to blow
a gasket.

"You watched me undress last night, you . . . you . . . damn dog!"

"Sookie," he said, persuasively. "Listen to me."

Another thought struck me. "Oh Sam. Bill will kill you." I sat on
the slipper chair in the corner by the bathroom door. I put my elbows
on my knees and hung my head. "Oh, no," I said. "No, no, no."

He was kneeling in front of me. The wirey red-gold hair of his
head was duplicated on his chest and trailed in a line down to . . . I
shut my eyes again.

"Sookie, I was worried when Arlene told me you were going to
be alone," Sam began.

"Didn't she tell you about Bubba?"

"Bubba?"

"This vampire Bill left watching the house."

"Oh. Yeah, she said he reminded her of some singer."

"Well, his name is Bubba. He likes to drain animals for fun."

I had the satisfaction of seeing (through my fingers) Sam turn pale.

"Well, isn't it lucky you let me in, then," he said finally.

Suddenly recalled to his guise of the night before, I said, "What are you, Sam?"

"I'm a shapeshifter. I thought it was time you knew."

"Did you have to do it quite like that?"

"Actually," he said, embarrassed, "I had planned on waking up and getting out before you opened your eyes. I just overslept. Running around on all fours kind of tires you out."

"I thought people just changed into wolves."

"Nope. I can change into anything."

I was so interested I dropped my hands and tried to just stare at his face. "How often?" I asked. "Do you get to pick?"

"I have to at the full moon," he explained. "Other times, I have to will it; it's harder and it takes longer. I turn into whatever animal I saw before I changed. So I keep a dog book open to a picture of a collie on my coffee table. Collies are big, but nonthreatening."

"So, you could be a bird?"

"Yeah, but flying is hard. I'm always scared I'm going to get fried on a power line, or fly into a window."

"Why? Why did you want me to know?"

"You seemed to handle Bill being a vampire really well. In fact, you seemed to enjoy it. So I thought I would see if you could handle my . . . condition."

"But what you are," I said abruptly, off on a mental tangent, "can't be explained by a virus! I mean, you utterly change!"

He didn't say anything. He just looked at me, the eyes now blue, but just as intelligent and observant.

"Being a shapeshifter is definitely supernatural. If that is, then other things can be. So . . ." I said, slowly, carefully, "Bill hasn't got a virus at all. Being a vampire, it really can't be explained by an allergy to silver or garlic or sunlight . . . that's just so much bullshit the vampires are spreading around, propaganda, you might say . . . so they can be more easily accepted, as sufferers from a terrible disease. But really they're . . . they're really . . ."

I dashed into the bathroom and threw up. Luckily, I made it to the toilet.

"Yeah," Sam said from the doorway, his voice sad. "I'm sorry, Sookie. But Bill doesn't just have a virus. He's really, really dead."

I WASHED MY face and brushed my teeth twice. I sat down on the edge of the bed, feeling too tired to go further. Sam sat beside me. He put his arm around me comfortingly, and after a moment I nestled closer, laying my cheek in the hollow of his neck.

"You know, once I was listening to NPR," I said, completely at random. "They were broadcasting a piece about cryogenics, about how lots of people are opting to just freeze their head because it's so much cheaper than getting your whole body frozen."

"Ummm?"

"Guess what song they played for the closing?"

"What, Sookie?"

" 'Put Your Head on My Shoulder.' "

Sam made a choking noise, then doubled over with laughter.

"Listen, Sam," I said, when he'd calmed down. "I hear what you're telling me, but I have to work this out with Bill. I love Bill. I am loyal to him. And he isn't here to give his point of view."

"Oh, this isn't about me trying to woo you away from Bill. Though that would be great." And Sam smiled his rare and brilliant smile. He seemed much more relaxed with me now that I knew his secret.

"Then what is it about?"

"This is about keeping you alive until the murderer is caught."

"So that's why you woke up naked in my bed? For my protection?"

He had the grace to look ashamed. "Well, maybe I could have planned it better. But I did think you needed someone with you, since Arlene told me Bill was out of town. I knew you wouldn't let me spend the night here as a human."

"Will you rest easy now that you know Bubba is watching the house at night?"

"Vampires are strong, and ferocious," Sam conceded. "I guess this Bubba owes Bill something, or he wouldn't be doing him a favor. Vampires aren't big on doing each other favors. They have a lot of structure in their world."

I should have paid more attention to what Sam was saying, but I was thinking I'd better not explain about Bubba's origins.

"If there's you, and Bill, I guess there must be lots of other things outside of nature," I said, realizing what a treasure trove of thought awaited me. Since I'd met Bill, I hadn't felt so much need to hoard neat things up for future contemplation, but it never hurt to be prepared. "You'll have to tell me sometime." Big Foot? The Loch Ness Monster? *I'd* always believed in the Loch Ness monster.

"Well, I guess I better be getting back home," Sam said. He looked at me hopefully. He was still naked.

"Yes, I think you better. But—oh, dang it—you . . . oh, hell." I stomped upstairs to look for some clothes. It seemed to me Jason had a couple of things in an upstairs closet he kept here for some emergency.

Sure enough, there was a pair of blue jeans and a work shirt in the first upstairs bedroom. It was already hot up there, under the tin roof, because the upstairs was on a separate thermostat. I came back down, grateful to feel the cool conditioned air.

"Here," I said, handing Sam the clothes. "I hope they fit well enough." He looked as though he wanted to start our conversation back up, but I was too aware now that I was clad in a thin nylon nightgown and he was clad in nothing at all.

"On with the clothes," I said firmly. "And you get dressed out in the living room." I shooed him out and shut the door behind him. I thought it would be insulting to lock the door, so I didn't. I did get dressed in record time, pulling on clean underwear and the denim skirt and yellow shirt I'd had on the night before. I dabbed on my makeup, put on some earrings, and brushed my hair up into a ponytail, putting a yellow squnchy over the elastic band. My morale rose as I looked in the mirror. My smile turned into a frown when I thought I heard a truck pulling into the front yard.

I came out of the bedroom like I'd been fired from a cannon, hoping like hell Sam was dressed and hiding. He'd done one better. He'd changed back into a dog. The clothes were scattered on the floor, and I swept them up and stuffed them into the closet in the hall.

"Good boy!" I said enthusiastically and scratched behind his ears. Dean responded by sticking his cold black nose up my skirt. "Now you cut that out," I said, and looked through the front window. "It's Andy Bellefleur," I told the dog.

Andy jumped out of his Dodge Ram, stretched for a long second, and headed for my front door. I opened it, Dean by my side.

I eyed Andy quizzically. "You look like you been up all night long, Andy. Can I make you some coffee?"

The dog stirred restlessly beside me.

"That would be great," he said. "Can I come in?"

"Sure." I stood aside. Dean growled.

"You got a good guard dog, there. Here, fella. Come here." Andy squatted to hold out a hand to the collie, whom I simply could not think of as Sam. Dean sniffed Andy's hand, but wouldn't give it a lick. Instead, he kept between me and Andy.

"Come on back to the kitchen," I said, and Andy stood and followed me. I had the coffee on in a jiffy and put some bread in the toaster. Assembling the cream and sugar and spoons and mugs took a few more minutes, but then I had to face why Andy was here. His face was drawn; he looked ten years older than I knew him to be. This was no courtesy call.

"Sookie, were you here last night? You didn't work?"

"No, I didn't. I was here except for a quick trip in to Merlotte's."

"Was Bill here any of that time?"

"No, he's in New Orleans. He's staying in that new hotel in the French Quarter, the one just for vampires."

"You're sure that's where he is."

"Yes." I could feel my face tighten. The bad thing was coming.

"I've been up all night," Andy said.

"Yes."

"I've just come from another crime scene."

"Yes." I went into his mind. "Amy Burley?" I stared at his eyes, trying to make sure. "Amy who worked at the Good Times Bar?" The name at the top of yesterday's pile of prospective barmaids, the name I'd left for Sam. I looked down at the dog. He lay on the floor with his muzzle between his paws, looking as sad and stunned as I felt. He whined pathetically.

Andy's brown eyes were boring a hole in me. "How'd you know?"

"Cut the crap, Andy, you know I can read minds. I feel awful. Poor Amy. Was it like the others?"

"Yes," he said. "Yes, it was like the others. But the puncture marks were fresher."

I thought of the night Bill and I had had to go to Shreveport to answer Eric's summons. Had Amy given Bill blood that night? I couldn't even count how many days ago that had been, my schedule had been so thrown off by all the strange and terrible events of the past few weeks.

I sat down heavily in a wooden kitchen chair, shaking my head absently for a few minutes, amazed at the turn my life had taken.

Amy Burley's life had no more turns to take. I shook the odd spell of apathy off, rose and poured the coffee.

"Bill hasn't been here since night before last," I said.

"And you were here all night?"

"Yes, I was. My dog can tell you," and I smiled down at Dean, who whined at being noticed. He came over to lay his fuzzy head on my knees while I drank my coffee. I smoothed his ears.

"Did you hear from your brother?"

"No, but I got a funny phone call, from someone who said he was at Merlotte's." After the words left my mouth I realized the caller must have been Sam, luring me over to Merlotte's so he could maneuver himself into accompanying me home. Dean yawned, a big jaw-cracking yawn that let us see every one of his white sharp teeth.

I wished I'd kept my mouth shut.

But now I had to explain the whole thing to Andy, who was slumped only half-awake in my kitchen chair, his plaid shirt wrinkled and blotched with coffee stains, his khakis shapeless through long wear. Andy was longing for bed the way a horse longs for his own stall.

"You need to get some rest," I said gently. There was something sad about Andy Bellefleur, something daunted.

"It's these murders," he said, his voice unsteady from exhaustion. "These poor women. And they were all the same in so many ways."

"Uneducated, blue-collar women who worked in bars? Didn't mind having a vampire lover from time to time?"

He nodded, his eyes drooping shut.

"Women just like me, in other words."

His eyes opened then. He was aghast at his error. "Sookie . . ."

"I understand, Andy," I said. "In some respects, we are all alike, and if you accept the attack on my grandmother as intended for me, well, I guess then I'm the only survivor."

I wondered who the murderer had left to kill. Was I the only one alive who met his criteria? That was the scariest thought I'd had all day.

Andy was practically nodding over his coffee cup.

"Why don't you go lie down in the other bedroom?" I suggested quietly. "You have to have some sleep. You're not safe to drive, I wouldn't think."

"That's kind of you," Andy said, his voice dragging. He sounded a little surprised, like kindness wasn't something he expected from me. "But I have to get home, set my alarm. I can sleep for maybe three hours."

"I promise I'll wake you up," I said. I didn't want Andy sleeping in my house, but I didn't want him to have a wreck on the way to his house, either. Old Mrs. Bellefleur would never forgive me, and probably Portia wouldn't either. "You come lie down in this room." I led him to my old bedroom. My single bed was neatly made up. "You just lie down on top of the bed, and I'll set the alarm." I did, while he watched. "Now, get a little sleep. I have one errand to run, and I'll be right back." Andy didn't offer any more resistance, but sat heavily on the bed even as I shut the door.

The dog had been padding after me while I got Andy situated, and now I said to him, in a quite different tone, "You go get dressed right *now*!"

Andy stuck his head out the bedroom door. "Sookie, who are you talking to?"

"The dog," I answered instantly. "He always gets his collar, and I put it on every day."

"Why do you ever take it off?"

"It jingles at night, keeps me up. You go to bed, now."

"All right." Looking satisfied at my explanation, Andy shut the door again.

I retrieved Jason's clothes from the closet, put them on the couch in front of the dog, and sat with my back turned. But I realized I could see in the mirror over the mantel.

The air grew hazy around the collie, seemed to hum and vibrate with energy, and then the form began to change within that electric concentration. When the haze cleared, there was Sam kneeling on the floor, buck-naked. Wow, what a bottom. I had to make myself close my eyes, tell myself repeatedly that I had not been unfaithful to Bill. Bill's butt, I told myself staunchly, was every bit as neat.

"I'm ready," Sam's voice said, so close behind me that I jumped. I stood up quickly and turned to face him, and found his face about six inches from mine.

"Sookie," he said hopefully, his hand landing on my shoulder, rubbing and caressing it.

I was angry because half of me wanted to respond.

"Listen here, buddy, you could have told me about yourself any time in the past few years. We've known each other what, four years? Or even more! And yet, Sam, despite the fact that I see you almost daily, you wait until Bill is interested in me, before you even . . ." and unable to think how to finish, I threw my hands up in the air.

Sam drew back, which was a good thing.

"I didn't see what was in front of me until I thought it might be taken away," he said, his voice quiet.

I had nothing to say to that. "Time to go home," I told him. "And we better get you there without anyone seeing you. I mean it."

This was chancy enough without some mischievous person like Rene seeing Sam in my car in the early morning and drawing wrong conclusions. And passing them on to Bill.

So off we went, Sam hunched down in the backseat. I pulled cautiously behind Merlotte's. There was a truck there; black, with pink and aqua flames down the sides. Jason's.

"Uh-oh," I said.

"What?" Sam's voice was somewhat muffled by his position.

"Let me go look," I said, beginning to be anxious. Why would Jason park over here in the employees' parking area? And it seemed to me there was a shape in the truck.

I opened my door. I waited for the sound to alert the figure in the truck. I watched for evidence of movement. When nothing happened, I began to walk across the gravel, as frightened as I'd ever been in the light of day.

When I got closer to the window, I could see that the figure inside was Jason. He was slumped behind the wheel. I could see that his shirt was stained, that his chin was resting on his chest, that his hands were limp on the seat on either side of him, that the mark on his handsome face was a long red scratch. I could see a videotape resting on the truck dashboard, unlabelled.

"Sam," I said, hating the fear in my voice. "Please come here."

Quicker than I could believe, Sam was beside me, then reaching past me to unlatch the truck door. Since the truck had apparently been sitting there for several hours—there was dew on its hood—with the windows closed, in the early summer, the smell that rolled out was pretty strong and compounded of at least three elements: blood, sex, and liquor.

"Call the ambulance!" I said urgently as Sam reached in to feel for Jason's pulse. Sam looked at me doubtfully. "Are you sure you want to do that?" he asked.

"Of course! He's unconscious!"

"Wait, Sookie. Think about this."

And I might have reconsidered in just a minute, but at that moment Arlene pulled up in her beat-up blue Ford, and Sam sighed and went into his trailer to phone.

I was so naive. That's what comes of being a law-abiding citizen for nearly every day of my life.

I rode with Jason to the tiny local hospital, oblivious to the police looking very carefully at Jason's truck, blind to the squad car following the ambulance, totally trusting when the emergency room doctor sent me home, telling me he'd call me when Jason regained consciousness. The doctor told me, eyeing me curiously, that Jason was apparently sleeping off the effects of alcohol or drugs. But Jason had never drunk that much before, and Jason didn't use drugs: our cousin Hadley's descent into the life of the streets had made a profound impression on both of us. I told the doctor all that, and he listened, and he shooed me off.

Not knowing what to think, I went home to find that Andy Bellefleur had been roused by his pager. He'd left me a note telling me that, and nothing else. Later on, I found that he'd actually been in the hospital while I was there, and waited until I was gone out of consideration for me before he'd handcuffed Jason to the bed.

Chapter 12

Sᴀᴍ ᴄᴀᴍᴇ ᴛᴏ give me the news about eleven o'clock. "They're going to arrest Jason as soon as he comes to, Sookie, which looks like being soon." Sam didn't tell me how he came to know this, and I didn't ask.

I stared at him, tears running down my face. Any other day, I might have thought of how plain I look when I cry, but today was not a day I cared about my outsides. I was all in a knot, frightened for Jason, sad about Amy Burley, full of anger the police were making such a stupid mistake, and underneath it all, missing my Bill.

"They think it looks like Amy Burley put up a fight. They think he got drunk after he killed her."

"Thanks, Sam, for warning me." My voice came from way faraway. "You better go to work, now."

After Sam had seen that I needed to be alone, I called information and got the number of Blood in the Quarter. I punched in the numbers, feeling somehow I was doing a bad thing, but I couldn't think how or why.

"Bloooooood . . . in the Quarter," announced a deep voice dramatically. "Your coffin away from home."

Geez. "Good morning. This is Sookie Stackhouse calling from Bon Temps," I said politely. "I need to leave a message for Bill Compton. He's a guest there."

"Fang or human?"

"Ah . . . fang."

"Just one minute, please."

The deep voice came back on the line after a moment. "What is the message, madam?"

That gave me pause.

"Please tell Mr. Compton that . . . my brother has been arrested, and I would appreciate it if he could come home as soon as his business is completed."

"I have that down." The sound of scribbling. "And your name again?"

"Stackhouse. Sookie Stackhouse."

"All right, miss. I'll see to it that he gets your message."

"Thanks."

And that was the only action I could think of to take, until I realized it would be much more practical to call Sid Matt Lancaster. He did his best to sound appalled to hear Jason was going to be arrested, said he'd hurry over to the hospital as soon as he got out of court that afternoon, and that he'd report back to me.

I drove back to the hospital to see if they'd let me sit with Jason until he became conscious. They wouldn't. I wondered if he was already conscious, and they weren't telling me. I saw Andy Bellefleur at the other end of the hall, and he turned and walked the other way.

Damn coward.

I went home because I couldn't think of anything to do. I realized it wasn't a workday for me anyway, and that was a good thing, though I didn't really care too much at that point. It occurred to me that I wasn't handling this as well as I ought, that I had been much steadier when Gran had died.

But that had been a finite situation. We would bury Gran, her killer would be arrested, we would go on. If the police seriously believed that Jason had killed Gran in addition to the other women, then the world was such a bad and chancy place that I wanted no part of it.

But I realized, as I sat and looked in front of me that long, long afternoon, that it was naivete like that that had led to Jason's arrest. If I'd just gotten him into Sam's trailer and cleaned him up, hidden the film until I found out what it contained, above all not called the ambulance . . . that had been what Sam had been thinking when he'd looked at me so doubtfully. However, Arlene's arrival had kind of wiped out my options.

I thought the phone would start ringing as soon as people heard.

But no one called.

They didn't know what to say.

Sid Matt Lancaster came about four-thirty.

Without any preliminary, he told me, "They've arrested him. For first-degree murder."

I closed my eyes. When I opened them, Sid was regarding me

with a shrewd expression on his mild face. His conservative black-framed glasses magnified his muddy brown eyes, and his jowls and sharp nose made him look a little like a bloodhound.

"What does he say?" I asked.

"He says that he was with Amy last night."

I sighed.

"He says they went to bed together, that he had been with Amy before. He says he hadn't seen Amy in a long time, that the last time they were together Amy was acting jealous about the other women he was seeing, really angry. So he was surprised when she approached him last night in Good Times. Jason says Amy acted funny all night, like she had an agenda he didn't know about. He remembers having sex with her, he remembers them lying in bed having a drink afterward, then he remembers nothing until he woke up in the hospital."

"He was set up," I said firmly, thinking I sounded exactly like a bad made-for-TV movie.

"Of course." Sid Matt's eyes were as steady and assured as if he'd been at Amy Burley's place last night.

Hell, maybe he had.

"Listen, Sid Matt." I leaned forward and made him meet my eyes. "Even if I could somehow believe that Jason had killed Amy, and Dawn, and Maudette, I could never believe he would raise his finger to hurt my grandmother."

"All right, then." Sid Matt prepared to meet my thoughts, fair and square, his entire body proclaimed it. "Miss Sookie, let's just assume for a minute that Jason did have some kind of involvement in those deaths. Perhaps, the police might think, your friend Bill Compton killed your grandmother since she was keeping you two apart."

I tried to give the appearance of considering this piece of idiocy. "Well, Sid Matt, my grandmother liked Bill, and she was pleased I was seeing him."

Until he put his game face back on, I saw stark disbelief in the lawyer's eyes. He wouldn't be at all happy if his daughter was seeing a vampire. He couldn't imagine a responsible parent being anything but appalled. And he couldn't imagine trying to convince a jury that my grandmother had been pleased I was dating a guy who wasn't even alive, and furthermore was over a hundred years older than me.

Those were Sid Matt's thoughts.

"Have you met Bill?" I asked.

He was taken aback. "No," he admitted. "You know, Miss Sookie, I'm not for this vampire stuff. I think it's taking a chink out of a wall we should keep built up, a wall between us and the so-called virus-infected. I think God intended that wall to be there, and I for one will hold up my section."

"The problem with that, Sid Matt, is that I personally was created straddling that wall." After a lifetime of keeping my mouth shut about my "gift," I found that if it would help Jason, I'd shake it in anybody's face.

"Well," Sid Matt said bravely, pushing his glasses up on the bridge of his sharp nose, "I am sure the Good Lord gave you this problem I've heard about for a reason. You have to learn how to use it for his glory."

No one had ever quite put it that way. That was an idea to chew over when I had time.

"I've made us stray from the subject, I'm afraid, and I know your time is valuable." I gathered my thoughts. "I want Jason out on bail. There is nothing but circumstantial evidence tying him to Amy's murder, am I right?"

"He's admitted to being with the victim right before the murder, and the videotape, one of the cops hinted to me pretty strongly, shows your brother having sex with the victim. The time and date on the film indicate it was made in the hours before her death, if not minutes."

Damn Jason's peculiar bedroom preferences. "Jason doesn't drink much at all. He smelled of liquor in the truck. I think it was just spilled over him. I think a test will prove that. Maybe Amy gave him some narcotic in the drink she fixed him."

"Why would she do that?"

"Because, like so many women, she was mad at Jason because she wanted him so much. My brother is able to date almost anyone he wants. No, I'm using that euphemism."

Sid Matt looked surprised I knew the word.

"He could go to bed with almost anyone he wanted. A dream life, most guys would think." Weariness descended on me like fog. "Now there he sits in the jail."

"You think another man did this to him? Framed him for this murder?"

"Yes, I do." I leaned forward, trying to persuade this skeptical lawyer by the force of my own belief. "Someone envious of him. Someone who knows his schedule, who kills these women when Jason's off work. Someone who knows Jason had had sex with these gals. Someone who knows he likes to make tapes."

"Could be almost anyone," Jason's lawyer said practically.

"Yep," I said sadly. "Even if Jason was nice enough to keep quiet about exactly who he'd been with, all anyone'd have to do is see who he left a bar with at closing time. Just being observant, maybe having asked about the tapes on a visit to his house . . ." My brother might be somewhat immoral, but I didn't think he'd show those videos to anyone else. He might tell another man that he liked to make the videos, though. "So this man, whoever he is, made some kind of deal with Amy, knowing she was mad at Jason. Maybe he told her he was going to play a practical joke on Jason or something."

"Your brother's never been arrested before," Sid Matt observed.

"No." Though it had been a near thing, a couple of times, to hear Jason tell it.

"No record, upstanding member of the community, steady job. There may be a chance I can get him out on bail. But if he runs, you'll lose everything."

It truly had never occurred to me that Jason might skip bail. I didn't know anything about arranging for bail, and I didn't know what I'd have to do, but I wanted Jason out of that jail. Somehow, staying in jail until the legal processes had been gone through before the trial . . . somehow, that would make him look guiltier.

"You find out about it and let me know what I have to do," I said. "In the meantime, can I go see him?"

"He'd rather you didn't," Sid Matt said.

That hurt dreadfully. "Why?" I asked, trying really hard not to tear up again.

"He's ashamed," said the lawyer.

The thought of Jason feeling shame was fascinating.

"So," I said, trying to move along, suddenly tired of this unsatisfactory meeting. "You'll call me when I can actually do something?"

Sid Matt nodded, his jowls trembling slightly with the movement. I made him uneasy. He sure was glad to be leaving me.

The lawyer drove off in his pickup, clapping a cowboy hat on his head when he was still in sight.

When it was full dark, I went out to check on Bubba. He was sitting under a pin oak, bottles of blood lined up beside him, empties on one side, fulls on the other.

I had a flashlight, and though I knew Bubba was there, it was still a shock to see him in the beam of light. I shook my head. Something really had gone wrong when Bubba "came over," no doubt about it. I was sincerely glad I couldn't read Bubba's thoughts. His eyes were crazy as hell.

"Hey, sugar," he said, his Southern accent as thick as syrup. "How you doing? You come to keep me company?"

"I just wanted to make sure you were comfortable," I said.

"Well, I could think of places I'd be more comfortable, but since you're Bill's girl, I ain't about to talk about them."

"Good," I said firmly.

"Any cats around here? I'm getting mighty tired of this bottled stuff."

"No cats. I'm sure Bill will be back soon, and then you can go home." I started back toward the house, not feeling comfortable enough in Bubba's presence to prolong the conversation, if you could call it that. I wondered what thoughts Bubba had during his long watchful nights; I wondered if he remembered his past.

"What about that dog?" he called after me.

"He went home," I called back over my shoulder.

"Too bad," Bubba said to himself, so softly I almost didn't hear him.

I got ready for bed. I watched television. I ate some ice cream, and I even chopped up a Heath Bar for a topping. None of my usual comfort things seemed to work tonight. My brother was in jail, my boyfriend was in New Orleans, my grandmother was dead, and someone had murdered my cat. I felt lonely and sorry for myself all the way around.

Sometimes you just have to roll in it.

Bill didn't return my call.

That added fuel to the flame of my misery. He'd probably found some accommodating whore in New Orleans, or some fang-banger, like the ones who hung around Blood in the Quarter every night, hoping for a vampire "date."

If I were a drinking woman, I would have gotten drunk. If I'd been a casual woman, I would have called lovely JB du Rone and had sex with him. But I'm not anything so dramatic or drastic, so I just ate ice cream and watched old movies on TV. By an eerie coincidence, *Blue Hawaii* was on.

I finally went to bed about midnight.

A shriek outside my bedroom window woke me up. I sat up straight in bed. I heard thumps, and thuds, and finally a voice I was sure was Bubba's shouting, "Come back here, sucker!"

When I hadn't heard anything in a couple of minutes, I pulled on a bathrobe and went to the front door. The yard, lit by the security light, was empty. Then I glimpsed movement to the left, and when I stuck my head out the door, I saw Bubba, trudging back to his hideout.

"What happened?" I called softly.

Bubba changed direction and slouched over to the porch.

"Sure enough, some sumbitch, scuse me, was sneaking around

the house," Bubba said. His brown eyes were glowing, and he looked more like his former self. "I heard him minutes before he got here, and I thought I'd catch ahold of him. But he cut through the woods to the road, and he had a truck parked there."

"Did you get a look?"

"Not enough of one to describe him," Bubba said shamefacedly. "He was driving a pickup, but I couldn't even tell what color it was. Dark."

"You saved me, though," I said, hoping my very real gratitude showed in my voice. I felt a swell of love for Bill, who had arranged my protection. Even Bubba looked better than he had before. "Thanks, Bubba."

"Aw, think nothing of it," he said graciously, and for that moment he stood up straight, kind of tossed his head back, had that sleepy smile on his face . . . it *was* him, and I'd opened my mouth to say his name, when Bill's warning came back to shut my mouth.

JASON MADE BAIL the next day.

It cost a fortune. I signed what Sid Matt told me to, though mostly the collateral was Jason's house and truck and his fishing boat. If Jason had ever been arrested before, even for jaywalking, I don't think he would have been permitted to post bond.

I was standing on the courthouse steps wearing my horrible, sober, navy blue suit in the heat of the late morning. Sweat trickled down my face and ran between my lips in that nasty way that makes you want to go jump in the shower. Jason stopped in front of me. I hadn't been sure he would speak. His face was years older. Real trouble had come to sit on his shoulder, real trouble that would not go away or ease up, like grief did.

"I can't talk to you about this," he said, so softly I could barely hear him. "You know it wasn't me. I've never been violent beyond a fight or two in a parking lot over some woman."

I touched his shoulder, let my hand drop when he didn't respond. "I never thought it was you. I never will. I'm sorry I was fool enough to call 911 yesterday. If I'd realized that wasn't your blood, I'd have taken you into Sam's trailer and cleaned you up and burned the tape. I was just so scared that was your blood." And I felt my eyes fill. This was no time to cry, though, and I tightened up all over, feeling my face tense. Jason's mind was a mess, like a mental pigsty. In it bubbled an unhealthy brew compounded of regrets, shame at his sexual habits being made public, guilt that he didn't feel worse about Amy being killed, horror that anyone in the town would think he'd killed his own grandmother while lying in wait for his sister.

"We'll get through this," I said helplessly.

"We'll get through this," he repeated, trying to make his voice sound strong and assured. But I thought it would be awhile, a long while, before Jason's assurance, that golden certainty that had made him irresistible, returned to his posture and his face and his speech.

Maybe it never would.

We parted there, at the courthouse. We had nothing more to say.

I sat in the bar all day, looking at the men who came in, reading their minds. Not one of them was thinking of how he'd killed four women and gotten away with it so far. At lunchtime Hoyt and Rene walked in the door and walked back out when they saw me sitting. Too embarrassing for them, I guess.

Finally, Sam made me leave. He said I was so creepy that I was driving away any customers who might give me useful information.

I trudged out the door and into the glaring sun. It was about to set. I thought about Bubba, about Bill, about all those creatures that were coming out of their deep sleep to walk the surface of the earth.

I stopped at the Grabbit Kwik to buy some milk for my morning cereal. The new clerk was a kid with pimples and a huge Adam's apple, who stared at me eagerly as if he was trying to make a print in his head of how I looked, the sister of a murderer. I could tell he could hardly wait for me to leave the store so he could use the phone to call his girlfriend. He was wishing he could see the puncture marks on my neck. He was wondering if there was any way he could find out how vampires did it.

This was the kind of trash I had to listen to, day in, day out. No matter how hard I concentrated on something else, no matter how high I kept my guard, how broad I kept my smile, it seeped through.

I reached home just when it was getting dark. After putting away the milk and taking off my suit, I put on a pair of shorts and a black Garth Brooks T-shirt and tried to think of some goal for the evening. I couldn't settle down enough to read; and I needed to go to the library and change my books anyway, which would be a real ordeal under the circumstances. Nothing on TV was good, at least tonight. I thought I might watch *Braveheart* again: Mel Gibson in a kilt is always a mood raiser. But it was just too bloody for my frame of mind. I couldn't bear for that gal get her throat cut again, even though I knew when to cover my eyes.

I'd gone into the bathroom to wash off my sweaty makeup when, over the sound of the running water, I thought I heard a yowl outside.

I turned the faucets off. I stood still, almost feeling my antenna twitch, I was listening so intently. What . . . ? Water from my wet face trickled onto my T-shirt.

No sound. No sound at all.

I crept toward the front door because it was closest to Bubba's watch point in the woods.

I opened the door a little. I yelled, "Bubba?"

No answer.

I tried again.

It seemed to me even the locusts and toads were holding their breaths. The night was so silent it might hold anything. Something was prowling out there, in the darkness.

I tried to think, but my heart was hammering so hard it interfered with the process.

Call the police, first.

I found that was not an option. The phone was dead.

So I could either wait in this house for trouble to come to me, or I could go out into the woods.

That was a tough one. I bit into my lower lip while I went around the house turning out the lamps, trying to map out a course of action. The house provided some protection: locks, walls, nooks, and crannies. But I knew any really determined person could get in, and then I would be trapped.

Okay. How could I get outside without being seen? I turned off the outside lights, for a start. The back door was closer to the woods, so that was the better choice. I knew the woods pretty well. I should be able to hide in them until daylight. I could go over to Bill's house, maybe; surely his phone was working, and I had a key.

Or I could try to get to my car and start it. But that pinned me down to a particular place for particular seconds.

No, the woods seemed the better choice to me.

In one of my pockets I tucked Bill's key and a pocketknife of my grandfather's that Gran had kept in the living-room table drawer, handy for opening packages. I tucked a tiny flashlight in the other pocket. Gran kept an old rifle in the coat closet by the front door. It had been my dad's when he was little, and she mostly had used it for shooting snakes; well, I had me a snake to shoot. I hated the damn rifle, hated the thought of using it, but now seemed to be the time.

It wasn't there.

I could hardly believe my senses. I felt all through the closet.

He'd been in my house!

But it hadn't been broken into.

Someone I'd invited in. Who'd been here? I tried to list them all as I went to the back door, my sneakers retied so they wouldn't have any spare shoelaces to step on. I skinned my hair into a ponytail sloppily, almost one handed, so it wouldn't get in my face, and twisted a rubber band around it. But all the time I thought about the stolen rifle.

Who'd been in my house? Bill, Jason, Arlene, Rene, the kids, Andy Bellefleur, Sam, Sid Matt; I was sure I'd left them all alone for a minute or two, perhaps long enough to stick the rifle outside to retrieve later.

Then I remembered the day of the funeral. Almost everyone I knew had been in and out of the house when Gran had died, and I couldn't remember if I'd seen the rifle since then. But it would have been hard to have casually strolled out of the crowded, busy house with a rifle. And if it had vanished then, I thought I would have noticed its absence by now. In fact, I was almost sure I would have.

I had to shove that aside now and concentrate on outwitting whatever was out there in the dark.

I opened the back door. I duckwalked out, keeping as low as I could, and gently eased the door nearly shut behind me. Rather than use the steps, I straightened one leg and tapped the ground while squatting on the porch; I shifted my weight to it, pulled the other leg behind me. I crouched again. This was a lot like playing hide and seek with Jason in the woods when we were kids.

I prayed I was not playing hide and seek with Jason again.

I used the tub full of flowers that Gran had planted as cover first, then I crept to her car, my second goal. I looked up in the sky. The moon was new, and since the night was clear the stars were out. The air was heavy with humidity, and it was still hot. My arms were slick with sweat in minutes.

Next step, from the car to the mimosa tree.

I wasn't as quiet this time. I tripped over a stump and hit the ground hard. I bit the inside of my mouth to keep from crying out. Pain shot through my leg and hip, and I knew the edges of the ragged stump had scraped my thigh pretty severely. Why hadn't I come out and sawed that stump off clean? Gran had asked Jason to do it, but he'd never found the time.

I heard, sensed, movement. Throwing caution to the winds, I leaped up and dashed for the trees. Someone crashed through the edge of the woods to my right and headed for me. But I knew where I was going, and in a vault that amazed me, I'd seized the low branch of our favorite childhood climbing tree and pulled myself up. If I lived until the next day, I'd have severely strained muscles, but it would be worth it. I balanced on the branch, trying to keep my breathing quiet, when I wanted to pant and groan like a dog dreaming.

I wished this were a dream. Yet here I undeniably was, Sookie Stackhouse, waitress and mind reader, sitting on a branch in the woods in the dead of night, armed with nothing more than a pocket knife.

Movement below me; a man glided through the woods. He had a length of cord hanging from one wrist. Oh, Jesus. Though the moon was almost full, his head stayed stubbornly in the shadow of the tree, and I couldn't tell who it was. He passed underneath without seeing me.

When he was out of sight, I breathed again. As quietly as I could, I scrambled down. I began working my way through the woods to the road. It would take awhile, but if I could get to the road maybe I could flag someone down. Then I thought of how seldom the road got traveled; it might be better to work my way across the cemetery to Bill's house. I thought of the cemetery at night, of the murderer looking for me, and I shivered all over.

Being even more scared was pointless. I had to concentrate on the here and now. I watched every foot placement, moving slowly. A fall would be noisy in this undergrowth, and he'd be on me in a minute.

I found the dead cat about ten yards south east of my perching tree. The cat's throat was a gaping wound. I couldn't even tell what color its fur had been in the bleaching effect of the moonlight, but the dark splotches around the little corpse were surely blood. After five more feet of stealthy movement, I found Bubba. He was unconscious or dead. With a vampire it was hard to tell the difference. But with no stake through his heart, and his head still on, I could hope he was only unconscious.

Someone had brought Bubba a drugged cat, I figured. Someone who had known Bubba was guarding me and had heard of Bubba's penchant for draining cats.

I heard a crackle behind me. The snap of a twig. I glided into the shadow of the nearest large tree. I was mad, mad and scared, and I wondered if I would die this night.

I might not have the rifle, but I had a built-in tool. I closed my eyes and reached out with my mind.

Dark tangle, red, black. Hate.

I flinched. But this was necessary, this was my only protection. I let down every shred of defense.

Into my head poured images that made me sick, made me terrified. Dawn, asking someone to punch her, then finding out that he'd got one of her hose in his hand, was stretching it between his fingers, preparing to tighten it around her neck. A flash of Maudette, naked and begging. A woman I'd never seen, her bare back to me, bruises and welts covering it. Then my grandmother—my grandmother—in our familiar kitchen, angry and fighting for her life.

I was paralyzed by the shock of it, the horror of it. Whose thoughts were these? I had an image of Arlene's kids, playing on my living room floor; I saw myself, and I didn't look like the person I saw in my own mirror. I had huge holes in my neck, and I was lewd; I had a knowing leer on my face, and I patted the inside of my thigh suggestively.

I was in the mind of Rene Lenier. This was how Rene saw me.

Rene was mad.

Now I knew why I'd never been able to read his thoughts explicitly; he kept them in a secret hole, a place in his mind he kept hidden and separate from his conscious self.

He was seeing an outline behind a tree now and wondering if it looked like the outline of a woman.

He was seeing me.

I bolted and ran west toward the cemetery. I couldn't listen to his head anymore, because my own head was focused so fixedly on running, dodging the obstacles of trees, bushes, fallen limbs, a little gully where rain had collected. My strong legs pumped, my arms swung, and my breath sounded like the wheezing of a bagpipe.

I broke from the woods and was in the cemetery. The oldest portion of the graveyard was farther north toward Bill's house, and it had the best places of concealment. I bounded over headstones, the modern kind, set almost flush with the ground, no good for hiding. I leaped over Gran's grave, the earth still raw, no stone yet. Her killer followed me. I turned to look, to see how close he was, like a fool, and in the moonlight I saw Rene's rough head of hair clearly as he gained on me.

I ran down into the gentle bowl the cemetery formed, then began sprinting up the other side. When I thought there were enough large headstones and statues between me and Rene, I dodged behind a tall granite column topped with a cross. I remained standing, flattening myself against the cold hardness of the stone. I clamped a hand across my own mouth to silence my sobbing effort to get air in my lungs. I made myself calm enough to try to listen to Rene; but his thoughts were not even coherent enough to decipher, except the rage he felt. Then a clear concept presented itself.

"Your sister," I yelled. "Is Cindy still alive, Rene?"

"Bitch!" he screamed, and I knew in that second that the first woman to die had been Rene's sister, the one who liked vampires, the one he was supposedly still visiting from time to time, according to Arlene. Rene had killed Cindy, his waitress sister, while she was still wearing her pink-and-white hospital cafeteria uniform. He'd strangled her with her apron strings. And he'd had sex with her, after she was dead. She'd sunk so low, she wouldn't mind her own brother, he'd thought, as much as he was capable of thinking. Anyone who'd let a vampire do that deserved to die. And he'd hidden her body from shame. The others weren't his flesh and blood; it had been all right to let them lie.

I'd gotten sucked down into Rene's sick interior like a twig dragged down by a whirlpool, and it made me stagger. When I came back into my own head, he was on me. He hit me in the face as hard as he could, and he expected me to go down. The blow broke my nose and hurt so bad I almost blanked out, but I didn't collapse. I hit him back. My lack of experience made my blow ineffectual. I just thumped him in the ribs, and he grunted, but in the next instant he retaliated.

His fist broke my collarbone. But I didn't fall.

He hadn't known how strong I was. In the moonlight, his face was shocked when I fought back, and I thanked the vampire blood I'd taken. I thought of my brave grandmother, and I launched myself at him, grabbing him by the ears and attempting to hit his head against the granite column. His hands shot up to grip my forearms, and he tried to pull me away so I'd loose my grip. Finally he succeeded, but I could tell from his eyes he was surprised and more on guard. I tried to knee him, but he anticipated me, twisting just far enough away to dodge me. While I was off-balance, he pushed, and I hit the ground with a teeth-chattering thud.

Then he was straddling me. But he'd dropped the cord in our struggle, and while he held my neck with one hand, he was groping with the other for his method of choice. My right arm was pinned, but my left was free, and I struck and clawed at him. He had to ignore this, had to look for the strangling cord because that was part of his ritual. My scrabbling hand encountered a familiar shape.

Rene, in his work clothes, was still wearing his knife on his belt. I yanked the snap open and pulled the knife from its sheath, and while he was still thinking, "I should have taken that off," I sank the knife into the soft flesh of his waist, angling up. And I pulled it out.

He screamed, then.

He staggered to his feet, twisting his upper torso sideways, trying with both hands to stanch the blood that was pouring from the wound.

I scuttered backward, getting up, trying to put distance between myself and man who was a monster just as surely as Bill was.

Rene screamed. "Aw, Jesus, woman! What you done to me? Oh, God, it hurts!"

That was rich.

He was scared now, frightened of discovery, of an end to his games, of an end to his vengeance.

"Girls like you deserve to die," he snarled. "I can feel you in my head, you freak!"

"Who's the freak around here?" I hissed. "Die, you bastard."

I didn't know I had it in me. I stood by the headstone in a crouch, the bloody knife still clutched in my hand, waiting for him to charge me again.

He staggered in circles, and I watched, my face stony. I closed my mind to him, to his feeling his death crawl up behind him. I stood ready to knife him a second time when he fell to the ground. When I was sure he couldn't move, I went to Bill's house, but I didn't run. I told myself it was because I couldn't: but I'm not sure. I kept seeing my grandmother, encapsuled in Rene's memory forever, fighting for her life in her own house.

I fished Bill's key out of my pocket, almost amazed it was still there.

I turned it somehow, staggered into the big living room, felt for the phone. My fingers touched the buttons, managed to figure out which was the nine and where the one was. I pushed the numbers hard enough to make them beep, and then, without warning, I checked out of consciousness.

I KNEW I was in the hospital: I was surrounded by the clean smell of hospital sheets.

The next thing I knew was that I hurt all over.

And someone was in the room with me. I opened my eyes, not without effort.

Andy Bellefleur. His square face was even more fatigued than the last time I'd seen him.

"Can you hear me?" he said.

I nodded, just a tiny movement, but even that sent a wave of pain through my head.

"We got him," he said, and then he proceeded to tell me a lot more, but I fell back asleep.

It was daylight when I woke again, and this time, I seemed to be much more alert.

Someone in the room.

"Who's here?" I said, and my voice came out in a painful rasp.

Kevin rose from the chair in the corner, rolling a crossword puzzle magazine and sticking it into his uniform pocket.

"Where's Kenya?" I whispered.

He grinned at me unexpectedly. "She was here for a couple of hours," he explained. "She'll be back soon. I spelled her for lunch."

His thin face and body formed one lean line of approval. "You are one tough lady," he told me.

"I don't feel tough," I managed.

"You got hurt," he told me as if I didn't know that.

"Rene."

"We found him out in the cemetery," Kevin assured me. "You stuck him pretty good. But he was still conscious, and he told us he'd been trying to kill you."

"Good."

"He was real sorry he hadn't finished the job. I can't believe he spilled the beans like that, but he was some kind of hurting and he was some kind of scared, by the time we got to him. He told us the whole thing was your fault because you wouldn't just lie down to die like the others. He said it must run in your genes, because your grandmother . . ." Here Kevin stopped short, aware that he was on upsetting ground.

"She fought, too," I whispered.

Kenya came in then, massive, impassive, and holding a steaming Styrofoam cup of coffee.

"She's awake," Kevin said, beaming at his partner.

"Good." Kenya sounded less overjoyed about it. "She say what happened? Maybe we should call Andy."

"Yeah, that's what he said to do. But he's just been asleep four hours."

"The man said call."

Kevin shrugged, went to the phone at the side of the bed. I eased off into a doze as I heard him speaking, but I could hear him murmur with Kenya as they waited. He was talking about his hunting dogs. Kenya, I guess, was listening.

Andy came in, I could feel his thoughts, the pattern of his brain. His solid presence came to roost by my bed. I opened my eyes as he was bending to look at me. We exchanged a long stare.

Two pair of feet in regulation shoes moved out into the hall.

"He's still alive," Andy said abruptly. "And he won't stop talking."

I made the briefest motion of my head, indicating a nod, I hoped.

"He says this goes back to his sister, who was seeing a vampire.

She evidently got so low on blood that Rene thought she'd turn into a vamp herself if he didn't stop her. He gave her an ultimatum, one evening in her apartment. She talked back, said she wouldn't give up her lover. She was tying her apron around her, getting ready to go to work as they were arguing. He yanked it off her, strangled her . . . did other stuff."

Andy looked a little sick.

"I know," I whispered.

"It seems to me," Andy began again, "that somehow he decided he'd feel justified in doing that horrible thing if he convinced himself that everyone in his sister's situation deserved to die. In fact, the murders here are very similar to two in Shreveport that haven't been solved up until now, and we're expecting Rene to touch on those while he's rambling along. If he makes it."

I could feel my lips pressing together in horrified sympathy for those other poor women.

"Can you tell me what happened to you?" Andy asked quietly. "Go slow, take your time, and keep your voice down to a whisper. Your throat is badly bruised."

I had figured that out for myself, thanks very much. I murmured my account of the evening, and I didn't leave anything out. Andy had switched on a little tape recorder after asking me if that was all right. He placed it on the pillow close to my mouth when I indicated the device was okay with me, so he'd have the whole story.

"Mr. Compton still out of town?" he asked me, after I'd finished.

"New Orleans," I whispered, barely able to speak.

"We'll look in Rene's house for the rifle, now that we know it's yours. It'll be a nice piece of corroborative evidence."

Then a gleaming young woman in white came into the room, looked at my face, and told Andy he'd have to come back some other time.

He nodded at me, gave me an awkward pat on the hand, and left. He gave the doctor a backward glance of admiration. She was sure worth admiring, but she was also wearing a wedding ring, so Andy was once again too late.

She thought he seemed too serious and grim.

I didn't want to hear this.

But I didn't have enough energy to keep everyone out of my head.

"Miss Stackhouse, how are you feeling?" the young woman asked a little too loudly. She was brunette and lean, with wide brown eyes and a full mouth.

"Like hell," I whispered.

"I can imagine," she said, nodding repeatedly while looking me over. I somehow didn't think she could. I was willing to bet she'd never been beaten up by a multiple murderer in a graveyard.

"You just lost your grandmother, too, didn't you?" she asked sympathetically. I nodded, just a fraction of an inch.

"My husband died about six months ago," she said. "I know about grief. It's tough being brave, isn't it?"

Well, well, well. I let my expression ask a question.

"He had cancer," she explained. I tried to look my condolences without moving anything, which was nearly impossible.

"Well," she said, standing upright, returning to her brisk manner, "Miss Stackhouse, you're sure gonna live. You have a broken collarbone, and two broken ribs, and a broken nose."

Shepherd of Judea! No wonder I felt bad.

"Your face and neck are severely bruised. Of course, you could tell your throat was hurt."

I was trying to imagine what I looked like. Good thing I didn't have a mirror handy.

"And you have lots of relatively minor bruises and cuts on your legs and arms." She smiled. "Your stomach is fine, and your feet!"

Hohoho. Very funny.

"I have prescribed pain medication for you, so when you start feeling bad, just ring for the nurse."

A visitor stuck his head in the door behind her. She turned, blocking my view, and said, "Hello?"

"This Sookie's room?"

"Yes, I was just finishing her examination. You can come in." The doctor (whose name was Sonntag, by her nameplate) looked questioningly at me to get my permission, and I managed a tiny "Sure."

JB du Rone drifted to my bedside, looking as lovely as the cover model on a romance novel. His tawny hair gleamed under the fluorescent lights, his eyes were just the same color, and his sleeveless shirt showed muscle definition that might have been chiseled with a—well, with a chisel. He was looking down at me, and Dr. Sonntag was drinking him in.

"Hey, Sookie, you feelin' all right?" he asked. He lay a finger gently on my cheek. He kissed an unbruised spot on my forehead.

"Thanks," I whispered. "I'll be okay. Meet my doctor."

JB turned his wide eyes on Dr. Sonntag, who practically tripped over her own feet to introduce herself.

"Doctors weren't this pretty when I was getting my shots," JB said sincerely and simply.

"You haven't been to a doctor since you were a kid?" Dr. Sonntag said, amazed.

"I never get sick." He beamed at her. "Strong as an ox."

And the brain of one. But Dr. Sonntag probably had smarts enough for two.

She couldn't think of any reason for lingering, though she cast a wistful glance over her shoulder as she left.

JB bent down to me and said earnestly, "Can I bring you anything, Sookie? Nabs or something?"

The thought of trying to eat crackers made tears come to my eyes. "No thanks," I breathed. "The doctor's a widow."

You could change subjects on JB without him wondering why.

"Wow," he said, impressed. "She's smart and single."

I wiggled my eyebrows in a significant way.

"You think I oughtta ask her out?" JB looked as thoughtful as it was possible for him to be. "That might be a good idea." He smiled down at me. "Long as *you* won't date me, Sookie. You're always number one to me. You just crook your little finger, and I'll come running."

What a sweet guy. I didn't believe in his devotion for a minute, but I did believe he knew how to make a woman feel good, even if she was as sure as I was that I looked breathtakingly bad. I felt pretty bad, too. Where were those pain pills? I tried to smile at JB.

"You're hurting," he said. "I'll send the nurse down here."

Oh, good. The reach to the little button had seemed longer and longer as I tried to get my arm to move.

He kissed me again as he left and said, "I'll go track that doctor of yours down, Sookie. I better ask her some more questions about your recovery."

After the nurse injected some stuff into my IV drip, I was just looking forward to feeling no pain when the door opened again.

My brother came in. He stood by my bed for a long time, staring at my face. He said finally, heavily, "I talked to the doctor for a minute before she left for the cafeteria with JB. She told me what-all was wrong with you." He walked away from me, took a turn around the room, came back. More staring. "You look like hell."

"Thanks," I whispered.

"Oh, yeah, your throat. I forgot."

He started to pat me, thought the better of it.

"Listen, Sis, I gotta say thank you, but it's got me down that you stood in for me when it came time to fight."

If I could have, I'd have kicked him.

Stood in for him, hell.

"I owe you big, Sis. I was so dumb, thinking Rene was a good friend."

Betrayed. He felt betrayed.

Then Arlene came in, to make things just peachy keen.

She was a mess. Her hair was in a red tangle, she had no makeup, and her clothes were chosen at random. I'd never seen Arlene without her hair curled and her makeup loud and bright.

She looked down at me—boy, would I be glad when I could stand up again—and for a second her face was hard as granite, but when she really took in my face, she began to crumble.

"I was so mad at you, I didn't believe it, but now that I'm seeing you and what he did . . . oh, Sookie, can you ever forgive me?"

Geez, I wanted her out of here. I tried to telegraph this to Jason, and for once I got through, because he put an arm around her shoulders and led her out. Arlene was sobbing before she reached the door. "I didn't know . . ." she said, barely coherent. "I just didn't know!"

"Hell, neither did I," Jason said heavily.

I took a nap after trying to ingest some delicious green gelatin.

My big excitement of the afternoon was walking to the bathroom, more or less by myself. I sat in the chair for ten minutes, after which I was more than ready to get back in bed. I looked in the mirror concealed in the rolling table and was very sorry I had.

I was running a little temperature, just enough to make me shivery and tender-skinned. My face was blue and gray and my nose was swollen double. My right eye was puffy and almost closed. I shuddered, and even that hurt. My legs . . . oh, hell, I didn't even want to check. I lay back very carefully and wanted this day to be over. Probably four days from now I'd feel just great. Work! When could I go back to work?

A little knock at the door distracted me. Another damn visitor. Well, this was someone I didn't know. An older lady with blue hair and red-framed glasses wheeled in a cart. She was wearing the yellow smock the hospital volunteers called Sunshine Ladies had to don when they were working.

The cart was covered with flowers for the patients in this wing.

"I'm delivering you a load of best wishes!" the lady said cheerfully.

I smiled, but the effect must have been ghastly because her own cheer wavered a little.

"These are for you," she said, lifting a potted plant decorated with a red ribbon. "Here's the card, honey. Let's see, these are for you, too . . ." This was an arrangement of cut flowers, featuring pink rosebuds and pink carnations and white baby's breath. She plucked the card from that bowl, too. Surveying the cart, she said, "Now, aren't you the lucky one! Here are some more for you!!"

The focus of the third floral tribute was a bizarre red flower I'd never seen before, surrounded by a host of other, more familiar blooms. I looked at this one doubtfully. The Sunshine Lady dutifully presented me with the card from the plastic prongs.

After she'd smiled her way out of the room, I opened the little envelopes. It was easier to move when I was in a better mood, I noticed wryly.

The potted plant was from Sam and "all your coworkers at Merlotte's" read the card, but it was written in Sam's handwriting. I touched the glossy leaves and wondered where I'd put it when I took it home. The cut flowers were from Sid Matt Lancaster and Elva Deene Lancaster—pooey. The arrangement centered with the peculiar red blossom (I decided that somehow the flower looked almost obscene, like a lady's private part) was definitely the most interesting of the three. I opened the card with some curiosity. It bore only a signature, "Eric."

That was all I needed. How the hell had he heard I was in the hospital? Why hadn't I heard from Bill?

After some delicious red gelatin for supper, I focused on the television for a couple of hours, since I hadn't anything to read, even if my eyes had been up to it. My bruises grew more charming every hour, and I felt weary to my bones, despite the fact that I'd only walked once to the bathroom and twice around my room. I switched off the television and turned onto my side. I fell asleep, and in my dreams the pain from my body seeped in and made me have nightmares. I ran in my dreams, ran through the cemetery, afraid for my life, falling over stones, into open graves, encountering all the people I knew who lay there: my father and mother, my grandmother, Maudette Pickens, Dawn Green, even a childhood friend who'd been killed in a hunting accident. I was looking for a particular headstone; if I found it, I was home free. They would all go back into their graves and leave me alone. I ran from this one to that one, putting my hand on each one, hoping it would be the right stone. I whimpered.

"Sweetheart, you're safe," came a familiar cool voice.

"Bill," I muttered. I turned to face a stone I hadn't yet touched. When I lay my fingers on it, they traced the letters "William Erasmus Compton." As if I'd been dashed with cold water, my eyes flew open, I drew in a breath to scream, and my throat gave a great throb of pain. I choked on the extra air, and the pain of the coughing, which pretty much hurt every single thing I'd broken, completed my awakening. A hand slipped under my cheek, the cool fingers feeling wonderfully good against my hot skin. I tried not to whimper, but a little noise made its way through my teeth.

"Turn to the light, darling," Bill said, his voice very light and casual.

I'be been sleeping with my back to the light the nurse had left on, the one in the bathroom. Now I rolled obediently to my back and looked up at my vampire.

Bill hissed.

"I'll kill him," he said, with a simple certainty that chilled me to the bone.

There was enough tension in the room to send a fleet of the nervous running for their tranquilizers.

"Hi, Bill," I croaked. "Glad to see you, too. Where you been so long? Thanks for returning all my calls."

That brought him up short. He blinked. I could feel him making an effort to calm himself.

"Sookie," he said. "I didn't call because I wanted to tell you in person what has happened." I couldn't read the expression on his face. If I'd had to take a shot, I would've said he looked proud of himself.

He paused, scanned all visible portions of me.

"This doesn't hurt," I croaked obligingly, extending my hand to him. He kissed that, lingered over it in a way that sent a faint tingle through my body. Believe me, a faint tingle was more than I'd thought I was capable of.

"Tell me what has been done to you," he commanded.

"Then lean down so I can whisper. This really hurts."

He pulled a chair close to the bed, lowered the bed rail, and lay his chin on his folded arms. His face was maybe four inches from mine.

"Your nose is broken," he observed.

I rolled my eyes. "Glad you spotted that," I whispered. "I'll tell the doctor when she comes in."

His gaze narrowed. "Stop trying to deflect me."

"Okay. Nose broken, two ribs, a collarbone."

But Bill wanted to examine me all over, and he pulled the sheet down. My mortification was complete. Of course, I was wearing an awful hospital gown, in itself a downer, and I hadn't bathed properly, and my face was several different shades, and my hair hadn't been brushed.

"I want to take you home," he announced, after he'd run his

hands all over and minutely examined each scrape and cut. The Vampire physician.

I motioned with my hand to make him bend down. "No," I breathed. I pointed to the drip bag. He eyed it with some suspicion, but of course he had to know what one was.

"I can take it out," he said.

I shook my head vehemently.

"You don't want me to take care of you?"

I puffed out my breath in exasperation, which hurt like hell.

I made a writing motion with my hand, and Bill searched the drawers until he found a notepad. Oddly enough, he had a pen. I wrote, "They'll let me out of the hospital tomorrow if my fever doesn't go high."

"Who'll take you home?" he asked. He was standing by the bed again, and looking down at me with stern disapproval, like a teacher whose best pupil happens to be chronically tardy.

"I'll get them to call Jason, or Charlsie Tooten," I wrote. If things had been different, I would have written Arlene's name automatically.

"I'll be there at dark," he said.

I looked up into his pale face, the clear whites of his eyes almost shining in the gloomy room.

"I'll heal you," he offered. "Let me give you some blood."

I remembered the way my hair had lightened, remembered that I was almost twice as strong as I'd ever been. I shook my head.

"Why not?" he said, as if he'd offered me a drink of water when I was thirsty and I'd said no. I thought maybe I'd hurt his feelings.

I took his hand and guided it to my mouth. I kissed the palm gently. I held the hand to my better cheek.

"People notice I am changing," I wrote, after a moment. "I notice I am changing."

He bowed his head for a moment, and then looked at me sadly.

"You know what happened?" I wrote.

"Bubba told me part of it," he said, and his face grew scary as he mentioned the half-witted vampire. "Sam told me the rest, and I went to the police department and read the police reports."

"Andy let you do that?" I scribbled.

"No one knew I was there," he said carelessly.

I tried to imagine that, and it gave me the creeps.

I gave him a disapproving look.

"Tell me what happened in New Orleans," I wrote. I was beginning to feel sleepy again.

"You will have to know a little about us," he said hesitantly.

"Woo woo, secret vampire stuff!!" I croaked.

It was his turn to give me disapproving.

"We're a little organized," he told me. "I was trying to think of ways to keep us safe from Eric." Involuntarily, I looked at the red flower arrangement.

"I knew if I were an official, like Eric, it would be much more difficult for him to interfere with my private life."

I looked encouraging, or at least I tried to.

"So I attended the regional meeting, and though I have never been involved in our politics, I ran for an office. And, through some concentrated lobbying, I won!"

This was absolutely amazing. Bill was a *union rep*? I wondered about the concentrated lobbying, too. Did that mean Bill had killed all the opposition? Or that he'd bought the voters a bottle of A positive apiece?

"What is your job?" I wrote slowly, imagining Bill sitting in a meeting. I tried to look proud, which seemed to be what Bill was looking for.

"I'm the Fifth Area investigator," he said. "I'll tell you what that means when you're home. I don't want to wear you out."

I nodded, beaming at him. I sure hoped he didn't take it into his head to ask me who all the flowers were from. I wondered if I had to write Eric a thank-you note. I wondered why my mind was going off on all these tangents. Must be the pain medication.

I gestured to Bill to draw close. He did, his face resting on the bed next to mine. "Don't kill Rene," I whispered.

He looked cold, colder, coldest.

"I may have already done the job. He's in intensive care. But even if he lives, there's been enough murder. Let the law do it. I don't want any more witchhunts coming after you. I want us to have peace." It was becoming very difficult to talk. I took his hand in both of mine, held it again to my least-bruised cheek. Suddenly, how much I had missed him became a solid lump lodged in my chest, and I held out my arms. He sat carefully on the edge of the bed, and leaning toward me, he carefully, carefully, slid his arms under me and pulled me up to him, a fraction of an inch at a time, to give me time to tell him if it hurt.

"I won't kill him," Bill said finally, into my ear.

"Sweetheart," I breathed, knowing his sharp hearing could pick it up. "I missed you." I heard his quick sigh, and his arms tightened a little, his hands began their gentle stroking down my back. "I wonder how quickly you can heal," he said, "without my help?"

"Oh, I'll try to hurry," I whispered. "I'll bet I surprise the doctor as it is."

A collie trotted down the corridor, looked in the open door, said, "Rowwf," and trotted away. Astonished, Bill turned to glance out into the corridor. Oh, yeah, it was the full moon, tonight—I could see it out of the window. I could see something else, too. A white face appeared out of the blackness and floated between me and the moon. It was a handsome face, framed by long golden hair. Eric the Vampire grinned at me and gradually disappeared from my view. He was flying.

"Soon we'll be back to normal," Bill said, laying me down gently so he could switch out the light in the bathroom. He glowed in the dark.

"Right," I whispered. "Yeah. Back to normal."

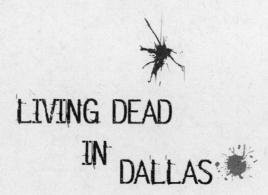

LIVING DEAD IN DALLAS

This book is dedicated to all the people
who told me they enjoyed Dead Until Dark.
Thanks for the encouragement.

My thanks go to Patsy Asher of Remember the Alibi in San Antonio, Texas; Chloe Green of Dallas; and the helpful cyber-friends I've made on DorothyL, who answered all my questions promptly and enthusiastically. I have the greatest job in the world.

Chapter 1

ANDY BELLEFLEUR WAS as drunk as a skunk. This wasn't normal for Andy—believe me, I know all the drunks in Bon Temps. Working at Sam Merlotte's bar for several years has pretty much introduced me to all of them. But Andy Bellefleur, native son and detective on Bon Temps's small police force, had never been drunk in Merlotte's before. I was mighty curious as to why tonight was an exception.

Andy and I aren't friends by any stretch of the imagination, so I couldn't ask him outright. But other means were open to me, and I decided to use them. Though I try to limit employing my disability, or gift, or whatever you want to call it, to find out things that might have an effect on me or mine, sometimes sheer curiosity wins out.

I let down my mental guard and read Andy's mind. I was sorry.

Andy had had to arrest a man that morning for kidnapping. He'd taken his ten-year-old neighbor to a place in the woods and raped her. The girl was in the hospital, and the man was in jail, but the damage that had been dealt was irreparable. I felt weepy and sad. It was a crime that touched too closely on my own past. I liked Andy a little better for his depression.

"Andy Bellefleur, give me your keys," I said. His broad face turned up to me, showing very little comprehension. After a long pause while my meaning filtered through to his addled brain, Andy fumbled in the pocket of his khakis and handed me his heavy key ring. I put another bourbon-and-Coke on the bar in front of him. "My treat," I said, and went to the phone at the end of the bar to call Portia, Andy's sister. The Bellefleur siblings lived in a decaying large white two-story antebellum, formerly quite a showplace, on the prettiest strect in the nicest area of Bon Temps. On Magnolia Creek Road, all the homes faced the strip of park through which ran the stream, crossed here and there by decorative bridges for foot traffic only; a road ran on both sides. There were a few other old homes on Magnolia Creek Road, but they were all in better repair than the Bellefleur place, Belle Rive. Belle Rive was just too much for Portia, a lawyer, and Andy, a cop, to maintain, since the money to support such a home and its grounds was long since gone. But their grandmother, Caroline, stubbornly refused to sell.

Portia answered on the second ring.

"Portia, this is Sookie Stackhouse," I said, having to raise my voice over the background noise in the bar.

"You must be at work."

"Yes. Andy's here, and he's three sheets to the wind. I took his keys. Can you come get him?"

"Andy had too much to drink? That's rare. Sure, I'll be there in ten minutes," she promised, and hung up.

"You're a sweet girl, Sookie," Andy volunteered unexpectedly.

He'd finished the drink I'd poured for him. I swept the glass out of sight and hoped he wouldn't ask for more. "Thanks, Andy," I said. "You're okay, yourself."

"Where's . . . boyfriend?"

"Right here," said a cool voice, and Bill Compton appeared just behind Andy. I smiled at him over Andy's drooping head. Bill was about five foot ten, with dark brown hair and eyes. He had the broad shoulders and hard muscular arms of a man who's done manual labor for years. Bill had worked a farm with his father, and then for himself, before he'd gone to be a soldier in the war. That would be the Civil War.

"Hey, V. B.!" called Charlsie Tooten's husband, Micah. Bill raised a casual hand to return the greeting, and my brother, Jason, said, "Evening, Vampire Bill," in a perfectly polite way. Jason, who had not exactly welcomed Bill into our little family circle, had turned over a whole new leaf. I was sort of mentally holding my breath, waiting to see if his improved attitude was permanent.

"Bill, you're okay for a bloodsucker," Andy said judiciously, rotating on his bar stool so he could face Bill. I upgraded my opinion of Andy's drunkenness, since he had never otherwise been enthusiastic about the acceptance of vampires into America's mainstream society.

"Thanks," Bill said dryly. "You're not too bad for a Bellefleur." He leaned across the bar to give me a kiss. His lips were as cool as his voice. You had to get used to it. Like when you laid your head on his chest, and you didn't hear a heartbeat inside. "Evening, sweetheart," he said in his low voice. I slid a glass of the Japanese-developed synthetic B negative across the bar, and he knocked it back and licked his lips. He looked pinker almost immediately.

"How'd your meeting go, honey?" I asked. Bill had been in Shreveport the better part of the night.

"I'll tell you later."

I hoped his work-related story was less distressing than Andy's. "Okay. I'd appreciate it if you'd help Portia get Andy to her car. Here she comes now," I said, nodding toward the door.

For once, Portia was not wearing the skirt, blouse, jacket, hose, and low-heeled pumps that constituted her professional uniform. She'd changed to blue jeans and a ragged Sophie Newcomb sweatshirt. Portia was built as squarely as her brother, but she had long, thick, chestnut hair. Keeping it beautifully tended was Portia's one signal that she hadn't given up yet. She plowed single-mindedly through the rowdy crowd.

"Well, he's soused, all right," she said, evaluating her brother. Portia was trying to ignore Bill, who made her very uneasy. "It doesn't happen often, but if he decides to tie one on, he does a good job."

"Portia, Bill can carry him to your car," I said. Andy was taller than Portia and thick in body, clearly too much of a burden for his sister.

"I think I can handle him," she told me firmly, still not looking toward Bill, who raised his eyebrows at me.

So I let her get one arm around him and try to hoist him off the stool. Andy stayed perched. Portia glanced around for Sam Merlotte, the bar owner, who was small and wiry in appearance but very strong. "Sam's bartending at an anniversary party at the country club," I said. "Better let Bill help."

"All right," the lawyer said stiffly, her eyes on the polished wood of the bar. "Thanks very much."

Bill had Andy up and moving toward the door in seconds, in spite of Andy's legs tending to turn to jelly. Micah Tooten jumped up to open the door, so Bill was able to sweep Andy right out into the parking lot.

"Thanks, Sookie," Portia said. "Is his bar tab settled up?"

I nodded.

"Okay," she said, slapping her hand on the bar to signal she was out of there. She had to listen to a chorus of well-meant advice as she followed Bill out the front door of Merlotte's.

That was how Detective Andy Bellefleur's old Buick came to sit in the parking lot at Merlotte's all night and into the next day. The Buick had certainly been empty when Andy had gotten out to enter the bar, he would later swear. He'd also testify that he'd had been so preoccupied by his internal turmoil that he'd forgotten to lock the car.

At some point between eight o'clock, when Andy had arrived at Merlotte's, and ten the next morning, when I arrived to help open the bar, Andy's car acquired a new passenger.

This one would cause considerable embarrassment for the policeman.

This one was dead.

I SHOULDN'T HAVE been there at all. I'd worked the late shift the night before, and I should've worked the late shift again that night. But Bill had asked me if I could switch with one of my coworkers, because he needed me to accompany him to Shreveport, and Sam hadn't objected. I'd asked my friend Arlene if she'd work my shift. She was due a day off, but she always wanted to earn the better tips we got at night, and she agreed to come in at five that afternoon.

By all rights, Andy should've collected his car that morning, but he'd been too hung over to fool with getting Portia to run him over to Merlotte's, which was out of the way to the police station. She'd told him she would pick him up at work at noon, and they'd eat lunch at the bar. Then he could retrieve his car.

So the Buick, with its silent passenger, waited for discovery far longer than it should have.

I'd gotten about six hours' sleep the night before, so I was feeling pretty good. Dating a vampire can be hard on your equilibrium if you're truly a daytime person, like me. I'd helped close the bar, and left for home with Bill by one o'clock. We'd gotten in Bill's hot tub together, then done other things, but I'd gotten to bed by a little after two, and I didn't get up until almost nine. Bill had long been in the ground by then.

I drank lots of water and orange juice and took a multivitamin and iron supplement for breakfast, which was my regimen since Bill had come into my life and brought (along with love, adventure, and excitement) the constant threat of anemia. The weather was getting cooler, thank God, and I sat on Bill's front porch wearing a cardigan and the black slacks we wore to work at Merlotte's when it was too cool for shorts. My white golf shirt had MERLOTTE'S BAR embroidered on the left breast.

As I skimmed the morning paper, with one part of my mind I was recording the fact that the grass was definitely not growing as fast. Some of the leaves appeared to be beginning to turn. The high school football stadium might be just about tolerable this coming Friday night.

The summer just hates to let go in Louisiana, even northern Louisiana. Fall begins in a very halfhearted way, as though it might quit at any minute and revert to the stifling heat of July. But I was on the alert, and I could spot traces of fall this morning. Fall and winter meant longer nights, more time with Bill, more hours of sleep.

So I was cheerful when I went to work. When I saw the Buick sitting all by its lonesome in front of the bar, I remembered Andy's surprising binge the night before. I have to confess, I smiled when I thought of how he'd be feeling today. Just as I was about to drive around in back and park with the other employees, I noticed that Andy's rear passenger door was open just a little bit. That would make his dome light stay on, surely? And his battery would run down. And he'd be angry, and have to come in the bar to call the tow truck, or ask someone to jump him . . . so I put my car in park and slid out, leaving it running. That turned out to be an optimistic error.

I shoved the door to, but it would only give an inch. So I pressed my body to it, thinking it would latch and I could be on my way. Again, the door would not click shut. Impatiently, I yanked it all the way open to find out what was in the way. A wave of smell gusted out into the parking lot, a dreadful smell. Dismay clutched at my throat, because the smell was not unknown to me. I peered into the backseat of the car, my hand covering my mouth, though that hardly helped with the smell.

"Oh, man," I whispered. "Oh, shit." Lafayette, the cook for one shift at Merlotte's, had been shoved into the backseat. He was naked. It was Lafayette's thin brown foot, its toenails painted a deep crimson, that had kept the door from shutting, and it was Lafayette's corpse that smelled to high heaven.

I backed away hastily, then scrambled into my car and drove around back behind the bar, blowing my horn. Sam came running out of the employee door, an apron tied around his waist. I turned off my car and was out of it so quick I hardly realized I'd done it, and I wrapped myself around Sam like a static-filled sock.

"What is it?" Sam's voice said in my ear. I leaned back to look at him, not having to gaze up too much since Sam is a smallish man. His reddish gold hair was gleaming in the morning sun. He has true-blue eyes, and they were wide with apprehension.

"It's Lafayette," I said, and began crying. That was ridiculous and silly and no help at all, but I couldn't help it. "He's dead, in Andy Bellefleur's car."

Sam's arms tightened behind my back and drew me into his body once more. "Sookie, I'm sorry you saw it," he said. "We'll call the police. Poor Lafayette."

Being a cook at Merlotte's does not exactly call for any extraordinary culinary skill, since Sam just offers a few sandwiches and fries, so there's a high turnover. But Lafayette had lasted longer than most, to my surprise. Lafayette had been gay, flamboyantly gay, makeup-and-long-fingernails gay. People in northern Louisiana are less tolerant of that than New Orleans people, and I expect Lafayette, a man of color, had had a doubly hard time of it. Despite—or because of—his difficulties, he was cheerful, entertainingly mischievous, clever, and actually a good cook. He had a special sauce he steeped hamburgers in, and people asked for Burgers Lafayette pretty regular.

"Did he have family here?" I asked Sam. We eased apart self-consciously and went into the building, to Sam's office.

"He had a cousin," Sam said, as his fingers punched 9-1-1. "Please come to Merlotte's on Hummingbird Road," he told the dispatcher. "There's a dead man in a car here. Yes, in the parking lot, in the front of the place. Oh, and you might want to alert Andy Bellefleur. It's his car."

I could hear the squawk on the other end of the line from where I stood.

Danielle Gray and Holly Cleary, the two waitresses on the morning shift, came through the back door laughing. Both divorced women in their midtwenties, Danielle and Holly were lifelong friends who seemed to be quite happy working their jobs as long as they were together. Holly had a five-year-old son who was at kindergarten, and Danielle had a seven-year-old daughter and a boy too young for school, who stayed with Danielle's mother while Danielle was at Merlotte's. I would never be any closer to the two women—who, after all, were around my age—because they were careful to be sufficient unto themselves.

"What's the matter?" Danielle asked when she saw my face. Her own, narrow and freckled, became instantly worried.

"Why's Andy's car out front?" Holly asked. She'd dated Andy Bellefleur for a while, I recalled. Holly had short blond hair that hung around her face like wilted daisy petals, and the prettiest skin I'd ever seen. "He spend the night in it?"

"No," I said, "but someone else did."

"Who?"

"Lafayette's in it."

"Andy let a black queer sleep in his car?" This was Holly, who was the blunt straightforward one.

"What happened to him?" This was Danielle, who was the smarter of the two.

"We don't know," Sam said. "The police are on the way."

"You mean," Danielle said, slowly and carefully, "that he's dead."

"Yes," I told her. "That's exactly what we mean."

"Well, we're set to open in an hour." Holly's hands settled on her round hips. "What are we gonna do about that? If the police let us open, who's gonna cook for us? People come in, they'll want lunch."

"We better get ready, just in case," Sam said. "Though I'm thinking we won't get to open until sometime this afternoon." He went into his office to begin calling substitute cooks.

It felt strange to be going about the opening routine, just as if Lafayette were going to mince in any minute with a story about some party he'd been to, the way he had a few days before. The sirens came shrieking down the county road that ran in front of Merlotte's. Cars crunched across Sam's gravel parking lot. By the time we had the chairs down, the tables set, and extra silverware rolled in napkins and ready to replace used settings, the police came in.

Merlotte's is out of the city limits, so the parish sheriff, Bud Dearborn, would be in charge. Bud Dearborn, who'd been a good friend of my father's, was gray-haired now. He had a mashed-in face, like a human Pekinese, and opaque brown eyes. As he came in the front door of the bar, I noticed Bud was wearing heavy boots and his Saints cap. He must have been called in from working on his farm. With Bud was Alcee Beck, the only African American detective on the parish force. Alcee was so black that his white shirt gleamed in contrast. His tie was knotted precisely, and his suit was absolutely correct. His shoes were polished and shining.

Bud and Alcee, between them, ran the parish . . . at least some of the more important elements that kept it functional. Mike Spencer, funeral home director and parish coroner, had a heavy hand in local affairs, too, and he was a good friend of Bud's. I was willing to bet Mike was already out in the parking lot, pronouncing poor Lafayette dead.

Bud Spencer said, "Who found the body?"

"I did." Bud and Alcee changed course slightly and headed toward me.

"Sam, can we borrow your office?" Bud asked. Without waiting for Sam's response, he jerked his head to indicate I should go in.

"Sure, go right ahead," my boss said dryly. "Sookie, you okay?"

"Fine, Sam." I wasn't sure that was true, but there wasn't anything Sam could do about it without getting into trouble, and all to no avail. Though Bud gestured to me to sit down, I shook my head as he and Alcee settled themselves in the office chairs. Bud, of course, took Sam's big chair, while Alcee made do with the better extra chair, the one with a little padding left.

"Tell us about the last time you saw Lafayette alive," Bud suggested.

I thought about it.

"He wasn't working last night," I said. "Anthony was working, Anthony Bolivar."

"Who is that?" Alcee's broad forehead wrinkled. "Don't recognize the name."

"He's a friend of Bill's. He was passing through, and he needed a job. He had the experience." He'd worked in a diner during the Great Depression.

"You mean the short-order cook at Merlotte's is a *vampire*?"

"So?" I asked. I could feel my mouth getting stubborn, and my brows drawing in, and I knew my face was getting mad. I was trying hard not to read their minds, trying hard to stay completely out of this, but it wasn't easy. Bud Dearborn was average, but Alcee projected his thoughts like a lighthouse sends a signal. Right now he was beaming disgust and fear.

In the months before I'd met Bill, and found that he treasured that disability of mine—my gift, as he saw it—I'd done my best to pretend to myself and everyone else that I couldn't really "read" minds. But since Bill had liberated me from the little prison I'd built for myself, I'd been practicing and experimenting, with Bill's encouragement. For him, I had put into words the things I'd been feeling for years. Some people sent a clear, strong message, like Alcee. Most people were more off-and-on, like Bud Dearborn. It depended a lot on how strong their emotions were, how clear-headed they were, what the weather was, for all I knew. Some people were murky as hell, and it was almost impossible to tell what they were thinking. I could get a reading of their moods, maybe, but that was all.

I had admitted that if I was touching people while I tried to read their thoughts, it made the picture clearer—like getting cable, after having only an antenna. And I'd found that if I "sent" a person relaxing images, I could flow through his brain like water.

There was nothing I wanted less than to flow through Alcee Beck's mind. But absolutely involuntarily I was getting a full picture of Alcee's deeply superstitious reaction to finding out there was a vampire working at Merlotte's, his revulsion on discovering I was the woman he'd heard about who was dating a vampire, his deep conviction that the openly gay Lafayette had been a disgrace to the black community.

Alcee figured someone must have it in for Andy Bellefleur, to have parked a gay black man's carcass in Andy's car. Alcee was wondering if Lafayette had had AIDS, if the virus could have seeped into Andy's car seat somehow and survived there. He'd sell the car, if it were his.

If I'd touched Alcee, I would have known his phone number and his wife's bra size.

Bud Dearborn was looking at me funny. "Did you say something?" I asked.

"Yeah. I was wondering if you had seen Lafayette in here during the evening. Did he come in to have a drink?"

"I never saw him here." Come to think of it, I'd never seen Lafayette have a drink. For the first time, I realized that though the lunch crowd was mixed, the night bar patrons were almost exclusively white.

"Where did he spend his social time?"

"I have no idea." All Lafayette's stories were told with the names changed to protect the innocent. Well, actually, the guilty.

"When did you see him last?"

"Dead, in the car."

Bud shook his head in exasperation. "Alive, Sookie."

"Hmmm. I guess . . . three days ago. He was still here when I got here to work my shift, and we said hello to each other. Oh, he told me about a party he'd been to." I tried to recall his exact words. "He said he'd been to a house where there were all kinds of sex hijinks going on."

The two men gaped at me.

"Well, that's what he said! I don't know how much truth was in it." I could just see Lafayette's face as he'd told me about it, the coy way he kept putting his finger across his lips to indicate he wasn't telling me any names or places.

"Didn't you think someone should know about that?" Bud Dearborn looked stunned.

"It was a private party. Why should I tell anyone about it?"

But that kind of party shouldn't happen in their parish. Both men were glaring at me. Through compressed lips, Bud said, "Did Lafayette tell you anything about drugs being used at this get-together?"

"No, I don't remember anything like that."

"Was this party at the home of someone white, or someone black?"

"White," I said, and then wished I'd pled ignorance. But Lafayette had been really impressed by the home—though not because it was large or fancy. Why had he been so impressed? I wasn't too sure what would constitute impressive for Lafayette, who had grown up poor and stayed that way, but I was sure he'd been talking about the home of someone white, because he'd said, "All the pictures on the walls, they all white as lilies and smiling like alligators." I didn't offer that comment to the police, and they didn't ask further.

When I'd left Sam's office, after explaining why Andy's car had been in the parking lot in the first place, I went back to stand behind the bar. I didn't want to watch the activity out in the parking lot, and there weren't any customers to wait on because the police had the entrances to the lot blocked off.

Sam was rearranging the bottles behind the bar, dusting as he went, and Holly and Danielle had plunked themselves down at a table in the smoking section so Danielle could have a cigarette.

"How was it?" Sam asked.

"Not much to it. They didn't like hearing about Anthony working here, and they didn't like what I told them about the party Lafayette was bragging about the other day. Did you hear him telling me? The orgy thing?"

"Yeah, he said something to me about that, too. Must have been a big evening for him. If it really happened."

"You think Lafayette made it up?"

"I don't think there are too many biracial, bisexual parties in Bon Temps," he said.

"But that's just because no one invited you to one," I said pointedly. I wondered if I really knew at all what went on in our little town. Of all the people in Bon Temps, I should be the one to know the ins and the outs, since all that information was more or less readily available to me, if I chose to dig for it. "At least, I assume that's the case?"

"That's the case," Sam said, smiling at me a little as he dusted a bottle of whiskey.

"I guess my invitation got lost in the mail, too."

"You think Lafayette came back here last night to talk more to you or me about this party?"

I shrugged. "He may have just arranged to meet someone in the parking lot. After all, everyone knows where Merlotte's is. Had he gotten his paycheck?" It was the end of the week, when Sam normally paid us.

"No. Maybe he'd come in for that, but I'd have given it to him at work the next day. Today."

"I wonder who invited Lafayette to that party."

"Good question."

"You don't reckon he'd have been dumb enough to try to black-mail anyone, do you?"

Sam rubbed the fake wood of the bar with a clean rag. The bar was already shining, but he liked to keep his hands busy, I'd noticed. "I don't think so," he said, after he'd thought it over. "No, they sure asked the wrong person. You know how indiscreet Lafayette was. Not only did he tell us that he went to such a party—and I'm betting he wasn't supposed to—he might have wanted to build more on it than the other, ah, participants, would feel comfortable with."

"Like, keep in contact with the people at the party? Give them a sly wink in public?"

"Something like that."

"I guess if you have sex with someone, or watch them having sex, you feel pretty much like you're their equal." I said this doubtfully, having limited experience in that area, but Sam was nodding.

"Lafayette wanted to be accepted for what he was more than anything else," he said, and I had to agree.

Chapter 2

Wᴇ ʀᴇᴏᴘᴇɴᴇᴅ ᴀᴛ four-thirty, by which time we were all as bored as we could possibly be. I was ashamed of that, since after all, we were there because a man we knew had died, but it was undeniable that after straightening up the storeroom, cleaning out Sam's office, and playing several hands of bourre (Sam won five dollars and change) we were all ready to see someone new. When Terry Bellefleur, Andy's cousin and a frequent substitute barman or cook at Merlotte's, came through the back door, he was a welcome sight.

I guess Terry was in his late fifties. A Vietnam vet, he'd been a prisoner of war for a year and a half. Terry had some obvious facial scarring, and my friend Arlene told me that the scars on his body were even more drastic. Terry was redheaded, though he was graying a little more each month, it seemed like.

I'd always been fond of Terry, who bent over backward to be kind to me—except when he was in one of his black moods. Everyone knew not to cross Terry Bellefleur when he was in one of his moods. Terry's dark days were inevitably preceded by nightmares of the worst kind, as his neighbors testified. They could hear Terry hollering on the night-mare nights.

I never, never read Terry's mind.

Terry looked okay today. His shoulders were relaxed, and his eyes didn't dart from side to side. "You okay, sweet thing?" he asked, patting my arm sympathetically.

"Thanks, Terry, I'm fine. Just sorry about Lafayette."

"Yeah, he wasn't too bad." From Terry, that was high praise. "Did his job, always showed up on time. Cleaned the kitchen good. Never a bad word." Functioning on that level was Terry's highest ambition. "And then he dies in Andy's Buick."

"I'm afraid Andy's car is kind of . . ." I groped for the blandest term.

"It's cleanable, he said." Terry was anxious to close that subject.

"Did he tell you what had happened to Lafayette?"

"Andy says it looks like his neck was broken. And there was some, ah, evidence that he'd been . . . messed with." Terry's brown eyes flickered away, revealing his discomfort. "Messed with" meant something violent and sexual to Terry.

"Oh. Gosh, how awful." Danielle and Holly had come up behind me, and Sam, with another sack of garbage he'd cleaned out of his office, paused on his way to the Dumpster out back.

"He didn't look that . . . I mean, the car didn't look that . . ."

"Stained?"

"Right."

"Andy thinks he was killed somewhere else."

"Yuck," said Holly. "Don't talk about it. That's too much for me."

Terry looked over my shoulder at the two women. He had no great love for either Holly or Danielle, though I didn't know why and had made no effort to learn. I tried to leave people privacy, especially now that I had better control over my own ability. I heard the two moving away, after Terry had kept his gaze trained on them for a few seconds.

"Portia came and got Andy last night?" he asked.

"Yes, I called her. He couldn't drive. Though I'm betting he wishes I'd let him, now." I was just never going to be number one on Andy Bellefleur's popularity list.

"She have trouble getting him to her car?"

"Bill helped her."

"Vampire Bill? Your boyfriend?"

"Uh-huh."

"I hope he didn't scare her," Terry said, as if he didn't remember I was still there.

I could feel my face squinching up. "There's no reason on earth why Bill would ever scare Portia Bellefleur," I said, and something about the way I said it penetrated Terry's fog of private thought.

"Portia ain't as tough as everyone thinks she is," Terry told me. "You, on the other hand, are a sweet little éclair on the outside and a pit bull on the inside."

"I don't know whether I should feel flattered, or whether I should sock you in the nose."

"There you go. How many women—or men, for that matter—would say such a thing to a crazy man like me?" And Terry smiled, as a ghost would smile. I hadn't known how conscious of his reputation Terry was, until now.

I stood on tiptoe to give him a kiss on the scarred cheek, to show him I wasn't scared of him. As I sank back to my heels, I realized that wasn't exactly true. Under some circumstances, not only would I be quite wary of this damaged man, but I might become very frightened indeed.

Terry tied the strings of one of the white cook's aprons and began to open up the kitchen. The rest of us got back into the work mode. I wouldn't have long to wait tables, since I was getting off at six tonight to get ready to drive to Shreveport with Bill. I hated for Sam to pay me for the time I'd spent lollygagging around Merlotte's today, waiting to work; but straightening the storeroom and cleaning out Sam's office had to count for something.

As soon as the police opened up the parking lot, people began streaming in, in as heavy a flow as a small town like Bon Temps ever gets. Andy and Portia were among the first in, and I saw Terry look out the hatch from the kitchen at his cousins. They waved at him, and he raised a spatula to acknowledge their greeting. I wondered how close a cousin Terry actually was. He wasn't a first cousin, I was sure. Of course, here you could call someone your cousin or your aunt or your uncle with little or no blood relation at all. After my mother and father had died in a flash flood that swept their car off a bridge, my mother's best friend tried to come by my Gran's every week or two with a little present for me; and I'd called her Aunt Patty my whole life.

I answered all the customers' questions if I had time, and served hamburgers and salads and chicken breast strips—and beer—until I felt dazed. When I glanced at the clock, it was time for me to go. In the ladies' room I found my replacement, my friend Arlene. Arlene's flaming red hair (two shades redder this month) was arranged in an elaborate cluster of curls on the back of her head, and her tight pants let the world know she'd lost seven pounds. Arlene had been married four times, and she was on the lookout for number five.

We talked about the murder for a couple of minutes, and I briefed her on the status of my tables, before I grabbed my purse from Sam's office and scooted out the back door. It wasn't quite dark when I pulled up to my house, which is a quarter mile back in the woods off a seldom-traveled parish road. It's an old house, parts of it dating back a hundred and forty-plus years, but it's been altered and added onto so often we don't count it as an antebellum house. It's just an old farmhouse, anyway. My grandmother, Adele Hale Stackhouse, left me this house, and I treasured it. Bill had spoken of me moving into his place, which sat on a hill just across the cemetery from my home, but I was reluctant to leave my own turf.

I yanked off my waitress outfit and opened my closet. If we were going over to Shreveport on vampire business, Bill would want me to dress up a little. I couldn't quite figure that out, since he didn't want anyone else making a pass at me, but he always wanted me to look extra pretty when we were going to Fangtasia, a vampire-owned bar catering mainly to tourists.

Men.

I couldn't make up my mind, so I hopped in the shower. Thinking about Fangtasia always made me tense. The vampires who owned it were part of the vampire power structure, and once they'd discovered my unique talent, I'd become a desirable acquisition to them. Only Bill's determined entry into the vampire self-governing system had kept me safe; that is, living where I wanted to live, working at my chosen job. But in return for that safety, I was still obliged to show up when I was summoned, and to put my telepathy to use for them. Milder measures than their former choices (torture and terror) were what "mainstreaming" vampires needed. The hot water immediately made me feel better, and I relaxed as it beat on my back.

"Shall I join you?"

"Shit, Bill!" My heart pounding a mile a minute, I leaned against the shower wall for support.

"Sorry, sweetheart. Didn't you hear the bathroom door opening?"

"No, dammit. Why can't you just call 'Honey, I'm home,' or something?"

"Sorry," he said again, not sounding very sincere. "Do you need someone to scrub your back?"

"No, thank you," I hissed. "I'm not in the back-scrubbing kind of mood."

Bill grinned (so I could see his fangs were retracted) and pulled the shower curtain closed.

When I came out of the bathroom, towel wrapped around me more or less modestly, he was stretched out on my bed, his shoes neatly lined up on the little rug by the night table. Bill was wearing a dark blue long-sleeved shirt and khakis, with socks that matched the shirt and polished loafers. His dark brown hair was brushed straight back, and his long sideburns looked retro.

Well, they were, but more retro than most people could ever have imagined.

He has high arched brows and a high-bridged nose. His mouth is the kind you see on Greek statues, at least the ones I've seen in pictures. He died a few years after the end of the Civil War (or the War of Northern Aggression, as my grandmother always called it).

"What's the agenda for tonight?" I asked. "Business, or pleasure?"

"Being with you is always pleasure," Bill said.

"We're going to Shreveport for what reason?" I asked, since I know a dodgy answer when I hear one.

"We were summoned."

"By?"

"Eric, of course."

Now that Bill had run for, and accepted, a position as Area 5 investigator, he was at Eric's beck and call—and under Eric's protection. That meant, Bill had explained, that anyone attacking Bill would also have to deal with Eric, and it meant that Bill's possessions were sacred to Eric. Which included me. I wasn't thrilled to be numbered among Bill's possessions, but it was better than some of the alternatives.

I made a face in the mirror.

"Sookie, you made a deal with Eric."

"Yeah," I admitted, "I did."

"So you must stick by it."

"I plan on it."

"Wear those tight blue jeans that lace up the sides," Bill suggested.

They weren't denim at all, but some kind of stretchy stuff. Bill just loved me in those jeans, which came down low. More than once, I had wondered if Bill had some kind of Britney Spears fantasy thing going on. Since I was fully aware that I looked good in the jeans, I pulled them on, and a dark blue-and-white-checked short-sleeved shirt that buttoned up the front and stopped about two inches below my bra. Just to exhibit a little independence (after all, he'd better remember I was my own woman) I brushed my hair into a ponytail high up on my head. I pinned a blue bow over the elastic band and slapped on a little makeup. Bill glanced at his watch once or twice, but I took my time. If he was so all-fired concerned about how I was going to impress his vampire friends, he could just wait for me.

Once we were in the car and on our way west to Shreveport, Bill said, "I started a new business venture today."

Frankly, I'd been wondering where Bill's money came from. He never seemed rich: he never seemed poor. But he never worked, either; unless it was on the nights we weren't together.

I was uneasily aware that any vampire worth his salt could become wealthy; after all, when you can control the minds of humans to some extent, it's not that difficult to persuade them to part with money or stock tips or investment opportunities. And until vampires gained the legal right to exist, they hadn't had to pay taxes, see. Even the U.S. government had to admit it couldn't tax the dead. But if you gave them rights, Congress had figured, and gave them the vote, then you could obligate them into paying taxes.

When the Japanese had perfected the synthetic blood that actually enabled vampires to "live" without drinking human blood, it had been possible for vampires to come out of the coffin. "See, we don't have to victimize mankind to exist," they could say. "We are not a threat."

But I knew Bill's big thrill was when he drank from me. He might have a pretty steady diet of LifeFlow (the most popular marketing name for the synthetic blood) but nipping my neck was incomparably better. He could drink some bottled A positive in front of a whole bar full of people, but if he planned on a mouthful of Sookie Stackhouse, we had better by golly be in private, the effect was that different. Bill didn't get any kind of erotic thrill from a wineglass of LifeFlow.

"So what's this new business?" I asked.

"I bought the strip mall by the highway, the one where LaLaurie's is."

"Who owned that?"

"The Bellefleurs originally owned the land. They let Sid Matt Lancaster do a development deal for them."

Sid Matt Lancaster had acted as my brother's lawyer before. He'd been around for donkey's years and had way more clout than Portia.

"That's good for the Bellefleurs. They've been trying to sell that for a couple of years. They need the cash, bad. You bought the land and the strip mall? How big a parcel of land is that?"

"Just an acre, but it's in a good location," Bill said, in a business-like voice that I'd never heard before.

"That same strip's got LaLaurie's, and a hair salon, and Tara's Togs?" Aside from the country club, LaLaurie's was the only restaurant with any pretensions in the Bon Temps area. It was where you took your wife for your twenty-fifth wedding anniversary, or your boss when you wanted a promotion, or a date you really, really wanted to impress. But it didn't make a lot of money, I'd heard.

I have no inkling of how to run a business, or manage business dealings, having been just a step or two ahead of poor all my life. If my parents hadn't had the good fortune to find a little oil on their land and save all the money from it before the oil ran out, Jason and Gran and I would've had a hand-to-mouth time of it. At least twice, we had been close to selling my parents' place, just to keep up Gran's house and taxes, while she raised the two of us.

"So, how does that work? You own the building that houses those three businesses, and they pay you rent?"

Bill nodded. "So now, if you want to get something done to your hair, go to Clip and Curl."

I'd only been to a hairdresser once in my life. If the ends got ragged, I usually went over to Arlene's trailer and she trimmed them evenly. "Do you think my hair needs something done to it?" I asked uncertainly.

"No, it's beautiful." Bill was reassuringly positive. "But if you should want to go, they have, ah, manicures, and hair-care products." He said "hair-care products" as if it were in a foreign language. I stifled a smile.

"And," he continued, "take anyone you want to LaLaurie's, and you won't have to pay."

I turned in my seat to stare at him.

"And Tara knows that if you come in, she will put any clothes you buy on my account."

I could feel my temper creak and give way. Bill, unfortunately, could not. "So, in other words," I said, proud of the evenness of my voice, "they know to indulge the boss's fancy woman."

Bill seemed to realize he'd made a mistake. "Oh, Sookie," he began, but I wasn't having any of it. My pride had risen up and whopped me in the face. I don't lose my temper a lot, but when I do, I make a good job of it.

"Why can't you just send me some damn flowers, like anyone else's boyfriend? Or some candy. I like candy. Just buy me a Hallmark card, why don't you? Or a kitten or a scarf!"

"I meant to give you something," he said cautiously.

"You've made me feel like a kept woman. And you've certainly given the people who work at those businesses the impression I am."

As far as I could tell in the dim dashboard light, Bill looked like he was trying to figure out the difference. We were just past the turn-off to Mimosa Lake, and I could see the deep woods on the lake side of the road in Bill's headlights.

To my complete surprise, the car coughed and stopped dead. I took it as a sign.

Bill would've locked the doors if he'd known what I was going to do, because he certainly looked startled when I scrambled out of the car and marched over to the woods by the road.

"Sookie, get back in here right now!" Bill was mad now, by God. Well, it had taken him long enough.

I shot him the bird as I stepped into the woods.

I knew if Bill wanted me in the car, I'd be in the car, since Bill's about twenty times stronger and faster than me. After a few seconds in the darkness, I almost wished he'd catch up with me. But then my pride gave a twitch, and I knew I'd done the right thing. Bill seemed to be a little confused about the nature of our relationship, and I wanted him to get it straight in his head. He could just take his sorry ass to Shreveport and explain my absence to his superior, Eric. By golly, that'd show him.

"Sookie," Bill called from the road, "I'm going to go to the nearest service station to get a mechanic."

"Good luck," I muttered under my breath. A service station with a full-time mechanic, open at night? Bill was thinking of the fifties, or some other era.

"You're acting like a child, Sookie," Bill said. "I could come to get you, but I'm not going to waste the time. When you're calm, come get in the car and lock it. I'm going now." Bill had his pride, too.

To my mingled relief and concern, I heard the faint footfalls along the road that meant Bill was running at vampire speed. He'd really left.

He probably thought *he* was teaching *me* a lesson. When it was just the opposite. I told myself that several times. After all, he'd be back in a few minutes. I was sure. All I had to do was be sure I didn't stumble far enough through the woods to fall into the lake.

It was *really dark* in the pines. Though the moon was not full, it was a cloudless night, and the shadows in the trees were pitch black in contrast with the cool remote glow of the open spaces.

I made my way back to the road, then took a deep breath and began marching back toward Bon Temps, the opposite direction from Bill. I wondered how many miles we'd put between us and Bon Temps before Bill had begun our conversation. Not so very many, I reassured myself, and patted myself on the back that I was wearing sneakers, not high-heeled sandals. I hadn't brought a sweater, and the exposed skin between my cropped top and my low-cut blue jeans felt goose-pimply. I began to run down the shoulder in an easy jog. There weren't any streetlights, so I would have been in bad shape if it weren't for the moonlight.

Just about the time I recalled that there was someone out there who'd murdered Lafayette, I heard footsteps in the woods parallel to my own path.

When I stopped, the movement in the trees did also.

I'd rather know now. "Okay, who's there?" I called. "If you're going to eat me, let's just get it over with."

A woman stepped out of the woods. With her was a razorback, a feral hog. Its tusks gleamed from the shadows. In her left hand she carried a sort of stick or wand, with a tuft of something on its end.

"Great," I whispered to myself. "Just great." The woman was as scary as the razorback. I was sure she wasn't a vampire, because I could feel the activity in her mind; but she was sure some supernatural being, so she didn't send a clear signal. I could snatch the tenor of her thoughts anyway. She was amused.

That couldn't be good.

I hoped the razorback was feeling friendly. They were very rarely seen around Bon Temps, though every now and then a hunter would spot one; even more rarely bring one down. That was a picture-in-the-paper occasion. This hog smelled, an awful and distinctive odor.

I wasn't sure which to address. After all, the razorback might not be a true animal at all, but a shapeshifter. That was one thing I'd learned in the past few months. If vampires, so long thought of as thrilling fiction, actually did exist, so did other things that we'd regarded as equally exciting fiction.

I was really nervous, so I smiled.

She had long snarled hair, an indeterminate dark in the uncertain light, and she was wearing almost nothing. She had a kind of shift on, but it was short and ragged and stained. She was barefoot. She smiled back at me. Rather than scream, I grinned even more brightly.

"I have no intention of eating you," she said.

"Glad to hear it. What about your friend?"

"Oh, the hog." As if she'd just noticed it, the woman reached over and scratched the razorback's neck, like I would a friendly dog's. The ferocious tusks bobbed up and down. "She'll do what I tell her," the woman said casually. I didn't need a translator to understand the threat. I tried to look equally casual as I glanced around the open space where I stood, hoping to locate a tree that I could climb if I had to. But all the trunks close enough for me to reach in time were bare of branches; they were the loblolly pines grown by the millions in our neck of the woods, for their lumber. The branches start about fifteen feet up.

I realized what I should've thought of sooner; Bill's car stopping there was no accident, and maybe even the fight we'd had was no coincidence.

"You wanted to talk to me about something?" I asked her, and in turning to her I found she'd come several feet closer. I could see her face a little better now, and I was in no wise reassured. There was a stain around her mouth, and when it opened as she spoke, I could see the teeth had dark margins; Miss Mysterious had been eating a raw mammal. "I see you've already had supper," I said nervously, and then could've slapped myself.

"Mmmm," she said. "You are Bill's pet?"

"Yes," I said. I objected to the terminology, but I wasn't in much position to take a stand. "He would be really awfully upset if anything happened to me."

"As if a vampire's anger is anything to me," she said offhandedly.

"Excuse me, ma'am, but what are you? If you don't mind me asking."

She smiled again, and I shuddered. "Not at all. I'm a maenad."

That was something Greek. I didn't know exactly what, but it was wild, female, and lived in nature, if my impressions were correct.

"That's very interesting," I said, grinning for all I was worth. "And you are out here tonight because . . . ?"

"I need a message taken to Eric Northman," she said, moving closer. This time I could see her do it. The hog snuffled along at her side as if she were tied to the woman. The smell was indescribable. I could see the little brushy tail of the razorback—it was switching back and forth in a brisk, impatient sort of way.

"What's the message?" I glanced up at her—and whirled to run as quickly as I could. If I hadn't ingested some vampire blood at the beginning of the summer, I couldn't have turned in time, and I would've taken the blow on my face and chest instead of my back. It felt exactly as though someone very strong had swung a heavy rake and the points had caught in my skin, gone deeper, and torn their way across my back.

I couldn't keep to my feet, but pitched forward and landed on my stomach. I heard her laughing behind me, and the hog snuffling, and then I registered the fact that she had gone. I lay there crying for a minute or two. I was trying not to shriek, and I found myself panting like a woman in labor, attempting to master the pain. My back hurt like hell.

I was mad, too, with the little energy I could spare. I was just a living bulletin board to that bitch, that maenad, whatever the hell she was. As I crawled, over twigs and rough ground, pine needles and dust, I grew angrier and angrier. I was shaking all over from the pain and the rage, dragging myself along, until I didn't feel I was worth killing, I was such a mess. I'd begun the crawl back to the car, trying to head back to the likeliest spot for Bill to find me, but when I was almost there I had second thoughts about staying out in the open.

I'd been assuming the road meant help—but of course, it didn't. I'd found out a few minutes before that not everyone met by chance was in a helping kind of mood. What if I met up with something else, something hungry? The smell of my blood might be attracting a predator at this very moment; a shark is said to be able to detect the tiniest particles of blood in the water, and a vampire is surely the shark's land equivalent.

So I crawled inside the tree line, instead of staying out beside the road where I'd be visible. This didn't seem like a very dignified or meaningful place to die. This was no Alamo, or Thermopylae. This was just a spot in the vegetation by a road in northern Louisiana. I was probably lying in poison ivy. I would probably not live long enough to break out, though.

I expected every second that the pain would begin to abate, but it only increased. I couldn't prevent the tears from coursing down my cheeks. I managed not to sob out loud, so I wouldn't attract any more attention, but it was impossible to keep completely still.

I was concentrating so desperately on maintaining my silence that I almost missed Bill. He was pacing along the road looking into the woods, and I could tell by the way he was walking that he was alert to danger. Bill knew something was wrong.

"Bill," I whispered, but with his vampire hearing, it was like a shout.

He was instantly still, his eyes scanning the shadows. "I'm here," I said, and swallowed back a sob. "Watch out." I might be a living booby trap.

In the moonlight, I could see that his face was clean of emotion, but I knew he was weighing the odds, just as I was. One of us had to move, and I realized if I came out into the moon glow, at least Bill could see more clearly if anything attacked.

I stuck my hands out, gripped the grass, and pulled. I couldn't even get up to my knees, so this progress was my best speed. I pushed a little with my feet, though even that use of my back muscles was excruciating. I didn't want to look at Bill while I moved toward him, because I didn't want to soften at the sight of his rage. It was an almost palpable thing.

"What did this to you, Sookie?" he asked softly.

"Get me in the car. Please, get me out of here," I said, doing my best to hold myself together. "If I make a lot of noise, she might come back." I shivered all over at the thought. "Take me to Eric," I said, trying to keep my voice even. "She said this was a message for Eric Northman."

Bill squatted beside me. "I have to lift you," he told me.

Oh, no. I started to say, "There must be some other way," but I knew there wasn't. Bill knew better than to hesitate. Before I could anticipate the pain to its full extent, he scooted an arm under me and applied his other hand to my crotch, and in an instant he had me dangling across his shoulder.

I screamed out loud. I tried not to sob after that, so Bill could listen for an attack, but I didn't manage that very well. Bill began to run along the road, back to the car. It was running already, its engine idling smoothly. Bill flung open the back door and tried to feed me gently but quickly onto the backseat of the Cadillac. It was impossible not to cause me more pain by doing this, but he made the attempt.

"It was her," I said, when I could say anything coherent. "It was her who made the car stop and made me get out." I was keeping an open mind about whether she'd caused the fight to begin with.

"We'll talk about it in a little while," he said. He sped toward Shreveport, at the highest speed he could, while I clawed at the upholstery in an attempt to keep control over myself.

All I remember about that ride was that it was at least two years long.

Bill got me to the back door of Fangtasia somehow, and kicked it to get attention.

"What?" Pam sounded hostile. She was a pretty blond vampire I'd met a couple of times before, a sensible sort of individual with considerable business acumen. "Oh, Bill. What's happened? Oh, yum, she's bleeding."

"Get Eric," Bill said.

"He's been waiting in here," she began, but Bill strode right by her with me bouncing on his shoulder like a bag of bloody game. I was so out of it by that time that I wouldn't have cared if he'd carried me onto the dance floor of the bar out front, but instead, Bill blew into Eric's office laden with me and rage.

"This is on your account," Bill snarled, and I moaned as he shook me as though he were drawing Eric's attention to me. I hardly see how Eric could have been looking anywhere else, since I was a full-grown female and probably the only bleeding woman in his office.

I would have loved to faint, to pass right out. But I didn't. I just sagged over Bill's shoulder and hurt. "Go to hell," I mumbled.

"What, my darling?"

"Go to *hell.*"

"We must lay her on her stomach on the couch," Eric said. "Here, let me . . ." I felt another pair of hands grip my legs, Bill sort of turned underneath me, and together they deposited me carefully on the broad couch that Eric had just bought for his office. It had that new smell, and it was leather. I was glad, staring at it from the distance of half an inch, that he hadn't gotten cloth upholstery. "Pam, call the doctor." I heard footsteps leave the room, and Eric crouched down to look into my face. It was quite a crouch, because Eric, tall and broad, looks exactly like what he is, a former Viking.

"What has happened to you?" he asked.

I glared at him, so incensed I could hardly speak. "I am a message to you," I said, almost in a whisper. "This woman in the woods made Bill's car stop, and maybe even made us argue, and then she came up to me with this hog."

"A *pig*?" Eric could not have been more astonished if I'd said she had a canary up her nose.

"Oink, oink. Razorback. Wild pig. And she said she wanted to send you a message, and I turned in time to keep her from getting my face, but she got my back, and then she left."

"Your face. She would have gotten your face," Bill said. I saw his hands clenching by his thighs, and the back of him as he began pacing around the office. "Eric, her cuts are not so deep. What's wrong with her?"

"Sookie," Eric said gently, "what did this woman look like?"

His face was right by mine, his thick golden hair almost touching my face.

"She looked nuts, I'll tell you how she looked. And she called you Eric Northman."

"That's the last name I use for human dealings," he said. "By looking nuts, you mean she looked . . . how?"

"Her clothes were all ragged and she had blood around her mouth and in her teeth, like she'd just eaten something raw. She was carrying this kind of wand thing, with something on the end of it. Her hair was long and tangled . . . look, speaking of hair, my hair is getting stuck to my back." I gasped.

"Yes, I see." Eric began trying to separate my long hair from my wounds, where blood was acting as an adherent as it thickened.

Pam came in then, with the doctor. If I had hoped Eric meant a regular doctor, like a stethoscope and tongue depressor kind of person, I was once again doomed to disappointment. This doctor was a dwarf, who hardly had to bend over to look me in the eyes. Bill hovered, vibrating with tension, while the small woman examined my wounds. She was wearing a pair of white pants and a tunic, just like doctors at the hospital; well, just like doctors used to, before they started wearing that green color, or blue, or whatever crazy print came their way. Her face was full of her nose, and her skin was olive. Her hair was golden brown and coarse, incredibly thick and wavy. She wore it clipped fairly short. She put me in mind of a hobbit. Maybe she *was* a hobbit. My understanding of reality had taken several raps to the head in the past few months.

"What kind of doctor are you?" I asked, though it took some time for me to collect myself enough.

"The healing kind," she said in a surprisingly deep voice. "You have been poisoned."

"So that's why I keeping thinking I'm gonna die," I muttered.

"You will, quite soon," she said.

"Thanks a lot, Doc. What can you do about that?"

"We don't have a lot of choices. You've been poisoned. Have you ever heard of Komodo dragons? Their mouths are teeming with bacteria. Well, maenad wounds have the same toxic level. After a dragon has bitten you, the creature tracks you for hours, waiting for the bacteria to kill you. For maenads, the delayed death adds to the fun. For Komodo dragons, who knows?"

Thanks for the National Geographic side trip, Doc. "What can you do?" I asked, through gritted teeth.

"I can dose the exterior wounds. But your bloodstream has been compromised, and your blood must be removed and replaced. That is a job for the vampires." The good doctor seemed positively jolly at the prospect of everyone working together. On me.

She turned to the gathered vamps. "If only one of you takes the poisoned blood, that one will be pretty miserable. It's the element of magic that the maenad imparts. The Komodo dragon bite would be no problem for you guys." She laughed heartily.

I hated her. Tears streamed down my face from the pain.

"So," she continued, "when I'm finished, each of you take a turn, removing just a little. Then we'll give her a transfusion."

"Of human blood," I said, wanting to make that perfectly clear. I'd had to have Bill's blood once to survive massive injuries and once to survive an examination of sorts, and I'd had another vampire's blood by accident, unlikely as that sounds. I'd been able to see changes in me after that blood ingestion, changes I didn't want to amplify by taking another dose. Vampire blood was the drug of choice among the wealthy now, and as far as I was concerned, they could have it.

"If Eric can pull some strings and get the human blood," the dwarf said. "At least half the transfusion can be synthetic. I'm Dr. Ludwig, by the way."

"I can get the blood, and we owe her the healing," I heard Eric say, to my relief. I would have given a lot to see Bill's face, at that moment. "What is your type, Sookie?" Eric asked.

"O positive," I said, glad my blood was so common.

"That shouldn't be a problem," Eric said. "Can you take care of that, Pam?"

Again, a sense of movement in the room. Dr. Ludwig bent forward and began licking my back. I shrieked.

"She's the doctor, Sookie," Bill said. "She will heal you this way."

"But she'll get poisoned," I said, trying to think of an objection that wouldn't sound homophobic and sizist. Truly, I didn't want anyone licking my back, female dwarf or large male vampire.

"She is the healer," Eric said, in a rebuking kind of way. "You must accept her treatment."

"Oh, all right," I said, not even caring how sullen I sounded. "By the way, I haven't heard an 'I'm sorry' from you yet." My sense of grievance had overwhelmed my sense of self-preservation.

"I am sorry that the maenad picked on you."

I glared at him. "Not enough," I said. I was trying hard to hang on to this conversation.

"Angelic Sookie, vision of love and beauty, I am prostrate that the wicked evil maenad violated your smooth and voluptuous body, in an attempt to deliver a message to me."

"That's more like it." I would have taken more satisfaction in Eric's words if I hadn't been jabbed with pain just then. (The doctor's treatment was not exactly comfortable.) Apologies had better be either heartfelt or elaborate, and since Eric didn't have a heart to feel (or at least I hadn't noticed it so far) he might as well distract me with words.

"I take it the message means that she's going to war with you?" I asked, trying to ignore the activities of Dr. Ludwig. I was sweating all over. The pain in my back was excruciating. I could feel tears trickling down my face. The room seemed to have acquired a yellow haze; everything looked sickly.

Eric looked surprised. "Not exactly," he said cautiously. "Pam?"

"It's on the way," she said. "This is bad."

"Start," Bill said urgently. "She's changing color."

I wondered, almost idly, what color I'd become. I couldn't hold my head off the couch anymore, as I'd been trying to do to look a little more alert. I laid my cheek on the leather, and immediately my sweat bound me to the surface. The burning sensation that radiated through my body from the claw marks on my back grew more intense, and I shrieked because I just couldn't help it. The dwarf leaped from the couch and bent to examine my eyes.

She shook her head. "Yes, if there's to be any hope," she said, but she sounded very far away to me. She had a syringe in her hand. The last thing I registered was Eric's face moving closer, and it seemed to me he winked.

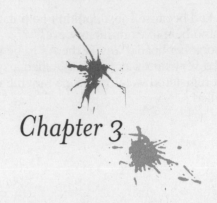

Chapter 3

I OPENED MY eyes with great reluctance. I felt that I'd been sleeping in a car, or that I'd taken a nap in a straight-back chair; I'd definitely dozed off somewhere inappropriate and uncomfortable. I felt groggy, and I ached all over. Pam was sitting on the floor a yard away, her wide blue eyes fixed on me.

"It worked," she commented. "Dr. Ludwig was right."

"Great."

"Yes, it would have been a pity to lose you before we'd gotten a chance to get some good out of you," she said with shocking practicality. "There are many other humans associated with us the maenad could have picked, and those humans are far more expendable."

"Thanks for the warm fuzzies, Pam," I muttered. I felt the last degree of nasty, as if I'd been dipped in a vat of sweat and then rolled in the dust. Even my teeth felt scummy.

"You're welcome," she said, and she almost smiled. So Pam had a sense of humor, not something vampires were noted for. You never saw vampire stand-up comedians, and human jokes just left vampires cold, ha-ha. (Some of *their* humor could give you nightmares for a week.)

"What happened?"

Pam relaced her fingers around her knee. "We did as Dr. Ludwig said. Bill, Eric, Chow, and I all took a turn, and when you were almost dry we began the transfusion."

I thought about that for a minute, glad I'd checked out of consciousness before I could experience the procedure. Bill always took blood when we were making love, so I associated it with the height of erotic activity. To have "donated" to so many people would have been extremely embarrassing to me if I'd been there for it, so to speak. "Who's Chow?" I asked.

"See if you can sit up," Pam advised. "Chow is our new bartender. He is quite a draw."

"Oh?"

"Tattoos," Pam said, sounding almost human for a moment. "He's tall for an Asian, and he has a wonderful set of . . . tattoos."

I tried to look like I cared. I pushed up, feeling a certain tenderness that made me very cautious. It was like my back was covered with wounds that had just healed, wounds that might break open again if I weren't careful. And that, Pam told me, was exactly the case.

Also, I had no shirt on. Or anything else. Above the waist. Below, my jeans were still intact, though remarkably nasty.

"Your shirt was so ragged we had to tear it off," Pam said, smiling openly. "We took turns holding you on our laps. You were much admired. Bill was furious."

"Go to hell" was all I could think of to say.

"Well, as to that, who knows?" Pam shrugged. "I meant to pay you a compliment. You must be a modest woman." She got up and opened a closet door. There were shirts hanging inside; an extra store for Eric, I assumed. Pam pulled one off a hanger and tossed it to me. I reached up to catch it and had to admit that movement was comparatively easy.

"Pam, is there a shower here?" I hated to pull the pristine white shirt over my grimy self.

"Yes, in the storeroom. By the employees' bathroom."

It was extremely basic, but it was a shower with soap and a towel. You had to step right out into the storeroom, which was probably just fine with the vampires, since modesty is not a big issue with them. When Pam agreed to guard the door, I enlisted her help in pulling off the jeans and shucking my shoes and socks. She enjoyed the process a little too much.

It was the best shower I'd ever had.

I had to move slowly and carefully. I found I was as shaky as though I'd passed through a grave illness, like pneumonia or a virulent strain of the flu. And I guess I had. Pam opened the door enough to pass me some underwear, which was a pleasant surprise, at least until I dried myself and prepared to struggle into it. The underpants were so tiny and lacy they hardly deserved to be called panties. At least they were white. I knew I was better when I caught myself wishing I could see how I looked in a mirror. The underpants and the white shirt were the only garments I could bear to put on. I came out barefoot, to find that Pam had rolled up the jeans and everything else and stuffed them in a plastic bag so I could get them home to the wash. My tan looked extremely brown against the white of the snowy shirt. I walked very slowly back to Eric's office and fished in my purse for my brush. As I began to try to work through the tangles, Bill came in and took the brush from my hand.

"Let me do that, darling," he said tenderly. "How are you? Slide off the shirt, so I can check your back." I did anxiously hoping there weren't cameras in the office—though from Pam's account, I might as well relax.

"How does it look?" I asked him over my shoulder.

Bill said briefly, "There will be marks."

"I figured." Better on my back than on my front. And being scarred was better than being dead.

I slipped the shirt back on, and Bill began working on my hair, a favorite thing for him. I grew tired very quickly and sat in Eric's chair while Bill stood behind me.

"So why did the maenad pick me?"

"She would have been waiting for the first vampire to come through. That I had you with me—so much easier to hurt—that was a bonus."

"Did she cause our fight?"

"No, I think that was just chance. I still don't understand why you got so angry."

"I'm too tired to explain, Bill. We'll talk about it tomorrow, okay?"

Eric came in, along with a vampire I knew must be Chow. Right away I could see why Chow would bring in customers. He was the first Asian vampire I'd seen, and he was extremely handsome. He was also covered—at least the parts I could see—with that intricate tattooing that I'd heard members of the Yakuza favored. Whether Chow had been a gangster when he was human or not, he was certainly sinister now. Pam slid through the door after another minute had passed, saying, "All locked up. Dr. Ludwig left, too."

So Fangtasia had closed its doors for the night. It must be two in the morning, then. Bill continued to brush my hair, and I sat in the office chair with my hands on my thighs, acutely conscious of my inadequate clothing. Though, come to think of it, Eric was so tall his shirt covered as much of me as some of my short sets. I guess it was the French-cut bikini panties underneath that made me so embarrassed. Also, no bra. Since God was generous with me in the bosom department, there's no mistaking when I leave off a bra.

But no matter if my clothes showed more of me than I wanted, no matter if all of these people had seen even more of my boobs than they could discern now, I had to mind my manners.

"Thank you all for saving my life," I said. I didn't succeed in sounding warm, but I hope they could tell I was sincere.

"It was truly my pleasure," said Chow, with an unmistakable leer in his voice. He had a trace of an accent, but I don't have enough experience with the different characteristics of the many strains of Asians to tell you where he came from originally. I am sure "Chow" was not his complete name, either, but it was all the other vampires called him. "It would have been perfect, without the poison."

I could feel Bill tense behind me. He laid his hands on my shoulders, and I reached up to put my fingers over his.

Eric said, "It was worth ingesting the poison." He held his fingers to his lips and kissed them, as if praising the bouquet of my blood. Ick.

Pam smiled. "Any time, Sookie."

Oh, just fantastic. "You, too, Bill," I said, leaning my head back against him.

"It was my privilege," he said, controlling his temper with an effort.

"You two had a fight before Sookie's encounter with the maenad?" Eric asked. "Is that what I heard Sookie say?"

"That's our business," I snapped, and the three vampires smiled at each other. I didn't like that one bit. "By the way, why did you want us to come over here tonight, anyway?" I asked, hoping to get off of the topic of Bill and me.

"You remember your promise to me, Sookie? That you would use your mental ability to help me out, as long as I let the humans involved live?"

"Of course I remember." I am not one to forget a promise, especially one made to a vampire.

"Since Bill has been appointed investigator of Area 5, we have not had a lot of mysteries. But Area 6, in Texas, has need of your special asset. So we have loaned you out."

I realized I'd been rented, like a chainsaw or backhoe. I wondered if the vampires of Dallas had had to put down a deposit against damage.

"I won't go without Bill." I looked Eric steadily in the eye. Bill's fingers gave me a little squeeze, so I knew I'd said the right thing.

"He'll be there. We drove a hard bargain," Eric said, smiling broadly. The effect was really disconcerting, because he was happy about something, and his fangs were out. "We were afraid they might keep you, or kill you, so an escort was part of our deal all along. And who better than Bill? If anything should render Bill incapable of guarding you, we will send another escort right out. And the vampires of Dallas have agreed to providing a car and chauffeur, lodgings and meals, and of course, a nice fee. Bill will get a percentage of that."

When I'd be doing the work? "You must work out your financial arrangement with Bill," Eric said smoothly. "I am sure he will at least recompense you for your time away from your bar job."

Had Ann Landers ever covered "When Your Date Becomes Your Manager"?

"Why a maenad?" I asked, startling all of them. I hoped I was pronouncing the word correctly. "Naiads are water and dryads are trees, right? So why a maenad, out there in the woods? Weren't maenads just women driven mad by the god Bacchus?"

"Sookie, you have unexpected depths," Eric said, after an appreciable pause. I didn't tell him I'd learned that from reading a mystery. Let him think I read ancient Greek literature in the original language. It couldn't hurt.

Chow said, "The god entered some women so completely that they became immortal, or very close to it. Bacchus was the god of the grape, of course, so bars are very interesting to maenads. In fact, so interesting that they don't like other creatures of the darkness becoming involved. Maenads consider that the violence sparked by the consumption of alcohol belongs to them; that's what they feed off, now that no one formally worships their god. And they are attracted to pride."

That rang a chime. Hadn't Bill and I both been feeling our pride, tonight?

"We had only heard rumors one was in the area," Eric said. "Until Bill brought you in."

"So what was she warning you of? What does she want?"

"Tribute," Pam said. "We think."

"What kind?"

Pam shrugged. It seemed that was the only answer I was going to get.

"Or what?" I asked. Again with the stares. I gave a deep sigh of exasperation. "What's she gonna do if you don't pay her tribute?"

"Send her madness." Bill sounded worried.

"Into the bar? Merlotte's?" Though there were plenty of bars in the area.

The vampires eyed each other.

"Or into one of us," Chow said. "It has happened. The Halloween massacre of 1876, in St. Petersburg."

They all nodded solemnly. "I was there," Eric said. "It took twenty of us to clean up. And we had to stake Gregory, it took all of us to do that. The maenad, Phryne, received tribute after that, you can be sure."

For the vampires to stake one of their own, things had to be pretty serious. Eric had staked a vampire who had stolen from him, and Bill had told me Eric had had to pay a severe penalty. Who to, Bill hadn't said, and I hadn't asked. There were some things I could live quite well without knowing.

"So you'll give a tribute to this maenad?"

They were exchanging thoughts on this, I could tell. "Yes," Eric said. "It is better if we do."

"I guess maenads are pretty hard to kill," Bill said, a question in his voice.

Eric shuddered. "Oh, yes," he said. "Oh, yes."

DURING OUR RIDE back to Bon Temps, Bill and I were silent. I had a lot of questions about the evening, but I was tired from my bones out to my skin.

"Sam should know about this," I said, as we stopped at my house.

Bill came around to open my door. "Why, Sookie?" He took my hand to pull me from the car, knowing that I could barely walk.

"Because . . ." and then I stopped dead. Bill knew Sam was supernatural, but I didn't want to remind him. Sam owned a bar, and we had been closer to Bon Temps than Shreveport when the maenad had interfered.

"He owns a bar, but he should be all right," Bill said reasonably. "Besides, the maenad said the message was for Eric."

That was true.

"You think too much about Sam to suit me," Bill said, and I gaped up at him.

"You're jealous?" Bill was very wary when other vampires seemed to be admiring me, but I'd assumed that was just territorial. I didn't know how to feel about this new development. I'd never had anyone feel jealous of my attentions before.

Bill didn't answer, in a very snitty way.

"Hmmm," I said thoughtfully. "Well, well, well." I was smiling to myself as Bill helped me up the steps and through the old house, into my room; the room my grandmother had slept in for so many years. Now the walls were painted pale yellow, the woodwork was off-white, the curtains were off-white with bright flowers scattered over them. The bed had a matching cover.

I went into the bathroom for a moment to brush my teeth and take care of necessities, and came out still in Eric's shirt.

"Take it off," Bill said.

"Look, Bill, normally I'd be hot to trot, but tonight—"

"I just hate to see you in his shirt."

Well, well, *well*. I could get used to this. On the other hand, if he carried it to extremes, it could be a nuisance.

"Oh, all right," I said, making a sigh he could hear from yards away. "I guess I'll just have to take this ole shirt off." I unbuttoned it slowly, knowing Bill's eyes were watching my hands move down the buttons, pulling the shirt apart a little more each time. Finally, I doffed it and stood there in Pam's white underwear.

"Oh," Bill breathed, and that was tribute enough for me. Maenads be damned, just seeing Bill's face made me feel like a goddess.

Maybe I'd go to Foxy Femme Lingerie in Ruston my next day off. Or maybe Bill's newly acquired clothing store carried lingerie?

Explaining to sam that I needed to go to Dallas wasn't easy. Sam had been wonderful to me when I'd lost my grandmother, and I counted him as a good friend, a great boss, and (every now and then) a sexual fantasy. I just told Sam that I was taking a little vacation; God knows, I'd never asked for one before. But he pretty much had figured out what the deal was. Sam didn't like it. His brilliant blue eyes looked hot and his face stony, and even his red-blond hair seemed to sizzle. Though he practically muzzled himself to keep from saying so, Sam obviously thought Bill should not have agreed to my going. But Sam didn't know all the circumstances of my dealings with the vampires, just as only Bill, of the vampires I knew, realized that Sam was a shapeshifter. And I tried not to remind Bill. I didn't want Bill thinking about Sam any more than he already did. Bill might decide Sam was an enemy, and I definitely didn't want Bill to do that. Bill is a really bad enemy to have.

I am good at keeping secrets and keeping my face blank, after years of reading unwanted items out of peoples' minds. But I have to confess that compartmentalizing Bill and Sam took a lot of energy.

Sam had leaned back in his chair after he'd agreed to give me the time off, his wiry build hidden by a big kingfisher-blue Merlotte's Bar tee shirt. His jeans were old but clean, and his boots were heavy-soled and ancient. I was sitting on the edge of the visitor's chair in front of Sam's desk, the office door shut behind me. I knew no one could be standing outside the door listening; after all, the bar was as noisy as usual, with the jukebox wailing a zydeco tune and the bellowing of people who'd had a few drinks. But still, when you talked about something like the maenad, you wanted to lower your voice, and I leaned across the desk.

Sam automatically mimicked my posture, and I put my hand on his arm and said in a whisper, "Sam, there's a maenad out by the Shreveport road." Sam's face went blank for a long second before he whooped with laughter.

Sam didn't get over his convulsions for at least three minutes, during which time I got pretty mad. "I'm sorry," he kept saying, and off he'd go again. You know how irritating that can be when you're the one who triggered it? He came around the desk, still trying to smother his chuckles. I stood because he was standing, but I was fuming. He grasped my shoulders. "I'm sorry, Sookie," he repeated. "I've never seen one, but I've heard they're nasty. Why does this concern you? The maenad, that is."

"Because she's not happy, as you would know if you could see the scars on my back," I snapped, and his face changed then, by golly.

"You were hurt? How did this happen?"

So I told him, trying to leave some of the drama out of it, and toning down the healing process employed by the vampires of Shreveport. He still wanted to see the scars. I turned around, and he pulled up my tee shirt, not past bra strap level. He didn't make a sound, but I felt a touch on my back, and after a second I realized Sam had kissed my skin. I shivered. He pulled the tee shirt over my scars and turned me around.

"I'm very sorry," he said, with complete sincerity. He wasn't laughing now, wasn't even close to it. He was awful close to me. I could practically feel the heat radiating from his skin, electricity crackling through the small fine hairs on his arms.

I took a deep breath. "I'm worried she'll turn her attention to you," I explained. "What do maenads want as tribute, Sam?"

"My mother used to tell my father that they love a proud man," he said, and for a moment I thought he was still teasing me. But I looked at his face, and he was not. "Maenads love nothing more than to tear a proud man down to size. Literally."

"Yuck," I said. "Anything else satisfy them?"

"Large game. Bears, tigers, so on."

"Hard to find a tiger in Louisiana. Maybe you could find a bear, but how'd you get it to the maenad's territory?" I pondered this for a while, but didn't come to any answer. "I assume she'd want it alive," I said, a question in my voice.

Sam, who seemed to have been watching me instead of thinking over the problem, nodded, and then he leaned forward and kissed me.

I should have seen it coming.

He was so warm after Bill, whose body never got up to warm. Tepid, maybe. Sam's lips actually felt hot, and his tongue, too. The kiss was deep, intense, unexpected; like the excitement you feel when someone gives you a present you didn't know you wanted. His arms were around me, mine were around him, and we were giving it everything we had, until I came back to earth.

I pulled away a little, and he slowly raised his head from mine.

"I do need to get out of town for a little while," I said.

"Sorry, Sookie, but I've been wanting to do that for years."

There were a lot of ways I could go from that statement, but I ratcheted up my determination and took the high road. "Sam, you know I am . . ."

"In love with Bill," he finished my sentence.

I wasn't completely sure I was in love with Bill, but I loved him, and I had committed myself to him. So to simplify the matter, I nodded in agreement.

I couldn't read Sam's thoughts clearly, because he was a supernatural being. But I would have been a dunce, a telepathic null, not to feel the waves of frustration and longing that rolled off of him.

"The point I was trying to make," I said, after a minute, during which time we disentangled and stepped away from each other, "is that if this maenad takes a special interest in bars, this is a bar run by someone who is not exactly run-of-the-mill human, like Eric's bar in Shreveport. So you better watch out."

Sam seemed to take heart that I was warning him, seemed to get some hope from it. "Thanks for telling me, Sookie. The next time I change, I'll be careful in the woods."

I hadn't even thought of Sam encountering the maenad in his shape-shifting adventures, and I had to sit down abruptly as I pictured that.

"Oh, no," I told him emphatically. "Don't change at all."

"It's full moon in four days," Sam said, after a glance at the calendar. "I'll have to. I've already got Terry scheduled to work for me that night."

"What do you tell him?"

"I tell him I have a date. He hasn't looked at the calendar to figure out that every time I ask him to work, it's a full moon."

"That's something. Did the police come back any more about Lafayette?"

"No." Sam shook his head. "And I hired a friend of Lafayette's, Khan."

"As in Sher Khan?"

"As in Chaka Khan."

"Okay, but can he cook?"

"He's been fired from the Shrimp Boat."

"What for?"

"Artistic temperament, I gather." Sam's voice was dry.

"Won't need much of that around here," I observed, my hand on the doorknob. I was glad Sam and I had had a conversation, just to ease down from our tense and unprecedented situation. We had never embraced each other at work. In fact, we'd only kissed once, when Sam brought me home after our single date months before. Sam was my boss, and starting something with your boss is always a bad idea. Starting something with your boss when your boyfriend is a vampire is another bad idea, possibly a fatal idea. Sam needed to find a woman. Quickly.

When I'm nervous, I smile. I was beaming when I said, "Back to work," and stepped through the door, shutting it behind me. I had a muddle of feelings about everything that had happened in Sam's office, but I pushed it all away, and prepared to hustle some drinks.

There was nothing unusual about the crowd that night in Merlotte's. My brother's friend Hoyt Fortenberry was drinking with some of his cronies. Kevin Prior, whom I was more accustomed to seeing in uniform, was sitting with Hoyt, but Kevin was not having a happy evening. He looked as though he'd rather be in his patrol car with his partner, Kenya. My brother, Jason, came in with his more and more frequent arm decoration, Liz Barrett. Liz always acted glad to see me, but she never tried to ingratiate herself, which earned her high points in my book. My grandmother would have been glad to know Jason was dating Liz so often. Jason had played the scene for years, until the scene was pretty darned tired of Jason. After all, there is a finite pool of women in Bon Temps and its surrounding area, and Jason had fished that pool for years. He needed to restock.

Besides, Liz seemed willing to ignore Jason's little brushes with the law.

"Baby sis!" he said in greeting. "Bring me and Liz a Seven-and-Seven apiece, would you?"

"Glad to," I said, smiling. Carried away on a wave of optimism, I listened in to Liz for a moment; she was hoping that very soon Jason would pop the question. The sooner the better, she thought, because she was pretty sure she was pregnant.

Good thing I've had years of concealing what I was thinking. I brought them each a drink, carefully shielding myself from any other stray thoughts I might catch, and tried to think what I should do. That's one of the worst things about being telepathic; things people are thinking, not talking about, are things other people (like me) really don't want to know. Or shouldn't want to know. I've heard enough secrets to choke a camel, and believe me, not a one of them was to my advantage in any way.

If Liz was pregnant, the last thing she needed was a drink, no matter who the baby's daddy was.

I watched her carefully, and she took a tiny sip from her glass. She wrapped her hand around it to partially hide it from public view. She and Jason chatted for a minute, then Hoyt called out to him, and Jason swung around on the bar stool to face his high school buddy. Liz stared down at her drink, as if she'd really like to gulp it in one swallow. I handed her a similar glass of plain 7UP and whisked the mived drink away.

Liz's big round brown eyes gazed up at me in astonishment. "Not for you," I said very quietly. Liz's olive complexion turned as white as it could. "You have good sense," I said. I was struggling to explain why I'd intervened, when it was against my personal policy to act on what I learned in such a surreptitious way. "You have good sense, you can do this right."

Jason turned back around then, and I got a call for another pitcher from one of my tables. As I moved out from behind the bar to answer the summons, I noticed Portia Bellefleur in the doorway. Portia peered around the dark bar as though she were searching for someone. To my astonishment, that someone turned out to be me.

"Sookie, do you have a minute?" she asked.

I could count the personal conversations I'd had with Portia on one hand, almost on one finger, and I couldn't imagine what was on her mind.

"Sit over there," I said, nodding at an empty table in my area. "I'll be with you in a minute."

"Oh, all right. And I'd better order a glass of wine, I guess. Merlot."

"I'll have it right there." I poured her glass carefully, and put it on a tray. After checking visually to make sure all my customers looked content, I carried the tray over to Portia's table and sat opposite her. I perched on the edge of the chair, so anyone who ran out of a drink could see I was fixing to hop up in just a second.

"What can I do for you?" I reached up to check that my ponytail was secure and smiled at Portia.

She seemed intent on her wineglass. She turned it with her fingers, took a sip, positioned it on the exact center of the coaster. "I have a favor to ask you," she said.

No shit, Sherlock. Since I'd never had a casual conversation with Portia longer than two sentences, it was obvious she needed something from me.

"Let me guess. You were sent here by your brother to ask me to listen in on people's thoughts when they're in the bar, so I can find out about this orgy thing Lafayette went to." Like I hadn't seen that coming.

Portia looked embarrassed, but determined. "He would never have asked you if he wasn't in serious trouble, Sookie."

"He would never have asked me because he doesn't like me. Though I've never been anything but nice to him his whole life! But now, it's okay to ask me for help, because he really needs me."

Portia's fair complexion was turning a deep unbecoming red. I knew it wasn't very pleasant of me to take out her brother's problems on her, but she had, after all, agreed to be the messenger. You know what happens to messengers. That made me think of my own messenger role the night before, and I wondered if I should be feeling lucky today.

"I wasn't for this," she muttered. It hurt her pride, to ask a favor of a barmaid; a Stackhouse, to boot.

Nobody liked me having a "gift." No one wanted me to use it on her. But everyone wanted me to find out something to her advantage, no matter how I felt about sifting through the thoughts (mostly unpleasant and irrelevant) of bar patrons to glean pertinent information.

"You'd probably forgotten that just recently Andy arrested my brother for murder?" Of course he'd had to let Jason go, but still.

If Portia had turned any redder she'd have lit a fire. "Just forget it, then," she said, scraping together all her dignity. "We don't need help from a freak like you, anyway."

I had touched her at the quick, because Portia had always been courteous, if not warm.

"Listen to me, Portia Bellefleur. I'll listen a little. Not for you or your brother, but because I liked Lafayette. He was a friend of mine, and he was always sweeter to me than you or Andy."

"I don't like you."

"I don't care."

"Darling, is there a problem?" asked a cool voice from behind me.

Bill. I reached with my mind, and felt the relaxing empty space right behind me. Other minds just buzzed like bees in a jar, but

Bill's was like a globe filled with air. It was wonderful. Portia stood up so abruptly that her chair almost went over backwards. She was frightened of even being close to Bill, like he was a venomous snake or something.

"Portia was just asking me for a favor," I said slowly, aware for the first time that our little trio was attracting a certain amount of attention from the crowd.

"In return for the many kind things the Bellefleurs have done for you?" Bill asked. Portia snapped. She whirled around to stalk out of the bar. Bill watched her leave with the oddest expression of satisfaction.

"Now I have to find out what that was about," I said, and leaned back against him. His arms circled me and drew me back closer to him. It was like being cuddled by a tree.

"The vampires in Dallas have made their arrangements," Bill said. "Can you leave tomorrow evening?"

"What about you?"

"I can travel in my coffin, if you're willing to make sure I'm unloaded at the airport. Then we'll have all night to find out what it is the Dallas vampires want us to do."

"So I'll have to take you to the airport in a hearse?"

"No, sweetheart. Just get yourself there. There's a transportation service that does that kind of thing."

"Just takes vampires places in daytime?"

"Yes, they're licensed and bonded."

I'd have to think about that for a while. "Want a bottle? Sam has some on the heater."

"Yes, please, I'd like some O positive."

My blood type. How sweet. I smiled at Bill, not my strained normal grin, but a true smile from my heart. I was so lucky to have him, no matter how many problems we had as a couple. I couldn't believe I'd kissed someone else, and I blotted out that idea as soon as it skittered across my mind.

Bill smiled back, maybe not the most reassuring sight, since he was happy to see me. "How soon can you get off?" he asked, leaning closer.

I glanced down at my watch. "Thirty minutes," I promised.

"I'll be waiting for you." He sat at the table Portia had vacated, and I brought him the blood, *tout de suite*.

Kevin drifted over to talk to him, ended up sitting down at the table. I was near enough only twice to catch fragments of the conversation; they were talking about the types of crimes we had in our small town, and the price of gas, and who would win the next sheriff's election. It was so normal! I beamed with pride. When Bill had first started coming into Merlotte's, the atmosphere had been on the strained side. Now, people came and went casually, speaking to Bill or only nodding, but not making a big issue of it either way. There were enough legal issues facing vampires without the social issues involved, too.

As Bill drove me home that night, he seemed to be in an excited mood. I couldn't account for that until I figured out that he was pleased about his visit to Dallas.

"Got itchy feet?" I asked, curious and not too pleased about his sudden case of travel lust.

"I have traveled for years. Staying in Bon Temps these months has been wonderful," he said as he reached over to pat my hand, "but naturally I like to visit with others of my own kind, and the vampires of Shreveport have too much power over me. I can't relax when I'm with them."

"Were vampires this organized before you went public?" I tried not to ask questions about vampire society, because I was never sure how Bill would react, but I was really curious.

"Not in the same way," he said evasively. I knew that was the best answer I'd get from him, but I sighed a little anyway. Mr. Mystery. Vampires still kept limits clearly drawn. No doctor could examine them, no vampires could be required to join the armed forces. In returned for these legal concessions, Americans had demanded that vampires who were doctors and nurses—and there were more than a few—had to hang up their stethoscopes, because humans were too leery of a blood-drinking health care professional. Even though, as far as humans knew, vampirism was an extreme allergic reaction to a combination of various things, including garlic and sunlight.

Though I was a human—albeit a weird one—I knew better. I'd been a lot happier when I believed Bill had some classifiable illness. Now, I knew that creatures we'd shoved off into the realm of myth and legend had a nasty habit of proving themselves real. Take the maenad. Who'd have believed an ancient Greek legend would be strolling through the woods of northern Louisiana?

Maybe there really *were* fairies at the bottom of the garden, a phrase I remembered from a song my grandmother had sung when she hung out the clothes on the line.

"Sookie?" Bill's voice was gently persistent.

"What?"

"You were thinking mighty hard about something."

"Yes, just wondering about the future," I said vaguely. "And the flight. You'll have to fill me in on all the arrangements, and when I have to be at the airport. And what clothes should I take?"

Bill began to turn that over in his head as we pulled up in the driveway in front of my old house, and I knew he would take my request seriously. It was one of the many good things about him.

"Before you pack, though," he said, his dark eyes solemn under the arch of his brows, "there is something else we have to discuss."

"What?" I was standing in the middle of my bedroom floor, staring in the open closet door, when his words registered.

"Relaxation techniques."

I swung around to face him, my hands on my hips. "What on earth are you talking about?"

"This." He scooped me up in the classic Rhett Butler carrying stance, and though I was wearing slacks rather than a long red— negligee? gown?—Bill managed to make me feel like I was as beautiful, as unforgettable, as Scarlett O'Hara. He didn't have to traipse up any stairs, either; the bed was very close. Most evenings, Bill took things very slow, so slow I thought I would start screaming before we came to the point, so to speak. But tonight, excited by the trip, by the imminent excursion, Bill's speed had greatly accelerated. We reached the end of the tunnel together, and as we lay together during the little aftershocks following successful love, I wondered what the vampires of Dallas would make of our association.

I'd only been to Dallas once, on a senior trip to Six Flags, and it hadn't been a wonderful time for me. I'd been clumsy at protecting my mind from the thoughts eternally broadcasting from other brains, I'd been unprepared for the unexpected pairing of my best friend, Marianne, and a classmate named Dennis Engelbright, and I'd never been away from home before.

This would be different, I told myself sternly. I was going at the request of the vampires of Dallas; was that glamorous, or what? I was needed because of my unique skills. I should focus on not calling my quirks a disability. I had learned how to control my telepathy, at least to have much more precision and predictability. I had my own man. No one would abandon me.

Still, I have to admit that before I went to sleep, I cried a few tears for the misery that had been my lot.

Chapter 4

I<small>T WAS AS</small> hot as the six shades of hell in Dallas, especially on the pavement at the airport. Our brief few days of fall had relapsed back into summer. Torch-hot gusts of air bearing all the sounds and smells of the Dallas–Fort Worth airport—the workings of small vehicles and airplanes, their fuel and their cargo—seemed to accumulate around the foot of the ramp from the cargo bay of the plane I'd been waiting for. I'd flown a regular commercial flight, but Bill had had to be shipped specially.

I was flapping my suit jacket, trying to keep my underarms dry, when the Catholic priest approached me.

Initially, I was so respectful of his collar that I didn't object to his approach, even though I didn't really want to talk to anyone. I had just emerged from one totally new experience, and I had several more such hurdles ahead of me.

"Can I be of some service to you? I couldn't help but notice your situation," the small man said. He was soberly clothed in clerical black, and he sounded chock-full of sympathy. Furthermore, he had the confidence of someone used to approaching strangers and being received politely. He had what I thought was sort of an unusual haircut for a priest, though; his brown hair was longish, and tangled, and he had a mustache, too. But I only noticed this vaguely.

"My situation?" I asked, not really paying attention to his words. I'd just glimpsed the polished wood coffin at the edge of the cargo hold. Bill was such a traditionalist; metal would have been more practical for travel. The uniformed attendants were rolling it to the head of the ramp, so they must have put wheels under it somehow. They'd promised Bill it would get to its destination without a scratch. And the armed guards behind me were insurance that no fanatic would rush over and tear the lid off. That was one of the extras Anubis Air had plugged in its ad. Per Bill's instructions, I'd also specified that he be first off the plane.

So far, so good.

I cast a look at the dusky sky. The lights around the field had come on minutes ago. The black jackal's head on the airplane's tail looked savage in the harsh light, which created deep shadows where none had been. I checked my watch again.

"Yes. I'm very sorry."

I glanced sideways at my unwanted companion. Had he gotten on the plane in Baton Rouge? I couldn't remember his face, but then, I'd been pretty nervous the whole flight. "Sorry," I said. "For what? Is there some kind of problem?"

He looked elaborately astonished. "Well," he said, nodding his head toward the coffin, which was now descending on the ramp on a roller system. "Your bereavement. Was this a loved one?" He edged a little closer to me.

"Well, sure," I said, poised between puzzlement and aggravation. Why was he out here? Surely the airline didn't pay a priest to meet every person traveling with a coffin? Especially one being unloaded from Anubis Air. "Why else would I be standing here?"

I began to worry.

Slowly, carefully, I slid down my mental shields and began to examine the man beside me. I know, I know: an invasion of his privacy. But I was responsible for not only my own safety, but Bill's.

The priest, who happened to be a strong broadcaster, was thinking about approaching nightfall as intently as I was, and with a lot more fear. He was hoping his friends were where they were supposed to be.

Trying not to show my increasing anxiety, I looked upward again. Deep into dusk, there was only the faintest trace of light remaining in the Texas sky.

"Your husband, maybe?" He curved his fingers around my arm.

Was this guy creepy, or what? I glanced over at him. His eyes were fixed on the baggage handlers who were clearly visible in the hold of the plane. They were wearing black and silver jumpsuits with the Anubis logo on the left chest. Then his gaze flickered down to the airline employee on the ground, who was preparing to guide the coffin onto the padded, flat-bedded baggage cart. The priest wanted . . . what did he want? He was trying to catch the men all looking away, preoccupied. He didn't want them to see. While he . . . what?

"Nah, it's my boyfriend," I said, just to keep our pretence up. My grandmother had raised me to be polite, but she hadn't raised me to be stupid. Surreptitiously, I opened my shoulder bag with one hand and extracted the pepper spray Bill had given me for emergencies. I held the little cylinder down by my thigh. I was edging away from the false priest and his unclear intentions, and his hand was tightening on my arm, when the lid of the coffin swung open.

The two baggage handlers in the plane had swung down to the ground. Now they bowed deeply. The one who'd guided the coffin onto the cart said, "Shit!" before he bowed, too (new guy, I guess). This little piece of obsequious behavior was also an airline extra, but I considered it way over the top.

The priest said, "Help me, Jesus!" But instead of falling to his knees, he jumped to my right, seized me by the arm holding the spray, and began to yank at me.

At first, I thought he felt he was trying to remove me from the danger represented by the opening coffin, by pulling me to safety. And I guess that was what it looked like to the baggage handlers, who were wrapped up in their role-playing as Anubis Air attendants. The upshot was, they didn't help me, even though I yelled, "Let go!" at the top of my well-developed lungs. The "priest" kept yanking at my arm and trying to run, and I kept digging in my two-inch heels and pulling back. I flailed at him with my free hand. I'm not letting anyone haul me off somewhere I don't want to go, not without a good fight.

"Bill!" I was really frightened. The priest was not a big man, but he was taller and heavier than me, and almost as determined. Though I was making his struggle as hard as possible, inch by inch he was moving me toward a staff door into the terminal. A wind had sprung up from nowhere, a hot dry wind, and if I sprayed the chemicals they would blow right back in my face.

The man inside the coffin sat up slowly, his large dark eyes taking in the scene around him. I caught a glimpse of him running a hand over his smooth brown hair.

The staff door opened and I could tell there was someone right inside, reinforcements for the priest.

"Bill!"

There was a whoosh through the air around me, and all of a sudden the priest let go and zipped through the door like a rabbit at a greyhound track. I staggered and would have landed on my butt if Bill hadn't slowed to catch me.

"Hey, baby," I said, incredibly relieved. I yanked at the jacket of my new gray suit, and felt glad I'd put on some more lipstick when the plane landed. I looked in the direction the priest had taken. *"That* was pretty weird." I tucked the pepper spray back in my purse.

"Sookie," Bill said, "are you all right?" He leaned down to give me a kiss, ignoring the awed whispers of the baggage handlers at work on a charter plane next to the Anubis gate. Even though the world at large had learned two years ago that vampires were not only the stuff of legends and horror movies, but truly led a centuries-long existence among us, lots of people had never seen a vampire in the flesh.

Bill ignored them. Bill is good at ignoring things that he doesn't feel are worth his attention.

"Yes, I'm fine," I said, a little dazed. "I don't know why he was trying to grab me."

"He misunderstood our relationship?"

"I don't think so. I think he knew I was waiting for you and he was trying to get me away before you woke up."

"We'll have to think about this," said Bill, master of the understatement. "Other than this bizarre incident, how did the evening go?"

"The flight was all right," I said, trying not to stick my bottom lip out.

"Did anything else untoward happen?" Bill sounded just a wee bit dry. He was quite aware that I considered myself put-upon.

"I don't know what normal is for airplane trips, never having done it before," I said tartly, "but up until the time the priest appeared, I'd say things pretty much ran smooth." Bill raised one eyebrow in that superior way he has, so I'd elaborate. "I don't think that man was really a priest at all. What did he meet the plane for? Why'd he come over to talk to me? He was just waiting till everyone working on the plane was looking in another direction."

"We'll talk about it in a more private place," my vampire said, glancing at the men and women who'd begun to gather around the plane to check out the commotion. He stepped over to the uniformed Anubis employees, and in a quiet voice he chastised them for not coming to my help. At least, I assumed that was the burden of his conversation, from the way they turned white and began to babble. Bill slid an arm around my waist and we began to stroll to the terminal.

"Send the coffin to the address on the lid," Bill called back over his shoulder. "The Silent Shore Hotel." The Silent Shore was the only hotel in the Dallas area that had undergone the extensive renovation necessary to accommodate vampire patrons. It was one of the grand old downtown hotels, the brochure had said, not that I'd ever seen downtown Dallas or any of its grand old hotels before.

We stopped in the stairwell of a grubby little flight leading up to the main passenger concourse. "Now, tell me," he demanded. I glanced up at him while I related the odd little incident from start to finish. He was very white. I knew he must be hungry. His eyebrows looked black against the pallor of his skin, and his eyes looked an even darker brown than they really were.

He help open a door and I passed through into the bustle and confusion of one of the biggest airports in the world.

"You didn't listen to him?" I could tell Bill didn't mean with my ears.

"I was still pretty heavily shielded from the plane," I said. "And by the time I got concerned, began to try to read him, you came out of your coffin and he took off. I had the funniest feeling, before he ran . . ." I hesitated, knowing this was far-fetched.

Bill just waited. He's not one to waste words. He lets me finish what I'm saying. We stopped walking for a second, edged over to the wall.

"I felt like he was there to kidnap me," I said. "I know that sounds nuts. Who would know who I am, here in Dallas? Who would know to be meeting the plane? But that's definitely the impression I got." Bill took my warm hands in his cool ones.

I looked up into Bill's eyes. I'm not that short, and he's not that tall, but I still have to look up at him. And it's a little pride issue with me, that I can meet his eyes and not get glamoured. Sometimes I wish Bill *could* give me a different set of memories—for example, I wouldn't mind forgetting about the maenad—but he can't.

Bill was thinking over what I'd said, filing it away for future reference. "So the flight itself was boring?" he asked.

"Actually, it was pretty exciting," I admitted. "After I made sure the Anubis people had stowed you on their plane, and I was boarded on mine, the woman showed us what to do when we crashed. I was sitting on the row with the emergency exit. She said to switch if we didn't think we could handle that. But I think I could, don't you? Handle an emergency? She brought me a drink and a magazine." I seldom got waited on myself, being a barmaid by profession, you might say, so I really enjoyed being served.

"I'm sure you can handle just about anything, Sookie. Were you frightened when the plane took off?"

"No. I was just a little worried about this evening. Aside from that, it went fine."

"Sorry I couldn't be with you," he murmured, his cool and liquid voice flowing around me. He pressed me against his chest.

"That's okay," I said into his shirt, mostly meaning it. "First time flying, you know, it's kind of nerve-wracking. But it went all right. Until we landed."

I might grouse and I might moan, but I was truly glad Bill had risen in time to steer me through the airport. I was feeling more and more like the poor country cousin.

We didn't talk any more about the priest, but I knew Bill hadn't forgotten. He walked me through collecting our luggage and finding transportation. He would've parked me somewhere and arranged it all, except, as he reminded me frequently, I'd have to do this on my own sometime, if our business demanded we land somewhere in full daylight.

Despite the fact that the airport seemed incredibly crowded, full of people who all appeared heavily burdened and unhappy, I managed to follow the signs with a little nudge from Bill, after reinforcing my mental shields. It was bad enough, getting washed with the weary misery of the travelers, without listening to their specific laments. I directed the porter with our luggage (which Bill could easily have carried under one arm) to the taxi stand, and Bill and I were on our way to the hotel within forty minutes of Bill's emergence. The Anubis people had sworn up and down that his coffin would be delivered within three hours.

We'd see. If they didn't make it, we got a free flight.

I'd forgotten the sprawl of Dallas, in the seven years since I'd graduated from high school. The lights of the city were amazing, and the busyness. I stared out of the windows at everything we passed, and Bill smiled at me with an irritating indulgence.

"You look very pretty, Sookie. Your clothes are just right."

"Thanks," I said, relieved and pleased. Bill had insisted that I needed to look "professional," and after I'd said, "Professional what?" he'd given me one of those looks. So I was wearing a gray suit over a white shell, with pearl earrings and a black purse and heels. I'd even smoothed my hair back into a twisted shape at the back of my head with one of those Hairagamis I'd ordered from TV. My friend Arlene had helped me. To my mind, I looked like a professional, all right—a professional funeral home attendant—but Bill seemed to approve. And I'd charged the whole outfit to him at Tara's Togs, since it was a legitimate business expense. So I couldn't complain about the cost.

I'd have been more comfortable in my barmaid's outfit. Give me shorts and a T-shirt over a dress and hose any day. And I could've been wearing my Adidas with my barmaid uniform, not these damn heels. I sighed.

The taxi pulled up to the hotel, and the driver got out to extract our luggage. There was enough of it for three days. If the vampires of Dallas had followed my directions, I could wind this up and we could go back to Bon Temps tomorrow night, to live there unmolested and uninvolved in vampire politics—at least until the next time Bill got a phone call. But it was better to bring extra clothes than to count on that.

I scooted across the seat to emerge after Bill, who was paying the driver. A uniformed bellboy from the hotel was loading the luggage onto a rolling cart. He turned his thin face to Bill and said, "Welcome to Silent Shore Hotel, sir! My name is Barry, and I'll . . ." Then Bill stepped forward, the light from the lobby door spilling onto his face. "I'll be your porter," Barry finished weakly.

"Thank you," I said, to give the boy, who couldn't be more than eighteen, a second to compose himself. His hands were a little trembly. I cast a mental net out to check the source of his distress.

To my startled delight, I realized (after a quick rummage in Barry's head) that he was a telepath, like me! But he was at the level of organization and development I'd been when I was, maybe, twelve years old. He was a mess, that boy. He couldn't control himself at all, and his shields were a shambles. He was heavy into denial. I didn't know whether to grab him and hug him, or smack him upside the head. Then I realized his secret was not mine to give away. I glanced off in another direction, and shifted from one foot to another, as if I were bored.

"I'll just follow you with your luggage," Barry mumbled, and Bill smiled at him gently. Barry smiled tentatively back, and then got busy bringing in the cart. It had to be Bill's appearance that unnerved Barry, since he couldn't read Bill's mind, the great attraction of the undead for people like me. Barry was going to have to learn how to relax around vampires, since he'd agreed to work at a hotel that catered to them.

Some people think all vampires look terrifying. To me, it depends on the vampire. I remember thinking, when I first met Bill, that he looked incredibly different; but I hadn't been frightened.

The one that was waiting for us in the lobby of Silent Shores, now, *she* was scary. I bet she made ole Barry wet his pants. She approached after we'd checked in, as Bill was putting his credit card back in his wallet (you just try applying for a credit card when you're a hundred sixty years old; that process had been a *bear*) and I sidled a little closer to him as he tipped Barry, hoping she wouldn't notice me.

"Bill Compton? The detective from Louisiana?" Her voice was as calm and cool as Bill's, with considerably less inflection. She had been dead a long time. She was as white as paper and as flat as a board, and her thin ankle-length blue-and-gold dress didn't do a thing for her except accentuate both whiteness and flatness. Light brown hair (braided and long enough to tap her butt) and glittery green eyes emphasized her otherness.

"Yes." Vampires don't shake hands, but the two made eye contact and gave each other a curt nod.

"This is the woman?" She had probably gestured toward me with one of those lightning quick movements, because I caught a blur from the corner of my eyes.

"This is my companion and coworker, Sookie Stackhouse," Bill said.

After a moment, she nodded to show she was picking up the hint. "I am Isabel Beaumont," she said, "and after you take your luggage to your room and take care of your needs, you are to come with me."

Bill said, "I have to feed."

Isabel swiveled an eye toward me thoughtfully, no doubt wondering why I wasn't supplying blood for my escort, but it was none of her business. She said, "Just punch the telephone button for room service."

MEASLY OLD MORTAL me would just have to order from the menu. But as I considered the time frame, I realized I'd feel much better if I waited to eat after this evening's business was finished.

After our bags had been put in the bedroom (big enough for the coffin and a bed), the silence in the little living room became uncomfortable. There was a little refrigerator well stocked with PureBlood, but this evening Bill would want the real thing.

"I have to call, Sookie," Bill said. We'd gone over this before the trip.

"Of course." Without looking at him, I retreated into the bedroom and shut the door. He might have to feed off someone else so I could keep my strength up for coming events, but I didn't have to watch it or like it. After a few minutes, I heard a knock on the corridor door and I heard Bill admit someone—his Meal on Wheels. There was a little murmur of voices and then a low moan.

Unfortunately for my tension level, I had too much common sense to do something like throw my hairbrush or one of the damn high heels across the room. Maybe retaining some dignity figured in there, too; and a healthy sense of how much temperament Bill would put up with. So I unpacked my suitcase and laid my makeup out in the bathroom, using the facility even though I didn't feel especially needy. Toilets were optional in the vampire world, I'd learned, and even if a functional facility was available in a house occupied by vampires, occasionally they forgot to stock toilet paper.

Soon I heard the outer door open and close again, and Bill knocked lightly before coming into the bedroom. He looked rosy and his face was fuller.

"Are you ready?" he asked. Suddenly, the fact that I was going out on my first real job for the vampires hit me, and I felt scared all over again. If I wasn't a success, my life would become out-and-out perilous, and Bill might become even deader than he was now. I nodded, my throat dry with fear.

"Don't bring your purse."

"Why not?" I stared down at it, astonished. Who could object?

"Things can be hidden in purses." Things like stakes, I assumed. "Just slip a room key into . . . does that skirt have a pocket?"

"No."

"Well, slip the key into your underthings."

I raised my hem so Bill could see exactly what underthings I had to tuck something into. I enjoyed the expression on his face more than I can say.

"Those are . . . would that be a . . . thong?" Bill seemed a little preoccupied all of a sudden.

"It would. I didn't see the need to be professional down to the skin."

"And what skin it is," Bill murmured. "So tan, so . . . smooth."

"Yep, I figured I didn't need to wear any hose." I tucked the plastic rectangle—the "key"—under one of the side straps.

"Oh, I don't think it'll stay there," he said, his eyes large and luminous. "We might get separated, so you definitely need to take it with you. Try another spot."

I moved it somewhere else.

"Oh, Sookie. You'll never get at it in a hurry there. We have . . . ah, we have to go." Bill seemed to shake himself out of his trance.

"All right, if you insist," I said, smoothing the skirt of the suit over my "underthings."

He gave me a dark look, patted his pockets like men do, just to make sure they got everything. It was an oddly human gesture, and it touched me in a way I couldn't even describe to myself. We gave each other a sharp nod and walked down the corridor to the elevator. Isabel Beaumont would be waiting, and I had a distinct feeling she wasn't used to that.

The ancient vampire, who looked no more than thirty-five, was standing exactly where we'd left her. Here at the Silent Shore Hotel, Isabel felt free to be her vampire self, which included immobile downtime. People fidget. They are compelled to look engaged in an activity, or purposeful. Vampires can just occupy space without feeling obliged to justify it. As we came out of the elevator, Isabel looked exactly like a statue. You could have hung your hat on her, though you'd have been sorry.

Some early warning system kicked in when we were within six feet of the vamp. Isabel's eyes flicked in our direction and her right hand moved, as though someone had thrown her "on" switch. "Come with me," she said, and glided out the main door. Barry could hardly open it for her fast enough. I noticed he had enough training to cast his eyes down as she passed. Everything you've heard about meeting vampires' eyes is true.

Predictably, Isabel's car was a black Lexus loaded with options. Vampires won't go around in any Geo. Isabel waited until I'd buckled my seat belt (she and Bill didn't bother to use them) before pulling away from the curb, which surprised me. Then we were driving through Dallas, down a main thoroughfare. Isabel seemed to be the strong silent type, but after we'd been in the car for maybe five minutes, she seemed to shake herself, as if she had been reminded she had orders.

We began a curve to the left. I could see some sort of grassy area, and a vague shape that would be some kind of historical marker, maybe. Isabel pointed to her right with a long bony finger. "The Texas School Book Depository," she said, and I understood she felt obliged to inform me. That meant she had been ordered to do so, which was very interesting. I followed her finger eagerly, taking in as much of the brick building as I could see. I was surprised it didn't look more notable.

"That's the grassy knoll?" I breathed, excited and impressed. It was like I'd happened upon the *Hindenburg* or some other fabled artifact.

Isabel nodded, a barely perceptible movement that I only caught because her braid jerked. "There is a museum in the old depository," she said.

Now, that was something I'd like to see in the daytime. If we were here long enough, I'd walk or maybe find out how to catch a cab while Bill was in his coffin.

Bill smiled over his shoulder at me. He could pick up on my slightest mood, which was wonderful about eighty percent of the time.

We drove for at least twenty more minutes, leaving business areas and entering residential. At first the structures were modest and boxy; but gradually, though the lots didn't seem that much larger, the houses began to grow as if they'd taken steroids. Our final destination was a huge house shoehorned onto a small lot. With its little ruffle of land around the cube of the house, it looked ridiculous, even in the dark.

I sure could have stood a longer ride and more delay.

We parked on the street in front of the mansion, for so it seemed to me. Bill opened my door for me. I stood for a moment, reluctant to start the—project. I knew there were vampires inside, lots of them. I knew it the same way I would be able to discern that humans were waiting. But instead of positive surges of thought, the kind I'd get to indicate people, I got mental pictures of . . . how can I put it? There were holes in the air inside the house. Each hole represented a vampire. I went a few feet down the short sidewalk to the front door, and there, finally, I caught a mental whiff of human.

The light over the door was on, so I could tell the house was of beige brick with white trim. The light, too, was for my benefit; any vampire could see far better than the sharpest-eyed human. Isabel led the way to the front door, which was framed in graduating arches of brick. There was a tasteful wreath of grapevines and dried flowers on the door, which almost disguised the peephole. This was clever main-streaming. I realized there was nothing apparent in this house's appearance to indicate that it was any different from any of the other oversized houses we'd passed, no outward indication that within lived vampires.

But they were there, in force. As I followed Isabel inside, I counted four in the main room onto which the front door opened, and there were two in the hall and at least six in the vast kitchen, which looked designed to produce meals for twenty people at a time. I knew immediately that the house had been purchased, not built, by a vampire, because vampires always plan tiny kitchens, or leave the kitchen out entirely. All they need is a refrigerator, for the synthetic blood, and a microwave, to heat it up. What are they going to cook?

At the sink, a tall, lanky human was washing a few dishes, so perhaps some humans did live here. He half-turned as we passed through, and nodded to me. He was wearing glasses and his shirtsleeves were rolled up. I didn't have a chance to speak, because Isabel was ushering us into what appeared to be the dining room.

Bill was tense. I might not be able to read his mind, but I knew him well enough to interpret the set of his shoulders. No vampire is ever comfortable entering another vamp's territory. Vampires have as many rules and regulations as any other society; they just try to keep them secret. But I was figuring things out.

Among all the vampires in the house, I quickly spotted the leader. He was one of those sitting at the long table in the large dining room. He was a total geek. That was my first impression. Then I realized that he was carefully disguised as a geek: he was quite . . . other. His sandy hair was slicked back, his physique was narrow and unimpressive, his black-rimmed glasses were sheer camouflage, and his pinstriped oxford cloth shirt was tucked into cotton-polyester blend pants. He was pale—well, duh—and freckled, with invisible eyelashes and minimal eyebrows.

"Bill Compton," the geek said.

"Stan Davis," Bill said.

"Yeah, welcome to the city." There was a faint trace of foreign accent in the geek's voice. *He used to be Stanislaus Davidowitz,* I thought, and then wiped my mind clean like a slate. If any of them found out that every now and then I picked a stray thought out of the silence of their minds, I'd be bloodless before I hit the floor.

Even Bill didn't know that.

I packed the fear down in the cellar of my mind as the pale eyes fixed on me and scrutinized me feature by feature.

"She comes in an agreeable package," he said to Bill, and I supposed that was meant to be a compliment, a pat on the back, for Bill.

Bill inclined his head.

Vampires didn't waste time saying a lot of things humans would under similar circumstances. A human executive would ask Bill how Eric, his boss, was doing; would threaten Bill a little in case I didn't perform; would maybe introduce Bill and me to at least the more important people in the room. Not Stan Davis, head vampire. He lifted his hand, and a young Hispanic vampire with bristly black hair left the room and returned with a human girl in tow. When she saw me, she gave a screech and lunged, trying to break free of the grip the vampire had on her upper arm.

"Help me," she shrieked. "You have to help me!"

I knew right away that she was stupid. After all, what could I do against a roomful of vampires? Her appeal was ridiculous. I told myself that several times, very fast, so I could go through with what I had to do.

I caught her eyes, and held up my finger to tell her to be silent. Once she'd looked at me, locked on to me, she obeyed. I don't have the hypnotic eyes of a vamp, but I don't look the least bit threatening. I look exactly like the girl you'd see in a low-paying job any place in any town in the South: blond and bosomy and tan and young. Possibly, I don't look very bright. But I think it's more that people (and vampires) assume that if you're pretty and blond and have a low-paying job, you are ipso facto dumb.

I turned to Stan Davis, very grateful that Bill was right behind me. "Mr. Davis, you understand that I need more privacy when I question this girl. And I have to know what you need from her."

The girl began to sob. It was slow and heartrending, and almost unbelievably irritating under the circumstances.

Davis's pale eyes fastened on mine. He was not trying to glamour me, or subdue me; he was just examining me. "I understood your escort knew the terms of my agreement with his leader," Stan Davis said. All right, I got the point. I was beneath contempt since I was a human. My talking to Stan was like a chicken talking to the buyer from KFC. But still, I had to know our goal. "I'm aware you met Area 5's conditions," I said, keeping my voice as steady as I could, "and I'm going to do my best. But without a goal, I can't get started."

"We need to know where our brother is," he said, after a pause.

I tried not to look as astonished as I felt.

As I've said, some vampires, like Bill, live by themselves. Others feel more secure in a cluster, called a nest. They call each other brother and sister when they've been in the same nest for a while, and some nests lasted decades. (One in New Orleans has lasted two centuries.) I knew from Bill's briefing before we left Louisiana that the Dallas vampires lived in an especially large nest.

I'm no brain surgeon, but even I realized that for a vampire as powerful as Stan to be missing one of his nest brothers was not only very unusual, it was humiliating.

Vampires like to be humiliated about as much as people do.

"Explain the circumstances, please," I said in my most neutral voice.

"My brother Farrell has not returned to his nest for five nights," Stan Davis said.

I knew they would have checked Farrell's favorite hunting grounds, have asked every other vampire in the Dallas nest to find out if Farrell had been seen. Nevertheless, I opened my mouth to ask, as humans are compelled to do. But Bill touched my shoulder, and I glanced behind me to see a tiny headshake. My questions would be taken as a serious insult.

"This girl?" I asked instead. She was still quiet, but she was shivering and shaking. The Hispanic vampire seemed to be the only thing holding her up.

"Works in the club where he was last seen. It's one we own, The Bat's Wing." Bars were favorite enterprises for vampires, naturally, because their heaviest traffic came at night. Somehow, fanged all-night dry cleaners didn't have the same allure that a vampire-studded bar did.

In the past two years, vampire bars had become the hottest form of nightlife a city could boast. The pathetic humans who became obsessed with vampires—fangbangers—hung out in vampire bars, often in costumes, in the hopes of attracting the attention of the real thing. Tourists came in to gape at the undead and the fangbangers. These bars weren't the safest place to work.

I caught the eyes of the Hispanic vampire, and indicated a chair on my side of the long table. He eased the girl into it. I looked down at her, preparing to slide into her thoughts. Her mind had no protection whatsoever. I closed my eyes.

Her name was Bethany. She was twenty-one, and she had thought of herself as a wild child, a real bad girl. She had had no idea what trouble that could get her into, until now. Getting a job at the Bat's Wing had been the rebellious gesture of her life, and it might just turn out to be fatal.

I turned my eyes back to Stan Davis. "You understand," I said, taking a great risk, "that if she yields the information you want, she goes free, unharmed." He'd said he understood the terms, but I had to be sure.

Bill heaved a sigh behind me. Not a happy camper. Stan Davis's eyes actually glowed for a second, so angry was he. "Yes," he said, biting out the words, his fangs half out, "I agreed." We met each other's eyes for a second. We both knew that even two years ago, the vampires of Dallas would have kidnapped Bethany and tortured her until they had every scrap of information she had stored in her brain, and some she'd made up.

Mainstreaming, going public with the fact of their existence, had many benefits—but it also had its price. In this instance, the price was my service.

"What does Farrell look like?"

"Like a cowboy." Stan said this without a trace of humor. "He wears one of those string ties, jeans, and shirts with fake pearl snaps."

The Dallas vampires didn't seem to be into haute couture. Maybe

I could have worn my barmaid outfit after all. "What color hair and eyes?"

"Brown hair going gray. Brown eyes. A big jaw. About . . . five feet, eleven inches." Stan was translating from some other method of measurement. "He would look about thirty-eight, to you," Stan said. "He's clean-shaven, and thin."

"Would you like me to take Bethany somewhere else? You got a smaller room, less crowded?" I tried to look agreeable, because it seemed like such a good idea.

Stan made a movement with his hand, almost too fast for me to detect, and in a second—literally—every vampire, except Stan himself and Bill, had left the kitchen. Without looking, I knew that Bill was standing against the wall, ready for anything. I took a deep breath. Time to start this venture.

"Bethany, how are you?" I said, making my voice gentle.

"How'd you know my name?" she asked, slumping down in her seat. It was a breakfast nook chair on wheels, and I rolled it out from the table and turned it to face the one I now settled in. Stan was still sitting at the head of the table, behind me, slightly to my left.

"I can tell lots of things about you," I said, trying to look warm and omniscient. I began picking thoughts out of the air, like apples from a laden tree. "You had a dog named Woof when you were little, and your mother makes the best coconut cake in the world. Your dad lost too much money at a card game one time, and you had to hock your VCR to help him pay up, so your mom wouldn't find out."

Her mouth was hanging open. As much as it was possible, she had forgotten the fact that she was in terrible danger. "That's amazing, you're as good as the psychic on TV, the one in the ads!"

"Well, Bethany, I'm not a psychic," I said, a little too sharply. "I'm a telepath, and what I do is read your thoughts, even some you maybe didn't know you had. I'm going to relax you, first, and then we're going to remember the evening you worked at the bar—not tonight, but five nights ago." I glanced back at Stan, who nodded.

"But I wasn't thinking about my mother's cake!" Bethany said, stuck on what had struck her.

I tried to suppress my sigh.

"You weren't aware of it, but you did. It slid across your mind when you looked at the palest vampire—Isabel—because her face was as white as the icing for the cake. And you thought of how much you missed your dog when you were thinking of how your parents would miss you."

I knew that was a mistake as soon as the words went out of my mouth, and sure enough, she began crying again, recalled to her present circumstances.

"So what are you here for?" she asked between sobs.

"I'm here to help you remember."

"But you said you're not psychic."

"And I'm not." Or was I? Sometimes I thought I had a streak mixed in with my other "gift," which was what the vampires thought it was. I had always thought of it as more of a curse, myself, until I'd met Bill. "Psychics can touch objects and get information about the wearers. Some psychics see visions of past or future events. Some psychics can communicate with the dead. I'm a telepath. I can read some peoples' thoughts. Supposedly, I can send thoughts, too, but I've never tried that." Now that I'd met another telepath, the attempt was an exciting possibility, but I stowed that idea away to explore at my leisure. I had to concentrate on the business at hand.

As I sat knee to knee with Bethany, I was making a series of decisions. I was new to the idea of using my "listening in" to some purpose. Most of my life had been spent struggling *not* to hear. Now, hearing was my job, and Bethany's life probably depended on it. Mine almost certainly did.

"Listen, Bethany, here's what we're going to do. You're going to remember that evening, and I'm going to go through it with you. In your mind."

"Will it hurt?"

"No, not a bit."

"And after that?"

"Why, you'll go."

"Go home?"

"Sure." With an amended memory that wouldn't include me, or this evening, courtesy of a vampire.

"They won't kill me?"

"No way."

"You promise?"

"I do." I managed to smile at her.

"Okay," she said, hesitantly. I moved her a little, so she couldn't see Stan over my shoulder. I had no idea what he was doing. But she didn't need to see that white face while I was trying to get her to relax.

"You're pretty," she said suddenly.

"Thanks, and back at you." At least, she might be pretty under better circumstances. Bethany had a mouth that was too small for her face, but that was a feature some men found attractive, since it looked like she was always puckered up. She had a great quantity of brown hair, thick and bushy, and a thin body with small breasts. Now that another woman was looking at her, Bethany was worried about her wrinkled clothes and stale makeup.

"You look fine," I said quietly, taking her hands into mine. "Now, we're just gonna hold hands here for a minute—I swear I'm not making a pass." She giggled, and her fingers relaxed a little more. Then I began my spiel.

This was a new wrinkle for me. Instead of trying to avoid using my telepathy, I'd been trying to develop it, with Bill's encouragement. The human staff at Fangtasia had acted as guinea pigs. I'd found out, almost by accident, that I could hypnotize people in a jiffy. It didn't put them under my spell or anything, but it let me into their minds with a frightening ease. When you can tell what really relaxes someone, by reading his or her mind, it's relatively easy to relax that person right into a trancelike state.

"What do you enjoy the most, Bethany?" I asked. "Do you get a massage every now and then? Or maybe you like getting your nails done?" I looked in Bethany's mind delicately. I selected the best channel for my purpose.

"You're getting your hair fixed," I said, keeping my voice soft and even, "by your favorite hairdresser . . . Jerry. He's combed it and combed it, there's not a tangle left. He's sectioned it off, so carefully, because your hair is so thick. It's gonna take him a long time to cut it, but he's looking forward to it, because your hair is healthy and shiny. Jerry's lifting a lock, and trimming it . . . the scissors give a little snick. A little bit of hair falls on the plastic cape and slides off to the floor. You feel his fingers in your hair again. Over and over, his fingers move in your hair, lift a lock, snip it. Sometimes he combs it again, to see if he got it even. It feels so good, just sitting and having someone work on your hair. There's no one else . . ." No, wait. I'd raised a hint of unease. "There's only a few people in the shop, and they're just as busy as Jerry. Someone's got a blow dryer going. You can barely hear voices murmuring in the next booth. His fingers run through, lift, snip, comb, over and over . . ."

I didn't know what a trained hypnotist would say about my technique, but it worked for me this time, at least. Bethany's brain was in a restful, fallow state, just waiting to be given a task. In the same even voice I said, "While he's working on your hair, we're going to walk through that night at work. He won't stop cutting, okay? Start with getting ready to go to the bar. Don't mind me, I'm just a puff of air right behind your shoulder. You might hear my voice, but it's coming from another booth in that beauty salon. You won't even be able to hear what I'm saying unless I use your name." I was informing Stan as well as reassuring Bethany. Then I submerged deeper into the girl's memory.

Bethany was looking at her apartment. It was very small, fairly neat, and she shared it with another Bat's Wing employee, who went by the name Desiree Dumas. Desiree Dumas, as seen by Bethany, looked exactly like her made-up name: a self-designated siren, a little too plump, a little too blond, and convinced of her own eroticism.

Taking the waitress through this experience was like watching a film, a really dull one. Bethany's memory was almost too good. Skipping over the boring parts, like Bethany and Desiree's argument over the relative merits of two brands of mascara, what Bethany remembered was this: she had prepared for work as she always did, and she and Desiree had ridden together to their job. Desiree worked in the gift shop section of the Bat's Wing. Dressed in a red bustier and black boots, she hawked vampire souvenirs for big bucks. Wearing artificial fangs, she posed for pictures with tourists for a good tip. Bony and shy Bethany was a humble waitress; for a year she'd been waiting for an opening in the more congenial gift shop, where she wouldn't make the big tips but her base salary would be higher, and she could sit down when she wasn't busy. Bethany hadn't gotten there yet. Big grudge against Desiree, there, on Bethany's part; irrelevant, but I heard myself telling Stan about it as if it were crucial information.

I had never been this deep into someone else's mind. I was trying to weed as I went, but it wasn't working. Finally, I just let it all come. Bethany was completely relaxed, still getting that haircut. She had excellent visual recall, and she was as deeply engaged as I was in the evening she'd spent at work.

In her mind, Bethany served synthetic blood to only four vampires: a red-haired female; a short, stocky Hispanic female with eyes as black as pitch; a blond teenager with ancient tattoos; and a brown-haired man with a jutting jaw and a bolo tie. There! Farrell was embedded in Bethany's memory. I had to suppress my surprise and recognition, and try to steer Bethany with more authority.

"That's the one, Bethany," I whispered. "What do you remember about him?"

"Oh, him," Bethany said out loud, startling me so much I almost jumped out of my chair. In her mind, she turned to look at Farrell, thinking of him. He'd had two synthetic bloods, O positive, and he'd left her a tip.

There was a crease between Bethany's eyebrows as she became focused on my request. She was trying hard now, searching her memory. Bits of the evening began to compact, so she could reach the parts containing the memory of the brown-haired vampire. "He went back to the bathroom with the blond," she said, and I saw in her mind the image of the blond tattooed vampire, the very young-looking one. If I'd been an artist, I could have drawn him.

"Young vampire, maybe sixteen. Blond, tattoo," I murmured to Stan, and he looked surprised. I barely caught that, having so much to concentrate on—this was like trying to juggle—but I did think surprise was the flash of feeling on Stan's face. That was puzzling.

"Sure he was a vampire?" I asked Bethany.

"He drank the blood," she said flatly. "He had that pale skin. He gave me the creeps. Yes, I'm sure."

And he'd gone into the bathroom with Farrell. I was disturbed. The only reason a vampire would enter a bathroom was if there were a human inside he wanted to have sex with, or drink from, or (any vamp's favorite) do both simultaneously. Submerging myself again in Bethany's recollections, I watched her serve a few more customers, no one I recognized, though I got as good a look as I could at the other patrons. Most of them seemed like harmless tourist types. One of them, a dark-complexioned man with a bushy mustache, seemed familiar, so I tried to note his companions: a tall, thin man with shoulder-length blond hair and a squatty woman with one of the worst haircuts I'd ever seen.

I had some questions to ask Stan, but I wanted to finish up with Bethany first. "Did the cowboy-looking vampire come out again, Bethany?"

"No," she said after a perceptible pause. "I didn't see him again." I checked her carefully for blank spots in her mind; I could never replace what had been erased, but I might know if her memory had been tampered with. I found nothing. And she was trying to remember, I could tell. I could sense her straining to recall another glimpse of Farrell. I realized, from the sense of her straining, that I was losing control of Bethany's thoughts and memories.

"What about the young blond one? The one with the tattoos?"

Bethany pondered that. She was about half out of her trance now. "I didn't see him neither," she said. A name slid through her head.

"What's that?" I asked, keeping my voice very quiet and calm.

"Nothing! Nothing!" Bethany's eyes were wide open now. Her haircut was over: I'd lost her. My control was far from perfect.

She wanted to protect someone; she wanted him not to go through the same thing she was going through. But she couldn't stop herself from thinking the name, and I caught it. I couldn't quite understand why she thought this man would know something else, but she did. I knew no purpose would be served by letting her know I'd picked up on her secret, so I smiled at her and told Stan, without turning to look at him, "She can go. I've gotten everything."

I absorbed the look of relief on Bethany's face before I turned to look at Stan. I was sure he realized I had something up my sleeve, and I didn't want him to say anything. Who can tell what a vampire is thinking when the vamp is being guarded? But I had the distinct feeling Stan understood me.

He didn't speak out loud, but another vampire came in, a girl who'd been about Bethany's age when she went over. Stan had made a good choice. The girl leaned over Bethany, took her hand, smiled with fangs fully retracted, and said, "We'll take you home now, okay?"

"Oh, great!" Bethany's relief was written in neon on her forehead. "Oh, great," she said again, less certainly. "Ah, you really are going to my house? You . . ."

But the vampire had looked directly into Bethany's eyes and now she said, "You won't remember anything about today or this evening except the party."

"Party?" Bethany's voice sounded sluggish. Only mildly curious.

"You went to a party," the vampire said as she led Bethany from the room. "You went to a great party, and you met a cute guy there. You've been with him." She was still murmuring to Bethany as they went out. I hoped she was giving her a good memory.

"What?" Stan asked, when the door shut behind the two.

"Bethany thought the club bouncer would know more. She watched him go into the men's room right on the heels of your friend Farrell and the vampire you didn't know." What *I* didn't know, and hardly liked to ask Stan, was whether vampires ever had sex with each other. Sex and food were so tied together in the vampire life system that I couldn't imagine a vampire having sex with someone nonhuman, that is, someone he couldn't get blood from. Did vampires ever take blood from each other in noncrisis situations? I knew if a vampire's life was at stake (har de har) another vampire would donate blood to revive the damaged one, but I had never heard of another situation involving blood exchange. I hardly liked to ask Stan. Maybe I'd broach the subject with Bill, when we got out of this house.

"What you uncovered in her mind was that Farrell was at the bar, and that he went into the toilet room with another vampire, a young male with long blond hair and many tattoos," Stan summarized. "The bouncer went into the toilet while the two were in there."

"Correct."

There was a sizeable pause while Stan made up his mind about what to do next. I waited, delighted not to hear one word of his inner debate. No flashes, no glimpses.

At least such momentary glimpses into a vampire mind were extremely rare. And I'd never had one from Bill; I hadn't known it was possible for some time after I'd been introduced to the vampiric world. So his company remained pure pleasure to me. It was possible, for the first time in my life, to have a normal relationship with a male. Of course, he wasn't a *live* male, but you couldn't have everything.

As if he knew I'd been thinking of him, I felt Bill's hand on my shoulder. I put my own over it, wishing I could get up and give him a full-length hug. Not a good idea in front of Stan. Might make him hungry.

"We don't know the vampire who went in with Farrell," Stan said, which seemed a little bit of an answer after all that thinking. Maybe he'd imagined giving me a longer explanation, but decided I wasn't smart enough to understand the answer. I would rather be underestimated than overrated any day. Besides, what real difference did it make? But I filed my question away under facts I needed to know.

"So, who's the bouncer at the Bat's Wing?"

"A man called Re-Bar," Stan said. There was a trace of distaste in the way he said it. "He is a fangbanger."

So Re-Bar had his dream job. Working with vampires, working for vampires, and being around them every night. For someone who had gotten fascinated by the undead, Re-Bar had hit a lucky streak. "What could he do if a vampire got rowdy?" I asked, out of sheer curiosity.

"He was only there for the human drunks. We found that a vampire bouncer tended to overuse his strength."

I didn't want to think about that too much. "Is Re-Bar here?"

"It will take a short time," Stan said, without consulting anyone in his entourage. He almost certainly had some kind of mind contact with them. I'd never seen that before, and I was sure Eric couldn't approach Bill mentally. It must be Stan's special gift.

While we waited, Bill sat down in the chair next to me. He reached over and took my hand. I found it very comforting, and loved Bill for it. I kept my mind relaxed, trying to maintain energy for the questioning ahead. But I was beginning to frame some worries, very serious worries, about the situation of the vampires of Dallas. And I was concerned about the glimpse I'd had of the bar patrons, especially the man I'd thought I recognized.

"Oh, no," I said sharply, suddenly recalling where I'd seen him. The vampires shot to full alert. "What, Sookie?" Bill asked.

Stan looked like he'd been carved from ice. His eyes actually glowed green, I wasn't just imagining it.

I stumbled all over my words in my haste to explain what I was thinking. "The priest," I told Bill. "The man that ran away at the airport, the one who tried to grab me. He was at the bar." The different clothes and setting had fooled me when I was deep into Bethany's memory, but now I was sure.

"I see," Bill said slowly. Bill seems to have almost total recall, and I could rely on him to have the man's face imprinted in his memory.

"I didn't think he was really a priest then, and now I know he was at the bar the night Farrell vanished," I said. "Dressed in regular clothes. Not, ah, the white collar and black shirt."

There was a pregnant pause.

Stan said, delicately, "But this man, this pretend priest, at the bar, even with two human companions, he could not have taken Farrell if Farrell didn't want to go."

I looked directly down at my hands and didn't say one word. I didn't want to be the one to say this out loud. Bill, wisely, didn't speak either. At last, Stan Davis, head vampire of Dallas, said, "Someone went in the bathroom with Farrell, Bethany recalled. A vampire I didn't know."

I nodded, keeping my gaze directed elsewhere.

"Then this vampire must have helped to abduct Farrell."

"Is Farrell gay?" I asked, trying to sound as if my question had just oozed out of the walls.

"He prefers men, yes. You think—"

"I don't think a thing." I shook my head emphatically, to let him know how much I wasn't thinking. Bill squeezed my fingers. Ouch.

The silence was tense until the teenage-looking vamp returned with a burly human, one I'd seen in Bethany's memories. He didn't look like Bethany saw him, though; through her eyes, he was more robust, less fat; more glamorous, less unkempt. But he was recognizable as Re-Bar.

It was apparent to me immediately that something was wrong with the man. He followed after the girl vamp readily enough, and he smiled at everyone in the room; but that was off, wasn't it? Any human who sensed vampire trouble would be worried, no matter how clear his conscience. I got up and went over to him. He watched me approach with cheerful anticipation.

"Hi, buddy," I said gently, and shook his hand. I dropped it as soon as I decently could. I took a couple of steps back. I wanted to take some Advil and lie down.

"Well," I said to Stan, "he sure enough has a hole in his head."

Stan examined Re-Bar's skull with a skeptical eye. "Explain," he said.

"How ya doin', Mr. Stan?" Re-Bar asked. I was willing to bet no one had ever spoken to Stan Davis that way, at least not in the past five hundred years or so.

"I'm fine, Re-Bar. How are you?" I gave Stan credit for keeping it calm and level.

"You know, I just feel great," Re-Bar said, shaking his head in wonderment. "I'm the luckiest sumbitch on earth—'scuse me, lady."

"You're excused." I had to force the words out.

Bill said, "What has been done to him, Sookie?"

"He's had a hole burned in his head," I said. "I don't know how else to explain it, exactly. I can't tell how it was done, because I've never seen it before, but when I look in his thoughts, his memories, there's just a big old ragged hole. It's like Re-Bar needed a tiny tumor removed, but the surgeon took his spleen and maybe his appendix, too, just to be sure. You know when y'all take away someone's memory, you replace it with another one?" I waved a hand to show I meant all vampires. "Well, someone took a chunk out of Re-Bar's mind, and didn't replace it with anything. Like a lobotomy," I added, inspired. I read a lot. School was tough for me with my little problem, but reading by myself gave me a means of escape from my situation. I guess I'm self-educated.

"So whatever Re-Bar knew about Farrell's disappearance is lost," Stan said.

"Yep, along with a few components of Re-Bar's personality and a lot of other memories."

"Is he still functional?"

"Why, yeah, I guess so." I'd never encountered anything like this, never even realized it was possible. "But I don't know how effective a bouncer he'll be," I said, trying to be honest.

"He was hurt while he was working for us. We'll take care of him. Maybe he can clean the club after it closes," Stan said. I could tell from Stan's voice that he wanted to be sure I was marking this down mentally; that vampires could be compassionate, or at least fair.

"Gosh, that would be great!" Re-Bar beamed at his boss. "Thanks, Mr. Stan."

"Take him back home," Mr. Stan told his minion. She departed directly, with the lobotomized man in tow.

"Who could've done such a crude job on him?" Stan wondered. Bill did not reply, since he wasn't there to stick his neck out, but to guard me and do his own detecting when it was required. A tall red-haired female vampire came in, the one who'd been at the bar the night Farrell was taken.

"What did you notice the evening Farrell vanished?" I asked her, without thinking about protocol. She snarled at me, her white teeth standing out against her dark tongue and brilliant lipstick.

Stan said, "Cooperate." At once her face smoothed out, all expression vanishing like wrinkles in a bedspread when you run your hand over it.

"I don't remember," she said finally. So Bill's ability to recall what he'd seen in minute detail was a personal gift. "I don't remember seeing Farrell more than a minute or two."

"Can you do the same thing to Rachel that you did to the barmaid?" Stan asked.

"No," I said immediately, my voice maybe a little too emphatic. "I can't read vampire minds at all. Closed books."

Bill said, "Can you remember a blond—one of us—who looks about sixteen years old? One with ancient blue tattooing on his arms and torso?"

"Oh, yes," red-haired Rachel said instantly. "The tattoos were from the time of the Romans, I think. They were crude but interesting. I wondered about him, because I hadn't seen him coming here to the house to ask Stan for hunting privileges."

So vamps passing through someone else's territory were required to sign in at the visitors' center, so to speak. I filed that away for future reference.

"He was with a human, or at least had some conversation with him," the red-haired vampire continued. She was wearing blue jeans and a green sweater that looked incredibly hot to me. But vamps don't worry about the actual temperature. She looked at Stan, then Bill, who made a beckoning gesture to indicate he wanted whatever memories she had. "The human was dark-haired, and had a mustache, if I am recalling him correctly." She made a gesture with her hands, an open-fingered sweep that seemed to say, "They're all so much alike!"

After Rachel left, Bill asked if there was a computer in the house. Stan said there was, and looked at Bill with actual curiosity when Bill asked if he could use it for a moment, apologizing for not having his laptop. Stan nodded. Bill was about to leave the room when he hesitated and looked back at me. "Will you be all right, Sookie?" he asked.

"Sure." I tried to sound confident.

Stan said, "She will be fine. There are more people for her to see."

I nodded, and Bill left. I smiled at Stan, which is what I do when I'm strained. It's not a happy smile, but it's better than screaming.

"You and Bill have been together for how long?" Stan asked.

"For a few months." The less Stan knew about us, the happier I'd be.

"You are content with him?"

"Yes."

"You love him?" Stan sounded amused.

"None of your business," I said, grinning. "Did you mention there were more people I needed to check?"

Following the same procedure I had with Bethany, I held a variety of hands and checked a boring bunch of brains. Bethany had definitely been the most observant person in the bar. These people—another barmaid, the human bartender, and a frequent patron (a fangbanger) who'd actually volunteered for this—had dull boring thoughts and limited powers of recollection. I did find out the bartender fenced stolen household goods on the side, and after the guy had left, I recommended to Stan that he get another employee behind the bar, or he'd be sucked into any police investigation. Stan seemed more impressed by this than I hoped he'd be. I didn't want him to get too enamored of my services.

Bill returned as I finished up the last bar employee, and he looked just a little pleased, so I concluded he'd been successful. Bill had been spending most of his waking hours on the computer lately, which had not been too popular an idea with me.

"The tattooed vampire," Bill said when Stan and I were the only two left in the room, "is named Godric, though for the past century he's gone by Godfrey. He's a renouncer." I don't know about Stan, but I was impressed. A few minutes on the computer, and Bill had done a neat piece of detective work.

Stan looked appalled, and I suppose I looked puzzled.

"He's allied himself with radical humans. He plans to commit sui-cide," Bill told me in a soft voice, since Stan was wrapped in thought. "This Godfrey plans to meet the sun. His existence has turned sour on him."

"So he's gonna take someone with him?" Godfrey would expose Farrell along with himself?

"He has betrayed us to the Fellowship," Stan said.

Betrayed is a word that packs a lot of melodrama, but I didn't dream of smirking when Stan said it. I'd heard of the Fellowship, though I'd never met anyone who claimed to actually belong to it. What the Klan was to African Americans, the Fellowship of the Sun was to vampires. It was the fastest-growing cult in America.

Once again, I was in deeper waters than I could swim in.

Chapter 5

THERE WERE LOTS of humans who hadn't liked discovering they shared the planet with vampires. Despite the fact that they had always done so—without knowing it—once they believed that vampires were real, these people were bent on the vampires' destruction. They weren't any choosier about their methods of murder than a rogue vampire was about his.

Rogue vampires were the backward-looking undead; they hadn't wanted to be made known to humans any more than the humans wanted to know about them. Rogues refused to drink the synthetic blood that was the mainstay of most vampires' diets these days. Rogues believed the only future for vampires lay in a return to secrecy and invisibility. Rogue vampires would slaughter humans for the fun of it, now, because they actually welcomed a return of persecution of their own kind. Rogues saw it as a means of persuading mainstream vampires that secrecy was best for the future of their kind; and then, too, persecution was a form of population control.

Now I learned from Bill that there were vampires who became afflicted with terrible remorse, or perhaps ennui, after a long life. These renouncers planned to "meet the sun," the vampire term for committing suicide by staying out past daybreak.

Once again, my choice of boyfriend had led me down paths I never would have trod otherwise. I wouldn't have needed to know any of this, would never have even dreamed of dating someone definitely deceased, if I hadn't been born with the disability of telepathy. I was kind of a pariah to human guys. You can imagine how impossible it is to date someone whose mind you can read. When I met Bill, I began the happiest time of my life. But I'd undoubtedly encountered more trouble in the months I'd known him than I had in my entire twenty-five years previously. "So, you're thinking Farrell is already dead?" I asked, forcing myself to focus on the current crisis. I hated to ask, but I needed to know.

"Maybe," Stan said after a long pause.

"Possibly they're keeping him somewhere," said Bill. "You know how they invite the press to these . . . ceremonies."

Stan stared into space for a long moment. Then he stood. "The same man was in the bar and at the airport," he said, almost to himself. Stan, the geeky head vampire of Dallas, was pacing now, up and down the room. It was making me nuts, though saying so was out of the question. This was Stan's house, and his "brother" was missing. But I'm not one for long, brooding silences. I was tired, and I wanted to go to bed.

"So," I said, doing my best to sound brisk, "how'd they know I was going to be there?"

If there's anything worse than having a vampire stare at you, it's having two vampires stare at you.

"To know you were coming ahead of time . . . there is a traitor," Stan said. The air in the room began to tremble and crackle with the tension he was producing.

But I had a less dramatic idea. I picked up a notepad lying on the table and wrote, "MAYBE YOU'RE BUGGED." They both glared at me as if I'd offered them a Big Mac. Vampires, who individually have incredible and various powers, are sometimes oblivious to the fact that humans have developed some powers of their own. The two men gave each other a look of speculation, but neither of them offered any practical suggestion.

Well, to heck with them. I'd only seen this done in movies, but I figured if someone had planted a bug in this room, they'd done it in a hurry and they'd been scared to death. So the bug would be close and not well hidden. I shrugged off the gray jacket and kicked off my shoes. Since I was a human and had no dignity to lose in Stan's eyes, I dropped below the table and began crawling down its length, pushing the rolling chairs away as I went. For about the millionth time, I wished I'd worn slacks.

I'd gotten about two yards from Stan's legs when I saw something odd. There was a dark bump adhering to the underside of the blond wood of the table. I looked at it as closely as I could without a flashlight. It was not old gum.

Having found the little mechanical device, I didn't know what to do. I crawled out, somewhat dustier for the experience, and found myself right at Stan's feet. He held out his hand and I took it reluctantly. Stan pulled gently, or it seemed gently, but suddenly I was on my feet facing him. He wasn't very tall, and I looked more into his eyes than I really wanted. I held up my finger in front of my face to be sure he was paying attention. I pointed under the table.

Bill left the room in a flash. Stan's face grew even whiter, and his eyes blazed. I looked anywhere but directly at him. I didn't want to be the sight filling his eyes while he digested the fact that someone had planted a bug in his audience chamber. He had indeed been betrayed, just not in the fashion he'd expected.

I cast around in my mind for something to do that would help. I beamed at Stan. Reaching up automatically to straighten my ponytail, I realized my hair was still in its roll on the back of my head, though considerably less neat. Fiddling with it gave me a good excuse to look down.

I was considerably relieved when Bill reappeared with Isabel and the dishwashing man, who was carrying a bowl of water. "I'm sorry, Stan," Bill said. "I'm afraid Farrell is already dead, if you go by what we have discovered this evening. Sookie and I will return to Louisiana tomorrow, unless you need us further." Isabel pointed to the table, and the man set the bowl down.

"You might as well," Stan replied, in a voice as cold as ice. "Send me your bill. Your master, Eric, was quite adamant about that. I will have to meet him someday." His tone indicated the meeting would not be pleasant for Eric.

Isabel said abruptly, "You stupid human! You've spilled my drink!" Bill reached past me to snatch the bug from under the table and drop it in the water, and Isabel, walking even more smoothly to keep the water from slopping over the sides of the bowl, left the room. Her companion remained behind.

That had been disposed of simply enough. And it was at least possible that whoever had been listening in had been fooled by that little bit of dialogue. We all relaxed, now that the bug was gone. Even Stan looked a little less frightening.

"Isabel says you have reason to think Farrell might have been abducted by the Fellowship," the man said. "Maybe this young lady and I could go to the Fellowship Center tomorrow, and try to find out if there're plans for any kind of ceremony soon."

Bill and Stan regarded him thoughtfully.

"That's a good idea," Stan said. "A couple would seem less noticeable."

"Sookie?" Bill asked.

"Certainly none of you can go," I said. "I think maybe we could at least get the layout of the place. If you think there's really a chance Farrell's being held there." If I could find out more about the situation at the Fellowship Center, maybe I could keep the vampires from attacking. They sure weren't going to go down to the police station to file a missing persons report to prod the police into searching the Center. No matter how much the Dallas vampires wanted to remain within the boundaries of human law so they could successfully reap the benefits of mainstreaming, I knew that if a Dallas vampire was being held captive in the Center, humans would die right, left, and sideways. I could maybe prevent that from happening, and locate the missing Farrell, too.

"If this tattooed vampire is a renouncer and plans to meet the sun, taking Farrell with him, and if this is being arranged through the Fellowship, then this pretend priest who tried to grab you at the airport must work for them. They know you now," Bill pointed out. "You would have to wear your wig." He smiled with gratification. The wig had been his idea.

A wig in this heat. Oh, hell. I tried not to look petulant. After all, it would be better to have an itchy head than to be identified as a woman who associated with vampires, while I was visiting a Fellowship of the Sun Center. "It would be better if there were another human with me," I admitted, sorry as I was to involve anyone else in danger.

"This is Isabel's current man," Stan said. He was silent for a minute, and I guessed he was "beaming" at her, or however he contacted his underlings.

Sure enough, Isabel glided in. It must be handy, being able to summon people like that. You wouldn't need an intercom, or a telephone. I wondered how far away other vamps could be and still receive his message. I was kind of glad Bill couldn't signal me without words, because I'd feel too much like his slave girl. Could Stan summon humans the way he called his vamps? Maybe I didn't really want to know.

The man reacted to Isabel's presence the way a bird dog does when he senses quail. Or maybe it was more like a hungry man who gets served a big steak, and then has to wait for grace. You could almost see his mouth water. I hoped I didn't look like that when I was around Bill.

"Isabel, your man has volunteered to go with Sookie to the Fellowship of the Sun Center. Can he be convincing as a potential convert?"

"Yes, I think he can," Isabel said, staring into the man's eyes.

"Before you go—are there visitors this evening?"

"Yes, one, from California."

"Where is he?"

"In the house."

"Has he been in this room?" Naturally, Stan would love the bug-planter to be a vamp or human he didn't know.

"Yes."

"Bring him."

A good five minutes later, Isabel returned with a tall blond vampire in tow. He must have been six foot four, or maybe even more. He was brawny, clean-shaven, and he had a mane of wheat-colored hair. I looked down at my feet immediately, just as I sensed Bill going immobile.

Isabel said, "This is Leif."

"Leif," Stan said smoothly, "welcome to my nest. This evening we have a problem here."

I stared at my toes, wishing more than I'd ever wished anything that I could be completely alone with Bill for two minutes and find out what the hell was going on, because this vampire wasn't any "Leif," and he wasn't from California.

It was Eric.

Bill's hand came into my line of vision and closed around mine. He gave my fingers a very careful little squeeze, and I returned it. Bill slid his arm around me, and I leaned against him. I needed to relax, by golly.

"How may I help you?" Eric—no, Leif, for the moment—asked courteously.

"It seems that someone has entered this room and performed an act of spying."

That seemed a nice way to put it. Stan wanted to keep the bugging a secret for right now, and in view of the fact that there surely was a traitor here, that was probably a great idea.

"I am a visitor to your nest, and I have no problem with you or any of yours."

Leif's calm and sincere denial was quite impressive, given that I knew for a fact that his whole presence was an imposture to further some unfathomable vampire purpose.

"Excuse me," I said, sounding as frail and human as I possibly could.

Stan looked quite irritated at the interruption, but screw him.

"The, uh, item, would have had to be put in here earlier than today," I said, trying to sound like I was sure Stan had already thought of this fact. "To get the details of our arrival in Dallas."

Stan was staring at me with no expression whatsoever.

In for a penny, in for a pound. "And excuse me, but I am really worn out. Could Bill take me back to the hotel now?"

"We will have Isabel take you back by yourself," Stan said dismissively.

"No, sir."

Behind the fake glasses, Stan's pale eyebrows flew up. "No?" He sounded as though he'd never heard the word.

"By the terms of my contract, I don't go anywhere without a vampire from my area. Bill is that vampire. I go nowhere without him, at night."

Stan gave me another good long stare. I was glad I had found the bug and proved myself useful otherwise, or I wouldn't last long in Stan's bailiwick. "Go," he said, and Bill and I didn't waste any time. We couldn't help Eric if Stan came to suspect him, and we might quite possibly give him away. I would be by far the more likely to do that by some word or gesture, with Stan watching me. Vampires have studied humans for centuries, in the way predators learn as much as they can about their prey.

Isabel came out with us, and we got back into her Lexus for the ride back to the Silent Shore Hotel. The streets of Dallas, though not empty, were at least much quieter than when we'd arrived at the nest hours earlier. I estimated it was less than two hours until dawn.

"Thank you," I said politely when we pulled under the porte cochere of the hotel.

"My human will come to get you at three o'clock in the afternoon," Isabel told me.

Repressing the urge to say, "Yes, ma'am!" and click my heels together, I just told her that would be fine. "What's his name?" I asked.

"His name is Hugo Ayres," she said.

"Okay." I already knew that he was a quick man with an idea. I went into the lobby and waited for Bill. He was only seconds behind me, and we went up in the elevator in silence.

"Do you have your key?" he asked me at the room door.

I had been half-asleep. "Where's yours?" I asked, none too graciously.

"I'd just like to see you recover yours," he said.

Suddenly I was in a better mood. "Maybe you'd like to find it," I suggested.

A male vampire with a waist-length black mane strolled down

the hall, his arm around a plump girl with a head of curly red hair. When they'd entered a room farther down the hall, Bill began searching for the key.

He found it pretty fast.

Once we'd gotten inside, Bill picked me up and kissed me at length. We needed to talk, since a lot had happened during this long night, but I wasn't in the mood and he wasn't, either.

The nice thing about skirts, I discovered, was that they just slide up, and if you were only wearing a thong underneath, it could vanish in a jiffy. The gray jacket was on the floor, the white shell was discarded, and my arms were locked around Bill's neck before you could say, "Screw a vampire."

Bill was leaning against the sitting room wall trying to open his slacks with me still wrapped around him when there was a knock at the door.

"Damn," he whispered in my ear. "Go away," he said, somewhat louder. I wriggled against him and his breath caught in his throat. He pulled the bobby pins and the Hairagami out of my hair to let it roll down my back.

"I need to talk to you," said a familiar voice, somewhat muffled by the thick door.

"No," I moaned. "Say it isn't Eric." The only creature in the world we *had* to admit.

"It's Eric," said the voice.

I unlocked my legs from around Bill's waist, and he gently lowered me to the floor. In a real snit, I stomped into the bedroom to put on my bathrobe. To hell with rebuttoning all those clothes.

I came back out as Eric was telling Bill that Bill had done well this evening.

"And, of course, you were marvelous, Sookie," Eric said, taking in the pink, short bathrobe with a comprehensive glance. I looked up at him—and up, and up—and wished him at the bottom of the Red River, spectacular smile, golden hair, and all.

"Oh," I said malignantly, "thanks so much for coming up to tell us this. We couldn't have gone to bed without a pat on the back from *you.*"

Eric looked as blandly delighted as he possibly could. "Oh, dear," he said. "Did I interrupt something? Would these—well, this—be yours, Sookie?" He held up the black string that had formerly been one side of my thong.

Bill said, "In a word, yes. Is there anything else you would like to discuss with us, Eric?" Ice would've been surprised by how cold Bill could sound.

"We haven't got time tonight," Eric said regretfully, "since daylight is so soon, and there are things I need to see to before I sleep. But to-morrow night we must meet. When you find out what Stan wants you to do, leave me a note at the desk, and we'll make an arrangement."

Bill nodded. "Good-bye, then," he said.

"You don't want a nightcap?" Was he hoping to be offered a bot-tle of blood? Eric's eyes went to the refrigerator, then to me. I was sorry I was wearing a thin nylon robe instead of something bulky and chenille. "Warm from the vessel?" Bill maintained a stony silence.

His gaze lingering on me until the last minute, Eric stepped through the door and Bill locked it behind him.

"You think he's listening outside?" I asked Bill, as he untied the sash of my robe.

"I don't care," Bill said, and bent his head to other things.

WHEN I GOT up, about one o'clock in the afternoon, the hotel had a silent feel to it. Of course, most of the guests were sleeping. Maids would not come into a room during the day. I had noted the security last night—vampire guards. The daytime would be different, since daytime guarding was what the guests were paying so heavily for. I called room service for the first time in my life and ordered breakfast. I was as hungry as a horse, since I hadn't eaten last night at all. I was showered and wrapped up in my robe when the waiter knocked on the door, and after I'd made sure he was who he said he was, I let him in.

After my attempted abduction at the airport the day before, I wasn't taking anything for granted. I held the pepper spray down by my side as the young man laid out the food and the coffeepot. If he took one step toward the door behind which Bill slept in his coffin, I would zap him. But this fellow, Arturo, had been well trained, and his eyes never even strayed toward the bedroom. He never looked di-rectly at me, either. He was thinking about me, though, and I wished I'd put on a bra before I let him in.

When he'd gone—and as Bill had instructed me, I added a tip to the room ticket I signed—I ate everything he'd brought: sausage and pancakes and a bowl of melon balls. Oh gosh, it tasted good. The syrup was real maple syrup, and the fruit was just ripe enough. The sausage was wonderful. I was glad Bill wasn't around to watch and make me feel uncomfortable. He didn't really like to see me eat, and he hated it if I ate garlic.

I brushed my teeth and hair and got my makeup situated. It was time to prepare for my visit to the Fellowship Center. I sectioned my hair and pinned it up, and got the wig out of its box. It was short and brown and really undistinguished. I had thought Bill was nuts when he'd suggested I get a wig, and I still wondered why it had occurred to him I might need one, but I was glad to have it. I had a pair of glasses like Stan's, serving the same camouflaging purpose, and I put them on. There was a little magnification in the bottom part, so I could legitimately claim they were reading glasses.

What did fanatics wear to go to a fanatic gathering place? In my limited experience, fanatics were usually conservative in dress, either because they were too preoccupied with other concerns to think about it or because they saw something evil in dressing stylishly. If I'd been at home I'd have run to Wal-Mart and been right on the money, but I was here in the expensive, windowless Silent Shores. However, Bill had told me to call the front desk for anything I needed. So I did.

"Front desk," said a human who was trying to copy the smooth cool voice of an older vampire. "How may I help you?" I felt like telling him to give it up. Who wants an imitation when the real thing is under the roof?

"This is Sookie Stackhouse in three-fourteen. I need a long denim skirt, size eight, and a pastel flowered blouse or knit top, same size."

"Yes, ma'am," he said, after a longish pause. "When shall I have those for you?"

"Soon." Gee, this was a lot of fun. "As a matter of fact, the sooner the better." I was getting into this. I loved being on someone else's expense account.

I watched the news while I waited. It was the typical news of any American city: traffic problems, zoning problems, homicide problems.

"A woman found dead last night in a hotel Dumpster has been identified," said a newscaster, his voice appropriately grave. He bent down the corners of his mouth to show serious concern. "The body of twenty-one-year-old Bethany Rogers was found behind the Silent Shore Hotel, famous for being Dallas's first hotel catering to the undead. Rogers had been killed by a single gunshot wound to the head. Police described the murder as 'execution-style.' Detective Tawny Kelner told our reporter that police are following up several leads." The screen image shifted from the artificially grim face to a genuinely grim one. The detective was in her forties, I thought, a very short woman with a long braid down her back. The camera shot swiveled to include the reporter, a small dark man with a sharply tailored suit. "Detective Kelner, is it true that Bethany Rogers worked at a vampire bar?"

The detective's frown grew even more formidable. "Yes, that's true," she said. "However, she was employed as a waitress, not an entertainer." An entertainer? What did entertainers do at the Bat's Wing? "She had only been working there a couple of months."

"Doesn't the site used to dump her body indicate that there's some kind of vampire involvement?" The reporter was more persistent than I would've been.

"On the contrary, I believe the site was chosen to send a message to the vampires," Kelner snapped, and then looked as if she regretted speaking. "Now, if you'll excuse me . . ."

"Of course, detective," the reporter said, a little dazed. "So, Tom," and he turned to face the camera, as if he could see through it back to the anchor in the station, "that's a provocative issue."

Huh?

The anchor realized the reporter wasn't making any sense, too, and quickly moved to another topic.

Poor Bethany was dead, and there wasn't anyone I could discuss that with. I pushed back tears; I hardly felt I had a right to cry for the girl. I couldn't help but wonder what had happened to Bethany Rogers last night after she'd been led from the room at the vampire nest. If there'd been no fang marks, surely a vampire hadn't killed her. It would be a rare vampire who could pass up the blood.

Sniffling from repressed tears and miserable with dismay, I sat on the couch and hunted through my purse to find a pencil. At last, I unearthed a pen. I used it to scratch up under the wig. Even in the air-conditioned dark of the hotel, it itched. In thirty minutes, there was a knock at the door. Once again, I looked through the peephole. There was Arturo again, with garments draped across his arm.

"We'll return the ones you don't want," he said, handing me the bundle. He tried not to stare at my hair.

"Thanks," I said, and tipped him. I could get used to this in a hurry.

It wasn't long until I was supposed to be meeting the Ayres guy, Isabel's honey bun. Dropping the robe where I stood, I looked at what Arturo'd brought me. The pale peachy blouse with the off-white flowers, that would do, and the skirt . . . hmmm. He hadn't been able to find denim, apparently, and the two he'd brought were khaki. That would be all right, I figured, and I pulled one on. It looked too tight for the effect I needed, and I was glad he'd brought another style. It was just right for the image. I slid my feet into flat sandals, put some tiny earrings in my pierced ears, and I was good to go. I even had a battered straw purse to carry with the ensemble. Unfortunately, it was my regular purse. But it fit right in. I dumped out my identifying items, and wished I had thought of that earlier instead of at the last minute. I wondered what other crucial safety measures I might have forgotten.

I stepped out into the silent corridor. It was exactly as it had been the night before. There were no mirrors and no windows, and the feeling of enclosure was complete. The dark red of the carpet and the federal blue, red, and cream of the wallpaper didn't help. The elevator snicked open when I touched the call button, and I rode down by myself. No elevator music, even. The Silent Shore was living up to its name.

There were armed guards on either side of the elevator, when I reached the lobby. They were looking at the main doors to the hotel. Those doors were obviously locked. There was a television set mounted by the doors, and it showed the sidewalk outside of the doors. Another television set showed a wider view.

I thought a terrible attack must be imminent and I froze, my heart racing, but after a few seconds of calm I figured out they must be there all the time. This was why vampires stayed here, and at other similar specialty hotels. No one would get past these guards to the elevators. No one would make it into the hotel rooms where sleeping and helpless vampires lay. This was why the fee for the hotel was exorbitant. The two guards on duty at the moment were both huge, and wearing the black livery of the hotel. (Ho, hum. Everyone seemed to think vampires were obsessed with black.) The guards' sidearms seemed gigantic to me, but then, I'm not too familiar with guns. The men glanced at me and then went back to their bored forward stare.

Even the desk clerks were armed. There were shotguns on racks behind the counter. I wondered how far they would go to protect their guests. Would they really shoot other humans, intruders? How would the law handle it?

A man wearing glasses sat in one of the padded chairs that punctuated the marble floor of the lobby. He was about thirty, tall and lanky, with sandy hair. He was wearing a suit, a lightweight summer khaki suit, with a conservative tie and penny loafers. The dishwasher, sure enough.

"Hugo Ayres?" I asked.

He sprang up to shake my hand. "You must be Sookie? But your hair . . . last night, you were blond?"

"I am. I'm wearing a wig."

"It looks very natural."

"Good. Are you ready?"

"My car's outside." He touched my back briefly to point me in the right direction, as if I wouldn't see the doors otherwise. I appreciated the courtesy, if not the implication. I was trying to get a feel for Hugo Ayres. He wasn't a broadcaster.

"How long have you been dating Isabel?" I asked as we buckled up in his Caprice.

"Ah, um, I guess about eleven months," Hugo Ayres said. He had big hands, with freckles on the back. I was surprised he wasn't living in the suburbs with a wife with streaked hair and two sandy children.

"Are you divorced?" I asked impulsively. I was sorry when I saw the grief cross his face.

"Yes," he said. "Pretty recently."

"Too bad." I started to ask about the children, decided it was none of my business. I could read him well enough to know he had a little girl, but I couldn't discover her name and age.

"Is it true you can read minds?" he asked.

"Yes, it's true."

"No wonder you're so attractive to them."

Well, *ouch,* Hugo. "That's probably a good part of the reason," I said, keeping my voice flat and even. "What's your day job?"

"I'm a lawyer," Hugo said.

"No wonder you're so attractive to them," I said, in the most neutral voice I could manage.

After a longish silence, Hugo said, "I guess I deserved that."

"Let's move on past it. Let's get a cover story."

"Could we be brother and sister?"

"That's not out of the question. I've seen brother and sister teams that looked less like each other than we do. But I think boyfriend-girlfriend would account for the gaps in our knowledge of each other more, if we get separated and questioned. I'm not predicting that'll happen, and I'd be amazed if it did, but as brother and sister we'd have to know all about each other."

"You're right. Why don't we say that we met at church? You just moved to Dallas, and I met you in Sunday school at Glen Craigie Methodist. That's actually my church."

"Okay. How about I'm manager of a . . . restaurant?" From working at Merlotte's, I thought I could be convincing in the role if I wasn't questioned too intensively.

He looked a little surprised. "That's just different enough to sound good. I'm not much of an actor, so if I just stick to being me, I'll be okay."

"How did you meet Isabel?" Of course I was curious.

"I represented Stan in court. His neighbors sued to have the vampires barred from the neighborhood. They lost." Hugo had mixed feelings about his involvement with a vampire woman, and wasn't entirely sure he should've won the court case, either. In fact, Hugo was deeply ambivalent about Isabel.

Oh, good, that made this errand much more frightening. "Did that get in the papers? The fact that you represented Stan Davis?"

He looked chagrined. "Yes, it did. Dammit, someone at the Center might recognize my name. Or me, from my picture being in the papers."

"But that might be even better. You can tell them you saw the error of your ways, after you'd gotten to know vampires."

Hugo thought that over, his big freckled hands moving restlessly on the steering wheel. "Okay," he said finally. "Like I said, I'm not much of an actor, but I think I can bring that off."

I acted all the time, so I wasn't too worried about myself. Taking a drink order from a guy while pretending you don't know whether he's speculating on whether you're blond all the way down can be excellent acting training. You can't blame people—mostly—for what they're thinking on the inside. You have to learn to rise above it.

I started to suggest to the lawyer that he hold my hand if things got tense today, to send me thoughts that I could act on. But his ambivalence, the ambivalence that wafted from him like a cheap cologne, gave me pause. He might be in sexual thrall to Isabel, he might even love her and the danger she represented, but I didn't think his heart and mind were wholly committed to her.

In an unpleasant moment of self-examination, I wondered if the same could be said of Bill and me. But now was not the time and place to ponder this. I was getting enough from Hugo's mind to wonder if he were completely trustworthy in terms of this little mission of ours. It was just a short step from there to wondering how safe I was in his company. I also wondered how much Hugo Ayres actually knew about me. He hadn't been in the room when I'd been working the night before. Isabel hadn't struck me as a chatterer. It was possible he didn't know much about me.

The four-lane road, running through a huge suburb, was lined with all the usual fast-food places and chain stores of all kinds. But gradually, the shopping gave way to residences, and the concrete to greenery. The traffic seemed unrelenting. I could never live in a place this size, cope with this on a daily basis.

Hugo slowed and put on his turn signal when we came to a major intersection. We were about to turn into the parking lot of a large church; at least, it had formerly been a church. The sanctuary was huge, by Bon Temps standards. Only Baptists could count that kind of attendance, in my neck of the woods, and that's if all their congregations joined together. The two-story sanctuary was flanked by two long one-story wings. The whole building was white-painted brick, and all the windows were tinted. There was a chemically green lawn surrounding the whole, and a huge parking lot.

The sign on the well-tended lawn read THE FELLOWSHIP OF THE SUN CENTER—Only Jesus Rose from the Dead.

I snorted as I opened my door and emerged from Hugo's car. "That right there is false," I pointed out to my companion. "Lazarus rose from the dead, too. Jerks can't even get their scripture right."

"You better banish that attitude from your head," Hugo warned me, as he got out and hit the lock button. "It'll make you careless. These people are dangerous. They've accepted responsibility, publicly, for handing over two vampires to the Drainers, saying at least humanity can benefit from the death of a vampire in some way."

"They deal with Drainers?" I felt sick. Drainers followed an extremely hazardous profession. They trapped vampires, wound them around with silver chains, and drained the blood from them for sale on the black market. "These people in here have handed over vampires to the Drainers?"

"That's what one of their members said in a newspaper interview. Of course, the leader was on the news the next day, denying the report vehemently, but I think that was just smokescreen. The Fellowship kills vampires any way they can, thinks they're unholy and an abomination, and they're capable of anything. If you're a vampire's best friend, they can bring tremendous pressure to bear. Just remember that, every time you open your mouth in here."

"You, too, Mr. Ominous Warning."

We walked to the building slowly, looking it over as we went. There were about ten other cars in the parking lot, ranging from aging and dented to brand new and upscale. My favorite was a pearly white Lexus, so nice it might almost have belonged to a vampire.

"Someone's doing well out of the hate business," Hugo observed. "Who's the head of this place?"

"Guy named Steve Newlin."

"Bet this is his car."

"That would account for the bumper sticker."

I nodded. It read TAKE THE *UN* OUT OF *UNDEAD*. Dangling from the mirror inside was a replica—well, maybe a replica—of a stake.

This was a busy place, for a Saturday afternoon. There were children using the swing set and jungle gym in a fenced yard to the side of the building. The kids were being watched by a bored teenager, who looked up every now and then from picking at his nails. Today was not as hot as the day before—summer was losing its doomed last stand, and thank God for that—and the door of the building was propped open to take advantage of the beautiful day and moderate temperature.

Hugo took my hand, which made me jump until I realized he was trying to make us look loverlike. He had zero interest in me personally, which was fine with me. After a second's adjustment we managed to look fairly natural. The contact made Hugo's mind just that more open to me, and I could tell that he was anxious but resolute. He found touching me distasteful, which was a little bit too strong a feeling for me to feel comfortable about; lack of attraction was peachy, but this actual distaste made me uneasy. There was something behind that feeling, some basic attitude . . . but there were people ahead of us, and I pulled my mind back to my job. I could feel my lips pull into their smile.

Bill had been careful to leave my neck alone last night, so I didn't have to worry about concealing any fang marks, and in my new outfit and on this lovely day it was easier to look carefree as we nodded at a middle-aged couple who were on their way out.

We passed into the dimness of the building, into what must have been the Sunday school wing of the church. There were fresh signs outside the rooms up and down the corridor, signs that read BUDGETING AND FINANCE, ADVERTISING, and most ominously, MEDIA RELATIONS.

A woman in her forties came out of a door farther down the hall, and turned to face us. She looked pleasant, even sweet, with lovely skin and short brown hair. Her definitely pink lipstick matched her definitely pink fingernails, and her lower lip was slightly pouty, which gave her an unexpectedly sensuous air; it sat with odd provocation on her pleasantly round body. A denim skirt and a knit shirt, neatly tucked in, were the echo of my own outfit, and I patted myself on the back mentally.

"Can I help you?" she asked, looking hopeful.

"We want to find out more about the Fellowship," Hugo said, and he seemed every bit as nice and sincere as our new friend. She had on a nametag, I noticed, which read S. NEWLIN.

"We're glad you're here," she said. "I'm the wife of the director, Steve Newlin? I'm Sarah?" She shook hands with Hugo, but not with me. Some women don't believe in shaking hands with another woman, so I didn't worry about it.

We exchanged pleasedtomeetyou's, and she waved a manicured

hand toward the double doors at the end of the hall. "If you'll just come with me, I'll show you where we get things done." She laughed a little, as if the idea of meeting goals was a touch ludicrous.

All of the doors in the hall were open, and within the rooms there was evidence of perfectly open activity. If the Newlins' organization was keeping prisoners or conducting covert ops, it was accomplishing its goals in some other part of the building. I looked at everything as hard as I could, determined to fill myself with information. But so far the interior of the Fellowship of the Sun was as blindingly clean as the outside, and the people hardly seemed sinister or devious.

Sarah covered ground ahead of us with an easy walk. She clutched a bundle of file folders to her chest and chattered over her shoulder as she moved at a pace that seemed relaxed, but actually was a bit challenging. Hugo and I, abandoning the handholding, had to step out to keep up.

This building was proving to be far larger than I'd estimated. We'd entered at the far end of one wing. Now we crossed the large sanctuary of the former church, set up for meetings like any big hall, and we passed into the other wing. This wing was divided into fewer and larger rooms; the one closest to the sanctuary was clearly the office of the former pastor. Now it had a sign on the door that read G. STEVEN NEWLIN, DIRECTOR.

This was the only closed door I'd seen in the building.

Sarah knocked and, having waited for a moment, entered. The tall, lanky man behind the desk stood to beam at us with an air of pleased expectancy. His head didn't seem quite big enough for his body. His eyes were a hazy blue, his nose was on the beaky side, and his hair was almost the same dark brown as his wife's, with a threading of gray. I don't know what I'd been expecting in a fanatic, but this man was not it. He seemed a little amused by his own life.

He'd been talking to a tall woman with iron gray hair. She was wearing a pair of slacks and a blouse, but she looked as if she'd have been more comfortable in a business suit. She was formidably made up, and she was less than pleased about something—maybe our interruption.

"What can I do for you today?" Steve Newlin asked, indicating that Hugo and I should be seated. We took green leather armchairs pulled up opposite his desk, and Sarah, unasked, plopped down in a smaller chair that was against the wall on one side. "Excuse me, Steve," she said to her husband. "Listen, can I get you two some coffee? Soda?"

Hugo and I looked at each other and shook our heads.

"Honey, this is—oh, I didn't even ask your names?" She looked at us with charming ruefulness.

"I'm Hugo Ayres, and this is my girlfriend, Marigold."

Marigold? Was he *nuts?* I kept my smile pasted on my face with an effort. Then I saw the pot of marigolds on the table beside Sarah, and at least I could understand his selection. We'd certainly made a large mistake already; we should have talked about this on the drive over. It stood to reason that if the Fellowship was responsible for the bug, the Fellowship knew the name of Sookie Stackhouse. Thank God Hugo had figured that out.

"Don't we know Hugo Ayres, Sarah?" Steve Newlin's face had the perfect quizzical expression—brow slightly wrinkled, eyebrows raised inquiringly, head tilted to one side.

"Ayres?" said the gray-haired woman. "By the way, I'm Polly Blythe, the Fellowship ceremonies officer."

"Oh, Polly, I'm sorry, I got sidetracked." Sarah tilted her head right back. Her forehead wrinkled, too. Then it smoothed out and she beamed at her husband. "Wasn't an Ayres the lawyer representing the vampires in University Park?"

"So he was," Steve said, leaning back in his chair and crossing his long legs. He waved to someone passing by in the corridor and wrapped his laced fingers around his knee. "Well, it's very interesting that you're paying us a call, Hugo. Can we hope that you've seen the other side of the vampire question?" Satisfaction rolled off Steve Newlin like scent off a skunk.

"It's appropriate that you should put it that way—" Hugo began, but Steve's voice just kept rolling on:

"The bloodsucking side, the dark side of vampire existence? Have you found that they want to kill us all, dominate us with their foul ways and empty promises?"

I knew my eyes were as round as plates. Sarah was nodding thoughtfully, still looking as sweet and bland as a vanilla pudding. Polly looked as if she were having some really grim kind of orgasm. Steve said—and he was still smiling—"You know, eternal life on this earth may sound good, but you'll lose your soul and eventually, when we catch up with you—maybe not me, of course, maybe my son, or eventually my granddaughter—we'll stake you and burn you and then you'll be in true hell. And it won't be any the better for having been put off. God has a special corner for vampires who've used up humans like toilet tissue and then flushed . . ."

Well, ick. This was going downhill in a hurry. And what I was getting off of Steve was just this endless, gloating satisfaction, along with a heavy dash of cleverness. Nothing concrete or informative.

"Excuse me, Steve," said a deep voice. I swiveled in my chair to see a handsome black-haired man with a crewcut and a bodybuilder's muscles. He smiled at all of us in the room with the same goodwill they were all showing. It had impressed me earlier. Now, I thought it was just creepy. "Our guest is asking for you."

"Really? I'll be there in a minute."

"I wish you would come now. I'm sure your guests wouldn't mind waiting?" Black Crewcut glanced at us appealingly. Hugo was thinking of some deep place, a flash of thought which seemed very peculiar to me.

"Gabe, I'll be there when I've finished with our visitors," Steve said very firmly.

"Well, Steve . . ." Gabe wasn't willing to give up that easily, but he got a flash from Steve's eyes and Steve sat up and uncrossed his legs, and Gabe got the message. He shot Steve a look that was anything but worshipful, but he left.

That exchange was promising. I wondered if Farrell was behind some locked door, and I could picture myself returning to the Dallas nest, telling Stan exactly where his nest brother was trapped. And then . . .

Uh-oh. And then Stan would come and attack the Fellowship of the Sun and kill all the members and free Farrell, and then . . .

Oh dear.

"WE JUST WANTED to know if you have some upcoming events we can attend, something that'll give us an idea of the scope of the programs here." Hugo's voice sounded mildly inquiring, nothing more. "Since Miss Blythe is here, maybe she can answer that."

I noticed Polly Blythe glanced at Steve before she spoke, and I noticed that his face remained shuttered. Polly Blythe was very pleased to be asked to give information, and she was very pleased about Hugo and me being there at the Fellowship.

"We do have some upcoming events," the gray-haired woman said. "Tonight, we're having a special lock-in, and following that, we have a Sunday dawn ritual."

"That sounds interesting," I said. "Literally, at dawn?"

"Oh, yes, exactly. We call the weather service and everything," Sarah said, laughing.

Steve said, "You'll never forget one of our dawn services. It's inspiring beyond belief."

"What kind of—well, what happens?" Hugo asked.

"You'll see the evidence of God's power right before you," Steve said, smiling.

That sounded really, really ominous. "Oh, Hugo," I said. "Doesn't that sound exciting?"

"It sure does. What time does the lock-in start?"

"At six-thirty. We want our members to get here before *they* rise."

For a second I envisioned a tray of rolls set in some warm place. Then I realized Steve meant he wanted members to get here before the vampires rose for the night.

"But what about when your congregation goes home?" I could not refrain from asking.

"Oh, you must not have gone to a lock-in as a teenager!" Sarah said. "It's loads of fun. Everyone comes and brings their sleeping bags, and we eat and have games and Bible readings and a sermon, and we all spend the night actually in the church." I noticed that the Fellowship was a church, in Sarah's eyes, and I was pretty sure that reflected the view of the rest of the management. If it looked like a church, and functioned like a church, then it was a church, no matter what its tax status was.

I'd been to a couple of lock-ins as a teenager, and I'd scarcely been able to endure the experience. A bunch of kids locked in a building all night, closely chaperoned, provided with an endless stream of movies and junk food, activities and sodas. I had suffered through the mental bombardment of teenage hormone-fueled ideas and impulses, the shrieking and the tantrums.

This would be different, I told myself. These would be adults, and purposeful adults, at that. There weren't likely to be a million bags of chips around, and there might be decent sleeping arrangements. If Hugo and I came, maybe we'd get a chance to search around the building and rescue Farrell, because I was sure that he was the one who was going to get to meet the dawn on Sunday, whether or not he got to choose.

Polly said, "You'd be very welcome. We have plenty of food and cots."

Hugo and I looked at each other uncertainly.

"Why don't we just go tour the building now, and you can see all there is to see? Then you can make up your minds," Sarah suggested. I took Hugo's hand, got a wallop of ambivalence. I was filled with dismay at Hugo's torn emotions. He thought, *Let's get out of here.*

I jettisoned my previous plans. If Hugo was in such turmoil, we didn't need to be here. Questions could wait until later. "We should go back to my place and pack our sleeping bags and pillows," I said brightly. "Right, baby?"

"And I've got to feed the cat," Hugo said. "But we'll be back here at . . . six-thirty, you said?"

"Gosh, Steve, don't we have some bedrolls left in the supply room? From when that other couple came to stay here for a while?"

"We'd love to have you stay until everyone gets here," Steve urged us, his smile as radiant as ever. I knew we were being threatened, and I knew we needed to get out, but all I was receiving from the Newlins psychically was a wall of determination. Polly Blythe seemed to actually be almost—gloating. I hated to push and probe, now that I was aware they had some suspicion of us. If we could just get out of here right now, I promised myself I'd never come back. I'd give up this detecting for the vampires, I'd just tend bar and sleep with Bill.

"We really do need to go," I said with firm courtesy. "We are so impressed with you all here, and we want to come to the lock-in tonight, but there is still enough time before then for us to get some of our errands done. You know how it is when you work all week. All those little things pile up."

"Hey, they'll still be there when the lock-in ends tomorrow!" Steve said. "You need to stay, both of you."

There wasn't any way to get out of here without dragging everything out into the open. And I wasn't going to be the first one to do that, not while there was any hope left we could get out. There were lots of people around. We turned left when we came out of Steve Newlin's office, and with Steve ambling behind us, and Polly to our right, and Sarah ahead of us, we went down the hall. Every time we passed an open door, someone inside would call, "Steve, can I see you for a minute?" or "Steve, Ed says we have to change the wording on this!" But aside from a blink or a minor tremor in his smile, I could not see much reaction from Steve Newlin to these constant demands.

I wondered how long this movement would last if Steve were removed. Then I was ashamed of myself for thinking this, because what I meant was, if Steve were killed. I was beginning to think either Sarah or Polly would be able to step into his shoes, if they were allowed, because both seemed made of steel.

All the offices were perfectly open and innocent, if you considered the premise on which the organization was founded to be innocent. These all looked like average, rather cleaner-cut-than-normal, Americans, and there were even a few people who were non-Caucasian.

And one nonhuman.

We passed a tiny, thin Hispanic woman in the hall, and as her eyes flicked over to us, I caught a mental signature I'd only felt once before. Then, it came from Sam Merlotte. This woman, like Sam, was a shapeshifter, and her big eyes widened as she caught the waft of "difference" from me. I tried to catch her gaze, and for a minute we stared at each other, me trying to send her a message, and her trying not to receive it.

"Did I tell you the first church to occupy this site was built in the early sixties?" Sarah was saying, as the tiny woman went on down the hall at a fast clip. She glanced back over her shoulder, and I met her eyes again. Hers were frightened. Mine said, "Help."

"No," I said, startled at the sudden turn in the conversation.

"Just a little bit more," Sarah coaxed. "We'll have seen the whole church." We'd come to the last door at the end of the corridor. The corresponding door on the other wing had led to the outside. The wings had seemed to be exactly balanced from the outside of the church. My observations had obviously been faulty, but still . . .

"It's certainly a large place," said Hugo agreeably. Whatever ambivalent emotions had been plaguing him seemed to have subsided. In fact, he no longer seemed at all concerned. Only someone with no psychic sense at all could fail to be worried about this situation.

That would be Hugo. No psychic sense at all. He looked only interested when Polly opened the last door, the door flat at the end of the corridor. It should have led outside.

Instead, it led down.

Chapter 6

"You know, I have a touch of claustrophobia," I said instantly. "I didn't know many Dallas buildings had a basement, but I have to say, I just don't believe I want to see it." I clung to Hugo's arm and tried to smile in a charming but self-deprecating way.

Hugo's heart was beating like a drum because he was scared shitless—I'll swear he was. Faced with those stairs, somehow his calm was eroding again. What was with Hugo? Despite his fear, he gamely patted my shoulder and smiled apologetically at our companions. "Maybe we should go," he murmured.

"But I really think you should see what we've got underground. We actually have, a bomb shelter," Sarah said, almost laughing in her amusement. "And it's fully equipped, isn't it, Steve?"

"Got all kinds of things down there," Steve agreed. He still looked relaxed, genial, and in charge, but I no longer saw those as benign characteristics. He stepped forward, and since he was behind us, I had to step forward or risk him touching me, which I found I very much did not want.

"Come on," Sarah said enthusiastically. "I'll bet Gabe's down here, and Steve can go on and see what Gabe wanted while we look at the rest of the facility." She trotted down the stairs as quickly as she'd moved down the hall, her round butt swaying in a way I probably would have considered cute if I hadn't been just on the edge of terrified.

Polly waved us down ahead of her, and down we went. I was going along with this because Hugo seemed absolutely confident that no harm would come to him. I was picking that up very clearly. His earlier fear had completely abated. It was as though he'd resigned himself to some program, and his ambivalence had vanished. Vainly, I wished he were easier to read. I turned my focus on Steve Newlin, but what I got from him was a thick wall of self-satisfaction.

We moved farther down the stairs, despite the fact that my steps had slowed, and then become slower again. I could tell Hugo was convinced that he would get to walk back up these stairs: after all, he was a civilized person. These were all civilized people.

Hugo really couldn't imagine that anything irreparable could happen to him, because he was a middle-class white American with a college education, as were all the people on the stairs with us.

I had no such conviction. I was not a wholly civilized person.

That was a new and interesting thought, but like many of my ideas that afternoon, it had to be stowed away, to be explored at leisure. If I ever had leisure again.

At the base of the stairs there was another door, and Sarah knocked on it in a pattern. Three fast, skip, two fast, my brain recorded. I heard locks shooting back.

Black Crewcut—Gabe—opened the door. "Hey, you brought me some visitors," he said enthusiastically. "Good show!" His golf shirt was tucked neatly into his pleated Dockers, his Nikes were new and spotless, and he was shaved as clean as a razor could get. I was willing to bet he did fifty push-ups every morning. There was an undercurrent of excitement in his every move and gesture; Gabe was really pumped about something.

I tried to "read" the area for life, but I was too agitated to concentrate.

"I'm glad you're here, Steve," Gabe said. "While Sarah is showing our visitors the shelter, maybe you can give our guest room a look-see." He nodded his head to the door in the right side of the narrow concrete hall. There was another door at the end of it, and a door to the left.

I hated it down here. I had pleaded claustrophobia to get out of this. Now that I had been coerced into coming down the stairs, I was finding that it was a true failing of mine. The musty smell, the glare of the artificial light, and the sense of enclosure . . . I hated it all. I didn't want to stay here. My palms broke out in a sweat. My feet felt anchored to the ground. "Hugo," I whispered. "I don't want to do this." There was very little act in the desperation in my voice. I didn't like to hear it, but it was there.

"She really needs to get back upstairs," Hugo said apologetically. "If you all don't mind, we'll just go back up and wait for you there."

I turned around, hoping this would work, but I found myself

looking up into Steve's face. He wasn't smiling anymore. "I think you two need to wait in the other room over there, until I'm through with my business. Then, we'll talk." His voice brooked no discussion, and Sarah opened the door to disclose a bare little room with two chairs and two cots.

"No," I said, "I can't do that," and I shoved Steve as hard as I could. I am very strong, very strong indeed, since I've had vampire blood, and despite his size, he staggered. I nipped up the stairs as fast as I could move, but a hand closed around my ankle, and I fell most painfully. The edges of the stairs hit me everywhere, across my left cheekbone, my breasts, my hipbones, my left knee. It hurt so much I almost gagged.

"Here, little lady," said Gabe, hauling me to my feet.

"What have you—how could you hurt her like that?" Hugo was sputtering, genuinely upset. "We come here thinking of joining your group, and this is the way you treat us?"

"Drop the act," Gabe advised, and he twisted my arm behind my back before I had gotten my wits back from the fall. I gasped with the new pain, and he propelled me into the room, at the last minute grabbing my wig and yanking it off my head. Hugo stepped in behind me, though I gasped, *"No!"* and then they shut the door behind him.

And we heard it lock.

And that was that.

"Sookie," HUGO SAID, "there's a dent across your cheekbone."

"No shit," I muttered weakly.

"Are you badly hurt?"

"What do you think?"

He took me literally. "I think you have bruises and maybe a concussion. You didn't break any bones, did you?"

"Not but one or two," I said.

"And you're obviously not hurt badly enough to cut out the sarcasm," Hugo said. If he could be angry with me, it would make him feel better, I could tell, and I wondered why. But I didn't wonder too hard. I was pretty sure I knew.

I was lying on one of the cots, an arm across my face, trying to keep private and do some thinking. We hadn't been able to hear much happening in the hall outside. Once I thought I'd heard a door opening, and we'd heard muted voices, but that was all. These walls were built to withstand a nuclear blast, so I guess the quiet was to be expected.

"Do you have a watch?" I asked Hugo.

"Yes. It's five-thirty."

A good two hours until the vampires rose.

I let the quiet go on. When I knew hard-to-read Hugo must have relapsed into his own thoughts, I opened my mind and I listened with complete concentration.

Not supposed to happen like this, don't like this, surely everything'll be okay, what about when we need to go to the bathroom, I can't haul it out in front of her, maybe Isabel won't ever know, I should have known after that girl last night, how can I get out of this still practicing law, if I begin to distance myself after tomorrow maybe I can kind of ease out of it . . .

I pressed my arm against my eyes hard enough to hurt, to stop myself from jumping up and grabbing a chair and beating Hugo Ayres senseless. At present, he didn't fully understand my telepathy, and neither did the Fellowship, or they wouldn't have left me in here with him.

Or maybe Hugo was as expendable to them as he was to me. And he certainly would be to the vampires; I could hardly wait to tell Isabel that her boy toy was a traitor.

That sobered up my bloodlust. When I realized what Isabel would do to Hugo, I realized that I would take no real satisfaction in it if I witnessed it. In fact, it would terrify me and sicken me.

But part of me thought he richly deserved it.

To whom did this conflicted lawyer owe fealty?

One way to find out.

I sat up painfully, pressed my back against the wall. I would heal pretty fast—the vampire blood, again—but I was still a human, and I still felt awful. I knew my face was badly bruised, and I was willing to believe my cheekbone was fractured. The left side of my face was swelling something fierce. But my legs weren't broken, and I could still run, given the chance; that was the main thing.

Once I was braced and as comfortable as I was going to get, I said, "Hugo, how long have you been a traitor?"

He flushed an incredible red. "To whom? To Isabel, or to the human race?"

"Take your pick."

"I betrayed the human race when I took the side of the vampires in court. If I'd had any idea of what they were . . . I took the case sight unseen, because I thought it would be an interesting legal challenge. I have always been a civil rights lawyer, and I was convinced vampires had the same civil rights as other people."

Mr. Floodgates. "Sure," I said.

"To deny them the right to live anywhere they wanted to, that was un-American, I thought," Hugo continued. He sounded bitter and world-weary.

He hadn't *seen* bitter, yet.

"But you know what, Sookie? Vampires aren't American. They aren't even black or Asian or Indian. They aren't Rotarians or Baptists. They're all just plain vampires. That's their color and their religion and their nationality."

Well, that was what happened when a minority went underground for thousands of years. Duh.

"At the time, I thought if Stan Davis wanted to live on Green Valley Road, or in the Hundred-Acre Wood, that was his right as an American. So I defended him against the neighborhood association, and I won. I was real proud of myself. Then I got to know Isabel, and I took her to bed one night, feeling real daring, really the big man, the emancipated thinker."

I stared at him, not blinking or saying a word.

"As you know, the sex is great, the best. I was in thrall to her, couldn't get enough. My practice suffered. I started seeing clients only in the afternoon, because I couldn't get up in the morning. I couldn't make my court dates in the morning. I couldn't leave Isabel after dark."

This sounded like an alcoholic's tale, to me. Hugo had become addicted to vampiric sex. I found the concept fascinating and repellent.

"I started doing little jobs she found for me. This past month, I've been going over there and doing the housekeeping chores, just so I can hang around Isabel. When she wanted me to bring the bowl of water into the dining room, I was excited. Not at doing such a menial task—I'm a *lawyer*, for God's sake! But because the Fellowship had called me, asked me if I could give them any insight into what the vampires of Dallas intended to do. At the time they called, I was mad at Isabel. We'd had a fight about the way she treated me. So I was open to listening to them. I'd heard your name pass between Stan and Isabel, so I passed it on to the Fellowship. They have a guy who works for Anubis Air. He found out when Bill's plane was coming in, and they tried to grab you at the airport so they could find out what the vamps wanted with you. What they'd do to get you back. When I came in with the bowl of water, I heard Stan or Bill call you by name, so I knew they'd missed you at the airport. I felt like I had something to tell them, to make up for losing the bug I'd put in the conference room."

"You betrayed Isabel," I said. "And you betrayed me, though I'm human, like you."

"Yes," he said. He didn't look me in the eyes.

"What about Bethany Rogers?"

"The waitress?"

He was stalling. "The dead waitress," I said.

"They took her," he said, shaking his head from side to side, as if he were actually saying, No, they couldn't have done what they did. "They took her, and I didn't know what they were going to do. I knew she was the only one who'd seen Farrell with Godfrey, and I'd told them that. When I got up today and I heard she'd been found dead, I just couldn't believe it."

"They abducted her after you told them she'd been at Stan's. After you told them she was the only true witness."

"Yes, they must have."

"You called them last night."

"Yes, I have a cell phone. I went out in the backyard and I called. I was really taking a chance, because you know how well the vamps can hear, but I called." He was trying to convince himself that had been a brave, bold thing to do. Place a phone call from vamp headquarters to lay the finger on poor, pathetic Bethany, who'd ended up shot in an alley.

"She was shot after you betrayed her."

"Yes, I . . . I heard that on the news."

"Guess who did that, Hugo."

"I . . . just don't know."

"Sure you do, Hugo. She'd been an eyewitness. And she was a lesson, a lesson to the vampires. 'This is what we'll do to people who work for you or make their living from you, if they go against the Fellowship.' What do you think they're going to do with you, Hugo?"

"I've been helping them," he said, surprised.

"Who else knows that?"

"No one."

"So who would die? The lawyer that helped Stan Davis live where he wanted."

Hugo was speechless.

"If you're so all-fired important to them, how come you're in this room with me?"

"Because up until now, you didn't know what I'd done," he

pointed out. "Up until now, it was possible you would give me other information we could use against them."

"So now, now that I know what you are, they'll let you out. Right? Why don't you try it and see? I'd much rather be alone."

Just then a small aperture in the door opened. I hadn't even known it was there, having been preoccupied while I was out in the hall. A face appeared at the opening, which measured perhaps ten inches by ten inches.

It was a familiar face. Gabe, grinning. "How you doing in there, you two?"

"Sookie needs a doctor," Hugo said. "She's not complaining, but I think her cheekbone is broken." He sounded reproachful. "And she knows about my alliance with the Fellowship, so you might as well let me out."

I didn't know what Hugo thought he was doing, but I tried to look as beaten as possible. That was pretty easy.

"I have me an idea," Gabe said. "I've gotten kind of bored down here, and I don't expect Steve or Sarah—or even old Polly—will be coming back down here any time soon. We got another prisoner over here, Hugo, might be glad to see you. Farrell? You meet him over at the headquarters of the Evil Ones?"

"Yes," said Hugo. He looked very unhappy about this turn of the conversation.

"You know how fond Farrell's gonna be of you? And he's gay, too, a queer bloodsucker. We're so deep underground that he's been waking up early. So I thought I might just put you in there with him, while I have me a little fun with the female traitor, here." And Gabe smiled at me in a way that made my stomach lurch.

Hugo's face was a picture. A real picture. Several things crossed my mind, pertinent things to say. I forewent the doubtful pleasure. I needed to save my energy.

One of my Gran's favorite adages popped into my mind irresistibly as I looked at Gabe's handsome face. "Pretty is as pretty does," I muttered, and began the painful process of getting to my feet to defend myself. My legs might not be broken, but my left knee was surely in bad shape. It was already badly discolored and swollen.

I wondered if Hugo and I together could take Gabe down when he opened the door, but as soon as it swung outward, I saw he'd armed himself with a gun and a black, menacing-looking object I decided might be a stun gun.

"Farrell!" I called. If he were awake, he'd hear me; he was a vampire.

Gabe jumped, looked at me suspiciously.

"Yes?" came a deep voice from the room farther down the hall. I heard chains clink as the vampire moved. Of course, they'd have to chain him with silver. Otherwise he could rip the door off its hinges.

"Stan sent us!" I yelled, and then Gabe backhanded me with the hand that held the gun. Since I was against the wall, my head bounced off it. I made an awful noise, not quite a scream but too loud for a moan.

"Shut up, bitch!" Gabe screamed. He was pointing the gun at Hugo and had the stun gun held at the ready a few inches from me. "Now, Lawyer, you get out here in the hall. Keep away from me, you hear?"

Hugo, sweat pouring down his face, edged past Gabe and into the hall. I was having a hard time tracking what was happening, but I noticed that in the narrow width Gabe had to maneuver, he came very close to Hugo on his way to open Farrell's cell. Just when I thought he was far enough down the hall for me to make it, he told Hugo to close my cell door, and though I frantically shook my head at Hugo, he did so.

I don't think Hugo even saw me. He was turned completely inward. Everything inside him was collapsing, his thoughts were in chaos. I'd done my best for him by telling Farrell we were from Stan, which in Hugo's case was stretching it considerably, but Hugo was too frightened or disillusioned or ashamed to show any backbone. Considering his deep betrayal, I was very surprised I'd bothered. If I hadn't held his hand and seen the images of his children, I wouldn't have.

"There's nothing to you, Hugo," I said. His face reappeared at the still-open window momentarily, his face white with distress of all kinds, but then he vanished. I heard a door open, I heard the clink of chains, and I heard a door close.

Gabe had forced Hugo into Farrell's cell. I took deep breaths, one right after another, until I felt I might hyperventilate. I picked up one of the chairs, a plastic one with four metal legs, the kind you've sat on a million times in churches and meetings and classrooms. I held it liontamer style, with the legs facing outward. It was all I could think of to do. I thought of Bill, but that was too painful. I thought of my brother, Jason, and I wished he were there with me. It had been a long time since I'd wished that about Jason.

The door opened. Gabe was already smiling as he came in. It was a nasty smile, letting all the ugliness leak out of his soul through his mouth and eyes. This really was his idea of a good time.

"You think that little chair is going to keep you safe?" he asked.

I wasn't in the mood for talking, and I didn't want to listen to the snakes in his mind. I closed myself off, contained myself tightly, bracing myself.

He'd holstered the gun, but kept the stun gun in his hand. Now, such was his confidence, he put it in a little leather pouch on his belt, on the left side. He seized the legs of the chair and began to yank the chair from side to side.

I charged.

I almost had him out the door, so unexpected was my strong counterattack, but at the last minute he managed to twist the legs sideways, so that they couldn't pass through the narrow doorway. He stood against the wall on the other side of the hall, panting, his face red.

"Bitch," he hissed, and came at me again, and this time he tried to pull the chair out of my hands altogether. But as I've said before, I've had vampire blood, and I didn't let him have it. And I didn't let him have me.

Without my seeing it, he'd drawn the stun gun and, quick as a snake, he reached over the chair and touched it to my shoulder.

I didn't collapse, which he expected, but I went down on my knees, still holding the chair. While I was still trying to figure out what had happened to me, he yanked the chair from my hands, and knocked me backwards.

I could hardly move, but I could scream and lock my legs together, and I did.

"Shut up!" he yelled, and since he was touching me, I could tell that he really wanted me unconscious, he would enjoy raping me while I was unconscious; in fact, that was his ideal.

"Don't like your women awake," I panted, "do you?" He stuck a hand between us and yanked open my blouse.

I heard Hugo's voice, yelling, as if that would do any good. I bit at Gabe's shoulder.

He called me a bitch again, which was getting old. He'd opened his own pants, now he was trying to pull up my skirt. I was fleetingly glad I'd bought a long one.

"You afraid they'll complain, if they're awake?" I yelled. "Let me go, get off me! Get off, get off, *get off!*" Finally, I'd unpinned my arms. In a moment, they'd recovered enough from the electric jolt to function. I formed two cups with my hands. As I screamed at him, I clapped my hands over his ears.

He roared, and reared back, his own hands going to his head. He was so full of rage it escaped him and washed over me; it felt like bathing in fury. I knew then that he would kill me if he could, no matter what reprisals he faced. I tried to roll to one side, but he had me pinned with his legs. I watched as his right hand formed a fist, which seemed as big as a boulder to me. And with a sense of doom, I watched the arc of that fist as it descended to my face, knowing this one would knock me out and it would be all over. . . .

And it didn't happen.

Up in the air Gabe went, pants open and dick hanging out, his fist landing on air, his shoes kicking at my legs.

A short man was holding Gabe up in the air; not a man, I realized at second glance, a teenager. An ancient teenager.

He was blond and shirtless, and his arms and chest were covered with blue tattoos. Gabe was yelling and flailing, but the boy stood calmly, his face expressionless, until Gabe ran down. By the time Gabe was silent, the boy had transferred his grip to a kind of bear hug encircling Gabe's waist, and Gabe was hanging forward.

The boy looked down at me dispassionately. My blouse had been torn open, and my bra was ripped down the middle.

"Are you badly hurt?" the boy asked, almost reluctantly.

I had a savior, but not an enthusiastic one.

I stood up, which was more of a feat than it sounds. It took me quite a while. I was trembling violently from the emotional shock. When I was upright, I was on an eye level with the boy. In human years, he would've been about sixteen when he'd been made vampire. There was no telling how many years ago that had been. He must be older than Stan, older than Isabel. His English was clear, but heavily accented. I had no idea what kind of accent it was. Maybe his original language was not even spoken anymore. What a lonely feeling that would be.

"I'll mend," I said. "Thank you." I tried to rebutton my blouse—there were a few remaining buttons—but my hands were shaking too badly. He wasn't interested in seeing my skin, anyway. It didn't do a thing for him. His eyes were quite dispassionate.

"Godfrey," Gabe said. His voice was thready. "Godfrey, she was trying to escape."

Godfrey shook him, and Gabe shut up.

So, Godfrey was the vampire I'd seen through Bethany's eyes—the only eyes that could remember seeing him at the Bat's Wing that evening. The eyes that were no longer seeing anything.

"What do you intend to do?" I asked him, keeping my voice quiet and even.

Godfrey's pale blue eyes flickered. He didn't know.

He'd gotten the tattoos while he was alive, and they were very strange, symbols whose meaning had been lost centuries ago, I was willing to bet. Probably some scholar would give his eyeteeth to have a look at those tattoos. Lucky me, I was getting to see them for nothing.

"Please let me out," I said with as much dignity as I could muster. "They'll kill me."

"But you consort with vampires," he said.

My eyes darted from one side to another, as I tried to figure this one out.

"Ah," I said hesitantly. "You're a vampire, aren't you?"

"Tomorrow I atone for my sin publicly," Godfrey said. "Tomorrow I greet the dawn. For the first time in a thousand years, I will see the sun. Then I will see the face of God."

Okay. "You chose," I said.

"Yes."

"But I didn't. I don't want to die." I spared a glance for Gabe's face, which was quite blue. In his agitation, Godfrey was squeezing Gabe much tighter than he ought to. I wondered if I should say something.

"You do consort with vampires," Godfrey accused, and I switched my gaze back to his face. I knew I'd better not let my concentration wander again.

"I'm in love," I said.

"With a vampire."

"Yes. Bill Compton."

"All vampires are damned, and should all meet the sun. We're a taint, a blot on the face of the earth."

"And these people"—I pointed upward to indicate I meant the Fellowship—"these people are better, Godfrey?"

The vampire looked uneasy and unhappy. He was starving, I noticed; his cheeks were almost concave, and they were as white as paper. His blond hair almost floated around his head, it was so electric, and his eyes looked like blue marbles against his pallor. "They, at least, are human, part of God's plan," he said quietly. "Vampires are an abomination."

"Yet you've been nicer to me than this human." Who was dead, I realized, as I glanced down at his face. I tried not to flinch, and refocused on Godfrey, who was much more important to my future.

"But we take the blood of the innocents." Godfrey's pale blue eyes fixed on mine.

"Who is innocent?" I asked rhetorically, hoping I didn't sound too much like Pontius Pilate asking, What is truth? when he knew damn well.

"Well, children," Godfrey said.

"Oh, you . . . fed on children?" I put my hand over my mouth.

"I killed children."

I couldn't think of a thing to say for a long time. Godfrey stood there, looking at me sadly, holding Gabe's body in his arms, forgotten.

"What stopped you?" I asked.

"Nothing will stop me. Nothing but my death."

"I'm so sorry," I said inadequately. He was suffering, and I was truly sorry for that. But if he'd been human, I'd have said he deserved the electric chair without thinking twice.

"How soon is it until dark?" I asked, not knowing what else to say.

Godfrey had no watch, of course. I assumed he was up only because he was underground and he was very old. Godfrey said, "An hour."

"Please let me go. If you help me, I can get out of here."

"But you will tell the vampires. They will attack. I will be prevented from meeting the dawn."

"Why wait till the morning?" I asked, suddenly irritated. "Walk outside. Do it now."

He was astounded. He dropped Gabe, who landed with a thud. Godfrey didn't even spare him a glance. "The ceremony is planned for dawn, with many believers there to witness it," he explained. "Farrell will also be brought up to face the sun."

"What part would I have played in this?"

He shrugged. "Sarah wanted to see if the vampires would exchange one of their own for you. Steve had other plans. His idea was to lash you to Farrell, so that when he burned, so would you."

I was stunned. Not that Steve Newlin had had the idea, but that he thought it would appeal to his congregation, for that was what they were. Newlin was further over the top than even I had guessed. "And you think lots of people would enjoy seeing that, a young woman executed without any kind of trial? That they would think it was a valid religious ceremony? You think the people who planned this terrible death for me are truly religious?"

For the first time, he seemed a shade doubtful. "Even for humans, that seems a little extreme," he agreed. "But Steve thought it would be a powerful statement."

"Well, sure it would be a powerful statement. It would say, 'I'm nuts.' I know this world has plenty of bad people and bad vampires, but I don't believe the majority of the people in this country, or for that matter just here in Texas, would be edified by the sight of a screaming woman burning to death."

Godfrey looked doubtful. I could see I was voicing thoughts that had occurred to him, thoughts he had denied to himself he was entertaining. "They have called the media," he said. It was like the protest of a bride slated to marry a groom she suddenly doubted. But the invitations have been sent out, Mother.

"I'm sure they have. But it'll be the end of their organization, I can tell you that flat out. I repeat, if you really want to make a statement that way, a big 'I'm sorry,' then you walk out of this church right now and stand on the lawn. God'll be watching, I promise you. That's who you should care about."

He struggled with it; I'll give him that.

"They have a special white robe for me to wear," he said. (But I've already bought the dress and reserved the church.)

"Big damn deal. If we're arguing clothes, you don't really want to do it. I bet you'll chicken out."

I had definitely lost sight of my goal. When the words came out of my mouth, I regretted them.

"You will see," he said firmly.

"I don't want to see, if I'm tied to Farrell at the time. I am not evil, and I don't want to die."

"When was the last time you were in church?" He was issuing me a challenge.

"About a week ago. And I took Communion, too." I was never happier to be a churchgoer, because I couldn't have lied about that.

"Oh." Godfrey looked dumbfounded.

"See?" I felt I was robbing him of all his wounded majesty by this argument, but dammit, I didn't want to die by burning. I wanted Bill, wanted him with a longing so intense I hoped it would pop his coffin open. If only I could tell him what was going on. . . . "Come on," said Godfrey, holding out his hand.

I didn't want to give him a chance to rethink his position, not after this long do-si-do, so I took his hand and stepped over Gabe's prone form out into the hall. There was an ominous lack of conversation from Farrell and Hugo, and to tell the truth, I was too scared to call out to find out what was going on with them. I figured if I could get out, I could rescue them both, anyway.

Godfrey sniffed the blood on me, and his face was swept with longing. I knew that look. But it was devoid of lust. He didn't care a thing for my body. The link between blood and sex is very strong for all vampires, so I considered myself lucky that I was definitely adult in form. I inclined my face to him out of courtesy. After a long hesitation, he licked the trickle of blood from the cut on my cheekbone. He closed his eyes for a second, savoring the taste, and then we started for the stairs.

With a great deal of help from Godfrey, I made it up the steep flight. He used his free arm to punch in a combination on the door, and swung it open. "I've been staying down here, in the room at the end," he explained, in a voice that was hardly more than a disturbance of the air.

The corridor was clear, but any second someone might come out of one of the offices. Godfrey didn't seem to fear that at all, but I did, and I was the one whose freedom was at stake. I didn't hear any voices; apparently the staff had gone home to get ready for the lock-in, and the lock-in guests had not yet started arriving. Some of the office doors were closed, and the windows in the offices were the only means of sunlight getting to the hall. It was dark enough for Godfrey to be comfortable, I assumed, since he didn't even wince. There was bright artificial light coming from under the main office door.

We hurried, or at least tried to, but my left leg was not very cooperative. I wasn't sure what door Godfrey was heading toward, perhaps double doors I'd seen earlier at the back of the sanctuary. If I could get safely out of those, I wouldn't have to traverse the other wing. I didn't know what I'd do when I got outside. But being outside would definitely be better than being inside. Just as we reached the open doorway to the next-to-last office on the left, the one from which the tiny Hispanic woman had come, the door to Steve's office opened. We froze. Godfrey's arm around me felt like an iron band. Polly stepped out, still facing into the room. We were only a couple of yards away.

". . . bonfire," she was saying.

"Oh, I think we've got enough," Sarah's sweet voice said. "If everyone returned their attendance cards, we'd know for sure. I can't believe how bad people are about not replying. It's so inconsiderate, after we made it as easy as possible for them to tell us whether or not they'd be here!"

An argument about etiquette. Gosh, I wished Miss Manners were here to give me advice on this situation. *I was an uninvited guest of a small church, and I left without saying good-bye. Am I obliged to write a thank-you note, or may I simply send flowers?*

Polly's head began turning, and I knew any moment she would

see us. Even as the thought formed, Godfrey pushed me into the dark empty office.

"Godfrey! What are you doing up here?" Polly didn't sound frightened, but she didn't sound happy, either. It was more like she'd found the yardman in the living room, making himself at home.

"I came to see if there is anything more I need to do."

"Isn't it awfully early for you to be awake?"

"I am very old," he said politely. "The old don't need as much sleep as the young."

Polly laughed. "Sarah," she said brightly, "Godfrey's up!"

Sarah's voice sounded closer, when she spoke. "Well, hey, Godfrey!" she said, in an identical bright tone. "Are you excited? I bet you are!"

They were talking to a thousand-year-old vampire like he was a child on his birthday eve.

"Your robe's all ready," Sarah said. "All systems go!"

"What if I changed my mind?" Godfrey asked.

There was a long silence. I tried to breathe very slowly and quietly. The closer it got to dark the more I could imagine I had a chance of getting out of this.

If I could telephone . . . I glanced over at the desk in the office. There was a telephone on it. But wouldn't the buttons in the offices light up, the buttons for that line, if I used the phone? At the moment, it would make too much noise.

"You changed your mind? Can this be possible?" Polly asked. She was clearly exasperated. "You came to us, remember? You told us about your life of sin, and the shame you felt when you killed children and . . . did other things. Has any of this changed?"

"No," Godfrey said, sounding more thoughtful than anything else. "None of this has changed. But I see no need to include any humans in this sacrifice of mine. In fact, I believe that Farrell should be left to make his own peace with God. We shouldn't force him into immolation."

"We need to get Steve back here," Polly said to Sarah in an undertone.

After that, I just heard Polly, so I assumed Sarah had gone back into the office to call Steve.

One of the lights on the phone lit up. Yep, that was what she was doing. She'd know if I tried to use one of the other lines. Maybe in a minute.

Polly was trying sweet reason with Godfrey. Godfrey was not talking much, himself, and I had no idea what was going through his head. I stood helplessly, pressed against the wall, hoping no one would come into the office, hoping no one would go downstairs and raise the alarm, hoping Godfrey wouldn't have yet another change of heart.

Help, I said in my mind. If only I could call for help that way, through my other sense!

A flicker of an idea crossed my mind. I made myself stand calmly, though my legs were still trembling with shock, and my knee and face hurt like the six shades of hell. Maybe I *could* call someone: Barry, the bellboy. He was a telepath, like me. He could be able to hear me. Not that I'd ever made such an attempt before—well, I'd never met another telepath, had I? I tried desperately to locate myself in relation to Barry, assuming he was at work. This was about the same time we'd arrived from Shreveport, so he might be. I pictured my location on the map, which luckily I'd looked up with Hugo—though I knew now that he had been pretending not to know where the Fellowship Center was—and I figured we were southwest of the Silent Shore Hotel.

I was in new mental territory. I gathered up what energy I had and tried to roll it into a ball, in my mind. For a second, I felt absolutely ridiculous, but when I thought of getting free of this place and these people, there was very little to gain in not being ridiculous. I thought to Barry. It's hard to peg down exactly how I did it, but I projected. Knowing his name helped, and knowing his location helped.

I decided to start easy. *Barry Barry Barry Barry . . .*

What do you want? He was absolutely panicked. This had never happened to him before.

I've never done this either. I hoped I sounded reassuring. *I need help. I'm in big trouble.*

Who are you?

Well, that would help. Stupid me. *I'm Sookie, the blond who came in last night with the brown-haired vampire. Third-floor suite.*

The one with the boobs? Oh, sorry.

At least he'd apologized. *Yes. The one with the boobs. And the boyfriend.*

So, what's the matter?

Now, all this sounds very clear and organized, but it wasn't words. It was like we were sending each other emotional telegrams and pictures.

I tried to think how to explain my predicament. *Get my vampire as soon as he wakes.*

And then?

Tell him I'm in danger. Dangerdangerdanger . . .

Okay, I get the idea. Where?

Church. I figured that would be shorthand for the Fellowship Center. I couldn't think how to convey that to Barry.

He knows where?

He knows where. Tell him, Go down the stairs.

Are you for real? I didn't know there was anyone else . . .

I'm for real. Please, help me.

I could feel a complicated bundle of emotions racing through Barry's mind. He was scared of talking to a vampire, he was frightened that his employers would discover he had a "weird brain thing," he was just excited that there was someone like him. But mostly he was scared of this part of him that had puzzled and frightened him for so long.

I knew all those feelings. *It's okay, I understand,* I told him. *I wouldn't ask if I wasn't going to be killed.*

Fear struck him again, fear of his own responsibility in this. I should never have added that.

And then, somehow, he erected a flimsy barrier between us, and I wasn't sure what Barry was going to do.

WHILE I'D BEEN concentrating on Barry, things had been moving right along in the hall. When I began listening again, Steve had returned. He, too, was trying to be reasonable and positive with Godfrey.

"Now, Godfrey," he was saying, "if you didn't want to do this, all you had to do was say so. You committed to it, we all did, and we've moved forward with every expectation that you would keep to your word. A lot of people are going to be very disappointed if you lose your commitment to the ceremony."

"What will you do with Farrell? With the man Hugo, and the blond woman?"

"Farrell's a vampire," said Steve, still the voice of sweet reason. "Hugo and the woman are vampires' creatures. They should go to the sun, too, tied to a vampire. That is the lot they chose in their lives, and it should be their lot in death."

"I am a sinner, and I know it, so when I die my soul will go to God," Godfrey said. "But Farrell does not know this. When he dies, he won't have a chance. The man and woman, too, have not had a chance to repent their ways. Is it fair to kill them and condemn them to hell?"

"We need to go into my office," Steve said decisively.

And I realized, finally, that that was what Godfrey had been aiming for all along. There was a certain amount of foot shuffling, and I heard Godfrey murmur, "After you," with great courtesy.

He wanted to be last so he could shut the door behind him.

My hair finally felt dry, freed from the wig that had drenched it in sweat. It was hanging around my shoulders in separate locks, because I'd been silently unpinning it during the conversation. It had seemed a casual thing to be doing, while listening to my fate being settled, but I had to keep occupied. Now I cautiously pocketed the bobby pins, ran my fingers through the tangled mess, and prepared to sneak out of the church.

I peered cautiously from the doorway. Yes, Steve's door was closed. I tiptoed out of the dark office, took a left, and continued to the door leading into the sanctuary. I turned its knob very quietly and eased it open. I stepped into the sanctuary, which was very dusky. There was just enough light from the huge stained-glass windows to help me get down the aisle without falling over the pews.

Then I heard voices, getting louder, coming from the far wing. The lights in the sanctuary came on. I dove into a row and rolled under the pew. A family group came in, all talking loudly, the little girl whining about missing some favorite show on television because she had to go to the stinky old lock-in.

That got her a slap on the bottom, sounded like, and her father told her she was lucky she was going to get to see such an amazing evidence of the power of God. She was going to see salvation in action.

Even under the circumstances, I took issue with that. I wondered if this father really understood that his leader planned for the congregation to watch two vampires burn to death, at least one of them clutching a human who would also burn. I wondered how the little girl's mental health would fare after that "amazing evidence of the power of God."

To my dismay, they proceeded to put their sleeping bags up against a wall on the far side of the sanctuary, still talking. At least this was a family that communicated. In addition to the whiny little girl, there were two older kids, a boy and a girl, and like true siblings they fought like cats and dogs.

A pair of small flat red shoes trotted by the end of my pew and disappeared through the door into Steve's wing. I wondered if the group in his office was still debating.

The feet went by again after a few seconds, this time going very fast. I wondered about that, too.

I waited about five more minutes, but nothing else happened.

From now on, there would be more people coming in. It was now or never. I rolled out from under the pew and got up. By my good fortune, they were all looking down at their task when I stood up, and I began walking briskly to the double doors at the back of the church. By their sudden silence, I knew they'd spotted me.

"Hi!" called the mother. She rose to her feet beside her bright blue sleeping bag. Her plain face was full of curiosity. "You must be new at the Fellowship. I'm Francie Polk."

"Yes," I called, trying to sound cheerful. "Gotta rush! Talk to you later!"

She drew closer. "Have you hurt yourself?" she asked. "You— excuse me—you look awful. Is that blood?"

I glanced down at my blouse. There were some small stains on my chest.

"I had a fall," I said, trying to sound rueful. "I need to go home and do a little first aid, change my clothes, like that. I'll be back!"

I could see the doubt on Francie Polk's face. "There's a first aid kit in the office, why don't I just run and get that?" she asked.

Because I don't want you to. "You know, I need to get a fresh blouse, too," I said. I wrinkled my nose to show my low opinion of going around in a spotted blouse all evening.

Another woman had come in the very doors I was hoping to go out of, and she stood listening to the conversation, her dark eyes darting back and forth from me to the determined Francie.

"Hey, girl!" she said in a lightly accented voice, and the little Hispanic woman, the shapeshifter, gave me a hug. I come from a hugging culture, and it was automatic to hug her right back. She gave me a meaningful pinch while we were clenched.

"How are you?" I asked brightly. "It's been too long."

"Oh, you know, same old same old," she said. She beamed up at me, but there was caution in her eyes. Her hair was a very dark brown, rather than black, and it was coarse and abundant. Her skin was the color of a milky caramel, and she had dark freckles. Generous lips were painted an outstanding fuchsia. She had big white teeth, flashing at me in her wide smile. I glanced down at her feet. Flat red shoes.

"Hey, come outside with me while I have a cigarette," she said.

Francie Polk was looking more satisfied.

"Luna, can't you see your friend needs to go to the doctor?" she said righteously.

"You do have a few bumps and bruises," Luna said, examining me. "Have you fallen down again, girl?"

"You know Mama always tells me, 'Marigold, you're as clumsy as an elephant.' "

"That mama of yours," Luna said, shaking her head in disgust. "Like that would make you less clumsy!"

"What can you do?" I said, shrugging. "If you'll excuse us, Francie?"

"Well, sure," she said. "I'll see you later, I guess."

"Sure will," said Luna. "I wouldn't miss it for anything."

And with Luna, I strolled out of the Fellowship of the Sun meeting hall. I concentrated ferociously on keeping my gait even, so Francie wouldn't see me limp and become even more suspicious.

"Thank God," I said, when we were outside.

"You knew me for what I was," she said rapidly. "How did you know?"

"I have a friend who's a shapeshifter."

"Who is he?"

"He's not local. And I won't tell you without his consent."

She stared at me, all pretence of friendship dropped in that instant.

"Okay, I respect that," she said. "Why are you here?"

"What's it to you?"

"I just saved your ass."

She had a point, a good point. "Okay. I am a telepath, and I was hired by your vampire area leader to find out what had become of a missing vampire."

"That's better. But it ain't *my* area leader. I'm a supe, but I ain't no freaking vampire. What vamp did you deal with?"

"I don't need to tell you that."

She raised her eyebrows.

"I don't."

She opened her mouth as if to yell.

"Yell away. There're some things I just won't tell. What's a supe?"

"A supernatural being. Now, you listen to me," Luna said. We were walking through the parking lot now, and cars were beginning to pull in regularly from the road. She did a lot of smiling and waving, and I tried to at least look happy. But the limp was no longer concealable, and my face was swelling like a bitch, as Arlene would say.

Gosh, I was homesick all of a sudden. But I thrust that feeling away to pay attention to Luna, who clearly had things to tell me.

"You tell the vampires *we* have this place under surveillance—"

" 'We' being who?"

" 'We' being the shapeshifters of the greater Dallas area."

"You guys are organized? Hey, that's great! I'll have to tell . . . my friend."

She rolled her eyes, clearly not impressed with my intellect. "Listen here, missy, you tell the vampires that as soon as the Fellowship figures out about us, they will be on us, too. And we aren't going to mainstream. We're underground for good. Stupid freakin' vampires. So we're keeping an eye on the Fellowship."

"If you're keeping such a good eye, how come you didn't call the vampires and tell them about Farrell being in the basement? And about Godfrey?"

"Hey, Godfrey wants to kill himself, no skin off our teeth. He came to the Fellowship; they didn't go to him. They about peed their pants, they were so glad to have him, after they got over the shock of sitting in the same room with one of the damned."

"What about Farrell?"

"I didn't know who was down there," Luna admitted. "I knew they'd captured someone, but I'm not exactly in the inner circle yet, and I couldn't find out who. I even tried buttering up that asshole Gabe, but that didn't help."

"You'll be pleased to know that Gabe is dead."

"Hey!" She smiled genuinely for the first time. "That *is* good news."

"Here's the rest. As soon as I get in touch with the vampires, they're going to be here to get Farrell. So if I were you, I wouldn't go back to the Fellowship tonight."

She chewed on her lower lip for a minute. We were at the far end of the parking lot.

"In fact," I said, "it would be perfect if you would give me a lift to the hotel."

"Well, I'm not in the business of making your life perfect," she snarled, recalled to her tough cookie persona. "I got to get back in that church before the shit hits the fan, and get some papers out. Think about this, girl. What are the vampires gonna do with Godfrey? Can they let him live? He's a child molester and a serial killer; so many times over you couldn't even count. He can't stop, and he knows it."

So there was a good side to the church . . . it gave vampires like Godfrey a venue to commit suicide while being watched?

"Maybe they should just put it on pay-per-view," I said.

"They would if they could." Luna was serious. "Those vampires trying to mainstream, they're pretty harsh to anyone who might upset their plan. Godfrey's no poster boy."

"I can't solve every problem, Luna. By the way, my real name is Sookie. Sookie Stackhouse. Anyway, I've done what I could. I did the job I was hired to do, and now I have to get back and report. Godfrey lives or Godfrey dies. I think Godfrey will die."

"You better be right," she said ominously.

I couldn't figure out why it was my fault if Godfrey changed his mind. I had just questioned his chosen venue. But maybe she was right. I might have some responsibility, here.

It was all just too much for me.

"Good-bye," I said, and began limping along the back of the parking lot to the road. I hadn't gotten far when I heard a hue and cry arise from the church, and all the outside lights popped on. The sudden glare was blinding.

"Maybe I won't go back in the Fellowship Center after all. Not a good idea," Luna said from the window of a Subaru Outback. I scrambled into the passenger's seat, and we sped toward the nearest exit onto the four-lane road. I fastened my seat belt automatically.

But as swiftly as we had moved, others had moved even more swiftly. Various family vehicles were being positioned to block the exits from the parking lot.

"Crap," said Luna.

We sat idling for a minute while she thought.

"They'll never let me out, even if we hide you somehow. I can't get you back into the church. They can search the parking lot too easily." Luna chewed on her lip some more.

"Oh, freak this job, anyway," she said, and threw the Outback into gear. She drove conservatively at first, trying to attract as little attention as possible. "These people wouldn't know what religion was if it bit them in the ass," she said. Up by the church, Luna drove over the curb separating the parking lot from the lawn. Then we were flooring it over the lawn, circling the fenced play area, and I discovered I was grinning from ear to ear, though it hurt to do so.

"Yee-hah!" I yelled, as we hit a sprinkler head on the lawn watering system. We flew across the front yard of the church, and, out of sheer shock, no one was pursuing us. They'd organize themselves in a minute, though, the die-hards. Those people who didn't espouse the more extreme measures of this Fellowship were going to get a real wake-up call tonight.

Sure enough, Luna looked in her rearview mirror and said, "They've unblocked the exits, and someone's coming after us." We pulled out into traffic on the road running in front of the church, another major four-lane road, and horns honked all around at our sudden entry into the traffic flow.

"Holy shit," Luna said. She slowed down to a reasonable speed and kept looking in her rearview mirror. "It's too dark now, I can't tell which headlights are them."

I wondered if Barry had alerted Bill.

"You got a cell phone?" I asked her.

"It's in my purse, along with my driver's license, which is still sitting in my office in the church. That's how I knew you were loose. I went in my office, smelled your scent. Knew you'd been hurt. So I went outside and scouted around, and when I couldn't find you, I came back in. We're damn lucky I had my keys in my pocket."

God bless shapeshifters. I felt wistful about the phone, but it couldn't be helped. I suddenly wondered where my purse was. Probably back in the Fellowship of the Sun office. At least I'd taken all my i.d. out of it.

"Should we stop at a pay phone, or the police station?"

"If you call the police, what are they going to do?" asked Luna, in the encouraging voice of someone leading a small child to wisdom.

"Go to the church?"

"And what will happen then, girl?"

"Ah, they'll ask Steve why he was holding a human prisoner?"

"Yep. And what will he say?"

"I don't know."

"He'll say, 'We never held her prisoner. She got into some kind of argument with our employee Gabe, and he ended up dead. Arrest her!' "

"Oh. You think?"

"Yeah, I think."

"What about Farrell?"

"If the police start coming in, you can better believe they've got someone detailed to hustle down to the basement and stake him. By the time the cops get there, no more Farrell. They could do the same to Godfrey, if he wouldn't back them up. He would probably stand still for it. He wants to die, that Godfrey."

"Well, what about Hugo?"

"You think Hugo is going to explain how come he got locked in a basement there? I don't know what that jerk would say, but he won't tell the truth. He's led a double life for months now, and he can't say whether his head is on straight or not."

"So we can't call the police. Who can we call?"

"I got to get you with your people. You don't need to meet mine. They don't want to be known, you understand?"

"Sure."

"You have to be something weird yourself, huh? To recognize us."

"Yes."

"So what are you? Not a vamp, for sure. Not one of us, either."

"I'm a telepath."

"You are! No shit! Well, woooo woooo," Luna said, imitating the traditional ghost sound.

"No more woo woo than you are," I said, feeling I could be pardoned for sounding a bit testy.

"Sorry," she said, not meaning it. "Okay, here's the plan—"

But I didn't get to hear what the plan was, because at that moment we were hit from the rear.

THE NEXT THING I knew, I was hanging upside down in my seat belt. A hand was reaching in to pull me out. I recognized the fingernails; it was Sarah. I bit her.

With a shriek, the hand withdrew. "She's obviously out of it," I heard Sarah's sweet voice gabbling to someone else, someone unconnected with the church, I realized, and knew I had to act.

"Don't you listen to her. It was her car that hit us," I called. "Don't you let her touch me."

I looked over at Luna, whose hair now touched the ceiling. She was awake but not talking. She was wriggling around, and I figured she was trying to undo her seat belt.

There was lots of conversation outside the window, most of it contentious.

"I tell you, I am her sister, and she is just drunk," Polly was telling someone.

"I am not. I demand to have a sobriety test right now," I said, in as dignified a voice as I could manage, considering that I was shocked silly and hanging upside down. "Call the police immediately, please, and an ambulance."

Though Sarah began spluttering, a heavy male voice said, "Lady, doesn't sound like she wants you around. Sounds like she's got some good points."

A man's face appeared in the window. He was kneeling and bent sideways to see in. "I've called nine-one-one," the heavy voice said. He was disheveled and stubbly and I thought he was beautiful.

"Please stay here till they come," I begged.

"I will," he promised, and his face vanished.

There were more voices now. Sarah and Polly were getting shrill. They'd hit our car. Several people had witnessed it. Them claiming to be sisters or whatever didn't go over well with this crowd. Also, I gathered, they had two Fellowship males with them who were being less than endearing.

"Then we'll just go," Polly said, fury in her voice.

"No, you won't," said my wonderful belligerent male. "You gotta trade insurance with them, anyway."

"That's right," said a much younger male voice. "You just don't want to pay for getting their car fixed. And what if they're hurt? Don't you have to pay their hospital?"

Luna had managed to unbuckle herself, and she twisted when she fell to the roof that was now the floor of the car. With a suppleness I could only envy, she worked her head out of the open window, and then began to brace her feet against whatever purchase she could find. Gradually, she began to wriggle her way out of the window. One of the purchases happened to be my shoulder, but I didn't even peep. One of us needed to be free.

There were exclamations outside as Luna made her appearance, and then I heard her say, "Okay, which one of you was driving?"

Various voices chimed in, some saying one, some saying another, but they all knew Sarah and Polly and their henchmen were the perpetrators and Luna was a victim. There were so many people around that when yet another car of men from the Fellowship pulled up, there wasn't any way they could just haul us off. God bless the American spectator, I thought. I was in a sentimental mood.

The paramedic that ended up extricating me from the car was the cutest guy I'd ever seen. His name was Salazar, according to his bar pin, and I said, "Salazar," just to be sure I could say it. I had to sound it out carefully.

"Yep, that's me," he said while lifting my eyelid to look at my eye. "You're kinda banged up, lady."

I started to tell him that I'd had some of these injuries before the car accident, but then I heard Luna say, "My calendar flew off the dashboard and hit her in the face."

"Be a lot safer if you'd keep your dash clear, ma'am," said a new voice with a flat twang to it.

"I hear you, Officer."

Officer? I tried to turn my head and got admonished by Salazar. "You just keep still till I finish looking you over," he said sternly.

"Okay." After a second I said, "The police are here?"

"Yes, ma'am. Now, what hurts?"

We went through a whole list of questions, most of which I was able to answer.

"I think you're going to be fine, ma'am, but we need to take you and your friend to the hospital just to check you out." Salazar and his partner, a heavy Anglo woman, were matter-of-fact about this necessity.

"Oh," I said anxiously, "we don't need to go to the hospital, do we, Luna?"

"Sure," she said, as surprised as she could be. "We have to get you X-rayed, honey bunch. I mean, that cheek of yours looks bad."

"Oh." I was a little stunned by this turn of events. "Well, if you think so."

"Oh, yeah."

So Luna walked to the ambulance, and I was loaded in on a gurney, and with siren blaring, we started off. My last view before Salazar shut the doors was of Polly and Sarah talking to a very tall policeman. Both of them looked very upset. That was good.

The hospital was like all hospitals. Luna stuck to me like white to rice, and when we were in the same cubicle and a nurse entered to take down still more details, Luna said, "Tell Dr. Josephus that Luna Garza and her sister are here."

The nurse, a young African American woman, gave Luna a doubtful look, but said, "Okay," and left immediately.

"How'd you do that?" I asked.

"Get a nurse to stop filling out charts? I asked for this hospital on purpose. We've got someone at every hospital in the city, but I know our man here best."

"Our?"

"Us. The Two-Natured."

"Oh." The shapeshifters. I could hardly wait to tell Sam about this.

"I'm Dr. Josephus," said a calm voice. I raised my head to see that a spare, silver-haired man had stepped into our curtained area. His hair was receding and he had a sharp nose on which a pair of wire-rimmed glasses perched. He had intent blue eyes, magnified by his glasses.

"I'm Luna Garza, and this is my friend, ah, Marigold." Luna said this as if she were a different person. In fact, I glanced over to see if it was the same Luna. "We met with misfortune tonight in the line of duty."

The doctor looked at me with some mistrust.

"She is worthy," Luna said with great solemnity. I didn't want to ruin the moment by giggling, but I had to bite the inside of my mouth.

"You need X rays," the doctor said after looking at my face and examining my grotesquely swollen knee. I had various abrasions and bruises, but those were my only really significant injuries.

"Then we need them very quickly, and then we need out of here in a secure way," Luna said in a voice that would brook no denial.

No hospital had ever moved so quickly. I could only suppose that Dr. Josephus was on the board of directors. Or maybe he was the chief of staff. The portable X-ray machine was wheeled in, the X rays were taken, and in a few minutes Dr. Josephus told me that I had a hairline fracture of the cheekbone which would mend on its own. Or I could see a plastic surgeon when the swelling had gone down. He gave me a prescription for pain pills, a lot of advice, and an ice pack for my face and another for my knee, which he called "wrenched."

Within ten minutes after that, we were on our way out of the hospital. Luna was pushing me in a wheelchair, and Dr. Josephus was leading us through a kind of service tunnel. We passed a couple of employees on their way in. They appeared to be poor people, the kind who take low-paying jobs like hospital janitor and cook. I couldn't believe the massively self-assured Dr. Josephus had ever come down this tunnel before, but he seemed to know his way, and the staff didn't act startled at the sight of him. At the end of the tunnel, he pushed open a heavy metal door.

Luna Garza nodded to him regally, said, "Many thanks," and wheeled me out into the night. There was a big old car parked out there. It was dark red or dark brown. As I looked around a little more, I realized that we were in an alley. There were big trash bins lining the wall, and I saw a cat pouncing on something—I didn't want to know what—between two of the bins. After the door whooshed pneumatically shut behind us, the alley was quiet. I began to feel afraid again.

I was incredibly tired of being afraid.

Luna went over to the car, opened the rear door, and said something to whoever was inside. Whatever answer she got, it made her angry. She expostulated in another language.

There was further argument.

Luna stomped back to me. "You have to be blindfolded," she said, obviously certain I would take great offense.

"No problem," I said, with a sweep of one hand to indicate how trifling a matter this was.

"You don't mind?"

"No. I understand, Luna. Everyone likes his privacy."

"Okay, then." She hurried back to the car and returned with a scarf in her hands, of green and peacock blue silk. She folded it as if we were going to play pin-the-tail, and tied it securely behind my head. "Listen to me," she said in my ear, "these two are tough. You watch it." Good. I wanted to be more frightened.

She rolled me over to the car and helped me in. I guess she wheeled the chair back to the door to await pickup; anyway, after a minute she got in the other side of the car.

There were two presences in the front seat. I felt them mentally, very delicately, and discovered both were shapeshifters; at least, they had the shapeshifter feel to their brains, the semiopaque snarly tangle I got from Sam and Luna. My boss, Sam, usually changes into a collie. I wondered what Luna preferred. There was a difference about these two, a pulsing sort of heaviness. The outline of their heads seemed subtly different, not exactly human.

There was only silence for a few minutes, while the car bumped out of the alley and drove through the night.

"Silent Shore Hotel, right?" said the driver. She sounded kind of growly. Then I realized it was almost the full moon. Oh, hell. They had to change at the full moon. Maybe that was why Luna had kicked over the traces so readily at the Fellowship tonight, once it got dark. She had been made giddy by the emergence of the moon.

"Yes, please," I said politely.

"Food that talks," said the passenger. His voice was even closer to a growl.

I sure didn't like that, but had no idea how to respond. There was just as much for me to learn about shapeshifters as there was about vampires, apparently.

"You two can it," Luna said. "This is my guest."

"Luna hangs with puppy chow," said the passenger. I was beginning to really not like this guy.

"Smells more like hamburger to me," said the driver. "She's got a scrape or two, doesn't she, Luna?"

"Y'all are giving her a great impression of how civilized we are," Luna snapped. "Show some control. She's already had a bad night. She's got a broken bone, too."

And the night wasn't even halfway over yet. I shifted the ice pack I was holding to my face. You can only stand so much freezing cold on your sinus cavity.

"Why'd Josephus have to send for freakin' werewolves?" Luna muttered into my ear. But I knew they'd heard; Sam heard everything, and he was by no means as powerful as a true werewolf. Or at least, that was my evaluation. To tell you the truth, until this moment, I hadn't been sure werewolves actually existed.

"I guess," I said tactfully and audibly, "he thought they could defend us best if we're attacked again."

I could feel the creatures in the front seat prick up their ears. Maybe literally.

"We were doing okay," Luna said indignantly. She twitched and fidgeted on the seat beside me like she'd drunk sixteen cups of coffee.

"Luna, we got rammed and your car got totaled. We were in the emergency room. 'Okay' in what sense?"

Then I had to answer my own question. "Hey, I'm sorry, Luna. You got me out of there when they would've killed me. It's not your fault they rammed us."

"You two have a little roughhouse tonight?" asked the passenger, more civilly. He was spoiling for a fight. I didn't know if all werewolves were as feisty as this guy, or if it was just his nature.

"Yeah, with the fucking Fellowship," Luna said, more than a trace of pride in her voice. "They had this chick stuck in a cell. In a dungeon."

"No shit?" asked the driver. She had the same hyper pulsing to her—well, I just had to call it her aura, for lack of a better word.

"No shit," I said firmly. "I work for a shifter, at home," I added, to make conversation.

"No kidding? What's the business?"

"A bar. He owns a bar."

"So, are you far from home?"

"Too far," I said.

"This little bat saved your life tonight, for real?"

"Yes." I was absolutely sincere about that. "Luna saved my life." Could they mean that literally? Did Luna shapeshift into a . . . oh golly.

"Way to go, Luna." There was a fraction more respect in the deeper growly voice.

Luna found the praise pleasant, as she ought to, and she patted my hand. In a more agreeable silence, we drove maybe five more minutes, and then the driver said, "The Silent Shore, coming up."

I breathed out a long sigh of relief.

"There's a vampire out front, waiting."

I almost ripped off the blindfold, before I realized that would be a really tacky thing to do. "What does he look like?"

"Very tall, blond. Big head of hair. Friend or foe?"

I had to think about that. "Friend," I said, trying not to sound doubtful.

"Yum, yum," said the driver. "Does he cross-date?"

"I don't know. Want me to ask?"

Luna and the passenger both made gagging sounds. "You can't date a deader!" Luna protested. "Come on, Deb—uh, girl!"

"Oh, okay," said the driver. "Some of them aren't so bad. I'm pulling into the curb, little Milkbone."

"That would be you," Luna said in my ear.

We came to a stop, and Luna leaned over me to open my door. As I stepped out, guided and shoved by her hands, I heard an exclamation from the sidewalk. Quick as a wink Luna slammed the door shut behind me. The car full of shapeshifters pulled away from the curb with a screech of tires. A howl trailed behind it in the thick night air.

"Sookie?" said a familiar voice.

"Eric?"

I was fumbling with the blindfold, but Eric just grabbed the back of it and pulled. I had acquired a beautiful, if somewhat stained, scarf. The front of the hotel, with its heavy blank doors, was brilliantly lit in the dark night, and Eric looked remarkably pale. He was wearing an absolutely conventional navy blue pinstripe suit, of all things.

I was actually glad to see him. He grabbed my arm to keep me from wobbling and looked down at me with an unreadable face. Vampires were good at that. "What has happened to you?" he said.

"I got . . . well, it's hard to explain in a second. Where is Bill?"

"First he went to the Fellowship of the Sun to get you out. But we heard along the way, from one of us who is a policeman, that you had been involved in an accident and gone to a hospital. So then he went to the hospital. At the hospital, he found out you had left outside the proper channels. No one would tell him anything, and he couldn't threaten them properly." Eric looked extremely frustrated. The fact that he had to live within human laws was a constant irritant to Eric, though he greatly enjoyed the benefits. "And then there was no trace of you. The doorman had only heard the once from you, mentally."

"Poor Barry. Is he all right?"

"The richer for several hundred dollars, and quite happy about it," Eric said in a dry voice. "Now we just need Bill. What a lot of trouble you are, Sookie." He pulled a cell phone out of his pocket and punched in a number. After what seemed a long time, it was answered.

"Bill, she is here. Some shapeshifters brought her in." He looked me over. "Battered, but walking." He listened some more. "Sookie, do you have your key?" he asked. I felt in the pocket of my skirt where I'd stuffed the plastic rectangle about a million years ago.

"Yes," I said, and simply could not believe that something had gone right. "Oh, wait! Did they get Farrell?"

Eric held up his hand to indicate he'd get to me in a minute. "Bill, I'll take her up and start doctoring." Eric's back stiffened. "Bill," he said and there was a world of threat in his voice. "All right then. Goodbye." He turned back to me as if there'd been no interruption.

"Yes, Farrell is safe. They raided the Fellowship."

"Did . . . did many people get hurt?"

"Most of them were too frightened to approach. They scattered and went home. Farrell was in an underground cell with Hugo."

"Oh, yes, Hugo. What happened to Hugo?"

My voice must have been very curious, because Eric looked at me sideways while we were progressing toward the elevator. He was matching my pace, and I was limping very badly.

"May I carry you?" he asked.

"Oh, I don't think so. I've made it this far." I would've taken Bill up on the offer instantly. Barry, at the bell captain's desk, gave me a little wave. He would've run up to me if I hadn't been with Eric. I gave him what I hoped was a significant look, to say I'd talk to him again later, and then the elevator door dinged open and we got on. Eric punched the floor button and leaned against the mirrored wall of the car opposite me. In looking at him, I got a look at my own reflection.

"Oh, no," I said, absolutely horrified. "Oh, no." My hair had been flattened by the wig, and then combed out with my fingers, so it was a disaster. My hands went up to it, helplessly and painfully, and my mouth shook with suppressed tears. And my hair was the least of it. I had visible bruises ranging from mild to severe on most of my body, and that was just the part you could see. My face was swollen and discolored on one side. There was a cut in the middle of the bruise over my cheekbone. My blouse was missing half its buttons, and my skirt was ripped and filthy. My right arm was ridged with bloody lumps.

I began crying. I looked so awful; it just broke what was left of my spirit.

To his credit, Eric didn't laugh, though he may have wanted to. "Sookie, a bath and clean clothes and you will be put to rights," he said as if he were talking to a child. To tell you the truth, I didn't feel much older at the moment.

"The werewolf thought you were cute," I said, and sobbed some more. We stepped out of the elevator.

"The werewolf? Sookie, you have had adventures tonight." He gathered me up like an armful of clothes and held me to him. I got his lovely suit jacket wet and snotty, and his pristine white shirt was spotless no more.

"Oh, I'm so sorry!" I held back and looked at his ensemble. I swabbed it with the scarf.

"Don't cry again," he said hastily. "Just don't start crying again, and I won't mind taking this to the cleaners. I won't even mind getting a whole new suit."

I thought it was pretty amusing that Eric, the dread master vampire, was afraid of weeping women. I sniggered through the residual sobs.

"Something funny?" he asked.

I shook my head.

I slid my key in the door and we went in. "I'll help you into the tub if you like, Sookie," Eric offered.

"Oh, I don't think so." A bath was what I wanted more than anything else in the world, that and to never put on these clothes again, but I sure wasn't taking a bath with Eric anywhere around.

"I'll bet you are a treat, naked," Eric said, just to boost my spirits.

"You know it. I'm just as tasty as a big éclair," I said, and carefully settled into a chair. "Though at the moment I feel more like boudain." Boudain is Cajun sausage, made of all kinds of things, none of them elegant. Eric pushed over a straight chair and lifted my leg to elevate the knee. I resettled the ice pack on it and closed my eyes. Eric called down to the desk for some tweezers, a bowl, and some antiseptic ointment, plus a rolling chair. The items arrived within ten minutes. This staff was good.

There was a small desk by one wall. Eric moved it over to the right side of my chair, lifted my arm, and laid it over the top of the desk. He switched on the lamp. After swabbing off my arm with a wet washcloth, Eric began removing the lumps. They were tiny pieces of glass from Luna's Outback's window. "If you were an ordinary girl, I could glamour you and you wouldn't feel this," he commented. "Be brave." It hurt like a bitch, and tears streamed down my face the whole time he worked. I worked hard keeping silent.

At last, I heard another key in the door, and I opened my eyes. Bill glanced at my face, winced, and then examined what Eric was doing. He nodded approvingly to Eric.

"How did this happen?" he asked, laying the lightest of touches on my face. He pulled the remaining chair closer and sat in it. Eric continued with his work.

I began to explain. I was so tired my voice faltered from time to time. When I got to the part about Gabe, I didn't have enough wits to tone the episode down, and I could see Bill was holding on to his temper with iron control. He gently lifted my blouse to peer at the ripped bra and the bruises on my chest, even with Eric there. (He looked, of course.)

"What happened to this Gabe?" Bill asked, very quietly.

"Well, he's dead," I said. "Godfrey killed him."

"You saw Godfrey?" Eric leaned forward. He hadn't said a thing up till this point. He'd finished doctoring my arm. He'd put antibiotic ointment all over it as if he were protecting a baby from diaper rash.

"You were right, Bill. He was the one who kidnapped Farrell, though I didn't get any details. And Godfrey stopped Gabe from raping me. Though I got to say, I had gotten in a few good licks myself."

"Don't brag," said Bill with a small smile. "So, the man is dead." But he didn't seem satisfied.

"Godfrey was very good in stopping Gabe and helping me get out. Specially since he just wanted to think about meeting the dawn. Where is he?"

"He ran into the night during our attack on the Fellowship," Bill explained. "None of us could catch him."

"What happened at the Fellowship?"

"I'll tell you, Sookie. But let's say good night to Eric, and I will tell you while I bathe you."

"Okay," I agreed. "Good night, Eric. Thanks for the first aid."

"I think those are the main points," Bill said to Eric. "If there is more, I'll come to your room later."

"Good." Eric looked at me, his eyes half open. He'd had a lick or two at my bloody arm while he doctored it and the taste seemed to have intoxicated him. "Rest well, Sookie."

"Oh," I said, my eyes opening all the way suddenly. "You know, we owe the shapeshifters."

Both the vampires stared at me. "Well, maybe not you guys, but I sure do."

"Oh, they'll put in a claim," Eric predicted. "Those shapeshifters never perform any service for free. Good night, Sookie. I am glad you weren't raped and killed." He gave his sudden flashing grin, and looked a lot more like himself.

"Gee, thanks a lot," I said, my eyes closing again. "Night."

When the door had closed behind Eric, Bill gathered me up out of the chair and took me in the bathroom. It was about as big as most hotel bathrooms, but the tub was adequate. Bill ran it full of hot water and very carefully took off my clothes.

"Just toss 'em, Bill," I said.

"Maybe I will, at that." He was eyeing the bruises again, his lips pressed together in a straight line.

"Some of these are from the fall on the stairs, and some are from the car accident," I explained.

"If Gabe wasn't dead I would find him and kill him," Bill said, mostly to himself. "I would take my time." He lifted me as easily as if I were a baby and put me in the bath, and began washing me with a cloth and a bar of soap.

"My hair is so nasty."

"Yes, it is, but we may have to take care of your hair in the morning. You need sleep."

Beginning with my face, Bill gently scrubbed me all the way down. The water became discolored with dirt and old blood. He checked my arm thoroughly, to make sure Eric had gotten all the glass. Then he emptied the tub and refilled it, while I shivered. This time, I got clean. After I moaned about my hair a second time, he gave in. He wet my head and shampooed my hair, rinsing it laboriously. There is nothing more wonderful than feeling head-to-toe clean after you've been filthy, having a comfortable bed with clean sheets, being able to sleep in it in safety.

"Tell me about what happened at the Fellowship," I said as he carried me to the bed. "Keep me company."

Bill inserted me under the sheet and crawled in the other side. He slid his arm under my head and scooted close. I carefully touched my forehead to his chest and rubbed it.

"By the time we got there, it was like a disrupted anthill," he said. "The parking lot was full of cars and people, and more kept arriving for the—all-night sleepover?"

"Lock-in," I murmured, carefully turning on my right side to burrow against him.

"There was a certain amount of turmoil when we arrived. Almost all of them piled into their cars and left as fast as traffic would allow. Their leader, Newlin, tried to deny us entrance to the Fellowship hall—surely that was a church at one time?—and he told us we would burst into flames if we entered, because we were the damned." Bill snorted. "Stan picked him up and set him aside. And into the church we went, Newlin and his woman trailing right behind us. Not a one of us burst into flames, which seemed to shake up the people a great deal."

"I'll bet," I mumbled into his chest.

"Barry told us that when he communicated with you, he had the sense you were 'down'—below ground level. He thought he picked up the word 'stairs' from you. There were six of us—Stan, Joseph Velasquez, Isabel, and others—and it took us perhaps six minutes to eliminate all the possibilities and find the stairs."

"What did you do about the door?" It had had stout locks, I remembered.

"We ripped it from its hinges."

"Oh." Well, that would provide quick access, sure enough.

"I thought you were still down there, of course. When I found the room with the dead man, who had his pants open . . ." He paused a long moment. "I was sure you had been there. I could smell you in the air still. There was a smear of blood on him, your blood, and I found other traces of it around. I was very worried."

I patted him. I felt too tired and weak to pat very vigorously, but it was the only consolation I had to offer at the moment.

"Sookie," he said very carefully, "is there anything more you want to tell me?"

I was too sleepy to figure this one through. "No," I said and yawned. "I think I pretty much covered my adventures earlier."

"I thought maybe since Eric was in the room earlier, you wouldn't want to say everything?"

I finally heard the other shoe drop. I kissed his chest, over his heart. "Godfrey really was in time."

There was a long silence. I looked up to see Bill's face set so rigidly that he looked like a statue. His dark eyelashes stood out against his pallor with amazing clarity. His dark eyes seemed bottomless. "Tell me the rest," I said.

"Then we went farther into the bomb shelter and found the larger room, along with an extended area full of supplies—food and guns—where it was obvious another vampire had been staying."

I hadn't seen that part of the bomb shelter, and I certainly had no plans to revisit it to view what I'd missed.

"In the second cell we found Farrell and Hugo."

"Was Hugo alive?"

"Just barely." Bill kissed my forehead. "Luckily for Hugo, Farrell likes his sex with younger men."

"Maybe that was why Godfrey chose Farrell to abduct, when he decided to make an example of another sinner."

Bill nodded. "That is what Farrell said. But he had been without sex and blood for a long time, and he was hungry in every sense. Without the silver manacles, Hugo would have . . . had a bad time. Even with silver on his wrists and ankles, Farrell was able to feed from Hugo."

"Did you know that Hugo was the traitor?"

"Farrell heard your conversation with him."

"How—oh, right, vampire hearing. Stupid me."

"Farrell would also like to know what you did to Gabe to make him scream."

"Clapped him over the ears." I cupped one hand to show him.

"Farrell was delighted. This Gabe was one of those men who enjoys power over others. He subjected Farrell to many indignities."

"Farrell's just lucky he's not a woman," I said. "Where is Hugo now?"

"He is somewhere safe."

"Safe for who?"

"Safe for vampires. Away from the media. They would enjoy Hugo's story all too much."

"What are they gonna do with him?"

"That's for Stan to decide."

"Remember the deal we had with Stan? If humans are found guilty by evidence of mine, they don't get killed."

Bill obviously didn't want to debate me on this now. His face shut down. "Sookie, you have to go to sleep now. We'll talk about it when you get up."

"But by then he may be dead."

"Why should you care?"

"Because that was the deal! I know Hugo is a shit, and I hate him, too, but I feel sorry for him; and I don't think I can be implicated in his death and live with a clear conscience."

"Sookie, he will still be alive when you get up. We'll talk about it then."

I felt sleep pulling me under like the undertow of the surf. It was hard to believe it was only two o'clock in the morning.

"Thanks for coming after me."

Bill said, after a pause, "First you weren't at the Fellowship, just traces of your blood and dead rapist. When I found you weren't at the hospital, that you had been spirited out of there somehow . . ."

"Mmmmh?"

"I was very, very scared. No one had any idea where you were. In fact, while I stood there talking to the nurse who admitted you, your name went off the computer screen."

I was impressed. Those shapeshifters were organized to an amazing degree. "Maybe I should send Luna some flowers," I said, hardly able to get the words out of my mouth.

Bill kissed me, a very satisfying kiss, and that was the last thing I remembered.

Chapter 7

I TURNED OVER laboriously and peered at the illuminated clock on the bedside table. It was not yet dawn, but dawn would come soon. Bill was in his coffin already: the lid was closed. Why was I awake? I thought it over.

There was something I had to do. Part of me stood back in amazement at my own stupidity as I pulled on some shorts and a T-shirt and slid my feet into sandals. I looked even worse in the mirror, to which I gave only a sideways glance. I stood with my back to it to brush my hair. To my astonishment and pleasure, my purse was sitting on the table in the sitting room. Someone had retrieved it from the Fellowship headquarters the night before. I stuck my plastic key in it and made my way painfully down the silent halls.

Barry was not on duty anymore, and his replacement was too well trained to ask me what the hell I was doing going around looking like something a train had dragged in. He got me a cab and I told the driver where I needed to go. The driver looked at me in the rearview mirror. "Wouldn't you rather go to a hospital?" he suggested uneasily.

"No. I've already been." That hardly seemed to reassure him.

"Those vampires treat you so bad, why do you hang around them?"

"People did this to me," I said. "Not vampires."

We drove off. Traffic was light, it being nearly dawn on a Sunday morning. It only took fifteen minutes to get to the same place I'd been the night before, the Fellowship parking lot.

"Can you wait for me?" I asked the driver. He was a man in his sixties, grizzled and missing a front tooth. He wore a plaid shirt with snaps instead of buttons.

"I reckon I can do that," he said. He pulled a Louis L'Amour western out from under his seat and switched on a dome light to read.

Under the glare of the sodium lights, the parking lot showed no visible traces of the events of the night before. There were only a couple of vehicles remaining, and I figured they'd been abandoned the night before. One of these cars was probably Gabe's. I wondered if Gabe had had a family; I hoped not. For one thing, he was such a sadist he must have made their lives miserable, and for another, for the rest of their lives they'd have to wonder how and why he'd died. What would Steve and Sarah Newlin do now? Would there be enough members left of their Fellowship to carry on? Presumably the guns and provisions were still in the church. Maybe they'd been stockpiling against the apocalypse.

Out of the dark shadows next to the church a figure emerged. Godfrey. He was still bare-chested, and he still looked like a fresh-faced sixteen. Only the alien character of the tattoos and his eyes gave the lie to his body.

"I came to watch," I said, when he was close to me, though maybe "bear witness" would have been more accurate.

"Why?"

"I owe it to you."

"I am an evil creature."

"Yes, you are." There just wasn't any getting around that. "But you did a good thing, saving me from Gabe."

"By killing one more man? My conscience hardly knew the difference. There have been so many. At least I spared you some humiliation."

His voice grabbed at my heart. The growing light in the sky was still so faint that the parking lot security lights remained on, and by their glow I examined the young, young face.

All of a sudden, absurdly, I began to cry.

"That's nice," Godfrey said. His voice was already remote. "Someone to cry for me at the end. I had hardly expected that." He stepped back to a safe distance.

And then the sun rose.

WHEN I GOT back in the cab, the driver stowed away his book.

"They have a fire going over there?" he asked. "I thought I saw some smoke. I almost came to see what was happening."

"It's out now," I said.

* * *

I MOPPED AT my face for a mile or so, and then I stared out the window as the stretches of city emerged from the night.

Back at the hotel, I let myself into our room again. I pulled off my shorts, lay down on the bed, and just as I was preparing myself for a long period of wakefulness, I fell deep asleep.

Bill woke me up at sundown, in his favorite way. My T-shirt was pushed up, and his dark hair brushed my chest. It was like waking up halfway down the road, so to speak; his mouth was sucking so tenderly on half of what he told me was the most beautiful pair of breasts in the world. He was very careful of his fangs, which were fully down. That was only one of the evidences of his arousal. "Do you feel up to doing this, enjoying it, if I am very, very careful?" he whispered against my ear.

"If you treat me like I was made of glass," I murmured, knowing that he could.

"But that doesn't feel like glass," he said, his hand moving gently. "That feels warm. And wet."

I gasped.

"That much? Am I hurting you?" His hand moved more forcefully.

"Bill" was all I could say. I put my lips on his, and his tongue began a familiar rhythm.

"Lie on your side," he whispered. "I will take care of everything." And he did.

"Why were you partly dressed?" he asked, later. He'd gotten up to get a bottle of blood from the refrigerator in the room, and he'd warmed it in the microwave. He hadn't taken any of my blood, in consideration of my weakened state.

"I went to see Godfrey die."

His eyes glowed down at me. "What?"

"Godfrey met the dawn." The phrase I had once considered embarrassingly melodramatic flowed quite naturally from my mouth.

There was a long silence.

"How did you know he would? How did you know where?"

I shrugged as much as you can while you're lying in a bed. "I just figured he'd stick with his original plan. He seemed pretty set on it. And he'd saved my life. It was the least I could do."

"Did he show courage?"

I met Bill's eyes. "He died very bravely. He was eager to go."

I had no idea what Bill was thinking. "We have to go see Stan," he said. "We'll tell him."

"Why do we have to go see Stan again?" If I hadn't been such a mature woman, I would've pouted. As it was, Bill gave me one of those looks.

"You have to tell him your part, so he can be convinced we've performed our service. Also, there's the matter of Hugo."

That was enough to make me gloomy. I was so sore the idea of any more clothes than necessary touching my skin made me feel ill, so I pulled on a long sleeveless taupe dress made out of a soft knit and slid my feet carefully into sandals, and that was my outfit. Bill brushed my hair and put in my earrings for me, since raising my arms was uncomfortable, and he decided I needed a gold chain. I looked like I was going to a party at the outpatient ward for battered women. Bill called down for a rental car to be brought around. When the car had arrived in the underground garage, I had no idea. I didn't even know who had arranged for it. Bill drove. I didn't look out the window anymore. I was sick of Dallas.

When we got to the house on Green Valley Road it looked as quiet as it had two nights ago. But after we'd been admitted, I found it was abuzz with vampires. We'd arrived in the midst of a welcome-home party for Farrell, who was standing in the living room with his arm around a handsome young man who might be all of eighteen. Farrell had a bottle of TrueBlood O negative in one hand, and his date had a Coke. The vampire looked almost as rosy as the boy.

Farrell had never actually seen me, so he was delighted to make my acquaintance. He was clad from head to toe in western regalia, and as he bowed over my hand, I expected to hear spurs clink.

"You are so lovely," he said extravagantly, waving the bottle of synthetic blood, "that if I slept with women, you would receive my undivided attention for a week. I know you are self-conscious about your bruises, but they only set off your beauty."

I couldn't help laughing. Not only was I walking like I was about eighty, my face was black-and-blue on the left side.

"Bill Compton, you are one lucky vampire," Farrell told Bill.

"I am well aware of that," Bill said, smiling, though somewhat coolly.

"She is brave and beautiful!"

"Thanks, Farrell. Where's Stan?" I decided to break this stream of praise. Not only did it make Bill antsy, but Farrell's young companion was getting entirely too curious. My intention was to relate this story once again, and only once.

"He's in the dining room," the young vampire said, the one who'd brought poor Bethany into the dining room when we'd been here before. This must be Joseph Velasquez. He was maybe five foot eight, and his Hispanic ancestry gave him the toast-colored complexion and dark eyes of a don, while his vampire state gave him an unblinking stare and the instant willingness to do damage. He was scanning the room, waiting for trouble. I decided he was sort of the sergeant at arms of the nest. "He will be glad to see both of you."

I glanced around at all the vampires and the sprinkling of humans in the large rooms of the house. I didn't see Eric. I wondered if he'd gone back to Shreveport. "Where's Isabel?" I asked Bill, keeping my voice quiet.

"Isabel is being punished," he said, almost too softly to hear. He didn't want to talk about this any louder, and when Bill thought that was a wise idea, I knew I better shut up. "She brought a traitor into the nest, and she has to pay a price for that."

"But—"

"Shhh."

We came into the dining room to find it as crowded as the living room. Stan was in the same chair, wearing virtually the same outfit he had been wearing last time I saw him. He stood up when we entered, and from the way he did this, I understood this was supposed to mark our status as important.

"Miss Stackhouse," he said formally, shaking my hand with great care. "Bill." Stan examined me with his eyes, their washed-out blue not missing a detail of my injuries. His glasses had been mended with Scotch tape. Stan was nothing if not thorough with his disguise. I thought I'd send him a pocket-protector for Christmas.

"Please tell me what happened to you yesterday, omitting nothing," Stan said.

This reminded me irresistibly of Archie Goodwin reporting to Nero Wolfe. "I'll bore Bill," I said, hoping to get out of this recitation.

"Bill will not mind being bored for a little."

There was no getting around this. I sighed, and began with Hugo picking me up from the Silent Shore Hotel. I tried to leave Barry's name out of my narrative, since I didn't know how he'd feel about being known by the vampires of Dallas. I just called him "a bellboy at the hotel." Of course, they could learn who he was if they tried.

When I got to the part where Gabe sent Hugo into Farrell's cell and then tried to rape me, my lips yanked up in a tight grin. My face felt so taut that I thought it might crack.

"Why does she do that?" Stan asked Bill, as though I weren't there.

"When she is tense . . ." Bill said.

"Oh." Stan looked at me even more thoughtfully. I reached up and began to pull my hair into a ponytail. Bill handed me an elastic band from his pocket, and with considerable discomfort, I held the hair in a tight hank so I could twist the band around it three times.

When I told Stan about the help the shapeshifters had given me, he leaned forward. He wanted to know more than I told, but I would not give any names away. He was intensely thoughtful after I told him about being dropped off at the hotel. I didn't know whether to include Eric or not; I left him out, completely. He was supposed to be from California. I amended my narrative to say I'd gone up to our room to wait for Bill.

And then I told him about Godfrey.

To my amazement, Stan could not seem to absorb Godfrey's death. He made me repeat the story. He swiveled in his chair to face the other way while I spoke. Behind his back, Bill gave me a reassuring caress. When Stan turned back to us, he was wiping his eyes with a red-stained handkerchief. So it was true that vampires could cry. And it was true that vampire tears were bloody.

I cried right along with him. For his centuries of molesting and killing children, Godfrey had deserved to die. I wondered how many humans were in jail for crimes Godfrey had committed. But Godfrey had helped me, and Godfrey had carried with him the most tremendous load of guilt and grief I'd ever encountered.

"What resolution and courage," Stan said admiringly. He hadn't been grieved at all, but lost in admiration. "It makes me weep." He said this in such a way that I knew it was meant to be a great tribute. "After Bill identified Godfrey the other night, I made some inquiries and found he had belonged to a nest in San Francisco. His nest mates will be grieved to hear of this. And of his betrayal of Farrell. But his courage in keeping his word, in fulfilling his plan!" It seemed to overwhelm Stan.

I just ached all over. I rummaged in my purse for a small bottle of Tylenol, and poured two out in my palm. At Stan's gesture, the young vampire brought me a glass of water, and I said, "Thank you," to his surprise.

"Thank you for your efforts," Stan said quite abruptly, as if he'd suddenly recalled his manners. "You have done the job we hired you to do, and more. Thanks to you we discovered and freed Farrell in time, and I'm sorry you sustained so much damage in the process."

That sounded mighty like dismissal.

"Excuse me," I said, sliding forward in the chair. Bill made a sudden movement behind me, but I disregarded him.

Stan raised his light eyebrows at my temerity. "Yes? Your check will be mailed to your representative in Shreveport, as per our agreement. Please stay with us this evening as we celebrate Farrell's return."

"Our agreement was that if what I discovered resulted in a human being found at fault, that human would not be punished by the vampires but would be turned over to the police. For the court system to deal with. Where is Hugo?"

Stan's eyes slid from my face to focus on Bill's behind me. He seemed to be silently asking Bill why he couldn't control his human better.

"Hugo and Isabel are together," said Stan cryptically.

I *so* didn't want to know what that meant. But I was honor-bound to see this through. "So you are not going to honor your agreement?" I said, knowing that was a real challenge to Stan.

There should be an adage, proud as a vampire. They all are, and I'd pinked Stan in his pride. The implication that he was dishonorable enraged the vampire. I almost backed down, his face grew so scary. He really had nothing human left about him after a few seconds. His lips drew away from his teeth, his fangs extended, and his body hunched and seemed to elongate.

After a moment he stood, and with a curt little jerk of his hand, indicated I should follow him. Bill helped me up, and we trailed after Stan as he walked deeper into the house. There must have been six bedrooms in the place, and all the doors to them were closed. From behind one door came the unmistakable sounds of sex. To my relief, we passed that door by. We went up the stairs, which was quite uncomfortable for me. Stan never looked back and never slowed down. He went up the stairs at exactly the same pace at which he walked. He stopped at a door that looked like all the others. He unlocked it. He stood aside and gestured to me to go in.

That was something I didn't want to do—oh, so much. But I had to. I stepped forward and looked in.

Except for the dark blue wall-to-wall, the room was bare. Isabel was chained to the wall on one side of the room—with silver, of course. Hugo was on the other. He was chained, too. They were both awake, and they both looked at the doorway, naturally.

Isabel nodded as if we'd met in the mall, though she was naked. I saw that her wrists and ankles were padded to prevent the silver from burning her, though the chains would still keep her weak.

Hugo was naked, too. He could not take his eyes off Isabel. He barely glanced at me to see who I was before his gaze returned to her. I tried not to be embarrassed, because that seemed such a petty consideration; but I think it was the first time I'd seen another naked adult in my life, besides Bill.

Stan said, "She cannot feed off him, though she is hungry. He cannot have sex with her, though he is addicted. This is their punishment, for months. What would happen to Hugo in human courts?"

I considered. What had Hugo actually done that was indictable?

He'd deceived the vampires in that he'd been in the Dallas nest under false pretenses. That is, he actually loved Isabel, but he'd betrayed her compadres. Hmmm. No law about that.

"He bugged the dining room," I said. That was illegal. At least, I thought it was.

"How long in jail would he get for that?" Stan asked.

Good question. Not much, was my guess. A human jury might feel bugging a vampire hangout was even justified. I sighed, sufficient answer for Stan.

"What other time would Hugo serve?" he asked.

"He got me to the Fellowship under false pretenses . . . not illegal. He . . . well, he . . ."

"Exactly."

Hugo's infatuated gaze never shifted from Isabel.

Hugo had caused and abetted evil, just as surely as Godfrey had committed evil.

"How long will you keep them there?" I asked.

Stan shrugged. "Three or four months. We will feed Hugo, of course. Not Isabel."

"And then?"

"We'll unchain him first. He will get a day's head start."

Bill's hand clamped down on my wrist. He didn't want me to ask any more questions.

Isabel looked at me and nodded. This seemed fair to her, she was saying. "All right," I said, holding my palms forward in the "Stop" position. "All right." And I turned and made my way slowly and carefully down the stairs.

I had lost some integrity, but for the life of me, I couldn't figure out what I could do differently. The more I tried to think about it, the more confused I got. I am not used to thinking through moral issues. Things are bad to do, or they aren't.

Well, there was a gray area. That's where a few things fell, like sleeping with Bill though we weren't married or telling Arlene her dress looked good, when in fact it made her look like hell. Actually, I couldn't marry Bill. It wasn't legal. But then, he hadn't asked me.

My thoughts wandered in a dithery circle around the miserable couple in the upstairs bedroom. To my amazement, I felt much sorrier for Isabel than for Hugo. Hugo, after all, was guilty of active evil. Isabel was only guilty of negligence.

I had a lot of time to maunder on and on through similar dead-end thought patterns, since Bill was having a rip-roaring good time at the party. I'd only been to a mixed vampire and human party once or twice before, and it was a mixture that was still uneasy after two years of legally recognized vampirism. Open drinking—that is, bloodsucking— from humans was absolutely illegal, and I am here to tell you that in Dallas's vampire headquarters, that law was strictly observed. From time to time, I saw a couple vanish for a while upstairs, but all the humans seemed to come back in good health. I know, because I counted and watched.

Bill had mainstreamed for so many months that apparently it was a real treat for him to get together with other vampires. So he was deep in conversation with this vamp or that, reminiscing about Chicago in the twenties or investment opportunities in various vampire holdings around the world. I was so shaky physically that I was content to sit on a soft couch and watch, sipping from time to time at my Screwdriver. The bartender was a pleasant young man, and we talked bars for a little while. I should have been enjoying my break from waiting tables at Merlotte's, but I would gladly have dressed in my uniform and taken orders. I wasn't used to big changes in my routine.

Then a woman maybe a little younger than me plopped down on the couch beside me. Turned out she was dating the vampire who acted as sergeant at arms, Joseph Velasquez, who'd gone to the Fellowship Center with Bill the night before. Her name was Trudi Pfeiffer. Trudi had hair done in deep red spikes, a pierced nose and tongue, and macabre makeup, including black lipstick. She told me proudly its color was called Grave Rot. Her jeans were so low I wondered how she got up and down in them. Maybe she wore them so low-cut to show off her navel ring. Her knit top was cropped very short. The outfit I'd worn the night the maenad had gotten me paled in comparison. So, there was lots of Trudi to see.

When you talked to her, she wasn't as bizarre as her appearance led you to believe. Trudi was a college student. I discovered, through absolutely legitimate listening, that she believed herself to be waving the red flag at the bull, by dating Joseph. The bull was her parents, I gathered.

"They would even rather I dated someone *black*," she told me proudly.

I tried to look appropriately impressed. "They really hate the dead scene, huh?"

"Oh, do they ever." She nodded several times and waved her black fingernails extravagantly. She was drinking Dos Equis. "My mom always says, 'Can't you date someone *alive*?'" We both laughed.

"So, how are you and Bill?" She waggled her eyebrows up and down to indicate how significant the question was.

"You mean . . . ?"

"How's he in bed? Joseph is un-fucking-believable."

I can't say I was surprised, but I was dismayed. I cast around in my mind for a minute. "I'm glad for you," I finally said. If she'd been my good friend Arlene, I might have winked and smiled, but I wasn't about to discuss my sex life with a total stranger, and I really didn't want to know about her and Joseph.

Trudi lurched up to get another beer, and remained in conversation with the bartender. I shut my eyes in relief and weariness, and felt the couch depress beside me. I cut my gaze to the right to see what new companion I had. Eric. Oh, great.

"How are you?" he asked.

"Better than I look." That wasn't true.

"You've seen Hugo and Isabel?"

"Yes." I looked at my hands folded in my lap.

"Appropriate, don't you think?"

I thought that Eric was trying to provoke me.

"In a way, yes," I said. "Assuming Stan sticks to his word."

"You didn't say that to him, I hope." But Eric looked only amused.

"No, I didn't. Not in so many words. You're all so damn proud."

He looked surprised. "Yes, I guess that's true."

"Did you just come to check up on me?"

"To Dallas?"

I nodded.

"Yes." He shrugged. He was wearing a knit shirt in a pretty tan-and-blue pattern, and the shrug made his shoulders look massive. "We are loaning you out for the first time. I wanted to see that things went smoothly without being here in my official capacity."

"Do you think Stan knows who you are?"

He looked interested in the idea. "It's not far-fetched," he said at last. "He would probably have done the same thing in my place."

"Do you think from now on, you could just let me stay at home, and leave me and Bill alone?" I asked.

"No. You are too useful," he said. "Besides, I'm hoping that the more you see me, the more I'll grow on you."

"Like a fungus?"

He laughed, but his eyes were fixed on me in a way that meant business. Oh, hell.

"You look especially luscious in that knit dress with nothing underneath," Eric said. "If you left Bill and came to me of your own free will, he would accept that."

"But I'm not going to do any such thing," I said, and then something caught at the edges of my consciousness.

Eric started to say something else to me, but I put my hand across his mouth. I moved my head from side to side, trying to get the best reception; that's the best way I can explain it.

"Help me up," I said.

Without a word, Eric stood and gently pulled me to my feet. I could feel my eyebrows draw together.

They were all around us. They circled the house.

Their brains were wound up to fever pitch. If Trudi hadn't been babbling earlier, I might have heard them as they crept up to circle the house.

"Eric," I said, trying to catch as many thoughts as I could, hearing a countdown, oh, God!

"Hit the floor!" I yelled at the top of my lungs.

Every vampire obeyed.

So when the Fellowship opened fire, it was the humans that died.

Chapter 8

A YARD AWAY, Trudi was cut down by a shotgun blast.

The dyed dark red of her hair turned another shade of red and her open eyes stared at me forever. Chuck, the bartender, was only wounded, since the structure of the bar itself offered him some protection.

Eric was lying on top of me. Given my sore condition, that was very painful, and I started to shove at him. Then I realized that if he were hit with bullets, he would most likely survive. But I wouldn't. So I accepted his shelter gratefully for the horrible minutes of the first wave of the attack, when rifles and shotguns and handguns were fired into the suburban mansion over and over.

Instinctively, I shut my eyes while the blasting lasted. Glass shattered, vampires roared, humans screamed. The noise battered at me, just as the tidal wave of scores of brains at high gear washed over me. When it began to taper off, I looked up into Eric's eyes. Incredibly, he was excited. He smiled at me. "I knew I'd get on top of you somehow," he said.

"Are you trying to make me mad so I'll forget how scared I am?"

"No, I'm just opportunistic."

I wiggled, trying to get out from under him, and he said, "Oh, do that again. It felt great."

"Eric, that girl I was just talking to is about three feet away from us with part of her head missing."

"Sookie," he said, suddenly serious, "I've been dead for a few hundred years. I am used to it. But she is not quite gone. There is a spark. Do you want me to bring her over?"

I was shocked speechless. How could I make that decision? And while I thought about it, he said, "She is gone."

While I stared up at him, the silence became complete. The only noise in the house was the sobbing of Farrell's wounded date, who was pressing both hands to his reddened thigh. From outside came the remote sounds of vehicles pulling out in a hurry up and down the quiet suburban street. The attack was over. I seemed to be having trouble breathing, and figuring out what I should do next. Surely there was something, some action, I should be taking?

This was as close to war as I would ever come.

The room was full of the survivors' screams and the vampires' howls of rage. Bits of stuffing from the couch and chairs floated in the air like snow. There was broken glass on everything and the heat of the night poured into the room. Several of the vampires were already up and giving chase, Joseph Velasquez among them, I noticed.

"No excuse to linger," Eric said with a mock sigh, and lifted off of me. He looked down at himself. "My shirts always get ruined when I am around you."

"Oh shit, Eric." I got to my knees with clumsy haste. "You're bleeding. You got hit. Bill! Bill!" My hair was slithering around my shoulders as I turned from side to side searching the room. The last time I'd noticed him he'd been talking to a black-haired vampire with a pronounced widow's peak. She'd looked something like Snow White, to me. Now I half-stood to search the floor and I saw her sprawled close to a window. Something was protruding from her chest. The window had been hit by a shotgun blast, and some splinters had flown into the room. One of them had pierced her chest and killed her. Bill was not in sight, among the living or the dead.

Eric pulled off his sodden shirt and looked down at his shoulder. "The bullet is right inside the wound, Sookie," Eric said, through clenched teeth. "Suck it out."

"What?" I gaped at him.

"If you don't suck it out, it will heal inside my flesh. If you are so squeamish, go get a knife and cut."

"But I can't do that." My tiny party purse had a pocketknife inside, but I had no idea where I'd put it down, and I couldn't gather my thoughts to search.

He bared his teeth at me. "I took this bullet for you. You can get it out for me. You are no coward."

I forced myself to steady. I used his discarded shirt as a swab. The bleeding was slowing, and by peering into the torn flesh, I could just see the bullet. If I'd had long fingernails like Trudi, I'd have been able to get it out, but my fingers are short and blunt, and my nails are clipped close. I sighed in resignation.

The phrase "biting the bullet" took on a whole new meaning as I bent to Eric's shoulder.

Eric gave a long moan as I sucked, and I felt the bullet pop into my mouth. He'd been right. The rug could hardly be stained any worse than it already was, so though it made me feel like a real heathen, I spat the bullet onto the floor along with most of the blood in my mouth. But some of it, inevitably, I swallowed. His shoulder was already healing. "This room reeks of blood," he whispered.

"Well, there," I said, and looked up. "That was the grossest—"

"Your lips are bloody." He seized my face in both hands and kissed me.

It's hard not to respond when a master of the art of kissing is laying one on you. And I might have let myself enjoy it—well, enjoy it more—if I hadn't been so worried about Bill; because let's face it, brushes with death have that effect. You want to reaffirm the fact that you're alive. Though vampires actually aren't, it seems they are no more immune to that syndrome than humans, and Eric's libido was up because of the blood in the room.

But I was worried about Bill, and I was shocked by the violence, so after a long hot moment of forgetting the horror around me, I pulled away. Eric's lips were bloody now. He licked them slowly. "Go look for Bill," he said in a thick voice.

I glanced at his shoulder again, to see the hole had begun to close. I picked up the bullet off the carpet, tacky as it was with blood, and wrapped it in a scrap from Eric's shirt. It seemed like a good memento, at the time. I really don't know what I was thinking. There were still the injured and dead on the floor in the room, but most of those who were still alive had help from other humans or from two vampires who hadn't joined in the chase.

Sirens were sounding in the distance.

The beautiful front door was splintered and pitted. I stood to one side to open it, just in case there was a lone vigilante in the yard, but nothing happened. I peered around the doorframe.

"Bill?" I called. "Are you okay?"

Just then he sauntered back in the yard looking positively rosy.

"Bill," I said, feeling old and grim and gray. A dull horror, that really was just a deep disappointment, filled the pit of my stomach.

He stopped in his tracks.

"They fired at us and killed some of us," he said. His fangs gleamed, and he was shiny with excitement.

"You just killed somebody."

"To defend us."

"To get vengeance."

There was a clear difference between the two, in my mind, at that moment. He seemed nonplussed.

"You didn't even wait to see if I was okay," I said. Once a vampire, always a vampire. Tigers can't change their stripes. You can't teach an old dog new tricks. I heard every warning anyone had ever fed me, in the warm drawl of home.

I turned and went back into the house, walking obliviously through the bloodstains and chaos and mess as if I saw such things every day. Some of the things I saw I didn't even register I'd seen, until the next week when my brain would suddenly throw out a picture for my viewing: maybe a closeup of a shattered skull, or a spouting artery. What was important to me at the moment was that I find my purse. I found that purse in the second place I looked. While Bill fussed with the wounded so he wouldn't have to talk to me, I walked out of that house and got in that rental car and, despite my anxiety, I drove. Being at this house was worse than the fear of big city traffic. I pulled away from the house right before the police got there.

After I'd driven a few blocks, I parked in front of a library and extricated the map from the glove compartment. Though it took twice as long as it should have, since my brain was so shell-shocked it was almost not functioning, I figured out how to get to the airport.

And that's where I went. I followed the signs that said RENTAL CARS and I parked the car and left the keys in it and walked away. I got a seat on the next flight to Shreveport, which was leaving within the hour. I thanked God I had my own credit card.

Since I'd never done it before, it took me a few minutes to figure out the pay phone. I was lucky enough to get hold of Jason, who said he'd meet me at the airport.

I was home in bed by early morning.

I didn't start crying until the next day.

Chapter 9

WE'D FOUGHT BEFORE, Bill and I. I'd gotten fed up before, tired of the vampirey stuff I had to learn to accommodate, frightened of getting in deeper. Sometimes, I just wanted to see humans for a while.

So for over three weeks, that was what I did. I didn't call Bill; he didn't call me. I knew he was back from Dallas because he left my suitcase on my front porch. When I unpacked it, I found a black velvet jeweler's box tucked in the side pocket. I wish I'd had the strength to keep from opening it, but I didn't. Inside was a pair of topaz earrings, and a note that said, "To go with your brown dress." Which meant the taupe knit thing I'd worn to the vampires' headquarters. I stuck my tongue out at the box, and drove over to his house that afternoon to leave it in his mailbox. He'd finally gone out and bought me a present, and here I had to return it.

I didn't even try to "think things through." I figured my brain would clear up in a while, and then I would know what to do.

I did read the papers. The vampires of Dallas and their human friends were now martyrs, which probably suited Stan down to the ground. The Dallas Midnight Massacre was being touted in all the newsmagazines as the perfect example of a hate crime. Legislatures were being pressured to pass all kinds of laws that would never make it onto the books, but it made people feel better to think they might; laws that would provide vampire-owned buildings with federal protection, laws that would permit vampires to hold certain elected positions (though no one yet suggested a vampire could run for the U.S. Senate or serve as a representative). There was even a motion in the Texas legislature to appoint a vampire as legal executioner of the state. After all, a Senator Garza was quoted as saying, "Death by vampire bite is at least supposed to be painless, and the vampire receives nutrition from it."

I had news for Senator Garza. Vampire bites were only pleasant by the will of the vampire. If the vampire didn't glamour you first, a serious vampire bite (as opposed to a love nip) hurt like hell.

I wondered if Senator Garza was related to Luna, but Sam told me that "Garza" was as common among Americans of Mexican descent as "Smith" was among Americans of English stock.

Sam didn't ask why I wanted to know. That made me feel a little forlorn, because I was used to feeling important to Sam. But he was preoccupied these days, on the job and off. Arlene said she thought he was dating someone, which was a first, as far as any of us could remember. Whoever she was, none of us got to see her, which was strange in and of itself. I tried to tell him about the shapeshifters of Dallas, but he just smiled and found an excuse to go do something else.

My brother, Jason, dropped by the house for lunch one day. It wasn't like it had been when my grandmother was alive. Gran would have a huge meal on the table at lunchtime, and then we'd just eat sandwiches at night. Jason had come by pretty frequently then; Gran had been an excellent cook. I managed to serve him meatloaf sandwiches and potato salad (though I didn't tell him it was from the store), and I had some peach tea fixed, which was lucky.

"What's with you and Bill?" he asked bluntly, when he was through. He'd been real good about not asking on the drive back from the airport.

"I got mad at him," I said.

"Why?"

"He broke a promise to me," I said. Jason was trying hard to act like a big brother, and I should try to accept his concern instead of getting mad. It occurred to me, not for the first time, that possibly I had a pretty hot temper. Under some circumstances. I locked my sixth sense down firmly, so I would only hear what Jason was actually saying.

"He's been seen over in Monroe."

I took a deep breath. "With someone else?"

"Yes."

"Who?"

"You're not going to believe this. Portia Bellefleur."

I couldn't have been more surprised if Jason had told me Bill had been dating Hillary Clinton (though Bill *was* a Democrat). I stared at my brother as if he'd suddenly announced he was Satan. The only things Portia Bellefleur and I had in common were a birthplace, female organs, and long hair. "Well," I said blankly. "I don't know whether to pitch a fit or laugh. What do you make of that?"

Because if anyone knew about man-woman stuff, it was Jason. At least, he knew about it from the man's point of view.

"She's your opposite," he said, with undue thoughtfulness. "In every way that I can think of. She's real educated, she comes from an, I guess you'd call it, aristocratic background, and she's a lawyer. Plus, her brother's a cop. And they go to symphonies and shit."

Tears prickled at my eyes. I would have gone to a symphony with Bill, if he'd ever asked me.

"On the other hand, you're smart, you're pretty, and you're willing to put up with his little ways." I wasn't exactly sure what Jason meant by that, and thought it better not to ask. "But we sure ain't aristocracy. You work in a bar, and your brother works on a road crew." Jason smiled at me lopsidedly.

"We've been here as long as the Bellefleurs," I said, trying not to sound sullen.

"I know that, and you know that. And Bill sure knows that, because he was alive then." True enough.

"What's happening about the case against Andy?" I asked.

"No charges brought against him yet, but the rumors are flying around town thick and fast about this sex club thing. Lafayette was so pleased to have been asked; evidently he mentioned it to quite a few people. They say that since the first rule of the club is Keep Silent, Lafayette got whacked for his enthusiasm."

"What do you think?"

"I think if anyone was forming a sex club around Bon Temps, they woulda called me," he said, dead serious.

"You're right," I said, struck again by how sensible Jason could be. "You'd be number one on the list." Why hadn't I thought of that before? Not only did Jason have a reputation as a guy who'd heated up many a bed, he was both very attractive and unmarried.

"The only thing I can think of," I said slowly, "Lafayette was gay, as you well know."

"And?"

"And maybe this club, if it exists, only accepts people who are all right with that."

"You might have a point there," Jason said.

"Yes, Mr. Homophobe."

Jason smiled and shrugged. "Everybody's got a weak point," he said. "Plus, as you know, I've been going out with Liz pretty steady. I think anyone with a brain would see Liz ain't about to share a napkin, much less a boyfriend."

He was right. Liz's family notoriously took "Neither a borrower nor a lender be" to a complete extreme.

"You are a piece of work, brother," I said, focusing on his short-comings, rather than those of Liz's folks. "There are so many worse things to be than gay."

"Such as?"

"Thief, traitor, murderer, rapist . . ."

"Okay, okay, I get the idea."

"I hope you do," I said. Our differences grieved me. But I loved Jason anyway; he was all I had left.

I saw Bill out with Portia that same night. I caught a glimpse of them together in Bill's car, driving down Claiborne Street. Portia had her head turned to Bill, talking; he was looking straight ahead, expressionless, as far as I could tell. They didn't see me. I was coming from the automated teller at the bank, on my way to work.

Hearing of and seeing directly are two very different things. I felt an overwhelming surge of rage; and I understood how Bill had felt, when he'd seen his friends dying. I wanted to kill someone. I just wasn't sure who I wanted to kill.

Andy was in the bar that evening, sitting in Arlene's section. I was glad, because Andy looked bad. He was not clean-shaven, and his clothes were rumpled. He came up to me as he was leaving, and I could smell the booze. "Take him back," he said. His voice was thick with anger. "Take the damn vampire back so he'll leave my sister alone."

I didn't know what to say to Andy Bellefleur. I just stared at him until he stumbled out of the bar. It crossed my mind that people wouldn't be as surprised to hear of a dead body in his car now as they had been a few weeks ago.

The next night I had off, and the temperature dropped. It was a Friday, and suddenly I was tired of being alone. I decided to go to the high school football game. This is a townwide pastime in Bon Temps, and the games are discussed thoroughly on Monday morning in every store in town. The film of the game is shown twice on a local-access channel, and boys who show promise with pigskin are minor royalty, more's the pity.

You don't show up at the game all disheveled.

I pulled my hair back from my forehead in an elastic band and used my curling iron on the rest, so I had thick curls hanging around my shoulders. My bruises were gone. I put on complete makeup, down to the lip liner. I put on black knit slacks and a black-and-red sweater. I wore my black leather boots, and my gold hoop earrings, and I pinned a red-and-black bow to hide the elastic band in my hair. (Guess what our school colors are.)

"Pretty good," I said, viewing the result in my mirror. "Pretty *damn* good." I gathered up my black jacket and my purse and drove into town.

The stands were full of people I knew. A dozen voices called to me, a dozen people told me how cute I looked, and the problem was . . . I was miserable. As soon as I realized this, I pasted a smile on my face and searched for someone to sit with.

"Sookie! Sookie!" Tara Thornton, one of my few good high school friends, was calling me from high up in the stands. She made a frantic beckoning gesture, and I smiled back and began to hike up, speaking to more people along the way. Mike Spencer, the funeral home director, was there, in his favorite western regalia, and my grandmother's good friend Maxine Fortenberry, and her grandson Hoyt, who was a buddy of Jason's. I saw Sid Matt Lancaster, the ancient lawyer, bundled up beside his wife.

Tara was sitting with her fiancé, Benedict Tallie, who was inevitably and regrettably called "Eggs." With them was Benedict's best friend, JB du Rone. When I saw JB, my spirits began to rise, and so did my repressed libido. JB could have been on the cover of a romance novel, he was so lovely. Unfortunately, he didn't have a brain in his head, as I'd discovered on our handful of dates. I'd often thought I'd hardly have to put up any mental shield to be with JB, because he had no thoughts to read.

"Hey, how ya'll doing?"

"We're great!" Tara said, with her party-girl face on. "How about you? I haven't seen you in a coon's age!" Her dark hair was cut in a short pageboy, and her lipstick could have lit a fire, it was so hot. She was wearing off-white and black with a red scarf to show her team spirit, and she and Eggs were sharing a drink in one of the paper cups sold in the stadium. It was spiked; I could smell the bourbon from where I stood. "Move over, JB, and let me sit with you," I said with an answering smile.

"Sure, Sookie," he said, looking very happy to see me. That was one of JB's charms. The others included white perfect teeth, an absolutely straight nose, a face so masculine yet so handsome that it made you want to reach out and stroke his cheeks, and a broad chest and trim waist. Maybe not quite as trim as it used to be, but then, JB was human, and that was a Good Thing. I settled in between Eggs and JB, and Eggs turned to me with a sloppy smile.

"Want a drink, Sookie?"

I am kind of spare on drinking, since I see its results every day. "No, thank you," I said. "How you been doing, Eggs?"

"Good," he said, after considering. He'd had more to drink than Tara. He'd had too much to drink.

We talked about mutual friends and acquaintances until the kick-off, after which the game was the sole topic of conversation. The Game, broadly, because every game for the past fifty years lay in the collective memory of Bon Temps, and this game was compared to all other games, these players to all others. I could actually enjoy this occasion a little, since I had developed my mental shielding to such an extent. I could pretend people were exactly what they said, since I was absolutely not listening in.

JB snuggled closer and closer, after a shower of compliments on my hair and my figure. JB's mother had taught him early on that appreciated women are happy women, and it was a simple philosophy that had kept JB's head above water for some time.

"You remember that doctor at that hospital, Sookie?" he asked me suddenly, during the second quarter.

"Yes. Dr. Sonntag. Widow." She'd been young to be a widow, and younger to be a doctor. I'd introduced her to JB.

"We dated for a while. Me and a doctor," he said wonderingly.

"Hey, that's great." I'd hoped as much. It had seemed to me that Dr. Sonntag could sure use what JB had to offer, and JB needed . . . well, he needed someone to take care of him.

"But then she got rotated back to Baton Rouge," he told me. He looked a little stricken. "I guess I miss her." A health care system had bought our little hospital, and the emergency room doctors were brought in for four months at a stretch. His arm tightened around my shoulders. "But it's awful good to see you," he reassured me.

Bless his heart. "JB, you could go to Baton Rouge to see her," I suggested. "Why don't you?"

"She's a doctor. She doesn't have much time off."

"She'd make time off for you."

"Do you think so?"

"Unless she's an absolute idiot," I told him.

"I might do that. I did talk to her on the phone the other night. She did say she wished I was there."

"That was a pretty big hint, JB."

"You think?"

"I sure do."

He looked perkier. "Then I'm fixing to drive to Baton Rouge tomorrow," he said again. He kissed my cheek. "You make me feel good, Sookie."

"Well, JB, right back at you." I gave him a peck on the lips, just a quick one.

Then I saw Bill staring a hole in me.

He and Portia were in the next section of seats, close to the bottom. He had twisted around and was looking up at me.

If I'd planned it, it couldn't have worked out better. This was a magnificent Screw-him moment.

And it was ruined.

I just wanted him.

I turned my eyes away and smiled at JB, and all the time what I wanted was to meet with Bill under the stands and have sex with him right then and there. I wanted him to pull down my pants and get behind me. I wanted him to make me moan.

I was so shocked at myself I didn't know what to do. I could feel my face turning a dull red. I could not even pretend to smile.

After a minute, I could appreciate that this was almost funny. I had been brought up as conventionally as possible, given my unusual disability. Naturally, I'd learned the facts of life pretty early since I could read minds (and, as a child, had no control over what I absorbed). And I'd always thought the idea of sex was pretty interesting, though the same disability that had led to me learning so much about it theoretically had kept me from putting that theory into practice. After all, it's hard to get really involved in sex when you know your partner is wishing you were Tara Thornton instead (for example), or when he's hoping you remembered to bring a condom, or when he's criticizing your body parts. For successful sex, you have to keep your concentration fixed on what your partner's *doing*, so you can't get distracted by what he's *thinking*.

With Bill, I couldn't hear a single thing. And he was so experienced, so smooth, so absolutely dedicated to getting it right. It appeared I was as much a junkie as Hugo.

I sat through the rest of the game, smiling and nodding when it seemed indicated, trying not to look down and to my left, and finding after the halftime show was over that I hadn't heard a single song the band had played. Nor had I noticed Tara's cousin's twirling solo. As the crowd moved slowly to the parking lot after the Bon Temps Hawks had won, 28–18, I agreed to drive JB home. Eggs had sobered some by then, so I was pretty sure he and Tara would be okay; but I was relieved to see Tara take the wheel.

JB lived close to downtown in half a duplex. He asked me very sweetly to come in, but I told him I had to get home. I gave him a big hug, and I advised him to call Dr. Sonntag. I still didn't know her first name.

He said he would, but then, with JB, you couldn't really tell.

Then I had to stop and get gas at the only late-night gas station, where I had a long conversation with Arlene's cousin Derrick (who was brave enough to take the night shift), so I was a little later getting home than I had planned.

As I unlocked the front door, Bill came out of the darkness. Without a word, he grabbed my arm and turned me to him, and then he kissed me. In a minute we were pressed against the door with his body moving rhythmically against mine. I reached one hand behind myself to fumble with the lock, and the key finally turned. We stumbled into the house, and he turned me to face the couch. I gripped it with my hands and, just as I'd imagined, he pulled down my pants, and then he was in me.

I made a hoarse noise I'd never heard come from my throat before. Bill was making noises equally as primitive. I didn't think I could form a word. His hands were under my sweater, and my bra was in two pieces. He was relentless. I almost collapsed after the first time I came. "No," he growled when I was flagging, and he kept pounding. Then he increased the pace until I was almost sobbing, and then my sweater tore, and his teeth found my shoulder. He made a deep, awful sound, and then, after long seconds, it was over.

I was panting as if I'd run a mile, and he was shivering, too. Without bothering to refasten his clothing, he turned me around to face him, and he bent his head to my shoulder again to lick the little wound. When it had stopped bleeding and begun healing, he took off everything I had on, very slowly. He cleaned me below; he kissed me above.

"You smell like him" was the only thing he said. He proceeded to erase that smell and replace it with his own.

Then we were in the bedroom, and I had a moment to be glad I'd changed the sheets that morning before he bent his mouth to mine again.

If I'd had doubts up until then, I had them no longer. He was not sleeping with Portia Bellefleur. I didn't know what he was up to, but he did not have a true relationship with her. He slid his arms underneath me and held me to him as tightly as possible; he nuzzled my neck, kneaded my hips, ran his fingers down my thighs, and kissed the backs of my knees. He bathed in me. "Spread your legs for me, Sookie," he whispered, in his cold dark voice, and I did. He was ready again, and he was rough with it, as if he were trying to prove something.

"Be sweet," I said, the first time I had spoken.

"I can't. It's been too long, next time I'll be sweet, I swear," he said, running his tongue down the line of my jaw. His fangs grazed my neck. Fangs, tongue, mouth, fingers, manhood; it was like being made love to by the Tasmanian Devil. He was everywhere, and everywhere in a hurry.

When he collapsed on top of me, I was exhausted. He shifted to lie by my side, one leg draped over mine, one arm across my chest. He might as well have gotten out a branding iron and had done with it, but it wouldn't have been as much fun for me.

"Are you okay?" he mumbled.

"Except for having run into a brick wall a few times," I said indistinctly.

We both drifted off to sleep for a little, though Bill woke first, as he always did at night. "Sookie," he said quietly. "Darling. Wake up."

"Oo," I said, slowly coming to consciousness. For the first time in weeks, I woke with the hazy conviction that all was right with the world. With slow dismay, I realized that things were far from right. I opened my eyes. Bill's were right above me.

"We have to talk," he said, stroking the hair back from my face.

"So talk." I was awake now. What I was regretting was not the sex, but having to discuss the issues between us.

"I got carried away in Dallas," he said immediately. "Vampires do, when the chance to hunt presents itself so obviously. We were attacked. We have the right to hunt down those who want to kill us."

"That's returning to days of lawlessness," I said.

"But vampires hunt, Sookie. It is our nature," he said very seriously. "Like leopards; like wolves. We are not human. We can pretend to be, when we're trying to live with people . . . in your society. We can sometimes remember what it was like to be among you, one of you. But we are not the same race. We are no longer of the same clay."

I thought this over. He'd told me this, over and over, in different words, since we'd begun seeing each other.

Or maybe, he'd been seeing me, but I hadn't been seeing him: clearly, truly. No matter how often I thought I'd made my peace with his otherness, I realized that I still expected him to react as he would if he were JB du Rone, or Jason, or my church pastor.

"I think I'm finally getting this," I said. "But you got to realize, sometimes I'm not going to like that difference. Sometimes I have to get away and cool down. I'm really going to try. I really love you." Having done my best to promise to meet him halfway, I was reminded of my own grievance. I grabbed his hair and rolled him over so I was looking down at him. I looked right in his eyes.

"Now, you tell me what you're doing with Portia."

Bill's big hands rested on my hips as he explained.

"She came to me after I got back from Dallas, the first night. She had read about what happened there, wondered if I knew anyone who'd been there that day. When I said that I had been there myself—I didn't mention you—Portia said she had information that some of the arms used in the attack had come from a place in Bon Temps, Sheridan's Sport Shop. I asked her how she had heard this; she said as a lawyer, she couldn't say. I asked her why she was so concerned, if there wasn't anything further she'd tell me about it; she said she was a good citizen and hated to see other citizens persecuted. I asked her why she came to me; she said I was the only vampire she knew."

I believed that like I believed Portia was a secret belly dancer.

I narrowed my eyes as I worked this through. "Portia doesn't care one damn thing about vampire rights," I said. "She might want to get in your pants, but she doesn't care about vampire legal issues."

" 'Get in my pants?' What a turn of phrase you have."

"Oh, you've heard that before," I said, a little abashed.

He shook his head, amusement sparkling in his face. "Get in my pants," he repeated, sounding it out slowly. "I would be in your pants, if you had any on." He rubbed his hands up and down to demonstrate.

"Cut that out," I said. "I'm trying to think."

His hands were pressing my hips, then releasing, moving me back and forth on him. I began to have difficulty forming thoughts.

"Stop, Bill," I said. "Listen, I think Portia wants to be seen with you so she might be asked to join that supposed sex club here in Bon Temps."

"Sex club?" Bill said with interest, not stopping in the least.

"Yes, didn't I tell you . . . oh, Bill, no . . . Bill, I'm still worn out from last . . . Oh. Oh, God." His hands had gripped me with their great strength, and moved me purposefully, right onto his stiffness. He began rocking me again, back and forth. "Oh," I said, lost in the moment. I began to see colors floating in front of my eyes, and then I was being rocked so fast I couldn't keep track of my motion. The end came at the same time for both of us, and we clung together panting for several minutes.

"We should never separate again," Bill said.

"I don't know, this makes it almost worth it."

A little aftershock rippled his body. "No," he said. "This is wonderful, but I would rather just leave town for a few days, than fight with you again." He opened his eyes wide. "Did you really suck a bullet from Eric's shoulder?"

"Yeah, he said I had to get it out before his flesh closed over it."

"Did he tell you he had a pocketknife in his pocket?"

I was taken aback. "No. Did he? Why would he do that?"

Bill raised his eyebrows, as if I had said something quite ridiculous.

"Guess," he said.

"So I would suck on his shoulder? You can't mean that."

Bill just maintained the skeptical look.

"Oh, Bill. I fell for it. Wait a minute—he got shot! That bullet could have hit me, but instead it hit him. He was guarding me."

"How?"

"Well, by lying on top of me . . ."

"I rest my case." There was nothing old-fashioned about Bill at the moment. On the other hand, there was a pretty old-fashioned look on his face.

"But, Bill . . . you mean he's that devious?"

Again with the raised eyebrows.

"Lying on top of me is not such a big treat," I protested, "that someone should take a bullet for it. Geez. That's nuts!"

"It got some of his blood in you."

"Only a drop or two. I spit the rest out," I said.

"A drop or two is enough when you are as old as Eric is."

"Enough for what?"

"He will know some things about you, now."

"What, like my dress size?"

Bill smiled, not always a relaxing sight. "No, like how you are feeling. Angry, horny, loving."

I shrugged. "Won't do him any good."

"Probably it is not too important, but be careful from now on," Bill warned me. He seemed quite serious.

"I still can't believe someone would put themselves in a position to take a bullet for me just in the hopes I'd ingest a drop of blood getting the bullet out. That's ridiculous. You know, it seems like to me you introduced this subject so I'd quit bugging you about Portia, but I'm not going to. I think Portia believes if she's dating you, someone will ask her to go to this sex club, since if she's willing to ball a vampire, she's willing to do anything. They *think*," said hastily after looking at

Bill's face. "So Portia figures she'll go, she'll learn stuff, she'll find out who actually killed Lafayette, Andy'll be off the hook."

"That's a complicated plot."

"Can you refute it?" I was proud to use *refute*, which had been on my Word of the Day calendar.

"As a matter of fact, I can't." He became immobile. His eyes were fixed and unblinking, and his hands relaxed. Since Bill doesn't breathe, he was absolutely still.

Finally he blinked. "It would have been better if she had told me the truth to begin with."

"You better not have had sex with her," I said, finally admitting to myself that the bare possibility had made me nearly blind with jealousy.

"I wondered when you were going to ask me," he said calmly. "As if I would ever bed a Belleflcur. No, she has not the slightest desire to have sex with me. She even has a hard time pretending she wants to at some later date. Portia is not much of an actress. Most of the time we are together, she takes me on wild goose chases to find this cache of arms the Fellowship has stowed here, saying all the Fellowship sympathizers are hiding them."

"So why'd you go along with any of this?"

"There's something about her that's honorable. And I wanted to see if you would be jealous."

"Oh, I see. Well, what do you think?"

"I think," he said, "I had better never see you within a yard of that handsome moron again."

"JB? I'm like his sister," I said.

"You forget, you've had my blood, and I can tell what you are feeling," Bill said. "I don't think you feel exactly like a sister to him."

"That would explain why I'm here in bed with you, right?"

"You love me."

I laughed, up against his throat.

"It's close to dawn," he said. "I have to go."

"Okay, baby." I smiled up at him as he gathered up his clothes. "Hey, you owe me a sweater and a bra. Two bras. Gabe tore one, so that was a work-related clothes injury. And you tore one last night, plus my sweater."

"That's why I bought a women's clothing store," he said smoothly. "So I could rip if the spirit moves me."

I laughed and lay back down. I could sleep for a couple more hours. I was still smiling when he let himself out of my house, and I woke up in the middle of the morning with a lightness in my heart that hadn't been there for a long time. (Well, it felt like a long time.) I walked, somewhat gingerly, into the bathroom to soak in a tubful of hot water. When I began to wash, I felt something in my earlobes. I stood up in the tub and looked over at the mirror above the sink. He'd put the topaz earrings in while I was asleep.

Mr. Last Word.

SINCE OUR REUNION had been secret, it was I who got invited to the club first. It had never occurred to me that that might happen; but after it did, I realized that if Portia had figured she might be invited after going with a vampire, I was even primer meat.

To my surprise and disgust, the one to broach the subject was Mike Spencer. Mike was the funeral home director and the coroner in Bon Temps, and we had not always had a completely cordial relationship. However, I'd known him all my life and was used to offering him respect, a hard habit to break. Mike was wearing his funeral home duds when he came in to Merlotte's that evening, because he'd come from Mrs. Cassidy's visitation. A dark suit, white shirt, subdued striped tie, and polished wing tips changed Mike Spencer from the guy who really preferred bolo ties and pointy-toed cowboy boots.

Since Mike was at least twenty years older than me, I'd always related to him as an elder, and it shocked me silly when he approached me. He was sitting by himself, which was unusual enough to be noteworthy. I brought him a hamburger and a beer. As he paid me, he said casually, "Sookie, some of us are getting together at Jan Fowler's lake house tomorrow night and we wondered if we could get you to come."

I am fortunate I have a well-schooled face. I felt as if a pit had opened beneath my feet, and I was actually a little nauseated. I understood immediately, but I couldn't quite believe it. I opened my mind to him, while my mouth was saying, "You said 'some of us'? Who would that be, Mr. Spencer?"

"Why don't you call me Mike, Sookie?" I nodded, looking inside his head all the while. Oh, geez Louise. Ick. "Well, some of your friends will be there. Eggs, and Portia, and Tara. The Hardaways."

Tara and Eggs . . . that really shocked me.

"So, what goes on at these parties? Is this just a drinking and dancing type thing?" This was not an unreasonable question. No matter how many people knew I was supposed to be able to read minds, they almost never believed it, no matter how much evidence to the contrary they'd witnessed. Mike simply could not believe that I could receive the images and concepts floating in his mind.

"Well, we get a little wild. We thought since you'd broken up with your boyfriend, that you might want to come let your hair down a little."

"Maybe I'll come," I said, without enthusiasm. It wouldn't do to look eager. "When?"

"Oh, ten o'clock tomorrow night."

"Thanks for the invite," I said, as if remembering my manners, and then sauntered off with my tip. I thought furiously, in the odd moments I had to myself during the rest of my shift.

What good could my going serve? Could I really learn anything that would solve the mystery of Lafayette's death? I didn't like Andy Bellefleur much, and now I liked Portia even less, but it wasn't fair that Andy might be prosecuted, his reputation ruined, for something that wasn't his fault. On the other hand, it stood to reason that no one present at a party at the lake house would trust me with any deep dark secrets until I'd become a regular, and I just couldn't stomach that. I wasn't even sure I could get through one gathering. The last thing in the world I wanted to see was my friends and my neighbors "letting their hair down." I didn't want to see them let down their hair, or anything else.

"What's the matter, Sookie?" Sam asked, so close to me that I jumped.

I looked at him, wishing that I could ask what he thought. Sam was strong and wiry, and he was clever, too. The bookkeeping, the ordering, the maintenance and planning, he never seemed to be taxed with any of it. Sam was a self-sufficient man, and I liked and trusted him.

"I'm just in a little quandary," I said. "What's up with you, Sam?"

"I got an interesting phone call last night, Sookie."

"Who from?"

"A squeaky woman in Dallas."

"Really?" I found myself smiling, really, not the grin I used to cover my nerves. "Would that be a lady of Mexican descent?"

"I believe so. She spoke of you."

"She's feisty," I said.

"She's got a lot of friends."

"Kind of friends you'd want to have?"

"I already have some good friends," Sam said, squeezing my hand briefly. "But it's always nice to know people who share your interests."

"So, are you driving over to Dallas?"

"I just might. In the meantime, she's put me in touch with some people in Ruston who also . . ."

Change their appearance when the moon is full, I finished mentally.

"How did she trace you? I didn't give her your name, on purpose, because I didn't know if you'd want me to."

"She traced you," Sam said. "And she found out who your boss was through local . . . people."

"How come you had never hooked up with them on your own?"

"Until you told me about the maenad," Sam said, "I never realized that there were so many more things I had to learn."

"Sam, you haven't been hanging around with her?"

"I've spent a few evenings in the woods with her, yes. As Sam, and in my other skin."

"But she's so evil," I blurted.

Sam's back stiffened. "She's a supernatural creature like me," he said evenly. "She's neither evil nor good, she just is."

"Oh, bullshit." I couldn't believe I was hearing this from Sam. "If she's feeding you this line, then she wants something from you." I remembered how beautiful the maenad had been, if you didn't mind bloodstains. And Sam, as a shapeshifter, wouldn't. "Oh," I said, comprehension sweeping me. Not that I could read Sam's mind clearly, since he was a supernatural creature, but I could get a lock on his emotional state, which was—embarrassed, horny, resentful, and horny.

"Oh," I said again, somewhat stiffly. "Excuse me, Sam. I didn't mean to speak ill of someone you . . . you, ah . . ." I could hardly say, "are screwing," however apropos it might be. "You're spending time with," I finished lamely. "I'm sure she's lovely once you get to know her. Of course, the fact that she cut my back to bloody ribbons may have something to do with my prejudice against her. I'll try to be more open-minded." And I stalked off to take an order, leaving Sam open-mouthed behind me.

I left a message on Bill's answering machine. I didn't know what Bill intended to do about Portia, and I guessed there was a possibility someone else would be there when he played his messages, so I said, "Bill, I got invited to that party tomorrow night. Let me know if you think I should go." I didn't identify myself, since he'd know my voice. Possibly, Portia had left an identical message, an idea that just made me furious.

When I drove home that night, I half-hoped Bill would be waiting to ambush me again in an erotic way, but the house and yard were silent. I perked up when I noticed the light on my answering machine was blinking.

"Sookie," said Bill's smooth voice, "stay out of the woods. The maenad was dissatisfied with our tribute. Eric will be in Bon Temps tomorrow night to negotiate with her, and he may call you. The—other people—of Dallas, the ones who helped you, are asking for outrageous recompense from the vampires of Dallas, so I am going over there on Anubis to meet with them, with Stan. You know where I'll be staying."

Yikes. Bill wouldn't be in Bon Temps to help me, and he was out of my reach. Or was he? It was one in the morning. I called the number I'd put in my address book, for the Silent Shore, Bill had not yet checked in, though his coffin (which the concierge referred to as his "baggage") had been put in his room. I left a message, which I had to phrase so guardedly that it might be incomprehensible.

I was really tired, since I hadn't gotten much sleep the night before, but I had no intention of going to the next night's party alone. I sighed deeply, and called Fangtasia, the vampire bar in Shreveport.

"You've reached Fantasia, where the undead live again every night," said a recording of Pam's voice. Pam was a co-owner. "For bar hours, press one. To make a party reservation, press two. To talk to a live person or a dead vampire, press three. Or, if you were intending to leave a humorous prank message on our answering machine, know this: we will find you."

I pressed three.

"Fangtasia," Pam said, as if she were bored more completely than anyone had ever been bored.

"Hi," I said, weighing in on the perky side to counteract the ennui. "This is Sookie, Pam. Is Eric around?"

"He is enthralling the vermin," Pam said. I took that to mean Eric was sprawling in a chair on the main floor of the bar, looking gorgeous and dangerous. Bill had told me that some vampires were under contract to Fangtasia, to put in one or two appearances a week of a stated duration, so the tourists would keep coming. Eric, as an owner, was there almost every night. There was another bar where vampires went of their own accord, a bar a tourist would never enter. I'd never been in it, because frankly, I see enough of bars while I'm at work.

"Could you take him the phone, please, ma'am?"

"Oh, all right," she said grudgingly. "I hear you had quite a time in Dallas," she said as she walked. Not that I could hear her steps, but the noise in the background ebbed and flowed.

"Unforgettable."

"What did you think of Stan Davis?"

Hmmm. "He's one of a kind."

"I like that nerdy, geeky look myself."

I was glad she wasn't there to see the astonished look I gave the telephone. I'd never realized Pam liked guys, too. "He certainly didn't seem to be dating anyone," I said, I hoped casually.

"Ah. Maybe I'll take a vacation to Dallas soon."

It was also news to me that vampires were interested in each other. I'd never actually seen two vampires together.

"I am here," Eric said.

"And I am here." I was a little amused at Eric's phone answering technique.

"Sookie, my little bullet-sucker," he said, sounding fond and warm.

"Eric, my big bullshitter."

"You want something, my darling?"

"I'm not your darling, and you know it, for one thing. For another— Bill said you were coming over here tomorrow night?"

"Yes, to tromp up in the woods looking for the maenad. She finds our offerings of vintage wine and a young bull inadequate."

"You took her live bull?" I was momentarily sidetracked by the vision of Eric herding a cow into a trailer and driving it to the shoulder of the interstate and shooing it into the trees.

"Yes, indeed we did. Pam and Indira and I."

"Was it fun?"

"Yes," he said, sounding faintly surprised. "It had been several centuries since I dealt with livestock. Pam is a city girl. Indira had too much awe of the bull to be a lot of help. But if you like, the next time I have to transport animals I will give you a call, and you can go along."

"Thanks, that would be lovely," I said, feeling pretty confident that was a call I'd never get. "The reason I called you is that I need you to go to a party with me tomorrow night."

A long silence.

"Bill is no longer your bedmate? The differences you developed in Dallas are permanent?"

"What I should have said is, 'I need a bodyguard for tomorrow night.' Bill's in Dallas." I was smacking myself on the forehead with the heel of my hand. "See, there's a long explanation, but the situation is that I need to go to a party tomorrow night that's really just a . . . well, it's a . . . kind of orgy thing? And I need someone with me in case . . . just in case."

"That's fascinating," Eric said, sounding fascinated. "And since I'm going to be in the neighborhood, you thought I might do as an escort? To an orgy?"

"You can look almost human," I said.

"This is a human orgy? One that excludes vampires?"

"It's a human orgy that doesn't know a vampire is coming."

"So, the more human I look the less frightening I'll be?"

"Yes, I nccd to read their thoughts. Pick their brains. And if I get them thinking about a certain thing, and pick their brains, then we can get out of there." I'd just had a great idea about how to get them to think about Lafayette. Telling Eric was going to be the problem.

"So you want me to go to a human orgy, where I will not be welcome, and you want us to leave before I get to enjoy myself?"

"Yes," I said, almost squeaking in my anxiety. In for a penny, in for a pound. "And . . . do you think you could pretend to be gay?"

There was a long silence. "What time do I need to be there?" Eric asked softly.

"Um. Nine-thirty? So I can brief you?"

"Nine-thirty at your house."

"I am carrying the phone back," Pam informed me. "What did you say to Eric? He is shaking his head back and forth with his eyes shut."

"Is he laughing, even a little bit?"

"Not that I can tell," Pam said.

Chapter 10

BILL DIDN'T CALL back that night, and I left for work before sun-set the next day. He'd left a message on the answering machine when I came home to dress for the "party."

"Sookie, I had a hard time making out what the situation was, from your very guarded message," he said. His usually calm voice was defi-nitely on the unhappy side. Miffed. "If you are going to this party, don't go alone, whatever you do. It isn't worth it. Get your brother or Sam to go with you."

Well, I'd gotten someone even stronger to go with me, so I should be feeling pretty virtuous. Somehow, I didn't think that my having Eric with me would reassure Bill.

"Stan Davis and Joseph Velasquez send their regards, and Barry the bellhop."

I smiled. I was sitting cross-legged on my bed wearing only an old chenille bathrobe, giving my hair a brushing while I listened to my messages.

"I haven't forgotten Friday night," Bill said, in the voice that always made me shiver. "I will never forget."

"So what happened Friday night?" Eric asked.

I shrieked. Once I could feel my heart was going to stay in my chest cavity, I scrambled off the bed and strode over to him with my fists balled.

"You are old enough to know you don't come in someone's house without knocking on the door and having it answered. Besides, when did I ever invite you inside?" I had to have extended the invitation, or else Eric couldn't have crossed the threshold.

"When I stopped by last month to see Bill. I did knock," Eric said, trying his best to look wounded. "You didn't answer, and I thought I heard voices, so I came in. I even called your name."

"You may have whispered my name." I was still furious. "But you acted bad, and you know it!"

"What are you wearing to the party?" Eric asked, effectively changing the subject. "If this is to be an orgy, what does a good girl like you wear?"

"I just don't know," I said, deflated by the reminder. "I'm sure I'm supposed to look like the kind of girl who goes to orgies, but I've never been to one and I have no idea how to start out, though I have a pretty clear idea of how I'm supposed to end up."

"I have been to orgies," he offered.

"Why does that not surprise me? What do you wear?"

"The last time I wore an animal hide; but this time I settled for this." Eric had been wearing a long trench coat. Now he threw it off dramatically, and I could only stand and stare. Normally, Eric was a blue-jeans-and-T-shirt kind of guy. Tonight, he wore a pink tank top and Lycra leggings. I don't know where he got them; I didn't know any company made Lycra leggings in Men's X-tra Large Tall. They were pink and aqua, like the swirls down the sides of Jason's truck.

"Wow," I said, since it was all I could think of to say. "Wow. That's some outfit." When you've got a big guy wearing Lycra it doesn't leave a whole lot to the imagination. I resisted the temptation to ask Eric to turn around.

"I don't believe I could be convincing as a queen," Eric said, "but I decided this sent such a mixed signal, almost anything was possible." He fluttered his eyelashes at me. Eric was definitely enjoying this.

"Oh, yes," I said, trying to find somewhere else to look.

"Shall I go through your drawers and find something for you to wear?" Eric suggested. He had actually opened the top drawer of my bureau before I said, "No, no! I'll find something!" But I couldn't find anything more informally sexy than shorts and a tee shirt. However, the shorts were some I had left over from my junior high days, and they encased me "like a caterpillar embraces a butterfly," Eric said poetically.

"More like Daisy Dukes," I muttered, wondering if the lace pattern of my bikini underwear would be imprinted on my butt for the rest of my life. I wore a matching steel blue bra with a dipping white tank top that exposed a lot of the decoration on the bra. This was one of my replacement bras, and Bill hadn't even gotten to see it yet, so I sure hoped nothing happened to it. My tan was still holding up, and I wore my hair loose.

"Hey, our hair's the same color," I said, eyeing us side by side in the mirror.

"Sure is, girlfriend." Eric grinned at me. "But are you blond all the way down?"

"Don't you wish you knew?"

"Yes," he said simply.

"Well, you'll just have to wonder."

"I am," he said. "Blond everywhere."

"I could tell as much from your chest hair."

He raised my arm to check my armpit. "You silly women, shaving your body hair," he said, dropping my arm.

I opened my mouth to say something else on the topic, suddenly realized that would lead to disaster, and said instead, "We need to go."

"Aren't you going to wear perfume?" He was sniffing all the bottles on top of my dressing table. "Oh, wear this!" He tossed me a bottle and I caught it without thinking. His eyebrows flew up. "You have had more vampire blood than I thought, Miss Sookie."

"Obsession," I said, looking at the bottle. "Oh, okay." Carefully not responding to his observation, I dabbed a little bit of Obsession between my breasts and behind my knees. I figured that way I was covered from head to toe.

"What is our agenda, Sookie?" Eric asked, eyeing this procedure with interest.

"What we're going to do is go to this stupid so-called sex party and do as little as possible in that line while I gather information from the minds of the people there."

"Pertaining to?"

"Pertaining to the murder of Lafayette Reynold, the cook at Merlotte's Bar."

"And why are we doing this?"

"Because I liked Lafayette. And to clear Andy Bellefleur of the suspicion that he murdered Lafayette."

"Bill knows you are trying to save a Bellefleur?"

"Why do you ask that?"

"You know Bill hates the Bellefleurs," Eric said, as if that were the best-known fact in Louisiana.

"No," I said. "No, I didn't know that at all." I sat down on the chair by my bed, my eyes fixed on Eric's face. "Why?"

"You'll have to ask Bill that, Sookie. And this is the only reason we're going? You're not cleverly using this as an excuse to make out with me?"

"I'm not that clever, Eric."

"I think you deceive yourself, Sookie," Eric said with a brilliant smile.

I remembered he could now sense my moods, according to Bill. I wondered what Eric knew about me that I didn't know.

"Listen, Eric," I began, as we went out the door and across the porch. Then I had to stop and cast around in my mind for how to say what I wanted to say.

He waited. The evening had been cloudy, and the woods felt closer around the house. I knew the night just seemed oppressive because I was going to go to an event personally distasteful to me. I was going to learn things about people that I didn't know and didn't want to know. It seemed stupid to be seeking the kind of information that I'd spent my life learning how to block out. But I felt a sort of public service obligation to Andy Bellefleur to discover the truth; and I respected Portia, in an odd way, for her willingness to subject herself to something unpleasant in order to save her brother. How Portia could feel a genuine distaste for Bill was simply incomprehensible to me, but if Bill said she was frightened of him, it was true. This coming evening, the idea of seeing the true secret face of people I'd known forever was just as frightening to me.

"Don't let anything happen to me, okay?" I said to Eric directly. "I have no intention of getting intimate with any of those people. I guess I'm scared that something will happen, someone will go too far. Even for the sake of Lafayette's murder being avenged, I won't willingly have sex with any of those people." That was my real fear, one I hadn't admitted to myself until this moment: that some cog would slip, some safeguard fail, and I would be a victim. When I'd been a child, something had happened to me, something that I could neither prevent nor control, something incredibly vile. I would almost rather die than be subjected to abuse like that again. That was why I'd fought so hard against Gabe and been so relieved when Godfrey had killed him.

"You trust me?" Eric sounded surprised.

"Yes."

"That's . . . crazy, Sookie."

"I don't think so." Where that surety had come from, I didn't know, but it was there. I pulled on a thigh-length heavy sweater I had brought out with me.

Shaking his blond head, his trench coat drawn close around him, Eric opened the door to his red Corvette. I would be arriving at the orgy in style.

I gave Eric directions to Mimosa Lake, and I filled him in as much as I could on the background of this series of events as we drove (flew) down the narrow two-lane. Eric drove with great zest and élan—and the recklessness of someone extremely hard to kill.

"Remember, I'm mortal," I said, after going around a curve at a speed that made me wish my fingernails were long enough to bite.

"I think about that often," Eric said, his eyes fixed on the road ahead of him.

I didn't know what to make of that, so I let my mind drift to relaxing things. Bill's hot tub. The nice check I would get from Eric when the check from the Dallas vampires cleared. The fact that Jason had dated the same woman several months in a row, which might mean he was serious about her, or might mean he'd run through all the available women (and a few who shouldn't have been) in Renard Parish. That it was a beautiful, cool night and I was riding in a wonderful car.

"You are happy," Eric said.

"Yes. I am."

"You will be safe."

"Thanks. I know I will."

I pointed to the little sign marked FOWLER that indicated a driveway almost hidden by a stand of myrtle and hawthorn. We turned down a short, rutted gravel driveway lined with trees. It canted sharply downhill. Eric frowned as the Corvette lurched along the deep ruts. By the time the drive leveled out into the clearing where the cabin stood, the slope was enough to render the roof a little below the height of the road around the lake. There were four cars parked on the beaten dirt in front of the cabin. The windows were open to admit the sharp cool of the evening, but the shades were drawn. I could hear voices drifting out, though I couldn't make out words. I was suddenly, deeply reluctant to enter Jan Fowler's cabin.

"I could be bisexual?" Eric asked. It didn't seem to bother him; he seemed, if anything, amused. We stood by Eric's car, facing each other, my hands stuffed in the sweater pockets.

"Okay." I shrugged. Who cared? This was make believe. I caught a movement out of the corner of my eye. Someone was watching us through a partially raised shade. "We're being watched."

"Then I'll act friendly."

We were out of the car by that time. Eric bent, and without yanking me to him, set his mouth on mine. He didn't grab me, so I felt fairly relaxed. I'd known that at the very minimum I'd have to kiss other people. So I set my mind to it.

Maybe I had natural talent, which had been nurtured by a great teacher. Bill had pronounced me an excellent kisser, and I wanted to do him proud.

Judging from the state of Eric's Lycra, I succeeded.

"Ready to go in?" I asked, doing my best to keep my eyes above his chest.

"Not really," Eric said. "But I suppose we have to. At least I look in the mood."

Though it was dismaying to think that this was the second time I had kissed Eric and that I had enjoyed it more than I should, I could feel a smile twitch the corners of my mouth as we crossed the bumpy ground of the clearing. We went up the steps to a large wooden deck, strewn with the usual aluminum folding chairs and a large gas grill. The screen door screeched as Eric pulled it open, and I knocked lightly on the inner door. "Who is it?" Jan's voice said.

"It's Sookie and a friend," I answered.

"Oh, goodie! Come on in!" she called.

When I pushed open the door, all the faces in the room were turned toward us. The welcoming smiles turned to startled looks as Eric came in behind me.

Eric stepped to my side, his coat over his arm, and I almost hooted at the variety of expressions. After the shock of realizing Eric was vampire, which everyone in the room did after a minute or so, eyes flickered up and down the length of Eric's body, taking in the panorama.

"Hey, Sookie, who's your friend?" Jan Fowler, a multiple divorcée in her thirties, was wearing what looked like a lace slip. Jan's hair was streaked and professionally tousled, and her makeup would have seemed in place on stage, though for a cabin by Mimosa Lake the effect was a bit much. But as hostess, I guess she felt she could wear what she wanted to her own orgy. I slid out of my sweater and endured the embarrassment of receiving the same scrutiny Eric had been given.

"This is Eric," I said. "I hope you don't mind me bringing a friend?"

"Oh, the more the merrier," she said with undoubted sincerity. Her eyes never rose to Eric's face. "Eric, what can I get you to drink?"

"Blood?" Eric asked hopefully.

"Yeah, I think I've got some O here," she said, unable to tear her gaze away from the Lycra. "Sometimes we . . . pretend." She raised her eyebrows significantly, and kind of leered at Eric.

"No need to pretend anymore," he said, giving her back look for look. On his way to join her at the refrigerator, he managed to stroke Eggs's shoulder, and Eggs's face lit up.

Oh. Well, I'd known I'd learn some things. Tara, beside him, was sulking, her dark brows drawn down over dark eyes. Tara was wearing a bra and panties of shrieking red, and she looked pretty good. Her toenails and fingernails were painted so they matched, and so did her lipstick. She'd come prepared. I met her eyes, and she looked away. It didn't take a mind reader to recognize shame.

Mike Spencer and Cleo Hardaway were on a dilapidated couch against the left-hand wall. The whole cottage, basically one large room with a sink and stove against the right-hand wall and a walled-in bathroom in the far corner, was furnished in cast-offs, because in Bon Temps that was what you did with your old furniture. However, most lake cabins would not have featured such a thick soft rug and such a lot of pillows tossed around at random, and there would not have been such thick shades drawn at all the windows. Plus, the knickknacks strewn around on that soft rug were simply nasty. I didn't even know what some of them were.

But I pasted a cheerful smile on my face, and hugged Cleo Hardaway, as I usually did when I saw her. Granted, she had always been wearing more clothes when she ran the high school cafeteria. But panties were more than Mike was wearing, which was not a stitch.

Well, I'd known it would be bad, but I guess you just can't prepare yourself for some sights. Cleo's huge milk-chocolate brown boobs were glistening with some kind of oil, and Mike's private parts were equally shiny. I didn't even want to think about that.

Mike tried to grab my hand, probably to assist with the oil, but I slithered away and edged over to Eggs and Tara.

"I sure never thought you'd come," Tara said. She was smiling, too, but not real happily. In fact, she looked pretty damn miserable. Maybe the fact that Tom Hardaway was kneeling in front of her smooching up the inside of her leg had something to do with that. Maybe it was Eggs's obvious interest in Eric. I tried to meet Tara's eyes, but I felt sick.

I'd only been here five minutes, but I was willing to bet this was the longest five minutes of my life.

"Do you do this real often?" I asked Tara, absurdly. Eggs, his eyes on Eric's bottom while Eric stood talking at the refrigerator with Jan, began fumbling with the button on my shorts. Eggs had been drinking again. I could smell it. His eyes were glassy and his jaw was slack. "Your friend is really big," he said, as if his mouth were watering, and maybe it was.

"Lots bigger than Lafayette," I whispered, and his gaze jerked up to meet mine. "I figured he'd be welcome."

"Oh, yes," Eggs said, deciding not to confront my statement. "Yes, Eric's . . . very large. It's good to have some diversity."

"This is as rainbow as Bon Temps gets," I said, trying hard not to sound perky. I endured Eggs's continued struggle with the button. This had been a big mistake. Eggs was just thinking about Eric's butt. And other things about Eric.

Speaking of the devil, he snugged up behind me and ran his arms around me, pulling me to him and removing me from Eggs's clumsy fingers. I leaned back into Eric, really glad he was there. I realized that was because I *expected* Eric to misbehave. But seeing people you'd known all your life act like this, well, it was deeply disgusting. I wasn't too sure I could keep my face from showing this, so I wiggled against Eric, and when he made a happy sound, I turned in his arms to face him. I put my arms up around his neck and raised my face. He happily complied with my silent suggestion. With my face concealed, my mind was free to roam. I opened myself up mentally, just as Eric parted my lips with his tongue, so I felt completely unguarded. There were some strong "senders" in that room, and I no longer felt like myself, but like a pipeline for other people's overwhelming needs.

I could taste the flavor of Eggs's thoughts. He was remembering Lafayette, thin brown body, talented fingers, and heavily made up eyes. He was remembering Lafayette's whispered suggestions. Then he was choking those happy memories off with more unpleasant ones, Lafayette protesting violently, shrilly . . .

"Sookie," Eric said in my ear, so low that I don't think another person in the room could've heard him. "Sookie, relax. I have you."

I made my hand stroke his neck. I found that someone else was behind Eric, sort of making out with him from behind.

Jan's hand reached around Eric and began rubbing my rear. Since she was touching me, her thoughts were absolutely clear; she was an exceptional "sender." I flicked through her mind like the pages of a book, and read nothing of interest. She was only thinking of Eric's anatomy, and worrying about her own fascination with Cleo's chest. Nothing there for me.

I reached in another direction, wormed into the head of Mike Spencer, found the nasty tangle I'd expected, found that as he rolled Cleo's breasts in his hands he was seeing other brown flesh, limp and lifeless. His own flesh rose as he remembered this. Through his memories I saw Jan asleep on the lumpy couch, Lafayette's protest that if they didn't stop hurting him he would tell everyone what he'd done and with whom, and then Mike's fists descending, Tom Hardaway kneeling on the thin dark chest . . .

I had to get out of here. I couldn't bear it, even if I hadn't just learned what I needed to know. I didn't see how Portia could have endured it, either, especially since she would have had to stay to learn anything, not having the "gift" I had.

I felt Jan's hand massaging my ass. This was the most joyless excuse for sex I had ever seen: sex separated from mind and spirit, from love or affection. Even simple liking.

According to my four-times-married friend Arlene, men had no problem with this. Evidently, some women didn't either.

"I have to get out," I breathed into Eric's mouth. I knew he could hear me.

"Go along with me," he replied, and it was almost as if I was hearing him in my head.

He lifted me and slung me over his shoulder. My hair trailed down almost to the middle of his thigh.

"We're going outside for a minute," he told Jan, and I heard a big smacking noise. He'd given her a kiss.

"Can I come, too?" she asked, in a breathless Marlene Dietrich voice. It was lucky my face wasn't showing.

"Give us a minute. Sookie is still a little shy," Eric said in a voice as full of promise as a tub of a new flavor of ice cream.

"Warm her up good," Mike Spencer said in a muffled voice. "We all want to see our Sookie fired up."

"She will be hot," Eric promised.

"Hot damn," said Tom Hardaway, from between Tara's legs.

Then, bless Eric, we were out the door and he laid me out on the hood of the Corvette. He lay on top of me, but most of his weight was supported by his hands resting on the hood on either side of my shoulders.

He was looking down at me, his face clamped down like a ship's deck during a storm. His fangs were out. His eyes were wide. Since the whites were so purely white, I could see them. It was too dark to see the blue of his eyes, even if I'd wanted to.

I didn't want. "That was . . ." I began, and had to stop. I took a deep breath. "You can call me a goody two-shoes if you want to, and I wouldn't blame you, after all this was my idea. But you know what I think? I think that's awful. Do men really like that? Do women, for that matter? Is it fun to have sex with someone you don't even like?"

"Do you like me, Sookie?" Eric asked. He rested more heavily on me and moved a little.

Uh-oh. "Eric, remember why we're here?"

"They're watching."

"Even if they are, remember?"

"Yes, I remember."

"So we need to go."

"Do you have any evidence? Do you know what you wanted to find out?"

"I don't have any more evidence than I had before tonight, not evidence you can hand out in court." I made myself put my arms around his ribs. "But I know who did it. It was Mike, Tom, and maybe Cleo."

"This is interesting," Eric said, with a complete lack of sincerity. His tongue flicked into my ear. I happen to particularly like that, and I could feel my breathing speed up. Maybe I wasn't as immune to uninvolved sex as I'd thought. But then, I liked Eric, when I wasn't afraid of him.

"No, I just hate this," I said, reaching some inner conclusion. "I don't like any part of this." I shoved Eric hard, though it didn't make a bit of difference. "Eric, you listen to me. I've done everything for Lafayette and Andy Bellefleur I can, though it's precious little. He'll just have to go from here on the little snatches I caught. He's a cop. He can find court evidence. I'm not selfless enough to go any further with this."

"Sookie," Eric said. I didn't think he'd heard a word. "Yield to me."

Well, that was pretty direct.

"No," I said, in the most definite voice I could summon. "No."

"I will protect you from Bill."

"You're the one that's gonna need protection!" When I reflected on that sentence, I was not proud of it.

"You think Bill is stronger than me?"

"I am not having this conversation." Then I proceeded to have it. "Eric, I appreciate your offering to help me, and I appreciate your willingness to come to an awful place like this."

"Believe me, Sookie, this little gathering of trash is nothing, nothing, compared to some of the places I have been."

And I believed him utterly. "Okay, but it's awful to me. Now, I realize that I should've known this would, ah, rouse your expectations, but you know I did not come out here tonight to have sex with anyone. Bill is my boyfriend." Though the words *boyfriend* and *Bill* sounded ludicrous in the same sentence, "boyfriend" was Bill's function in my world, anyway.

"I am glad to hear it," said a cool, familiar voice. "This scene would make me wonder, otherwise."

Oh, great.

Eric rose up off of me, and I scrambled off the hood of the car and stumbled in the direction of Bill's voice.

"Sookie," he said, when I drew near, "it's getting to where I just can't let you go anywhere alone."

As far as I could tell in the poor lighting, he didn't look very glad to see me. But I couldn't blame him for that. "I sure made a big mistake," I said, from the bottom of my heart. I hugged him.

"You smell like Eric," he said into my hair. Well, hell, I was forever smelling like other men to Bill. I felt a flood of misery and shame, and I realized things were about to happen.

But what happened was not what I expected.

Andy Bellefleur stepped out of the bushes with a gun in his hand. His clothes looked torn and stained, and the gun looked huge.

"Sookie, step away from the vampire," he said.

"No." I wrapped myself around Bill. I didn't know if I was protecting him or he was protecting me. But if Andy wanted us separated, I wanted us joined.

There was a sudden surge of voices on the porch of the cabin. Someone clearly had been looking out of the window—I had kind of wondered if Eric had made that up—because, though no voices had been raised, the showdown in the clearing had attracted the attention of the revelers inside. While Eric and I had been in the yard, the orgy had progressed. Tom Hardaway was naked, and Jan, too. Eggs Tallie looked drunker.

"You smell like Eric," Bill repeated, in a hissing voice.

I reared back from him, completely forgetting about Andy and his gun. And I lost my temper.

This is a rare thing, but not as rare as it used to be. It was kind of exhilarating. "Yeah, uh-huh, and I can't even tell what you smell like! For all I know you've been with six women! Hardly fair, is it?"

Bill gaped at me, stunned. Behind me, Eric started laughing. The crowd on the sundeck was silently enthralled. Andy didn't think we should all be ignoring the man with the gun.

"Stand together in a group," he bellowed. Andy had had a lot to drink.

Eric shrugged. "Have you ever dealt with vampires, Bellefleur?" he asked.

"No," Andy said. "But I can shoot you dead. I have silver bullets."

"That's—" I started to say, but Bill's hand covered my mouth. Silver bullets were only definitely fatal to werewolves, but vampires also had a terrible reaction to silver, and a vampire hit in a vital place would certainly suffer.

Eric raised an eyebrow and sauntered over to the orgiasts on the deck. Bill took my hand, and we joined them. For once, I would have loved to know what Bill was thinking.

"Which one of you was it, or was it all of you?" Andy bellowed.

We all kept silent. I was standing by Tara, who was shivering in her red underwear. Tara was scared, no big surprise. I wondered if knowing Andy's thoughts would help any, and I began to focus on him. Drunks don't make for good reading, I can tell you, because they only think about stupid stuff, and their ideas are quite unreliable. Their memories are shaky, too. Andy didn't have too many thoughts at the moment. He didn't like anyone in the clearing, not even himself, and he was determined to get the truth out of someone.

"Sookie, come here," he yelled.

"No," Bill said very definitely.

"I have to have her right here beside me in thirty seconds, or I shoot—her!" Andy said, pointing his gun right at me.

"You will not live thirty seconds after, if you do," Bill said.

I believed him. Evidently Andy did, too.

"I don't care," Andy said. "She's not much loss to the world."

Well, that made me mad all over again. My temper had begun to die down, but that made it flare up in a big way.

I yanked free from Bill's hand and stomped down the steps to the yard. I wasn't so blind with anger that I ignored the gun, though I was sorely tempted to grab Andy by his balls and squeeze. He'd still shoot me, but he'd hurt, too. However, that was as self-defeating as drinking was. Would the moment of satisfaction be worth it?

"Now, Sookie, you read the minds of those people and you tell me which one did it," Andy ordered. He gripped the back of my neck with his big hands, like I was an untrained puppy, and swiveled me around to face the deck.

"What the hell do you think I was doing here, you stupid shit? Do you think this is the way I like to spend my time, with assholes like these?"

Andy shook me by my neck. I am very strong, and there was a good chance that I could break free from him and grab the gun, but it was not close enough to a sure thing to make me comfortable. I decided to wait for a minute. Bill was trying to tell me something with his face, but I wasn't sure what it was. Eric was trying to cop a feel from Tara. Or Eggs. It was hard to tell.

A dog whined at the edge of the woods. I rolled my eyes in that direction, unable to turn my head. Well, great. Just great.

"That's my collie," I told Andy. "Dean, remember?" I could have used some human-shaped help, but since Sam had arrived on the scene in his collie persona, he'd have to stay that way or risk exposure.

"Yeah. What's your dog doing out here?"

"I don't know. Don't shoot him, okay?"

"I'd never shoot a dog," he said, sounding genuinely shocked.

"Oh, but me, it's okay," I said bitterly.

The collie padded over to where we were standing. I wondered what was on Sam's mind. I wondered if he retained much human thinking while he was in his favorite form. I rolled my eyes toward the gun, and Sam/Dean's eyes followed mine, but how much comprehension was in there, I just couldn't estimate.

The collie began to growl. His teeth were bared and he was glaring at the gun.

"Back up, dog," Andy said, annoyed.

If I could just hold Andy still for a minute, the vampires could get him. I tried to work out all the moves in my mind. I'd have to grab his gun hand with both of my hands and force it up. But with Andy holding me out from him like this, that wasn't going to be easy.

"No, sweetheart," Bill said.

My eyes flashed over to him. I was considerably startled. Bill's eyes moved from my face to behind Andy. I could take a hint.

"Oh, who is being held like a little cub?" inquired a voice behind Andy.

Oh, this was just *peachy*.

"It is my messenger!" The maenad sauntered around Andy in a wide circle and came to stand to his right, a few feet before him. She was not between Andy and the group on the deck. She was clean tonight, and wearing nothing at all. I guessed she and Sam had been out in the woods making whoopee, before they heard the crowd. Her black hair fell in a tangled mass all the way to her hips. She didn't seem cold. The rest of us (except the vampires) were definitely feeling the nip in the air. We'd come dressed for an orgy, not an outdoors party.

"Hello, messenger," the maenad said to me. "I forgot to introduce myself last time, my canine friend reminds me. I am Callisto."

"Miss Callisto," I said, since I had no idea what to call her. I would have nodded, but Andy had hold of my neck. It was sure beginning to hurt.

"Who is this stalwart brave gripping you?" Callisto moved a little closer.

I had no idea what Andy looked like, but everyone on the deck was enthralled and terrified, Eric and Bill excepted. They were easing back, away from the humans. This wasn't good.

"This is Andy Bellefleur," I croaked. "He has a problem."

I could tell from the way my skin crawled that the maenad had eased forward a little.

"You have never seen anything like me, have you?" she said to Andy.

"No," Andy admitted. He sounded dazed.

"Am I beautiful?"

"Yes," he said, without hesitation.

"Do I deserve tribute?"

"Yes," he said.

"I love drunkenness, and you are very drunk," Callisto said happily. "I love pleasures of the flesh, and these people are full of lust. This is my kind of place."

"Oh, good," Andy said uncertainly. "But one of these people is a murderer, and I need to know which."

"Not just one," I muttered. Reminded I was on the end of his arm, Andy shook me again. I was getting really tired of this.

The maenad had gotten close enough now to touch me. She gently stroked my face, and I smelled earth and wine on her fingers.

"You are not drunk," she observed.

"No, ma'am."

"And you have not had the pleasures of the flesh this evening."

"Oh, just give me time," I said.

She laughed. It was a high, whooping laugh. It went on and on.

Andy's grip loosened, as he grew more and more disconcerted by the maenad's nearness. I don't know what the people on the deck thought they saw. But Andy knew he was seeing a creature of the night. He let go of me, quite suddenly.

"Come on up here, new girl," called Mike Spencer. "Let's have a look at you."

I was on a heap on the ground by Dean, who was licking my face enthusiastically. From that point of view, I could see the maenad's arm snake around Andy's waist. Andy transferred his gun to his left hand so he could return the compliment.

"Now, what did you want to know?" she asked Andy. Her voice was calm and reasonable. She idly waved the long wand with the tuft

on the end. It was called a thyrsis; I'd looked *maenad* up in the ency-
clopedia. Now I could die educated.

"One of those people killed a man named Lafayette, and I want
to know which one," Andy said with the belligerence of the drunk.

"Of course you do, my darling," the maenad crooned. "Shall I find
out for you?"

"Please," he begged.

"All right." She scanned the people, and crooked her finger at
Eggs. Tara held on to his arm to try to keep him with her, but he lurched
down the steps and over to the maenad, grinning foolishly all the while.

"Are you a girl?" Eggs asked.

"Not by any stretch of the imagination," Callisto said. "You have
had a lot of wine." She touched him with the thyrsis.

"Oh, yeah," he agreed. He wasn't smiling anymore. He looked
into Callisto's eyes, and he shivered and shook. Her eyes were glowing. I looked at Bill, and saw he had his own eyes focused on the
ground. Eric was looking at the hood of his car. Ignored by everyone,
I began to crawl toward Bill.

This was a fine kettle of fish.

The dog paced beside me, nosing me anxiously. I felt he wanted
me to move faster. I reached Bill's legs and gripped them. I felt his
hand on my hair. I was scared to make the large movement of rising
to my feet.

Callisto wrapped her thin arms around Eggs and began to whisper to him. He nodded and whispered back. She kissed him, and he
went rigid. When she left him to glide over to the deck, he stood absolutely still, staring into the woods.

She stopped by Eric, who was closer to the deck than we were. She
looked him up and down, and smiled that terrifying smile again. Eric
looked at her chest fixedly, careful not to meet her eyes. "Lovely," she
said, "just lovely. But not for me, you beautiful piece of dead meat."

Then she was up amongst the people on the deck. She took a deep
breath, inhaling the scents of drinking and sex. She sniffed as if she
were following a trail, and then she swung to face Mike Spencer. His
middle-aged body did not fare well in the chilly air, but Callisto seemed
delighted with him.

"Oh," she said as happily as though she'd just gotten a present,
"you're so proud! Are you a king? Are you a great soldier?"

"No," Mike said. "I own a funeral home." He didn't sound too
sure. "What are you, lady?"

"Have you ever seen anything like me before?"

"No," he said, and all the others shook their heads.

"You don't remember my first visit?"

"No, ma'am."

"But you've made me an offering before."

"I have? An offering?"

"Oh, yes, when you killed the little black man. The pretty one. He was a lesser child of mine, and a fitting tribute for me. I thank you for leaving him outside the drinking place; bars are my particular delight. Could you not find me in the woods?"

"Lady, we didn't make no offering," Tom Hardaway said, his dark skin all over goose pimples and his penis gone south.

"I saw you," she said.

Everything fell silent then. The woods around the lake, always full of little noises and tiny movements, became still. I very carefully rose to my feet beside Bill.

"I love the violence of sex, I love the reek of drink," she said dreamily. "I can run from miles away to be there for the end."

The fear pouring out of their heads began to fill mine up, and run out. I covered my face with my hands. I threw up the strongest shields I could fashion, but I could still barely contain the terror. My back arched, and I bit my tongue to keep from making a sound. I could feel the movement as Bill turned to me, and then Eric was by his side and they were both mashing me between them. There is not a thing erotic about being pressed between two vampires under those circumstances. Their own urgent desire for my silence fed the fear, because what would frighten vampires? The dog pressed against our legs as if he offered us protection.

"You hit him during sex," the maenad said to Tom. "You hit him, because you are proud, and his subservience disgusted and excited you." She stretched her bony hand to caress Tom's dark face. I could see the whites of his eyes. "And you"—she patted Mike with her other hand—"you beat him, too, because you were seized with the madness. Then he threatened to tell." Her hand left Tom and rubbed his wife, Cleo. Cleo had thrown on a sweater before she went out, but it wasn't buttoned.

Since she had avoided notice, Tara began backing up. She was the only one who wasn't paralyzed by fear. I could feel the tiny spark of hope in her, the desire to survive. Tara crouched under a wrought-iron table on the deck, made herself into a little ball, and squeezed her eyes shut. She was making a lot of promises to God about her future behavior, if he'd get her out of this. That poured into my mind, too. The reek of fear from the others built to a peak, and I could feel my body go into tremors as they broadcast so heavily that it broke through all my barriers. I had nothing left of myself. I was only fear. Eric and Bill locked arms with each other, to hold me upright and immobile between them.

Jan, in her nudity, was completely ignored by the maenad. I can only suppose that there was nothing in Jan that appealed to the creature; Jan was not proud, she was pathetic, and she hadn't had a drink that night. She embraced sex out of other needs than the need for its loss of self—needs that had nothing to do with leaving one's mind and body for a moment of wonderful madness. Trying, as always, to be the center of the group, Jan reached out with a would-be flirty smile and took the maenad's hand. Suddenly she began to convulse, and the noises coming from her throat were horrible. Foam came from her mouth, and her eyes rolled up. She collapsed to the deck, and I could hear her heels drumming the wood.

Then the silence resumed. But something was brewing a few yards away in the little group on the deck: something terrible and fine, something pure and horrible. Their fear was subsiding, and my body began to calm again. The awful pressure eased in my head. But as it ebbed, a new force began to build, and it was indescribably beautiful and absolutely evil.

It was pure madness, it was mindless madness. From the maenad poured the berserker rage, the lust of pillage, the hubris of pride. I was overwhelmed when the people on the deck were overwhelmed, I jerked and thrashed as the insanity rolled off Callisto and into their brains, and only Eric's hand across my mouth kept me from screaming as they did. I bit him and tasted his blood, and heard him grunt at the pain.

It went on and on and on, the screaming, and then there were awful wet sounds. The dog, pressed against our legs, whimpered.

Suddenly, it was over.

I felt like a dancing puppet whose strings have suddenly been severed. I went limp. Bill laid me down on Eric's car hood again. I opened my eyes. The maenad looked down at me. She was smiling again, and she was drenched in blood. It was like someone had poured a bucket of red paint over her head; her hair was drenched, as was every bit of her bare body, and she reeked of the copper smell, enough to set your teeth on edge.

"You were close," she said to me, her voice as sweet and high as a flute. She moved a little more deliberately, as if she'd eaten a heavy meal. "You were very close. Maybe as close as you'll ever come, maybe not. I've never seen anyone maddened by the insanity of others. An entertaining thought."

"Entertaining for you, maybe," I gasped. The dog bit my leg to bring me to myself. She looked down at him.

"My dear Sam," she murmured. "Darling, I must leave you."

The dog looked up at her with intelligent eyes.

"We've had some good nights running through the woods," she said, and stroked his head. "Catching little rabbits, little coons."

The dog wagged his tail.

"Doing other things."

The dog grinned and panted.

"But it's time for me to go, darling. The world is full of woods and people that need to learn their lesson. I must be paid tribute. They mustn't forget me. I'm owed," she said, in her sated voice, "owed the madness and death." She began to drift to the edge of the woods.

"After all," she said over her shoulder, "it can't always be hunting season."

Chapter 11

Even if I'd wanted to, I couldn't have walked over to see what was on the deck. Bill and Eric seemed subdued, and when vampires seem subdued, it means you don't really want to go investigate.

"We'll have to burn the cabin," Eric said from a few yards away. "I wish Callisto had taken care of her own mess."

"She never has," Bill said. "that I have heard. It is the madness. What does true madness care about discovery?"

"Oh, I don't know," Eric said carelessly. He sounded as if he was lifting something. There was a heavy thud. "I have seen a few people who were definitely mad and quite crafty with it."

"That's true," Bill said. "Shouldn't we leave a couple of them on the porch?"

"How can you tell?"

"That's true, too. It's a rare night I can agree with you this much."

"She called me and asked me to help." Eric was responding to the subtext rather than the statement.

"Then, all right. But you remember our agreement."

"How can I forget?"

"You know Sookie can hear us."

"Quite all right with me," Eric said, and laughed. I stared up at the night and wondered, not too curiously, what the hell they were talking about. It's not like I was Russia, to be parceled out to the strongest dictator. Sam was resting beside me, back in his human form, and stark naked. At the moment, I could not have cared less. The cold didn't bother Sam, since he was a shapeshifter.

"Whoops, here's a live one," Eric called.

"Tara," Sam called.

Tara scrambled down the steps of the deck and over to us. She flung her arms around me and began sobbing. With tremendous weariness, I held her and let her boo-hoo. I was still in my Daisy Duke outfit, and she was in her fire-engine lingerie. We were like big white water lilies in a cold pond, we two. I made myself straighten up and hold Tara.

"Would there be a blanket in that cabin, you think?" I asked Sam. He trotted over to the steps, and I noticed the effect was interesting from behind. After a minute, he trotted back—wow, this view was even more arresting—and wrapped a blanket around the two of us.

"I must be gonna live," I muttered.

"Why do you say that?" Sam was curious. He didn't seem unduly surprised by the events of the night.

I could hardly tell him it was because I'd watched him bounce around, so I said, "How are Eggs and Andy?"

"Sounds like a radio show," Tara said suddenly, and giggled. I didn't like the sound of it.

"They're still standing where she left them," Sam reported. "Still staring."

"I'm—still—staring," Tara sang, to the tune of Elton's "I'm Still Standing."

Eric laughed.

He and Bill were just about to start the fire. They strolled over to us for a last-minute check.

"What car did you come in?" Bill asked Tara.

"Ooo, a vampire," she said. "You're Sookie's honey, aren't you? Why were you at the game the other night with a dog like Portia Bellefleur?"

"She's kind, too," Eric said. He looked down at Tara with a sort of beneficent but disappointed smile, like a dog breeder regarding a cute, but inferior, puppy.

"What car did you come in?" Bill asked again. "If there is a sensible side to you, I want to see it now."

"I came in the white Camaro," she said, quite soberly. "I'll drive it home. Or maybe I better not. Sam?"

"Sure, I'll drive you home. Bill, you need my help here?"

"I think Eric and I can cope. Can you take the skinny one?"

"Eggs? I'll see."

Tara gave me a kiss on the cheek and began picking her way across the yard to her car. "I left the keys in it," she called.

"What about your purse?" The police would surely wonder if they found Tara's purse in a cabin with a lot of bodies.

"Oh . . . it's in there."

I looked at Bill silently, and he went in to fetch the purse. He returned with a big shoulder bag, large enough to contain not only makeup and everyday items, but also a change of clothing.

"This is yours?"

"Yes, thanks," Tara said, taking the bag from him as if she were afraid his fingers might touch hers. She hadn't been so picky earlier in the evening, I thought.

Eric was carrying Eggs to her car. "He will not remember any of this," Eric told Tara as Sam opened the back door of the Camaro so Eric could lay Eggs inside.

"I wish I could say the same." Her face seemed to sag on its bones under the weight of the knowledge of what had happened this night. "I wish I'd never seen that thing, whatever she is. I wish I'd never come here, to start with. I hated doing this. I just thought Eggs was worth it." She gave a look to the inert form in the backseat of her car. "He's not. No one is."

"I can remove your memory, too." Eric made the offer offhandedly.

"No," she said. "I need to remember some of this, and it's worth carrying the burden of the rest." Tara sounded twenty years older. Sometimes we can grow up all in a minute; I'd done that when I was about seven and my parents died. Tara had done that this night.

"But they're all dead, all but me and Eggs and Andy. Aren't you afraid we'll talk? Are you gonna come after us?"

Eric and Bill exchanged glances. Eric moved a little closer to Tara. "Look, Tara," he began, in a very reasonable voice, and she made the mistake of glancing up. Then, once her gaze was fixed, Eric began to erase the memory of the night. I was just too tired to protest, as if that would do any good. If Tara could even raise the question, she shouldn't be burdened with the knowledge. I hoped she wouldn't repeat her mistakes, having been separated from the knowledge of what they had cost her; but she couldn't be allowed to tell tales.

Tara and Eggs, driven by Sam (who had borrowed Eggs's pants), were on their way back to town when Bill began arranging a natural-looking fire to consume the cabin. Eric was apparently counting bones up on the deck, to make sure the bodies there were complete enough to reassure the investigators. He went across the yard to check on Andy.

"Why does Bill hate the Bellefleurs so much?" I asked him again.

"Oh, that's an old story," Eric said. "Back from before Bill had even changed over." He seemed satisfied by Andy's condition and went back to work.

I heard a car approaching, and Bill and Eric both appeared in the yard instantly. I could hear a faint crackle from the far side of the cabin. "We can't start the fire from more than one place, or they may be able to tell it wasn't natural," Bill said to Eric. "I hate these strides in police science."

"If we hadn't decided to go public, they'd have to blame it on one of them," Eric said. "But as it is, we are such attractive scapegoats . . . it's galling, when you think of how much stronger we are."

"Hey, guys, I'm not a Martian, I'm a human, and I can hear you just fine," I said. I was glaring at them, and they were looking perhaps one-fiftieth embarrassed, when Portia Bellefleur got out of her car and ran to her brother. "What have you done to Andy?" she said, her voice harsh and cracking. "You damn vampires." She pulled the collar of Andy's shirt this way and that, looking for puncture marks.

"They saved his life," I told her.

Eric looked at Portia for a long moment, evaluating her, and then he began to search the cars of the dead revelers. He'd gotten their car keys, which I didn't want to picture.

Bill went over to Andy and said, "Wake up," in the quietest voice, so quiet it could hardly be heard a few feet away.

Andy blinked. He looked over at me, confused that I wasn't still in his grasp, I guess. He saw Bill, so close to him, and he flinched, expecting retaliation. He registered that Portia was at his side. Then he looked past Bill at the cabin.

"It's on fire," he observed, slowly.

"Yes," Bill said. "They are all dead, except the two who've gone back into town. They knew nothing."

"Then . . . these people did kill Lafayette?"

"Yes," I said. "Mike, and the Hardaways, and I guess maybe Jan knew about it."

"But I haven't got any proof."

"Oh, I think so," Eric called. He was looking down into the trunk of Mike Spencer's Lincoln.

We all moved to the car to see. Bill's and Eric's superior vision made it easy for them to tell there was blood in the trunk, blood and some stained clothes and a wallet. Eric reached down and carefully flipped the wallet open.

"Can you read whose it is?" Andy asked.

"Lafayette Reynold," Eric said.

"So if we just leave the cars like this, and we leave, the police will find what's in the trunk and it'll all be over. I'll be clear."

"Oh, thank God!" Portia said, and gave a kind of sobbing gasp. Her plain face and thick chestnut hair caught a gleam of moonlight filtering through the trees. "Oh, Andy, let's go home."

"Portia," Bill said, "look at me."

She glanced up at him, then away. "I'm sorry I led you on like that," she said rapidly. She was ashamed to apologize to a vampire, you could tell. "I was just trying to get one of the people who came here to invite me, so I could find out for myself what was going on."

"Sookie did that for you," Bill said mildly.

Portia's gaze darted over to me. "I hope it wasn't too awful, Sookie," she said, surprising me.

"It was really horrible," I said. Portia cringed. "But it's over."

"Thank you for helping Andy," Portia said bravely.

"I wasn't helping Andy. I was helping Lafayette," I snapped.

She took a deep breath. "Of course," she said, with some dignity. "He was your coworker."

"He was my *friend*," I corrected.

Her back straightened. "Your friend," she said.

The fire was catching in the cabin now, and soon there would be police and firefighters. It was definitely time to leave.

I noticed neither Eric nor Bill offered to remove any memories from Andy.

"You better get out of here," I said to him. "You better go back to your house, with Portia, and tell your grandmama to swear you were there all night."

Without a word, brother and sister piled into Portia's Audi and left. Eric folded himself into the Corvette for the drive back to Shreveport, and Bill and I went through the woods to Bill's car, concealed in the trees across the road. He earned me, as he enjoyed doing. I have to say, I enjoyed it, too, on occasion. This was definitely one of the occasions.

It wasn't far from dawn. One of the longest nights of my life was about to come to a close. I lay back against the seat of the car, tired beyond reckoning.

"Where did Callisto go?" I asked Bill.

"I have no idea. She moves from place to place. Not too many maenads survived the loss of the god, and the ones that did find woods, and roam them. They move before their presence is discovered. They're crafty like that. They love war and its madness. You'll never find them far from a battlefield. I think they'd all move to the Middle East if there were more woods."

"Callisto was here because . . . ?"

"Just passing through. She stayed maybe two months, now she'll work her way . . . who knows? To the Everglades, or up the river to the Ozarks."

"I can't understand Sam, ah, palling around with her."

"That's what you call it? Is that what we do, pal around?"

I reached over and poked him in the arm, which was like pressing on wood. "You," I said.

"Maybe he just wanted to walk on the wild side," Bill said. "After all, it's hard for Sam to find someone who can accept his true nature." Bill paused significantly.

"Well, that can be hard to do," I said. I recalled Bill coming back in the mansion in Dallas, all rosy, and I gulped. "But people in love are hard to pry apart." I thought of how I'd felt when I'd heard he'd been seeing Portia, and I thought of how I'd reacted when I'd seen him at the football game. I stretched my hand over to rest on his thigh and I gave it a gentle squeeze.

With his eyes on the road, he smiled. His fangs ran out a little.

"Did you get everything settled with the shapeshifters in Dallas?" I asked after a moment.

"I settled it in an hour, or rather Stan did. He offered them his ranch for the nights of the full moon, for the next four months."

"Oh, that was nice of him."

"Well, it doesn't cost him anything exactly. And he doesn't hunt, so the deer need culling anyway, as he pointed out."

"Oh," I said in acknowledgment, and then after a second, "ooooh."

"They hunt."

"Right. Gotcha."

When we got back to my house, it didn't lack much till dawn. Eric would just make it to Shreveport, I figured. While Bill showered, I ate some peanut butter and jelly, since I hadn't had anything for more hours than I could add up. Then I went and brushed my teeth.

At least he didn't have to rush off. Bill had spent several nights the month before creating a place for himself at my house. He'd cut out the bottom of the closet in my old bedroom, the one I'd used for years before my grandmother died and I'd started using hers. He'd made the whole closet floor into a trapdoor, so he could open it, climb in, and pull it shut after him, and no one would be the wiser but me. If I was still up when he went to earth, I put an old suitcase in the closet and a couple of pairs of shoes to make it look more natural. Bill kept a box in the crawl space to sleep in, because it was mighty nasty down there. He didn't often stay there, but it had come in handy from time to time.

"Sookie," Bill called from my bathroom. "Come, I have time to scrub you."

"But if you scrub me, I'll have a hard time getting to sleep."

"Why?"

"Because I'll be frustrated."

"Frustrated?"

"Because I'll be clean but . . . unloved."

"It is close to dawn," Bill admitted, his head poking around the shower curtain. "But we'll have our time tomorrow night."

"If Eric doesn't make us go somewhere else," I muttered, when his head was safely under the cascade of water. As usual, he was using up most of my hot. I wriggled out of the damn shorts and resolved to throw them away tomorrow. I pulled the tee shirt over my head and stretched out on my bed to wait for Bill. At least my new bra was intact. I turned on one side, and closed my eyes against the light coming from the half-closed bathroom door.

"Darling?"

"You out of the shower?" I asked drowsily.

"Yes, twelve hours ago."

"What?" My eyes flew open. I looked at the windows. They were not pitch black, but very dark.

"You fell asleep."

I had a blanket over me, and I was still wearing the steel blue bra and panty set. I felt like moldy bread. I looked at Bill. He was wearing nothing at all.

"Hold that thought," I said and paid a visit to the bathroom. When I came back, Bill was waiting for me on the bed, propped on one elbow.

"Did you notice the outfit you got me?" I rotated to give him the full benefit of his generosity.

"It's lovely, but you may be slightly overdressed for the occasion."

"What occasion would that be?"

"The best sex of your life."

I felt a lurch of sheer lust down low. But I kept my face still. "And can you be sure it will be the best?"

"Oh, yes," he said, his voice becoming so smooth and cold it was like running water over stones. "I can be sure, and so can you."

"Prove it," I said, smiling very slightly.

His eyes were in the shadows, but I could see the curve of his lips as he smiled back. "Gladly," he said.

Some time later, I was trying to recover my strength, and he was draped over me, an arm across my stomach, a leg across mine. My mouth was so tired it could barely pucker to kiss his shoulder. Bill's tongue was gently licking the tiny puncture marks on my shoulder.

"You know what we need to do?" I said, feeling too lazy to move ever again.

"Um?"

"We need to get the newspaper."

After a long pause, Bill slowly unwrapped himself from me and strolled to the front door. My paperwoman pulls up my driveway and tosses it in the general direction of the porch because I pay her a great big tip on that understanding.

"Look," said Bill, and I opened my eyes. He was holding a foil-wrapped plate. The paper was tucked under his arm.

I rolled off the bed and we went automatically to the kitchen. I pulled on my pink robe as I padded after Bill. He was still natural, and I admired the effect.

"There's a message on the answering machine," I said, as I put on some coffee. The most important thing done, I rolled back the aluminum foil and saw a two-layer cake with chocolate icing, studded with pecans in a star pattern on the top.

"That's old Mrs. Bellefleur's chocolate cake," I said, awe in my voice.

"You can tell whose it is by looking?"

"Oh, this is a famous cake. It's a legend. Nothing is as good as Mrs. Bellefleur's cake. If she enters it in the county fair, the ribbon's as good as won. And she brings it when someone dies. Jason said it was worth someone dying, just to get a piece of Mrs. Bellefleur's cake."

"What a wonderful smell," Bill said, to my amazement. He bent down and sniffed. Bill doesn't breathe, so I haven't exactly figured out how he smells, but he does. "If you could wear that as a perfume, I would eat you up."

"You already did."

"I would do it a second time."

"I don't think I could stand it." I poured myself a cup of coffee. I stared at the cake, full of wonderment. "I didn't even know she knew where I live."

Bill pressed the message button on my answering machine. "Miss Stackhouse," said the voice of a very old, very Southern, aristocrat. "I knocked on your door, but you must have been busy. I left a chocolate cake for you, since I didn't know what else to do to thank you for what Portia tells me you've done for my grandson Andrew. Some

people have been kind enough to tell me that the cake is good. I hope
you enjoy it. If I can ever be of service to you, just give me a call."
     "Didn't say her name."
     "Caroline Holliday Bellefleur expects everyone to know who
she is."
     "Who?"
     I looked up at Bill, who was standing by the window. I was sitting
at the kitchen table, drinking coffee from one of my grandmother's
flowered cups.
     "Caroline Holliday Bellefleur."
     Bill could not get any paler, but he was undoubtedly stunned. He
sat down very abruptly into the chair across from me. "Sookie, do me
a favor."
     "Sure, baby. What is it?"
     "Go over to my house and get the Bible that is in the glass-fronted
bookshelf in the hallway."
     He seemed so upset, I grabbed my keys and drove over in my
bathrobe, hoping I wouldn't meet anyone along the way. Not too many
people live out on our parish road, and none of them were out at four
in the morning.
     I let myself into Bill's house and found the Bible exactly where
he'd said. I eased it out of the bookcase very carefully. It was obviously
quite old. I was so nervous carrying it up the steps to my house that I
almost tripped. Bill was sitting where I'd left him. When I'd set the
Bible in front of him, he stared at it for a long minute. I began to wonder if he could touch it. But he didn't ask for help, so I waited. His hand
reached out and the white fingers caressed the worn leather cover. The
book was massive, and the gold lettering on the cover was ornate.
     Bill opened the book with gentle fingers and turned a page. He
was looking at a family page, with entries in faded ink, made in several different handwritings.
     "I made these," he said in a whisper. "These here." He pointed at
a few lines of writing.
     My heart was in my throat as I came around the table to look over
his shoulder. I put my own hand on his shoulder, to link him to the
here and now.
     I could barely make out the writing.
     William Thomas Compton, his mother had written, or perhaps his
father. *Born April 9, 1840.* Another hand had written *Died November
25, 1868.*
     "You have a birthday," I said, of all the stupid things to say. I'd
never thought of Bill having a birthday.

"I was the second son," Bill said. "The only son who grew up."

I remembered that Robert, Bill's older brother, had died when he was twelve or so, and two other babies had died in infancy. There all these births and deaths were recorded, on the page under Bill's fingers.

"Sarah, my sister, died childless." I remembered that. "Her young man died in the war. All the young men died in the war. But I survived, only to die later. This is the date of my death, as far as my family is concerned. It's in Sarah's handwriting."

I held my lips pressed tight, so I wouldn't make a sound. There was something about Bill's voice, the way he touched the Bible that was almost unbearable. I could feel my eyes fill with tears.

"Here is the name of my wife," he said, his voice quieter and quieter.

I bent over again to read, *Caroline Isabelle Holliday.* For one second, the room swung sideways, until I realized it just could not be.

"And we had children," he said. "We had three children."

Their names were there, too. *Thomas Charles Compton, b. 1859.* She'd gotten pregnant right after they'd married, then.

I would never have Bill's baby.

Sarah Isabelle Compton, b. 1861. Named after her aunt (Bill's sister) and her mother. She'd been born around the time Bill had left for the war. *Lee Davis Compton, b. 1866.* A homecoming baby. *Died 1867,* a different hand had added.

"Babies died like flies then," Bill whispered. "We were so poor after the war, and there wasn't any medicine."

I was about to take my sad weepy self out of the kitchen, but then I realized that if Bill could stand this, I pretty much had to.

"The other two children?" I asked.

"They lived," he said, the tension in his face easing a little. "I had left then, of course. Tom was only nine when I died, and Sarah was seven. She was towheaded, like her mother." Bill smiled a little, a smile that I'd never seen on his face before. He looked quite human. It was like seeing a different being sitting here in my kitchen, not the same person I'd made love with so thoroughly not an hour earlier. I pulled a Kleenex out of the box on the baker's rack and dabbed at my face. Bill was crying, too, and I handed him one. He looked at it in surprise, as if he'd expected to see something different—maybe a monogrammed cotton handkerchief. He patted his own cheeks. The Kleenex turned pink.

"I hadn't ever looked to see what became of them," he said wonderingly. "I cut myself off so thoroughly. I never came back, of course, while there was any chance any one of them would be alive. That would be too cruel." He read down the page.

"My descendant Jessie Compton, from whom I received my house, was the last of my direct line," Bill told me. "My mother's line, too, has thinned down, until the remaining Loudermilks are only distantly related to me. But Jessie did descend from my son Tom, and apparently, my daughter Sarah married in 1881. She had a baby in—Sarah had a baby! She had four babies! But one of them was born dead."

I could not even look at Bill. Instead, I looked at the window. It had begun raining. My grandmother had loved her tin roof, so when it had had to be replaced, we'd gotten tin again, and the drumming of the rain was normally the most relaxing sound I knew. But not tonight.

"Look, Sookie," Bill said, pointing. "Look! My Sarah's daughter, named Caroline for her grandmother, married a cousin of hers, Matthew Phillips Holliday. And her second child was Caroline Holliday." His face was glowing.

"So old Mrs. Bellefleur is your great-granddaughter."

"Yes," he said unbelievingly.

"So Andy," I continued, before I could think twice about it, "is your, ah, great-great-great-grandson. And Portia . . ."

"Yes," he said, less happily.

I had no idea what to say, so for once, I said nothing. After a minute, I got the feeling it might be better if I made myself scarce, so I tried to slip by him to get out of the small kitchen.

"What do they need?" he asked me, seizing my wrist.

Okay. "They need money," I said instantly. "You can't help them with their personality problems, but they are cash-poor in the worst possible way. Old Mrs. Bellefleur won't give up that house, and it's eating every dime."

"Is she proud?"

"I think you could tell from her phone message. If I hadn't known her middle name was Holliday, I would have thought it was 'Proud.'" I eyed Bill. "I guess she comes by it natural."

Somehow, now that Bill knew he could do something for his descendants, he seemed to feel much better. I knew he would be reminiscing for a few days, and I would not grudge him that. But if he decided to take up Portia and Andy as permanent causes, that might be a problem.

"You didn't like the name Bellefleur before this," I said, surprising myself. "Why?"

"When I spoke to your grandmother's club, you remember, the Descendants of the Glorious Dead?"

"Yes, sure."

"And I told the story, the story of the wounded soldier out in the field, the one who kept calling for help? And how my friend Tolliver Humphries tried to rescue him?"

I nodded.

"Tolliver died in the attempt," Bill said bleakly. "And the wounded soldier resumed calling for help after his death. We managed to retrieve him during the night. His name was Jebediah Bellefleur. He was seventeen years old."

"Oh my gosh. So that was all you knew of the Bellefleurs until today."

Bill nodded.

I tried to think of something of significance to say. Something about cosmic plans. Something about throwing your bread upon the waters. What goes around, comes around?

I tried to leave again. But Bill caught my arm, pulled me to him. "Thank you, Sookie."

That was the last thing I had expected him to say. "Why?"

"You made me do the right thing with no idea of the eventual reward."

"Bill, I can't make you do anything."

"You made me think like a human, like I was still alive."

"The good you do is in you, not in me."

"I am a vampire, Sookie. I have been a vampire far longer than I was human. I have upset you many times. To tell the truth, sometimes I can't understand why you do what you do sometimes, because it's been so long since I was a person. It's not always comfortable to remember what it was like to be a man. Sometimes I don't want to be reminded."

These were deep waters for me. "I don't know if I'm right or wrong, but I don't know how to be different," I said. "I'd be miserable if it wasn't for you."

"If anything happens to me," Bill said, "you should go to Eric."

"You've said that before," I told him. "If anything happens to you, I don't have to go to anyone. I'm my own person. I get to make up my mind what I want to do. You've got to make sure nothing happens to you."

"We'll be having more trouble from the Fellowship in the years to come," Bill said. "Actions will have to be taken that may be repugnant to you as a human. And there are the dangers attached to your job." He didn't mean waiting tables.

"We'll cross that bridge when we get to it." Sitting on Bill's lap was a real treat, especially since he was still naked. My life had not exactly been full of treats until I met Bill. Now every day held a treat, or two.

In the low-lit kitchen, with the coffee smelling as beautiful (in its own way) as the chocolate cake did, and the rain drumming on the roof, I was having a beautiful moment with my vampire, what you might call a warm human moment.

But maybe I shouldn't call it that, I reflected, rubbing my cheek against Bill's. This evening, Bill had looked quite human. And I— well, I had noticed while we made love on our clean sheets, that in the darkness Bill's skin had been glowing in its beautiful otherworldly way.

And mine had, too.

CLUB DEAD

*This book is dedicated to my middle child,
Timothy Schulz, who told me flatly
he wanted a book all to himself.*

ACKNOWLEDGMENTS

My thanks to Lisa Weissenbuehler, Kerie L. Nickel, Marie La Salle, and the incomparable Doris Ann Norris for their input on car trunks, great and small. My further thanks to Janet Davis, Irene, and Sonya Socklin, Also cybercitizens of DorothyL, for their information on bars, bourree (a card game), and the parish governments of Louisiana. Joan Coffey was most gracious with supplying information about Jackson. The wonderful and obliging Jane Lee drove me patiently around Jackson for many hours, entering thoroughly into the spirit of finding the perfect location for a vampire bar.

Chapter 1

Bɪʟʟ ᴡᴀs ʜᴜɴᴄʜᴇᴅ over the computer when I let myself in his house. This was an all-too-familiar scenario in the past month or two. He'd torn himself away from his work when I came home, until the past couple of weeks. Now it was the keyboard that attracted him.

"Hello, sweetheart," he said absently, his gaze riveted to the screen. An empty bottle of type O TrueBlood was on the desk beside the keyboard. At least he'd remembered to eat.

Bill, not a jeans-and-tee kind of guy, was wearing khakis and a plaid shirt in muted blue and green. His skin was glowing, and his thick dark hair smelled like Herbal Essence. He was enough to give any woman a hormonal surge. I kissed his neck, and he didn't react. I licked his ear. Nothing.

I'd been on my feet for six hours straight at Merlotte's Bar, and every time some customer had under-tipped, or some fool had patted my fanny, I'd reminded myself that in a short while I'd be with my boyfriend, having incredible sex and basking in his attention.

That didn't appear to be happening.

I inhaled slowly and steadily and glared at Bill's back. It was a wonderful back, with broad shoulders, and I had planned on seeing it bare with my nails dug into it. I had counted on that very strongly. I exhaled, slowly and steadily.

"Be with you in a minute," Bill said. On the screen, there was a snapshot of a distinguished man with silver hair and a dark tan. He looked sort of Anthony Quinn-type sexy, and he looked powerful. Under the picture was a name, and under that was some text. "Born 1756 in Sicily," it began. Just as I opened my mouth to comment that vampires *did* appear in photographs despite the legend, Bill twisted around and realized I was reading.

He hit a button and the screen went blank.

I stared at him, not quite believing what had just happened.

"Sookie," he said, attempting a smile. His fangs were retracted, so he was totally not in the mood in which I'd hoped to find him; he wasn't thinking of me carnally. Like all vampires, his fangs are only fully extended when he's in the mood for the sexy kind of lust, or the feeding-and-killing kind of lust. (Sometimes, those lusts all get kind of snarled up, and you get your dead fang-bangers. But that element of danger is what attracts most fang-bangers, if you ask me.) Though I've been accused of being one of those pathetic creatures that hang around vampires in the hope of attracting their attention, there's only one vampire I'm involved with (at least voluntarily) and it was the one sitting right in front of me. The one who was keeping secrets from me. The one who wasn't nearly glad enough to see me.

"Bill," I said coldly. Something was Up, with a capital *U*. And it wasn't Bill's libido. (Libido had just been on my Word-A-Day calendar.)

"You didn't see what you just saw," he said steadily. His dark brown eyes regarded me without blinking.

"Uh-huh," I said, maybe sounding just a little sarcastic. "What are you up to?"

"I have a secret assignment."

I didn't know whether to laugh or stalk away in a snit. So I just raised my eyebrows and waited for more. Bill was the investigator for Area 5, a vampire division of Louisiana. Eric, the head of Area 5, had never given Bill an "assignment" that was secret from me before. In fact, I was usually an integral part of the investigation team, however unwilling I might be.

"Eric must not know. None of the Area 5 vampires can know."

My heart sank. "So—if you're not doing a job for Eric, who are you working for?" I knelt because my feet were so tired, and I leaned against Bill's knees.

"The queen of Louisiana," he said, almost in a whisper.

Because he looked so solemn, I tried to keep a straight face, but it was no use. I began to laugh, little giggles that I couldn't suppress.

"You're serious?" I asked, knowing he must be. Bill was almost always a serious kind of fellow. I buried my face on his thigh so he couldn't see my amusement. I rolled my eyes up for a quick look at his face. He was looking pretty pissed.

"I am as serious as the grave," Bill said, and he sounded so steely, I made a major effort to change my attitude.

"Okay, let me get this straight," I said in a reasonably level tone. I sat back on the floor, cross-legged, and rested my hands on my knees. "You work for Eric, who is the boss of Area 5, but there is also a queen? Of Louisiana?"

Bill nodded.

"So the state is divided up into Areas? And she's Eric's superior, since he runs a business in Shreveport, which is in Area 5."

Again with the nod. I put my hand over my face and shook my head. "So, where does she live, Baton Rouge?" The state capital seemed the obvious place.

"No, no. New Orleans, of course."

Of *course*. Vampire central. You could hardly throw a rock in the Big Easy without hitting one of the undead, according to the papers (though only a real fool would do so). The tourist trade in New Orleans was booming, but it was not exactly the same crowd as before, the hard-drinking, rollicking crowd who'd filled the city to party hearty. The newer tourists were the ones who wanted to rub elbows with the un-dead; patronize a vampire bar, visit a vampire prostitute, watch a vampire sex show.

This was what I'd heard; I hadn't been to New Orleans since I was little. My mother and father had taken my brother, Jason, and me. That would have been before I was seven, because that's when they died.

Mama and Daddy died nearly twenty years before vampires had appeared on network television to announce the fact that they were actually present among us, an announcement that had followed on the Japanese development of synthetic blood that actually maintained a vampire's life without the necessity of drinking from humans.

The United States vampire community had let the Japanese vampire clans come forth first. Then, simultaneously, in most of the nations of the world that had television—and who doesn't these days?—the announcement had been made in hundreds of different languages, by hundreds of carefully picked personable vampires.

That night, two and half years ago, we regular old live people learned that we had always lived with monsters among us.

"But"—the burden of this announcement had been—"now we can come forward and join with you in harmony. You are in no danger from us anymore. We don't need to drink from you to live."

As you can imagine, this was a night of high ratings and tremendous uproar. Reaction varied sharply, depending on the nation.

The vampires in the predominantly Islamic nations had fared the worst. You don't even want to know what happened to the undead spokesman in Syria, though perhaps the female vamp in Afghanistan died an even more horrible—and final—death. (What were they thinking, selecting a female for that particular job? Vampires could be so smart, but they sometimes didn't seem quite in touch with the present world.)

Some nations—France, Italy, and Germany were the most notable—refused to accept vampires as equal citizens. Many—like Bosnia, Argentina, and most of the African nations—denied any status to the vampires, and declared them fair game for any bounty hunter. But America, England, Mexico, Canada, Japan, Switzerland, and the Scandinavian countries adopted a more tolerant attitude.

It was hard to determine if this reaction was what the vampires had expected or not. Since they were still struggling to maintain a foothold in the stream of the living, the vampires remained very secretive about their organization and government, and what Bill was telling me now was the most I'd ever heard on the subject.

"So, the Louisiana queen of the vampires has you working on a secret project," I said, trying to sound neutral. "And this is why you have lived at your computer every waking hour for the past few weeks."

"Yes," Bill said. He picked up the bottle of TrueBlood and tipped it up, but there were only a couple of drops left. He went down the hall into the small kitchen area (when he'd remodeled his old family home, he'd pretty much left out the kitchen, since he didn't need one) and extracted another bottle from the refrigerator. I was tracking him by sound as he opened the bottle and popped it into the microwave. The microwave went off, and he reentered, shaking the bottle with his thumb over the top so there wouldn't be any hot spots.

"So, how much more time do you have to spend on this project?" I asked—reasonably, I thought.

"As long as it takes," he said, less reasonably. Actually, Bill sounded downright irritable.

Hmmm. Could our honeymoon be over? Of course I mean figurative honeymoon, since Bill's a vampire and we can't be legally married, practically anywhere in the world.

Not that he's asked me.

"Well, if you're so absorbed in your project, I'll just stay away until it's over," I said slowly.

"That might be best," Bill said, after a perceptible pause, and I felt like he'd socked me in the stomach. In a flash, I was on my feet and pulling my coat back over my cold-weather waitress outfit—black slacks, white boat-neck long-sleeved tee with "Merlotte's" embroidered over the left breast. I turned my back to Bill to hide my face.

I was trying not to cry, so I didn't look at him even after I felt Bill's hand touch my shoulder.

"I have to tell you something," Bill said in his cold, smooth voice. I stopped in the middle of pulling on my gloves, but I didn't think I could stand to see him. He could tell my backside.

"If anything happens to me," he continued (and here's where I should have begun worrying), "you must look in the hiding place I built at your house. My computer should be in it, and some disks. Don't tell anyone. If the computer isn't in the hiding place, come over to my house and see if it's here. Come in the daytime, and come armed. Get the computer and any disks you can find, and hide them in my hidey-hole, as you call it."

I nodded. He could see that from the back. I didn't trust my voice.

"If I'm not back, or if you don't get word from me, in say . . . eight weeks—yes, eight weeks, then tell Eric everything I said to you today. And place yourself under his protection."

I didn't speak. I was too miserable to be furious, but it wouldn't be long before I reached meltdown. I acknowledged his words with a jerk of my head. I could feel my ponytail switch against my neck.

"I am going to . . . Seattle soon," Bill said. I could feel his cool lips touch the place my ponytail had brushed.

He was lying.

"When I come back, we'll talk."

Somehow, that didn't sound like an entrancing prospect. Somehow, that sounded ominous.

Again I inclined my head, not risking speech because I was actually crying now. I would rather have died than let him see the tears.

And that was how I left him, that cold December night.

THE NEXT DAY, on my way to work, I took an unwise detour. I was in that kind of mood where I was rolling in how awful everything was. Despite a nearly sleepless night, something inside me told me I could probably make my mood a little worse if I drove along Magnolia Creek Road: so sure enough, that's what I did.

The old Bellefleur mansion, Belle Rive, was a beehive of activity, even on a cold and ugly day. There were vans from the pest control company, a kitchen design firm, and a siding contractor parked at the kitchen entrance to the antebellum home. Life was just humming for

Caroline Holliday Bellefleur, the ancient lady who had ruled Belle Rive and (at least in part) Bon Temps for the past eighty years. I wondered how Portia, a lawyer, and Andy, a detective, were enjoying all the changes at Belle Rive. They had lived with their grandmother (as I had lived with mine) for all their adult lives. At the very least, they had to be enjoying her pleasure in the mansion's renovation.

My own grandmother had been murdered a few months ago.

The Bellefleurs hadn't had anything to do with it, of course. And there was no reason Portia and Andy would share the pleasure of this new affluence with me. In fact, they both avoided me like the plague.

They owed me, and they couldn't stand it. They just didn't know how *much* they owed me.

The Bellefleurs had received a mysterious legacy from a relative who had "died mysteriously over in Europe somewhere," I'd heard Andy tell a fellow cop while they were drinking at Merlotte's. When she dropped off some raffle tickets for Gethsemane Baptist Church's Ladies' Quilt, Maxine Fortenberry told me Miss Caroline had combed every family record she could unearth to identify their benefactor, and she was still mystified at the family's good fortune.

She didn't seem to have any qualms about spending the money, though.

Even Terry Bellefleur, Portia and Andy's cousin, had a new pickup sitting in the packed dirt yard of his double-wide. I liked Terry, a scarred Viet Nam vet who didn't have a lot of friends, and I didn't grudge him a new set of wheels.

But I thought about the carburetor I'd just been forced to replace in my old car. I'd paid for the work in full, though I'd considered asking Jim Downey if I could just pay half and get the rest together over the next two months. But Jim had a wife and three kids. Just this morning I'd been thinking of asking my boss, Sam Merlotte, if he could add to my hours at the bar. Especially with Bill gone to "Seattle," I could just about live at Merlotte's, if Sam could use me. I sure needed the money.

I tried real hard not to be bitter as I drove away from Belle Rive. I went south out of town and then turned left onto Hummingbird Road on my way to Merlotte's. I tried to pretend that all was well; that on his return from Seattle—or wherever—Bill would be a passionate lover again, and Bill would treasure me and make me feel valuable once more. I would again have that feeling of belonging with someone, instead of being alone.

Of course, I had my brother, Jason. Though as far as intimacy and companionship goes, I had to admit that he hardly counted.

But the pain in my middle was the unmistakable pain of rejection. I knew the feeling so well, it was like a second skin.

I sure hated to crawl back inside it.

Chapter 2

I TESTED THE doorknob to make sure I'd locked it, turned around, and out of the corner of my eye glimpsed a figure sitting in the swing on my front porch. I stifled a shriek as he rose. Then I recognized him.

I was wearing a heavy coat, but he was in a tank top; that didn't surprise me, really.

"El—" Uh-oh, close call. "Bubba, how are you?" I was trying to sound casual, carefree. I failed, but Bubba wasn't the sharpest tool in the shed. The vampires admitted that bringing him over, when he'd been so very close to death and so saturated with drugs, had been a big mistake. The night he'd been brought in, one of the morgue attendants happened to be one of the undead, and also happened to be a huge fan. With a hastily constructed and elaborate plot involving a murder or two, the attendant had "brought him over"—made Bubba a vampire. But the process doesn't always go right, you know. Since then, he's been passed around like idiot royalty. Louisiana had been hosting him for the past year.

"Miss Sookie, how you doin'?" His accent was still thick and his face still handsome, in a jowly kind of way. The dark hair tumbled over his forehead in a carefully careless style. The heavy sideburns were brushed. Some undead fan had groomed him for the evening.

"I'm just fine, thank you," I said politely, grinning from ear to ear. I do that when I'm nervous. "I was just fixing to go to work," I added, wondering if it was possible I would be able to simply get in my car and drive away. I thought not.

"Well, Miss Sookie, I been sent to guard you tonight."

"You have? By who?"

"By Eric," he said proudly. "I was the only one in the office when he got a phone call. He tole me to get my ass over here."

"What's the danger?" I peered around the clearing in the woods in which my old house stood. Bubba's news made me very nervous.

"I don't know, Miss Sookie. Eric, he tole me to watch you tonight till one of them from Fangtasia gets here—Eric, or Chow, or Miss Pam, or even Clancy. So if you go to work, I go with you. And I take care of anyone who bothers you."

There was no point in questioning Bubba further, putting strain on that fragile brain. He'd just get upset, and you didn't want to see that happen. That was why you had to remember not to call him by his former name . . . though every now and then he would sing, and that was a moment to remember.

"You can't come in the bar," I said bluntly. That would be a disaster. The clientele of Merlotte's is used to the occasional vampire, sure, but I couldn't warn *everyone* not to say his name. Eric must have been desperate; the vampire community kept mistakes like Bubba out of sight, though from time to time he'd take it in his head to wander off on his own. Then you got a "sighting," and the tabloids went crazy.

"Maybe you could sit in my car while I work?" The cold wouldn't affect Bubba.

"I got to be closer than that," he said, and he sounded immovable.

"Okay, then, how about my boss's office? It's right off the bar, and you can hear me if I yell."

Bubba still didn't look satisfied, but finally, he nodded. I let out a breath I didn't realize I'd been holding. It would be easiest for me to stay home, call in sick. However, not only did Sam expect me to show up, but also, I needed the paycheck.

The car felt a little small with Bubba in the front seat beside me. As we bumped off my property, through the woods and out to the parish road, I made a mental note to get the gravel company to come dump some more gravel on my long, meandering driveway. Then I canceled that order, also mentally. I couldn't afford that right now. It'd have to wait until spring. Or summer.

We turned right to drive the few miles to Merlotte's, the bar where I work as a waitress when I'm not doing Heap Big Secret Stuff for the vampires. It occurred to me when we were about halfway there that I hadn't seen a car Bubba could've used to drive to my house. Maybe he'd flown? Some vamps could. Though Bubba was the least talented vampire I'd met, maybe he had a flair for it.

A year ago I would've asked him, but not now. I'm used to hanging around with the undead now. Not that I'm a vampire. I'm a telepath. My life was hell on wheels until I met a man whose mind I couldn't read. Unfortunately, I couldn't read his mind because he was dead. But Bill and I had been together for several months now, and until recently, our relationship had been real good. And the other vampires need me, so I'm safe—to a certain extent. Mostly. Sometimes.

Merlotte's didn't look too busy, judging from the half-empty parking lot. Sam had bought the bar about five years ago. It had been failing—maybe because it had been cut out of the forest, which loomed all around the parking lot. Or maybe the former owner just hadn't found the right combination of drinks, food, and service.

Somehow, after he renamed the place and renovated it, Sam had turned balance sheets around. He made a nice living off it now. But tonight was a Monday night, not a big drinking night in our neck of the woods, which happened to be in northern Louisiana. I pulled around to the employee parking lot, which was right in front of Sam Merlotte's trailer, which itself is behind and at right angles to the employee entrance to the bar. I hopped out of the driver's seat, trotted through the storeroom, and peeked through the glass pane in the door to check the short hall with its doors to the rest rooms and Sam's office. Empty. Good. And when I knocked on Sam's door, he was behind his desk, which was even better.

Sam is not a big man, but he's very strong. He's a strawberry blond with blue eyes, and he's maybe three years older than my twenty-six. I've worked for him for about that many years. I'm fond of Sam, and he's starred in some of my favorite fantasies; but since he dated a beautiful but homicidal creature a couple of months before, my enthusiasm has somewhat faded. He's for sure my friend, though.

"'Scuse me, Sam," I said, smiling like an idiot.

"What's up?" He closed the catalog of bar supplies he'd been studying.

"I need to stash someone in here for a little while."

Sam didn't look altogether happy. "Who? Has Bill gotten back?"

"No, he's still traveling." My smile got even brighter. "But, um, they sent another vampire to sort of guard me? And I need to stow him in here while I work, if that's okay with you."

"Why do you need to be guarded? And why can't he just sit out in the bar? We have plenty of TrueBlood." TrueBlood was definitely proving to be the front-runner among competing blood replacements. "Next best to the drink of life," its first ad had read, and vampires had responded to the ad campaign.

I heard the tiniest of sounds behind me, and I sighed. Bubba had gotten impatient.

"Now, I asked you—" I began, starting to turn, but never got further. A hand grasped my shoulder and whirled me around. I was facing a man I'd never seen before. He was cocking his fist to punch me in the head.

Though the vampire blood I had ingested a few months ago (to save my life, let me point out) has mostly worn off—I barcly glow in the dark at all now—I'm still quicker than most people. I dropped and rolled into the man's legs, which made him stagger, which made it easier for Bubba to grab him and crush his throat.

I scrambled to my feet and Sam rushed out of his office. We stared at each other, Bubba, and the dead man.

Well, now we were really in a pickle.

"I've kilt him," Bubba said proudly. "I saved you, Miss Sookie."

Having the Man from Memphis appear in your bar, realizing he's become a vampire, and watching him kill a would-be assailant— well, that was a lot to absorb in a couple of minutes, even for Sam, though he himself was more than he appeared.

"Well, so you have," Sam said to Bubba in a soothing voice. "Do you know who he was?"

I had never seen a dead man—outside of visitation at the local funeral home—until I'd started dating Bill (who of course was technically dead, but I mean human dead people).

It seems I run across them now quite often. Lucky I'm not too squeamish.

This particular dead man had been in his forties, and every year of that had been hard. He had tattoos all over his arms, mostly of the poor quality you get in jail, and he was missing some crucial teeth. He was dressed in what I thought of as biker clothes: greasy blue jeans and a leather vest, with an obscene T-shirt underneath.

"What's on the back of the vest?" Sam asked, as if that would have significance for him.

Bubba obligingly squatted and rolled the man to his side. The way the man's hand flopped at the end of his arm made me feel pretty queasy. But I forced myself to look at the vest. The back was decorated with a wolf's head insignia. The wolf was in profile, and seemed to be howling. The head was silhouetted against a white circle, which I decided was supposed to be the moon. Sam looked even more worried when he saw the insignia. "Werewolf," he said tersely. That explained a lot.

The weather was too chilly for a man wearing only a vest, if he wasn't a vampire. Weres ran a little hotter than regular people, but mostly they were careful to wear coats in cold weather, since Were society was still secret from the human race (except for lucky, lucky me, and probably a few hundred others). I wondered if the dead man had left a coat out in the bar hanging on the hooks by the main entrance; in which case, he'd been back here hiding in the men's room, waiting for me to appear. Or maybe he'd come through the back door right after me. Maybe his coat was in his vehicle.

"You see him come in?" I asked Bubba. I was maybe just a little light-headed.

"Yes, ma'am. He must have been waiting in the big parking lot for you. He drove around the corner, got out of his car, and went in the back just a minute after you did. You hightailed it through the door, and then he went in. And I followed him. You mighty lucky you had me with you."

"Thank you, Bubba. You're right; I'm lucky to have you. I wonder what he planned to do with me." I felt cold all over as I thought about it. Had he just been looking for a lone woman to grab, or did he plan on grabbing me specifically? Then I realized that was dumb thinking. If Eric had been alarmed enough to send a bodyguard, he must have known there was a threat, which pretty much ruled out me being targeted at random. Without comment, Bubba strode out the back door. He returned in just a minute.

"He's got him some duct tape and gags on the front seat of his car," Bubba said. "That's where his coat is. I brought it to put under his head." He bent to arrange the heavily padded camouflage jacket around the dead man's face and neck. Wrapping the head was a real good idea, since the man was leaking a little bit. When he had finished his task, Bubba licked his fingers.

Sam put an arm around me because I had started shaking.

"This is strange, though," I was saying, when the door to the hall from the bar began to open. I glimpsed Kevin Pryor's face. Kevin is a sweet guy, but he's a cop, and that's the last thing we needed.

"Sorry, toilet's back-flowing," I said, and pushed the door shut on his narrow, astonished, face. "Listen, fellas, why don't I hold this door shut while you two take this guy and put him in his car? Then we can figure out what to do with him." The floor of the hall would need swabbing. I discovered the hall door actually locked. I'd never realized that.

Sam was doubtful. "Sookie, don't you think that we should call the police?" he asked.

A year ago I would have been on the phone dialing 911 before the corpse even hit the floor. But that year had been one long learning curve. I caught Sam's eye and inclined my head toward Bubba. "How do you think he'd handle jail?" I murmured. Bubba was humming the opening line to "Blue Christmas." "Our hands are hardly strong enough to have done this," I pointed out.

After a moment of indecision, Sam nodded, resigned to the inevitable. "Okay, Bubba, let's you and me tote this guy out to his car."

I ran to get a mop while the men—well, the vampire and the shape-shifter—carried Biker Boy out the back door. By the time Sam and Bubba returned, bringing a gust of cold air in their wake, I had mopped the hall and the men's bathroom (as I would if there really had been an overflow). I sprayed some air freshener in the hall to improve the environment.

It was a good thing we'd acted quickly, because Kevin was pushing open the door as soon as I'd unlocked it.

"Everything okay back here?" he asked. Kevin is a runner, so he has almost no body fat, and he's not a big guy. He looks kind of like a sheep, and he still lives with his mom. But for all that, he's nobody's fool. In the past, whenever I'd listened to his thoughts, they were either on police work, or his black amazon of a partner, Kenya Jones. Right now, his thoughts ran more to the suspicious.

"I think we got it fixed," Sam said. "Watch your feet, we just mopped. Don't slip and sue me!" He smiled at Kevin.

"Someone in your office?" Kevin asked, nodding his head toward the closed door.

"One of Sookie's friends," Sam said.

"I better get out there and hustle some drinks," I said cheerfully, beaming at them both. I reached up to check that my ponytail was smooth, and then I made my Reeboks move. The bar was almost empty, and the woman I was replacing (Charlsie Tooten) looked relieved. "This is one slow night," she muttered to me. "The guys at table six have been nursing that pitcher for an hour, and Jane Bodehouse has tried to pick up every man who's come in. Kevin's been writing something in a notebook all night."

I glanced at the only female customer in the bar, trying to keep the distaste off my face. Every drinking establishment has its share of alcoholic customers, people who open and close the place. Jane Bodehouse was one of ours. Normally, Jane drank by herself at home, but every two weeks or so she'd take it into her head to come in and pick up a man. The pickup process was getting more and more iffy, since not only was Jane in her fifties, but lack of regular sleep and proper nutrition had been taking a toll for the past ten years.

This particular night, I noticed that when Jane had applied her makeup, she had missed the actual perimeters of her eyebrows and lips. The result was pretty unsettling. We'd have to call her son to come get her. I could tell at a glance she couldn't drive.

I nodded to Charlsie, and waved at Arlene, the other waitress, who was sitting at a table with her latest flame, Buck Foley. Things were really dead if Arlene was off her feet. Arlene waved back, her red curls bouncing.

"How're the kids?" I called, beginning to put away some of the glasses Charlsie had gotten out of the dishwasher. I felt like I was acting real normal until I noticed that my hands were shaking violently.

"Doing great. Coby made the All-A honor roll and Lisa won the spelling bee," she said with a broad smile. To anyone who believed that a four-times married woman couldn't be good mother, I would point at Arlene. I gave Buck a quick smile, too, in Arlene's honor. Buck is about the average kind of guy Arlene dates, which is not good enough for her.

"That's great! They're smart kids, like their mama," I said.

"Hey, did that guy find you?"

"What guy?" Though I had a feeling I already knew.

"That guy in the motorcycle gear. He asked me was I the waitress dating Bill Compton, since he'd got a delivery for that waitress."

"He didn't know my name?"

"No, and that's pretty weird, isn't it? Oh my God, Sookie, if he didn't know your name, how could he have come from Bill?"

Possibly Coby's smarts had come through his daddy, since it had taken Arlene this long to figure that out. I loved Arlene for her nature, not her brain.

"So, what did you tell him?" I asked, beaming at her. It was my nervous smile, not my real one. I don't always know when I'm wearing it.

"I told him I liked my men warm and breathing," she said, and laughed. Arlene was occasionally completely tactless, too. I reminded myself to reevaluate why she was my good friend. "No, I didn't really say that. I just told him you would be the blond who came in at nine."

Thanks, Arlene. So my attacker had known who I was because my best friend had identified me; he hadn't known my name or where I lived, just that I worked at Merlotte's and dated Bill Compton. That was a little reassuring, but not a lot.

Three hours dragged by. Sam came out, told me in a whisper that he'd given Bubba a magazine to look at and a bottle of Life Support to sip on, and began to poke around behind the bar. "How come that guy was driving a car instead of a motorcycle?" Sam muttered in a low voice. "How come his car's got a Mississippi license plate?" He hushed when Kevin came up to check that we were going to call Jane's son, Marvin. Sam phoned while Kevin stood there so he could relay the son's promise to be at Merlotte's in twenty minutes. Kevin pushed off after that, his notebook tucked under his arm. I wondered if Kevin was turning into a poet, or writing his resume.

The four men who'd been trying to ignore Jane while sipping their pitcher at the speed of a turtle finished their beer and left, each dropping a dollar on the table by way of tip. Big spenders. I'd never get my driveway regraveled with customers like these.

With only half an hour to wait, Arlene did her closing chores and asked if she could go on and leave with Buck. Her kids were still with her mom, so she and Buck might have the trailer to themselves for a little while.

"Bill coming home soon?" she asked me as she pulled on her coat. Buck was talking football with Sam.

I shrugged. He'd called me three nights before, telling me he'd gotten to "Seattle" safely and was meeting with—whomever he was supposed to meet with. The Caller ID had read "Unavailable." I felt like that said quite a lot about the whole situation. I felt like that was a bad sign.

"You . . . missing him?" Her voice was sly.

"What do you think?" I asked, with a little smile at the corners of my mouth. "You go on home, have a good time."

"Buck is very good at good times," she said, almost leering.

"Lucky you."

So Jane Bodehouse was the only customer in Merlotte's when Pam arrived. Jane hardly counted; she was so out of it.

Pam is a vampire, and she is co-owner of Fangtasia, a tourist bar in Shreveport. She's Eric's second in command. Pam is blond, probably two hundred-plus years old, and actually has a sense of humor—not a vampire trademark. If a vampire can be your friend, she was as close as I'd gotten.

She sat on a bar stool and faced me over the shining expanse of wood.

This was ominous. I had *never* seen Pam anywhere but Fangtasia. "What's up?" I said by way of greeting. I smiled at her, but I was tense all over.

"Where's Bubba?" she asked, in her precise voice. She looked over my shoulder. "Eric's going to be angry if Bubba didn't make it here." For the first time, I noticed that Pam had a faint accent, but I couldn't pin it down. Maybe just the inflections of antique English.

"Bubba's in the back, in Sam's office," I said, focusing on her face. I wished the ax would go on and fall. Sam came to stand beside me, and I introduced them. Pam gave him a more significant greeting than she would have given a plain human (whom she might not have acknowledged at all), since Sam was a shape-shifter. And I expected to see a flicker of interest, since Pam is omnivorous in matters of sex, and Sam is an attractive supernatural being. Though vampires aren't well-known for facial expressions, I decided that Pam's was definitely unhappy.

"What's the deal?" I asked, after a moment of silence.

Pam met my gaze. We're both blue-eyed blonds, but that's like saying two animals are both dogs. That's as far as any resemblance went. Pam's hair was straight and pale, and her eyes were very dark. Now they were full of trouble. She looked at Sam, her stare signifi-cant. Without a word, he went over to help Jane's son, a worn-looking man in his thirties, shift Jane to the car.

"Bill's missing," Pam said, shooting from the conversational hip.

"No, he's not. He's in Seattle," I said. Willfully obtuse. I had learned that word from my Word-A-Day calendar only that morning, and here I was getting to use it.

"He lied to you."

I absorbed that, made a "come on" gesture with my hand.

"He's been in Mississippi all this time. He drove to Jackson."

I stared down at the heavily polyurethane-coated wood of the bar. I'd pretty much figured Bill had lied to me, but hearing it said out loud, baldly, hurt like hell. He'd lied to me, and he was missing.

"So . . . what are you going to do to find him?" I asked, and hated how unsteady my voice was.

"We're looking. We're doing everything we can," Pam said. "Who-ever got him may be after you, too. That's why Eric sent Bubba."

I couldn't answer. I was struggling to control myself.

Sam had returned, I suppose when he saw how upset I was. From about an inch behind my back, he said, "Someone tried to grab Sookie on her way into work tonight. Bubba saved her. The body's out behind the bar. We were going to move him after we'd closed."

"So quickly," Pam said. She sounded even unhappier. She gave Sam a once-over, nodded. He was a fellow supernatural being, though that was definitely second best to him being another vampire. "I'd better go over the car and see what I can find." Pam took it quite for granted that we'd dispose of the body ourselves rather than doing something more official. Vampires are having trouble accepting the authority of law enforcement and the obligation of citizens to notify the police when trouble arises. Though vamps can't join the armed services, they can become cops, and actually enjoy the hell out of the job. But vamp cops are often pariahs to the other undead.

I would a lot rather think about vampire cops than what Pam had just told me.

"When did Bill go missing?" Sam asked. His voice managed to stay level, but there was anger just under the surface.

"He was due in last night," Pam said. My head snapped up. I hadn't known that. Why hadn't Bill told me he was coming home? "He was going to drive into Bon Temps, phone us at Fangtasia to let us know he'd made it home, and meet with us tonight." This was practically babbling, for a vampire.

Pam punched in numbers on a cell phone; I could hear the little beeps. I listened to her resultant conversation with Eric. After relaying the facts, Pam told him, "She's sitting here. She's not speaking."

She pressed the phone into my hand. I automatically put it to my ear.

"Sookie, are you listening?" I knew Eric could hear the sounds of my hair moving over the receiver, the whisper of my breath.

"I can tell you are," he said. "Listen and obey me. For now, tell no one what's happened. Act just as normal. Live your life as you always do. One of us will be watching you all the time, whether you think so or not. Even in the day, we'll find some way to guard you. We will avenge Bill, and we will protect you."

Avenge Bill? So Eric was sure Bill was dead. Well, nonexistent.

"I didn't know he was supposed to be coming in last night," I said, as if that was the most important fact I'd learned.

"He had—bad news he was going to tell you," Pam said suddenly.

Eric overheard her and made a disgusted sound. "Tell Pam to shut up," he said, sounding overtly furious for the first time since I'd known him. I didn't see any need to relay the message, because I figured Pam had been able to hear him, too. Most vampires have very acute hearing.

"So you knew this bad news and you knew he was coming back," I said. Not only was Bill missing and possibly dead—permanently dead—but he had lied to me about where he was going and why, and he'd kept some important secret from me, something concerning me. The pain went so deep, I could not even feel the wound. But I knew I would later.

I handed the phone back to Pam, and I turned and left the bar.

I faltered as I was getting into my car. I should stay at Merlotte's to help dispose of the body. Sam wasn't a vampire, and he was only involved in this for my sake. This wasn't fair to him.

But after only a second's hesitation, I drove away. Bubba could help him, and Pam—Pam, who knew all, while I knew nothing.

Sure enough, I caught a glimpse of a white face in the woods when I got home. I almost called out to the watcher, invited the vampire in to at least sit on the couch during the night. But then I thought, No. I had to be by myself. None of this was any of my doing. I had no action to take. I had to remain passive, and I was ignorant through no will of my own.

I was as wounded and as angry as it was possible for me to be. Or at least I thought I was. Subsequent revelations would prove me wrong.

I stomped inside my house and locked the door behind me. A lock wouldn't keep the vampire out, of course, but lack of an invitation to enter would. The vampire could definitely keep any humans out, at least until dawn.

I put on my old long-sleeved blue nylon gown, and I sat at my kitchen table staring blankly at my hands. I wondered where Bill was now. Was he even walking the earth; or was he a pile of ashes in some barbecue pit? I thought of his dark brown hair, the thick feel of it beneath my fingers. I considered the secrecy of his planned return. After what seemed like a minute or two, I glanced at the clock on the stove. I'd been sitting at the table, staring into space, for over an hour.

I should go to bed. It was late, and cold, and sleeping would be the normal thing to do. But nothing in my future would be normal again. Oh, wait! If Bill were gone, my future *would* be normal.

No Bill. So, no vampires: no Eric, Pam, or Bubba.

No supernatural creatures: no Weres, shape-shifters, or maenads. I wouldn't have encountered them, either, if it hadn't been for my involvement with Bill. If he'd never come into Merlotte's, I'd just be waiting tables, listening to the unwanted thoughts of those around me: the petty greed, the lust, the disillusionment, the hopes, and the fantasies. Crazy Sookie, the village telepath of Bon Temps, Louisiana.

I'd been a virgin until Bill. Now the only sex I might possibly have would be with JB du Rone, who was so lovely that you could almost overlook the fact that he was dumb as a stump. He had so few thoughts that his companionship was nearly comfortable for me. I could even touch JB without receiving unpleasant pictures. But *Bill* . . . I found that my right hand was clenched in a fist, and I pounded it on the table so hard, it hurt like hell.

Bill had told me that if anything happened to him, I was to "go to" Eric. I'd never been sure if he was telling me that Eric would see to it that I received some financial legacy of Bill's, or that Eric would protect me from other vampires, or that I'd be Eric's . . . well, that I'd have to have the same relationship with Eric that I had with Bill. I'd told Bill I wasn't going to be passed around like a Christmas fruitcake.

But Eric had already come to me, so I didn't even have the chance to decide whether or not to follow Bill's last piece of advice.

I lost the trail of my thought. It had never been a clear one anyway.

Oh, Bill, where are you? I buried my face in my hands.

My head was throbbing with exhaustion, and even my cozy kitchen was chilly in this small hour. I rose to go to bed, though I knew I wouldn't sleep. I needed Bill with such gut-clenching intensity that I wondered if it was somehow abnormal, if I'd been enchanted by some supernatural power.

Though my telepathic ability provided immunity from the vampires' glamour, maybe I was vulnerable to another power? Or maybe I was just missing the only man I'd ever loved. I felt eviscerated, empty, and betrayed. I felt worse than I had when my grandmother had died, worse than when my parents had drowned. When my parents had died, I'd been very young, and maybe I hadn't fully comprehended, all at once, that they were permanently gone. It was hard to remember now. When my grandmother had died a few months ago, I had taken comfort in the ritual surrounding death in the South.

And I'd known they hadn't willingly left me.

I found myself standing in the kitchen doorway. I switched off the overhead light.

Once I was wrapped up in bed in the dark, I began crying, and I didn't stop for a long, long time. It was not a night to count my blessings. It was a night when every loss I'd ever had pressed hard on me. It did seem I'd had more bad luck than most people. Though I made a token attempt to fend off a deluge of self-pity, I wasn't too successful. It was pretty much twined in there with the misery of not knowing Bill's fate.

I wanted Bill to curl up against my back; I wanted his cool lips on my neck. I wanted his white hands running down my stomach. I wanted to talk to him. I wanted him to laugh off my terrible suspicions. I wanted to tell him about my day; about the stupid problem I was having with the gas company, and the new channels our cable company had added. I wanted to remind him that he needed a new washer on the sink in his bathroom, let him know that my brother, Jason, had found out he wasn't going to be a father after all (which was good, since he wasn't a husband, either).

The sweetest part of being a couple was sharing your life with someone else.

But my life, evidently, had not been good enough to share.

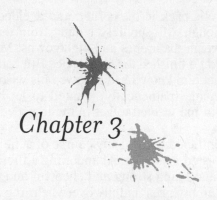

Chapter 3

WHEN THE SUN came up, I'd managed a half hour of sleep. I started to rise and make some coffee, but there didn't seem to be much point. I just stayed in bed. The phone rang during the morning, but I didn't pick it up. The doorbell rang, but I didn't answer it.

At some point toward the middle of the afternoon, I realized that there was one thing I had to do, the task Bill had insisted on my accomplishing if he was delayed. This situation exactly fit what he'd told me.

Now I sleep in the largest bedroom, formerly my grandmother's. I wobbled across the hall to my former room. A couple of months before, Bill had taken out the floor of my old closet and made it into a trapdoor. He'd established a lighttight hidey-hole for himself in the crawl space under the house. He'd done a great job.

I made sure I couldn't be seen from the window before I opened the closet door. The floor of the closet was bare of everything but the carpet, which was an extension of the one cut to fit the room. After I'd retracted the flap that covered the closet floor, I ran a pocketknife around the flooring and eventually pried it up. I looked down into the black box below. It was full: Bill's computer, a box of disks, even his monitor and printer.

So Bill had foreseen this might happen, and he'd hidden his work before he'd left. He'd had some faith in me, no matter how faithless he might have been himself. I nodded, and rolled the carpet back into place, fitting it carefully into the corners. On the floor of the closet I put out-of-season things—shoe boxes containing summer shoes, a beach bag filled with big sunbathing towels and one of my many tubes of suntan lotion, and my folding chaise that I used for tanning. I stuck a huge umbrella back in the corner, and decided that the closet looked realistic enough. My sundresses hung from the bar, along with some very lightweight bathrobes and nightgowns. My flare of energy faded as I realized I'd finished the last service Bill had asked of me, and I had no way to let him know I had followed his wishes.

Half of me (pathetically) wanted to let him know I'd kept the faith; half of me wanted to get in the toolshed and sharpen me some stakes.

Too conflicted to form any course of action, I crawled back to my bed and hoisted myself in. Abandoning a lifetime of making the best of things, and being strong and cheerful and practical, I returned to wallowing in my grief and my overwhelming sense of betrayal.

When I woke, it was dark again, and Bill was in bed with me. Oh, thank God! Relief swept over me. Now all would be well. I felt his cool body behind me, and I rolled over, half asleep, and put my arms around him. He eased up my long nylon gown, and his hand stroked my leg. I put my head against his silent chest and nuzzled him. His arms tightened around me, he pressed firmly against me, and I sighed with joy, inserting a hand between us to unfasten his pants. Everything was back to normal.

Except he smelled different.

My eyes flew open, and I pushed back against rock-hard shoulders. I let out a little squeak of horror.

"It's me," said a familiar voice.

"Eric, what are you doing here?"

"Snuggling."

"You son of a bitch! I thought you were Bill! I thought he was back!"

"Sookie, you need a shower."

"What?"

"Your hair is dirty, and your breath could knock down a horse."

"Not that I care what you think," I said flatly.

"Go get cleaned up."

"Why?"

"Because we have to talk, and I'm pretty sure you don't want to have a long conversation in bed. Not that I have any objection to being in bed with you"—he pressed himself against me to prove how little he objected—"but I'd enjoy it more if I were with the hygienic Sookie I've come to know."

Possibly nothing he could have said would have gotten me out of the bed faster than that. The hot shower felt wonderful to my cold body, and my temper took care of warming up my insides. It wasn't the first time Eric had surprised me in my own home. I was going to have to rescind his invitation to enter. What had stopped me from that drastic step before—what stopped me now—was the idea that if I ever needed help, and he couldn't enter, I might be dead before I could yell, "Come in!"

I'd entered the bathroom carrying my jeans and underwear and a red-and-green Christmas sweater with reindeer on it, because that's what had been at the top of my drawer. You only get a month to wear the darn things, so I make the most of it. I used a blow-dryer on my hair, wishing Bill were there to comb it out for me. He really enjoyed doing that, and I enjoyed letting him. At that mental image, I almost broke down again, but I stood with my head resting against the wall for a long moment while I gathered my resolve. I took a deep breath, turned to the mirror, and slapped on some makeup. My tan wasn't great this far into the cold season; but I still had a nice glow, thanks to the tanning bed at Bon Temps Video Rental.

I'm a summer person. I like the sun, and the short dresses, and the feeling you had many hours of light to do whatever you chose. Even Bill loved the smells of summer; he loved it when he could smell suntan oil and (he told me) the sun itself on my skin.

But the sweet part of winter was that the nights were much longer—at least, I'd thought so when Bill was around to share those nights with me. I threw my hairbrush across the bathroom. It made a satisfying clatter as it ricocheted into the tub. "You *bastard!*" I screamed at the top of my lungs. Hearing my voice saying such a thing out loud calmed me down as nothing else could have.

When I emerged from the bathroom, Eric was completely dressed. He had on a freebie T-shirt from one of the breweries that supplied Fangtasia ("This Blood's For You," it read) and blue jeans, and he had thoughtfully made the bed.

"Can Pam and Chow come in?" he asked.

I walked through the living room to the front door and opened it. The two vampires were sitting silently on the porch swing. They were in what I thought of as downtime. When vampires don't have anything in particular to do, they sort of go blank; retreat inside themselves, sitting or standing utterly immobile, eyes open but vacant. It seems to refresh them.

"Please come in," I said.

Pam and Chow entered slowly, looking around them with interest, as if they were on a field trip. Louisiana farmhouse, circa early twenty-first century. The house had belonged to our family since it was built over a hundred and sixty years ago. When my brother, Jason, had struck out on his own, he'd moved into the place my parents had built when they'd married. I'd stayed here, with Gran, in this much-altered, much-renovated house; and she'd left it to me in her will.

The living room had been the total original house. Other additions, like the modern kitchen and the bathrooms, were relatively new. The next floor, which was much smaller than the ground level, had been added in the early 1900s to accommodate a generation of children who all survived. I rarely went up there these days. It was awfully hot upstairs in the summer, even with the window air conditioners.

All my furniture was aged, styleless, and comfortable—absolutely conventional. The living room had couches and chairs and a television and a VCR, and then you passed through a hall that had my large bedroom with its own bath on one side, and a hall bathroom and my former bedroom and some closets—linen, coat—on the other. Through that passage, you were into the kitchen/dining area, which had been added on soon after my grandparents' wedding. After the kitchen, there was a big roofed back porch, which I'd just had screened in. The porch housed a useful old bench, the washer and dryer, and a bunch of shelves.

There was a ceiling fan in every room and a fly swatter, too, hung in a discreet spot on a tiny nail. Gran wouldn't turn on the air conditioner unless she absolutely had to.

Though they didn't venture upstairs, no detail escaped Pam and Chow on the ground floor.

By the time they settled at the old pine table where Stackhouses had eaten for a few generations, I felt like I lived in a museum that had just been cataloged. I opened the refrigerator and got out three bottles of TrueBlood, heated them up in the microwave, gave them a good shake, and plonked them down on the table in front of my guests.

Chow was still practically a stranger to me. He'd been working at Fangtasia only a few months. I assume he'd bought into the bar, as the previous bartender had. Chow had amazing tattoos, the dark blue Asian kind that are so intricate, they are like a set of fancy clothes. These were so different from my attacker's jailhouse decorations that it was hard to believe they were the same art form. I'd been told Chow's were Yakuza tattoos, but I had never had the nerve to ask him, especially since it wasn't exactly my business. However, if these were true Yakuza tats, Chow was not that old for a vampire. I'd looked up the Yakuza, and the tattooing was a (relatively) recent development in that criminal organization's long history. Chow had long black hair (no surprise there), and I'd heard from many sources that he was a tremendous draw

at Fangtasia. Most evenings, he worked shirtless. Tonight, as a conces-
sion to the cold, he was wearing a zipped red vest.

I couldn't help but wonder if he ever really felt naked; his body
was so thoroughly decorated. I wished I could ask him, but of course
that was out of the question. He was the only person of Asian descent
I had ever met, and no matter how you know individuals don't repre-
sent their whole race, you do kind of expect at least some of the gen-
eralizations to be valid. Chow did seem to have a strong sense of
privacy. But far from being silent and inscrutable, he was chattering
away with Pam, though in a language I couldn't understand. And he
smiled at me in a disconcerting way. Okay, maybe he was too far
from inscrutable. He was probably insulting the hell out of me, and I
was too dumb to know it.

Pam was dressed, as always, in sort of middle-class anonymous
clothes. This evening it was a pair of winter white knit pants and a
blue sweater. Her blond hair was shining, straight and loose, down
her back. She looked like Alice in Wonderland with fangs.

"Have you found out anything else about Bill?" I asked, when
they'd all had a swallow of their drinks.

Eric said, "A little."

I folded my hands in my lap and waited.

"I know Bill's been kidnapped," he said, and the room swam
around my head for a second. I took a deep breath to make it stop.

"Who by?" Grammar was the least of my worries.

"We aren't sure," Chow told me. "The witnesses are not agreeing."
His English was accented, but very clear.

"Let me at them," I said. "If they're human, I'll find out."

"If they were under our dominion, that would be the logical thing
to do," Eric said agreeably. "But, unfortunately, they're not."

Dominion, my foot. "Please explain." I was sure I was showing
extraordinary patience under the circumstances.

"These humans owe allegiance to the king of Mississippi."

I knew my mouth was falling open, but I couldn't seem to stop it.
"Excuse me," I said, after a long moment, "but I could have sworn
you said . . . the king? Of Mississippi?"

Eric nodded without a trace of a smile.

I looked down, trying to keep a straight face. Even under the circumstances, it was impossible. I could feel my mouth twitch. "For
real?" I asked helplessly. I don't know why it seemed even funnier that
Mississippi had a king—after all, Louisiana had a queen—but it did. I
reminded myself I wasn't supposed to know about the queen. Check.

The vampires looked at one another. They nodded in unison.

"Are you the king of Louisiana?" I asked Eric, giddy with all my mental effort to keep varying stories straight. I was laughing so hard that it was all I could do to keep upright in the chair. Possibly there was a note of hysteria.

"Oh, no," he said. "I am the sheriff of Area 5."

That really set me off. I had tears running down my face, and Chow was looking uneasy. I got up, made myself some Swiss Miss microwave hot chocolate, and stirred it with a spoon so it would cool off. I was calming down as I performed the little task, and by the time I returned to the table, I was almost sober.

"You never told me all this before," I said, by way of explanation. "You all have divided up America into kingdoms, is that right?"

Pam and Chow looked at Eric with some surprise, but he didn't regard them. "Yes," he said simply. "It has been so since vampires came to America. Of course, over the years the system's changed with the population. There were far fewer vampires in America for the first two hundred years, because the trip over was so perilous. It was hard to work out the length of the voyage with the available blood supply." Which would have been the crew, of course. "And the Louisiana Purchase made a great difference."

Well, of course it *would*. I stifled another bout of giggles. "And the kingdoms are divided into . . . ?"

"Areas. Used to be called fiefdoms, until we decided that was too behind the times. A sheriff controls each area. As you know, we live in Area 5 of the kingdom of Louisiana. Stan, whom you visited in Dallas, is sheriff of Area 6 in the kingdom of . . . in Texas."

I pictured Eric as the sheriff of Nottingham, and when that had lost amusement value, as Wyatt Earp. I was definitely on the light-headed side. I really felt pretty bad physically. I told myself to pack away my reaction to this information, to focus on the immediate problem. "So, Bill was kidnapped in daylight, I take it?"

Multiple nods all around.

"This kidnapping was witnessed by some humans who live in the kingdom of Mississippi." I just loved to say that. "And they're under the control of a vampire king?"

"Russell Edgington. Yes, they live in his kingdom, but a few of them will give me information. For a price."

"This king won't let you question them?"

"We haven't asked him yet. It could be Bill was taken on his orders."

That raised a whole new crop of questions, but I told myself to stay focused. "How can I get to them? Assuming I decide I want to."

"We've thought of a way you may be able to gather information from humans in the area where Bill disappeared," said Eric. "Not just people I have bribed to let me know what's happening there, but all the people that associated with Russell. It's risky. I had to tell you what I have, to make it work. And you may be unwilling. Someone's already tried to get you once. Apparently, whoever has Bill must not have much information about you yet. But soon, Bill will talk. If you're anywhere around when he breaks, they'll have you."

"They won't really need me then," I pointed out. "If he's already broken."

"That's not necessarily true," Pam said. They did some more of the enigmatic-gaze-swapping thing.

"Give me the whole story," I said. I noticed that Chow had finished his blood, so I got up to get him some more.

"As Russell Edgington's people tell it, Betty Jo Pickard, Edgington's second in command, was supposed to begin a flight to St. Louis yesterday. The humans responsible for taking her coffin to the airport took Bill's identical coffin by mistake. When they delivered the coffin to the hangar Anubis Airlines leases, they left it unguarded for perhaps ten minutes while they were filling out paperwork. During that time—they claim—someone wheeled the coffin, which was on a kind of gurney, out of the back of the hangar, loaded it onto a truck, and drove away."

"Someone who could penetrate Anubis security," I said, doubt heavy in my voice. Anubis Airlines had been established to transport vampires safely both day and night, and their guarantee of heavy security to guard the coffins of sleeping vampires was their big calling card. Of course, vampires don't have to sleep in coffins, but it sure is easy to ship them that way. There had been unfortunate "accidents" when vampires had tried to fly Delta. Some fanatic had gotten in the baggage hold and hacked open a couple of coffins with an ax. Northwest had suffered the same problem. Saving money suddenly didn't seem so attractive to the undead, who now flew Anubis almost exclusively.

"I'm thinking that someone could have mingled with Edgington's people, someone the Anubis employees thought was Edgington's, and Edgington's people thought belonged to Anubis. He could have wheeled Bill out as Edgington's people left, and the guards would be none the wiser."

"The Anubis people wouldn't ask to see papers? On a departing coffin?"

"They say they did see papers, Betty Jo Pickard's. She was on her way to Missouri to negotiate a trade agreement with the vampires of St. Louis." I had a blank moment of wondering what on earth the vampires of Mississippi could be trading with the vampires of Missouri, and then I decided I just didn't want to know.

"There was also extra confusion at the time," Pam was saying. "A fire started under the tail of another Anubis plane, and the guards were distracted."

"Oh, accidentally-on-purpose."

"I think so," Chow said.

"So, why would anyone want to snatch Bill?" I asked. I was afraid I knew. I was hoping they'd provide me with something else. Thank God Bill had prepared for this moment.

"Bill's been working on a little special project," Eric said, his eyes on my face. "Do you know anything about that?"

More than I wanted to. Less than I ought to.

"What project?" I said. I've spent my whole life concealing my thoughts, and I called on all my skill now. That life depended on my sincerity.

Eric's gaze flickered over to Pam, to Chow. They both gave some infinitesimal signal. He focused on me again, and said, "That is a little hard to believe, Sookie."

"How come?" I asked, anger in my voice. When in doubt, attack. "When do any of you exactly spill your emotional guts to a human? And Bill is definitely one of you." I infused that with as much rage as I could muster.

They did that eye-flicker thing at one another again.

"You think we'll believe that Bill didn't tell you what he was working on?"

"Yes, I think so. Because he didn't." I had more or less figured it out all by myself anyway.

"Here's what I'm going to do," Eric said finally. He looked at me from across the table, his blue eyes as hard as marbles and just as warm. No more Mr. Nice Vampire. "I can't tell if you're lying or not, which is remarkable. For your sake, I hope you are telling the truth. I could torture you until you told me the truth, or until I was sure you had been telling me the truth from the beginning."

Oh, brother. I took a deep breath, blew it out, and tried to think of an appropriate prayer. *God, don't let me scream too loud* seemed kind of weak and negative. Besides, there was no one to hear me besides the vampires, no matter how loudly I shrieked. When the time came, I might as well let it rip.

"But," Eric continued thoughtfully, "that might damage you too badly for the other part of my plan. And really, it doesn't make that much difference if you know what Bill has been doing behind our backs or not."

Behind their backs? Oh, *shit*. And now I knew whom to blame for my very deep predicament. My own dear love, Bill Compton.

"That got a reaction," Pam observed.

"But not the one I expected," Eric said slowly.

"I'm not too happy about the torture option." I was in so much trouble, I couldn't even begin to add it up, and I was so overloaded with stress that I felt like my head was floating somewhere above my body. "And I miss Bill." Even though at the moment I would gladly kick his ass, I did miss him. And if I could just have ten minutes' conversation with him, how much better prepared I would be to face the coming days. Tears rolled down my face. But there was more they had to tell me; more I had to hear, whether I wanted to or not. "I do expect you to tell me why he lied about this trip, if you know. Pam mentioned bad news."

Eric looked at Pam with no love in his eyes at all.

"She's leaking again," Pam observed, sounding a little uncomfortable. "I think before she goes to Mississippi, she should know the truth. Besides, if she has been keeping secrets for Bill, this will . . ."

Make her spill the beans? Change her loyalty to Bill? Force her to realize she has to tell us?

It was obvious that Chow and Eric had been all for keeping me in ignorance and that they were acutely unhappy with Pam for hinting to me that, though I supposedly didn't know it, all was not well with Bill and me. But they both eyed Pam intently for a long minute, and then Eric nodded curtly.

"You and Chow wait outside," Eric said to Pam. She gave him a very pointed look, and then they walked out, leaving their drained bottles sitting on the table. Not even a thank-you for the blood. Didn't even rinse the bottles out. My head felt lighter and lighter as I contemplated poor vampire manners. I felt my eyelids flicker, and it occurred to me that I was on the edge of fainting. I am not one of these frail gals who keels over at every little thing, but I felt I was justified right now. Plus, I vaguely realized I hadn't eaten in over twenty-four hours.

"Don't you do it," Eric said. He sounded definite. I tried to concentrate on his voice, and I looked at him.

I nodded to indicate I was doing my best.

He moved over to my side of the table, turned the chair Pam had occupied until it faced me and was very close. He sat and leaned over to me, his big white hand covering both of mine, still folded neatly in my lap. If he closed his hand, he could crush all my fingers. I'd never work as a waitress again.

"I don't enjoy seeing you scared of me," he said, his face too close to mine. I could smell his cologne—Ulysse, I thought. "I have always been very fond of you."

He'd always wanted to have sex with me.

"Plus, I want to fuck you." He grinned, but at this moment it didn't do a thing to me. "When we kiss . . . it's very exciting." We had kissed in the line of duty, so to speak, and not as recreation. But it had been exciting. How not? He was gorgeous, and he'd had several hundred years to work on his smooching technique.

Eric got closer and closer. I wasn't sure if he was going to bite me or kiss me. His fangs had run out. He was angry, or horny, or hungry, or all three. New vampires tended to lisp while they talked until they got used to their fangs; you couldn't even tell, with Eric. He'd had centuries of perfecting that technique, too.

"Somehow, that torture plan didn't make me feel very sexy," I told him.

"It did something for Chow, though," Eric whispered in my ear.

I wasn't shaking, but I should have been. "Could you cut to the chase here?" I asked. "Are you gonna torture me, or not? Are you my friend, or my enemy? Are you gonna find Bill, or let him rot?"

Eric laughed. It was short and unfunny, but it was better than him getting closer, at least at the moment. "Sookie, you are too much," he said, but not as though he found that particularly endearing. "I'm not going to torture you. For one thing, I would hate to ruin that beautiful skin; one day, I will see all of it."

I just hoped it was still on my body when that happened.

"You won't always be so afraid of me," he said, as if he were absolutely certain of the future. "And you won't always be as devoted to Bill as you are now. There is something I must tell you."

Here came the Big Bad. His cool fingers twined with mine, and without wanting to, I held his hand hard. I couldn't think of a word to say, at least a word that was safe. My eyes fixed on his.

"Bill was summoned to Mississippi," Eric told me, "by a vampire—a female—he'd known many years ago. I don't know if you've realized that vampires almost never mate with other vampires, for any longer than a rare one-night affair. We don't do this because it gives us power over each other forever, the mating and sharing of blood. This vampire . . ."

"Her name," I said.

"Lorena," he said reluctantly. Or maybe he wanted to tell me all along, and the reluctance was just for show. Who the heck knows, with a vampire.

He waited to see if I would speak, but I did not.

"She was in Mississippi. I am not sure if she regularly lives there, or if she went there to ensnare Bill. She had been living in Seattle for years, I know, because she and Bill lived there together for many years."

I had wondered why he'd picked Seattle as his fictitious destination. He hadn't just plucked it out of the air.

"But whatever her intention in asking him to meet her there . . . what excuse she gave him for not coming here . . . maybe he was just being careful of you . . ."

I wanted to die at that moment. I took a deep breath and looked down at our joined hands. I was too humiliated to look in Eric's eyes.

"He was—he became—instantly enthralled with her, all over again. After a few nights, he called Pam to say that he was coming home early without telling you, so he could arrange your future care before he saw you again."

"Future care?" I sounded like a crow.

"Bill wanted to make a financial arrangement for you."

The shock of it made me blanch. "Pension me off," I said numbly. No matter how well he had meant, Bill could not have offered me any greater offense. When he'd been in my life, it had never occurred to him to ask me how my finances were faring—though he could hardly *wait* to help his newly discovered descendants, the Bellefleurs.

But when he was going to be out of my life, and felt guilty for leaving pitiful, pitiable me—then he started worrying.

"He wanted . . ." Eric began, then stopped and looked closely at my face. "Well, leave that for now. I would not have told you any of this, if Pam hadn't interfered. I would have sent you off in ignorance, because then it wouldn't have been words from my mouth that hurt you so badly. And I would not have had to plead with you, as I'm going to plead."

I made myself listen. I gripped Eric's hand as if it were a lifeline.

"What I'm going to do—and you have to understand, Sookie, my hide depends on this, too . . ."

I looked him straight in the face, and he saw the rush of my surprise.

"Yes, my job, and maybe my life, too, Sookie—not just yours, and Bill's. I'm sending you a contact tomorrow. He lives in Shreveport, but he has a second apartment in Jackson. He has friends among the supernatural community there, the vampires, shifters, and Weres. Through him you can meet some of them, and their human employees."

I was not completely in my head right now, but I felt like I'd understand all this when I played it back. So I nodded. His fingers stroked mine, over and over.

"This man is a Were," Eric said carelessly, "so he is scum. But he is more reliable than some others, and he owes me a big personal favor."

I absorbed that, nodded again. Eric's long fingers seemed almost warm.

"He'll take you out and about in the vampire community in Jackson, and you can pick brains there among human employees. I know it's a long shot, but if there's something to discover, if Russell Edgington did abduct Bill, you may pick up a hint. The man who tried to abduct you was from Jackson, going by the bills in his car, and he was a Were, as the wolf's head on his vest indicates. I don't know why they came after you. But I suspect it means Bill is alive, and they wanted to grab you to use as leverage over him."

"Then I guess they should have abducted *Lorena*," I said.

Eric's eyes widened in appreciation.

"Maybe they already have her," he said. "But maybe Bill has realized it is Lorena who betrayed him. He wouldn't have been taken if she hadn't revealed the secret he had told her."

I mulled that over, nodded yet again.

"Another puzzle is why she happened to be there at all," Eric said. "I think I would have known if she'd been a regular member of the Mississippi group. But I'll be thinking about that in my spare time." From his grim face, Eric had already put in considerable brain time on that question. "If this plan doesn't work within about three days, Sookie, we may have to kidnap one of the Mississippi vampires in return. This would almost certainly lead to a war, and a war—even with Mississippi—would be costly in lives and money. And in the end, they would kill Bill anyway."

Okay, the weight of the world was resting on my shoulders. Thanks, Eric. I needed more responsibility and pressure.

"But know this: If they have Bill—if he is still alive—we will get him back. And you will be together again, if that's what you want."

Big *if.*

"To answer your question: I am your friend, and that will last as long as I can be your friend without jeopardizing my own life. Or the future of my area."

Well, that laid it on the line. I appreciated his honesty. "As long as it's convenient for you, you mean," I said calmly, which was both unfair and inaccurate. However, I thought it was odd that my characterization of his attitude actually seemed to bother him. "Let me ask you something, Eric."

He raised his eyebrows to tell me he was waiting. His hands traveled up and down my arms, absently, as if he wasn't thinking of what he was doing. The movement reminded me of a man warming his hands at a fire.

"If I'm understanding you, Bill was working on a project for the . . ." I felt a wild bubble of laughter rising, and I ruthlessly suppressed it. "For the queen of Louisiana," I finished. "But you didn't know about it. Is this right?"

Eric stared at me for a long moment, while he thought about what to tell me. "She told me she had work for Bill to do," he said. "But not what it was, or why he had to be the one to do it, or when it would be complete."

That would miff almost any leader, having his underling co-opted like that. Especially if the leader was kept in ignorance. "So, why isn't this queen looking for Bill?" I asked, keeping my voice carefully neutral.

"She doesn't know he's gone."

"Why is that?"

"We haven't told her."

Sooner or later he'd quit answering. "Why not?"

"She would punish us."

"Why?" I was beginning to sound like a two-year-old.

"For letting something happen to Bill, when he was doing a special project for her."

"What would that punishment be?"

"Oh, with her it's difficult to tell." He gave a choked laugh. "Something very unpleasant."

Eric was even closer to me, his face almost touching my hair. He was inhaling, very delicately. Vampires rely on smell, and hearing, much more than sight, though their eyesight is extremely accurate. Eric had had my blood, so he could tell more about my emotions than a vampire who hadn't. All bloodsuckers are students of the human emotional system, since the most successful predators know the habits of their prey.

Eric actually rubbed his cheek against mine. He was like a cat in his enjoyment of contact.

"Eric." He'd given me more information than he knew.

"Mmm?"

"Really, what will the queen do to you if you can't produce Bill on the date her project is due?"

My question got the desired result. Eric pulled away from me and looked down at me with eyes bluer than mine and harder than mine and colder than the Arctic waste.

"Sookie, you really don't want to know," he said. "Producing his work would be good enough. Bill's actual presence would be a bonus."

I returned his look with eyes almost as cold as his. "And what will I get in return for doing this for you?" I asked.

Eric managed to look both surprised and pleased. "If Pam hadn't hinted to you about Bill, his safe return would have been enough and you would have jumped at the chance to help," Eric reminded me.

"But now I know about Lorena."

"And knowing, do you agree to do this for us?"

"Yes, on one condition."

Eric looked wary. "What would that be?" he asked.

"If something happens to me, I want you to take her out."

He gaped at me for at least a whole second before he roared with laughter. "I would have to pay a huge fine," he said when he'd quit chortling. "And I'd have to accomplish it first. That's easier said than done. She's three hundred years old."

"You've told me that what will happen to you if all this comes unraveled would be pretty horrible," I reminded him.

"True."

"You've told me you desperately need me to do this for you."

"True."

"That's what I ask in return."

"You might make a decent vampire, Sookie," Eric said finally. "All right. Done. If anything happens to you, she'll never fuck Bill again."

"Oh, it's not just that."

"No?" Eric looked very skeptical, as well he might.

"It's because she betrayed him."

Eric's hard blue eyes met mine. "Tell me this, Sookie: Would you ask this of me if she were a human?" His wide, thin-lipped mouth, most often amused, was in a serious straight line.

"If she were a human, I'd take care of it myself," I said, and stood to show him to the door.

After Eric had driven away, I leaned against the door and laid my cheek against the wood. Did I mean what I'd told him? I'd long wondered if I were really a civilized person, though I kept striving to be one. I knew that at the moment I'd said I would take care of Lorena myself, I had meant it. There was something pretty savage inside me, and I'd always controlled it. My grandmother had not raised me to be a murderess.

As I plodded down the hall to my bedroom, I realized that my temper had been showing more and more lately. Ever since I'd gotten to know the vampires.

I couldn't figure out why that should be. They exerted tremendous control over themselves. Why should mine be slipping?

But that was enough introspection for one night.

I had to think about tomorrow.

Chapter 4

S<small>INCE IT SEEMED</small> I was going out of town, there was laundry to be done, and stuff in the refrigerator that needed throwing away. I wasn't particularly sleepy after spending so long in bed the preceding day and night, so I got out my suitcase, opened it, and tossed some clothes into the washer out on the freezing back porch. I didn't want to think about my own character any longer. I had plenty of other items to mull over.

Eric had certainly adopted a shotgun approach to bending me to his will. He'd bombarded me with many reasons to do what he wanted: intimidation, threat, seduction, an appeal for Bill's return, an appeal for his (and Pam's, and Chow's) life and/or well-being—to say nothing of my own health. "I might have to torture you, but I want to have sex with you; I need Bill, but I'm furious with him because he deceived me; I have to keep peace with Russell Edgington, but I have to get Bill back from him; Bill is my serf, but he's secretly working more for my boss."

Darn vampires. You can see why I'm glad their glamour doesn't affect me. It's one of the few positives my mind-reading ability has yielded me. Unfortunately, humans with psychic glitches are very attractive to the undead.

I certainly could not have foreseen any of this when I'd become attached to Bill. Bill had become almost as necessary to me as water; and not entirely because of my deep feelings for him, or my physical pleasure in his lovemaking. Bill was the only insurance I had against being annexed by another vampire, against my will.

After I'd run a couple of loads through the washer and dryer and folded the clothes, I felt much more relaxed. I was almost packed, and

I'd put in a couple of romances and a mystery in case I got a little time to read. I am self-educated from genre books.

I stretched and yawned. There was a certain peace of mind to be found in having a plan, and my uneasy sleep of the past day and night had not refreshed me as much as I thought. I might be able to fall asleep easily.

Even without help from the vampires, I could maybe find Bill, I thought, as I brushed my teeth and climbed into bed. But breaking him out of whatever prison he was in and making a successful escape, that was another question. And then I'd have to decide what to do about our relationship.

I woke up at about four in the morning with an odd feeling there was an idea just waiting to be acknowledged. I'd had a thought at some point during the night; it was the kind of idea that you just know has been bubbling in your brain, waiting to boil over.

Sure enough, after a minute the idea resurfaced. What if Bill had not been abducted, but had defected? What if he'd become so enamored or addicted to Lorena that he'd decided to leave the Louisiana vampires and join with the Mississippi group? Immediately, I had doubts that that had been Bill's plan; it would be a very elaborate one, with the leakage of informants to Eric concerning Bill's abduction, the confirmed presence of Lorena in Mississippi. Surely there'd be a less dramatic, and simpler, way to arrange his disappearance.

I wondered if Eric, Chow, and Pam were even now searching Bill's house, which lay across the cemetery from mine. They weren't going to find what they were looking for. Maybe they'd come back here. They wouldn't have to get Bill back at all, if they could find the computer files the queen wanted so badly. I fell to sleep out of sheer exhaustion, thinking I heard Chow laugh outside.

Even the knowledge of Bill's betrayal did not stop me from searching for him in my dreams. I must have rolled over three times, reaching out to see if he'd slid into bed with me, as he often did. And every time, the other side of the bed was empty and cold.

However, that was better than finding Eric there instead.

I was up and showering at first light, and I'd made a pot of coffee before the knock at the front door came.

"Who is it?" I stood to one side of the door as I asked.

"Eric sent me," a gruff voice said.

I opened the door and looked up. And looked up some more.

He was huge. His eyes were green. His tousled hair was curly and thick and black as pitch. His brain buzzed and pulsed with energy; kind of a red effect. Werewolf.

"Come on in. You want some coffee?"

Whatever he'd expected, it wasn't what he was seeing. "You bet, chere. You got some eggs? Some sausage?"

"Sure." I led him to the kitchen. "I'm Sookie Stackhouse," I said, over my shoulder. I bent over to get the eggs out of the refrigerator. "You?"

"Alcide," he said, pronouncing it *Al-see*, with the *d* barely sounded. "Alcide Herveaux."

He watched me steadily while I lifted out the skillet—my grandmother's old, blackened iron skillet. She'd gotten it when she got married, and fired it, like any woman worth her salt would do. Now it was perfectly seasoned. I turned the gas eye on at the stove. I cooked the sausage first (for the grease), plopped it on a paper towel on a plate and stuck it in the oven to keep warm. After asking Alcide how he wanted the eggs, I scrambled them and cooked them quickly, sliding them onto the warm plate. He opened the right drawer for the silverware on the first try, and poured himself some juice and coffee after I silently pointed out which cabinet contained the cups. He refilled my mug while he was at it.

He ate neatly. And he ate everything.

I plunged my hands into the hot, soapy water to clean the few dishes. I washed the skillet last, dried it, and rubbed some Crisco into the blackness, taking occasional glances at my guest. The kitchen smelled comfortably of breakfast and soapy water. It was a peculiarly peaceful moment.

This was anything but what I had expected when Eric had told me someone who owed him a favor would be my entrée into the Mississippi vampire milieu. As I looked out the kitchen window at the cold landscape, I realized that this was how I had envisioned my future; on the few occasions I'd let myself imagine a man sharing my house.

This was the way life was supposed to be, for normal people. It was morning, time to get up and work, time for a woman to cook breakfast for a man, if he had to go out and earn. This big rough man was eating real food. He almost certainly had a pickup truck sitting out in front of my house.

Of course, he was a werewolf. But a Were could live a more close-to-human life than a vampire.

On the other hand, what I didn't know about Weres could fill a book.

He finished, put his plate in the water in the sink, and washed and dried it himself while I wiped the table. It was as smooth as if we'd choreographed it. He disappeared into the bathroom for a minute while I ran over my mental list of things that had to be done before I left. I needed to talk to Sam, that was the main thing. I'd called my brother the night before to tell him I'd be gone for a few days. Liz had been at Jason's, so he hadn't really thought a lot about my departure. He'd agreed to pick up my mail and my papers for me.

Alcide came to sit opposite me at the table. I was trying to think about how we should talk about our joint task; I was trying to antici-pate any sore paws I might tread on. Maybe he was worrying about the same things. I can't read the minds of shape-shifters or werewolves with any consistency; they're supernatural creatures. I can reliably interpret moods, and pick up on the occasional clear idea. So the humans-with-a-difference are much less opaque to me than the vam-pires. Though I understand there's a contingent of shape-shifters and Weres who wants to change things, the fact of their existence still remains a secret. Until they see how publicity works out for the vam-pires, the supernaturals of the two-natured variety are ferocious about their privacy.

Werewolves are the tough guys of the shape-shifting world. They're shape-shifters by definition, but they're the only ones who have their own separate society, and they will not allow anyone else to be called "Were" in their hearing. Alcide Herveaux looked plenty tough. He was big as a boulder, with biceps that I could do pull-ups on. He would have to shave a second time if he planned on going out in the evening. He would fit right in on a construction site or a wharf.

He was a proper man.

"How are they forcing you to do this?" I asked.

"They have a marker of my dad's," he said. He put his massive hands on the table and leaned into them. "They own a casino in Shreve-port, you know?"

"Sure." It was a popular weekend excursion for people in this area, to go over to Shreveport or up to Tunica (in Mississippi, right below Memphis) and rent a room for a couple of nights, play the slots, see a show or two, eat lots of buffet food.

"My dad got in too deep. He owns a surveying company—I work for him—but he likes to gamble." The green eyes smoldered with rage. "He got in too deep in the casino in Louisiana, so your vamps own his marker, his debt. If they call it in, our company will go under." Were-wolves seemed to respect vampires about as much as vampires respect them. "So, to get the marker back, I have to help you hang around with the vamps in Jackson." He leaned back in the chair, looking me in the eyes. "That's not a hard thing, taking a pretty woman to Jackson and

out barhopping. Now that I've met you, I'm glad to do it, to get my father out from under the debt. But why the hell you want to do that? You
look like a real woman, not one of those sick bitches who get off on
hanging around the vamps."

This was a refreshingly direct conversation, after my conference
with the vampires. "I only hang around with one vampire, by choice,"
I said bitterly. "Bill, my—well, I don't know if he's even my boyfriend
anymore. It seems the vampires of Jackson may have kidnapped him.
Someone tried to grab me last night." I thought it only fair to let him
know. "Since the kidnapper didn't seem to know my name, just that I
worked at Merlotte's, I'll probably be safe in Jackson if no one figures
out I'm the woman who goes with Bill. I have to tell you, the man
who tried to grab me was a werewolf. And he had a Hinds County car
plate." Jackson was in Hinds County.

"Wearing a gang vest?" Alcide asked. I nodded. Alcide looked
thoughtful, which was a good thing. This was not a situation I took
lightly, and it was a good sign that he didn't, either. "There's a small
gang in Jackson made up of Weres. Some of the bigger shifters hang
around the edges of this gang—the panther, the bear. They hire themselves out to the vamps on a pretty regular basis."

"There's one less of them now," I said.

After a moment's digestion of that information, my new companion gave me a long, challenging stare. "So, what good is a little human gal going to do against the vampires of Jackson? You a martial
artist? You a great shot? You been in the Army?"

I had to smile. "No. You never heard my name?"

"You're famous?"

"Guess not." I was pleased that he didn't have any preconceptions
about me. "I think I'll just let you find out about me."

"Long as you're not gonna turn into a snake." He stood up. "You're
not a guy, are you?" That late-breaking thought made his eyes widen.

"No, Alcide. I'm a woman." I tried to say that matter-of-factly, but
it was pretty hard.

"I was willing to put money on that." He grinned at me. "If you're
not some kind of superwoman, what are you going to do when you
know where your man is?"

"I'm going to call Eric, the . . ." Suddenly I realized that telling
vampire secrets is a bad idea. "Eric is Bill's boss. He'll decide what to
do after that."

Alcide looked skeptical. "I don't trust Eric. I don't trust any of
'em. He'll probably double-cross you."

"How?"

"He might use your man as leverage. He might demand restitution, since they have one of his men. He might use your man's abduction as an excuse to go to war, in which case your man will be executed tout de suite."

I had not thought that far. "Bill knows stuff," I said. "Important stuff."

"Good. That may keep him alive." Then he saw my face, and chagrin ran across his own. "Hey, Sookie, I'm sorry. I don't think before I talk sometimes. We'll get him back, though it makes me sick to think of a woman like you with one of those bloodsuckers."

This was painful, but oddly refreshing.

"Thanks, I guess," I said, attempting a smile. "What about you? Do you have a plan about how to introduce me to the vampires?"

"Yeah. There's a nightclub in Jackson, close to the capitol. It's for Supes and their dates only. No tourists. The vamps can't make it pay on their own, and it's a convenient meeting place for them, so they let us lowlifes share the fun." He grinned. His teeth were perfect—white and sharp. "It won't be suspicious if I go there. I always drop in when I'm in Jackson. You'll have to go as my date." He looked embarrassed. "Uh, I better tell you, you seem like you're a jeans kind of person like me—but this club, they like you to dress kind of party style." He feared I had no fancy dresses in my closet; I could read that clearly. And he didn't want me to be humiliated by appearing in the wrong clothes. What a man.

"Your girlfriend won't be crazy about this," I said, angling for information out of sheer curiosity.

"She lives in Jackson, as a matter of fact. But we broke up a couple of months ago," he said. "She took up with another shape-shifter. Guy turns into a damn owl."

Was she *nuts*? Of course, there'd be more to the story. And of course, it fell into the category of "none of your business."

So without comment, I went to my room to pack my two party dresses and their accessories in a hanging bag. Both were purchases from Tara's Togs, managed (and now owned) by my friend Tara Thornton. Tara was real good about calling me when things went on clearance. Bill actually owned the building that housed Tara's Togs, and had told all the businesses housed in there to run a tab for me that he would pay, but I had resisted the temptation. Well, except for replacing clothes that Bill himself had ripped in our more thrilling moments.

I was very proud of both these dresses, since I'd never had anything like them before, and I zipped the bag shut with a smile.

Alcide stuck his head in the bedroom to ask if I was ready. He looked at the cream-and-yellow bed and curtains, and nodded approvingly. "I got to call my boss," I said. "Then we'll be good to go." I perched on the side of the bed and picked up the receiver.

Alcide propped himself against the wall by my closet door while I dialed Sam's personal number. His voice was sleepy when he answered, and I apologized for calling so early. "What's happening, Sookie?" he asked groggily.

"I have to go away for a few days," I said. "I'm sorry for not giving you more notice, but I called Sue Jennings last night to see if she'd work for me. She said yes, so I gave her my hours."

"Where are you going?" he asked.

"I have to go to Mississippi," I said. "Jackson."

"You got someone lined up to pick up your mail?"

"My brother. Thanks for asking."

"Plants to water?"

"None that won't live till I get back."

"Okay. Are you going by yourself?"

"No," I said hesitantly.

"With Bill?"

"No, he, uh, he hasn't shown up."

"Are you in trouble?"

"I'm just fine," I lied.

"Tell him a man's going with you," Alcide rumbled, and I gave him an exasperated look. He was leaning against the wall, and he took up an awful lot of it.

"Someone's there?" Sam's nothing if not quick on the uptake.

"Yes, Alcide Herveaux," I said, figuring it was a smart thing to tell someone who cared about me that I was leaving the area with this guy. First impressions can be absolutely false, and Alcide needed to be aware there was someone who would hold him accountable.

"Aha," Sam said. The name did not seem to be unfamiliar to him. "Let me talk to him."

"Why?" I can take a lot of paternalism, but I was about up to my ears.

"Hand over the damn phone." Sam almost never curses, so I made a face to show what I thought of his demand and gave the phone to Alcide. I stomped out to the living room and looked through the window. Yep. A Dodge Ram, extended cab. I was willing to bet it had everything on it that could be put on.

I'd rolled my suitcase out by its handle, and I'd slung my carrying bag over a chair by the door, so I just had to pull on my heavy jacket.

I was glad Alcide had warned me about the dress-up rule for the bar, since it never would have occurred to me to pack anything fancy. Stupid vampires. Stupid dress code.

I was Sullen, with a capital *S*.

I wandered back down the hall, mentally reviewing the contents of my suitcase, while the two shape-shifters had (presumably) a "man talk." I glanced through the doorway of my bedroom to see that Alcide, with the phone to his ear, was perched on the side of my bed where I'd been sitting. He looked oddly at home there.

I paced restlessly back into the living room and stared out the window some more. Maybe the two were having shape-shifting talk. Though to Alcide, Sam (who generally shifted into a collie, though he was not limited to that form) would rank as a lightweight, at least they were from the same branch of the tree. Sam, on the other hand, would be a little leery of Alcide; werewolves had a bad rep.

Alcide strode down the hall, safety shoes clomping on the hardwood floor. "I promised him I'd take care of you," he said. "Now, we'll just hope that works out." He wasn't smiling.

I had been tuning up to be aggravated, but his last sentence was so realistic that the hot air went out of me as if I'd been punctured. In the complex relationship between vampire, Were, and human, there was a lot of leeway for something to go wrong somewhere. After all, my plan was thin, and the vampires' hold over Alcide was tenuous. Bill might not have been taken unwillingly; he might be happy being held captive by a king, as long as the vampire Lorena was on site. He might be enraged that I had come to find him.

He might be dead.

I locked the door behind me and followed Alcide as he stowed my things in the extended cab of the Ram.

The outside of the big truck gleamed, but inside, it was the littered vehicle of a man who spent his working life on the road; a hard hat, invoices, estimates, business cards, boots, a first-aid kit. At least there wasn't any food trash. As we bumped down my eroded driveway, I picked up a rubber-banded sheaf of brochures whose cover read, "Herveaux and Son, AAA Accurate Surveys." I eased out the top one and studied it carefully as Alcide drove the short distance to interstate 20 to go east to Monroe, Vicksburg, and then to Jackson.

I discovered that the Herveauxes, father and son, owned a bi-state surveying company, with offices in Jackson, Monroe, Shreveport, and Baton Rouge. The home office, as Alcide had told me, was in Shreveport. There was a photo inside of the two men, and the older Herveaux was just as impressive (in a senior way) as his son.

"Is your dad a werewolf, too?" I asked, after I'd digested the information and realized that the Herveaux family was at least prosperous, and possibly rich. They'd worked hard for it, though; and they'd keep working hard, unless the older Mr. Herveaux could control his gambling.

"Both my parents," Alcide said, after a pause.

"Oh, sorry." I wasn't sure what I was apologizing for, but it was safer than not.

"That's the only way to produce a Were child," he said, after a moment. I couldn't tell if he was explaining to be polite, or because he really thought I should know.

"So how come America's not full of werewolves and shapeshifters?" I asked, after I'd considered his statement.

"Like must marry like to produce another, which is not always doable. And each union only produces one child with the trait. Infant mortality is high."

"So, if you marry another werewolf, one of your kids will be a werebaby?"

"The condition will manifest itself at the onset of, ah, puberty."

"Oh, that's awful. Being a teenager is tough enough."

He smiled, not at me, but at the road. "Yeah, it does complicate things."

"So, your ex-girlfriend . . . she a shifter?"

"Yeah. I don't normally date shifters, but I guess I thought with her it would be different. Weres and shifters are strongly attracted to each other. Animal magnetism, I guess," Alcide said, as an attempt at humor.

My boss, also a shifter, had been glad to make friends with other shifters in the area. He had been hanging out with a maenad ("dating" would be too sweet a word for their relationship), but she'd moved on. Now, Sam was hoping to find another compatible shifter. He felt more comfortable with a strange human, like me, or another shifter, than he did with regular women. When he'd told me that, he'd meant it as a compliment, or maybe just as a simple statement; but it had hurt me a little, though my abnormality had been borne in on me since I was very young.

Telepathy doesn't wait for puberty.

"How come?" I asked baldly. "How come you thought it would be different?"

"She told me she was sterile. I found out she was on birth control pills. Big difference. I'm not passing this along. Even a shifter and a werewolf may have a child who has to change at the full moon, though only kids of a pure couple—both Weres or both shifters—can change at will."

Food for thought, there. "So you normally date regular old girls. But doesn't it make it hard to date? Keeping secret such a big, ah, factor, in your life?"

"Yeah," he admitted. "Dating regular girls can be a pain. But I have to date someone." There was an edge of desperation to his rumbly voice.

I gave that a long moment's contemplation, and then I closed my eyes and counted to ten. I was missing Bill in a most elemental and unexpected way. My first clue had been the tug-below-the-waist I'd felt when I'd watched my tape of *The Last of the Mohicans* the week before and I'd fixated on Daniel Day-Lewis bounding through the forest. If I could appear from behind a tree before he saw Madeleine Stowe . . .

I was going to have to watch my step.

"So, if you bite someone, they won't turn into a werewolf?" I decided to change the direction of my thoughts. Then I remembered the last time Bill had bitten me, and felt a rush of heat through . . . oh, *hell.*

"That's when you get your wolf-man. Like the ones in the movies. They die pretty quick, poor people. And that's not passed along, if they, ah, engender children in their human form. If it's when they're in their altered form, the baby is miscarried."

"How interesting." I could not think of one other thing to say.

"But there's that element of the supernatural, too, just like with vampires," Alcide said, still not looking in my direction. "The tie-in of genetics and the supernatural element, that's what no one seems to understand. We just can't tell the world we exist, like the vampires did. We'd be locked up in zoos, sterilized, ghettoized—because we're sometimes animals. Going public just seems to make the vampires glamorous and rich." He sounded more than a little bitter.

"So how come you're telling me all this, right off the bat? If it's such a big secret?" He had given me more information in ten minutes than I'd had from Bill in months.

"If I'm going to be spending a few days with you, it will make my life a lot easier if you know. I figure you have your own problems, and it seems the vampires have some power over you, too. I don't think you'll tell. And if the worst happens, and I've been utterly wrong about you, I'll ask Eric to pay you a visit and wipe out your memory." He shook his head in baffled irritation. "I don't know why, really. I just feel like I know you."

I couldn't think of a response to that, but I had to speak. Silence would lend too much importance to his last sentence. "I'm sorry the vampires have a hold on your dad. But I have to find Bill. If this is the only way I can do it, this is what I have to do. I at least owe him that much, even if . . ." My voice trailed off. I didn't want to finish the sentence. All the possible endings were too sad, too final.

He shrugged, a large movement on Alcide Herveaux. "Taking a pretty girl to a bar isn't that big a deal," he reassured me again, trying to bolster my spirits.

In his position, I might not have been so generous. "Is your dad a constant gambler?"

"Only since my mother died," Alcide said, after a long pause.

"I'm sorry." I kept my eyes off his face in case he needed some privacy. "I don't have either of my parents," I offered.

"They been gone long?"

"Since I was seven."

"Who raised you?"

"My grandmother raised me and my brother."

"She still living?"

"No. She died this year. She was murdered."

"Tough." He was matter-of-fact.

"Yeah." I had one more question. "Did both your parents tell you about yourself?"

"No. My grandfather told me when I was about thirteen. He'd noticed the signs. I just don't know orphaned Weres get through it without guidance."

"That would be really rough."

"We try to keep aware of all the Weres breeding in the area, so no one will go unwarned."

Even a secondhand warning would be better than no warning at all. But still, such a session would be a major trauma in anyone's life.

We stopped in Vicksburg to get gas. I offered to pay for filling the tank, but Alcide told me firmly this could go on his books as a business expense, since he did in fact need to see some customers. He waved off my offer to pump the gas, too. He did accept the cup of coffee I bought him, with as many thanks as if it had been a new suit. It was a cold, bright day, and I took a brisk walk around the travel center to stretch my legs before climbing back into the cab of the truck.

Seeing the signs for the battlefield reminded me of one of the most taxing days I'd had as an adult. I found myself telling Alcide about my grandmother's favorite club, the Descendants of the Glorious Dead, and about their field trip to the battlefield two years before. I'd driven one car, Maxine Fortenberry (grandmother of one of my brother Jason's good buddies) another, and we'd toured at length. Each of the Descendants had brought a favorite text covering the siege, and an early stop at the visitors' center had gotten the Descendants all tanked up with maps and memorabilia. Despite the failure of Velda Cannon's Depends, we'd had a great time. We'd read every monument, we'd had a picnic lunch by the restored USS *Cairo,* and we'd gone home laden with souvenir booty and exhausted. We'd even gone into the Isle of Capri Casino for an hour of amazed staring, and some tentative slot machine feeding. It had been a very happy day for my grandmother, almost as happy a time as the evening she'd inveigled Bill into speaking at the Descendants meeting.

"Why did she want him to do that?" Alcide asked. He was smiling at my description of our supper stop at a Cracker Barrel.

"Bill's a vet," I said. "An Army vet, not an animal-doctor vet."

"So?" After a beat, he said, "You mean your boyfriend is a veteran of the *Civil War?*"

"Yeah. He was human then. He wasn't brought over until after the war. He had a wife and children." I could hardly keep calling him my boyfriend, since he'd been on the verge of leaving me for someone else.

"Who made him a vampire?" Alcide asked. We were in Jackson now, and he was making his way downtown to the apartment his company maintained.

"I don't know," I said. "He doesn't talk about it."

"That seems a little strange to me."

Actually, it seemed a little strange to me, too; but I figured it was something really personal, and when Bill wanted to tell me about it, he would. The relationship was very strong, I knew, between the older vampire and the one he'd "brought over."

"I guess he really isn't my boyfriend anymore," I admitted. Though "boyfriend" seemed a pretty pale term for what Bill had been to me.

"Oh, yeah?"

I flushed. I shouldn't have said anything. "But I still have to find him."

We were silent for a while after that. The last city I'd visited had been Dallas, and it was easy to see that Jackson was nowhere close to that size. (That was a big plus, as far as I was concerned.) Alcide pointed out the golden figure on the dome of the new capitol, and I admired it appropriately. I thought it was an eagle, but I wasn't sure, and I was a little embarrassed to ask. Did I need glasses? The building we were going to was close to the corner of High and State streets.

It was not a new building; the brick had started out a golden tan, and now it was a grimy light brown.

"The apartments here are larger than they are in new buildings," Alcide said. "There's a small guest bedroom. Everything should be all ready for us. We use the apartment cleaning service."

I nodded silently. I could not remember if I'd ever been in an apartment building before. Then I realized I had, of course. There was a two-story U-shaped apartment building in Bon Temps. I had surely visited someone there; in the past seven years, almost every single person in Bon Temps had rented a place in Kingfisher Apartments at some point in his or her dating career.

Alcide's apartment, he told me, was on the top floor, the fifth. You drove in from the street down a ramp to park. There was a guard at the garage entrance, standing in a little booth. Alcide showed him a plastic pass. The heavyset guard, who had a cigarette hanging out of his mouth, barely glanced at the card Alcide held out before he pressed a button to raise the barrier. I wasn't too impressed with the security. I felt like I could whip that guy, myself. My brother, Jason, could pound him into the pavement.

We scrambled out of the truck and retrieved our bags from the rudimentary backseat. My hanging bag had fared pretty well. Without asking me, Alcide took my small suitcase. He led the way to a central block in the parking area, and I saw a gleaming elevator door. He punched the button, and it opened immediately. The elevator creaked its way up after Alcide punched the button marked with a 5. At least the elevator was very clean, and when the door swished open, so were the carpet and the hall beyond.

"They went condo, so we bought the place," Alcide said, as if it was no big deal. Yes, he and his dad had made some money. There were four apartments per floor, Alcide told me.

"Who are your neighbors?"

"Two state senators own 501, and I'm sure they've gone home for the holiday season," he said. "Mrs. Charles Osburgh the Third lives in 502, with her nurse. Mrs. Osburgh was a grand old lady until the past year. I don't think she can walk anymore. Five-oh-three is empty right now, unless the realtor sold it this past two weeks." He unlocked the door to number 504, pushed it open, and gestured for me to enter ahead of him. I entered the silent warmth of the hall, which opened on my left into a kitchen enclosed by counters, not walls, so the eye was unobstructed in sweeping the living room/dining area. There was a door immediately on my right, which probably opened onto a coat closet, and another a little farther down, which led into a small bedroom with a neatly made-up double bed. A door past that revealed a small bathroom with white-and-blue tiles and towels hung just so on the racks.

Across the living room, to my left, was a door that led into a larger bedroom. I peered inside briefly, not wanting to seem overly interested in Alcide's personal space. The bed in that room was a king. I wondered if Alcide and his dad did a lot of entertaining when they visited Jackson.

"The master bedroom has its own bath," Alcide explained. "I'd be glad to let you have the bigger room, but the phone's in there, and I'm expecting some business calls."

"The smaller bedroom is just fine," I said. I peeked around a little more after my bags were stowed in my room.

The apartment was a symphony in beige. Beige carpet, beige furniture. Sort of oriental bamboo-y patterned wallpaper with a beige background. It was very quiet and very clean.

As I hung my dresses in the closet, I wondered how many nights I'd have to go to the club. More than two, and I'd have to do some shopping. But that was impossible, at the least imprudent, on my budget. A familiar worry settled hard on my shoulders.

My grandmother hadn't had much to leave me, God bless her, especially after her funeral expenses. The house had been a wonderful and unexpected gift.

The money she'd used to raise Jason and me, money that had come from an oil well that had petered out, was long gone. The fee I'd gotten paid for moonlighting for the Dallas vampires had mostly gone to buy the two dresses, pay my property taxes, and have a tree cut down because the previous winter's ice storm had loosened its roots and it had begun to lean too close to the house. A big branch had already fallen, damaging the tin roof a bit. Luckily, Jason and Hoyt Fortenberry had known enough about roofing to repair that for me.

I recalled the roofing truck outside of Belle Rive.

I sat on the bed abruptly. Where had that come from? Was I petty enough to be angry that my boyfriend had been thinking of a dozen different ways to be sure his descendants (the unfriendly and sometimes snooty Bellefleurs) prospered, while I, the love of his afterlife, worried herself to tears about her finances?

You bet, I was petty enough.

I should be ashamed of myself.

But later. My mind was not through toting up grievances.

As long as I was considering money (lack of), I wondered if it had even occurred to Eric when he dispatched me on this mission that since I'd be missing work, I wouldn't get paid. Since I wouldn't get paid, I couldn't pay the electric company, or the cable, or the phone, or my car insurance . . . though I had a moral obligation to find Bill, no matter what had happened to our relationship, right?

I flopped back on the bed and told myself that this would all work out. I knew, in the back of my mind, that all I had to do was sit down with Bill—assuming I ever got him back—and explain my situation to him, and he'd . . . he'd do something.

But I couldn't just take money from Bill. Of course, if we were married, it would be okay; husband and wife held all in common. But we couldn't get married. It was illegal.

And he hadn't asked me.

"Sookie?" a voice said from the doorway.

I blinked and sat up. Alcide was lounging against the jamb, his arms crossed over his chest.

"You okay?"

I nodded uncertainly.

"You missing him?"

I was too ashamed to mention my money troubles, and they weren't more important than Bill, of course. To simplify things, I nodded.

He sat beside me and put his arm around me. He was so warm. He smelled like Tide detergent, and Irish Spring soap, and man. I closed my eyes and counted to ten again.

"You miss him," he said, confirming. He reached across his body to take my left hand, and his right arm tightened around me.

You don't know *how I miss him,* I thought.

Apparently, once you got used to regular and spectacular sex, your body had a mind of its own (so to speak) when it was deprived of that recreation; to say nothing of missing the hugging and cuddling part. My body was begging me to knock Alcide Herveaux back onto the bed so it could have its way with him. *Right now.*

"I do miss him, no matter what problems we have," I said, and my voice came out tiny and shaky. I wouldn't open my eyes, because if I did, I might see on his face a tiny impulse, some little inclination, and that would be all it would take.

"What time do you think we should go to the club?" I asked, firmly steering in another direction.

He was so *warm.*

Other direction! "Would you like me to cook supper before we go?" Least I could do. I shot up off the bed like a bottle rocket; turned to face him with the most natural smile I could muster. Get out of close proximity, or jump his bones.

"Oh, let's go to the Mayflower Cafe. It looks like an old diner—it *is* an old diner—but you'll enjoy it. Everyone goes there—senators and carpenters, all kinds of people. They just serve beer, that okay?" I shrugged and nodded. That was fine with me. "I don't drink much," I told him.

"Me neither," he said. "Maybe because, every so often, my dad tends to drink too much. Then he makes bad decisions." Alcide seemed to regret having told me this. "After the Mayflower, we'll go to the club," Alcide said, much more briskly. "It gets dark real early these days, but the vamps don't show up till they've had some blood, picked up their dates, done some business. We should get there about ten. So we'll go out to eat about eight, if that suits you?"

"Sure, that'll be great." I was at a loss. It was only two in the afternoon. His apartment didn't need cleaning. There was no reason to cook. If I wanted to read, I had romance novels in my suitcase. But in my present condition, it was hardly likely to help my state of . . . mind.

"Listen, would it be okay if I ran out to visit some clients?" he asked.

"Oh, that would be fine." I thought it would be all to the good if he wasn't in my immediate vicinity. "You go do whatever you need to do. I have books to read, and there's the television." Maybe I could begin the mystery novel.

"If you want to . . . I don't know . . . my sister, Janice, owns a beauty shop about four blocks away, in one of the older neighborhoods. She married a local guy. You want to, you could walk over and get the works."

"Oh, I . . . well, that . . ." I didn't have the sophistication to think of a smooth and plausible refusal, when the glaring roadblock to such a treat was my lack of money.

Suddenly, comprehension crossed his face. "If you stopped by, it would give Janice the opportunity to look you over. After all, you're supposed to be my girlfriend, and she hated Debbie. She'd really enjoy a visit."

"You're being awful nice," I said, trying not to sound as confused and touched as I felt. "That's not what I expected."

"You're not what I expected, either," he said, and left his sister's shop number by the phone before heading out on his business.

Chapter 5

Janice Herveaux Phillips (married two years, mother of one, I learned quickly) was exactly what I might have expected of a sister of Alcide's. She was tall, attractive, plainspoken, and confident; and she ran her business efficiently.

I seldom went into beauty parlors. My gran had always done her own home perms, and I had never colored my hair or done anything else to it, besides a trim now and then. When I confessed this to Janice, who'd noticed I was looking around me with the curiosity of the ignorant, her broad face split in a grin. "Then you'll need everything," she said with satisfaction.

"No, no, no," I protested anxiously. "Alcide—."

"Called me on his cell phone and made it clear I was to give you the works," Janice said. "And frankly, honey, anyone who helps him recover from that Debbie is my best friend."

I had to smile. "But I'll pay," I told her.

"No, your money's no good here," she said. "Even if you break up with Alcide tomorrow, just getting him through tonight will be worth it."

"Tonight?" I began to have a sinking feeling that once again, I didn't know everything there was to know.

"I happen to know that tonight that bitch is going to announce her engagement at that club they go to," Janice said.

Okay, this time what I didn't know was something pretty major. "She's marrying the—man she took up with after she dumped Alcide?" (I barely stopped myself from saying, "The shape-shifter?")

"Quick work, huh? What could he have that my brother doesn't have?"

"I can't imagine," I said with absolutely sincerity, earning a quick smile from Janice. There was sure to be a flaw in her brother somewhere—maybe Alcide came to the supper table in his underwear, or picked his nose in public.

"Well, if you find out, you let me know. Now, let's get you going." Janice glanced around her in a businesslike way. "Corinne is going to give you your pedicure and manicure, and Jarvis is going to do your hair. You sure have a great head of it," Janice said in a more personal way.

"All mine, all natural," I admitted.

"No color?"

"Nope."

"You're the lucky one," Janice said, shaking her head.

That was a minority opinion.

Janice herself was working on a client whose silver hair and gold jewelry proclaimed she was a woman of privilege, and while this cold-faced lady examined me with indifferent eyes, Janice fired off some instructions to her employees and went back to Ms. Big Bucks.

I had never been so pampered in my life. And everything was new to me. Corinne (manicures and pedicures), who was as plump and juicy as one of the sausages I'd cooked that morning, painted my toenails and fingernails screaming red to match the dress I was going to wear. The only male in the shop, Jarvis, had fingers as light and quick as butterflies. He was thin as a reed and artificially platinum blond. Entertaining me with a stream of chatter, he washed and set my hair and established me under the dryer. I was one chair down from the rich lady, but I got just as much attention. I had a *People* magazine to read, and Corinne brought me a Coke. It was so nice to have people urging me to relax.

I was feeling kind of roasted under the dryer when the timer binged. Jarvis got me out from under it and set me back in his chair. After consulting with Janice, he whipped his preheated curling iron from a sort of holster mounted on the wall, and painstakingly arranged my hair in loose curls trailing down my back. I looked spectacular. Looking spectacular makes you happy. This was the best I'd felt since Bill had left.

Janice came over to talk every moment she was able. I caught myself forgetting that I wasn't Alcide's real girlfriend, with a real chance of becoming Janice's sister-in-law. This kind of acceptance didn't come my way too often.

I was wishing I could repay her kindness in some way, when a chance presented itself. Jarvis's station mirrored Janice's, so my back was to Janice's customer's back. Left on my own while Jarvis went to get a bottle of the conditioner he thought I should try, I watched (in the mirror) Janice take off her earrings and put them in a little china dish. I might never have observed what happened next if I hadn't picked up a clear covetous thought from the rich lady's head, which was, simply, "Aha!" Janice walked away to get another towel, and in the clear reflection, I watched the silver-haired customer deftly sweep up the earrings and stuff them into her jacket pocket, while Janice's back was turned.

By the time I was finished, I'd figured out what to do. I was just waiting to say good-bye to Jarvis, who'd had to go to the telephone; I knew he was talking to his mother, from the pictures I got from his head. So I slid out of my vinyl chair and walked over to the rich woman, who was writing a check for Janice.

"'Scuse me," I said, smiling brilliantly. Janice looked a little startled, and the elegant woman looked snooty. This was a client who spent a lot of money here, and Janice wouldn't want to lose her. "You got a smear of hair gel on your jacket. If you'll please just slide out of it for a second, I'll get it right off."

She could hardly refuse. I grasped the jacket shoulders and gently tugged, and she automatically helped me slide the green-and-red plaid jacket down her arms. I carried it behind the screen that concealed the hair-washing area, and wiped at a perfectly clean area just for verisimilitude (a great word from my Word of the Day calendar). Of course, I also extracted the earrings and put them in my own pocket.

"There you are, good as new!" I beamed at her and helped her into the jacket.

"Thanks, Sookie," Janice said, too brightly. She suspected something was amiss.

"You're welcome!" I smiled steadily.

"Yes, of course," said the elegant woman, somewhat confusedly. "Well, I'll see you next week, Janice."

She clicked on her high heels all the way out the door, not looking back. When she was out of sight, I reached in my pocket and held out my hand to Janice. She opened her hand under mine, and I dropped the earrings into her palm.

"Good God almighty," Janice said, suddenly looking about five years older. "I forgot and left something where she could reach it."

"She does this all the time?"

"Yeah. That's why we're about the fifth beauty salon she's patronized in the past ten years. The others put up with it for a while, but

eventually she did that one thing too many. She's so rich, and so educated, and she was brought up right. I don't know why she does stuff
like this."

We shrugged at each other, the vagaries of the white-collar
well-to-do beyond our comprehension. It was a moment of perfect
understanding. "I hope you don't lose her as a customer. I tried to be
tactful," I said.

"And I really appreciate that. But I would have hated losing those
earrings more than losing her as a client. My husband gave them to
me. They tend to pinch after a while, and I didn't even think when I
pulled them off."

I'd been thanked more than enough. I pulled on my own coat. "I
better be off," I said. "I've really enjoyed the wonderful treat."

"Thank my brother," Janice said, her broad smile restored. "And,
after all, you just paid for it." She held up the earrings.

I was smiling, too, as I left the warmth and camaraderie of the salon, but that didn't last too long. The thermometer had dropped and the
sky was getting darker by the minute. I walked the distance back to the
apartment building very briskly. After a chilly ride on a creaky elevator, I was glad to use the key Alcide had given me and step into the
warmth. I switched on a lamp and turned on the television for a little
company, and I huddled on the couch and thought about the pleasures
of the afternoon. Once I'd thawed out, I realized Alcide must have
turned down the thermostat. Though pleasant compared to the out-of-
doors, the apartment was definitely on the cool side.

The sound of the key in the door roused me out of my reverie,
and Alcide came in with a clipboard full of paperwork. He looked
tired and preoccupied, but his face relaxed when he saw me waiting.

"Janice called me to tell me you'd come by," he said. His voice
warmed up as he spoke. "She wanted me to say thank you again."

I shrugged. "I appreciate my hair and my new nails," I said. "I've
never done that before."

"You've never been to a beauty shop before?"

"My grandmother went every now and then. I had my ends
trimmed, once."

He looked as stunned as if I'd confessed I'd never seen a flush
toilet.

To cover my embarrassment, I fanned my nails out for his admiration. I hadn't wanted very long ones, and these were the shortest ones
Corinne could in all conscience manage, she had told me. "My toenails
match," I told my host.

"Let's see," he said.

I untied my sneakers and pulled off my socks. I held out my feet. "Aren't they pretty?" I asked.

He was looking at me kind of funny. "They look great," he said quietly.

I glanced at the clock on top of the television. "I guess I better go get ready," I said, trying to figure out how to take a bath without affecting my hair and nails. I thought of Janice's news about Debbie. "You're really ready to dress up tonight, right?"

"Sure," he said gamely.

"'Cause I'm going all out."

That interested him. "That would mean . . . ?"

"Wait and see." This was a nice guy, with a nice family, doing me a heavy-duty favor. Okay, he'd been coerced into it. But he was being extremely gracious to me, under any circumstances.

I ROLLED OUT of my room an hour later. Alcide was standing in the kitchen, pouring himself a Coke. It ran over the edge of the glass while he took me in.

That was a real compliment.

While Alcide mopped up the counter with a paper towel, he kept darting glances at me. I turned around slowly.

I was wearing red—screaming red, fire engine red. I was going to freeze most of the evening, because my dress didn't have any shoulders, though it did have long sleeves that you slid on separately. It zipped up the back. It flared below the hips, what there *was* below the hips. My grandmother would have flung herself across the doorsill to keep me from going out the door in this dress. I loved it. I had got it on extreme sale at Tara's Togs; I suspected Tara had kind of put it aside for me. Acting on a huge and unwise impulse, I'd bought the shoes and lipstick to go with it. And now the nails, thanks to Janice! I had a gray-and-black fringed silk shawl to wrap around myself, and a little bitty bag that matched my shoes. The bag was beaded.

"Turn around again," Alcide suggested a little hoarsely. He himself was wearing a conventional black suit with a white shirt and a green patterned tie that matched his eyes. Nothing, apparently, could tame his hair. Maybe he should have gone to Janice's beauty shop instead of me. He looked handsome and rough, though "attractive" might be a more accurate word than "handsome."

I rotated slowly. I wasn't confident enough to keep my eyebrows from arching in a silent question as I completed my turn.

"You look *mouthwatering*," he said sincerely. I released a breath I hadn't realized I'd been holding.

"Thanks," I said, trying not to beam like an idiot.

I had a trying time getting into Alcide's truck, what with the shortness of the dress and the highness of the heels, but with Alcide giving me a tactical boost, I managed.

Our destination was a small place on the corner of Capitol and Roach. It wasn't impressive from the outside, but the Mayflower Cafe was as interesting as Alcide had predicted. Some of the people at the tables scattered on the black-and-white tile floor were dressed to the nines, like Alcide and me. Some of them were wearing flannel and denim. Some had brought their own wine or liquor. I was glad we weren't drinking; Alcide had one beer, and that was it. I had iced tea. The food was really good, but not fancy. Dinner was long, drawn-out, and interesting. Lots of people knew Alcide, and they came by the table to say hello to him and to find out who I was. Some of these visitors were involved in the state government, some were in the building trade like Alcide, and some appeared to be friends of Alcide's dad's.

A few of them were not law-abiding men at all; even though I've always lived in Bon Temps, I know hoods when I see the product of their brains. I'm not saying they were thinking about bumping off anyone, or bribing senators, or anything specific like that. Their thoughts were greedy—greedy of money, greedy of me, and in one case, greedy of Alcide (to which he was completely oblivious, I could tell).

But most of all, these men—all of them—were greedy for power. I guess in a state capital, that lust for power was inevitable, even in as poverty-plagued a state as Mississippi.

The women with the greediest men were almost all extremely well groomed and very expensively dressed. For this one evening, I could match them, and I held my head up. One of them thought I looked like a high-priced whore, but I decided that was a compliment, at least for tonight. At least she thought I was expensive. One woman, a banker, knew Debbie the-former-girlfriend, and she examined me from head to toe, thinking Debbie would want a detailed description.

None of these people, of course, knew one thing about me. It was wonderful to be among people who had no idea of my background and upbringing, my occupation or my abilities. Determined to enjoy the feeling, I concentrated on not speaking unless I was spoken to, not spilling any food on my beautiful dress, and minding my manners, both table and social. While I was enjoying myself, I figured it would be a pity if I caused Alcide any embarrassment, since I was entering his life so briefly.

Alcide snatched the bill before I could reach it, and scowled at me when I opened my mouth to protest. I finally gave a little bob of my head. After that silent struggle, I was glad to observe that Alcide was a generous tipper. That raised him in my estimation. To tell the truth, he was entirely too high in my estimation already. I was on the alert to pick out something negative about the man. When we got back in Alcide's pickup—this time he gave me even more help when he boosted me up to the seat, and I was pretty confident he enjoyed the procedure—we were both quiet and thoughtful.

"You didn't talk much at supper," he said. "You didn't have a good time?"

"Oh, sure, I did. I just didn't think it was a real good time to start broadcasting any opinions."

"What did you think of Jake O'Malley?" O'Malley, a man in his early sixties with thick steel-colored eyebrows, had stood talking to Alcide for at least five minutes, all the while stealing little sideways glances at my boobs.

"I think he's planning on screwing you six ways from Sunday."

It was lucky we hadn't pulled away from the curb yet. Alcide switched on the overhead light and looked at me. His face was grim. "What are you talking about?" he asked.

"He's going to underbid you on the next job, because he's bribed one of the women in your office—Thomasina something?—to let him know what you all's bid is. And then—"

"What?"

I was glad the heater was running full blast. When werewolves got mad, you could feel it in the air around you. I had so hoped I wouldn't have to explain myself to Alcide. It had been so neat, being unknown.

"You are . . . what?" he asked, to make sure I understood him.

"Telepath," I said, kind of mumbling.

A long silence fell, while Alcide digested this.

"Did you hear *anything* good?" he asked, finally.

"Sure. Mrs. O'Malley wants to jump your bones," I told him, smiling brightly. I had to remind myself not to pull at my hair.

"That's good?"

"Comparatively," I said. "Better to be screwed physically than financially." Mrs. O'Malley was at least twenty years younger than Mr. O'Malley, and she was the most groomed person I'd ever seen. I was betting she brushed her eyebrows a hundred strokes a night.

He shook his head. I had no clear picture of what he was thinking. "What about me, you read me?"

Aha. "Shape-shifters are not so easy," I said. "I can't pick out a clear line of thought, more a general mood, intentions, sort of. I guess if you thought directly at me, I'd get it. You want to try? Think something at me."

The dishes I use at the apartment have a border of yellow roses.

"I wouldn't call them roses," I said doubtfully. "More like zinnias, if you ask me."

I could feel his withdrawal, his wariness. I sighed. Same old, same old. It sort of hurt, since I liked him. "But just to pick your own thoughts out of your head, that's a murky area," I said. "I can't consistently do that, with Weres and shifters." (A few Supes were fairly easy to read, but I saw no need to bring that up at this point in time.)

"Thank God."

"Oh?" I said archly, in an attempt to lighten the mood. "What are you afraid I'll read?"

Alcide actually grinned at me before he turned off the dome light and we pulled out of our parking space. "Never mind," he said, almost absently. "Never mind. So what you're going to be doing tonight is reading minds, to try to pick up clues about your vampire's whereabouts?"

"That's right. I can't read vampires; they don't seem to put out any brainwaves. That's just how I put it. I don't know how I do this, or if there's a scientific way to phrase it." I wasn't exactly lying: Undead minds really were unreadable—except for a little split second's glimpse every now and then (which hardly counted, and no one could know about). If vampires thought I could read their minds, not even Bill could save me. If he would.

Every time I forgot for a second that our relationship had radically changed, it hurt all over again to be reminded.

"So what's your plan?"

"I'm aiming for humans dating or serving local vampires. Humans were the actual abductors. He was snatched in daytime. At least, that's what they told Eric."

"I should have asked you about this earlier," he said, mostly to himself. "Just in case I hear something the regular way—through my ears—maybe you should tell me the circumstances."

As we drove by what Alcide said was the old train station, I gave him a quick summary. I caught a glimpse of a street sign reading "Amite" as we pulled up to an awning that stretched over a deserted length of sidewalk in the outskirts of downtown Jackson. The area directly under the awning was lit with a brilliant and cold light. Somehow that length of sidewalk seemed creepily ominous, especially since the rest of the street was dark. Uneasiness crawled down my back. I felt a deep reluctance to stop at that bit of sidewalk.

It was a stupid feeling, I told myself. It was just a stretch of cement. No beasts were in sight. After the businesses closed at five, downtown Jackson was not exactly teeming, even under ordinary circumstances. I was willing to bet that most of the sidewalks in the whole state of Mississippi were bare on this cold December night.

But there was something ominous in the air, a watchfulness laced with a charge of malice. The eyes observing us were invisible; but they were observing us, nonetheless. When Alcide climbed out of the truck and came around to help me down, I noticed that he left the keys in the ignition. I swung my legs outward and put my hands on his shoulders, my long silk stole wound firmly around me and trailing behind, fringe trembling in a gust of chilled air. I pushed off as he lifted, and then I was on the sidewalk.

The truck drove away.

I looked at Alcide sideways, to see if this was startling to him, but he looked quite matter-of-fact. "Vehicles parked in front would attract attention from the general public," he told me, his voice hushed in the vast silence of that coldly lit bit of pavement.

"They can come in? Regular people?" I asked, nodding toward the single metal door. It looked as uninviting as a door can look. There was no name anywhere on it, or on the building, for that matter. No Christmas decorations, either. (Of course, vampires don't observe holidays, except for Halloween. It's the ancient festival of Samhain dressed up in trappings that the vamps find delightful. So Halloween's a great favorite, and it's celebrated worldwide in the vamp community.)

"Sure, if they want to pay a twenty-dollar cover charge to drink the worst drinks in five states. Served by the rudest waiters. Very slowly."

I tried to smother my smile. This was not a smiley kind of place. "And if they stick that out?"

"There's no floor show, no one speaks to them, and if they last much longer, they find themselves out on the sidewalk getting into their car with no memory of how they got there."

He grasped the handle of the door and pulled it open. The dread that soaked the air did not seem to affect Alcide.

We stepped into a tiny hall that was blocked by another door after about four feet. There, again, I knew we were being watched, though I couldn't see a camera or a peephole anywhere.

"What's the name of this place?" I whispered.

"The vamp that owns it calls it Josephine's," he said, just as quietly. "But Weres call it Club Dead."

I thought about laughing, but the inner door opened just then. The doorman was a goblin.

I had never seen one before, but the word "goblin" popped into my mind as if I had a supernatural dictionary printed on the inside of my eyeballs. He was very short and very cranky-looking, with a knobby face and broad hands. His eyes were full of fire and malignance. He glared up at us as if customers were the last things he needed.

Why any ordinary person would walk into Josephine's after the cumulative effect of the haunted sidewalk, the vanishing vehicle, and the goblin at the door . . . well, some people are just born asking to be killed, I guess.

"Mr. Herveaux," the goblin said slowly, in a deep, growly voice. "Good to have you back. Your companion is . . . ?"

"Miss Stackhouse," Alcide said. "Sookie, this is Mr. Hob." The goblin examined me with glowing eyes. He looked faintly troubled, as if he couldn't quite fit me into a slot; but after a second, he stood aside to let us pass.

Josephine's was not very crowded. Of course, it was somewhat early for its patrons. After the eerie build-up, the large room looked almost disappointingly like any other bar. The serving area itself was in the middle of the room, a large square bar with a lift-up panel for the staff to go to and fro. I wondered if the owner had been watching reruns of *Cheers*. The glasses hung down, suspended on racks, and there were artificial plants and low music and dim lighting. There were polished bar stools set evenly all around the square. To the left of the bar was a small dance floor, and even farther left was a tiny stage for a band or a disc jockey. On the other three sides of the square were the usual small tables, about half of which were in use.

Then I spotted the list of ambiguous rules on the wall, rules designed to be understood by the regular habitués, but not by the occasional tourist. "No Changing on the Premises," one said sternly. (Weres and shifters could not switch from animal to human when they were at the bar; well, I could understand that.) "No Biting of Any Kind," said another. "No Live Snacks," read a third. Ick.

The vampires were scattered throughout the bar, some with others of their own kind, some with humans. There was a raucous party of shifters in the southeast corner, where several tables had been drawn together to accommodate the size of the party. The center of this group appeared to be a tall young woman with gleaming short black hair, an athletic build, and a long, narrow face. She was draped over a square man of her own age, which I guessed to be about twenty-eight. He had round eyes and a flat nose and the softest looking hair I'd ever seen—it was almost baby fine, and so light a blond, it was nearly white. I wondered if this were the engagement party, and I wondered if Alcide had known it was to take place. His attention was definitely focused on that group.

Naturally, I immediately checked out what the other women in the bar were wearing. The female vampires and the women with male vampires were dressed about at my level. The shifter females tended to dress down a bit more. The black-haired woman I'd pegged for Debbie was wearing a gold silk blouse and skintight brown leather pants, with boots. She laughed at some comment of the blond man's, and I felt Alcide's arm grow rigid under my fingers. Yep, this must be the ex-girlfriend, Debbie. Her good time had certainly escalated since she'd glimpsed Alcide's entrance.

Phony bitch, I decided in the time it takes to snap your fingers, and I made up my mind to behave accordingly. The goblin Hob led the way to an empty table within view of the happy party, and held out a chair for me. I nodded to him politely, and unwound my wrap, folding it and tossing it onto an empty chair. Alcide sat in the chair to my right, so he could put his back to the corner where the shifters were having such a raucous good time.

A bone-thin vampire came to take our order. Alcide asked my pleasure with an inclination of his head. "A champagne cocktail," I said, having no idea what one tasted like. I'd never gone to the trouble to mix myself one at Merlotte's, but now that I was in someone else's bar, I thought I'd give it a shot. Alcide ordered a Heineken. Debbie was casting many glances our way, so I leaned forward and smoothed back a lock of Alcide's curly black hair. He looked surprised, though of course Debbie couldn't see that.

"Sookie?" he said, rather doubtfully.

I smiled at him, not my nervous smile—because I wasn't, for once. Thanks to Bill, I now had a little confidence about my own physical attractiveness. "Hey, I'm your date, remember? I'm acting date-like," I told him.

The thin vampire brought our drinks just then, and I clinked my glass against his bottle. "To our joint venture," I said, and his eyes lit up. We sipped.

I loved champagne cocktails.

"Tell me more about your family," I said, because I enjoyed listening to his rumbly voice. I would have to wait until there were more humans in the bar before I began listening in to others' thoughts.

Alcide obligingly began telling me about how poor his dad had been when he started his surveying business, and how long it had taken for him to prosper. He was just beginning to tell me about his mother when Debbie sashayed up.

It had only been a matter of time.

"Hello, Alcide," she purred. Since he hadn't been able to see her coming, his strong face quivered. "Who's your new friend? Did you borrow her for the evening?"

"Oh, longer than that," I said clearly, and smiled at Debbie, a smile that matched her own for sincerity.

"Really?" If her eyebrows had crawled any higher, they'd have been in heaven.

"Sookie is a good friend," Alcide said impassively.

"Oh?" Debbie doubted his word. "It wasn't too long ago you told me you'd never have another 'friend' if you couldn't have . . . Well." She smirked.

I covered Alcide's huge hand with my own and gave her a look that implied much.

"Tell me," Debbie said, her lips curling in a skeptical way, "how do you like that birthmark of Alcide's?"

Who could have predicted she was willing to be a bitch so openly? Most women try to hide it, at least from strangers.

It's on my right butt cheek. It's shaped like a rabbit. Well, how nice. Alcide had remembered what I'd said, and he'd thought directly at me.

"I love bunnies," I said, still smiling, my hand drifting down Alcide's back to caress, very lightly, the top of his right buttock.

For a second, I saw sheer rage on Debbie's face. She was so focused, so controlled, that her mind was a lot less opaque than most shifters'. She was thinking about her owl fiancé, about how he wasn't as good in the sack as Alcide, but he had a lot of ready cash and he was willing to have children, which Alcide wasn't. And she was stronger than the owl, able to dominate him.

She was no demon (of course, her fiancé would have a really short shelf life if she *were*) but she was no sweetie, either.

Debbie still could have recovered the situation, but her discovery that I knew Alcide's little secret made her nuts. She made a big mistake.

She raked me over with a glare that would have paralyzed a lion. "Looks like you went to Janice's salon today," she said, taking in the casually tumbled curls, the fingernails. Her own straight black hair had been cut in asymmetrical clumps, tiny locks of different lengths, making her look a little like a dog in a very good show, maybe an Afghan. Her narrow face increased the resemblance. "Janice never sends anyone out looking like they live in this century."

Alcide opened his mouth, rage tensing all his muscles. I laid my hand on his arm.

"What do *you* think of my hair?" I asked softly, moving my head so it slithered over my bare shoulders. I took his hand and held it gently to the curls falling over my chest. Hey, I was pretty good at this! Sookie the sex kitten.

Alcide caught his breath. His fingers trailed through the length of my hair, and his knuckles brushed my collarbone. "I think it's beautiful," he said, and his voice was both sincere and husky.

I smiled at him.

"I guess instead of borrowing you, he rented you," Debbie said, goaded into irreparable error.

It was a terrible insult, to both of us. It took every bit of resolution I had to hang on to a ladylike self-control. I felt the primitive self, the truer me, swim nearly to the surface. We sat staling at the shifter, and she blanched at our silence. "Okay, I shouldn't have said that," she said nervously. "Just forget it."

Because she was a shifter, she'd beat me in a fair fight. Of course, I had no intention of fighting fair, if it came to that.

I leaned over and touched one red fingertip to her leather pants. "Wearing Cousin Elsie?" I asked.

Unexpectedly, Alcide burst into laughter. I smiled at him as he doubled over, and when I looked up, Debbie was stalking back to her party, who had fallen silent during our exchange.

I reminded myself to skip going to the ladies' room alone this evening.

BY THE TIME we ordered our second drinks, the place was full. Some Were friends of Alcide's came in, a large group—Weres like to travel in packs, I understand. Shifters, it depended on the animal they most often shifted to. Despite their theoretical versatility, Sam had told me that shape-shifters most often changed to the same animal every time, some creature they had a special affinity for. And they might call themselves by that animal: weredog, or werebat, or weretiger. But never just "Weres"—that term was reserved for the wolves. The true werewolves scorned such variance in form, and they didn't think much of shifters in general. They, the werewolves, considered themselves the cream of the shape-shifting world.

Shifters, on the other hand, Alcide explained, thought of were-wolves as the thugs of the supernatural scene. "And you do find a lot of us in the building trades," he said, as if he were trying hard to be fair. "Lots of Weres are mechanics, or brick masons, or plumbers, or cooks."

"Useful occupations," I said.

"Yes," he agreed. "But not exactly white-collar. So though we all cooperate with each other, to some extent, there's a lot of class discrimination."

A small group of Weres in motorcycle gear strode in. They wore the same sort of leather vest with wolf's heads on the back that had been worn by the man who'd attacked me at Merlotte's. I wondered if they'd started searching for their comrade yet. I wondered if they had a clearer idea of who they were looking for, what they'd do if they realized who I was. The four men ordered several pitchers of beer and began talking very secretively, heads close together and chairs pulled right up to the table.

A deejay—he appeared to be a vampire—began to play records at the perfect level; you could be sure what the song was, but you could still talk.

"Let's dance," Alcide suggested.

I hadn't expected that; but it would put me closer to the vampires and their humans, so I accepted. Alcide held my chair for me, and took my hand as we went over to the minuscule dance floor. The vampire changed the music from some heavy metal thing to Sarah McLachlan's "Good Enough," which is slow, but with a beat.

I can't sing, but I can dance; as it happened, Alcide could, too.

The good thing about dancing is that you don't have to talk for a while, if you feel chatted out. The bad thing is it makes you hyper-conscious of your partner's body. I had already been uncomfortably aware of Alcide's—excuse me—animal magnetism. Now, so close to him, swaying in rhythm with him, following his every move, I found myself in a kind of trance. When the song was over, we stayed on the little dance floor, and I kept my eyes on the floor. When the next song started up, a faster piece of music—though for the life of me I couldn't have told you what—we began dancing again, and I spun and dipped and moved with the werewolf.

Then the muscular squat man sitting at a bar stool behind us said to his vampire companion, "He hasn't talked yet. And Harvey called today. He said they searched the house and didn't find anything."

"Public place," said his companion, in a sharp voice. The vampire was a very small man—perhaps he'd become a vampire when men were shorter.

I knew they were talking about Bill, because the human was thinking of Bill when he said, "He hasn't talked." And the human was an exceptional broadcaster, both sound and visuals coming through clearly.

When Alcide tried to lead me away from their orbit, I resisted his lead. Looking up into his surprised face, I cut my eyes toward the couple. Comprehension filtered into his eyes, but he didn't look happy.

Dancing and trying to read another person's mind at the same time is not something I'd recommend. I was straining mentally, and my heart was pounding with shock at the glimpse of Bill's image. Luckily, Alcide excused himself to go to the men's room just then, parking me on a stool at the bar right by the vampire. I tried to keep looking around at different dancers, at the deejay, at anything but the man to the vampire's left, the man whose mind I was trying to pick through.

He was thinking about what he'd done during the day; he'd been trying to keep someone awake, someone who really needed to sleep—a vampire. Bill.

Keeping a vampire awake during the day was the worst kind of torture. It was difficult to do, too. The compulsion to sleep when the sun came up was imperative, and the sleep itself was like death.

Somehow, it had never crossed my mind—I guess since I'm an American—that the vampires who had snatched Bill might be resorting to evil means to get him to talk. If they wanted the information, naturally they weren't just going to wait around until Bill felt like telling them. Stupid me—dumb, dumb, dumb. Even knowing Bill had betrayed me, even knowing he had thought of leaving me for his vampire lover, I was struck deep with pain for him.

Engrossed in my unhappy thoughts, I didn't recognize trouble when it was standing right beside me. Until it grabbed me by the arm.

One of the Were gang members, a big dark-haired man, very heavy and very smelly, had grabbed hold of my arm. He was getting his greasy fingerprints all over my beautiful red sleeves, and I tried to pull away from him.

"Come to our table and let us get to know you, sweet thing," he said, grinning at me. He had a couple of earrings in one ear. I wondered what happened to them during the full moon. But almost immediately, I realized I had more serious problems to solve. The expression on his face was too frank; men just didn't look at women that way unless those women were standing on a street corner in hot pants and a bra: in other words, he thought I was a sure thing.

"No, thank you," I said politely. I had a weary, wary feeling that this wasn't going to be the end of it, but I might as well try. I'd had plenty of experience at Merlotte's with pushy guys, but I always had backup at Merlotte's. Sam wouldn't tolerate the servers being pawed or insulted.

"Sure, darlin'. You want to come see us," he said insistently.

For the first time in my life, I wished Bubba were with me.

I was getting far too used to people who bothered me meeting a bad end. And maybe I was getting too accustomed to having some of my problems solved by others.

I thought of scaring the Were by reading his mind. It would have been an easy read—he was wide open, for a Were. But not only were his thoughts boring and unsurprising (lust, aggression), if his gang was charged with searching for the girlfriend of Bill the vampire, and they knew she was a barmaid and a telepath, and they found a tele-path, well . . .

"No, I don't want to come sit with you," I said definitely. "Leave me alone." I slid off the stool so I wouldn't be trapped in one position.

"You don't have no man here. We're real men, honey." With his free hand, he cupped himself. Oh, charming. That really made me horny. "We'll keep you happy."

"You couldn't make me happy if you were Santa Claus," I said, stomping on his instep with all my strength. If he hadn't been wear-ing motorcycle boots, it might have been effective. As it was, I came close to breaking the heel of my shoe. I was mentally cursing my false nails because they made it hard to form a fist. I was going to hit him in the nose with my free hand; a blow to the nose really hurts badly. He'd have to let go.

He snarled at me, really snarled, when my heel hit his instep, but he didn't loosen his grip. His free hand seized my bare shoulder, and his fingers dug in.

I'd been trying to be quiet, hoping to resolve this without hubbub, but I was past that point right now. "Let *go!*" I yelled, as I made a heroic attempt to knee him in the balls. His thighs were heavy and his stance narrow, so I couldn't get a good shot. But I did make him flinch, and though his nails gouged my shoulder, he let go.

Part of this was due to the fact that Alcide had a hold on the scruff of his neck. And Mr. Hob stepped in, just as the other gang members surged around the bar to come to the aid of their buddy. The goblin who'd ushered us into the club doubled as the bouncer, it hap-pened. Though he looked like a very small man on the outside, he wrapped his arms around the biker's waist and lifted him with ease. The biker began shrieking, and the smell of burned flesh began to circulate in the bar. The rail-thin bartender switched on a heavy-duty exhaust fan, which helped a lot, but we could hear the screams of the biker all the way down a narrow dark hall I hadn't noticed before. It must lead to the rear exit of the building. Then there was a big clang, a yell, and the same clang sounding again. Clearly, the back door of the bar had been opened and the offender tossed outside.

Alcide swung around to face the biker's friends, while I stood shaking with reaction behind him. I was bleeding from the imprints of the biker's fingernails in the flesh of my shoulder. I needed some Neosporin, which was what my grandmother had put on every injury when I'd objected to Campho-Phenique. But any little first-aid concerns were going to have to wait: It looked as though we faced another fight. I glanced around for a weapon, and saw the bartender had gotten a baseball bat out and laid it on the bar. She was keeping a wary eye on the situation. I seized the bat and went to stand beside Alcide. I swung the bat into position and waited for the next move. As my brother, Jason, had taught me—based on his many fights in bars, I'm afraid—I picked out one man in particular, pictured myself swinging the bat and bringing it to strike on his knee, which was more accessible to me than his head. That would bring him down, sure enough.

Then someone stepped into the no-man's-land between Alcide and me and the Weres. It was the small vampire, the one who'd been talking with the human whose mind had been such a source of unpleasant information.

Maybe five feet five with his shoes on, he was also slight of build. When he'd died, he'd been in his early twenties, I guessed. Clean-shaven and very pale, he had eyes the color of bitter chocolate, a jarring contrast with his red hair.

"Miss, I apologize for this unpleasantness," he said, his voice soft and his accent heavily Southern. I hadn't heard an accent that thick since my great-grandmother had died twenty years ago.

"I'm sorry the peace of the bar has been disturbed," I said, summoning up as much dignity as I could while gripping a baseball bat. I'd instinctively kicked off my heels so I could fight. I straightened up from my fighting stance, and inclined my head to him, acknowledging his authority.

"You men should leave now," the little man said, turning to the group of Weres, "after apologizing to this lady and her escort."

They milled around uneasily, but none wanted to be the first to back down. One of them who was apparently younger and dumber than the others, was a blond with a heavy beard and a bandanna around his head in a particularly stupid-looking style. He had the fire of battle in his eyes; his pride couldn't handle the whole situation. The biker telegraphed his move before he'd even begun it, and quick as lightning I held out the bat to the vampire, who snatched it in a move so fast, I couldn't even glimpse it. He used it to break the werewolf's leg.

The bar was absolutely silent as the screaming biker was carried out by his friends. The Weres chorused, "Sorry, sorry," as they lifted the blond and removed him from of the bar.

Then the music started again, the small vampire returned the bat to the bartender, Alcide began checking me over for damage, and I began shaking.

"I'm fine," I said, pretty much just wanting everyone to look somewhere else.

"But you're bleeding, my dear," said the vampire.

It was true; my shoulder was trailing blood from the biker's fingernails. I knew etiquette. I leaned toward the vampire, offering him the blood.

"Thank you," he said instantly, and his tongue flicked out. I knew I would heal better and quicker with his saliva anyway, so I held quite still, though to tell the truth, it was like letting someone feel me up in public. Despite my discomfort, I smiled, though I know it can't have been a comfortable smile. Alcide held my hand, which was reassuring.

"Sorry I didn't come out quicker," he said.

"Not something you can predict." Lick, lick, lick. Oh, come on, I had to have stopped bleeding by now.

The vampire straightened, ran his tongue over his lips, and smiled at me. "That was quite an experience. May I introduce myself? I'm Russell Edgington."

Russell Edgington, the king of Mississippi; from the reaction of the bikers, I had suspected as much. "Pleased to meet you," I said politely, wondering if I should curtsey. But he hadn't introduced himself by his title. "I'm Sookie Stackhouse, and this is my friend Alcide Herveaux."

"I've known the Herveaux family for years," the king of Mississippi said. "Good to see you, Alcide. How's that father of yours?" We might have been standing in the Sunday sunlight outside the First Presbyterian Church, rather than in a vampire bar at midnight.

"Fine, thank you," Alcide said, somewhat stiffly. "We're sorry there was trouble."

"Not your fault," the vampire said graciously. "Men sometimes have to leave their ladies alone, and ladies are not responsible for the bad manners of fools." Edgington actually bowed to me. I had no idea what to do in response, but an even deeper head-inclination seemed safe. "You're like a rose blooming in an untended garden, my dear."

And you're full of bull hockey. "Thank you, Mr. Edgington," I said, casting my eyes down lest he read the skepticism in them. Maybe I should have called him "Your Highness"? "Alcide, I'm afraid I need to call it a night," I said, trying to sound soft and gentle and shaken. It was a little too easy.

"Of course, darlin'," he said instantly. "Let me get your wrap and purse." He began making his way to our table immediately, God bless him.

"Now, Miss Stackhouse, we want you to come back tomorrow night," Russell Edgington said. His human friend stood behind Edgington, his hands resting on Edgington's shoulders. The small vampire reached up and patted one of those hands. "We don't want you scared off by the bad manners of one individual."

"Thanks, I'll mention that to Alcide," I said, not letting any enthusiasm leak into my voice. I hoped I appeared subservient to Alcide without being spineless. Spineless people didn't last long around vampires. Russell Edgington believed he was projecting the appearance of an old-style Southern gentleman, and if that was his thing, I might as well feed it.

Alcide returned, and his face was grim. "I'm afraid your wrap had an accident," he said, and I realized he was furious. "Debbie, I guess."

My beautiful silk shawl had a big hole burned in it. I tried to keep my face impassive, but I didn't manage very well. Tears actually welled up in my eyes, I suppose because the incident with the biker had shaken me already.

Edgington, of course, was soaking this all in.

"Better the shawl than me," I said, attempting a shrug. I made the corners of my mouth turn up. At least my little purse appeared intact, though I hadn't had any more in it than a compact and a lipstick, and enough cash to pay for supper. To my intense embarrassment, Alcide shrugged out of his suit coat and held it for me to slide into. I began to protest, but the look on his face said he wasn't going to take no for an answer.

"Good night, Miss Stackhouse," the vampire said. "Herveaux, see you tomorrow night? Does your business keep you in Jackson?"

"Yes, it does," Alcide said pleasantly. "It was good to talk to you, Russell."

THE TRUCK WAS outside the club when we emerged. The sidewalk seemed no less full of menace than it had when we arrived. I wondered how all these effects were achieved, but I was too depressed to question my escort.

"You shouldn't have given me your coat, you must be freezing," I said, after we'd driven a couple of blocks.

"I have on more clothes than you," Alcide said.

He wasn't shivering like I was, even without his coat. I huddled in it, enjoying the silk lining, and the warmth, and his smell.

"I should never have left you by yourself with those jerks in the club."

"Everyone has to go to the bathroom," I said mildly.

"I should have asked someone else to sit with you."

"I'm a big girl. I don't need a perpetual guard. I handle little incidents like that all the time at the bar." If I sounded weary of it, I was. You just don't get to see the best side of men when you're a barmaid; even at a place like Merlotte's, where the owner watches out for his servers and almost all the clientele is local.

"Then you shouldn't be working there." Alcide sounded very definite.

"Okay, marry me and take me away from all this," I said, deadpan, and got a frightened look in return. I grinned at him. "I have to make my living, Alcide. And mostly, I like my job."

He looked unconvinced and thoughtful. It was time to change the subject.

"They've got Bill," I said.

"You know for sure."

"Yeah."

"Why? What does he know that Edgington would want to know so badly, badly enough to risk a war?"

"I can't tell you."

"But you do know?"

To tell him would be to say I trusted him. I was in the same kind of danger as Bill if it was known that I knew what he knew. And I'd break a lot faster.

"Yes," I said. "I know."

Chapter 6

WE WERE SILENT in the elevator. As Alcide unlocked his apartment, I leaned against the wall. I was a mess: tired, conflicted, and agitated by the fracas with the biker and Debbie's vandalism.

I felt like apologizing, but I didn't know what for.

"Good night," I said, at the door to my room. "Oh, here. Thanks." I shrugged out of his coat and held it out to him. He hung it over the back of one of the bar stools at the eat-in counter.

"Need help with your zipper?" he asked.

"It would be great if you could get it started." I turned my back to him. He'd zipped it up the last couple of inches when I was getting dressed, and I appreciated his thinking of this before he vanished into his room.

I felt his big fingers against my back, and the little hiss of the zipper. Then something unexpected happened; I felt him touch me again.

I shivered all over as his fingers trailed down my skin.

I didn't know what to do.

I didn't know what I wanted to do.

I made myself turn to face him. His face was as uncertain as mine.

"Worst possible time," I said. "You're on the rebound. I'm looking for my boyfriend; granted, he's my unfaithful boyfriend, but still . . ."

"Bad timing," he agreed, and his hands settled on my shoulders. Then he bent down and kissed me. It took about a half a second for my arms to go around his waist and his tongue to slide into my mouth. He kissed soft. I wanted to run my fingers through his hair and find out how broad his chest was and if his butt was really as high and round as it looked in his pants . . . oh, hell. I gently pushed back.

"Bad timing," I said. I flushed, realizing that with my dress half unzipped, Alcide could see my bra and the tops of my bosom easily. Well, it was good I had a pretty bra on.

"Oh, God," he said, having gotten an eyeful. He made a supreme effort and squeezed those green eyes shut. "Bad timing," he agreed again. "Though I can hope that, real soon, it might seem like better timing."

I smiled. "Who knows?" I said, and stepped back into my room while I could still make myself move in that direction. After shutting the door gently, I hung up the red dress, pleased it still looked good and unstained. The sleeves were a disaster, with greasy fingerprints and a little blood on them. I sighed regretfully.

I'd have to flit from door to door to use the bathroom. I didn't want to be a tease, and my robe was definitely short, nylon, and pink. So I scooted, because I could hear Alcide rummaging around in the kitchen. What with one thing and another, I was in the little bathroom for a while. When I came out, all the lights in the apartment were off except the one in my bedroom. I closed the shades, feeling a little silly doing so since no other building on the block was five stories high. I put on my pink nightgown, and crawled in the bed to read a chapter of my romance by way of calming down. It was the one where the heroine finally beds the hero, so it didn't work too well, but I did stop thinking about the biker's skin burning from contact with the goblin, and about Debbie's malicious narrow face. And about the idea of Bill being tortured.

The love scene (actually, the sex scene) steered my mind more toward Alcide's warm mouth.

I switched off the bedside lamp after I'd put my bookmark in my book. I snuggled down in the bed and piled the covers high on top of me, and felt—finally—warm and safe.

Someone knocked at my window.

I let out a little shriek. Then, figuring who it must be, I yanked on my robe, belted it, and opened the shades.

Sure enough, Eric was floating just outside. I switched on the lamp again, and struggled with the unfamiliar window.

"What the hell do you want?" I was saying, as Alcide dashed into the room.

I barely spared him a glance over my shoulder. "You better leave me alone and let me get some sleep," I told Eric, not caring if I sounded like an old scold, "and you better stop showing up outside places in the middle of the night and expecting me to let you in!"

"Sookie, let me in," Eric said.

"No! Well, actually, this is Alcide's place. Alcide, what you want to do?"

I turned to look at him for the first time, and tried not to let my mouth fall open. Alcide slept in those long drawstring pants, period. Whoa. If he'd been shirtless thirty minutes before, the timing might have seemed just perfect.

"What do you want, Eric?" Alcide asked, much more calmly than I had done.

"We need to talk," Eric said, sounding impatient.

"If I let him in now, can I rescind it?" Alcide asked me.

"Sure." I grinned at Eric. "Any moment, you can rescind it."

"Okay. You can come in, Eric." Alcide took the screen off the window, and Eric slid in feetfirst. I eased the window shut behind him. Now I was cold again. There was gooseflesh all over Alcide's chest, too, and his nipples . . . I forced myself to keep an eye on Eric.

Eric gave both of us a sharp look, his blue eyes as brilliant as sapphires in the lamplight. "What have you found out, Sookie?"

"The vampires here do have him."

Eric's eyes may have widened a little, but that was his only reaction. He appeared to be thinking intently.

"Isn't it a little dangerous for you to be on Edgington's turf, unannounced?" Alcide asked. He was doing his leaning-against-the-wall thing again. He and Eric were both big men and the room really seemed crowded all of a sudden. Maybe their egos were using up all the oxygen.

"Oh, yes," Eric said. "Very dangerous." He smiled radiantly.

I wondered if they'd notice if I went back to bed. I yawned. Two pairs of eyes swung to focus on me. "Anything else you need, Eric?" I asked.

"Do you have anything else to report?"

"Yes, they've tortured him."

"Then they won't let him go."

Of course not. You wouldn't let loose a vampire you'd tortured. You'd be looking over your shoulder for the rest of your life. I hadn't thought that through, but I could see its truth.

"You're going to attack?" I wanted to be nowhere around Jackson when that happened.

"Let me think on it," Eric said. "You are going back to the bar tomorrow night?"

"Yes, Russell invited us specifically."

"Sookie attracted his attention tonight," Alcide said.

"But that's perfect!" Eric said. "Tomorrow night, sit with the Edgington crew and pick their brains, Sookie."

"Well, that would never have occurred to me, Eric," I said, wonderingly. "Gosh, I'm glad you woke me up tonight to explain that to me."

"No problem," Eric said. "Anytime you want me to wake you up, Sookie, you have only to say."

I sighed. "Go away, Eric. Good night again, Alcide."

Alcide straightened, waiting for Eric to go back out the window. Eric waited for Alcide to leave.

"I rescind your invitation into my apartment," Alcide said, and abruptly Eric walked to the window, reopened it, and launched himself out. He was scowling. Once outside, he regained his composure and smiled at us, waving as he vanished downward.

Alcide slammed the window shut and let the blinds back down.

"No, there are lots of men who don't like me at all," I told him. He'd been easy to read that time, all right.

He gave me an odd look. "Is that so?"

"Yes, it is."

"If you say so."

"Most people, regular people, that is . . . they think I'm nuts."

"Is that right?"

"Yes, that's right! And it makes them very nervous to have me serve them."

He began laughing, a reaction that was so far from what I had intended that I had no idea what to say next.

He left the room, still more or less chuckling to himself.

Well, that had been weird. I turned out the lamp and took off the robe, tossing it across the foot of the bed. I snuggled between the sheets again, the blanket and spread pulled up to my chin. It was cold and bleak outside, but here I was, finally, warm and safe and alone.

Really, really alone.

THE NEXT MORNING, Alcide was already gone when I got up. Construction and surveying people get going early, naturally, and I was used to sleeping late because of my job at the bar and because I hung around with a vampire. If I wanted to spend time with Bill, it had to be at night, obviously.

There was a note propped up on the coffeepot. I had a slight headache since I am not used to alcohol and I'd had two drinks the night before—the headache was not quite a hangover, but I wasn't my normal cheerful self, either. I squinted at the tiny printing.

"Running errands. Make yourself at home. I'll be back in the afternoon."

For a minute I felt disappointed and deflated. Then I got a hold of myself. It wasn't like he'd called me up and scheduled this as a romantic weekend, or like we really knew each other. Alcide had had my company foisted on him. I shrugged, and poured myself a cup of coffee. I made some toast and turned on the news. After I'd watched one cycle of CNN headlines, I decided to shower. I took my time. What else was there to do?

I was in danger of experiencing an almost unknown state—boredom.

At home, there was always something to do, though it might not be something I particularly enjoyed. If you have a house, there's always some little job waiting for your attention. And when I was in Bon Temps, there was the library to go to, or the dollar store, or the grocery. Since I'd taken up with Bill, I'd also been running errands for him that could only be done in the daytime when offices were open.

As Bill crossed my mind, I was plucking a stray hair from my eyebrow line, leaning over the sink to peer in the bathroom mirror. I had to lay down the tweezers and sit on the edge of the tub. My feelings for Bill were so confused and conflicting, I had no hope of sorting them out anytime soon. But knowing he was in pain, in trouble, and I didn't know how to find him—that was a lot to bear. I had never supposed that our romance would go smoothly. It was an interspecies relationship, after all. And Bill was a lot older than me. But this aching chasm I felt now that he was gone—that, I hadn't ever imagined.

I pulled on some jeans and a sweater and made my bed. I lined up all my makeup in the bathroom I was using, and hung the towel just so. I would have straightened up Alcide's room if I hadn't felt it would be sort of impertinent to handle his things. So I read a few chapters of my book, and then decided I simply could not sit in the apartment any longer.

I left a note for Alcide telling him I was taking a walk, and then I rode down in the elevator with a man in casual clothes, lugging a golf bag. I refrained from saying, "Going to play golf?" and confined myself to mentioning that it was a good day to be outside. It was bright and sunny, clear as a bell, and probably in the fifties. It was a happy day, with all the Christmas decorations looking bright in the sun, and lots of shopping traffic.

I wondered if Bill would be home for Christmas. I wondered if

Bill could go to church with me on Christmas Eve, or if he would. I thought of the new Skil saw I'd gotten Jason; I'd had it on layaway at Sears in Monroe for months, and just picked it up a week ago. I had gotten a toy for each of Arlene's kids, and a sweater for Arlene. I really didn't have anyone else to buy a gift for, and that was pathetic. I decided I'd get Sam a CD this year. The idea cheered me. I love to give presents. This would have been my first Christmas with a boyfriend . . .

Oh, hell, I'd come full cycle, just like *Headline News.*

"Sookie!" called a voice.

Startled out of my dreary round of thoughts, I looked around to see that Janice was waving at me out of the door of her shop, on the other side of the street. I'd unconsciously walked the direction I knew. I waved back at her.

"Come on over!" she said.

I went down to the corner and crossed with the light. The shop was busy, and Jarvis and Corinne had their hands full with customers.

"Christmas parties tonight," Janice explained, while her hands were busy rolling up a young matron's black shoulder-length hair. "We're not usually open after noon on Saturdays." The young woman, whose hands were decorated with an impressive set of diamond rings, kept riffling through a copy of *Southern Living* while Janice worked on her head.

"Does this sound good?" she asked Janice. "Ginger meatballs?" One glowing fingernail pointed to the recipe.

"Kind of oriental?" Janice asked.

"Um, sort of." She read the recipe intently. "No one else would be serving them," she muttered. "You could stick toothpicks in 'em."

"Sookie, what are you doing today?" Janice asked, when she was sure her customer was thinking about ground beef.

"Just hanging out," I said. I shrugged. "Your brother's out running errands, his note said."

"He left you a note to tell you what he was doing? Girl, you should be proud. That man hasn't set pen to paper since high school." She gave me a sideways look and grinned. "You all have a good time last night?"

I thought it over. "Ah, it was okay," I said hesitantly. The dancing had been fun, anyway.

Janice burst out laughing. "If you have to think about it that hard, it must not have been a perfect evening."

"Well, no," I admitted. "There was like a little fight in the bar, and a man had to be evicted. And then, Debbie was there."

"How did her engagement party go?"

"There was quite a crowd at her table," I said. "But she came over after a while and asked a lot of questions." I smiled reminiscently. "She sure didn't like seeing Alcide with someone else!"

Janice laughed again.

"Who got engaged?" asked her customer, having decided against the recipe.

"Oh, Debbie Pelt? Used to go with my brother?" Janice said.

"I know her," said the black-haired woman, pleasure in her voice. "She used to date your brother, Alcide? And now she's marrying someone else?"

"Marrying Charles Clausen," Janice said, nodding gravely. "You know him?"

"Sure I do! We went to high school together. He's marrying Debbie Pelt? Well, better him than your brother," Black Hair said confidentially.

"I'd already figured that out," Janice said. "You know something I don't know, though?"

"That Debbie, she's into some weird stuff," Black Hair said, raising her eyebrows to mark deep significance.

"Like what?" I asked, hardly breathing as I waited to hear what would come out. Could it be that this woman actually knew about shape-shifting, about werewolves? My eyes met Janice's and I saw the same apprehension in them.

Janice knew about her brother. She knew about his world.

And she knew I did, too.

"Devil worship, they say," Black Hair said. "Witchcraft."

We both gaped at her reflection in the mirror. She had gotten the reaction she'd been looking for. She gave a satisfied nod. Devil worship and witchcraft weren't synonymous, but I wasn't going to argue with this woman; this was the wrong time and place.

"Yes, ma'am, that's what I hear. At every full moon, she and some friends of hers go out in the woods and do stuff. No one seems to know exactly what," she admitted.

Janice and I exhaled simultaneously.

"Oh, my goodness," I said weakly.

"Then my brother's well out of a relationship with her. We don't hold with such doings," Janice said righteously.

"Of course not," I agreed.

We didn't meet each other's eyes.

After that little passage, I made motions about leaving, but Janice asked me what I was wearing that night.

"Oh, it's kind of a champagne color," I said. "Kind of a shiny beige."

"Then the red nails won't do," Janice said. "Corinne!"

Despite all my protests, I left the shop with bronze finger- and toenails, and Jarvis worked on my hair again. I tried to pay Janice, but the most she would let me do was tip her employees.

"I've never been pampered so much in my life," I told her.

"What do you do, Sookie?" Somehow that hadn't come up the day before.

"I'm a barmaid," I said.

"That *is* a change from Debbie," Janice said. She looked thoughtful.

"Oh, yeah? What does Debbie do?"

"She's a legal assistant."

Debbie definitely had an educational edge. I'd never been able to manage college; financially, it would have been rough, though I could've found a way, I guess. But my disability had made it hard enough to get out of high school. A telepathic teenager has an extremely hard time of it, let me tell you. And I had so little control then. Every day had been full of dramas—the dramas of other kids. Trying to concentrate on listening in class, taking tests in a roomful of buzzing brains . . . the only thing I'd ever excelled in was homework.

Janice didn't seem to be too concerned that I was a barmaid, which was an occupation not guaranteed to impress the families of those you dated.

I had to remind myself all over again that this setup with Alcide was a temporary arrangement he'd never asked for, and that after I'd discovered Bill's whereabouts—right, Sookie, remember Bill, your *boyfriend?*—I'd never see Alcide again. Oh, he might drop into Merlotte's, if he felt like getting off the interstate on his way from Shreveport to Jackson, but that would be all.

Janice was genuinely hoping I would be a permanent member of her family. That was so nice of her. I liked her a lot. I almost found myself wishing that Alcide really liked me, that there was a real chance of Janice being my sister-in-law.

They say there's no harm in daydreaming, but there is.

Chapter 7

ALCIDE WAS WAITING for me when I got back. A pile of wrapped presents on the kitchen counter showed me how he'd spent at least part of his morning. Alcide had been completing his Christmas shopping.

Judging from his self-conscious look (Mr. Subtle, he wasn't), he'd done something he wasn't sure I'd like. Whatever it was, he wasn't ready to reveal it to me, so I tried to be polite and stay out of his head. As I was passing through the short hall formed by the bedroom wall and the kitchen counter, I sniffed something less than pleasant. Maybe the garbage needed to be tossed? What garbage could we have generated in our short stay that would produce that faint, unpleasant odor? But the past pleasure of my chat with Janice and the present pleasure of seeing Alcide made it easy to forget.

"You look nice," he said.

"I stopped in to see Janice." I was worried for fear he would think I was imposing on his sister's generosity. "She has a way of getting you to accept things you had no intention of accepting."

"She's good," he said simply. "She's known about me since we were in high school, and she's never told a soul."

"I could tell."

"How—? Oh, yeah." He shook his head. "You seem like the most regular person I ever met, and it's hard to remember you've got all this extra stuff."

No one had ever put it quite like that.

"When you were coming in, did you smell something strange by—" he began, but then the doorbell rang.

Alcide went to answer it while I took off my coat.

He sounded pleased, and I turned to face the door with a smile. The young man coming in didn't seem surprised to see me, and Alcide introduced him as Janice's husband, Dell Phillips. I shook his hand, expecting to be as pleased with him as I was with Janice.

He touched me as briefly as possible, and then he ignored me. "I wondered if you could come by this afternoon and help me set up our outside Christmas lights," Dell said—to Alcide, and Alcide only.

"Where's Tommy?" Alcide asked. He looked disappointed. "You didn't bring him by to see me?" Tommy was Janice's baby.

Dell looked at me, and shook his head. "You've got a woman here, it didn't seem right. He's with my mom."

The comment was so unexpected, all I could do was stand in silence. Dell's attitude had caught Alcide flat-footed, too. "Dell," he said, "don't be rude to my friend."

"She's staying in your apartment, that says more than friend," Dell said matter-of-factly. "Sorry, miss, this just isn't right."

"Judge not, that ye be not judged," I told him, hoping I didn't sound as furious as my clenched stomach told me I was. It felt wrong to quote the Bible when you were in a towering rage. I went into the guest bedroom and shut the door.

After I heard Dell Phillips leave, Alcide knocked on the door. "You want to play Scrabble?" he asked.

I blinked. "Sure."

"When I was shopping for Tommy, I picked up a game."

He'd already put it on the coffee table in front of the couch, but he hadn't been confident enough to unwrap it and set it up.

"I'll pour us a Coke," I said. Not for the first time, I noticed that the apartment was quite cool, though of course it was much warmer than outside. I wished I had brought a light sweater to put on, and I wondered if it would offend Alcide if I asked him to turn the heat up. Then I remembered how warm his skin was, and I figured he was one of those people who runs kind of hot. Or maybe all Weres were like that? I pulled on the sweatshirt I'd worn yesterday, being very careful when I eased it over my hair.

Alcide had folded himself onto the floor on one side of the table, and I settled on the other. It had been a long time since either of us played Scrabble, so we studied the rules for a while before we began the game.

Alcide had graduated from Louisiana Tech. I'd never been to college, but I read a lot, so we were about even on the extent of our vocabulary. Alcide was the better strategist. I seemed to think a little faster.

I scored big with "quirt," and he stuck his tongue out at me. I laughed, and he said, "Don't read my mind, that would be cheating."

"Of course I wouldn't do any such thing," I said demurely, and he scowled at me.

I lost—but only by twelve points. After a pleasantly quarrelsome rehash of the game, Alcide got up and took our glasses over to the kitchen. He put them down and began to search through the cabinets, while I stored the game pieces and replaced the lid.

"Where you want me to put this?" I asked.

"Oh, in the closet by the door. There are a couple of shelves in there."

I tucked the box under one arm and went to the closet. The smell I'd noticed earlier seemed to be stronger.

"You know, Alcide," I said, hoping I wasn't being tacky, "there's something that smells almost rotten, right around here."

"I'd noticed it, too. That's why I'm over here looking through the cabinets. Maybe there's a dead mouse?"

As I spoke, I was turning the doorknob.

I discovered the source of the smell.

"Oh, no," I said. "Oh, *nononono*."

"Don't tell me a rat got in there and died," Alcide said.

"Not a rat," I said. "A werewolf."

The closet had a shelf above a hanging bar, and it was a small closet, intended only for visitors' coats. Now it was filled by the swarthy man from Club Dead, the man who'd grabbed me by the shoulder. He was really dead. He'd been dead for several hours.

I didn't seem to be able to look away.

Alcide's presence at my back was an unexpected comfort. He stared over my head, his hands gripping my shoulders.

"No blood," I said in a jittery voice.

"His neck." Alcide was at least as shaken as I was.

His head really was resting on his shoulder, while still attached to his body. Ick, ick, ick. I gulped hard. "We should call the police," I said, not sounding very positive about the process. I noted the way the body had been stuffed into the closet. The dead man was almost standing up. I figured he'd been shoved in, and then whoever had done the shoving had forced the door closed. He'd sort of hardened in position.

"But if we call the police . . ." Alcide's voice trailed off. He took a deep breath. "They'll never believe we didn't do it. They'll interview his friends, and his friends will tell them he was at Club Dead last night, and they'll check it out. They'll find out he got into trouble for bothering you. No one will believe we didn't have a hand in killing him."

"On the other hand," I said slowly, thinking out loud, "do you think they'd mention a word about Club Dead?"

Alcide pondered that. He ran his thumb over his mouth while he thought. "You may be right. And if they couldn't bring up Club Dead, how could they describe the, uh, confrontation? You know what they'd do? They'd want to take care of the problem themselves."

That was an *excellent* point. I was sold: no police. "Then we need to dispose of him," I said, getting down to brass tacks. "How are we gonna do that?"

Alcide was a practical man. He was used to solving problems, starting with the biggest.

"We need to take him out to the country somewhere. To do that, we have to get him down to the garage," he said after a few moments' thought. "To do that, we have to wrap him up."

"The shower curtain," I suggested, nodding my head in the direction of the bathroom I'd used. "Um, can we close the closet and go somewhere else while we work this out?"

"Sure," Alcide said, suddenly as anxious as I was to stop looking at the gruesome sight before us.

So we stood in the middle of the living room and had a planning session. The first thing I did was turn off the heat in the apartment altogether, and open all the windows. The body had not made its presence known earlier only because Alcide liked the temperature kept cool, and because the closet door fit well. Now we had to disperse the faint but pervasive smell.

"It's five flights down, and I don't think I can carry him that far," Alcide said. "He needs to go at least some of the distance in the elevator. That's the most dangerous part."

We kept discussing and refining, until we felt we had a workable procedure. Alcide asked me twice if I was okay, and I reassured him both times; it finally dawned on me that he was thinking I might break into hysterics, or faint.

"I've never been able to afford to be too finicky," I said. "That's not my nature." If Alcide expected or wanted me to ask for smelling salts, or to beg him to save little me from the big bad wolf, he had the wrong woman.

I might be determined to keep my head, but that's not to say I felt exactly calm. I was so jittery when I went to get the shower curtain that I had to restrain myself from ripping it from the clear plastic rings. Slow and steady, I told myself fiercely. Breathe in, breathe out, get the shower curtain, spread it on the hall floor.

It was blue and green with yellow fish swimming serenely in even rows.

Alcide had gone downstairs to the parking garage to move his truck as close to the stair door as possible. He'd thoughtfully brought a pair of work gloves back up with him. While he pulled them on, he took a deep breath—maybe a mistake, considering the body's proximity. His face a frozen mask of determination, Alcide gripped the corpse's shoulders and gave a yank.

The results were dramatic beyond our imagining. In one stiff piece, the biker toppled out of the closet. Alcide had to leap to his right to avoid the falling body, which banged against the kitchen counter and then fell sideways onto the shower curtain.

"Wow," I said in a shaky voice, looking down at the result. "That turned out well."

The body was lying almost exactly as we wanted it. Alcide and I gave each other a sharp nod and knelt at each end. Acting in concert, we took one side of the plastic curtain and flipped it over the body, then the other. We both relaxed when the man's face was covered. Alcide had also brought up a roll of duct tape—real men always have duct tape in their trucks—and we used it to seal the wrapped body in the curtain. Then we folded the ends over, and taped them. Luckily, though a hefty guy, the Were hadn't been very tall.

We stood up and let ourselves have a little moment of recovery. Alcide spoke first. "It looks like a big green burrito," he observed.

I slapped a hand over my mouth to stifle a fit of the giggles.

Alcide's eyes were startled as he stared at me over the wrapped corpse. Suddenly, he laughed, too.

After we'd settled down, I asked, "You ready for phase two?"

He nodded, and I pulled on my coat and scooted past the body and Alcide. I went out to the elevator, closing the apartment door behind me very quickly, just in case someone passed by.

The minute I punched the button, a man appeared around the corner and came to stand by the elevator door. Perhaps he was a relative of old Mrs. Osburgh, or maybe one of the senators was making a flying trip back to Jackson. Whoever he was, he was well dressed and in his sixties, and he was polite enough to feel the obligation of making conversation.

"It's really cold today, isn't it?"

"Yes, but not as cold as yesterday." I stared at the closed doors, willing them to open so he would be gone.

"Did you just move in?"

I had never been so irritated with a courteous person before. "I'm visiting," I said, in the kind of flat voice that should indicate the conversation is closed.

"Oh," he said cheerfully. "Who?"

Luckily the elevator chose that moment to arrive and its doors snicked open just in time to save this too-genial man from getting his head snapped off. He gestured with a sweep of his hand, wanting me to precede him, but I took a step back, said, "Oh my gosh, I forgot my keys!" and walked briskly off without a backward glance. I went to the door of the apartment next to Alcide's, the one he'd told me was empty, and I knocked on the door. I heard the elevator doors close behind me, and I breathed a sigh of relief.

When I figured Mr. Chatty had had time to get to his car and drive out of the garage—unless he was talking the ears off the security guard—I recalled the elevator. It was Saturday, and there was no telling what people's schedules would be like. According to Alcide, many of the condos had been bought as an investment and were subleased to legislators, most of who would be gone for the pre-holidays. The year-round tenants, however, would be moving around in atypical ways, since it was not only the weekend, but also only two weekends before Christmas. When the creaky contraption came back to the fifth floor, it was empty.

I dashed back to 504, knocked twice on the door, and dashed back to the elevator to hold the doors open. Preceded by the legs of the corpse, Alcide emerged from the apartment. He moved as quickly as a man can while he's carrying a stiff body over his shoulder.

This was our most vulnerable moment. Alcide's bundle looked like nothing on this earth but a corpse wrapped in a shower curtain. The plastic kept the smell down, but it was still noticeable in the small enclosure. We made it down one floor safely, then the next. At the third floor, our nerve ran out. We stopped the elevator, and to our great relief it opened onto an empty corridor. I darted out and over to the stair door, holding it open for Alcide. Then I scampered down the stairs ahead of him, and looked through the pane of glass in the door to the garage.

"Whoa," I said, holding my hand up. A middle-aged woman and a teenage girl were unloading packages from the trunk of their Toyota, simultaneously having a vigorous disagreement. The girl had been invited to an all-night party. No, her mother said.

She had to go, all her friends would be there. No, her mother said.

But Mom, everyone else's mom was letting them go. No, her mother said.

"Please don't decide to take the stairs," I whispered.

But the argument raged on as they got in the elevator. I clearly heard the girl break her train of complaint long enough to say, "Ew, something smells in here!" before the doors closed.

"What's happening?" Alcide whispered.

"Nothing. Let's see if that lasts a minute longer."

It did, and I stepped out of the door and over to Alcide's truck, darting glances from side to side to make sure I was really alone. We weren't quite in sight of the security guard, who was in his little glass hut up the slope of the ramp.

I unlocked the back of Alcide's pickup; fortunately, his pickup bed had a cover. With one more comprehensive look around the garage, I hurried back to the stair door and rapped on it. After a second, I pulled it open.

Alcide shot out and over to his truck faster than I would have believed he could move, burdened as he was. We pushed as hard as we could, and the body slowly retreated into the truck bed. With tremendous relief, we slammed the tailgate shut and locked it.

"Phase two complete," Alcide said with an air that I would have called giddy if he hadn't been such a big man.

Driving through the streets of a city with a body in your vehicle is a terrifying exercise in paranoia.

"Obey every single traffic rule," I reminded Alcide, unhappy with how tense my voice sounded.

"Okay, okay," he growled, his voice equally tense.

"Do you think those people in that Jimmy are looking at us?"

"No."

It would obviously be a good thing for me to keep quiet, so I did. We got back on I-20, the same way we'd entered Jackson, and drove until there was no city, only farmland.

When we got to the Bolton exit, Alcide said, "This looks good."

"Sure," I said. I didn't think I could stand driving around with the body any longer. The land between Jackson and Vicksburg is pretty low and flat, mostly open fields broken up by a few bayous, and this area was typical. We exited the interstate and headed north toward the woods. After a few miles Alcide took a right onto a road that had needed repaving for years. The trees grew up on either side of the much-patched strip of gray. The bleak winter sky didn't stand a chance of giving much light with this kind of competition, and I shivered in the cab of the truck.

"Not too much longer," Alcide said. I nodded jerkily.

A tiny thread of a road led off to the left, and I pointed. Alcide braked, and we examined the prospect. We gave each other a sharp nod of approval. Alcide backed in, which surprised me; but I decided that it was a good idea. The farther we went into the woods, the more I liked our choice of venue. The road had been graveled not too long ago, so we wouldn't leave tire tracks, for one thing. And I thought the chances were good that this rudimentary road led to a hunting camp, which wouldn't be in much use now that deer season was over.

Sure enough, after we'd crunched a few yards down the track, I spotted a sign nailed to a tree. It proclaimed, "Kiley-Odum Hunt Club private property—KEEP OUT."

We proceeded down the track, Alcide backing slowly and carefully.

"Here," he said, when we'd gone far enough into the woods that it was almost certain we couldn't be seen from the road. He put the truck into Park. "Listen, Sookie, you don't have to get out."

"It'll be quicker if we work together."

He tried to give me a menacing glare, but I gave him a stone face right back, and finally, he sighed. "Okay, let's get this over with," he said.

The air was cold and wet, and if you stood still for a moment the chilling damp would creep into your bones. I could tell the temperature was taking a dive, and the bright sky of the morning was a fond memory. It was an appropriate day to dump a body. Alcide opened the back of the truck, we both pulled on gloves, and we grasped the bright blue-and-green bundle. The cheerful yellow fish looked almost obscene out here in the freezing woods.

"Give it everything you got," Alcide advised me, and on a count of three, we yanked with all our might. That got the bundle half out, and the end of it protruded over the tailgate in a nasty way. "Ready? Let's go again. One, two, three!" Again I yanked, and the body's own gravity shot it out of the truck and onto the road.

If we could have driven off then and there, I would have been much happier; but we had decided we had to take the shower curtain with us. Who was to say what fingerprints might be found somewhere on the duct tape or the curtain itself? There was sure to be other, microscopic evidence that I couldn't even imagine.

I don't watch the Discovery Channel for nothing.

Alcide had a utility knife, and I did let him have the honor of this particular task. I held open a garbage bag while he cut the plastic away and stuffed it into the opening. I tried not to look, but of course I did.

The body's appearance had not improved.

That job, too, was finished sooner than I expected. I half turned to get back in the truck, but Alcide stood, his face raised to the sky. He looked as if he was smelling the forest.

"Tonight's the full moon," he said. His whole body seemed to quiver. When he looked at me, his eyes looked alien. I couldn't say that they had changed in color or contour, but it was as if a different person was looking out of them.

I was very alone in the woods with a comrade who had suddenly taken on a whole new dimension. I fought conflicting impulses to scream, burst into tears, or run. I smiled brightly at him and waited. After a long, fraught pause, Alcide said, "Let's get back in the truck."

I was only too glad to scramble up into the seat.

"What do you think killed him?" I asked, when it seemed to me Alcide had had time to return to normal.

"I think someone gave his neck a big twist," Alcide said. "I can't figure out how he got into the apartment. I know I locked the door last night. I'm sure of it. And this morning it was locked again."

I tried to figure that out for a while, but I couldn't. Then I wondered what actually killed you if your neck was broken. But I decided that wasn't really a great thing to think about.

En route to the apartment, we made a stop at Wal-Mart. On a weekend this close to Christmas, it was swarming with shoppers. Once again, I thought, *I haven't gotten anything for Bill.*

And I felt a sharp pain in my heart as I realized that I might never buy Bill a Christmas present, not now, not ever.

We needed air fresheners, Resolve (to clean the carpet), and a new shower curtain. I packed my misery away and walked a little more briskly. Alcide let me pick out the shower curtain, which I actually enjoyed. He paid cash, so there wouldn't be any record of our visit.

I checked out my nails after we had climbed back in the truck. They were fine. Then I thought of how callous I must be, worrying about my fingernails. I'd just finished disposing of a dead man. For several minutes, I sat there feeling mighty unhappy about myself.

I relayed this to Alcide, who seemed more approachable now that we were back in civilization minus our silent passenger.

"Well, you didn't kill him," he pointed out. "Ah—did you?"

I met his green eyes, feeling only a little surprise. "No, I certainly did not. Did you?"

"No," he said, and from his expression I could tell he'd been waiting for me to ask him. It had never occurred to me to do so.

While I'd never suspected Alcide, of course someone had made the Were into a body. For the first time I tried to figure who could have stuffed the body in the closet. Up until this point, I'd just been busy trying to make the body go away.

"Who has keys?" I asked.

"Just Dad and me, and the cleaning woman who does most of the apartments in the building. She doesn't keep a key of her own. The building manager gives her one." We pulled around behind the row of stores, and Alcide tossed in the garbage bag containing the old shower curtain.

"That's a pretty short list."

"Yes," Alcide said slowly. "Yes, it is. But I know my dad's in Jackson. I talked to him on the phone this morning, right after I got up. The cleaning woman only comes in when we leave a message with the building manager. He keeps a copy of our key, hands it to her when she needs it, and she returns it to him."

"What about the security guard in the garage? Is he on duty all night?"

"Yes, because he's the only line of defense between people sneaking into the garage and taking the elevator. You've always come in that way, but there are actually front doors to the building that face onto the major street. Those front doors are locked all the time. There's no guard there, but you do have to have a key to get in."

"So if someone could sneak past the guard, they could ride up in the elevator to your floor, without being stopped."

"Oh, sure."

"And that someone would have to pick the lock to the door."

"Yes, and carry in a body, and stuff it in the closet. That sounds pretty unlikely," said Alcide.

"But that's apparently what happened. Oh, um . . . did you ever give Debbie a key? Maybe someone borrowed hers?" I tried hard to sound totally neutral. That probably didn't work too well.

Long pause.

"Yes, she had a key," Alcide said stiffly.

I bit down on my lips so I wouldn't ask the next question.

"No, I didn't get it back from her."

I hadn't even needed to ask.

Breaking a somewhat charged silence, Alcide suggested we eat a late lunch. Oddly enough, I found I was really hungry.

We ate at Hal and Mal's, a restaurant close to downtown. It was in an old warehouse, and the tables were just far enough apart to make our conversation possible without anyone calling the police.

"I don't think," I murmured, "that anyone could walk around your building with a body over his shoulder, no matter what the hour."

"We just did," he said, unanswerably. "I figure it had to have happened between, say, two a.m. and seven. We were asleep by two, right?"

"More like three, considering Eric's little visit."

Our eyes met. Eric. Eureka!

"But why would he have done that? Is he nuts about you?" Alcide asked bluntly.

"Not so much nuts," I muttered, embarrassed.

"Oh, wants to get in your pants."

I nodded, not meeting his eyes.

"Lot of that going around," Alcide said, under his breath.

"Huh," I said dismissively. "You're still hung up on that Debbie, and you know it."

We looked right at each other. Better to haul this out of the shadows now, and put it to rest.

"You can read my mind better than I thought," Alcide said. His broad face looked unhappy. "But she's not . . . Why do I care about her? I'm not sure I even like her. I like the hell out of you."

"Thanks," I said, smiling from my heart. "I like the hell out of you, too."

"We're obviously better for each other than either of the people we're dating are for us," he said.

Undeniably true. "Yes, and I would be happy with you."

"And I'd enjoy sharing my day with you."

"But it looks like we're not going to get there."

"No." He sighed heavily. "I guess not."

The young waitress beamed at us as we left, making sure Alcide noticed how well packed into her jeans she was.

"What I think I'll do," Alcide said, "is I'll do my best to yank Debbie out of me by the roots. And then I'll turn up on your doorstep, one day when you least expect it, and I'll hope by then you will have given up on your vampire."

"And then we'll be happy ever after?" I smiled.

He nodded.

"Well, that'll be something to look forward to," I told him.

Chapter 8

I WAS SO tired by the time we entered Alcide's apartment that I was sure all I was good for was a nap. It had been one of the longest days of my life, and it was only the middle of the afternoon.

But we had some housekeeping chores to do first. While Alcide hung the new shower curtain, I cleaned the carpet in the closet with Resolve, and opened one of the air fresheners and placed it on the shelf. We closed all the windows, turned on the heat, and breathed experimentally, our eyes locked on each other's.

The apartment smelled okay. We simultaneously breathed out a sigh of relief.

"We just did something really illegal," I said, still uneasy about my own immorality. "But all I really feel is happy we got away with it."

"Don't worry about not feeling guilty," Alcide said. "Something'll come along pretty soon that you'll feel guilty about. Save it up."

This was such good advice that I decided to try it. "I'm going to take a nap," I said, "so I'll be at least a little alert tonight." You didn't want to be slow on the uptake around vampires.

"Good idea," Alcide said. He cocked an eyebrow at me, and I laughed, shaking my head. I went in the smaller bedroom and shut the door, taking off my shoes and falling onto the bed with a feeling of quiet delight. I reached over the side of the bed after a moment, grabbed the fringe of the chenille bedspread, and wrapped it around me. In the quiet apartment, with the heating system blowing a steady stream of warm air into the bedroom, it took only a few minutes to fall asleep.

I woke all of a sudden, and I was completely awake. I knew there was someone else in the apartment. Maybe on some level I'd heard a knock on the front door; or maybe I'd registered the rumble of voices in the living room. I swung silently off the bed and padded to the door, my socks making no noise at all on the beige carpet. I had pushed my door to, but not latched it, and now I turned my head to position my ear at the crack.

A deep, gravelly voice said, "Jerry Falcon came to my apartment last night."

"I don't know him," Alcide replied. He sounded calm, but wary.

"He says you got him into trouble at Josephine's last night."

"I got him into trouble? If he's the guy who grabbed my date, he got himself into trouble!"

"Tell me what happened."

"He made a pass at my date while I was in the men's room. When she protested, he started manhandling her, and she drew attention to the situation."

"He hurt her?"

"Shook her up. And he drew some blood on her shoulder."

"A blood offense." The voice had become deadly serious.

"Yes."

So the fingernail gouges on my shoulder constituted a blood offense, whatever that was.

"And then?"

"I came out of the men's room, hauled him off of her. Then Mr. Hob stepped in."

"That explains the burns."

"Yes. Hob threw him out the back door. And that was the last I saw of him. You say his name is Jerry Falcon?"

"Yeah. He came right to my house then, after the rest of the boys left the bar."

"Edgington intervened. They were about to jump us."

"Edgington was there?" The deep voice sounded very unhappy.

"Oh, yes, with his boyfriend."

"How did Edgington get involved?"

"He told them to leave. Since he's the king, and they work for him from time to time, he expected obedience. But a pup gave him some trouble, so Edgington broke his knee, made the others carry the guy out. I'm sorry there was trouble in your city, Terence. But it was none of our doing."

"You've got guest privileges with our pack, Alcide. We respect you. And those of us who work for the vampires, well, what can I say? Not the best element. But Jerry is their leader, and he was shamed in front of his people last night. How much longer you going to be in our city?"

"Just one more night."

"And it's a full moon."

"Yeah, I know, I'll try to keep a low profile."

"What are you going to do tonight? Try to avoid the change, or come out to my hunting land with me?"

"I'll try to stay out of the moon, try to avoid stress."

"Then you'll keep out of Josephine's."

"Unfortunately, Russell pretty much demanded that we come back tonight. He felt apologetic that my date went through so much aggravation. He made a point of insisting she come back."

"Club Dead on a full-moon night, Alcide. This isn't wise."

"What am I gonna do? Russell calls the shots in Mississippi."

"I can understand. But watch out, and if you see Jerry Falcon there, you turn the other way. This is my city." The deep voice was heavy with authority.

"I understand, Packmaster."

"Good. Now that you and Debbie Pelt have broken up, I hope it's a while before we see you back here, Alcide. Give things a chance to settle down. Jerry's a vindictive son of a bitch. He'll do you an injury if he can, without starting a feud."

"He was the one who caused a blood offense."

"I know, but because of his long association with the vampires, Jerry has too good an opinion of himself. He doesn't always follow the pack traditions. He only came to me, as he should, because Edgington backed the other side."

Jerry wasn't going to be following any tradition anymore. Jerry was lying in the woods to the west.

While I'd napped, it had gotten dark outside. I heard a tap on the glass of the window. I jumped, of course, but then I padded across as quietly as I could. I opened the curtain and held a finger across my lips. It was Eric. I hoped no one on the street outside looked up. He smiled at me and motioned me to open the window. I shook my head vehemently and held my finger across my lips again. If I let Eric in now, Terence would hear, and my presence would be discovered. Terence, I knew instinctively, would not like to find he had been overheard. I tiptoed back to the door and listened. Good-byes were being said. I glanced back at the window, to see that Eric was watching me with great interest. I held up one finger to indicate it would just be a minute.

I heard the apartment door close. Moments later, there was a knock at my door. As I let Alcide in, I hoped I didn't have those funny creases on my face.

"Alcide, I heard most of that," I said. "I'm sorry I eavesdropped, but it did seem like it concerned me. Um, Eric is here."

"So I see," Alcide said unenthusiastically. "I guess I'd better let him in. Enter, Eric," he said, as he slid open the window.

Eric entered as smoothly as a tall man can enter a small window. He was wearing a suit, complete with vest and tie. His hair was slicked back into a ponytail. He was also wearing glasses.

"Are you in disguise?" I asked. I could hardly believe it.

"Yes, I am." He looked down at himself proudly. "Don't I look different?"

"Yes," I admitted. "You look just like Eric, dressed up for once."

"Do you like the suit?"

"Sure," I said. I have limited knowledge of men's clothes, but I was willing to bet this sort of olive-brown three-piece ensemble had cost more than I made in two weeks. Or four. I might not have picked this out for a guy with blue eyes, but I had to admit he looked spectacular. If they put out a vampire issue of *GQ*, he'd definitely be in the running for a photo shoot. "Who did your hair?" I asked, noticing for the first time that it had been braided in an intricate pattern.

"Oooh, jealous?"

"No, I thought maybe they could teach me how to do that to mine."

Alcide had had enough of fashion commentary. He said belligerently, "What do you mean by leaving the dead man in my closet?"

I have seldom seen Eric at a loss for words, but he was definitely speechless—for all of thirty seconds.

"It wasn't Bubba in the closet, was it?" he asked.

It was our turn to stand with mouths open, Alcide because he didn't know who the hell Bubba was, and me because I couldn't imagine what could have happened to the dazed vampire.

I hastily filled Alcide in on Bubba.

"So that explains all the sightings," he said, shaking his head from side to side. "Damn—they were all for real!"

"The Memphis group wanted to keep him, but it was just impossible," Eric explained. "He kept wanting to go home, and then there'd be incidents. So we started passing him around."

"And now you've lost him," Alcide observed, not too chagrined by Eric's problem.

"It's possible that the people who were trying to get to Sookie in Bon Temps got Bubba instead," Eric said. He tugged on his vest and looked down with some satisfaction. "So, who was in the closet?"

"The biker who marked Sookie last night," Alcide said. "He made a pretty rough pass at her while I was in the men's room."

"Marked her?"

"Yes, blood offense," Alcide said significantly.

"You didn't say anything about this last night." Eric raised an eyebrow at me.

"I didn't want to talk about it," I said. I didn't like the way that came out, kind of forlorn. "Besides, it wasn't much blood."

"Let me see."

I rolled my eyes, but I knew darn good and well that Eric wouldn't give up. I pulled my sweatshirt off my shoulder, along with my bra strap. Luckily, the sweatshirt was so old, the neck had lost its elasticity, and it afforded enough room. The fingernail gouges on my shoulder were crusted half-moons, puffy and red, though I'd scrubbed the area carefully the night before. I know how many germs are under fingernails. "See," I said. "No big deal. I was more mad than scared or hurt."

Eric kept his eyes on the little nasty wounds until I shrugged my clothes back into order. Then he switched his eyes to Alcide. "And he was dead in the closet?"

"Yes," Alcide said. "Had been dead for hours."

"What killed him?"

"He hadn't been bitten," I said. "He looked as though his neck might have been broken. We didn't feel like looking that closely. You're saying you aren't the guilty party?"

"No, though it would have been a pleasure to have done it."

I shrugged, not willing to explore that dark thought. "So, who put him there?" I asked, to get the discussion going again.

"And why?" Alcide asked.

"Would it be too much to ask where he is now?" Eric managed to look as if he were indulging two rowdy children.

Alcide and I shot each other glances. "Um, well, he's . . ." My voice trailed away.

Eric inhaled, sampling the apartment's atmosphere. "The body's not here. You called the police?"

"Well, no," I muttered. "Actually, we, ah . . ."

"We dumped him out in the country," Alcide said. There just wasn't a nice way to say it.

We had surprised Eric a second time. "Well," he said blankly. "Aren't you two enterprising?"

"We worked it all out," I said, maybe sounding a tad defensive.

Eric smiled. It was not a happy sight. "Yes, I'll bet you did."

"The packmaster came to see me today," Alcide said. "Just now, in fact. And he didn't know that Jerry was missing. In fact, Jerry went complaining to Terence after he left the bar last night, telling Terence he had a grievance against me. So he was seen and heard after the incident at Josephine's."

"So you may have gotten away with it."

"I think we did."

"You should have burned him," Eric said. "It would have killed any trace of your smell on him."

"I don't think anyone could pick out our smell," I told him. "Really and truly. I don't think we ever touched him with our bare skin."

Eric looked at Alcide, and Alcide nodded. "I agree," he said. "And I'm one of the two-natured."

Eric shrugged. "I have no idea who would have killed him and put him in the apartment. Obviously, someone wanted his death blamed on you."

"Then why not call the police from a pay phone and tell them there's a dead body in 504?"

"A good question, Sookie, and one I can't answer right now." Eric seemed to lose interest all of a sudden. "I will be at the club tonight. If I need to talk to you, Alcide, tell Russell that I am your friend from out of town, and I've been invited to meet Sookie, your new girl-friend."

"Okay," said Alcide. "But I don't understand why you want to be there. It's asking for trouble. What if one of the vamps recognizes you?"

"I don't know any of them."

"Why are you taking this chance?" I asked. "Why go there at all?"

"There may be something I can pick up on that you won't hear of, or that Alcide won't know because he is not a vampire," Eric said reasonably. "Excuse us for a minute, Alcide. Sookie and I have some business to discuss."

Alcide looked at me to make sure I was okay with this, before he nodded grudgingly and went out to the living room.

Eric said abruptly, "Do you want me to heal the marks on your shoulder?"

I thought of the ugly, crusty crescents, and I thought about the thin shoulder straps on the dress I'd brought to wear. I almost said yes, but then I had a second thought. "How would I explain that, Eric? The whole bar saw him grab me."

"You're right." Eric shook his head, his eyes closed, as if he were angry with himself. "Of course. You're not Were, you're not undead. How would you have healed so quickly?"

Then he did something else unexpected. Eric took my right hand with both of his and gripped it. He looked directly into my face. "I have searched Jackson. I have looked in warehouses, cemeteries, farmhouses, and anyplace that had a trace of vampire scent about it: every property Edgington owns, and some his followers own. I haven't found a trace of Bill. I am very afraid, Sookie, that it is becoming most likely that Bill is dead. Finally dead."

I felt like he'd smacked me in the middle of the forehead with a sledgehammer. My knees just folded, and if he hadn't moved quick as lightning, I'd have been on the floor. Eric sat on a chair that was in the corner of the room, and he gathered me up into a bundle in his lap. He said, "I've upset you too much. I was trying to be practical, and instead I was . . ."

"Brutal." I felt a tear trickle out of each eye.

Eric's tongue darted out, and I felt a tiny trace of moisture as he licked up my tears. Vampires just seem to like any body fluid, if they can't get blood, and that didn't particularly bother me. I felt glad someone was holding me in a comforting way, even if it was Eric. I sunk deeper into misery while Eric spent a few moments thinking.

"The only place I haven't checked is Russell Edgington's compound—his mansion, with its outbuildings. It would be amazing if Russell were rash enough to keep another vampire prisoner in his own home. But he's been king for a hundred years. It could be that he is that confident. Maybe I could sneak in over the wall, but I wouldn't come out again. The grounds are patrolled by Weres. It's very unlikely we'll get access to such a secure place, and he won't invite us in except in very unusual circumstances." Eric let all this sink in. "I think you must tell me what you know about Bill's project."

"Is that what all this holding and niceness is about?" I was furious. "You want to get some information out of me?" I leaped up, revitalized with wrath.

Eric jumped up himself and did his best to loom over me. "I think Bill is dead," he said. "And I'm trying to save my own life, and yours, you stupid woman." Eric sounded just as angry as I was.

"I will find Bill," I said, enunciating each world carefully. I wasn't sure how I was going to accomplish this, but I'd just do some very good spying tonight, and something would turn up. I am no Pollyanna, but I have always been optimistic.

"You can't make eyes at Edgington, Sookie. He's not interested in women. And if I flirted with him, he would be suspicious. A vampire mating with another—that's unusual. Edgington hasn't gotten where he is by being gullible. Maybe his second, Betty Joe, would be interested in me, but she is a vampire, too, and the same rule applies. I can't tell you how unusual Bill's fascination with Lorena is. In fact, we disapprove of vampires loving others of our kind."

I ignored his last two sentences. "How'd you find all this out?"

"I met up with a young female vampire last night, and her boyfriend also went to parties at Edgington's place."

"Oh, he's bi?"

Eric shrugged. "He's a werewolf, so I guess he's two-natured in more ways than one."

"I thought vamps didn't date werewolves, either."

"She is being perverse. The young ones like to experiment."

I rolled my eyes. "So, what you're saying is that I need to concentrate on getting an invitation into Edgington's compound, since there's nowhere else in Jackson that Bill can be hidden?"

"He could be somewhere else in the city," Eric said cautiously. "But I don't think so. The possibility is faint. Remember, Sookie, they've had him for days now." When Eric looked at me, what I saw in his face was pity.

That frightened me more than anything.

Chapter 9

I HAD THE shivery, shaky feeling that precedes walking into danger. This was the last night that Alcide could go to Club Dead: Terence had warned him away, very definitely. After this, I would be on my own, if I were even allowed into the club when Alcide did not escort me.

As I dressed, I found myself wishing I were going to an ordinary vampire bar, the kind where regular humans came to gape at the undead. Fangtasia, Eric's bar in Shreveport, was such a place. People would actually come through on tours, make an evening of wearing all black, maybe pouring on a little fake blood or inserting some cheesy fake fangs. They'd stare at the vampires carefully planted throughout the bar, and they'd thrill at their own daring. Every now and then, one of these tourists would step across the line that kept them safe. Maybe he'd make a pass at one of the vamps, or maybe he'd disrespect Chow, the bartender. Then, perhaps, that tourist would find out what he'd been messing with.

At a bar like Club Dead, all the cards were out on the table. Humans were the adornments, the frills. The supernaturals were the necessity.

I'd been excited this time the night before. Now I just felt a detached sort of determination, like I was on a powerful drug that divorced me from all my more ordinary emotions. I pulled on my hose and some pretty black garters that Arlene had given me for my birthday. I smiled as I thought of my red-haired friend and her incredible optimism about men, even after four marriages. Arlene would tell me to enjoy the minute, the second, with every bit of zest I could summon up. She would tell me I never knew what man I might meet, maybe tonight would be the magic night. Maybe wearing garters would change the course of my life, Arlene would tell me.

I can't say I exactly summoned up a smile, but I felt a little less grim as I pulled my dress over my head. It was the color of champagne. There wasn't much of it. I had on black heels and jet earrings, and I was trying to decide if my old coat would look too horrible, or if I should just freeze my butt off out of vanity. Looking at the very worn blue cloth coat, I sighed. I carried it into the living room over my arm. Alcide was ready, and he was standing in the middle of the room waiting for me. Just as I registered the fact that he was looking distinctly nervous, Alcide pulled one of the wrapped boxes out of the pile he'd collected during his morning shopping. He got that self-conscious look on his face, the one he'd been wearing when I'd returned to the apartment.

"I think I owe you this," he said. And handed me the large box.

"Oh, Alcide! You got me a present?" I know, I know, I was standing there holding the box. But you have to understand, this is not something that happens to me very often.

"Open it," he said gruffly.

I tossed the coat onto the nearest chair and I unwrapped the gift awkwardly—I wasn't used to my fake nails. After a little maneuvering, I opened the white cardboard box to find that Alcide had replaced my evening wrap. I pulled out the long rectangle slowly, savoring every moment. It was beautiful; a black velvet wrap with beading on the ends. I couldn't help but realize that it cost five times what I'd spent on the one that had been damaged.

I was speechless. That hardly ever happens to me. But I don't get too many presents, and I don't take them lightly. I wrapped the velvet around me, luxuriating in the feel of it. I rubbed my cheek against it.

"Thank you," I said, my voice wobbling.

"You're welcome," he said. "God, don't cry, Sookie. I meant you to be happy."

"I'm real happy," I said. "I'm not going to cry." I choked back the tears, and went to look at myself in the mirror in my bathroom. "Oh, it's beautiful," I said, my heart in my voice.

"Good, glad you like it," Alcide said brusquely. "I thought it was the least I could do." He arranged the wrap so that the material covered the red, scabbed marks on my left shoulder.

"You didn't owe me a thing," I said. "It's me that owes you." I could tell that my being serious worried Alcide just as much as my crying. "Come on," I said. "Let's go to Club Dead. We'll learn everything, tonight, and no one will get hurt."

Which just goes to prove I don't have second sight.

*   *   *

ALCIDE WAS WEARING a different suit and I a different dress, but Josephine's seemed just the same. Deserted sidewalk, atmosphere of doom. It was even colder tonight, cold enough for me to see my breath on the air, cold enough to make me pathetically grateful for the warmth of the velvet wrap. Tonight, Alcide practically leaped from the truck to the cover of the awning, not even helping me down, and then stood under it waiting for me.

"Full moon," he explained tersely. "It'll be a tense night."

"I'm sorry," I said, feeling helpless. "This must be awfully hard on you." If he hadn't been obliged to accompany me, he could have been off bounding through the woods after deer and bunnies. He shrugged my apology off. "There'll always be tomorrow night," he said. "That's almost as good." But he was humming with tension.

Tonight I didn't jump quite so much when the truck rolled away, apparently on its own, and I didn't even quiver when Mr. Hob opened the door. I can't say the goblin looked pleased to see us, but I couldn't tell you what his ordinary facial expression really meant. So he could have been doing emotional cartwheels of joy, and I wouldn't have known it.

Somehow, I doubted he was that excited about my second appearance in his club. Or was he the owner? It was hard to imagine Mr. Hob naming a club "Josephine's." "Dead Rotten Dog," maybe, or "Flaming Maggots," but not "Josephine's."

"We won't have trouble tonight," Mr. Hob told us grimly. His voice was bumpy and rusty, as if he didn't talk much, and didn't enjoy it when he did.

"It wasn't her fault," Alcide said.

"Nonetheless," Hob said, and left it at that. He probably felt he didn't need to say anything else, and he was right. The short, lumpy goblin jerked his head at a group of tables that had been pushed together. "The king is waiting for you."

The men stood as I reached the table. Russell Edgington and his special friend Talbot were facing the dance floor; and across from them were an older (well, he'd become undead when he was older) vampire, and a woman, who of course stayed seated. My gaze trailed over her, came back, and I shrieked with delight.

"Tara!"

My high school friend shrieked right back and jumped up. We gave each other a full frontal hug, rather than the slightly less enthusiastic half-hug that was our norm. We were both strangers in a strange land, here at Club Dead.

Tara, who is several inches taller than I am, has dark hair and eyes and olive skin. She was wearing a long-sleeved gold-and-bronze dress that shimmered as she moved, and she had on high, high heels. She had attained the height of her date.

Just as I was disengaging from the embrace and giving her a happy pat on the back, I realized that seeing Tara was the worst thing that could have happened. I went into her mind, and I saw that, sure enough, she was about to ask me why I was with someone who wasn't Bill.

"Come on, girlfriend, come to the ladies' with me for a second!" I said cheerfully, and she grabbed her purse, while giving her date a perfect smile, both promising and rueful. I gave Alcide a little wave, asked the other gentlemen to excuse us, and we walked briskly to the rest rooms, which were off the passage leading to the back door. The ladies' room was empty. I pressed my back against the door to keep other females out. Tara was facing me, her face lit up with questions.

"Tara, please, don't say anything about Bill or anything about Bon Temps."

"You want to tell me why?"

"Just . . ." I tried to think of something reasonable, couldn't. "Tara, it'll cost me my life if you do."

She twitched, and gave me a steady stare. Who wouldn't? But Tara had been through a lot in her life, and she was a tough, if wounded, bird. "I'm so happy to see you here," she said. "It was lonely being in this crowd by myself. Who's your friend? What is he?"

I always forgot that other people couldn't tell. And sometimes I nearly forgot that other people didn't know about Weres and shifters. "He's a surveyor," I said. "Come on, I'll introduce you."

"Sorry we left so quickly," I said, smiling brightly at all the men. "I forgot my manners." I introduced Tara to Alcide, who looked appropriately appreciative. Then it was Tara's turn. "Sook, this is Franklin Mott."

"A pleasure to meet you," I said, and extended my hand before I realized my faux pas. Vampires don't shake hands. "I beg your pardon," I said hastily, and gave him a little wave instead. "Do you live here in Jackson, Mr. Mott?" I was determined not to embarrass Tara.

"Please call me Franklin," he said. He had a wonderful mellow voice with a light Italion accent. When he had died, he had probably been in his late fifties or early sixties; his hair and mustache were iron gray, and his face was lined. He looked vigorous and very masculine. "Yes, I do, but I own a business that has a franchise in Jackson, one in Ruston, and one in Vicksburg. I met Tara at a gathering in Ruston."

Gradually we progressed through the social do-si-do of getting seated, explaining to the men how Tara and I had attended high school together, and ordering drinks. All the vampires, of course, ordered synthetic blood, and Talbot, Tara, Alcide, and I got mixed drinks. I decided another champagne cocktail would be good. The waitress, a shifter, was moving in an odd, almost slinking manner, and she didn't seem inclined to talk much. The night of the full moon was making itself felt in all kinds of ways.

There were far fewer of the two-natured in the bar this night of the moon cycle. I was glad to see Debbie and her fiancé were missing, and there were only a couple of the Were bikers. There were more vampires, and more humans. I wondered how the vampires of Jackson kept this bar a secret. Among the humans who came in with Supe dates, surely one or two were inclined to talk to a reporter or just tell a group of friends about the bar's existence?

I asked Alcide, and he said quietly, "The bar's spellbound. You wouldn't be able to tell anyone how to get here if you tried."

I'd have to experiment with that later, see if it worked. I wonder who did the spell casting, or whatever it was called. If I could believe in vampires and werewolves and shape-shifters, it was not too far a stretch to believe in witches.

I was sandwiched between Talbot and Alcide, so by way of making conversation I asked Talbot about secrecy. Talbot didn't seem averse to chatting with me, and Alcide and Franklin Mott had found they had acquaintances in common. Talbot had on too much cologne, but I didn't hold that against him. Talbot was a man in love, and furthermore, he was a man addicted to vampiric sex . . . the two states are not always combined. He was a ruthless, intelligent man who could not understand how his life had taken such an exotic turn. (He was a big broadcaster, too, which was why I could pick up so much of his life.)

He repeated Alcide's story about the spell on the bar. "But the way what happens here is kept a secret, that's different," Talbot said, as if he was considering a long answer and a short answer. I looked at his pleasant, handsome face and reminded myself that he knew Bill was being tortured, and he didn't care. I wished he would think about Bill again, so I could learn more; at least I would know if Bill was dead or alive. "Well, Miss Sookie, what goes on here is kept secret by terror and punishment."

Talbot said that with relish. He liked that. He liked that he had won the heart of Russell Edgington, a being who could kill easily, who deserved to be feared. "Any vampire or Were—in fact, any sort of supernatural creature, and you haven't seen quite a few of them, believe me—who brings in a human is responsible for that human's behavior. For example, if you were to leave here tonight and call a tabloid, it would be Alcide's bounden duty to track and kill you."

"I see." And indeed, I did. "What if Alcide couldn't bring himself to do that?"

"Then his life would be forfeit, and one of the bounty hunters would be commissioned to do the job."

Jesus Christ, Shepherd of Judea. "There are bounty hunters?" Alcide could have told me a lot more than he had; that was an unpleasant discovery. My voice may have been a little on the croaky side.

"Sure. The Weres who wear the motorcycle gear, in this area. In fact, they're asking questions around the bar tonight because . . ." His expression sharpened, became suspicious. "The man who was bothering you . . . did you see him again last night? After you left the bar?"

"No," I said, speaking the technical truth. I hadn't seen him again—last night. I knew what God thought about technical truths, but I also figured he expected me to save my own life. "Alcide and I, we went right back to the apartment. I was pretty upset." I cast my eyes down like a modest girl unused to approaches in bars, which was also a few steps away from the truth. (Though Sam keeps such incidents down to a minimum, and it was widely known I was crazy and therefore undesirable, I certainly had to put up with the occasional aggressive advance, as well as a certain amount of halfhearted passes from guys who got too drunk to care that I was supposed to be crazy.)

"You were sure plucky when it looked like there was going to be a fight," Talbot observed. Talbot was thinking that my courage last night didn't jibe with my demure demeanor this evening. Darn it, I'd overplayed my role.

"Plucky is the word for Sookie," Tara said. It was a welcome interruption. "When we danced together on stage, about a million years ago, she was the one who was brave, not me! I was shaking in my shoes."

Thank you, Tara.

"You danced?" asked Franklin Mott, his attention caught by the conversation.

"Oh, yes, and we won the talent contest," Tara told him. "What we didn't realize, until we graduated and had some experience in the world, was that our little routine was really, ah—"

"Suggestive," I said, calling a spade a spade. "We were the most innocent girls in our little high school, and there we were, with this dance routine we lifted straight off MTV."

"It took us years to understand why the principal was sweating so hard," Tara said, her smile just rascally enough to be charming. "As a matter of fact, let me go talk to the deejay right now." She sprang up and worked her way over to the vampire who'd set up his gear on the small stage. He bent over and listened intently, and then he nodded.

"Oh, no." I was going to be horribly embarrassed.

"What?" Alcide was amused.

"She's going to make us do it all over again."

Sure enough, Tara wiggled her way through the crowd to get back to me, and she was beaming. I had thought of twenty-five good reasons not to do what she wanted by the time she seized my hands and pulled me to my feet. But it was evident that the only way I could get out of this was to go forward. Tara had her heart set on this exhibition, and Tara was my friend. The crowd made a space as Pat Benatar's "Love Is a Battlefield" began to play.

Unfortunately, I remembered every bump and grind, every hip thrust.

In our innocence, Tara and I had planned our routine almost like pairs figure skating, so we were touching (or very near) during the whole thing. Could it have looked more like some lesbian tease act performed in a stripper bar? Not much. Not that I'd ever been to a stripper bar, or a porno movie house; but I assume the rise of communal lust I felt in Josephine's that night was similar. I didn't like being the object of it—but yet, I discovered I felt a certain flood of power.

Bill had informed my body about good sex, and I was sure that now I danced like I knew about enjoying sex—and so did Tara. In a perverse way, we were having an "I am woman, hear me roar" moment. And, by golly, love sure *was* a battlefield. Benatar was right about that.

We had our sides to the audience, Tara gripping my waist, for the last few bars, and we pumped our hips in unison, and brought our hands sweeping to the floor. The music stopped. There was a tiny second of silence, and then a lot of applause and whistling.

The vampires thought of the blood flowing in our veins, I was sure from the hungry looks on their faces—especially those lower main lines on our inner thighs. And I could hear that the werewolves were imagining how good we would taste. So I was feeling quite edible as I made my way back to our table. Tara and I were patted and complimented along the way, and we received many invitations. I

was halfway tempted to accept the dance offer of a curly-haired brunette vamp who was just about my size and cute as a bunny. But I just
smiled and kept on going.

Franklin Mott was delighted. "Oh, you were so right," he said as
he held Tara's chair for her. Alcide, I observed, remained seated and
glowered at me, forcing Talbot to lean over and pull my chair out for
me, an awkward and makeshift courtesy. (He did get a caress on the
shoulder from Russell for his gesture.) "I can't believe you girls didn't
get expelled," Talbot said, covering the awkward moment. I never
would have pegged Alcide for a possessive jerk.

"We had no clue," Tara protested, laughing. "None. We couldn't
understand what all the fuss was about."

"What bit your ass?" I asked Alcide, very quietly. But when I
listened carefully, I could pick out the source of his dissatisfaction.
He was resenting the fact that he had acknowledged to me that he still
had Debbie in his heart, because otherwise he'd make a determined
effort to share my bed tonight. He felt both guilty and angry about
that, since it was the full moon—come to think of it, his time of the
month. In a way.

"Not looking for your boyfriend too hard, are you?" he said
coldly, in a nasty undertone.

It was like he'd thrown a bucket of cold water in my face. It was a
shock, and it hurt terribly. Tears welled up in my eyes. It was also
completely obvious to everyone at the table that he had said something to upset me.

Talbot, Russell, and Franklin all gave Alcide level looks practically
laden with threat. Talbot's look was a weak echo of his lover's, so it
could be disregarded, but Russell was the king, after all, and Franklin
was apparently an influential vampire. Alcide recalled where he was,
and with whom.

"Excuse me, Sookie, I was just feeling jealous," he said, loud
enough for all at the table to hear. "That was really interesting."

"Interesting?" I said, as lightly as I could. I was pretty damn
mad, myself. I ran my fingers through his hair as I leaned over to his
chair. "Just interesting?" We smiled at each other quite falsely, but the
others bought it. I felt like taking a handful of that black hair and giving it a good hard yank. He might not be a mind reader like me, but
he could read that impulse loud and clear. Alcide had to force himself
not to flinch.

Tara stepped in once again to ask Alcide what his occupation
was—God bless her—and yet another awkward moment passed harm-
lessly by. I pushed my chair a little farther back from the circle around

the table and let my mind roam. Alcide had been right about the fact that I needed to be at work, rather than amusing myself; but I didn't see how I could have refused Tara something she enjoyed so much.

A parting of the bodies crowding the little dance floor gave me a glimpse of Eric, leaning against the wall behind the small stage. His eyes were on me, and they were full of heat. *There* was someone who wasn't pissed off at me, someone who had taken our little routine in the spirit in which it was offered.

Eric looked quite nice in the suit and glasses. The glasses made him seem somehow less threatening, I decided, and turned my mind to business. Fewer Weres and humans made it easier to listen in to each one, easier to track the thread of thought back to its owner. I closed my eyes to help me concentrate, and almost immediately I caught a snatch of inner monologue that shook me up.

"Martyrdom," the man was thinking. I knew the thinker was a man, and that his thoughts were coming from the area behind me, the area right around the bar. My head began to turn, and I stopped myself. Looking wouldn't help, but it was an almost irresistible impulse. I looked down instead, so the movements of the other patrons wouldn't distract me.

People don't really think in complete sentences, of course. What I'm doing, when I spell out their thoughts, is translating.

"When I die, my name will be famous," he thought. "It's almost here. God, please let it not hurt. At least he's here with me . . . I hope the stake's sharp enough."

Oh, *dammit.* The next thing I knew I was on my feet, walking away from the table.

I WAS INCHING along, blocking the noise of the music and the voices so I could listen sharply to what was being said silently. It was like walking underwater. At the bar, slugging back a glass of synthetic blood, was a woman with a poof of teased hair. She was dressed in a tight-bodiced dress with a full skirt fluffing out around it. Her muscular arms and broad shoulders looked pretty strange with the outfit; but I'd never tell her so, nor would any sane person. This had to be Betty Joe Pickard, Russell Edgington's second in command. She had on white gloves and pumps, too. All she needed was a little hat with a half-veil, I decided. I was willing to bet Betty Joe had been a big fan of Mamie Eisenhower's.

And standing behind this formidable vampire, also facing the bar, were two male humans. One was tall, and oddly familiar. His gray-threaded brown hair was long, but neatly combed. It looked like a regular men's haircut, allowed to grow however it wanted to grow. The hairstyle looked odd with his suit. His shorter companion had rough black hair, tousled and flecked with gray. This second man wore a sports coat that maybe came off the rack from JCPenney on a sale day.

And inside that cheap coat, in a specially sewn pocket, he carried a stake.

Horribly enough, I hesitated. If I stopped him, I would be revealing my hidden talent, and to reveal that would be to unmask my identity. The consequences of this revelation would depend on what Edgington knew about me; he apparently knew Bill's girlfriend was a barmaid at Merlotte's in Bon Temps, but not her name. That's why I'd been free to introduce myself as Sookie Stackhouse. If Russell knew Bill's girlfriend was a telepath, and he discovered I was a telepath, who knew what would happen then?

Actually, I could make a good guess.

As I dithered, ashamed and frightened, the decision was made for me. The man with the black hair reached inside his coat and the fanaticism roiling in his head reached fever pitch. He pulled out the long sharpened piece of ash, and then a lot happened.

I yelled, *"STAKE!"* and lunged for the fanatic's arm, gripping it desperately with both my hands. The vampires and their humans whirled around looking for the threat, and the shifters and Weres wisely scattered to the walls to leave the floor free for the vampires. The tall man beat at me, his big hands pounding at my head and shoulders, and his dark-haired companion kept twisting his arm, trying to free it from my grasp. He heaved from side to side to throw me off.

Somehow, in the melee, my eyes met those of the taller man, and we recognized each other. He was G. Steve Newlin, former leader of the Brotherhood of the Sun, a militant anti-vampire organization whose Dallas branch had more or less bit the dust after I'd paid it a visit. He was going to tell them who I was, I just knew it, but I had to pay attention to what the man with the stake was doing. I was staggering around on my heels, trying to keep my feet, when the assassin finally had a stroke of brilliance and transferred the stake from his pinned right hand to his free left.

With a final punch to my back, Steve Newlin dashed for the exit, and I caught a flash of creatures bounding in pursuit. I heard lots of yowling and tweeting, and then the black-haired man threw back his left arm and plunged the stake into my waist on my right side.

I let go of his arm then, and stared down at what he'd done to me. I looked back up into his eyes for a long moment, reading nothing there but a horror to mirror my own. Then Betty Joe Pickard swung back her gloved fist and hit him twice—boom-boom. The first blow snapped his neck. The second shattered his skull. I could hear the bones break.

And then he went down to the floor, and since my legs were tangled with his, I went down, too. I landed flat on my back.

I lay looking up at the ceiling of the bar, at the fan that was rotating solemnly above my head. I wondered why the fan was on in the middle of winter. I saw a hawk fly across the ceiling, narrowly avoiding the fan blades. A wolf came to my side and licked my face and whined, but turned and dashed away. Tara was screaming. I was not. I was so cold.

With my right hand, I covered the spot where the stake entered my body. I didn't want to see it, and I was scared I'd look down. I could feel the growing wetness around the wound.

"Call nine-one-one!" Tara yelled as she landed on her knees beside me. The bartender and Betty Joe exchanged a look over her head. I understood.

"Tara," I said, and it came out like a croak. "Honey, all the shifters are changing. It's full moon. The police can't come in here, and they'll come if anyone calls nine-one-one."

The shifter part just didn't seem to register with Tara, who didn't know such things were possible. "The vampires are not gonna let you die," Tara said confidently. "You just saved one of them!"

I wasn't so sure about that. I saw Franklin Mott's face above Tara. He was looking at me, and I could read his expression.

"Tara," I whispered, "you have to get out of here. This is getting crazy, and if there's any chance the police are coming, you can't be here."

Franklin Mott nodded in approval.

"I'm not going to leave you until you have help," Tara said, her voice full of determination. Bless her heart.

The crowd around me consisted of vampires. One of them was Eric. I could not decipher his face.

"The tall blond will help me," I told Tara, my voice barely a rasp. I pointed a finger at Eric. I didn't look at him for fear I'd read rejection in his eyes. If Eric wouldn't help me, I suspected I would lie here and die on this polished wood floor in a vampire bar in Jackson, Mississippi.

My brother, Jason, would be so pissed off.

Tara had met Eric in Bon Temps, but their introduction had been on a very stressful night. She didn't seem to identify the tall blond she'd met that night with the tall blond she saw tonight, wearing glasses and a suit and with his hair pulled back strictly into a braid.

"Please help Sookie," she said to him directly, as Franklin Mott almost yanked her to her feet.

"This young man will be *glad* to help your friend," Mott said. He gave Eric a sharp look that told Eric he damn well better agree.

"Of course. I'm a good friend of Alcide's," Eric said, lying without a blink.

He took Tara's place by my side, and I could tell after he was on his knees that he caught the smell of my blood. His face went even whiter, and his bones stood out starkly under his skin. His eyes blazed.

"You don't know how hard it is," he whispered to me, "not to bend over and lick."

"If you do, everyone else will," I said. "And they won't just lick, they'll bite." There was a German shepherd staring at me with luminous yellow eyes, just past my feet.

"That's the only thing stopping me."

"Who are you?" asked Russell Edgington. He was giving Eric a careful once-over. Russell was standing to my other side, and he bent over both of us. I had been loomed over enough, I can tell you that, but I was in no position to do a damn thing about it.

"I'm a friend of Alcide's," Eric repeated. "He invited me here tonight to meet his new girlfriend. My name is Leif."

Russell could look down at Eric, since Eric was kneeling, and his golden brown eyes bored into Eric's blue ones. "Alcide doesn't hang with many vampires," Russell said.

"I'm one of the few."

"We have to get this young lady out of here," Russell said.

The snarling a few feet away increased in intensity. There appeared to be a knot of animals gathered around something on the floor.

"Take that out of here!" roared Mr. Hob. "Out the back door! You know the rules!"

Two of the vampires lifted the corpse, for that was what the Weres and shifters were squabbling over, and carried it out the back door, followed by all the animals. So much for the black-haired fanatic.

Just this afternoon Alcide and I had disposed of a corpse. We'd never thought of just bringing it down to the club, laying it in the alley. Of course, this one was fresh.

". . . maybe has nicked a kidney," Eric was saying. I had been unconscious, or at least somewhere else, for a few moments.

I was sweating heavily, and the pain was excruciating. I felt a flash of chagrin when I realized I was sweating all over my dress. But possibly the big bloody hole had already ruined the dress anyway, huh?

"We'll take her to my place," Russell said, and if I hadn't been sure I was very badly hurt, I might have laughed. "The limo's on its way. I'm sure a familiar face would make her more comfortable, don't you agree?"

What I thought was, Russell didn't want to get his suit nasty picking me up. And Talbot probably couldn't lug me. Though the small vampire with curly black hair was still there, and still smiling, I would be awful bulky for him . . .

And I lost some more time.

"Alcide turned into a wolf and chased after the assassin's companion," Eric was telling me, though I didn't remember asking. I started to tell Eric who the companion was, and then I realized that I'd better not. "Leif," I muttered, trying to commit the name to memory. "Leif. I guess my garters are showing. Does that mean . . . ?"

"Yes, Sookie?"

. . . and I was out again. Then I was aware I was moving, and I realized that Eric was carrying me. Nothing had ever hurt so badly in my life, and I reflected, not for the first time, that I'd never even been in a hospital until I'd met Bill, and now I seemed to spend half my time battered or recovering from being battered. This was very significant and important.

A lynx padded out of the bar beside us. I looked down into the golden eyes. What a night this was turning out to be for Jackson. I hoped all the good people had decided to stay home tonight.

And then we were in the limo. My head was resting on Eric's thigh, and in the seat across from us sat Talbot, Russell, and the small curly-haired vampire. As we stopped at a light, a bison lumbered by.

"Lucky no one's out in downtown Jackson on a weekend night in December," Talbot was remarking, and Eric laughed.

We drove for what seemed like some time. Eric smoothed my skirt over my legs, and brushed my hair out of my face. I looked up at him, and . . .

". . . did she know what he was going to do?" Talbot was asking.

"She saw him pull the stake out, she said," Eric said mendaciously. "She was going to the bar to get another drink."

"Lucky for Betty Joe," Russell said in his smooth Southern drawl. "I guess she's still hunting the one that got away."

Then we pulled up into a driveway and stopped at a gate. A bearded vampire came up and peered in the window, looking at all the occupants carefully. He was far more alert than the indifferent guard at

Alcide's apartment building. I heard an electronic hum, and the gate opened. We went up a driveway (I could hear the gravel crunching) and then we swung around in front of a mansion. It was lit up like a birthday cake, and as Eric carefully extracted me from the limo, I could see we were under a porte cochere that was as fancy as all get-out. Even the carport had columns. I expected to see Vivian Leigh come down the steps.

I had a blank moment again, and then we were in the foyer. The pain seemed to be fading away, and its absence left me giddy.

As the master of this mansion, Russell's return was a big event, and when the inhabitants smelled fresh blood, they were doubly quick to come thronging. I felt like I'd landed in the middle of romance cover model contest. I had never seen so many cute men in one place in my life. But I could tell they were not for me. Russell was like the gay vampire Hugh Hefner, and this was the Playboy Mansion, with an emphasis on the "boy."

"Water, water, everywhere, nor any drop to drink," I said, and Eric laughed out loud. That was why I liked him, I thought rosily; he "got" me.

"Good, the shot's taking effect," said a white-haired man in a sports shirt and pleated trousers. He was human, and he might as well have had a stethoscope tattooed around his neck, he was so clearly a doctor. "Will you be needing me?"

"Why don't you stay for a while?" Russell suggested. "Josh will keep you company, I'm sure."

I didn't get to see what Josh looked like, because Eric was carrying me upstairs then.

"Rhett and Scarlet," I said.

"I don't understand," Eric told me.

"You haven't seen *Gone with the Wind*?" I was horrified. But then, why should a vampire Viking have seen that staple of the Southern mystique? But he'd read *The Rhyme of the Ancient Mariner*, which I had worked my way through in high school. "You'll have to watch it on video. Why am I acting so stupid? Why am I not scared?"

"That human doctor gave you a big dose of drugs," Eric said, smiling down at me. "Now I am carrying you to a bedroom so you can be healed."

"He's here," I told Eric.

His eyes flashed caution at me. "Russell, yes. But I'm afraid that Alcide made less than a stellar choice, Sookie. He raced off into the night after the other attacker. He should have stayed with you."

"Screw him," I said expansively.

"He wishes, especially after seeing you dance."

I wasn't feeling quite good enough to laugh, but it did cross my mind. "Giving me drugs maybe wasn't such a great idea," I told Eric. I had too many secrets to keep.

"I agree, but I am glad you're out of pain."

Then we were in a bedroom, and Eric was laying me on a gosh-to-goodness canopied four-poster. He took the opportunity to whisper, "Be careful," in my ear. And I tried to bore that thought into my drug-addled brain. I might blurt out the fact that I knew, beyond a doubt, that Bill was somewhere close to me.

Chapter 10

THERE WAS QUITE a crowd in the bedroom, I noticed. Eric had gotten me situated on the bed, which was so high, I might need a stepstool to get down. But it would be convenient for the healing, I had heard Russell comment, and I was beginning to worry about what constituted "the healing." The last time I'd been involved in a vampire "healing," the treatment had been what you might call nontraditional.

"What's gonna happen?" I asked Eric, who was standing at the side of the bed on my left, non-wounded, side.

But it was the vampire who had taken his place to my right who answered. He had a long, horsy face, and his blond eyebrows and eyelashes were almost invisible against his pallor. His bare chest was hairless, too. He was wearing a pair of pants, which I suspected were vinyl. Even in the winter, they must be, um, unbreathing. I wouldn't like to peel those suckers off. This vamp's saving grace was his lovely straight pale hair, the color of white corn.

"Miss Stackhouse, this is Ray Don," Russell said.

"How de do." Good manners would make you welcome anywhere, my gran had always told me.

"Pleased to meet you," he responded correctly. He had been raised right, too, though no telling when that had been. "I'm not going to ask you how you're doing, cause I can see you got a great big hole in your side."

"Kind of ironic, isn't it, that it was the human that got staked," I said socially. I hoped I would see that doctor again, because I sure wanted to ask him what he'd given me. It was worth its weight in gold.

Ray Don gave me a dubious look, and I realized I'd just shot out of his comfort zone, conversationally. Maybe I could give Ray Don a Word of the Day calendar, like Arlene gave me every Christmas.

"I'll tell you what's going to happen, Sookie," Eric said. "You know, when we start to feed and our fangs come out, they release a little anticoagulant?"

"Um-hum."

"And when we are ready to finish feeding, the fangs release a little coagulant and a little trace of the, the—"

"Stuff that helps you all heal so fast?"

"Yes, exactly."

"So, Ray Don is going to what?"

"Ray Don, his nest mates say, has an extra supply of all these chemicals in his body. This is his talent."

Ray Don beamed at me. He was proud of that.

"So he will start the process on a volunteer, and when he has fed, he will begin cleaning your wound and healing it."

What Eric had left out of this narrative was that at some point during this process, the stake was going to have to come out, and that no drug in the world could keep that from hurting like a son of a bitch. I realized that in one of my few moments of clarity.

"Okay," I said. "Let's get the show on the road."

The volunteer turned out to be a thin blond human teenager, who was no taller than me and probably no wider in the shoulders. He seemed to be quite willing. Ray Don gave him a big kiss before he bit him, which I could have done without, since I'm not into public displays of carnal affection. (When I say "big," I don't mean a loud smack, but the intense, moaning, tonsil-sucking kind.) When that was done, to both their satisfactions, Blondie inclined his head to one side, and the taller Ray Don sank his fangs in. There was much cleaving, and much panting—and even to drug-addled me, Ray Don's vinyl pants didn't leave enough to the imagination.

Eric watched without apparent reaction. Vampires seem, as a whole, to be extremely tolerant of any sexual preference; I guess there aren't that many taboos when you've been alive a few hundred years.

When Ray Don drew back from Blondie and turned to face the bed, he had a bloody mouth. My euphoria evaporated as Eric instantly sat on the bed and pinned my shoulders. The Big Bad Thing was coming.

"Look at me," he demanded. "Look at me, Sookie."

I felt the bed indent, and I assumed Ray Don was kneeling beside it and leaning over to my wound.

There was a jar in the torn flesh of my side that jolted me down to the marrow of my bones. I felt the blood leave my face and felt hysteria bubbling up my throat like my blood was leaving the wound.

"Don't, Sookie! Look at me!" Eric said urgently.

I looked down to see that Ray Don had grabbed the stake. Next he would . . .

I screamed over and over, until I didn't have the energy. I met Eric's eyes as I felt Ray Don's mouth sucking at the wound. Eric was holding my hands, and I was digging my nails into him like we were doing something else. He won't mind, I thought, as I realized I'd drawn blood.

And sure enough, he didn't. "Let go," he advised me, and I loosened my grip on his hands. "No, not of me," he said, smiling. "You can hold on to me as long as you want. Let go of the pain, Sookie. Let go. You need to drift away."

It was the first time I had relinquished my will to someone else. As I looked at him, it became easy, and I retreated from the suffering and uncertainty of this strange place.

The next thing I knew, I was awake. I was tucked in the bed, lying on my back, my formerly beautiful dress removed. I was still wearing my beige lace underwear, which was good. Eric was in the bed with me, which was not. He was really making a habit of this. He was lying on his side, his arm draped over me, one leg thrown over mine. His hair was tangled with my hair, and the strands were almost indistinguishable, the color was so similar. I contemplated that for a while, in a sort of misty, drifting state.

Eric was having downtime. He was in that absolutely immobile state into which vampires retreat when they have nothing else to do. It refreshes them, I think, reduces the wear and tear of the world that ceaselessly passes them by, year after year, full of war and famine and inventions that they must learn how to master, changing mores and conventions and styles that they must adopt in order to fit in. I pulled down the covers to check out my side. I was still in pain, but it was greatly reduced. There was a large circle of scar tissue on the site of the wound. It was hot and shiny and red and somehow glossy.

"It's much better," Eric said, and I gasped. I hadn't felt him rouse from his suspended animation.

Eric was wearing silk boxers. I would have figured him for a Jockey man.

"Thank you, Eric." I didn't care for how shaky I sounded, but an obligation is an obligation.

"For what?" His hand gently stroked my stomach.

"For standing by me in the club. For coming here with me. For not leaving me alone with all these people."

"How grateful are you?" he whispered, his mouth hovering over mine. His eyes were very alert now, and his gaze was boring into mine.

"That kind of ruins it, when you say something like that," I said, trying to keep my voice gentle. "You shouldn't want me to have sex with you just because I owe you."

"I don't really care why you have sex with me, as long as you do it," he said, equally gently. His mouth was on mine then. Try as I might to stay detached, I wasn't too successful. For one thing, Eric had had hundreds of years to practice his kissing technique, and he'd used them to good advantage. I snuck my hands up to his shoulders, and I am ashamed to say I responded. As sore and tired as my body was, it wanted what it wanted, and my mind and will were running far behind. Eric seemed to have six hands, and they were everywhere, encouraging my body to have its way. A finger slid under the elastic of my (minimal) panties, and glided right into me.

I made a noise, and it was not a noise of rejection. The finger began moving in a wonderful rhythm. Eric's mouth seemed bent on sucking my tongue down his throat. My hands were enjoying the smooth skin and the muscles that worked underneath it.

Then the window flew open, and Bubba crawled in.

"Miss Sookie! Mr. Eric! I tracked you down!" Bubba was proud.

"Oh, good for you, Bubba," Eric said, ending the kiss. I clamped my hand on his wrist, and pulled his hand away. He allowed me to do it. I am nowhere near as strong as the weakest vampire.

"Bubba, have you been here the whole time? Here in Jackson?" I asked, once I had some wits in my head. It was a good thing Bubba had come in, though Eric didn't think so.

"Mr. Eric told me to stick with you," Bubba said simply. He settled into a low chair tastefully upholstered in flowered material. He had a dark lock of hair falling over his forehead, and he was wearing a gold ring on every finger. "You get hurt bad at that club, Miss Sookie?"

"It's a lot better now," I said.

"I'm sorry I didn't do my job, but that little critter guarding the door wouldn't let me in. He didn't seem to know who I was, if you can believe that."

Since Bubba himself hardly remembered who he was, and had a real fit when he did, maybe it wasn't too surprising that a goblin wouldn't be current on American popular music.

"But I saw Mr. Eric carrying you out, so I followed you."

"Thank you, Bubba. That was real smart."

He smiled, in a slack and dim sort of way. "Miss Sookie, what you doing in bed with Mr. Eric if Bill is your boyfriend?"

"That's a real good question, Bubba," I said. I tried to sit up, but I couldn't do it. I made a little pain sound, and Eric cursed in another language.

"I am going to give her blood, Bubba," Eric said. "Let me tell you what I need you to do."

"Sure," Bubba said agreeably.

"Since you got over the wall and into the house without being caught, I need you to search this estate. We think Bill is here somewhere. They are keeping him prisoner. Don't try to free him. This is an order. Come back here and tell us when you have found him. If they see you, don't run. Just don't say anything. Nothing. Not about me, or Sookie, or Bill. Nothing more than, 'Hi, my name is Bubba.'"

"Hi, my name is Bubba."

"Right."

"Hi, my name is Bubba."

"Yes. That's fine. Now, you sneak, and you be quiet and invisible."

Bubba smiled at us. "Yes, Mr. Eric. But after that, I gotta go find me some food. I'm mighty hungry."

"Okay, Bubba. Go search now."

Bubba scrambled back out the window, which was on the second story. I wondered how he was going to get to the ground, but if he'd gotten into the window, I was sure he could get out of it.

"Sookie," Eric said, right in my ear. "We could have a long argument about you taking my blood, and I know everything you would say. But the fact is, dawn is coming. I don't know if you will be allowed to stay the day here or not. I will have to find shelter, here or elsewhere. I want you strong and able to defend yourself; at least able to move quickly."

"I know Bill is here," I said, after I'd thought this over for a moment. "And no matter what we almost just did—thank God for Bubba—I need to find Bill. The best time to get him out of here would be while all you vampires are asleep. Can he move at all during the daytime?"

"If he knows he is in great danger, he may be able to stagger," Eric said, slowly and thoughtfully. "Now I am even more sure you will need my blood, because you need strength. He will need to be covered thoroughly. You will need to take the blanket off this bed; it's thick. How will you get him out of here?"

"That's where you come in," I said. "After we do this blood thing, you need to go get me a car—a car with a great big trunk, like a Lincoln or a Caddy. And you need to get the keys to me. And you'll need to sleep somewhere else. You don't want to be here when they wake up and find their prisoner is gone." Eric's hand was resting quietly on my stomach, and we were still wrapped up together in the bedding. But the situation felt completely different.

"Sookie, where will you take him?"

"An underground place," I said uncertainly. "Hey, maybe Alcide's parking garage! That's better than being out in the open."

Eric sat up against the headboard. The silk boxers were royal blue. He spread his legs and I could see up the leg hole. Oh, Lord. I had to close my eyes. He laughed.

"Sit up with your back against my chest, Sookie. That will make you more comfortable."

He carefully eased me up against him, my back to his chest, and wrapped his arms around me. It was like leaning against a firm, cool, pillow. His right arm vanished, and I heard a little crunch sound. Then his wrist appeared in front of my face, blood running from the two wounds in his skin.

"This will cure you of everything," Eric said.

I hesitated, then derided myself for my foolish hesitation. I knew that the more of Eric's blood I had in me, the more he would know me. I knew that it would give him some kind of power over me. I knew that I would be stronger for a long time, and given how old Eric was, I would be very strong. I would heal, and I would feel wonderful. I would be more attractive. This was why vampires were preyed upon by Drainers, humans who worked in teams to capture vamps, chain them with silver, and drain their blood into vials, which sold for varying sums on the black market. Two hundred dollars had been the going price for one vial last year; God knows what Eric's blood would bring, since he was so old. Proving that provenance would definitely be a problem for the Drainer. Draining was an extremely hazardous occupation, and it was also extremely illegal.

Eric was giving me a great gift.

I have never been what you would call squeamish, thank goodness. I closed my mouth over the little wounds, and I sucked.

Eric moaned, and I could tell quickly that he was once again pleased to be in such close contact. He began to move a little, and there wasn't a lot I could do about it. His left arm was keeping me firmly clamped against him, and his right arm was, after all, feeding me. It was still hard not to be icked out by the process. But Eric was definitely having a good time, and since with every pull I felt better, it was hard to argue with myself that this was a bad thing to be doing. I tried not to think, and I tried not to move myself in response. I remembered the time I'd taken Bill's blood because I needed extra strength, and I remembered Bill's reaction.

Eric pressed against me even harder, and suddenly he said, "Ohhhhh," and relaxed all over. I felt wetness against my back, and I took one deep, last draw. Eric groaned again, a deep and guttural sound, and his mouth trailed down the side of my neck.

"Don't bite me," I said. I was holding on to the remnants of my sanity with difficulty. What had excited me, I told myself, was my memory of Bill; his reaction when I'd bitten him, his intense arousal. Eric just happened to be here. I couldn't have sex with a vampire, especially Eric, just because I found him attractive—not when there would be such dire consequences. I was just too strung out to enumerate those consequences to myself. I was an adult, I told myself sternly; true adults don't have sex just because the other person is skilled and pretty.

Eric's fangs scraped my shoulder.

I launched myself out of that bed like a rocket. Intending to locate a bathroom, I flung open the door to find the short brunette vampire, the one with the curly hair, standing just outside, his left arm draped with clothes, his right raised to knock.

"Well, look at you," he said, smiling. And he certainly was looking. He burned his candle at both ends, apparently.

"You needed to talk to me?" I leaned against the door frame, doing my best to look wan and frail.

"Yes, after we cut your beautiful dress off, Russell figured you'd need some clothes. I happened to have these in my closet, and since we're the same height . . ."

"Oh," I said faintly. I'd never shared clothes with a guy. "Well, thank you so much. This is very kind of you." And it was. He'd brought some sweats (powder blue) and socks, and a silk bathrobe, and even some fresh panties. I didn't want to think about that too closely.

"You seem better," the small man said. His eyes were admiring, but not in any real personal way. Maybe I'd overestimated my charms.

"I am very shaky," I said quietly. "I was up because I was on my way to the bathroom."

Curly's brown eyes flared, and I could tell he was looking at Eric over my shoulder. This view definitely was more to his taste, and his smile became frankly inviting. "Leif, would you like to share my coffin today?" he asked, practically batting his eyelashes.

I didn't dare turn to look at Eric. There was a patch on my back that was still wet. I was suddenly disgusted with myself. I'd had thoughts about Alcide, and more than had thoughts about Eric. I was not pleased with my moral fiber. It was no excuse that I knew Bill had been unfaithful to me, or at least it wasn't much of an excuse. It was probably also not an excuse that being with Bill had accustomed me to regular, spectacular sex. Or not much of an excuse.

It was time to pull my moral socks up and behave myself. Just deciding that made me feel better.

"I have to run an errand for Sookie," Eric was telling the curly-haired vamp. "I am not sure I'll return before daybreak, but if I do, you can be sure I'll seek you out." Eric was flirting back. While all this repartee was flying around me, I pulled on the silk robe, which was black and pink and white, all flowers. It was really outstanding. Curly spared me a glance, and seemed more interested than he had when I'd just appeared in my undies.

"Yum," he said simply.

"Again, thanks," I said. "Could you tell me where the nearest bathroom is?"

He pointed down the hall to a half-open door.

"Excuse me," I said to both of them, and reminded myself to walk slowly and carefully, as if I was still in pain, as I made my way down the hall. Past the bathroom, by maybe two doors, I could see the head of the staircase. Okay, I knew the way out now. That was actually a comfort.

The bathroom was just a regular old bathroom. It was full of the stuff that usually clutters bathrooms: hair dryers, hot curlers, deodorant, shampoo, styling gel. Some makeup. Brushes and combs and razors.

Though the counter was clean and orderly, it was apparent several people shared the room. I was willing to bet Russell Edgington's personal bathroom looked nothing like this one. I found some bobby pins and secured my hair on top of my head, and I took the quickest shower on record. Since my hair had just been washed that morning, which now seemed years ago and took forever to dry besides, I was glad to skip it in favor of scrubbing my skin vigorously with the scented soap in the built-in dish. There were clean towels in the closet, which was a relief.

I was back in the bedroom within fifteen minutes. Curly was gone, Eric was dressed, and Bubba was back.

Eric did not say one word about the embarrassing incident that had taken place between us. He eyed the robe appreciatively but silently.

"Bubba has scoped out the territory, Sookie," Eric said, clearly quoting.

Bubba was smiling his slightly lopsided smile. He was pleased with himself. "Miss Sookie, I found Bill," he said triumphantly. "He ain't in such good shape, but he's alive."

I sank into a chair with no forewarning. I was just lucky it was behind me. My back was still straight—but all of a sudden, I was sitting instead of standing. It was one more strange sensation in a night full of them.

When I was able to think of anything else, I noticed vaguely that Eric's expression was a bewildering blend of things: pleasure, regret, anger, satisfaction. Bubba just looked happy.

"Where is he?" My voice didn't even sound like my own.

"There's a big building in back of here, like a four-car garage, but it's got apartments on top of it and a room to the side."

Russell liked to keep his help handy.

"Are there other buildings? Could I get confused?"

"There's a swimming pool, Miss Sookie, and it's got a little building right by it for people to change into their bathing suits. And there's a great big toolshed, I think that's what it's for, but it's separate from the garage."

Eric said, "What part of the garage is he being kept in?"

Bubba said, "The room to the right side. I think maybe the garage used to be stables, and the room is where they kept the saddles and stuff. It isn't too big."

"How many are in there with him?" Eric was asking some good questions. I could not get over Bubba's assurance that Bill was still alive and that I was very close to him.

"They got three in there right now, Mr. Eric, two men and one woman. All three are vamps. She's the one with the knife."

I shrank inside myself. "Knife," I said.

"Yes'm, she's cut him up pretty bad."

This was no time to falter. I'd been priding myself on my lack of squeamishness earlier. This was the moment to prove I'd been telling the truth to myself.

"He's held out this long," I said.

"He has," Eric agreed. "Sookie, I will go to get a car. I'll try to park it back there by the stables."

"Do you think they'll let you back in?"

"If I take Bernard with me."

"Bernard?"

"The little one." Eric smiled at me, and his own smile was a little lopsided.

"You mean . . . Oh, if you take Curly with you, they'll let you back in because he lives here?"

"Yes. But I may have to stay here. With him."

"You couldn't, ah, get out of it?"

"Maybe, maybe not. I don't want to be caught here, rising, when they discover Bill is gone, and you with him."

"Miss Sookie, they'll put werewolves to guarding him during the day."

We both looked at Bubba simultaneously.

"Those werewolves that have been on your trail? They'll be guarding Bill when the vamps go to sleep."

"But tonight is the full moon," I said. "They'll be worn out when it's their turn to take over. If they show up at all."

Eric looked at me with some surprise. "You're right, Sookie. This is the best opportunity we're going to get."

We talked it over some more; perhaps I could act very weak and hole up in the house, waiting for a human ally of Eric's to arrive from Shreveport. Eric said he would call the minute he got out of the immediate area, on his cell phone.

Eric said, "Maybe Alcide could lend a hand tomorrow morning."

I have to admit, I was tempted by the idea of calling him in again. Alcide was big and tough and competent, and something hidden and weak in me suggested that surely Alcide would be able to manage everything better than I would. But my conscience gave an enormous twinge. Alcide, I argued, could not be involved further. He'd done his job. He had to deal with these people in a business way, and it would ruin him if Russell figured out his part in the escape of Bill Compton.

We couldn't spend any more time in discussion, because it lacked only two hours until dawn. With a lot of details still loose, Eric went to find Curly—Bernard—and coyly request his company on an errand to obtain a car I assumed he intended to rent, and what car rental place would be open at this hour was a mystery to me, but Eric didn't seem to anticipate any trouble. I tried to dismiss my doubts from my mind. Bubba agreed to go over Russell's wall again, as he'd entered, and find a place to go to ground for the day. Only the fact that this was the night of the full moon had saved Bubba's life, Eric said, and I was willing to believe it. The vampire guarding the gate might be good, but he couldn't be everywhere.

My job was to play weak until day, when the vampires would retire, and then somehow get Bill out of the stable and into the trunk of the car Eric would provide. They'd have no reason to stop me from leaving.

"This is maybe the worst plan I have ever heard," Eric said.

"You got that right, but it's all we have."

"You'll do great, Miss Sookie," Bubba told me encouragingly.

That's what I needed, a positive attitude. "Thank you, Bubba," I said, trying to sound as grateful as I felt. I was energized by Eric's blood. I felt like my eyes were shooting sparks and my hair was floating around my head in a electric halo.

"Don't get too carried away," Eric advised. He reminded me that this was a common problem with people who ingested black-market vampire blood. They attempted crazy things since they felt so strong, so invincible, and sometimes they just weren't up to the attempted feat—like the guy who tried to fight a whole gang at once, or the woman who took on an oncoming train. I took a deep breath, trying to impress his warning on my brain. What I wanted to do was lean out the window and see if I could crawl up the wall to the roof. Wow, Eric's blood was *awesome*. That was a word I'd never used before, but it was accurate. I'd never realized what a difference there would be between taking Bill's blood and taking Eric's.

There was a knock at the door, and we all looked at it as if we could see through it.

In an amazingly short time, Bubba was out the window, Eric was sitting in the chair by the bed, and I was in the bed trying to look weak and shaky.

"Come in," Eric called in a hushed voice, as befitted the companion of someone recuperating from a terrible wound.

It was Curly—that is, Bernard. Bernard was wearing jeans and a dark red sweater, and he looked good enough to eat. I closed my eyes and gave myself a stern lecture. The blood infusion had made me very lively.

"How is she doing?" Bernard asked, almost whispering. "Her color is better."

"Still in pain, but healing, thanks to the generosity of your king."

"He was glad to do it," Bernard said courteously. "But he will be, ah, best pleased if she can leave on her own tomorrow morning. He is sure by then her boyfriend will be back at his apartment after he has enjoyed the moon tonight. I hope this doesn't seem too brusque?"

"No, I can understand his concern," Eric said, being polite right back.

Apparently, Russell was afraid that I would stay for several days, cashing in on my act of heroism. Russell, unused to having human female houseguests, wanted me to go back to Alcide, when he was sure Alcide would be able to see after me. Russell was a little uneasy about an unknown woman wandering around his compound during the day, when he and all his retinue would be in their deep sleep.

Russell was quite right to worry about this.

"Then I'll go get her a car and park it in the area to the rear of the house, and she can drive herself out tomorrow. If you can arrange that she'll have safe passage through the front gates—I assume they are guarded during the day?—I will have fulfilled my obligation to my friend Alcide."

"That sounds very reasonable," Bernard said, giving me a fraction of the smile he was aiming at Eric. I didn't return it. I closed my eyes wearily. "I'll leave word at the gate when we go. My car okay? It's just a little old egg-beater, but it'll get us to . . . where did you want to go?"

"I'll tell you when we're on the road. It's close to the home of a friend of mine. He knows a man who'll loan me the car for a day or two."

Well, he'd found a way to obtain a car without a paper trail. Good.

I felt movement to my left. Eric bent over me. I knew it was Eric, because his blood inside me informed me so. This was really scary, and this was why Bill had warned me against taking blood from any vampire other than him. Too late. Rock and a hard place.

He kissed my cheek in a chaste, friend-of-the-boyfriend way. "Sookie," he said very quietly. "Can you hear me?"

I nodded just a trifle.

"Good. Listen, I am going to get you a car. I'll leave the keys up here by the bed when I get back. In the morning, you need to drive out of here and back to Alcide's. Do you understand?"

I nodded again. "Bye," I said, trying to make my voice drowsy. "Thank you."

"My pleasure," he said, and I heard the edge in his voice. With an effort, I kept my face straight.

It's hard to credit, but I actually fell asleep after they left. Bubba had evidently obeyed, and gone over the fence to arrange shelter for the day. The mansion became very quiet as the night's revelries drew to a close. I supposed the werewolves were off having their last howl somewhere. As I was drifting off, I wondered how the other shape-shifters had fared. What did they do with their clothes? Tonight's drama at Club Dead had been a fluke; I was sure they had a normal procedure. I wondered where Alcide was. Maybe he had caught that son of a bitch Newlin.

I woke up when I heard the chink of keys.

"I'm back," Eric said. His voice was very quiet, and I had to open my eyes a little to make sure he was actually there. "It's a white Lincoln. I parked out by the garage; there wasn't room inside, which is a real pity.

They wouldn't let me get any closer to confirm what Bubba said. Are you hearing me?"

I nodded.

"Good luck." Eric hesitated. "If I can disentangle myself, I'll meet you in the parking garage at first dark tonight. If you aren't there, I'll go back to Shreveport."

I opened my eyes. The room was dark, still; I could see Eric's skin glowing. Mine was, too. That scared the tar out of me. I had just stopped glowing from taking Bill's blood (in an emergency situation), when here came another crisis, and now I was shining like a disco ball. Life around vampires was just one continuous emergency, I decided.

"We'll talk later," Eric said ominously.

"Thanks for the car," I said.

Eric looked down at me. He seemed to have a hickey on his neck. I opened my mouth, and then shut it again. Better not to comment.

"I don't like having feelings," Eric said coldly, and he left.

That was a tough exit line to top.

Chapter 11

THERE WAS A line of light in the sky when I crept out of the mansion of the king of Mississippi. It was a little warmer this morning, and the sky was dark with not just night, but rain. I had a little roll of my belongings under my arm. Somehow my purse and my black velvet shawl had made it here to the mansion from the nightclub, and I had rolled my high heels in the shawl. The purse did have the key to Alcide's apartment in it, the one he'd loaned me, so I felt reassured that I could find shelter there if need be. I had the blanket from the bed folded neatly under my other arm. I'd made the bed up, so its loss would not be obvious for a little while.

What Bernard had not loaned me was a jacket. When I'd snuck out, I'd snagged a dark blue quilted jacket that had been hanging on the banister. I felt very guilty. I'd never stolen anything before. Now I had taken the blanket and the jacket. My conscience was protesting vigorously.

When I considered what I might have to do to get out of this compound, taking a jacket and a blanket seemed pretty mild. I told my conscience to shut up.

As I crept through the cavernous kitchen and opened the back door, my feet were sliding around in the elastic-sided slippers Bernard had included in the bundle of clothes he'd brought to my room. The socks and slippers were better than teetering in the heels, by a long shot.

I hadn't seen anyone so far. I seemed to have hit the magic time. Almost all the vampires were securely in their coffins, or beds, or in the ground, or whatever the heck they did during the day. Almost all the Were creatures, of whatever persuasion, were not back from their last night's binge or were already sleeping it off. But I was vibrating with tension, because at any moment this luck might run out.

Behind the mansion, there was indeed a smallish swimming pool, covered for the winter by a huge black tarp. It had weighted edges that extended far beyond the actual perimeter of the pool. The tiny pool house was completely dark. I moved silently down a pathway created with uneven flagstones, and after I passed through a gap in a dense hedge, I found myself in a paved area. With my enhanced vision, I was able to see instantly that I had found the courtyard in front of the former stables. It was a large edifice sided with white clapboards, and the second story (where Bubba had spotted apartments) had gable-style windows. Though his was the fanciest garage I had ever seen, the bays for cars did not have doors, but open archways. I could count four vehicles parked inside, from the limo to a Jeep. And there, on the right, instead of a fifth archway, there was a solid wall, and in it, a door.

Bill, I thought. *Bill.* My heart was pounding now. With an overwhelming sense of relief, I spotted the Lincoln parked close to the door. I turned the key in the driver's door, and it clicked open. When I opened the door, the dome light came on, but there didn't seem to be anyone here to see it. I tucked my little bundle of belongings on the passenger seat, and I eased the driver's door almost shut. I found a little switch and turned off the dome light. I took a precious minute to look at the dashboard, though I was so excited and terrified, it was hard to focus. Then I went to the rear of the vehicle and unlocked the trunk. It was just huge—but not clean, like the interior. I had the idea that Eric had gathered up all the large contents and tossed them in the trash, leaving the bottom littered with cigarette rolling papers, plastic bags, and spots of white powder on the floor. Hmmm. Well, okay. That couldn't be too important. Eric had stuck in two bottles of blood, and I moved them over to one side. The trunk was dirty, yes, but clear of anything that would cause Bill discomfort.

I took a deep breath, and clutched the blanket to my chest. Wrapped in its folds was the stake that had hurt me so badly. It was the only weapon I had, and despite its grisly appearance (it was still stained with my blood and a little tissue), I had retrieved it from the wastebasket and brought it with me. After all, I knew for sure it could cause damage.

The sky was a shade lighter, but when I felt raindrops on my face, I felt confident the darkness would last a little longer. I skulked my way to the garage. Creeping around surely looked suspicious, but I simply could not make myself stride purposefully over to the door.

The gravel made silence almost impossible, but still I tried to step lightly.

I put my ear to the door, listened with all my enhanced ability. I was picking up nothing. At least I knew there was no human inside. Turning the knob slowly, easing it back into position after I pushed, I stepped into the room.

The floor was wooden, and covered with stains. The smell was awful. I knew immediately that Russell had used this room for torture before. Bill was in the center of the room, lashed to a straight-back chair by silver chains.

After the confused emotions and unfamiliar surroundings of the past few days, I felt like the world suddenly came into focus.

Everything was clear. Here was Bill. I would save him.

And after I'd had a good look at him in the light of the naked bulb hanging from the ceiling, I knew I would do *anything* to save him.

I had never imagined anything so bad.

There were burn marks under the silver chains, which were draped all around him. I knew that silver caused unremitting agony to a vampire, and my Bill was suffering that now. He had been burned with other things, and cut, cut more than he could heal. He had been starved, and he had been denied sleep. He was slumped over now, and I knew he was taking what respite he could while his tormenters were gone. His dark hair was matted with blood.

There were two doors leading out of the windowless room. One, to my right, led to a dormitory of sorts. I could see some beds through the open doorway. There was a man passed out on one, just sprawled across the cot fully clothed. One of the werewolves, back after his monthly toot. He was snoring, and there were dark smears around his mouth that I didn't want to look at more closely. I couldn't see the rest of the room, so I couldn't be sure if there were others; it would be smart to assume there were.

The door at the rear of the room led farther back into the garage, perhaps to the stairs going up to the apartments. I couldn't spare the time to investigate. I had a feeling of urgency, impelling me to get Bill out as fast as I could. I was trembly with the need to hurry. So far, I had encountered enormous luck. I couldn't count on its holding.

I took two steps closer to Bill.

I knew when he smelled me, realized it was me.

His head snapped up and his eyes blazed at me. A terrible hope shone on his filthy face. I held up a finger; I stepped quietly over to the open door to the dormitory, and gently, gently, slid it almost shut. Then I glided behind him, looking down at the chains. There were two small padlocks, like the ones you put on your locker at school, holding the chains together. "Key?" I breathed in Bill's ear. He had an unbroken finger, and that was the one he used to point at the door I'd come in by. Two keys hung on a nail by the door, quite high from the floor, and always in Bill's sight. Of course they'd think of that. I put the blanket and stake on the floor by Bill's feet. I crept across the stained floor, and reached up as far as I could strain. I couldn't reach the keys. A vampire who could float would be able to get them. I reminded myself I was strong, strong from Eric's blood.

There was a shelf on the wall that held interesting things like pokers and pincers. Pincers! I stood on my tiptoes and lifted them off the shelf, trying hard to keep my gorge from rising when I saw they were crusted with—oh, horrible stuff. I held them up, and they were very heavy, but I managed to clamp them on the keys, work them forward off the nail, and lower the pincers until I could take the keys from their pointed ends. I exhaled a giant sigh of relief, as silently as you can exhale. That hadn't been so hard.

In fact, that was the last easy thing I encountered. I began the horrible task of unwrapping Bill, while trying to keep the movement of the chains as silent as I could. It was oddly difficult to unwind the shiny rope of links. In fact, they seemed to be sticking to Bill, whose whole body was rigid with tension.

Then I understood. He was trying not to scream out loud as the chains were pulled out of his charred flesh. My stomach lurched. I had to stop my task for a few precious seconds, and I had to inhale very carefully. If it was this hard for me to witness his agony, how much harder must it be for Bill to endure it?

I braced up my mental fortitude, and I began working again. My grandmother always told me women could do whatever they had to do, and once again, she was right.

There were literally yards of silver chain, and the careful unwinding took more time than I liked. *Any* time was more time than I liked. The danger lurked right over my shoulder. I was breathing disaster, in and out, with every breath. Bill was very weak, and struggling to stay awake now that the sun had risen. It helped that the day was so dark, but he would not be able to move much when the sun was high, no matter how dreary the day.

The last bit of chain slid to the floor.

"You have to stand up," I said in Bill's ear. "You just have to. I know it hurts. But I can't carry you." At least, I didn't think I could. "There's a big Lincoln outside, and the trunk is open. I'm putting you in the trunk, wrapped in this blanket, and we're driving out of here. Understand, babe?"

Bill's dark head moved a fraction of an inch.

Right then our luck ran out.

"Who the hell are you?" asked a heavily accented voice. Someone had come through the door at my back

Bill flinched under my hands. I whirled to face her, dipping to pick up the stake as I did so, and then she was on me.

I had talked myself into believing they were all in their coffins for the day, but this one was doing her best to kill me.

I would have been dead in a minute if she hadn't been as shocked as I was. I twisted my arm from her grasp and pivoted around Bill in his chair. Her fangs were all out, and she was snarling at me over Bill's head. She was a blond, like me, but her eyes were brown and her build was smaller; she was a tiny woman. She had dried blood on her hands, and I knew it was Bill's. A flame started up inside me. I could feel it flicker through my eyes.

"You must be his little human bitch whore," she said. "He was fucking me, all this time, you understand. The minute he saw me, he forgot about you, except for pity."

Well, Lorena wasn't elegant, but she knew where to sink the verbal knife. I batted the words aside, because she wanted to distract me. I shifted my grip on the stake to be ready, and she leaped across Bill to land on top of me.

As she moved, without a conscious decision I whipped up the stake and pointed it at an angle. As she came down on me, the sharp point went in her chest and out the other side. Then we were on the floor. I was still gripping the end of the stake, and she was holding herself off of me with her arms. She looked down at the wood in her chest, astonished. Then she looked in my eyes, her mouth agape, her fangs retracting. "No," she said. Her eyes went dull.

I used the stake to push her to my left side, and I scrambled up off the floor. I was panting, and my hands shook violently. She didn't move. The whole incident had been so swift and so quiet that it hardly felt real.

Bill's eyes went from the thing on the floor to me. His expression was unreadable. "Well," I told him, "I killed *her* ass."

Then I was on my knees beside her, trying not to vomit.

It took me more precious seconds to regain control of myself. I had a goal I had to meet. Her death would not do me a bit of good if I couldn't get Bill out of here before someone else came in. Since I had done something so horrible, I had to get something, some advantage out of it.

It would be a smart thing to conceal the body—which was beginning to shrivel—but that had to take second place to removing Bill. I wrapped the blanket around his shoulders as he sat slumped in the stained chair. I'd been afraid to look at his face since I'd done this thing.

"That was Lorena?" I whispered in Bill's ear, plagued by a sudden doubt. "She did this to you?"

He gave that tiny nod again.

Ding dong, the witch was dead.

After a pause, while I waited to feel something, the only thing I could think of was asking Bill why someone named Lorena would have a foreign accent. That was dumb, so I forgot about it.

"You got to wake up. You got to stay awake till I get you in the car, Bill." I was trying to keep a mental eye open for the Weres in the next room. One of them began snoring behind the closed door, and I felt the mental stir of another, one I hadn't been able to spot. I froze for several seconds, before I could feel that mind settle into a sleep pattern again. I took a deep, deep breath and pulled a flap of blanket over Bill's head. Then I got his left aim draped around my neck, and I heaved. He came up out of the chair, and though he gave a ragged hiss of pain, he managed to shuffle to the door. I was more than half carrying him, so I was glad to stop there and grab the knob and twist it. Then I almost lost hold of him, since he was literally sleeping on his feet.

Only the danger that we would be caught was stimulating him enough to afford movement.

The door opened, and I checked to make sure the blanket, which happened to be fuzzy and yellow, completely covered his head. Bill moaned and went almost completely limp when he felt the sunlight, weak and watery as it was. I began talking to him under my breath, cursing him and challenging him to move, telling him I could keep him awake if that bitch Lorena could, telling him I would beat him up if he didn't make it to the car.

Finally, with a tremendous effort that left me trembling, I got Bill to the trunk of the car. I pushed it open. "Bill, just sit on the lip here," I told him, tugging at him until he was facing me and sitting on the edge of the trunk. But the life left him completely at that point, and he simply collapsed backward. As he folded into the space, he made a deep pain noise that tore at my heart, and then he was absolutely silent and limp. It was always terrifying to see Bill die like that. I wanted to shake him, scream at him, pound on his chest.

There was no point in any of that.

I made myself shove all the sticking-out bits—a leg, an arm— into the trunk with him, and then I closed it. I allowed myself the luxury of a moment of intense relief.

Standing in the dim daylight in the deserted courtyard, I conducted a brief inner debate. Should I attempt to hide Lorena's body? Would such an effort be worth the time and energy?

I changed my mind about six times in the course of thirty seconds. I finally decided that yeah, it might be worth it. If there was no body to see, the Weres might suppose that Lorena had taken Bill somewhere for a little extra torture session. And Russell and Betty Joe would be dead to the world and unavailable to give instructions. I had no illusions that Betty Joe would be grateful enough to me to spare me, if I should get caught right now. A somewhat quicker death would be the most I could hope for.

My decision reached, back into that awful bloodstained room I went. Misery had soaked into the walls, along with the stains. I wondered how many humans, Weres, and vampires had been held prisoner in this room. Gathering up the chains as silently as I could, I stuffed them in Lorena's blouse, so anyone checking out the room might assume they were still around Bill. I looked around to see if there was any more cleanup I needed to do. There was so much blood in the room already, Lorena's made no difference.

Time to get her out of there.

To keep her heels from dragging and making noise, I had to lift her onto my shoulder. I had never done such a thing, and the procedure was awkward. Lucky for me she was so small, and lucky I'd practiced blocking things out of my mind all these years. Otherwise, the way Lorena dangled, completely limp, and the way she was beginning to flake away, would have freaked me out. I gritted my teeth, to hold back the bubble of hysteria starting up my throat.

It was raining heavily as I carried the body to the pool. Without Eric's blood, I could never have lifted the weighted edge of the pool cover, but I managed it with one hand and pushed what was left of Lorena into the pool with one foot. I was aware at any second that someone could look out the windows at the back of the mansion and see me, realize what I was doing—but if any of the humans living in the house did so, they decided to keep silent.

I was beginning to feel overwhelmingly weary. I trudged back down the flagstone path through the hedge to the car. I leaned on it for a minute, just breathing, gathering myself. Then I got in the driver's seat, and turned the key in the ignition. The Lincoln was the biggest car I'd ever driven, and one of the most luxurious cars I'd ever been in, but just at the moment I could take no interest or pleasure in it. I buckled my seat belt, adjusted the mirror and the seat, and looked at the dashboard carefully. I was going to need the windshield wipers, of course. This car was a new one, and the lights came on automatically, so that was one less worry.

I took a deep breath. This was at least phase three of the rescue of Bill. It was scary how much of this had happened by sheer chance, but the best-laid plans never take every happenstance into account anyway. Not possible. Generally, my plans tended to be what I called roomy.

I swung the car around and drove out of the courtyard. The drive swept in a graceful curve and went across the front of the main building. For the first time, I saw the facade of the mansion. It was as beautiful—white painted siding, huge columns—as I had imagined. Russell had spent a pretty penny renovating the place.

The driveway wound through grounds that still looked manicured even in their winter brown state, but that long driveway was all too short. I could see the wall ahead of me. There was the checkpoint at the gate, and it was manned. I was sweating despite the cold.

I stopped just before the gate. There was a little white cubicle to one side, and it was glass from waist level up. It extended inside and outside the wall, so guards could check both incoming and outgoing vehicles. I hoped it was heated, for the sake of the two Weres on duty. Both of them were wearing their leathers and looking mighty grumpy. They'd had a hard night, no doubt about it. As I pulled to a stop, I resisted an almost overwhelming temptation to plow right through those gates. One of the Weres came out. He was carrying a rifle, so it was a good thing I hadn't acted on that impulse.

"I guess Bernard told you all I'd be leaving this morning?" I said, after I'd rolled down my window. I attempted a smile.

"You the one who got staked last night?" My questioner was surly and stubbly, and he smelled like a wet dog.

"Yeah."

"How you feeling?"

"Better, thank you."

"You coming back for the crucifixion?"

Surely I hadn't heard him right. "Excuse me?" I asked faintly.

His companion, who'd come to stand in the hut's door, said, "Doug, shut up."

Doug glowered at his fellow Were, but he shrugged after the glower didn't have any effect. "Okay, you're cleared to go."

The gates opened, way too slowly to suit me. When they were wide, and the Weres had stepped back, I drove sedately through. I suddenly realized I had no idea which way to go, but it seemed correct to turn left, since I wanted to head back to Jackson. My subconscious was telling me we had turned right to enter the driveway the night before.

My subconscious was a big fat liar.

After five minutes, I was fairly positive I was lost, and the sun continued to rise, naturally, even through the mass of clouds. I couldn't remember how well the blanket covered Bill, and I wasn't sure how light-tight the trunk would be. After all, safe transportation of vampires was not something the carmakers would cover in their list of specs.

On the other hand, I told myself, the trunk would have to be waterproof—that was sure important—so lightproof couldn't be far behind. Nonetheless, it seemed vitally important to find a dark place to park the Lincoln for the remaining hours of the day. Though every impulse told me to drive hard and get as far away from the mansion as I could, just in case someone went checking for Bill and put two and two together, I pulled over to the side of the road and opened the glove compartment. God bless America! There was a map of Mississippi with an inset for Jackson.

Which would have helped if I'd had any idea where I was at the moment.

People making desperate escapes aren't supposed to get lost.

I took a few deep breaths. I pulled back out into the road and drove on until I saw a busy gas station. Though the Lincoln's tank was full (thank you, Eric) I pulled in and parked at one of the pumps. The car on the other side was a black Mercedes, and the woman pumping the gas was an intelligent-looking middle-aged woman dressed in casual, comfortable, nice clothes. As I got the windshield squeegee out of its vat of water, I said, "You wouldn't happen to know how to get back to I-20 from here, would you?"

"Oh, sure," she said. She smiled. She was the kind of person who just loves to help other people, and I was thanking my lucky stars I'd spotted her. "This is Madison, and Jackson is south of here. I-55 is maybe a mile over that way." She pointed west. "You take I-55 south, and you'll run right into I-20. Or, you could take . . ."

I was about to be overloaded with information. "Oh, that sounds perfect. Let me just do that, or I'll lose track."

"Sure, glad I could help."

"Oh, you surely did."

We beamed at each other, just two nice women. I had to fight an impulse to say, "There's a tortured vampire in my trunk," out of sheer giddiness. I had rescued Bill, and I was alive, and tonight we would be on our way back to Bon Temps. Life would be wonderfully trouble-free. Except, of course, for dealing with my unfaithful boyfriend, finding out if the werewolf's body we'd disposed of in Bon Temps had been found, waiting to hear the same about the werewolf who'd been stuffed in Alcide's closet, and waiting for the reaction of the queen of Louisiana to Bill's indiscretion with Lorena. His verbal indiscretion: I didn't think for one minute that she would care about his sexual activities.

Other than that, we were hunky-dory.

"Sufficient unto the day is the evil thereof," I told myself. That had been Gran's favorite Bible quotation. When I was about nine, I'd asked her to explain that to me, and she'd said, "Don't go looking for trouble; it's already looking for you."

Bearing that in mind, I cleared my mental decks. My next goal was simply to get back to Jackson and the shelter of the garage. I followed the instructions the kind woman had given me, and I had the relief of entering Jackson within a half hour.

I knew if I could find the state capitol, I could find Alcide's apartment building. I hadn't allowed for one-way streets, and I hadn't been paying awful close attention to directions when Alcide gave me my little tour of downtown Jackson. But there aren't that many five-story buildings in the whole state of Mississippi, even in the capital. After a tense period of cruising, I spotted it.

Now, I thought, *all my troubles will be over.* Isn't it dumb to think that? Ever?

I pulled into the area by the little guard cubicle, where you had to wait to be recognized while the guy flipped the switch, or punched the button, or whatever made the barrier lift up. I was terrified he might deny me entrance because I didn't have a special sticker, like Alcide did on his truck.

The man wasn't there. The cubicle was empty. Surely that was wrong? I frowned, wondering what to do. But here the guard came, in his heavy brown uniform, trudging up the ramp. When he saw I was waiting, he looked stricken, and hurried up to the car. I sighed. I would have to talk to him after all. I pushed the button that would lower my window.

"I'm sorry I was away from my post," he said instantly. "I had to, ah . . . personal needs."

I had a little leverage here.

"I had to go borrow me a car," I said. "Can I get a temporary sticker?" I looked at him in a way that clued him in to my mindset. That look said, "Don't hassle me about getting the sticker, and I won't say a word about you leaving your post."

"Yes, ma'am. That's apartment 504?"

"You have a wonderful memory," I said, and his seamed face flushed.

"Part of the job," he said nonchalantly, and handed me a laminated number that I stuck on the dashboard. "If you'll just hand that in when you leave for good, please? Or if you plan on staying, you'll have to fill out a form we can have on file, and we'll give you a sticker. Actually," he said, stumbling a little, embarrassed, "Mr. Herveaux will have to fill it out, as the property owner."

"Sure," I said. "No problem." I gave him a cheery wave, and he retreated to the cubicle to raise the barrier.

I drove into the dark parking garage, feeling that rush of relief that follows clearing a major hurdle.

Reaction set in. I was shaking all over when I took the keys out of the ignition. I thought I saw Alcide's pickup over a couple of rows, but I had parked as deeply in the garage as I could—in the darkest corner, away from all the other cars, as it happened. This was as far as I had planned. I had no idea what to do next. I hadn't really believed I would get this far. I leaned back in the comfortable seat just for a minute, to relax and stop shaking before I got out. I'd had the heater on full blast during my drive from the mansion, so it was toasty warm inside the car.

When I woke up, I'd been asleep for hours.

The car was cold, and I was colder, despite the stolen quilted jacket. I got out of the driver's seat stiffly, stretching and bending to relieve cramped joints.

Maybe I should check on Bill. He had gotten rolled around in the trunk, I was sure, and I needed to make sure he was covered.

Actually, I just wanted to see him again. My heart actually beat faster at the thought. I was a real idiot.

I checked my distance from the weak sunlight at the entrance; I was well away. And I had parked so the trunk opening was pointed away from that bit of sunlight.

Yielding to temptation, I stepped around to the back of the car. I turned the key in the lock, pulled it out and popped it in my jacket pocket, and watched as the lid rose.

In the dim garage, I couldn't see too well, and it was hard to make out even the fuzzy yellow blanket. Bill appeared to be pretty well concealed. I bent over a little more, so I could arrange a fold further over his head. I had only a second's warning, a scuff of a shoe against the concrete, and then I felt a forceful shove from behind.

I fell into the trunk on top of Bill.

An instant and extra shove brought my legs in, and the trunk slammed shut.

Now Bill and I were locked in the trunk of the Lincoln.

Chapter 12

DEBBIE. I FIGURED it had been Debbie. After I got over my initial flood of panic, which lasted longer than I wanted to admit, I tried to relive the few seconds carefully. I'd caught a trace of brain pattern, enough to inform me that my attacker was a shifter. I figured it must have been Alcide's former girlfriend—his not-so-former girlfriend, apparently, since she was hanging around his garage.

Had she been waiting for me to return to Alcide since the night before? Or had she met up with him at some point during the craziness of the full moon? Debbie had been even more angered by my escorting Alcide than I could have imagined. Either she loved him, or she was extremely possessive.

Not that her motivation was any big concern right now. My big concern was air. For the first time, I felt lucky that Bill didn't breathe.

I made my own breath slow and even. No deep, panicky gasps, no thrashing. I made myself figure things out. Okay, I'd entered the trunk probably about, hmm, one p.m. Bill would wake around five, when it was getting dark. Maybe he'd sleep a little longer, because he'd been so exhausted—but no later than six-thirty, for sure. When he was awake, he'd be able to get us out of here. Or would he? He was very weak. He'd been terribly injured, and his injuries would take a while in healing, even for a vampire. He would need rest and blood before he'd be up to par. And he hadn't had any blood in a week. As that thought passed through my mind, I suddenly felt cold.

Cold all over.

Bill would be hungry. Really, really hungry. Crazy hungry.

And here I was—fast food.

Would he know who I was? Would he realize it was me, in time to stop?

It hurt even worse to think that he might not care enough anymore—care enough about me—to stop. He might just keep sucking and sucking, until I was drained dry. After all, he'd had an affair with Lorena. He'd seen me kill her, right in front of his eyes. Granted, she'd betrayed and tortured him, and that should have doused his ardor, right there. But aren't relationships crazy anyway?

Even my grandmother would have said, "Oh, *shit.*"

Okay. I had stay calm. I had to breathe shallow and slow to save air. And I had to rearrange our bodies, so I could be more comfortable. I was relieved this was the biggest trunk I'd ever seen, because that made such a maneuver possible. Bill was limp—well, he was dead, of course. So I could sort of shove him without worrying too much about the consequences. The trunk was cold, too, and I tried to unwrap Bill a little bit so I could share the blanket.

The trunk was also quite dark. I could write the car designer a letter, and let him know I could vouch for its light-tightness, if that was how you'd put it. If I got out of here alive, that is. I felt the shape of the two bottles of blood. Maybe Bill would be content with that?

Suddenly, I remembered an article I'd read in a news magazine while I was waiting in the dentist's office. It was about a woman who'd been taken hostage and forced into the trunk of her own car, and she'd been campaigning ever since to have inside latches installed in trunks so any captive could release herself. I wondered if she'd influenced the people who made Lincolns. I felt all around the trunk, at least the parts I could reach, and I did feel a latch release, maybe; there was a place where wires were sticking into the trunk. But whatever handle they'd been attached to had been clipped off.

I tried pulling, I tried yanking to the left or right. Damn it, this just wasn't right. I almost went nuts, there in that trunk. The means of escape was in there with me, and I couldn't make it work. My fingertips went over and over the wires, but to no purpose.

The mechanism had been disabled.

I tried real hard to figure out how that could have happened. I am ashamed to confess, I wondered if somehow Eric knew I'd be shut in the trunk, and this was his way of saying, "That's what you get for preferring Bill." But I just couldn't believe that. Eric sure had some big blank moral blind spots, but I didn't think he'd do that to me. After all, he hadn't reached his stated goal of having me, which was the nicest way I could put it to myself.

Since I had nothing else to do but think, which didn't take up extra oxygen, as far as I knew, I considered the car's previous owner. It occurred to me that Eric's friend had pointed out a car that would be easy to steal; a car belonging to someone who was sure to be out late at night, someone who could afford a fine car, someone whose trunk would hold the litter of cigarette papers, powder, and Baggies.

Eric had liberated the Lincoln from a drug dealer, I was willing to bet. And that drug dealer had disabled the inner trunk release for reasons I didn't even want to think about too closely.

Oh, give me a break, I thought indignantly. (It was easy just then to forget the many breaks I'd had during the day.) Unless I got a final break, and got out of this trunk before Bill awoke, none of the others would exactly count.

It was a Sunday, and very close to Christmas, so the garage was silent. Maybe some people had gone home for the holidays, and the legislators had gone home to their constituency, and the other people were busy doing . . . Christmas, Sunday stuff. I heard one car leave while I lay there, and then I heard voices after a time; two people getting off the elevator. I screamed, and banged on the trunk lid, but the sound was swallowed up in the starting of a big engine. I quieted immediately, frightened of using more air than I could afford.

I'll tell you, time spent in the nearly pitch-black dark, in a confined space, waiting for something to happen—that's pretty awful time. I didn't have a watch on; I would have had to have one with those hands that light up, anyway. I never fell asleep, but I drifted into an odd state of suspension. This was mostly due to the cold, I expect. Even with the quilted jacket and the blanket, it was very cold in the trunk. Still, cold, unmoving, dark, silent. My mind drifted.

Then I was terrified.

Bill was moving. He stirred, made a pain noise. Then his body seemed to go tense. I knew he had smelled me.

"Bill," I said hoarsely, my lips almost too stiff with cold to move. "Bill, it's me, Sookie. Bill, are you okay? There's some bottled blood in here. Drink it *now.*"

He struck.

In his hunger, he made no attempt to spare me anything, and it hurt like the six shades of hell.

"Bill, it's me," I said, starting to cry. "Bill, it's me. Don't do this, honey. Bill, it's Sookie. There's TrueBlood in here."

But he didn't stop. I kept talking, and he kept sucking, and I was becoming even colder, and very weak. His arms were clamping me to him, and struggling was no use, it would only excite him more. His leg was slung over my legs.

"Bill," I whispered, thinking it was already maybe too late. With the little strength I had left, I pinched his ear with the fingers of my right hand. "Please listen, Bill."

"Ow," he said. His voice sounded rough; his throat was sore. He had stopped taking blood. Now another need was on him, one closely related to feeding. His hands pulled down my sweatpants, and after a lot of fumbling and rearranging and contorting, he entered me with no preparation at all. I screamed, and he clapped a hand over my mouth. I was crying, sobbing, and my nose was all stopped up, and I needed to breathe through my mouth. All restraint left me and I began fighting like a wildcat. I bit and scratched and kicked, not caring about the air supply, not caring that I would enrage him. I just had to have air.

After a few seconds, his hand fell away. And he stopped moving. I drew air in with a deep, shuddering gasp. I was crying in earnest, one sob after another.

"Sookie?" Bill said uncertainly. "Sookie?"

I couldn't answer.

"It's you," he said, his voice hoarse and wondering. "It's you. You were really there in that room?"

I tried to gather myself, but I felt very fuzzy and I was afraid I was going to faint. Finally, I was able to say, "Bill," in a whisper.

"It is you. Are you all right?"

"No," I said almost apologetically. After all, it was Bill who'd been held prisoner and tortured.

"Did I . . ." He paused, and seemed to brace himself. "Have I taken more blood than I should?"

I couldn't answer. I laid my head on his arm. It seemed too much trouble to speak.

"I seem to be having sex with you in a closet," Bill said in a subdued voice. "Did you, ah, volunteer?"

I turned my head from side to side, then let it loll on his arm again.

"Oh, no," he whispered. "Oh, no." He pulled out of me and fumbled around a lot for the second time. He was putting me back to rights; himself, too, I guess. His hands patted our surroundings. "Car trunk," he muttered.

"I need air," I said, in a voice almost too soft to hear.

"Why didn't you say so?" Bill punched a hole in the trunk. He *was* stronger. Good for him.

Cold air rushed in and I sucked it deep. Beautiful, beautiful oxygen.

"Where are we?" he asked, after a moment.

"Parking garage," I gasped. "Apartment building. Jackson." I was so weak, I just wanted to let go and float away.

"Why?"

I tried to gather enough energy to answer him. "Alcide lives here," I managed to mutter, eventually.

"Alcide who? What are we supposed to do now?"

"Eric's . . . coming. Drink the bottled blood."

"Sookie? Are you all right?"

I couldn't answer. If I could have, I might have said, "Why do you care? You were going to leave me anyway." I might have said, "I forgive you," though that doesn't seem real likely. Maybe I would have just told him that I'd missed him, and that his secret was still safe with me; faithful unto death, that was Sookie Stackhouse.

I heard him open a bottle.

As I was drifting off in a boat down a current that seemed to be moving ever faster, I realized that Bill had never revealed my name. I knew they had tried to find it out, to kidnap me and bring me to be tortured in front of him for extra leverage. And he hadn't told.

The trunk opened with a noise of tearing metal.

Eric stood outlined by the fluorescent lights of the garage. They'd come on when it got dark. "What are you two doing in here?" he asked.

But the current carried me away before I could answer.

"SHE'S COMING AROUND," Eric observed. "Maybe that was enough blood." My head buzzed for a minute, went silent again.

"She really is," he was saying next, and my eyes flickered open to register three anxious male faces hovering above me: Eric's, Alcide's, and Bill's. Somehow, the sight made me want to laugh. So many men at home were scared of me, or didn't want to think about me, and here were the three men in the world who wanted to have sex with me, or who at least had thought about it seriously; all crowding around the bed. I giggled, actually giggled, for the first time in maybe ten years. "The Three Musketeers," I said.

"Is she hallucinating?" Eric asked.

"I think she's laughing at us," Alcide said. He didn't sound unhappy about that. He put an empty TrueBlood bottle on the vanity table behind him. There was a large pitcher beside it, and a glass.

Bill's cool fingers laced with mine. "Sookie," he said, in that quiet voice that always sent shivers down my spine. I tried to focus on his face. He was sitting on the bed to my right.

He looked better. The deepest cuts were scars on his face, and the bruises were fading.

"They said, was I coming back for the crucifixion?" I told him.

"Who said that to you?" He bent over me, his face intent, dark eyes wide.

"Guards at the gate."

"The guards at the gates of the mansion asked you if you were coming back for a crucifixion tonight? This night?"

"Yes."

"Whose?"

"Don't know."

"I would have expected you to say, 'Where am I? What happened to me?' " Eric said. "Not ask whose crucifixion would be taking place—perhaps is taking place," he corrected himself, glancing at the clock by the bed.

"Maybe they meant mine?" Bill looked a little stunned by the idea. "Maybe they decided to kill me tonight?"

"Or perhaps they caught the fanatic who tried to stake Betty Joe?" Eric suggested. "He would be a prime candidate for crucifixion."

I thought it over, as much as I was able to reason through the weariness that kept threatening to overwhelm me. "Not the picture I got," I whispered. My neck was very, very sore.

"You were able to read something from the Weres?" Eric asked.

I nodded. "I think they meant Bubba," I whispered, and everyone in the room froze.

"That cretin," Eric said savagely, after he'd had time to process that. "They caught him?"

"Think so." That was the impression I'd gotten.

"We'll have to retrieve him," Bill said. "If he's still alive."

It was very brave for Bill to say he would go back in that compound. I would never have said that, if I'd been him.

The silence that had fallen was distinctly uneasy.

"Eric?" Bill's dark eyebrows arched; he was waiting for a comment.

Eric looked royally angry. "I guess you are right. We have the responsibility of him. I can't believe his home state is willing to execute him! Where is their loyalty?"

"And you?" Bill's voice was considerably cooler as he asked Alcide.

Alcide's warmth filled the room. So did the confused tangle of his thoughts. He'd spent part of last night with Debbie, all right.

"I don't see how I can," Alcide said desperately. "My business, my father's, depends on my being able to come here often. And if I'm on the outs with Russell and his crew, that would be almost impossible. It's going to be difficult enough when they realize Sookie must be the one who stole their prisoner."

"And killed Lorena," I added.

Another pregnant silence.

Eric began to grin. "You offed Lorena?" He had a good grasp of the vernacular, for a very old vampire.

It was hard to interpret Bill's expression. "Sookie staked her," he said. "It was a fair kill."

"She killed Lorena in a fight?" Eric's grin grew even broader. He was as proud as if he'd heard his firstborn reciting Shakespeare.

"Very *short* fight," I said, not wanting to take any credit that was not due me. If you could term it credit.

"Sookie killed a vampire," Alcide said, as if that raised me in his evaluation, too. The two vampires in the room scowled.

Alcide poured and handed me a big glass of water. I drank it, slowly and painfully. I felt appreciably better after a minute or two.

"Back to the original subject," Eric said, giving me another meaningful look to show me he had more to say about the killing of Lorena. "If Sookie has not been pegged as having helped Bill escape, she is the best choice to get us back on the grounds without setting off alarms. They might not be expecting her, but they won't turn her away, either, I'm sure. Especially if she says she has a message for Russell from the queen of Louisiana, or if she says she has something she wants to return to Russell . . ." He shrugged, as if to say surely we could make up a good story.

I didn't want to go back in there. I thought of poor Bubba, and tried to worry about his fate—which he might have already met—but I was just too weak to worry about it.

"Flag of truce?" I suggested. I cleared my throat. "Do the vampires have such a thing?"

Eric looked thoughtful. "Of course, then I'd have to explain who I am," he said.

Happiness had made Alcide a lot easier to read. He was thinking about how soon he could call Debbie.

I opened my mouth, reconsidered, shut it, opened it again. What the hell. "Know who pushed me in the trunk and slammed it shut?" I asked Alcide. His green eyes locked onto me. His face became still, contained, as if he was afraid emotion would leak out. He turned and left the room, pulling the door shut behind him. For the first time, I registered that I was back in the guest bedroom in his apartment.

"So, who did the deed, Sookie?" Eric asked.

"His ex-girlfriend. Not so ex, after last night."

"Why would she do that?" Bill asked.

There was another significant silence. "Sookie was represented as Alcide's new girlfriend to gain entrée to the club," Eric said delicately.

"Oh," Bill said. "Why did you need to go to the club?"

"You must have gotten hit on the head a few times, Bill," Eric said coldly. "She was trying to 'hear' where they had taken you."

This was getting too close to things Bill and I had to talk about alone.

"It's dumb to go back in there," I said. "What about a phone call?"

They both stared at me like I was turning into a frog.

"Well, what a good idea," Eric said.

THE PHONE, AS it turned out, was just listed under Russell Edgington's name; not "Mansion of Doom," or "Vampires R Us." I worked on getting my story straight as I downed the contents of a big opaque plastic mug. I hated the taste of the synthetic blood Bill insisted I drink, so he'd mixed it with apple juice, and I was trying not to look as I gulped it down.

They'd made me drink it straight when they'd gotten up to Alcide's apartment that evening; and I didn't ask them how. At least I knew why the clothes I'd borrowed from Bernard were really horrible now. I looked like I'd had my throat cut, instead of mangled by Bill's painful bite. It was still very sore, but it was better.

Of course I had been picked to make the call. I never met a man yet, above the age of sixteen, who liked to talk on the phone.

"Betty Joe Pickard, please," I said to the male voice that answered the phone.

"She's busy," he said promptly.

"I need to talk to her right now."

"She's otherwise engaged. May I take your number?"

"This is the woman who saved her life last night." No point beating around the bush. "I need to talk to her, right now. Tout de suite."

"I'll see."

There was a long pause. I could hear people walking by the phone from time to time, and I heard a lot of cheering that sounded as if it was coming from a distance. I didn't want to think about that too much. Eric, Bill, and Alcide—who had finally stomped back into the room when Bill had asked him if we could borrow his phone—were standing there making all kinds of faces at me, and I just shrugged back.

Finally, there was the click, click, click of heels on tile.

"I'm grateful, but you can't bank on this forever," Betty Jo Pickard said briskly. "We arranged for your healing, you had a place to stay to recuperate. We didn't erase your memory," she added, as if that was a little detail that had escaped her until just this moment. "What have you called to ask?"

"You have a vampire there, an Elvis impersonator?"

"So?" Suddenly she sounded very wary. "We caught an intruder within our walls last night, yes."

"This morning, after I left your place, I was stopped again," I said. We had figured this would sound convincing because I sounded so hoarse and weak.

There was a long silence while she thought through the implications. "You have a habit of being in the wrong place," she said, as if she were remotely sorry for me.

"They are getting me to call you now," I said carefully. "I am supposed to tell you that the vampire you have there, he's the real thing."

She laughed a little. "Oh, but . . ." she began. Then she fell silent. "You're shitting me, right?" Mamie Eisenhower would never have said *that,* I was willing to swear.

"Absolutely not. There was a vamp working in the morgue that night," I croaked. Betty Jo made a sound that came out between a gasp and a choke. "Don't call him by his real name. Call him 'Bubba.' And for goodness' sake, don't hurt him."

"But we've already . . . hold on!"

She ran. I could hear the urgent sound die away.

I sighed, and waited. After a few seconds, I was completely nuts with the two guys standing around looking down at me. I was strong enough to sit up, I figured.

Bill gently held me up, while Eric propped pillows behind my back. I was glad to see one of them had had the presence of mind to spread the yellow blanket over the bed so I wouldn't stain the bedspread. All this while, I'd held the phone clamped to my ear, and when it squawked, I was actually startled.

"We got him down in time," Betty Joe said brightly.

"The call came in time," I told Eric. He closed his eyes and seemed to be offering up a prayer. I wondered to whom Eric prayed. I waited for further instructions.

"Tell them," he said, "to just let him go, and he will take himself home. Tell them that we apologize for letting him stray."

I relayed that message from my "abductors."

Betty Jo was quick to dismiss the directions. "Would you ask if he could stay and sing to us a little? He's in pretty good shape," she said.

So I relayed *that*. Eric rolled his eyes. "She can ask him, but if he says no, she must take it to heart and not ask him anymore," he said. "It just upsets him, if he's not in the mood. And sometimes when he does sing, it brings back memories, and he gets, ah, obstreperous."

"All right," she said, after I'd explained. "We'll do our best. If he doesn't want to sing, we'll let him go right away." From the sound of it, she turned to someone by her. "He can sing, if he'll consent," she said, and the someone said, "Yippee!" Two big nights in a row for the crowd at the king of Mississippi's mansion, I guess.

Betty Joe said into the telephone, "I hope you get out of your difficulties. I don't know how whoever's got you got lucky enough to have the care of the greatest star in the world. Would he consider negotiating?"

She didn't know yet about the troubles that entailed. "Bubba" had an unfortunate predilection for cat blood, and he was addlepated, and he could only follow the simplest directions; though every now and then, he exhibited a streak of shrewdness. He followed directions quite literally.

"She wants permission to keep him," I told Eric. I was tired of being the go-between. But Betty Joe couldn't meet with Eric, or she'd know he was the supposed friend of Alcide's who'd helped me get to the mansion the night before.

This was all too complicated for me.

"Yes?" Eric said into the telephone. Suddenly he had an English accent. Mr. Master of Disguise. Soon he was saying things like, "He's a sacred trust," and, "You don't know what you're biting off," into the phone. (If I'd had any sense of humor that night, I would have thought the last statement was pretty funny.) After a little more conversation, he hung up, with a pleased air.

I was thinking how strange it was that Betty Joe hadn't indicated that anything else was amiss at the compound. She hadn't accused Bubba of taking their prisoner, and she hadn't commented on finding the body of Lorena. Not that she'd necessarily mention these things in a phone conversation with a human stranger; and, for that matter, not that there'd be much to find; vampires disintegrate pretty quickly. But the silver chains would still be in the pool, and maybe enough sludge to identify as the corpse of a vampire. Of course, why would anyone look under the pool cover? But surely someone had noticed their star prisoner was gone?

Maybe they were assuming Bubba had freed Bill while he was roaming the compound. We'd told him not to say anything, and he would follow that directive to the letter.

Maybe I was off the hook. Maybe Lorena would be completely dissolved by the time they started to clean the pool in the spring.

The topic of corpses reminded me of the body we'd found stuffed in the closet of this apartment. Someone sure knew where we were, and someone sure didn't like us. Leaving the body there was an attempt to tie us to the crime of murder, which, actually, I had committed. I just hadn't done that particular murder. I wondered if the body of Jerry Falcon had been discovered yet. The chance seemed remote. I opened my mouth to ask Alcide if it had been on the news, and then I closed it again. I lacked the energy to frame the sentence.

My life was spinning out of control. In the space of two days I'd hidden one corpse and created another one. And all because I'd fallen in love with a vampire. I gave Bill an unloving glance. I was so absorbed in my thoughts, I hardly heard the telephone. Alcide, who had gone into the kitchen, must have answered it on the first ring.

Alcide appeared in the door of the bedroom. "Move," he said, "you all have to move next door into the empty apartment. Quick, quick!"

Bill scooped me up, blanket and all. We were out the door and Eric was breaking the lock on the apartment next to Alcide's before you could say "Jack Daniels." I heard the slow grumble of the elevator arriving on the fifth floor as Bill closed the door behind us.

We stood stock-still in the empty cold living room of the barren apartment. The vampires were listening intently to what was going on next door. I began to shiver in Bill's arms.

To tell the truth, it felt great to be held by him, no matter how angry I had been at him, no matter how many issues we had to settle. To tell the truth, I had a dismayingly wonderful sense of homecoming. To tell the truth, no matter how battered my body was—and battered at his hands, or rather, his fangs—that body could hardly wait to meet up with his body again, buck naked, despite the terrible incident in the trunk. I sighed. I was disappointed in myself. I would have to stand up for my psyche, because my body was ready to betray me, big time. It seemed to be blacking out Bill's mindless attack.

Bill laid me on the floor in the smaller guest bedroom of this apartment as carefully as if I'd cost him a million dollars, and he swaddled me securely in the blanket. He and Eric listened at the wall, which was shared with Alcide's bedroom.

"What a bitch," Eric murmured. Oh. Debbie was back.

I closed my eyes. Eric made a little noise of surprise and I opened them again. He was looking at me, and there was that disconcerting amusement in his face again.

"Debbie stopped by his sister's house last night to grill her about you. Alcide's sister likes you very much," Eric said in a tiny whisper. "This angers the shape-shifter Debbie. She is insulting his sister in front of him."

Bill's face showed he was not so thrilled.

Suddenly every line in Bill's body became tense, as if someone had jammed Bill's finger in an electric socket. Eric's jaw dropped and he looked at me with an unreadable expression.

There was the unmistakable sound of a slap—even I could hear it—from the next room.

"Leave us for a moment," Bill said to Eric. I didn't like the sound of his voice.

I closed my eyes. I didn't think I was up to whatever would come next. I didn't want to argue with Bill, or upbraid him for his unfaithfulness. I didn't want to listen to explanations and excuses.

I heard the whisper of movement as Bill knelt beside me on the carpet. Bill stretched out beside me, turned on his side, and laid his arm across me.

"He just told this woman how good you are in bed," Bill murmured gently.

I came up from my prone position so fast that it tore my healing neck and gave me a twinge in my nearly healed side.

I clapped my hand to my neck and gritted my teeth so I wouldn't moan. When I could talk, I could only say, "He what? He *what*?" I was almost incoherent with anger. Bill gave me a piercing look, put his finger over his lips to remind me to be quiet.

"I *never* did," I whispered furiously. "But even if I had, you know what? It would serve you right, you betraying son of a bitch." I caught his eyes with mine and stared right into them. Okay, we were going to do this now.

"You're right," he murmured. "Lie down, Sookie. You are hurting."

"Of course I'm hurting," I whispered, and burst into tears. "And to have the others tell me, to hear that you were just going to pension me off and go live with her without even having the courage to talk to me about it yourself! Bill, how could you be capable of such a thing! I was idiot enough to think you really loved me!" With a savagery I could scarcely believe was coming from inside me, I tossed off the blanket and threw myself on him, my fingers scrabbling for his throat.

And to hell with the pain.

My hands could not circle his neck, but I dug in as hard as I could and I felt a red rage carry me away. I wanted to kill him.

If Bill had fought back, I could have kept it up, but the longer I squeezed, the more the fine rage ebbed away, leaving me cold and empty. I was straddling Bill, and he was prone on the floor, lying passively with his hands at his sides. My hands eased off of his neck and I used them to cover my face.

"I hope that hurt like hell," I said, my voice choking but clear enough.

"Yes," he said. "It hurt like hell."

Bill pulled me down to the floor by him, covered us both with the blanket. He gently pushed my head into the notch of his neck and shoulder.

We lay there in silence for what seemed like a long time, though maybe it was only minutes. My body nestled into his out of habit and out of a deep need; though I didn't know if the need was for Bill specifically, or the intimacy I'd only shared with him. I hated him. I loved him.

"Sookie," he said, against my hair, "I'm—"

"Hush," I said. "Hush." I huddled closer against him. I relaxed. It was like taking off an Ace bandage, one that had been wrapped too tight.

"You're wearing someone else's clothes," he whispered, after a minute or two.

"Yes, a vampire named Bernard. He gave me clothes to wear after my dress got ruined at the bar."

"At Josephine's?"

"Yes."

"How did your dress get ruined?"

"I got staked."

Everything about him went still. "Where? Did it hurt?" He folded down the blanket. "Show me."

"Of course it hurt," I said deliberately. "It hurt like hell." I lifted the hem of the sweatshirt carefully.

His fingers stroked the shiny skin. I would not heal like Bill. It might take a night or two more for him to become as smooth and perfect as he had been, but he would look just as before, despite a week of torture. I would have a scar the rest of my life, vampire blood or no vampire blood. The scar might not be as severe, and it was certainly forming at a phenomenal rate, but it was undeniably red and ugly, the flesh underneath it still tender, the whole area sore.

"Who did this to you?"

"A man. A fanatic. It's a long story."

"Is he dead?"

"Yeah. Betty Joe Pickard killed him with two big blows of her fist. It kind of reminded me of a story I read in elementary school, about Paul Bunyan."

"I don't know that story." His dark eyes caught mine.

I shrugged.

"As long as he's dead now." Bill had a good grip on that idea.

"Lots of people are dead now. All because of your program."

There was a long moment of silence.

Bill cast a glance at the door Eric had tactfully closed behind him. Of course, he was probably listening right outside, and like all vampires, Eric had excellent hearing. "It's safe?"

"Yes."

Bill's mouth was right by my ear. It tickled when he whispered, "Did they search my house?"

"I don't know. Maybe the vamps from Mississippi went in. I never had a chance to get over there after Eric and Pam and Chow came to tell me you'd been snatched."

"And they told you . . . ?"

"That you were planning on leaving me. Yes. They told me."

"I already got paid back for that piece of madness," Bill said.

"You might have been paid back enough to suit *you*," I said, "but I don't know if you've been paid back enough to suit *me*."

There was a long silence in the cold, empty room. It was quiet out in the living room, too. I hoped Eric had worked out what we were going to do next, and I hoped it involved going home. No matter what happened between Bill and me, I needed to be home in Bon Temps. I needed to go back to my job and my friends and I needed to see my brother. He might not be much, but he was what I had.

I wondered what was happening in the next apartment.

"When the queen came to me and said she'd heard I was working on a program that had never been attempted before, I was flattered," Bill told me. "The money she offered was very good, and she would have been within her rights not to offer any, since I am her subject."

I could feel my mouth twisting at hearing yet another reminder of how different Bill's world was from mine. "Who do you think told her?" I asked.

"I don't know. I don't really want to," Bill said. His voice sounded offhand, even gentle, but I knew better.

"You know I had been working on it for some time," Bill said, when he figured I wasn't going to say anything.

"Why?"

"Why?" He sounded oddly disconcerted. "Well, because it seemed like a good idea to me. Having a list of all America's vampires, and at least some of the rest of the world's? That was a valuable project, and actually, it was kind of fun to compile. And once I started doing research, I thought of including pictures. And aliases. And histories. It just grew."

"So you've been, um, compiling a—like a directory? Of vampires?"

"Exactly." Bill's glowing face lit up even brighter. "I just started one night, thinking how many other vampires I'd come across in my travels over the past century, and I started making a list, and then I started adding a drawing I'd done or a photograph I'd taken."

"So vampires do photograph? I mean, they show up in pictures?"

"Sure. We never liked to have our picture made, when photography became a common thing in America, because a picture was proof we'd been in a particular place at a particular time, and if we showed up looking exactly the same twenty years later, well, it was obvious what we were. But since we have admitted our existence, there is no point clinging to the old ways."

"I'll bet some vampires still do."

"Of course. There are some who still hide in the shadows and sleep in crypts every night."

(This from a guy who slept in the soil of the cemetery from time to time.)

"And other vampires helped you with this?"

"Yes," he said, sounding surprised. "Yes, a few did. Some enjoyed the exercise of memory . . . some used it as a reason to search for old acquaintances, travel to old haunts. I am sure that I don't have all the vampires in America, especially the recent immigrants, but I think I have probably eighty percent of them."

"Okay, so why is the queen so anxious to have this program? Why would the other vampires want it, once they learned about it? They could assemble all the same information, right?"

"Yes," he said. "But it would be far easier to take it from me. And as for why it's so desirable to have this program . . . wouldn't you like to have a booklet that listed all the other telepaths in the United States?"

"Oh, sure," I said. "I could get lots of tips on how to handle my problem, or maybe how to use it better."

"So, wouldn't it be good to have a directory of vampires in the United States, what they're good at, where their gifts lie?"

"But surely some vampires really wouldn't want to be in such a book," I said. "You've told me that some vamps don't want to come out, that they want to stay in the darkness and hunt secretly."

"Exactly."

"Those vamps are in there, too?"

Bill nodded.

"Do you want to get yourself staked?"

"I never realized how tempting this project would be to anyone else. I never thought of how much power it would give to the one who owned it, until others began trying to steal it."

Bill looked glum.

The sound of shouting in the apartment next door drew our attention.

Alcide and Debbie were at it again. They were really bad for each other. But some mutual attraction kept them ricocheting back to each other. Maybe, away from Alcide, Debbie was a nice person.

Nah, I couldn't bring myself to believe that. But maybe she was at least tolerable when Alcide's affections weren't an issue.

Of course they should separate. They should never be in the same room again.

And I had to take this to heart.

Look at me. Mangled, drained, staked, battered. Lying in a cold apartment in a strange city with a vampire who had betrayed me.

A big decision was standing right in front of my face, waiting to be recognized and enacted.

I shoved Bill away, and wobbled to my feet. I pulled on my stolen jacket. With his silence heavy at my back, I opened the door to the living room. Eric was listening with some amusement to the battle going on in the next apartment.

"Take me home," I said.

"Of course," he said. "Now?"

"Yes. Alcide can drop my things by when he goes back to Baton Rouge."

"Is the Lincoln drivable?"

"Oh, yes." I pulled the keys out of my pocket. "Here."

We walked out of the empty apartment and took the elevator down to the garage.

Bill didn't follow.

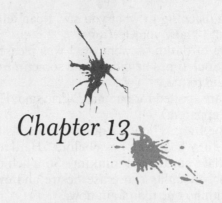

Chapter 13

ERIC CAUGHT UP with me as I was climbing into the Lincoln.

"I had to give Bill a few instructions about cleaning up the mess he caused," he said, though I didn't ask.

Eric was used to driving sports cars, and he had a few issues with the Lincoln.

"Had it occurred to you," he said, after we'd rolled out of the city's center, "that you tend to walk away when things between you and Bill become rocky? Not that I mind, necessarily, since I would be glad for you two to sever your association. But if this is the pattern you follow in your romantic attachments, I want to know now."

I thought of several things to say, discarded the first few, which would have blistered my grandmother's ears, and drew a deep breath.

"Firstly, Eric, what happens between Bill and me is just none of your damn business." I let that sink in for a few seconds. "Second, my relationship with Bill is the only one I've ever had, so I've never had any idea what I'm going to do even from day to day, much less establishing a policy." I paused to work on phrasing my next idea! "Third, I'm through with you all. I'm tired of seeing all this sick stuff. I'm tired of having to be brave, and having to do things that scare me, and having to hang out with the bizarre and the supernatural. I am just a regular person, and I just want to date regular people. Or at least people who are *breathing*."

Eric waited to see if I'd finished. I cast a quick glance over at him, and the streetlights illuminated his strong profile with its knife-edge nose. At least he wasn't laughing at me. He wasn't even smiling.

He glanced at me briefly before turning his attention back to the road. "I'm listening to what you say. I can tell you mean it. I've had your blood: I know your feelings."

A mile of darkness went by. I was pleased Eric was taking me seriously. Sometimes he didn't; and sometimes he didn't seem to care what he said to me.

"You are spoiled for humans," Eric said. His slight foreign accent was more apparent.

"Maybe I am. Though I don't see that as much of a loss, since I didn't have any luck with guys before." Hard to date, when you know exactly what your date is thinking. So much of the time, knowing a man's exact thoughts can erase desire and even liking. "But I'd be happier with no one than I am now."

I'd been considering the old Ann Landers rule of thumb: Would I be better off with him, or without him? My grandmother and Jason and I had read Ann Landers every day when Jason and I had been growing up. We'd discussed all Ann's responses to reader questions. A lot of the advice she'd ladled out had been intended to help women deal with guys like Jason, so he certainly brought perspective to the conversations.

Right at this moment, I was pretty darn sure I was better off without Bill. He'd used me and abused me, betrayed me and drained me.

He'd also defended me, avenged me, worshiped me with his body, and provided hours of uncritical companionship, a very major blessing.

Well, I just didn't have my scales handy. What I had was a heart full of hurt and a way to go home. We flew through the black night, wrapped in our own thoughts. Traffic was light, but this was an interstate, so of course there were cars around us from time to time.

I had no idea what Eric was thinking about, a wonderful feeling. He might be debating pulling over to the shoulder and breaking my neck, or he might be wondering what tonight's take at Fangtasia would add up to. I wanted him to talk to me. I wished he would tell me about his life before he became a vampire, but that's a real touchy subject with lots of vamps, and I wasn't about to bring it up tonight of all nights.

About an hour out of Bon Temps, we took an exit ramp. We were a little low on gas, and I needed to use the ladies' room. Eric had already begun to fill the tank as I eased my sore body carefully out of the car. He had dismissed my offer to pump the gas with a courteous, "No, thank you." One other car was filling up, and the woman, a peroxide blond about my age, hung up the nozzle as I got out of the Lincoln.

At one in the morning, the gas station/convenience store was almost empty besides the young woman, who was heavily made up and wrapped in a quilted coat. I spied a battered Toyota pickup parked by the side of the filling station, in the only shadow on the lot. Inside the pickup, two men were sitting, involved in a heated conversation.

"It's too cold to be sitting outside in a pickup," the dark-rooted blond said, as we went through the glass doors together. She gave an elaborate shiver.

"You'd think so," I commented. I was halfway down the aisle by the back of the store, when the clerk, behind a high counter on a raised platform, turned away from his little television to take the blond's money.

The door to the bathroom was hard to shut behind me, since the wooden sill had swollen during some past leakage. In fact, it probably didn't shut all the way behind me, since I was in something of a hurry. But the stall door shut and locked, and it was clean enough. In no hurry to get back in the car with the silent Eric, I took my time after using the facilities. I peered in the mirror over the sink, expecting I'd look like holy hell and not being contradicted by what I saw reflected there.

The mangled bite mark on my neck looked really disgusting, as though a dog had had hold of me. As I cleaned the wound with soap and wet paper towels, I wondered if having ingested vampire blood would give me a specific quantity of extra strength and healing, and then be exhausted, or if it was good for a certain amount of time like a time-release capsule, or what the deal was. After I'd had Bill's blood, I'd felt great for a couple of months.

I didn't have a comb or brush or anything, and I looked like something the cat dragged in. Trying to tame my hair with my fingers just made a bad thing worse. I washed my face and neck, and stepped back into the glare of the store. I hardly registered that once again the door didn't shut behind me, instead lodged quietly on the swollen sill. I emerged behind the last long aisle of groceries, crowded with Corn-Nuts and Lays Chips and Moon Pies and Scotch Snuf and Prince Albert in a can . . .

And two armed robbers up by the clerk's platform inside the door.

Holy Moses, why don't they just give these poor clerks shirts with big targets printed on them? That was my first thought, detached, as if I were watching a movie with a convenience store robbery. Then I snapped into the here and now, tuned in by the very real strain on the clerk's face. He was awfully young—a reedy, blotched teenager. And he was facing the two big guys with guns. His hands were in the air, and he was mad as hell. I would have expected blubbering for his life, or incoherence, but this boy was furious.

It was the fourth time he'd been robbed, I read fresh from his brain. And the third time at gunpoint. He was wishing he could grab the shotgun under the seat in his truck behind the store and blast these sumbitches to hell.

And no one acknowledged that I was there. They didn't seem to know.

Not that I was complaining, okay?

I glanced behind me, to verify that the door to the bathroom had stuck open again, so its sound would not betray me. The best thing for me to do would be to creep out the back door to this place, if I could find it, and run around the building to get Eric to call the police.

Wait a minute. Now that I was thinking of Eric, where was he? Why hadn't he come in to pay for the gas?

If it was possible to have a foreboding any more ominous than the one I already had, that fit the bill. If Eric hadn't come in yet, Eric wasn't coming. Maybe he'd decided to leave. Leave me.

Here.

Alone.

Just like Bill left you, my mind supplied helpfully. Well, thanks a hell of a lot, Mind.

Or maybe they'd shot him. If he'd taken a head wound . . . and there was no healing a heart that had taken a direct hit with a big-caliber bullet.

There was no point whatsoever in standing there worrying.

This was a typical convenience store. You came in the front door, and the clerk was behind a long counter to your right, up on a platform. The cold drinks were in the refrigerator case that took up the left wall. You were facing three long aisles running the width of the store, plus various special displays and stacks of insulated mugs and charcoal briquettes and birdseed. I was all the way at the back of the store and I could see the clerk (easily) and the crooks (just barely) over the top of the groceries. I had to get out of the store, preferably unseen. I spotted a splintered wooden door, marked "Employees Only" farther along the back wall. It was actually beyond the counter behind which the clerk stood. There was a gap between the end of the counter and the wall, and from the end of my aisle to the beginning of that counter, I'd be exposed.

Nothing would be gained by waiting.

I dropped to my hands and knees and began crawling. I moved slowly, so I could listen, too.

"You seen a blond come in here, about this tall?" the burlier of the two robbers was saying, and all of a sudden I felt faint.

Which blond? Me, or Eric? Or the peroxide blond? Of course, I couldn't see the height indication. Were they looking for a male vampire or a female telepath? Or . . . after all, I wasn't the only woman in the world who could get into trouble, I reminded myself.

"Blond woman come in here five minutes ago, bought some cigarettes," the boy said sullenly. Good for you, fella!

"Naw, that one done drove off. We want the one who was with the vampire."

Yep, that would be me.

"I didn't see no other woman," the boy said. I glanced up a little and saw the reflection off a mirror mounted up in the corner of the store. It was a security mirror so the clerk could detect shoplifters. I thought, *He can see me crouching here. He knows I'm here.*

God bless him. He was doing his best for me. I had to do my best for him. At the same time, if we could avoid getting shot, that would be a very good thing. And where the hell was Eric?

Blessing my borrowed sweatpants and slippers for being soft and silent, I crept deliberately toward the stained wooden "Employees Only" door. I wondered if it creaked. The two robbers were still talking to the clerk, but I blocked out their voices so I could concentrate on reaching the door.

I'd been scared before, plenty of times, but this was right up there with the scariest events of my life. My dad had hunted, and Jason and his buddies hunted, and I'd watched a massacre in Dallas. I knew what bullets could do. Now that I'd reached the end of the aisle, I'd come to the end of my cover.

I peered around the display counter's end. I had to cross about four feet of open floor to reach the partial shelter of the long counter that ran in front of the cash register. I would be lower and well hidden from the robbers' perspective, once I crossed that empty space.

"Car pulling in," the clerk said, and the two robbers automatically looked out the plate glass window to see. If I hadn't known what he was doing telepathically, I might have hesitated too long. I scuttled across the exposed linoleum faster than I would have believed possible.

"I don't see no car," said the less bulky man.

The clerk said, "I thought I heard the bell ring, the one that goes when a car drives across it."

I reached up and turned the knob on the door. It opened quietly.

"It rings sometimes when there ain't nobody there," the boy continued, and I realized he was trying to make noise and hold their attention so I could get out the door. God bless him, all over again.

I pushed the door a little wider, and duck-walked through. I was in a narrow passage. There was another door at the end of it, a door that presumably led to the area behind the convenience store. In the door was a set of keys. They wisely kept the back door locked. From one of a row of nails by the back door hung a heavy camo jacket. I poked my hand down in the pocket on the right and came up with the boy's keys. That was just a lucky guess. It happens. Clutching them to prevent their jingling, I opened the back door and stepped outside.

There was nothing out here but a battered pickup and a reeking Dumpster. The lighting was poor, but at least there was some light. The blacktop was cracked. Since it was winter, the weeds that had sprouted up from those cracks were dry and bleached. I heard a little sound to my left and drew in a shaky breath after I'd jumped about a foot. The sound was caused by a huge old raccoon, and he ambled off into the small patch of woods behind the store.

I exhaled just as shakily as I'd drawn the air in. I made myself focus on the bunch of keys. Unfortunately, there were about twenty. This boy had more keys than squirrels had acorns. No one on God's green earth could possibly use this many keys. I flicked through them desperately, and finally selected one that had GM stamped on a black rubber cover. I unlocked the door and reached into the musty interior, which smelled strongly of cigarettes and dogs. Yes, the shotgun was under the seat. I broke it open. It was loaded. Thank God Jason believed in self-defense. He'd showed me how to load and fire his new Benelli.

Despite my new protection, I was so scared, I wasn't sure I could get around to the front of the store. But I had to scout out the situation, and find out what had happened to Eric. I eased down the side of the building where the old Toyota truck was parked. Nothing was in the back, except a little spot that picked up a stray fraction of light. The shotgun cradled in one arm, I reached down to run a finger over it.

Fresh blood. I felt old and cold. I stood with my head bowed for a long moment, and then I braced myself.

I looked in the driver's window to find the cab was unlocked. Well, happy days. I opened the door quietly, glanced in. There was a sizeable open box on the front seat, and when I checked its contents, my heart sank so low, I thought it'd come out the bottom of my shoes. On the outside, the box was stamped "Contents: Two." Now it contained one silver mesh net, the kind sold in "mercenary" magazines, the kind always advertised as "vampire proof."

That was like calling a shark cage a sure deterrent from shark bites.

Where was Eric? I glanced over the immediate vicinity, but I saw no other trace. I could hear traffic whooshing by on the interstate, but the silence hung over this bleak parking lot.

My eyes lit on a pocketknife on the dash. Yahoo! Carefully placing the shotgun on the front seat, I scooped up the knife, opened it, and held it ready to sink into the tire. Then I thought twice. A wholehearted tire-slashing was proof someone had been out here while the robbers were inside. That might not be a good thing. I contented myself with poking a single hole in the tire. It was just a smallish hole that might have come from anything, I told myself. If they did drive off, they'd have to stop somewhere down the road. Then I pocketed the knife—I was certainly quite the thief lately—and returned to the shadows around the building. This hadn't taken as long as you might think, but still it had been several minutes since I'd assessed the situation in the convenience store.

The Lincoln was still parked by the pumps. The gas port was closed, so I knew Eric had finished refueling before something had happened to him. I sidled around the corner of the building, hugging its lines. I found good cover at the front, in the angle formed by the ice machine and the front wall of the store. I risked standing up enough to peek over the top of the machine.

The robbers had come up into the higher area where the clerk stood, and they were beating on him.

Hey, now. That had to stop. They were beating him because they wanted to know where I was hiding, was my guess; and I couldn't let someone else get beaten up on my behalf.

"Sookie," said a voice right behind me.

The next instant a hand clapped across my mouth just as I was about to scream.

"Sorry," Eric whispered. "I should have thought of a better way to let you know I was here."

"Eric," I said, when I could speak. He could tell I was calmer, and he moved his hand. "We gotta save him."

"Why?"

Sometimes vampires just astound me. Well, people, too, but tonight it was a vampire.

"Because he's getting beaten for our sakes, and they're probably gonna kill him, and it'll be our fault!"

"They're robbing the store," Eric said, as if I were particularly dim. "They had a new vampire net, and they thought they'd try it out on me. They don't know it yet, but it didn't work. But they're just opportunistic scum."

"They're looking for *us,*" I said furiously.

"Tell me," he whispered, and I did.

"Give me the shotgun," he said.

I kept a good grip on it. "You know how to use one of these things?"

"Probably as well as you." But he looked at it dubiously.

"That's where you're wrong," I told him. Rather than have a prolonged argument while my new hero was getting internal injuries, I ran in a crouch around the ice machine, the propane gas rack, and through the front door into the store. The little bell over the door rang like crazy, and though with all the shouting they didn't seem to hear it, they sure paid attention when I fired a blast through the ceiling over their heads. Tiles, dust, and insulation rained down.

It almost knocked me flat—but not quite. I leveled the gun right on them. They were frozen. It was like playing Swing the Statue when I was little. But not quite. The poor pimply clerk had a bloody face, and I was sure his nose was broken, and some of his teeth knocked loose.

I felt a fine rage break out behind my eyes. "Let the young man go," I said clearly.

"You gonna shoot us, little lady?"

"You bet your ass I am," I said.

"And if she misses, I will get you," said Eric's voice, above and behind me. A big vampire makes great backup.

"The vampire got loose, Sonny." The speaker was a thinnish man with filthy hands and greasy boots.

"I see that," said Sonny, the heavier one. He was darker, too. The smaller man's head was covered with that no-color hair, the kind people call "brown" because they have to call it something.

The young clerk pulled himself up out of his pain and fear and came around the counter as fast as he could move. Mixed with the blood on his face was a lot of white powder from me shooting into the ceiling. He looked a sight.

"I see you found my shotgun," he said as he passed by me, carefully not getting between the bad guys and me. He pulled a cell phone out of his pocket, and I heard the tiny beeps as he pressed numbers. His growlly voice was soon in staccato conversation with the police.

"Before the police get here, Sookie, we need to find out who sent these two imbeciles," Eric said. If I'd been them, I'd have been mighty

scared at the tone of his voice, and they seemed to be aware of what
an angry vampire could do. For the first time Eric stepped abreast of
me and then a little bit ahead, and I could see his face. Burns crisscrossed it like angry strings of poison ivy welts. He was lucky only
his face had been bare, but I doubt he was feeling very lucky.

"Come down here," Eric said, and he caught the eyes of Sonny.

Sonny immediately walked down from the clerk's platform and
around the counter while his companion was gaping.

"Stay," said Eric. The no-color man squeezed his eyes shut so he
couldn't glimpse Eric, but he opened them just a crack when he heard
Eric take a step closer, and that was enough. If you don't have any
extra abilities yourself, you just can't look a vampire in the eyes. If
they want to, they'll get you.

"Who sent you here?" Eric asked softly.

"One of the Hounds of Hell," Sonny said, with no inflection in his
voice.

Eric looked startled. "A member of the motorcycle gang," I explained carefully, mindful that we had a civilian audience who was
listening with great curiosity. I was getting a great amplification of
the answers through their brains.

"What did they tell you to do?"

"They told us to wait along the interstate. There are more fellas
waiting at other gas stations."

They'd called about forty thugs altogether. They'd outlaid a lot of
cash.

"What were you supposed to watch for?"

"A big dark guy and a tall blond guy. With a blond woman, real
young, with nice tits."

Eric's hand moved too fast for me to track. I was only sure he'd
moved when I saw the blood running down Sonny's face.

"You are speaking of my future lover. Be more respectful. Why
were you looking for us?"

"We were supposed to catch you. Take you back to Jackson."

"Why?"

"The gang suspected you mighta had something to do with Jerry
Falcon's disappearance. They wanted to ask you some questions
about it. They had someone watching some apartment building, seen
you two coming out in a Lincoln, had you followed part of the way.
The dark guy wasn't with you, but the woman was the right one, so
we started tracking you."

"Do the vampires of Jackson know anything about this plan?"

"No, the gang figured it was their problem. But they also got a lot of other problems, a prisoner escape and so on, and lots of people out sick. So what with one thing and another, they recruited a bunch of us to help."

"What are these men?" Eric asked me.

I closed my eyes and thought carefully. "Nothing," I said. "They're nothing." They weren't shifters, or Weres, or anything. They were hardly human beings, in my opinion, but nobody died and made me God.

"We need to get out of here," Eric said. I agreed heartily. The last thing I wanted to do was spend the night at the police station, and for Eric, that was an impossibility. There wasn't an approved vampire jail cell any closer than Shreveport. Heck, the police station in Bon Temps had just gotten wheelchair accessible.

Eric looked into Sonny's eyes. "We weren't here," he said. "This lady and myself."

"Just the boy," Sonny agreed.

Again, the other robber tried to keep his eyes tight shut, but Eric blew in his face, and just as a dog would, the man opened his eyes and tried to wiggle back. Eric had him in a second, and repeated his procedure.

Then he turned to the clerk and handed him the shotgun. "Yours, I believe," Eric said.

"Thanks," the boy said, his eyes firmly on the barrel of the gun. He aimed at the robbers. "I know you weren't here," he growled, keeping his gaze ahead of him. "And I ain't saying nothing to the police."

Eric put forty dollars on the counter. "For the gas," he explained. "Sookie, let's make tracks."

"A Lincoln with a big hole in the trunk does stand out," the boy called after us.

"He's right." I was buckling up and Eric was accelerating as we heard sirens, pretty close.

"I should have taken the truck," Eric said. He seemed pleased with our adventure, now that it was over.

"How's your face?"

"It's getting better."

The welts were not nearly as noticeable.

"What happened?" I asked, hoping this was not a very touchy subject.

He cast me a sideways glance. Now that we were back on the interstate, we had slowed down to the speed limit, so it wouldn't seem to any of the many police cars converging on the convenience store that we were fleeing.

"While you were tending to your human needs in the bathroom," he said, "I finished putting gas in the tank. I had hung up the pump and was almost at the door when those two got out of the truck and just tossed a net over me. It is very humiliating, that they were able to do that, two fools with a silver net."

"Your mind must have been somewhere else."

"Yes," he said shortly. "It was."

"So then what happened?" I asked, when it seemed he was going to stop there.

"The heavier one hit me with the butt of his gun, and it took me a small time to recover," Eric said.

"I saw the blood."

He touched a place on the back of his head. "Yes, I bled. After getting used to the pain, I snagged a corner of the net on the bumper of their truck and managed to roll out of it. They were inept in that, as well as robbery. If they had tied the net shut with silver chains, the result might have been different."

"So you got free?"

"The head blow was more of a problem than I thought at first," Eric said stiffly. "I ran along the back of the store to the water spigot on the other side. Then I heard someone coming out of the back. When I was recovered, I followed the sounds and found you." After a long moment's silence, Eric asked me what had happened in the store.

"They got me confused with the other woman who went in the store at the same time I went to the ladies' room," I explained. "They didn't seem to be sure I was in the store, and the clerk was telling them that there had been only one woman, and she'd gone. I could tell he had a shotgun in his truck—you know, I heard it in his head—and I went and got it, and I disabled their truck, and I was looking for you because I figured something had happened to you."

"So you planned to save me and the clerk, together?"

"Well . . . yeah." I couldn't understand the odd tone of his voice. "I didn't feel like I had a whole lot of choices there."

The welts were just pink lines now.

The silence still didn't seem relaxed. We were about forty minutes from home now. I started to let it drop. I didn't.

"You don't seem too happy about something," I said, a definite edge to my voice. My own temper was fraying around the edges. I *knew* I was heading in the wrong direction conversationally; I *knew* I should just be content with silence, however brooding and pregnant.

Eric took the exit for Bon Temps and turned south.

Sometimes, instead of going down the road less taken, you just charge right down the beaten path.

"Would there be something *wrong* with me rescuing the two of you?" We were driving through Bon Temps now. Eric turned east after the buildings along Main gradually thinned and vanished. We passed Merlotte's, still open. We turned south again, on a small parish road. Then we were bumping down my driveway.

Eric pulled over and killed the engine. "Yes," he said. "There is something wrong with that. And why the hell don't you get your driveway fixed?"

The string of tension that had stretched between us popped. I was out of the car in a New York minute, and he was, too. We faced each other across the roof of the Lincoln, though not much of me showed. I charged around it until I was right in front of him.

"Because I can't afford it, that's why! I don't have any money! And you all keep asking me to take time off from my job to do stuff for you! I can't! I can't do it anymore!" I shrieked. "I quit!"

There was a long moment of silence while Eric regarded me. My chest was heaving underneath my stolen jacket. Something felt funny, something was bothering me about the appearance of my house, but I was too het up to examine my worry.

"Bill . . ." Eric began cautiously, and it set me off like a rocket.

"He's spending all his money on the freaking Bellefleurs," I said, my tone this time low and venomous, but no less sincere. "He never thinks about giving me money. And how could I take it? It would make me a kept woman, and I'm not his whore, I'm his . . . I used to be his girlfriend."

I took a deep, shuddering breath, dismally aware that I was going to cry. It would be better to get mad again. I tried. "Where do you get off, telling them that I'm your . . . your lover? Where'd that come from?"

"What happened to the money you earned in Dallas?" Eric asked, taking me completely by surprise.

"I paid my property taxes with it."

"Did you ever think that if you told me where Bill's hiding his computer program, I would give you anything you asked for? Did you not realize that Russell would have paid you handsomely?"

I sucked in my breath, so offended, I hardly knew where to begin.

"I see you didn't think of those things."

"Oh, yeah, I'm just an angel." Actually, none of those things had occurred to me, and I was almost defensive they hadn't. I was shaking with fury, and all my good sense went out the window. I would feel the presence of other brains at work, and the fact that someone was in my place enraged me farther. The rational part of my mind crumpled under the weight of my anger.

"Someone's waiting in my house, Eric." I swung around and stomped over to my porch, finding the key I'd hidden under the rocker my grandmother had loved. Ignoring everything my brain was trying to tell me, ignoring the beginning of a bellow from Eric, I opened the front door and got hit with a ton of bricks.

Chapter 14

"WE GOT HER," said a voice I didn't recognize. I had been yanked to my feet, and I was swaying between two men who were holding me up.

"What about the vamp?"

"I shot him twice, but he's in the woods. He got away."

"That's bad news. Work fast."

I could sense that there were many men in the room with me, and I opened my eyes. They'd turned on the lights. They were in my house. They were in my home. As much as the blow to my jaw, that made me sick. Somehow, I'd assumed my visitors would be Sam or Arlene or Jason.

There were five strangers in my living room, if I was thinking clearly enough to count. But before I could form another idea, one of the men—and now I realized he was wearing a familiar leather vest—punched me in the stomach.

I didn't have enough breath to scream.

The two men holding me pulled me back upright.

"Where is he?"

"Who?" I really couldn't remember, at this point, what particular missing person he wanted me to locate. But, of course, he hit me again. I had a dreadful minute when I needed to gag but hadn't the air to do it. I was strangling and suffocating.

Finally, I drew in a long breath. It was noisy and painful and just heaven.

My Were interrogator, who had light hair shaved close to his scalp and a nasty little goatee, slapped me, hard, open-handed. My head rocked on my neck like a car on faulty shock absorbers. "Where's the vampire, bitch?" the Were said. He drew his fist back.

I couldn't take any more of this. I decided to speed things up. I pulled my legs up, and while the two at my sides kept desperate grips on my arms, I kicked the Were in front of me with both feet. If I hadn't had on bedroom slippers, it probably would have been more effective. I'm never wearing safety boots when I need them. But Nasty Goatee did stagger back, and then he came for me with my death in his eyes.

By then my legs had swung back to the floor, but I made them keep going backward, and threw my two captors completely off balance. They staggered, tried to recover, but their frantic footing was in vain. Down we all went, the Were along with us.

This might not be better, but it was an improvement over waiting to get hit.

I'd landed on my face, since my arms and hands weren't under my control. One guy did let go as we fell, and when I got that hand underneath me for leverage, I yanked away from the other man.

I'd gotten halfway to my feet when the Were, quicker than the humans, managed to grab my hair. He dealt a slap to my face while he wound my hair around his hand for a better grip. The other hired hands closed in, either to help the two on the floor to rise, or just to see me get battered.

A real fight is over in a few minutes because people wear out quick. It had been a very long day, and the fact was, I was ready to give up against these overwhelming odds. But I had a little pride and I went for the guy closest to me, a potbellied pig of a man with greasy dark hair. I dug my fingers into his face, trying to cause any damage I could, while I could.

The Were kneed me in the belly and I screamed, and the pig-man began to yell for the others to get me off of him, and the front door crashed open as Eric came in, blood covering his chest and right leg. Bill was right behind him.

They lost all control.

I saw firsthand what a vampire could do.

After a second, I realized my help would not be needed, and I decided the Goddess of Really Tough Gals would have to excuse me while I closed my eyes.

In two minutes, all the men in my living room were dead.

"SOOKIE? SOOKIE?" ERIC's voice was hoarse. "Do we need to take her to the hospital?" he asked Bill.

I felt cool fingers on my wrist, touching my neck. I almost explained that for once I was conscious, but it was just too hard. The floor seemed like a good place to be.

"Her pulse is strong," Bill reported. "I'm going to turn her over."

"She's alive?"

"Yes."

Eric's voice, suddenly closer, said, "Is the blood hers?"

"Yes, some of it."

He drew a deep, shuddering breath. "Hers is different."

"Yes," Bill said coldly. "But surely you are full by now."

"It's been a long time since I had real blood in quantity," Eric said, just exactly like my brother, Jason, would have remarked it had been a long time since he'd had blackberry cobbler.

Bill slid his hands underneath me. "For me, too. We'll need to put them all out in the yard," he said casually, "and clean up Sookie's house."

"Of course."

Bill began rolling me over, and I began crying. I couldn't help it. As strong as I wanted to be, all I could think of was my body. If you've ever been really beaten, you'll know what I mean. When you've been really beaten, you realize that you are just an envelope of skin, an easily penetrated envelope that holds together a lot of fluids and some rigid structures, which in their turn can simply be broken and invaded. I thought I'd been badly hurt in Dallas a few weeks before, but this felt worse. I knew that didn't mean it was worse; there was a lot of soft tissue damage. In Dallas, my cheekbone had been fractured and my knee twisted. I thought maybe the knee had been compromised all over again, and I thought maybe one of the slaps had rebroken the cheekbone. I opened my eyes, blinked, and opened them again. My vision cleared after a few seconds.

"Can you speak?" Eric said, after a long, long moment.

I tried, but my mouth was so dry, nothing came out.

"She needs a drink." Bill went to the kitchen, having to take a less than direct route, since there were a lot of obstructions in the way.

Eric's hands stroked back my hair. He'd been shot, I remembered, and I wanted to ask him how he felt, but I couldn't. He was sitting on his butt beside me, leaning on the cushions of my couch. There was blood on his face, and he looked pinker than I'd ever seen him, ruddy with health. When Bill returned with my water—he'd even added a straw—I looked at his face. Bill looked almost sunburned.

Bill held me up carefully and put the straw to my lips. I drank, and it was the best thing I'd ever tasted.

"You killed them all," I said in a creaky voice.

Eric nodded.

I thought of the circle of brutish faces that had surrounded me. I thought of the Were slapping me in the face.

"Good," I said. Eric looked a little amused, just for a second. Bill didn't look anything in particular.

"How many?"

Eric looked around vaguely, and Bill pointed a finger silently as he toted them up.

"Seven?" Bill said doubtfully. "Two in the yard and five in the house?"

"I was thinking eight," Eric murmured.

"Why did they come after you like that?"

"Jerry Falcon."

"Oh," said Bill, a different note in his voice. "Oh, yes. I've encountered him. In the torture room. He is first on my list."

"Well, you can cross him off," Eric said. "Alcide and Sookie disposed of his body in the woods yesterday."

"Did this Alcide kill him?" Bill looked down at me, reconsidered. "Or Sookie?"

"He says no. They found the corpse in the closet of Alcide's apartment, and they hatched a plan to hide his remains." Eric sounded like that had been kind of cute of us.

"My Sookie hid a corpse?"

"I don't think you can be too sure about that possessive pronoun."

"Where did you learn that term, Northman?"

"I took 'English as a Second Language' at a community college in the seventies."

Bill said, "She is mine."

I wondered if my hands would move. They would. I raised both of them, making an unmistakable one-fingered gesture.

Eric laughed, and Bill said, "Sookie!" in shocked admonishment.

"I think that Sookie is telling us she belongs to herself," Eric said softly. "In the meantime, to finish our conversation, whoever stuffed the corpse in the closet meant to saddle Alcide with the blame, since Jerry Falcon had made a blatant pass at Sookie in the bar the night before, and Alcide had taken umbrage."

"So all this plot might be directed at Alcide instead of us?"

"Hard to say. Evidently, from what the armed robbers at the gas station told us, what's remaining of the gang called in all the thugs they knew and stationed them along the interstate to intercept us on the way back. If they'd just called ahead, they wouldn't now be in jail for armed robbery. And I'm certainly sure that's where they are."

"So how'd these guys get here? How'd they know where Sookie lived, who she really was?"

"She used her own name at Club Dead. They didn't know the name of Bill's human girlfriend. You were faithful."

"I hadn't been faithful in other ways," Bill said bleakly. "I thought it was the least I could do for her."

And this was the guy whom I'd shot the bird. On the other hand, this was the guy who was talking like I wasn't in the room. And most importantly, this was the guy who'd had another "darling," for whom he'd planned to leave me flat.

"So the Weres may not know she was your girlfriend; they only know she was staying in the apartment with Alcide when Jerry disappeared. They know Jerry may have come by the apartment. This Alcide says that the packmaster in Jackson told Alcide to leave and not return for a while, but that he believed Alcide had not killed Jerry."

"This Alcide . . . he seemed to have a troubled relationship with his girlfriend."

"She is engaged to someone else. She believes he is attached to Sookie."

"And is he? He has the gall to tell this virago Debbie that Sookie is good in bed."

"He wanted to make her jealous. He has not slept with Sookie."

"But he likes her." Bill made it sound like a capital crime.

"Doesn't everyone?"

I said, with great effort, "You just killed a bunch of guys who didn't seem to like me at all." I was tired of them talking about me right above my head, as illuminating as it was. I was hurting real bad, and my living room was full of dead men. I was ready for both those situations to be remedied.

"Bill, how'd you get here?" I asked in a raspy whisper.

"My car. I negotiated a deal with Russell, since I didn't want to be looking over my shoulder for the rest of my existence. Russell was in a tantrum when I called him. Not only had I disappeared and Lorena vanished, but his hired Weres had disobeyed him and thus jeopardized business dealings Russell has with this Alcide and his father."

"Who was Russell angriest with?" Eric asked.

"Lorena, for letting me escape."

They had a good laugh over that one before Bill continued his story. Those vamps. A laugh a minute.

"Russell agreed to return my car and leave me alone if I would tell him how I'd escaped, so he could plug the hole I'd wiggled out of. And he asked me to put in a bid for him to share in the vampire directory."

If Russell had just done that in the first place, it would have saved everyone a lot of grief. On the other hand, Lorena would still be alive. So would the thugs who'd beaten me, and perhaps so would Jerry Falcon, whose death was still a mystery.

"So," Bill continued, "I sped down the highway, on the way to tell you two that the Weres and their hired hands were pursuing you, and that they had gone ahead to lie in wait. They had discovered, via the computer, that Alcide's girlfriend Sookie Stackhouse lived in Bon Temps."

"These computers are dangerous things," Eric said. His voice sounded weary, and I remembered the blood on his clothes. Eric had been shot twice, because he'd been with me.

"Her face is swelling," Bill said. His voice was both gentle and angry.

"Eric okay?" I asked wearily, figuring I could skip a few words if I got the idea across.

"I will heal," he said, from a great distance. "Especially since having all that good . . ."

And then I fell asleep, or passed out, or some blend of the two.

SUNSHINE. IT HAD been so long since I'd seen sunshine; I'd almost forgotten how good it looked.

I was in my own bed, and I was in my soft blue brushed-nylon nightgown, and I was wrapped up like a mummy. I really, really had to get up and get to the bathroom. Once I moved enough to establish how awful walking was going to be, only my bladder compelled me to get out of that bed.

I took tiny steps across the floor, which suddenly seemed as wide and empty as the desert. I covered it inch by painful inch. My toenails were still painted bronze, to match my nails. I had a lot of time to look at my toes as I made my journey.

Thank God I had indoor plumbing. If I'd had to make it into the yard to an outhouse, as my grandmother had as a child, I would've given up.

When I had completed my journey and pulled on a fleecy blue robe, I inched my way down the hall to the living room to examine the floor. I noticed along the way that the sun outside was brilliant and the sky was the deep rich blue of heaven. It was forty-two, said the thermometer Jason had given me on my birthday. He'd mounted it for me on the window frame, so I could just peek out to read it.

The living room looked real good. I wasn't sure how long the vampire cleaning crew had been at work the night before, but there were no body parts visible. The wood of the floor was gleaming, and the furniture looked spanky clean. The old throw rug was missing, but I didn't care. It had been no wonderful heirloom anyway, just a sort of pretty rug Gran had picked up at a flea market for thirty-five dollars. Why did I remember that? It didn't matter at all. And my grandmother was dead.

I felt the sudden danger of weeping, and I pushed it away. I wasn't going to fall back into a trough of self-pity. My reaction to Bill's unfaithfulness seemed faint and far away now; I was a colder woman, or maybe my protective hide had just grown thicker. I no longer felt angry with him, to my surprise. He'd been tortured by the woman— well, the vampire—he'd thought loved him. And she'd tortured him for financial gain—that was the worst.

To my startled horror, suddenly I relived the moment when the stake had gone in under her ribs, and I was feeling the movement of the wood as it plowed through her body.

I made it back to the hall bathroom just in time.

Okay, I'd killed someone.

I'd once hurt someone who was trying to kill me, but that had never bothered me: oh, the odd dream or two. But the horror of staking the vampire Lorena felt worse. She would've killed me a lot quicker, and I was sure it would have been no problem whatsoever for Lorena. She probably would've laughed her ass off.

Maybe that was what had gotten to me so much. After I'd sunk the stake in, I was sure I'd had a moment, a second, a flash of time in which I'd thought, *So there, bitch.* And it had been pure pleasure.

A couple of hours later, I'd discovered it was the early afternoon, and it was Monday. I called my brother on his cell phone, and he came by with my mail. When I opened my door, he stood for a long minute, looking me up and down.

"If he did that to you, I'm heading over there with a torch and a sharpened broom handle," he said.

"No, he didn't."

"What happened to the ones who did?"

"You better not think about it too much."

"At least he does some things right."

"I'm not gonna see him anymore."

"Uh-huh. I've heard that before."

He had a point. "For a while," I said firmly.

"Sam said you'd gone off with Alcide Herveaux."

"Sam shouldn't have told you."

"Hell, I'm your brother. I need to know who you're going around with."

"It was business," I said, trying a little smile on for size.

"You going into surveying?"

"You know Alcide?"

"Who doesn't, at least by name? Those Herveauxes, they're well known. Tough guys. Good to work for. Rich."

"He's a nice guy."

"He coming around anymore? I'd like to meet him. I don't want to be on a road crew working for the parish my whole life."

That was news to me. "Next time I see him, I'll call you. I don't know if he'll be stopping by anytime soon, but if he does, you'll know about it."

"Good." Jason glanced around. "What happened to the rug?"

I noticed a spot of blood on the couch, about where Eric had leaned. I sat down so my legs were covering it. "The rug? I spilled some tomato sauce on it. I was eating spaghetti out here while I watched TV."

"So you took it to get it cleaned?"

I didn't know how to answer. I didn't know if that was what the vampires had done with the rug, or if it'd had to be torched. "Yes," I said, with some hesitation. "But they may not be able to get the stain out, they said."

"New gravel looks good."

I stared at him in gape-mouthed surprise. "What?"

He looked at me as if I were a fool. "The new gravel. On the driveway. They did a good job, getting it level. Not a single pothole."

Completely forgetting the bloodstain, I heaved myself up from the couch with some difficulty and peered out the front window, this time really looking.

Not only was the driveway done, but also there was a new parking area in front of the house. It was outlined with landscaping timbers. The gravel was the very expensive kind, the kind that's supposed to interlock so it doesn't roll out of the desired area. I put my hand over my mouth as I calculated how much it had cost. "It's done like that all the way to the road?" I asked Jason, my voice hardly audible.

"Yeah, I saw the Burgess and Sons crew out here when I drove by earlier," he said slowly. "Didn't you fix it up to have it done?"

I shook my head.

"Damn, they did it by mistake?" Quick to rage, Jason flushed. "I'll call that Randy Burgess and ream his ass. Don't you pay the bill!

Here's the note that was stuck to the front door." Jason pulled a rolled receipt from his front pocket. "Sorry, I was going to hand that to you before I noticed your face."

I unrolled the yellow sheet and read the note scribbled across it. "Sookie—Mr. Northman said not to knock on your door, so I'm sticking this to it. You may need this in case something is wrong. Just call us. Randy."

"It's paid for," I said, and Jason calmed a little.

"The boyfriend? The ex?"

I remembered screaming at Eric about my driveway. "No," I said. "Someone else." I caught myself wishing the man who'd been so thoughtful had been Bill.

"You sure are getting around these days," Jason said. He didn't sound as judgmental as I expected, but then Jason was shrewd enough to know he could hardly throw many stones.

I said flatly, "No, I'm not."

He eyed me for a long moment. I met his gaze. "Okay," he said slowly. "Then someone owes you, big time."

"That would be closer to the truth," I said, and wondered in turn if I myself was being truthful. "Thanks for getting my mail for me, Big Bro. I need to crawl back in bed."

"No problem. You want to go to the doctor?"

I shook my head. I couldn't face the waiting room.

"Then you let me know if you need me to get you some groceries."

"Thanks," I said again, with more pleasure. "You're a good brother." To our mutual surprise, I stood on tiptoe and gave him a kiss on the cheek. He awkwardly put his arm around me, and I made myself keep the smile on my face, rather than wincing from the pain.

"Get back in bed, Sis," he said, shutting the door behind him carefully. I noticed he stood on the porch for a full minute, surveying all that premium gravel. Then he shook his head and got back into his pickup, always clean and gleaming, the pink and aqua flames startling against the black paint that covered the rest of the truck.

I watched a little television. I tried to eat, but my face hurt too much. I felt lucky when I discovered some yogurt in the refrigerator.

A big pickup pulled up to the front of the house about three o'clock. Alcide got out with my suitcase. He knocked softly.

He might be happier if I didn't answer, but I figured I wasn't in the business of making Alcide Herveaux happy, and I opened the door.

"Oh, Jesus Christ," he said, not irreverently, as he took me in.

"Come in," I said, through jaws that were getting so sore I could barely part them. I knew I'd said I'll call Jason if Alcide came by; but Alcide and I needed to talk.

He came in and stood looking at me. Finally, he put the suitcase back in my room, fixed me a big glass of iced tea with a straw in it, and put it on the table by the couch. My eyes filled with tears. Not everyone would have realized that a hot drink made my swollen face hurt.

"Tell me what happened, chere," he said, sitting on the couch beside me. "Here, put your feet up while you do." He helped me swivel sideways and lay my legs over his lap. I had plenty of pillows propped behind me, and I did feel comfortable, or as comfortable as I was going to feel for a couple of days.

I told him everything.

"So, you think they'll come after me in Shreveport?" he asked. He didn't seem to be blaming me for bringing all this on his head, which frankly I'd half expected.

I shook my head helplessly. "I just don't know. I wish we knew what had really happened. That might get them off our backs."

"Weres are nothing if not loyal," Alcide said.

I took his hand. "I know that."

Alcide's green eyes regarded me steadily.

"Debbie asked me to kill you," he said.

For a moment I felt cold down to my bones. "What did you tell her back?" I asked, through stiff lips.

"I told her she could go fuck herself, excuse my language."

"And how do you feel now?"

"Numb. Isn't that stupid? I'm pulling her out of me by the roots, though. I told you I would. I had to do it. It's like being addicted to crack. She's awful."

I thought of Lorena. "Sometimes," I said, and even to my own ears I sounded sad, "the bitch wins." Lorena was far from dead between Bill and me. Speaking of Debbie raised yet another unpleasant memory. "Hey, you told her we had been to bed together, when you two were fighting!"

He looked profoundly embarrassed, his olive skin flushing. "I'm ashamed of that. I knew she'd been having a good time with her fiancé; she bragged about it. I sort of used your name in vain when I was really mad. I apologize."

I could understand that, even though I didn't like it. I raised my eyebrows to indicate that wasn't quite enough.

"Okay, that was really low. A double apology and a promise to never do it again."

I nodded. I would accept that.

"I hated to hustle you all out of the apartment like that, but I didn't want her to see the three of you, in view of conclusions she might have drawn. Debbie can get really mad, and I thought if she saw you in conjunction with the vampires, she might hear a rumor that Russell was missing a prisoner and put two and two together. She might even be mad enough to call Russell."

"So much for loyalty among Weres."

"She's a shifter, not a Were," Alcide said instantly, and a suspicion of mine was confirmed. I was beginning to believe that Alcide, despite his stated conviction that he was determined to kept the Were gene to himself, would never be happy with anyone but another Were. I sighed: I tried to keep it a nice, quiet sigh. I might be wrong, after all.

"Debbie aside," I said, waving my hand to show how completely Debbie was out of our conversational picture, "*someone* killed Jerry Falcon and put him in your closet. That's caused me—and you—a lot more trouble that the original mission, which was searching for Bill. Who would do something like that? It would have to be someone really malicious."

"Or someone really stupid," Alcide said fairly.

"I know Bill didn't do it, because he was a prisoner. And I'd swear Eric was telling the truth when he said he didn't do it." I hesitated, hating to bring a name back up. "But what about Debbie? She's . . ." I stopped myself from saying "a real bitch," because only Alcide should call her that. "She was angry with you for having a date," I said mildly. "Maybe she would put Jerry Falcon in your closet to cause you trouble?"

"Debbie's mean and she can cause trouble, but she's never killed anyone," Alcide said. "She doesn't have the, the . . . grit for it, the sand. The will to kill."

Okay. Just call me Sandy.

Alcide must have read my dismay on my face. "Hey, I'm a Were," he said, shrugging. "I'd do it if I had to. Especially at the right time of the moon."

"So maybe a fellow pack member did him in, for reasons we don't know, and decided to lay the blame on you?" Another possible scenario.

"That doesn't feel right. Another Were would have—well, the body would've looked different." Alcide said, trying to spare my finer feelings. He meant the body would have been ripped to shreds. "And I think I would've smelled another Were on him. Not that I got that close."

We just didn't have any other ideas, though if I'd tape-recorded that conversation and played it back, I would have thought of another possible culprit easily enough.

Alcide said he had to get back to Shreveport, and I lifted my legs for him to rise. He got up, but went down on one knee by the head of the couch to tell me good-bye. I said the polite things, how nice it had been of him to give me a place to stay, how much I'd enjoyed meeting his sister, how much fun it had been to hide a body with him. No, I didn't really say that, but it crossed my mind, as I was being Gran's courteous product.

"I'm glad I met you," he said. He was closer to me than I'd thought, and he gave me a peck on the lips in farewell. But after the peck, which was okay, he returned for a longer good-bye. His lips felt so warm; and after a second, his tongue felt even warmer. His head turned slightly to get a better angle, and then he went at it again. His right hand hovered above me, trying to find a place to settle that wouldn't hurt me. Finally he covered my left hand with his. Oh boy, this was good. But only my mouth and my lower pelvis were happy. The rest of me hurt. His hand slid, in a questioning sort of way, up to my breast, and I gave a sharp gasp.

"Oh, God, I hurt you!" he said. His lips looked very full and red after the long kiss, and his eyes were brilliant.

I felt obliged to apologize. "I'm just so sore," I said.

"What did they do to you?" he asked. "Not just a few slaps across the face?"

He had imagined my swollen face was my most serious problem.

"I wish that had been it," I said, trying to smile.

He truly looked stricken. "And here I am, making a pass at you."

"Well, I didn't push you away," I said mildly. (I was too sore to push.) "And I didn't say, 'No, sir, how dare you force your attentions on me!'"

Alcide looked somewhat startled. "I'll come back by soon," he promised. "If you need anything, you call me." He fished a card out of his pocket and laid it on the table by the couch. "This has got my work number on it, and I'm writing my cell number on the back, and my home number. Give me yours." Obediently, I recited the numbers to him, and he wrote them down in, no kidding, a little black book. I didn't have the energy to make a joke.

When he was gone, the house felt extra empty. He was so big and so energetic—so alive—he filled large spaces with his personality and presence.

It was a day for me to sigh.

Having talked to Jason at Merlotte's, Arlene came by at half past five. She surveyed me, looked as if she were suppressing a lot of comments she really wanted to make, and heated me up some Campbell's. I let it cool before I ate it very carefully and slowly, and felt the better for it. She put the dishes in the dishwasher, and asked me if I needed any other help. I thought of her children waiting for her at home, and I said I was just fine. It did me good to see Arlene, and to know she was struggling with herself about speaking out of turn made me feel even better.

Physically, I was feeling more and more stiff. I made myself get up and walk a little (though it looked more like a hobble), but as my bruises became fully developed and the house grew colder, I began to feel much worse. This was when living alone really got to you, when you felt bad or sick and there was no one there.

You might feel a little sorry for yourself, too, if you weren't careful.

To my surprise, the first vampire to arrive after dark was Pam. Tonight she was wearing a trailing black gown, so she was scheduled to work at Fangtasia. Ordinarily, Pam shunned black; she was a pastels kind of female. She yanked at the chiffon sleeves impatiently.

"Eric says you may need a female to help you," she said impatiently. "Though why I am supposed to be your lady's maid, I don't know. Do you really need help, or is he just trying to curry favor with you? I like you well enough, but after all, I am vampire, and you are human."

That Pam, what a sweetie.

"You could sit and visit with me for a minute," I suggested, at a loss as to how to proceed. Actually, it would be nice to have help getting into and out of the bathtub, but I knew Pam would be offended to be asked to perform such a personal task. After all, she was vampire, I was human. . . .

Pam settled into the armchair facing the couch. "Eric says you can fire a shotgun," she said, more conversationally. "Would you teach me?"

"I'd be real glad to, when I'm better."

"Did you really stake Lorena?"

The shotgun lessons were more important than the death of Lorena, it seemed.

"Yes. She would've killed me."

"How'd you do it?"

"I had the stake that had been used on me."

Then Pam had to hear about that, and ask me how it felt, since I was the only person she knew who'd survived being staked, and then she asked me exactly how I'd killed Lorena, and there we were, back at my least favorite topic.

"I don't want to talk about it," I admitted.

"Why not?" Pam was curious. "You say she was trying to kill you."

"She was."

"And after she had done that, she would have tortured Bill more, until he broke, and you would have been dead, and it all would have been for nothing."

Pam had a point, a good one, and I tried to think about it as a practical step to have taken, rather than a desperate reflex.

"Bill and Eric will be here soon," Pam said, looking at her watch.

"I wish you had told me that earlier," I said, struggling to my feet.

"Got to brush your teeth and hair?" Pam was cheerfully sarcastic. "That's why Eric thought you might need my help."

"I think I can manage my own grooming, if you wouldn't mind heating up some blood in the microwave—of course, for yourself as well. I'm sorry, I wasn't being polite."

Pam gave me a skeptical look, but trotted off to the kitchen without further comment. I listened for a minute to make sure she knew how to operate a microwave, and I heard reassuringly unhesitating beeps as she punched in the numbers and hit Start.

Slowly and painfully, I washed off in the sink, brushed my hair and teeth, and put on some silky pink pajamas and a matching robe and slippers. I wished I had the energy to dress, but I just couldn't face underwear and socks and shoes.

There was no point putting on makeup over the bruises. There was no way I could cover them. In fact, I wondered why I'd gotten up from the couch to put myself through this much pain. I looked in the mirror and told myself I was an idiot to make any preparation for their arrival. I was just plain primping. Given my overall misery (mental and physical), my behavior was ridiculous. I was sorry I had felt the impulse, and even sorrier Pam had witnessed it.

But the first male caller I had was Bubba.

He was all decked out. The vampires of Jackson had enjoyed Bubba's company, it was apparent. Bubba was wearing a red jumpsuit with rhinestones on it (I wasn't too surprised one of the boy toys at the mansion had had one) complete with wide belt and half boots. Bubba looked good.

He didn't seem pleased, though. He seemed apologetic. "Miss Sookie, I'm sorry I lost you last night," he said right away. He brushed past Pam, who looked surprised. "I see something awful happened to you last night, and I wasn't there to stop it like Eric told me to be. I was having a good time in Jackson, those guys there really know how to throw themselves a party."

I had an idea, a blindingly simple idea. If I'd been in a comic strip, it would have shown itself as a lightning bolt over my head. "You've been watching me every night," I said, as gently as I could, trying hard to keep all excitement out of my voice. "Right?"

"Yes'm, ever since Mr. Eric told me to." He was standing straighter, his head full of carefully combed hair gelled into the familiar style. The guys at Russell's mansion had really worked hard on him.

"So you were out there the night we came back from the club? The first night?"

"You bet, Miss Sookie."

"Did you see anyone else outside the apartment?"

"I sure did." He looked proud.

Oh, boy. "Was this a guy in gang leathers?"

He looked surprised. "Yes'm, it was that guy hurt you in the bar. I seen him when the doorman threw him out back. Some of his buddies came around back there, and they were talking about what had happened. So I knew he'd offended you. Mr. Eric said not to come up to you or him in public, so I didn't. But I followed you back to the apartment, in that truck. Bet you didn't even know I was in the back."

"No, I sure didn't know you were in the back of the pickup. That was real smart. Now tell me, when you saw the Were later, what was he doing?"

"He had picked the lock on the apartment door by the time I snuck up behind him. I just barely caught that sucker in time."

"What did you do with him?" I smiled at Bubba.

"I broke his neck and stuffed him in the closet," Bubba said proudly. "I didn't have time to take the body anywhere, and I figured you and Mr. Eric could figure out what to do about it."

I had to look away. So simple. So direct. Solving that mystery had just taken asking the right person the right question.

Why hadn't we thought of it? You couldn't give Bubba orders and expect him to adapt them to circumstances. Quite possibly, he had saved my life by killing Jerry Falcon, since my bedroom was the first one the Were would have come to. I had been so tired when I finally got to bed, I might not have woken until it was too late.

Pam had been looking back and forth between us with a question on her face. I held up a hand to indicate I'd explain later, and I made myself smile at Bubba and tell him he'd done the right thing. "Eric will be so pleased," I said. And telling Alcide would be an interesting experience.

Bubba's whole face relaxed. He smiled, that upper lip curling just a little. "I'm glad to hear you say so," he said. "You got any blood? I'm mighty thirsty."

"Sure," I said. Pam was thoughtful enough to fetch the blood, and Bubba took a big swig.

"Not as good as a cat's," he observed. "But mighty fine just the same. Thank you, thank you very much."

Chapter 15

WHAT A COZY evening it was turning out to be—yours truly and four vampires, after Bill and Eric arrived separately but almost simultaneously. Just me and my buds, hanging at the house.

Bill insisted on braiding my hair for me, just so he could show his familiarity with my house and habits by going in the bathroom and getting my box of hair doodads. Then he put me on the ottoman in front of him as he sat behind me to brush and fix my hair. I have always found this a very soothing process, and it aroused memories of another evening Bill and I had begun just about the same way, with a fabulous finale. Of course, Bill was well aware he was pushing those memories to the fore.

Eric observed this with the air of one taking notes, and Pam sneered openly. I could not for the life of me understand why they all had to be here at the same time, and why they all didn't get sick of one another—and me—and go away. After a few minutes of having a comparative crowd in my house, I longed to be alone once more. Why had I thought I was lonely?

Bubba left fairly quickly, anxious to do some hunting. I didn't want to think too closely about that. When he'd left, I was able to tell the other vampires about what had really happened to Jerry Falcon.

Eric didn't seem too upset that his directions to Bubba had caused the death of Jerry Falcon, and I'd already admitted to myself that I couldn't be too wrought up about it, either. If it came down to him, or me, well, I liked me better. Bill was indifferent to Jerry's fate, and Pam thought the whole thing was funny.

"That he followed you to Jackson, when his instructions were just for here, for one night . . . that he kept following his instructions, no matter what! It's not very vampiric, but he's certainly a good soldier."

"It would have been much better if he'd told Sookie what he'd done and why he'd done it," Eric observed.

"Yes, a note would have been nice," I said sarcastically. "Anything would have been better than opening that closet and finding the body stuffed in there."

Pam hooted with laughter. I'd really found the way to tickle her funny bone. Wonderful.

"I can just see your face," she said. "You and the Were had to hide the body? That's priceless."

"I wish I'd known all this when Alcide was here today," I said. I'd closed my eyes when the full effect of the hair brushing had soothed me. But the sudden silence was delightful. At last, I was getting to amuse my own self a little bit.

Eric said, "Alcide Herveaux came here?"

"Yeah, he brought my bag. He stayed to help me out, seeing as how I'm banged up."

When I opened my eyes, because Bill had quit brushing, I caught Pam's eyes. She winked at me. I gave her a tiny smile.

"I unpacked your bag for you, Sookie," Pam said smoothly. "Where did you get that beautiful velvet shawl-thing?"

I pressed my lips together firmly. "Well, my first evening wrap got ruined at Club—I mean, at Josephine's. Alcide very kindly went shopping and bought it to surprise me . . . he said he felt responsible for the first one getting burned." I was delighted I'd carried it up to the apartment from its place on the front seat of the Lincoln. I didn't remember doing that.

"He has excellent taste, for a Were," Pam conceded. "If I borrow your red dress, can I borrow the shawl, too?"

I hadn't known Pam and I were on clothes-swapping terms. She was definitely up to mischief. "Sure," I said.

Shortly after that, Pam said she was leaving. "I think I'll run home through the woods," she said. "I feel like experiencing the night."

"You'll run all the way back to Shreveport?" I said, astonished.

"It won't be the first time," she said. "Oh, by the way, Bill, the queen called Fangtasia this evening to find out why you are late with her little job. She had been unable to reach you at your home for several nights, she said."

Bill resumed brushing my hair. "I will call her back later," he said. "From my place. She'll be glad to hear that I've completed it."

"You nearly lost everything," Eric said, his sudden outburst startling everyone in the room.

Pam slipped out the front door after she'd looked from Eric to Bill. That kind of scared me.

"Yes, I'm well aware of that," Bill said. His voice, always cool and sweet, was absolutely frigid. Eric, on the other hand, tended toward the fiery.

"You were a fool to take up with that she-demon again," Eric said.

"Hey, guys, I'm sitting right here," I said.

They both glared at me. They seemed determined to finish this quarrel, and I figured I would leave them to go at it. Once they were outside. I hadn't thanked Eric for the driveway yet, and I wanted to, but tonight was maybe not the time.

"Okay," I said. "I'd hoped to avoid this, but . . . Bill, I rescind your invitation into my house." Bill began walking backward to the door, a helpless look on his face, and my brush still in his hand. Eric grinned at him triumphantly. "Eric," I said, and his smile faded. "I rescind your invitation into my house." And backward he went, out my door and off my porch. The door slammed shut behind (or maybe in front of?) them.

I sat on the ottoman, feeling relief beyond words at the sudden silence. And all of a sudden, I realized that the computer program so desired by the queen of Louisiana, the computer program that had cost lives and the ruin of my relationship with Bill, was in my house . . . which not Eric, or Bill, or even the queen, could enter without my say-so.

I hadn't laughed so hard in weeks.

THE **Science Fiction** BOOK CLUB®

If you enjoyed this book…
Come visit our Web site at
www.sfbc.com
and find hundreds more:
- science fiction • fantasy
- the newest books
- the greatest classics

THE SCIENCE FICTION BOOK CLUB

has been bringing the best of science fiction and fantasy
to the doors of discriminating readers for over 50 years.
For a look at currently available books and details on how to join,
just visit us at the address above.

About the Author

Charlaine Harris has produced two mystery series in addition to her Sookie Stackhouse books. She lives in southern Arkansas with her husband, three children, two dogs, two ferrets, and a duck. An avid reader, mild cinemaphile, and occasional weightlifter, her favorite activity is cheering her children on in various sports while sitting on uncomfortable bleachers. Her website is www.charlaineharris.com.